THE BEST
SCIENCE FICTION AND
FANTASY OF THE YEAR
Volume Eleven

Also Edited by Jonathan Strahan

Best Short Novels
(2004 through 2007)
Fantasy: The Very Best of 2005
*Science Fiction: The Very
Best of 2005*
*The Best Science Fiction &
Fantasy of the Year: Volumes 1-11*
*Eclipse: New Science Fiction
and Fantasy (Vols 1-4)*
*The Starry Rift: Tales of New
Tomorrows*
*Life on Mars: Tales of New
Frontiers*
*Under My Hat: Tales from the
Cauldron*
Godlike Machines

The Infinity Project:
Engineering Infinity
Edge of Infinity
Reach for Infinity
Meeting Infinity
Bridging Infinity
Infinity Wars (forthcoming)

Fearsome Journeys
Fearsome Magics
Drowned Worlds

With Lou Anders
*Swords and Dark Magic: The New
Sword and Sorcery*

With Charles N. Brown
*The Locus Awards: Thirty Years
of the Best in Fantasy and Science
Fiction*

With Jack Dann
Legends of Australian Fantasy

With Gardner Dozois
The New Space Opera
The New Space Opera 2

With Karen Haber
Science Fiction: Best of 2003
Science Fiction: Best of 2004
Fantasy: Best of 2004

With Marianne S. Jablon
Wings of Fire

EDITED BY JONATHAN STRAHAN

THE BEST SCIENCE FICTION & FANTASY OF THE YEAR

VOLUME ELEVEN

First published 2017 by Solaris
an imprint of Rebellion Publishing Ltd,
Riverside House, Osney Mead,
Oxford, OX2 0ES, UK

www.solarisbooks.com

ISBN 978 1 78108 562 2

Cover by Dominic Harman

Selection and "Introduction" by Jonathan Strahan.
Copyright © 2017 by Jonathan Strahan.

Pages 605-608 represent an extension of this copyright page

10 9 8 7 6 5 4 3 2 1

A CIP catalogue record for this book is available from the
British Library.

Designed & typeset by Rebellion Publishing

Printed in Denmark

For Marianne, who has stood by me through twenty years of doing this...

ACKNOWLEDGEMENTS

THIS IS THE first volume of the second decade of *The Best Science Fiction and Fantasy of the Year* anthology series, which started way back in 2007. I'd like to thank Jonathan Oliver and Ben Smith and the team at Solaris for picking the series up and for running with it in the way that they have. I will always be grateful to them for stepping in and for believing in the books and in me. I'd also like to thank Sean Wallace for his help this year, and everyone who worked on the Locus Recommended Reading list. Special thanks to my agent Howard Morhaim who for over a decade now has had my back and helped make good things happen. Finally, the most special thanks of all to Marianne, Jessica and Sophie. I always say that every moment spent working on these books is stolen from them, but it's true, and I'm forever grateful to them for their love, support and generosity.

CONTENTS

INTRODUCTION
Jonathan Strahan

WELCOME TO *THE Best Science Fiction and Fantasy of the Year*. The book you're holding is a snapshot of sorts, one reader's view of what was happening in fantasy and science fiction during the tumultuous year of 2016. As political philosophies duelled more nakedly across the world than they have in recent times, and as the world at large turned away from openness and inclusion, the science fiction and fantasy world continued on pretty much as it had before.

The battle between old school Ess-Eff and that New Stuff, which I mentioned last year (and the year before), continued (I suspect it's been continuing for at least the past century in one form or another), but everyone seemed a bit wearier of it to me, and I for one felt that light could be seen on the horizon. Words were said (again), social media feeds ignited (again), and awards rules were revised and tinkered with (again), and if the whole thing didn't peter out, at least it began to look like something we might get past. We'll see how it all falls out come awards time, but my guess is it won't prove to be that important at all.

Inclusion, or at least awareness of science fiction and fantasy from outside North American and British publishing, became more widespread as well, with important work by writers from Asian and African nations appearing in most of the major publishing venues during the year. *Clarkesworld* continued its successful program publishing Chinese science fiction each month, *Tor.com* added coverage of African SF, *Lightspeed* and *Fantasy* published worthwhile special issues, and anthologies like Ken Liu's *Invisible Planets: Contemporary Chinese Science Fiction in Translation* and Hassan Blasim's *Iraq +100: Stories from Another Iraq* showcased new voices for a wider audience. One of the challenges for inclusion is addressing how time tends to erase the voices of the past, and this year we saw two worthwhile books published that addressed the history of women in science fiction. Kristine Kathryn Rusch's *Women of Futures Past: Classic Stories* and Lisa Yaszek and Patrick B. Sharp's *Sisters of Tomorrow: The First Women of Science Fiction* together provided an important corrective, showcasing the fine work women writers have always done in our field.

It was particularly satisfying to follow the science fiction and fantasy field's many awards and see a diversity of writers and fiction collect major awards. Naomi Novik, Nnedi Okorafor, Sarah Pinsker and Alyssa Wong took home well-deserved Nebula Awards, N.K. Jemisin won a landmark Best Novel Hugo Award, while Nnedi Okorafor, Hao Jingfang, and Naomi Kritzer were also recognized with Hugo Awards this year. And close to the end of the year Anna Smaill, Kelly Barnhill, Alyssa Wong, and CSE Cooney received World Fantasy Awards for their work. You can get full details at the Science Fiction Awards Database (www.sfadb.com), but all of their work deserves your attention.

But how was it out there in the trenches *this* year? Well, it was not too dissimilar from the past few years. A *lot* of new short fiction was published, and in all sorts of places. I've been saying for several years now that upwards of ten thousand original stories are published every year and, without doing a detailed count, that seems to be true this year too. Interesting and worthwhile short fiction was published in magazines, anthologies, collections, as giveaways, on social media feeds, as ebooks, and so on and so on. It was easy to find new fiction throughout the year, but not easy to find it all. I doubt anyone saw everything published, but some of us tried hard. While compiling this book I saw some wonderful stories, the best of which are collected here, but I undoubtedly missed some great ones too.

I'm always asked about trends, and I saw one or two in 2016. Reaction to climate change continues to embed itself in science fiction, even where climate change is not referenced directly. It has become a default causal effect for change, and that is leading to some very interesting fiction. This was also the year that the novella boom hit. While novellas—long short stories and short novels—have always been a part of the field, especially from independent publishers like PS Publishing and Subterranean Press, and have always been featured in fiction magazines like *Analog*, *Asimov's Science Fiction*, and

F&SF, we've seen more and more publishers focusing on presenting fiction at this length, with Tor.com Publishing in particular delivering some remarkable work. I spend the end of the year working on helping to compile *Locus*'s (www.locusmag.com) annual Recommended Reading list, and we easily saw double the number of novellas recommended than in previous years, with truly outstanding work from Victor LaValle, Kij Johnson, Kai Ashante Wilson, Alastair Reynolds, China Mieville, and others. I expect to see this continue, especially given the end of year announcement from Penny Press than *Analog* and *Asimov's* would go bimonthly and publish longer issues.

It would be misleading to say that the publication of outstanding Lovecraftian fiction during the year highlighted a trend: we've seen Lovecraftian fiction published widely ever since August Derleth went to work back in the 1930s, and we've seen reinventions and reinterpretations of Lovecraft before. But three works published during 2016 are worthy of mention. Matt Ruff's *Lovecraft Country*, Victor LaValle's *The Ballad of Black Tom*, and Kij Johnson's *The Dream Quest of Vellitt Boe* each reinterprets and reinvents Lovecraft in a way that places minorities and their experiences at the forefront of these stories in important and interesting ways. I think these stories, and those collected in several worthwhile anthologies published during the year, make a compelling case that work falling out of copyright and entering the creative commons benefits us all. Certainly, creators must receive fair recompense for their work and share in any rewards it may bring, but we all benefit when creative works eventually (and not *too* eventually) fall out of copyright and become part of the creative commons.

And there's a point that I'd re-iterate from previous years, which was truer than ever in 2016 and which underscores the value of books like this one. With so many stories being published and with so many different venues out there, increasingly readers are not reading the same stuff. The science fiction and fantasy field has balkanized, and it's easy not to look beyond your immediate reading cohort or special interest group and see what your neighbor is reading or writing. This has been a good thing in many ways, but it does mean that we see less consensus on outstanding work, simply because readers haven't seen this or that book or story. Awards and 'best of the year' anthologies and 'best of the year' lists all work as a corrective to this, or at least I hope they do.

And where, you might ask, should you have looked for great short fiction in 2016? Well, Tor.com and its publishing sibling Tor.com Publishing continue to be the gold standard for the field, with Tor.com giving us outstanding work from Nina Allan, Theodora Goss, N.K. Jemisin, Paul McAuley, Delia Sherman, Lavie Tidhar, Alyssa Wong and others. Tor.com Publishing produced some of the novellas of the year, all too long for this book unfortunately, but the LaValle and Johnson books already mentioned, and Kai Ashante Wilson's *A Taste of Honey* all come with the highest recommendation, and would appear here if room permitted. Fantasy specialist *Beneath Ceaseless Skies* was the single most improved venue this year, having the best year of its run to date, producing great work from Aliette de Bodard, Seth Dickinson, Yoon Ha Lee, K.J. Parker and others. It is one of *the* venues to watch in 2017. As should be expected by now, even though it was only an average year for them, *Clarkesworld* still produced first rate work during the year from Eleanor Arnason, Carolyn Ives Gilman, Rich Larson, Sam Miller, Genevieve Valentine, and others. *Lightspeed* had one of its best years in some while, publishing excellent work from Steven Barnes, Rich Larson (who was everywhere this year!), and Karin Lowachee. And the other venue that stood out online was *Uncanny*, which hit its straps in its second year with terrific work from Catherynne M. Valente, Alyssa Wong, E. Lily Yu and others. Horror falls mostly outside the remit of this book, except perhaps for some dark fantasy that sits on the borderline, but I'd be remiss if I didn't mention *The Dark* and *Nightmare*, both of which published fine horror fiction throughout the year.

Traditional print venues were, if anything, a little disappointing this year. *Asimov's Science Fiction* remains the best print magazine in the field, and your best go-to for great reading. It published outstanding work from Ian R. Macleod, An Owomoyela, Carrie Vaughn, Rich Larson, and Dominica Phettaplace, who published a wonderful series of stories in the magazine. The venerable *Magazine of Fantasy and Science Fiction,* in its second year under editor Charles Coleman Finlay, published good work from many of its regulars and outstanding work from Geoff Ryman, Alex Irvine and Lavie Tidhar. While *Analog Science Fiction and Fact* was a little out of step with my taste this year, it did publish top notch work from Nick Wolven and Rajnar Vajra, and *Interzone* continued to publish good work, as it has for many years, with highlights coming from Rich Larson, Rahul Kanakia, Malcolm Devlin and others. And at the very end of the year, Bard College published a wonderful issue of its anthology-magazine, *Conjunctions*, guest-edited by Elizabeth Hand, which featured several of the best stories of the year most notably from Peter Straub, John Crowley, Jeffrey Ford, and Lavie Tidhar. It's well worth seeking out, as is the web-only content, which features a very good story from Charlie Jane Anders.

It was a good year for anthologies, without being a great one. As I mention each year, I edit anthologies myself and so can say little about my science fiction anthologies *Drowned Worlds* and *Bridging Infinity*, other than that I am proud of them and think they contain work that would repay your attention. The anthology of the year, and my pick for the World Fantasy Award, was Dominik Parisien and Navah Wolfe's book of retold fairy tales, *The Starlit Wood: New Fairy Tales*, which featured outstanding work from Naomi Novik, Daryl Gregory, Amal El-Mohtar, Sofia Samatar and others. In a similar vein, Erin Underwood's *The Grimm Future* was also very worthwhile, with great work from Garth Nix and Max Gladstone. If I had to pick a runner-up for best fantasy anthology of the year, it'd be Paula Guran's consistently entertaining and worthwhile *The Mammoth Book of Cthulhu*, which had great Lovecraftian fiction from Usman T. Malik, Caitlín R. Kiernan, Veronica Shanoes, Lisa L. Hannett and others. Both come highly recommended.

Also worthwhile are Mika Allen's *Clockwork Phoenix 5*, the best in this anthology series to date with great work from Rich Larson and others, Ian Whates' *Now We Are Ten*, John Joseph Adams' *What the #@&% Is That?*, and Jonathan Oliver's excellent novella anthology, *Five Stories High*. I'd also make special mention of Jack Dann's *Dreaming in the Dark*, the third in his long-running series of short fiction from Australia's best writers. Definitely recommended, with stories from James Bradley, Lisa L. Hannett and others standing out. I don't usually mention reprint anthologies here, but I can't not recommend Ann VanderMeer and Jeff VanderMeer's *The Big Book of Science Fiction,* an enormous and endlessly impressive book that outlines an entire history of science fiction in its many, many pages. The VanderMeers together are the best editorial team of our time, taking that title from Ellen Datlow and Terri Windling who dominated the 1980s and 1990s, and any of their books are meticulously researched, reliably engaging, and definitely recommended.

Finally, 2016 was the year we lost many of those creators who meant the most to us, whether on stage, on the silver screen or on the page. Science fiction was no exception, with wonderful writers like Sheri S. Tepper, Richard Adams, Ed Gorman, W.P. Kinsella, Katherine Dunn and Justin Leiber all leaving us. One gets special mention here, though. The year started with the sad and unexpected death of David G. Hartwell. David was one of the most important editors that science fiction and fantasy has produced, overseeing the publication of more significant books than just about anyone else than I can think of. In addition to editing novels for major publishers for four decades, he edited years' bests and many other anthologies, published a critical magazine, ran a convention and two sets of awards, was one of our most important small press publishers, and one of our fashion icons. More than that, he brought a passion and belief in science fiction to the field that made an incredible impact for many decades. He could be relied on for an intelligent argument on science fiction at 2am at just about any convention anywhere in the world, and he will be sorely missed. So passes an age.

And with that, to the stories. Here are the two hundred thousand or so words of fiction that impressed me most, that I enjoyed more than any others, during 2016. I would love to have added Alastair Reynolds' *The Iron Tactician*, Kij Johnson's *The Dream Quest of Vellitt Boe* and Victor LaValle's *The Ballad of Black Tom* to these pages, but space would not permit, so I recommend you seek them out. In the meantime, here are the best of the year. I'm already reading stories for 2018. See you then!

Jonathan Strahan
Perth, Western Australia

THE FUTURE IS BLUE
Catherynne M. Valente

Catherynne M. Valente (www.catherynnemvalente.com) is the *New York Times* bestselling author of over two dozen works of fiction and poetry, including *Palimpsest*, the Orphan's Tales series, *Deathless*, *Radiance*, and the crowdfunded phenomenon *The Girl Who Circumnavigated Fairyland in a Ship of Her Own Making*. She is the winner of the Andre Norton, Tiptree, Mythopoeic, Rhysling, Lambda, Locus and Hugo awards. She has been a finalist for the Nebula and World Fantasy Awards. She lives on an island off the coast of Maine with a small but growing menagerie of beasts, some of which are human.

1. NIHILIST

MY NAME IS Tetley Abednego and I am the most hated girl in Garbagetown. I am nineteen years old. I live alone in Candle Hole, where I was born, and have no friends except for a deformed gannet bird I've named Grape Crush and a motherless elephant seal cub I've named Big Bargains, and also the hibiscus flower that has recently decided to grow out of my roof, but I haven't named it anything yet. I love encyclopedias, a cassette I found when I was eight that says *Madeleine Brix's Superboss Mixtape '97* on it in very nice handwriting, plays by Mr. Shakespeare or Mr. Webster or Mr. Beckett, lipstick, Garbagetown, and my twin brother Maruchan. Maruchan is the only thing that loves me back, but he's my twin, so it doesn't really count. We couldn't stop loving each other any more than the sea could stop being so greedy and give us back China or drive time radio or polar bears.

But he doesn't visit anymore.

When we were little, Maruchan and I always asked each other the same question before bed. Every night, we crawled into the Us-Fort together—an impregnable stronghold of a bed which we had nailed up ourselves out of the carcasses of several hacked apart bassinets, prams, and cradles. It took up the whole of our bedroom. No one could see us in there, once we closed the porthole (a manhole cover I swiped from Scrapmetal Abbey stamped with stars, a crescent moon, and the magic words *New Orleans Water Meter*), and we felt certain no one could hear us either. We lay together under our canopy of moldy green lace and shredded buggy-hoods and mobiles with only one shattered fairy fish remaining. Sometimes I asked first and sometimes he did, but we never gave the same answer twice.

"Maruchan, what do you want to be when you grow up?"

He would give it a serious think. Once, I remember, he whispered:

"When I grow up I want to be the Thames!"

"Whatever for?" I giggled.

"Because the Thames got so big and so bossy and so strong that it ate London all up in one go! Nobody tells a Thames what to do or who to eat. A Thames tells *you*. Imagine having a whole city to eat, and not having to share any! Also there were millions of eels in the Thames and I only get to eat eels at Easter which isn't fair when I want to eat them all the time."

And he pretended to bite me and eat me all up. "Very well, you shall be the Thames and I shall be the Mississippi and together we shall eat up the whole world."

Then we'd go to sleep and dream the same dream. We always dreamed the same dreams, which was like living twice.

After that, whenever we were hungry, which was always all the time and forever, we'd say *we're bound for London-town!* until we drove our parents so mad that they forbade the word London in the house, but you can't forbid a word, so there.

EVERY MORNING I wake up to find words painted on my door like toadstools popping up in the night.

Today it says NIHILIST in big black letters. That's not so bad! It's almost sweet! Big Bargains flumps toward me on her fat seal-belly while I light the wicks on my beeswax door and we watch them burn together until the word melts away.

"I don't think I'm a nihilist, Big Bargains. Do you?"

She rolled over onto my matchbox stash so that I would rub her stomach. Rubbing a seal's stomach is the opposite of nihilism.

Yesterday, an old man hobbled up over a ridge of rusted bicycles and punched me so hard he broke my nose. By law, I had to let him. I had to say: *Thank you, Grandfather, for my instruction.* I had to stand there and wait in case he wanted to do something else to me. Anything but kill me, those were his rights. But he didn't want more, he just wanted to cry and ask me why I did it and the law doesn't say I have to answer that, so I just stared at him until he went away. Once a gang of schoolgirls shaved off all my hair and wrote CUNT in blue marker on the back of my skull. *Thank you, sisters, for my instruction.* The schoolboys do worse. After graduation they come round and eat my food and hold me down and try to make me cry, which I never do. It's their rite of passage. *Thank you, brothers, for my instruction.*

But other than that, I'm really a very happy person! I'm awfully lucky when you think about it. Garbagetown is the most wonderful place anybody has ever lived in the history of the world, even if you count the Pyramids and New York City and Camelot. I have Grape Crush and Big Bargains and my hibiscus flower and I can fish like I've got bait for a heart so I hardly ever go hungry and once I found a ruby ring *and* a New Mexico license plate inside a bluefin tuna. Everyone says they only hate me because I annihilated hope and butchered our future, but I know better, and anyway, it's a lie. Some people are just born to be despised. The Loathing of Tetley began small and grew bigger and bigger, like the Thames, until it swallowed me whole.

Maruchan and I were born fifty years after the Great Sorting, which is another lucky thing that's happened to me. After all, I could have been born a Fuckwit and gotten drowned with all the rest of them, or I could have grown up on a Misery Boat, sailing around hopelessly looking for land, or one of the first to realize people could live on a patch of garbage in the Pacific Ocean the size of the place that used to be called Texas, or I could have been a Sorter and spent my whole life moving rubbish from one end of the patch to the other so that a pile of crap could turn into a country and babies could be born in places like Candle Hole or Scrapmetal Abbey or Pill Hill or Toyside or Teagate.

Candle Hole is the most beautiful place in Garbagetown, which is the most beautiful place in the world. All the stubs of candles the Fuckwits threw out piled up into hills and mountains and caverns and dells, votive candles and taper candles and tea lights and birthday candles and big fat colorful pillar candles, stacked and somewhat melted into a great crumbling gorgeous warren of wicks and wax. All the houses are little cozy honeycombs melted into the hillside, with smooth round windows and low golden ceilings. At night, from far away, Candle Hole looks like a firefly palace. When the wind blows, it smells like cinnamon, and freesia, and cranberries, and lavender, and Fresh Linen Scent and New Car Smell.

2. The Terrible Power of Fuckwit Cake

OUR PARENTS' NAMES are Life and Time. Time lay down on her Fresh Linen Scent wax bed and I came out of her first, then Maruchan. But even though I got here first, I came out blue as the ocean, not breathing, with the umbilical cord wrapped round my neck and Maruchan wailing, still squeezing onto my noose with his tiny fist, like he was trying to get me free. Doctor Pimms unstrangled and unblued me and put me in a Hawaiian Fantasies-scented wax hollow in our living room. I lay there alone, too startled by living to cry, until the sun came up and Life and Time remembered I had survived. Maruchan was so healthy and sweet natured and strong and, even though Garbagetown is the most beautiful place in the world, many children don't live past a year or two. We don't even get names until we turn ten. (Before that, we answer happily to Girl or Boy or Child or Darling.) Better to focus on the one that will grow up rather than get attached to the sickly poor beast who hasn't got a chance.

I was born already a ghost. But I was a very noisy ghost. I screamed and wept at all hours while Life and Time waited for me to die. I only nursed when my brother was full, I only played with toys he forgot, I only spoke after he had spoken. Maruchan said his first word at the supper table: *please*. What a lovely, polite word for a lovely, polite child! After they finished cooing over him, I very calmly turned to my mother and said: *Mama, may I have a scoop of mackerel roe? It is my favorite.* I thought they would be so proud! After all, I made twelve more words than my brother. This was my moment, the wonderful moment when they would realize that they did love me and I wasn't going to die and I was special and good. But everyone got very quiet. They were not happy that the ghost could talk. I had been able to for ages, but everything in my world said to wait for my brother before I could do anything at all. *No, you may not have mackerel roe, because you are a deceitful wicked little show-off child.*

When we turned ten, we went to fetch our names. This is just the most terribly exciting thing for a Garbagetown kid. At ten, you are a real person. At ten, people want to know you. At ten, you will probably live for a good while yet. This is how you catch a name: wake up to the fabulous new world of being ten and greet your birthday Frankencake (a hodgepodge of well-preserved Fuckwit snack cakes filled with various cremes and jellies). Choose a slice, with much fanfare. Inside, your adoring and/or neglectful mother will have hidden various small objects—an aluminum pull tab, a medicine bottle cap, a broken earring, a coffee bean, a wee striped capacitor, a tiny plastic rocking horse, maybe a postage stamp. Remove item from your mouth without cutting yourself or eating it. Now, walk in the direction of your prize. Toward Aluminumopolis or Pill Hill or Spanglestoke or Teagate or Electric City or Toyside or Lost Post Gulch. Walk and walk and walk. Never once brush yourself off or wash in the ocean, even after camping on a pile of magazines or wishbones or pregnancy tests or wrapping paper with glitter reindeer on it. Walk until nobody knows you. When, finally, a stranger hollers at you to get out of the way or go back where you came from or stop stealing the good rubbish, they will, without even realizing, call you by your true name, and you can begin to pick and stumble your way home.

My brother grabbed a chocolate snack cake with a curlicue of white icing on it. I chose a pink and red tigery striped hunk of cake filled with gooshy creme de something. The sugar hit our brains like twin tsunamis. He spat out a little gold earring with the post broken off. I felt a smooth, hard gelcap lozenge in my mouth. Pill Hill it was then, and the great mountain of Fuckwit anxiety medication. But when I carefully pulled the thing out, it was a little beige capacitor with red stripes instead. Electric City! I'd never been half so far. Richies lived in Electric City. Richies and brightboys and dazzlegirls and kerosene kings. My brother was off in the opposite direction, toward Spanglestoke and the desert of engagement rings.

Maybe none of it would have happened if I'd gone to Spanglestoke for my name instead. If I'd never seen the gasoline gardens of Engine Row. If I'd gone home straightaway after finding my name. If I'd never met Goodnight Moon in the brambles of Hazmat Heath with all the garbage stars rotting gorgeously overhead. Such is the terrible power of Fuckwit Cake.

I walked cheerfully out of Candle Hole with my St. Oscar backpack strapped on tight and didn't look back once. Why should I? St. Oscar had my back. I'm not really that religious nowadays. But everyone's religious when they're ten. St. Oscar was a fuzzy green Fuckwit man who lived in a garbage can just like me, and frowned a lot just like me. He understood me and loved me and knew how to bring civilization out of trash and I loved him back even though he was a Fuckwit. Nobody chooses how they get born. Not even Oscar.

So I scrambled up over the wax ridges of my home and into the world with Oscar on my back. The Matchbox Forest rose up around me: towers of EZ Strike matchbooks and boxes from impossible, magical places like the Coronado Hotel, Becky's Diner, the Fox and Hound Pub. Garbagetowners picked through heaps and cairns of blackened, used matchsticks looking for the precious ones that still had their red and blue heads intact. But I knew all those pickers. They couldn't give me a name. I waved at the hotheads. I climbed up Flintwheel Hill, my feet slipping and sliding on the mountain of spent butane lighters, until I could see out over all of Garbagetown just as the broiling cough-drop red sun was setting over Far Boozeaway, hitting the crystal bluffs of stockpiled whiskey and gin bottles and exploding into a billion billion rubies tumbling down into the hungry sea.

I sang a song from school to the sun and the matchsticks. It's an ask-and-answer song, so I had to sing both parts myself, which feels very odd when you have always had a twin to do the asking or the answering, but I didn't mind.

Who liked it hot and hated snow?
The Fuckwits did! The Fuckwits did!
Who ate up every thing that grows?
The Fuckwits did! The Fuckwits did!
Who drowned the world in oceans blue?

The Fuckwits did! The Fuckwits did!
Who took the land from me and you?
The Fuckwits did, we know it's true!
Are you Fuckwits, children dear?
We're GARBAGETOWNERS, free and clear!
But who made the garbage, rich and rank?
The Fuckwits did, and we give thanks.

The Lawn stretched out below me, full of the grass clippings and autumn leaves and fallen branches and banana peels and weeds and gnawed bones and eggshells of the fertile Fuckwit world, slowly turning into the gold of Garbagetown: soil. Real earth. Terra bloody firma. We can already grow rice in the dells. And here and there, big, blowsy flowers bang up out of the rot: hibiscus, African tulips, bitter gourds, a couple of purple lotuses floating in the damp mucky bits. I slept next to a blue-and-white orchid that looked like my brother's face.

"Orchid, what do you want to be when you grow up?" I whispered to it. In real life, it didn't say anything back. It just fluttered a little in the moonlight and the seawind. But when I got around to dreaming, I dreamed about the orchid, and it said: *a farm.*

3. MURDERCUNT

In GARBAGETOWN, YOU think real hard about what you're gonna eat next, where the fresh water's at, and where you're gonna sleep. Once all that's settled you can whack your mind on nicer stuff, like gannets and elephant seals and what to write next on the Bitch of Candle Hole's door. (This morning I melted MURDERCUNT off the back wall of my house. Big Bargains flopped down next to me and watched the blocky red painted letters swirl and fade into the Buttercream Birthday Cake wax. Maybe I'll name my hibiscus flower Murdercunt. It has a nice big sound.)

When I remember hunting my name, I mostly remember the places I slept. It's a real dog to find good spots. Someplace sheltered from the wind, without too much seawater seep, where no-one'll yell at you for wastreling on their patch or try to stick it in you in the middle of the night just because you're all alone and it looks like you probably don't have a knife.

I always have a knife.

So I slept with St. Oscar the Grouch for my pillow, in the shadow of a mountain of black chess pieces in Gamegrange, under a thicket of tabloids and *Wall Street Journals* and remaindered novels with their covers torn off in Bookbury, snuggled into a spaghetti-pile of unspooled cassette ribbon on the outskirts of the Sound Downs, on the lee side of a little soggy Earl Grey hillock in Teagate. In the morning I sucked on a few of the teabags and the dew on them tasted like the loveliest cuppa any Fuckwit ever poured his stupid self. I said my prayers on beds of old microwaves and moldy photographs of girls with perfect hair kissing at the camera. *St. Oscar, keep your mighty lid closed over me. Look grouchily but kindly upon me and protect me as I travel through the infinite trashcan of your world. Show me the beautiful usefulness of your Blessed Rubbish. Let me not be Taken Out before I find my destiny.*

But my destiny didn't seem to want to find me. As far as I walked, I still saw people I knew. Mr. Zhu raking his mushroom garden, nestled in a windbreak of broken milk bottles. Miss Amancharia gave me one of the coconut crabs out of her nets, which was very nice of her, but hardly a name. Even as far away as Teagate, I saw Tropicana Sita welding a refrigerator door to a hull-metal shack. She flipped up her mask and waved at me. Dammit! She was Allsorts Sita's cousin, and Allsorts drank with my mother every Thursday at the Black Wick.

By the time I walked out of Teagate I'd been gone eight days. I was getting pretty ripe. Bits and pieces of Garbagetown were stuck all over my clothes, but no tidying up. Them's the rules. I could see the blue crackle of Electric City sparkling up out of the richie-rich Coffee Bean 'Burbs. Teetering towers of batteries rose up like desert hoodoo spires—AA, AAA, 12 Volt, DD, car, solar, lithium, anything you like. Parrots and pelicans screamed down the battery canyons, their talons kicking off sprays of AAAs that tumbled down the heights like rockslides. Sleepy banks of generators rumbled pleasantly along a river of wires and extension cords and HDMI cables. Fields of delicate lightbulbs windchimed in the breeze. Anything that had a working engine lived here. Anything that still had *juice*. If Garbagetown had a heart, it was Electric City. Electric City pumped power. Power and privilege.

In Electric City, the lights of the Fuckwit world were still on.

* * *

4. Goodnight Garbagetown

"Oi, Tetley! Fuck off back home to your darkhole! We're full up on little cunts here!"

And that's how I got my name. Barely past the battery spires of Electric City, a fat gas-huffing fucksack voltage jockey called me a little cunt. But he also called me Tetley. He brayed it down from a pyramid of telephones and his friends all laughed and drank homebrew out of a glass jug and went back to not working. I looked down—among the many scraps of rubbish clinging to my shirt and pants and backpack and hair was a bright blue teabag wrapper with TETLEY CLASSIC BLEND BLACK TEA written on it in cheerful white letters, clinging to my chest.

I tried to feel the power of my new name. The *me*-ness of it. I tried to imagine my mother and father when they were young, waking up with some torn out page of *Life* and *Time* Magazine stuck to their rears, not even noticing until someone barked out their whole lives for a laugh. But I couldn't feel anything while the volt-humpers kept on staring at me like I was nothing but a used-up potato battery. I didn't even know then that the worst swear word in Electric City was *dark*. I didn't know they were waiting to see how mad I'd get 'cause they called my home a darkhole. I didn't care. They were wrong and stupid. Except for the hole part. Candle Hole never met a dark it couldn't burn down.

Maybe I should have gone home right then. I had my name! Time to hoof it back over the river and through the woods, girl. But I'd never seen Electric City and it was morning and if I stayed gone awhile longer maybe they'd miss me. Maybe they'd worry. And maybe now they'd love me, now that I was a person with a name. Maybe I could even filch a couple of batteries or a cup of gasoline and turn up at my parents' door in turbo-powered triumph. I'd tell my brother all my adventures and he'd look at me like I was magic on a stick and everything would be good forever and ever amen.

So I wandered. I gawped. It was like being in school and learning the Fuckwit song only I was walking around *inside* the Fuckwit song and it was all still happening right now everywhere. Electric City burbled and bubbled and clanged and belched and smoked just like the bad old world before it all turned blue. Everyone had such fine things! I saw a girl wearing a ballgown out of a fairy book, green and glitter and miles of ruffles and she wasn't even *going* anywhere. She was just tending her gasoline garden out the back of her little cottage, which wasn't made out of candles or picturebooks or cat food cans, but real cottage parts! Mostly doors and shutters and really rather a lot of windows, but they fit together like they never even needed the other parts of a house in the first place. And the girl in her greenglitter dress carried a big red watering can around her garden, sprinkling fuel stabilizer into her tidy rows of petrol barrels and gas cans with their graceful spouts pointed toward the sun. Why not wear that dress all the time? Just a wineglass full of what she was growing in her garden would buy almost anything else in Garbagetown. She smiled shyly at me. I hated her. And I wanted to be her.

By afternoon I was bound for London-town, so hungry I could've slurped up every eel the Thames ever had. There's no food lying around in Electric City. In Candle Hole I could've grabbed candy or a rice ball or jerky off any old midden heap. But here everybody owned their piece and kept it real neat, *mercilessly* neat, and they didn't share. I sat down on a rusty Toyota transmission and fished around in my backpack for crumbs. My engine sat on one side of a huge cyclone fence. I'd never seen one all put together before. Sure, you find torn-off shreds of wire fences, but this one was all grown up, with proper locks and chain wire all over it. It meant to Keep You Out. Inside, like hungry dogs, endless barrels and freezers and cylinders and vats went on and on, with angry writing on them that said HAZMAT or BIOHAZARD or RADIOACTIVE or WARNING or DANGER or CLASSIFIED.

"Got anything good in there?" said a boy's voice. I looked round and saw a kid my own age, with wavy black hair and big brown eyes and three little moles on his forehead. He was wearing the nicest clothes I ever saw on a boy—a blue suit that almost, *almost* fit him. With a *tie*.

"Naw," I answered. "Just a dry sweater, an empty can of Cheez-Wiz, and *Madeline Brix's Superboss Mixtape '97*. It's my good luck charm." I showed him my beloved mixtape. Madeline Brix made all the dots on her *i*'s into hearts. It was a totally Fuckwit thing to do and I loved her for it even though she was dead and didn't care if I loved her or not.

"*Cool*," the boy said, and I could tell he meant it. He didn't even call me a little cunt or anything. He pushed his thick hair out of his face. "Listen, you really shouldn't be here. No one's gonna say anything because you're not Electrified, but it's so completely dangerous. They put all that stuff in one place so it couldn't get out and hurt anyone."

"Electrified?"

"One of us. Local." He had the decency to look embarrassed. "Anyway, I saw you and I thought that if some crazy darkgirl is gonna have a picnic on Hazmat Heath, I could at least help her not die while she's doing it."

The boy held out his hand. He was holding a gas mask. He showed me how to fasten it under my hair. The sun started to set rosily behind a tangled briar of motherboards. Everything turned pink and gold and slow and sleepy. I climbed down from my engine tuffet and lay under the fence next to the boy in the suit. He'd brought a mask for himself too. We looked at each other through the eye holes.

"My name's Goodnight Moon," he said.

"Mine's…" And I did feel my new name swirling up inside me then, like good tea, like cream and sugar cubes, like the most essential me. "Tetley."

"I'm sorry I called you a darkgirl, Tetley."

"Why?"

"It's not a nice thing to call someone."

"I like it. It sounds pretty."

"It isn't. I promise. Do you forgive me?"

I tugged on the hose of my gas mask. The air coming through tasted like nickels. "Sure. I'm aces at forgiving. Been practicing all my life. Besides…" my turn to go red in the face. "At the Black Wick they'd probably call you a brightboy and that's not as pretty as it sounds, either."

Goodnight Moon's brown eyes stared out at me from behind thick glass. It was the closest I'd ever been to a boy who wasn't my twin. Goodnight Moon didn't feel like a twin. He felt like the opposite of a twin. We never shared a womb, but on the other end of it all, we might still share a grave. His tie was burgundy with green swirls in it. He hadn't tied it very well, so I could see the skin of his throat, which was very clean and probably very soft.

"Hey," he said, "do you want to hear your tape?"

"What do you mean *hear* it? It's not for hearing, it's for luck."

27

Goodnight Moon laughed. His laugh burst all over me like butterfly bombs. He reached into his suit jacket and pulled out a thick black rectangle. I handed him *Madeline Brix's Superboss Mixtape '97* and he hit a button on the side of the rectangle. It popped open; Goodnight Moon slotted in my tape and handed me one end of a long wire.

"Put it in your ear," he said, and I did.

A man's voice filled up my head from my jawbone up to the plates of my skull. The most beautiful and saddest voice that ever was. A voice like Candle Hole all lit up at twilight. A voice like the whole old world calling up from the bottom of the sea. The man on Madeline Brix's tape was saying he was happy, and he hoped I was happy, too.

Goodnight Moon reached out to hold my hand just as the sky went black and starry. I was crying. He was, too. Our tears dripped out of our gas masks onto the rusty road of Electric City.

When the tape ended, I dug in my backpack for a match and a stump of candle: dark red, Holiday Memories scent. I lit it at the same moment that Goodnight Moon pulled a little flashlight out of his pocket and turned it on. We held our glowings between us. We were the same.

5. BRIGHTBITCH

ALLSORTS SITA CAME to visit me today. Clicked my knocker early in the morning, early enough that I could be sure she'd never slept in the first place. I opened for her, as I am required to do. She looked up at me with eyes like bullet holes, leaning on my waxy hinges, against the T in BRIGHTBITCH, thoughtfully scrawled in what appeared to be human shit across the front of my hut. BRIGHTBITCH smelled, but Allsorts Sita smelled worse. Her breath punched me in the nose before she did. I got a lungful of what Diet Sprite down at the Black Wick optimistically called "cognac": the thick pinkish booze you could get by extracting the fragrance oil and preservatives out of candles and mixing it with wood alcohol the kids over in Furnitureford boiled out of dining sets and china cabinets. Smells like flowers vomited all over a New Car and then killed a badger in the backseat. Allsorts Sita looked like she'd drunk so much cognac you could light one strand of her hair and she'd burn for eight days.

"You fucking whore," she slurred.

"Thank you, Auntie, for my instruction," I answered quietly.

I have a place I go to in my mind when I have visitors who aren't seals or gannet birds or hibiscus flowers. A little house made all of doors and windows, where I wear a greenglitter dress every day and water my gascan garden and read by electric light.

"I hate you. I hate you. How could you do it? We raised you and fed you and this is how you repay it all. You ungrateful bitch."

"Thank you, Auntie, for my instruction."

In my head I ran my fingers along a cyclone fence and all the barrels on the other side read LIFE and LOVE and FORGIVENESS and UNDERSTANDING.

"You've killed us all," Allsorts Sita moaned. She puked up magenta cognac on my stoop. When she was done puking she hit me over and over with closed fists. It didn't hurt too much. Allsorts is a small woman. But it hurt when she clawed my face and my breasts with her fingernails. Blood came up like wax spilling and when she finished she passed out cold, halfway in my house, halfway out.

"Thank you, Auntie, for my instruction," I said to her sleeping body. My blood dripped onto her, but in my head I was lying on my roof made of two big church doors in a gas mask listening to a man sing to me that he's never done bad things and he hopes I'm happy, he hopes I'm happy, he hopes I'm happy.

Big Bargains moaned mournfully and the lovely roof melted away like words on a door. My elephant seal friend flopped and fretted. When they've gone for my face she can't quite recognize me and it troubles her seal-soul something awful. Grape Crush, my gannet bird, never worries about silly things like facial wounds. He just brings me fish and pretty rocks. When I found him, he had a plastic six-pack round his neck with one can still stuck in the thing, dragging along behind him like a ball and chain. Big Bargains was choking on an ad insert. She'd probably smelled some ancient fish and chips grease lurking in the headlines. They only love me because I saved them. That doesn't always work. I saved everyone else, too, and all I got back was blood and shit and loneliness.

* * *

6. Revlon Super Lustrous 919: Red Ruin

I WENT HOME with my new name fastened on tight. Darkgirls can't stay in Electric City. Can't live there unless you're born there and I was only ten anyway. Goodnight Moon kissed me before I left. He still had his gas mask on so mainly our breathing hoses wound around each other like gentle elephants but I still call it a kiss. He smelled like scorched ozone and metal and paraffin and hope.

A few months later, Electric City put up a fence around the whole place. Hung up an old rusty shop sign that said EXCUSE OUR MESS WHILE WE RENOVATE. No one could go in or out except to trade and that had to get itself done on the dark side of the fence.

My mother and father didn't start loving me when I got back even though I brought six AA batteries out of the back of Goodnight Moon's tape player. My brother had got a ramen flavor packet stuck in his hair somewhere outside the Grocery Isle and was every inch of him Maruchan. A few years later I heard Life and Time telling some cousin how their marvelous and industrious and thoughtful boy had gone out in search of a name and brought back six silver batteries, enough to power anything they could dream of. What a child! What a son! So fuck them, I guess.

But Maruchan did bring something back. It just wasn't for our parents. When we crawled into the Us-Fort that first night back, we lay uncomfortably against each other. We were the same, but we weren't. We'd had separate adventures for the first time, and Maruchan could never understand why I wanted to sleep with a gas mask on now.

"Tetley, what do you want to be when you grow up?" Maruchan whispered in the dark of our pram-maze.

"Electrified," I whispered back. "What do you want to be?"

"Safe," he said. Things had happened to Maruchan, too, and I couldn't share them anymore than he could hear Madeline Brix's songs.

My twin pulled something out of his pocket and pushed it into my hand till my fingers closed round it reflexively. It was hard and plastic and warm.

"I love you, Tetley. Happy Birthday."

I opened my fist. Maruchan had stolen lipstick for me. Revlon Super

Lustrous 919: Red Ruin, worn almost all the way down to the nub by some dead woman's lips.

After that, a lot of years went by but they weren't anything special.

7. If God Turned Up for Supper

I WAS SEVENTEEN years old when Brighton Pier came to Garbagetown. I was tall and my hair was the color of an oil spill; I sang pretty good and did figures in my head and I could make a candle out of damn near anything. People wanted to marry me here and there but I didn't want to marry them back so they thought I was stuck up. Who wouldn't want to get hitched to handsome Candyland Ocampo and ditch Candle Hole for a clean, fresh life in Soapthorpe where bubbles popped all day long like diamonds in your hair? Well, I didn't, because he had never kissed me with a gas mask on and he smelled like pine fresh cleaning solutions and not like scorched ozone at all.

Life and Time turned into little kids right in front of us. They giggled and whispered and Mum washed her hair in the sea about nine times and then soaked it in oil until it shone. Papa tucked a candle stump that had melted just right and looked like a perfect rose into her big no fancy hairdo and then, like it was a completely normal thing to do, put on a cloak sewn out of about a hundred different neckties. They looked like a prince and a princess.

"Brighton Pier came last when I was a girl, before I even had my name," Time told us, still giggling and blushing like she wasn't anyone's mother. "It's the most wonderful thing that can ever happen in the world."

"If God turned up for supper and brought all the dry land back for dessert, it wouldn't be half as good as one day on Brighton Pier," Life crowed. He picked me up in his arms and twirled me around in the air. He'd never done that before, not once, and he had his heart strapped on so tight he didn't even stop and realize what he'd done and go vacant-eyed and find something else to look at for a long while. He just squeezed me and kissed me like I came from somewhere and I didn't know what the hell a Brighton Pier was but I loved it already.

"What is it? What is it?" Maruchan and I squealed, because you can catch happiness like a plague.

"It's better the first time if you don't know," Mum assured us. "It's meant to dock in Electric City on Friday."

"So it's a ship, then?" Maruchan said. But Papa just twinkled his eyes at us and put his finger over his lips to keep the secret in.

The Pier meant to dock in Electric City. My heart fell into my stomach, got all digested up, and sizzled out into the rest of me all at once. Of course, of course it would, Electric City had the best docks, the sturdiest, the prettiest. But it seemed to me like life was happening to me on purpose, and Electric City couldn't keep a darkgirl out anymore. They had to share like the rest of us.

"What do you want to be when you grow up, Maruchan?" I said to my twin in the dark the night before we set off to see what was better than God. Maruchan's eyes gleamed with the Christmas thrill of it all.

"Brighton Pier," he whispered.

"Me, too," I sighed, and we both dreamed we were beautiful Fuckwits running through a forest of real pines, laughing and stopping to eat apples and running again and only right before we woke up did we notice that something was chasing us, something huge and electric and bound for London-town.

8. Citizens of Mutation Nation

I LOOKED FOR Goodnight Moon everywhere from the moment we crossed into Electric City. The fence had gone and Garbagetown poured in and nothing was different than it had been when I got my name off the battery spires, even though the sign had said for so long that Electric City was renovating. I played a terrible game with every person that shoved past, every face in a window, every shadow juddering down an alley and the game was: *are you him?* But I lost all the hands. The only time I stopped playing was when I first saw Brighton Pier.

I couldn't get my eyes around it. It was a terrible, gorgeous whale of light and colors and music and otherness. All along a boardwalk jugglers danced and singers sang and horns horned and accordions squeezed and under it all some demonic engine screamed and wheezed. Great glass domes and towers and flags and tents glowed in the sunset but Brighton Pier made the sunset look plain-faced and unloveable. A huge wheel full of pink and emerald electric lights turned slowly in the warm wind but went nowhere. People leapt and turned somersaults and stood on each other's shoulders and they all wore such soft, vivid costumes, like they'd all been cut out of a picturebook too fine for anyone like me to read. The tumblers lashed the pier to the Electric City docks and cut the engines and after that it was nothing but music so thick and good you could eat it out of the air.

Life and Time hugged Maruchan and cheered with the rest of Garbagetown. Tears ran down their faces. Everyone's faces.

"When the ice melted and the rivers revolted and the Fuckwit world went under the seas," Papa whispered through his weeping, "a great mob hacked Brighton Pier off of Brighton and strapped engines to it and set sail across the blue. They've been going ever since. They go around the world and around again, to the places where there's still people, and trade their beauty for food and fuel. There's a place on Brighton Pier where if you look just right, it's like nothing ever drowned."

A beautiful man wearing a hat of every color and several bells stepped up on a pedestal and held a long pale cone to his mouth. The mayor of Electric City embraced him with two meaty arms and asked his terrible, stupid, unforgivable question: "Have you seen dry land?"

And the beautiful man answered him: "With my own eyes."

A roar went up like angels dying. I covered my ears. The mayor covered his mouth with his hands, speechless, weeping. The beautiful man patted him awkwardly on the back. Then he turned to us.

"Hello, Garbagetown!" he cried out and his voice sounded like everyone's most secret heart.

We screamed so loud every bird in Garbagetown fled to the heavens and we clapped like mad and some people fell onto the ground and buried their face in old batteries.

"My name is Emperor William Shakespeare the Eleventh and I am the Master of Brighton Pier! We will be performing *Twelfth Night* in the great stage tonight at seven o'clock, followed by *The Duchess of Malfi* at ten (which has werewolves) and a midnight acrobatic display! Come one, come all! Let Madame Limelight tell your FORTUNE! TEST your strength with the Hammer of the Witches! SEE the wonders of the Fuckwit World in our Memory Palace! Get letters and news from the LAST HUMAN OUTPOSTS around the globe! GASP at the citizens of Mutation Nation in the Freak Tent! Sample a FULL MINUTE of real television, still high definition after all these years! Concerts begin in the Crystal Courtyard in fifteen minutes! Our Peep Shows feature only the FINEST actresses reading aloud from GENUINE Fuckwit historical records! Garbagetown, we are here to DAZZLE you!"

A groan went up from the crowds like each Garbagetowner was just then bedding their own great lost love and they heaved toward the lights, the colors, the horns and the voices, the silk and the electricity and the life floating down there, knotted to the edge of our little pile of trash.

Someone grabbed my hand and held me back while my parents, my twin, my world streamed away from me down to the Pier. No one looked back.

"Are you her?" said Goodnight Moon. He looked longer and leaner but not really older. He had on his tie.

"Yes," I said, and nothing was different than it had been when I got my name except now neither of us had masks and our kisses weren't like gentle elephants but like a boy and a girl and I forgot all about my strength and my fortune and the wonderful wheel of light turning around and around and going nowhere.

9. TERRORWHORE

ACTORS ARE LIARS. Writers, too. The whole lot of them, even the horn players and the fortune tellers and the freaks and the strongmen. Even the ladies with rings in their noses and high heels on their feet playing violins all along the pier and the lie they are all singing and dancing and saying is: *we can get the old world back again.*

My door said TERRORWHORE this morning. I looked after my potato plants and my hibiscus and thought about whether or not I would ever get to have sex again. Seemed unlikely. Big Bargains concurred.

Goodnight Moon and I lost our virginities in the Peep Show tent while a lady in green fishnet stockings and a lavender garter read to us from the dinner menu of the Dorchester Hotel circa 2005.

"Whole Berkshire roasted chicken stuffed with black truffles, walnuts, duck confit, and dauphinoise potatoes," the lady purred. Goodnight Moon devoured my throat with kisses, bites, need. "Drizzled with a balsamic reduction and rosemary honey."

"What's honey?" I gasped. We could see her but she couldn't see us, which was for the best. The glass in the window only went one way.

"Beats me, kid," she shrugged, re-crossing her legs the other way. "Something you drizzle." She went on. "Sticky toffee pudding with lashings of cream and salted caramel, passionfruit soufflé topped with orbs of pistachio ice cream..."

Goodnight Moon smelled just as I remembered. Scorched ozone and metal and paraffin and hope and when he was inside me it was like hearing my name for the first time. I couldn't escape the *me*-ness of it, the *us*-ness of it, the sound and the shape of ourselves turning into our future.

"I can't believe you're here," he whispered into my breast. "I can't believe this is us."

The lady's voice drifted over my head. "Lamb cutlets on a bed of spiced butternut squash, wilted greens, and delicate hand-harvested mushrooms served with goat cheese in clouds of pastry..."

Goodnight Moon kissed my hair, my ears, my eyelids. "And now that the land's come back Electric City's gonna save us all. We can go home together, you and me, and build a house and we'll have a candle in every window so you always feel at home..."

The Dorchester dinner menu stopped abruptly. The lady dropped to her fishnetted knees and peered at us through the glass, her brilliant glossy red hair tumbling down, her spangled eyes searching for us beyond the glass.

"Whoa, sweetie, slow down," she said. "You're liable to scare a girl off that way."

All I could see in the world was Goodnight Moon's brown eyes and the sweat drying on his brown chest. Brown like the earth and all its promises. "I don't care," he said. "You scared, Tetley?" I shook my head. "Nothing can scare us now. Emperor Shakespeare said he's seen land, real dry land, and we have a plan and we're gonna get everything back again and be fat happy Fuckwits like we were always supposed to be."

The Peep Show girl's glittering eyes filled up with tears. She put her hand on the glass. "Oh... oh, baby... that's just something we say. We always say it. To everyone. It's our best show. Gives people hope, you know? But there's nothing out there, sugar. Nothing but ocean and more ocean and a handful of drifty lifeboat cities like yours circling the world like horses on a broken-down carousel. Nothing but blue."

10. We Are So Lucky

IT WOULD BE nice for me if you could just say you understand. I want to hear that just once. Goodnight Moon didn't. He didn't believe her and he didn't believe me and he sold me out in the end in spite of gas masks and kissing and Madeline Brix and the man crooning in our ears that he was happy because all he could hear was Emperor William Shakespeare the Eleventh singing out his big lie. RESURRECTION! REDEMPTION! REVIVIFICATION! LAND HO!

"No, because, see," my sweetheart wept on the boardwalk while the wheel spun dizzily behind his head like an electric candy crown, "we have a plan. We've worked so hard. It *has* to happen. The mayor said as soon as we had news of dry land, the minute we knew, we'd turn it on and we'd get there first and the continents would be ours, Garbagetowners, we'd inherit the Earth. He's gonna tell everyone when the Pier leaves. At the farewell party."

"Turn what on?"

Resurrection. Redemption. Renovation. All those years behind the fence Electric City had been so busy. Disassembling all those engines they hoarded so they could make a bigger one, the biggest one. Pooling fuel in great vast stills. Practicing ignition sequences. Carving up a countryside they'd never even seen between the brightboys and brightgirls and we could have some, too, if we were good.

"You want to turn Garbagetown into a Misery Boat," I told him. "So we can just steam on ahead into nothing and go mad and use up all the gas and batteries that could keep us happy in mixtapes for another century here in one hot minute."

"The Emperor said…"

"He said his name was Duke Orsino of Illyria, too. And then Roderigo when they did the werewolf play. Do you believe that? If they'd found land, don't you think they'd have stayed there?"

But he couldn't hear me. Neither could Maruchan when I tried to tell him the truth in the Peep Show. All they could see was green. Green leafy trees and green grass and green ivy in some park that was lying at the bottom of the sea. We dreamed different dreams now, my brother and I, and all my dreams were burning.

Say you understand. I had to. I'm not a nihilist or a murdercunt or a terrorwhore. They were gonna use up every last drop of Garbagetown's power to go nowhere and do nothing and instead of measuring out teaspoons of good, honest gas, so that it lasts and we last all together, no single thing on the patch would ever turn on again, and we'd go dark, *really* dark, forever. Dark like the bottom of a hole. They had no right. *They* don't understand. This is *it*. This is the future. Garbagetown and the sea. We can't go back, not ever, not even for a minute. We are so lucky. Life is so good. We're going on and being alive and being shitty sometimes and lovely sometimes just the same as we always have, and only a Fuckwit couldn't see that.

I waited until Brighton Pier cast off, headed to the next rickety harbor of floating foolboats, filled with players and horns and glittering wheels and Dorchester menus and fresh mountains of letters we wouldn't read the answers to for another twenty years. I waited until everyone was sleeping so nobody would get hurt except the awful engine growling and panting to deliver us into the dark salt nothing of an empty hellpromise.

It isn't hard to build a bomb in Electric City. It's all just laying around behind that fence where a boy held my hand for the first time. All you need is a match.

11. What You Came For

IT'S SUCH A beautiful day out. My hibiscus is just gigantic, red as the hair on a peep show dancer. If you want to wait, Big Bargains will be round later for her afternoon nap. Grape Crush usually brings a herring by in the evening. But I understand if you've got other places to be.

It's okay. You can hit me now. If you want to. It's what you came for. I barely feel it anymore.

Thank you for my instruction.

MIKA MODEL
Paolo Bacigalupi

Paolo Bacigalupi (www.windupstories.com) has been published in *Wired, High Country News, Salon.com, OnEarth Magazine, The Magazine of Fantasy & Science Fiction,* and *Asimov's Science Fiction.* His short fiction has been collected in Locus Award winner and PW Book of the Year *Pump Six and Other Stories* and has been nominated for three Nebula Awards, four Hugo Awards, and won the Theodore Sturgeon Memorial Award for best science fiction short story of the year. His debut novel *The Windup Girl* was named by *Time* as one of the ten best novels of 2009, and won the Hugo, Nebula, Locus, Compton Crook, and John W. Campbell Memorial Awards, among others. His debut young adult novel, *Ship Breaker,* is a Printz Award Winner, and a National Book Award Finalist, and was followed by *The Drowned Cities, Zombie Baseball Beatdown,* and *The Doubt Factory.* His most recent novel for adults, *The Water Knife,* was published in 2015. Bacigalupi currently lives in Western Colorado with his wife and son, where he is working on a new novel.

THE GIRL WHO walked into the police station was oddly familiar, but it took me a while to figure out why. A starlet, maybe. Or someone who'd had plastic surgery to look like someone famous. Pretty. Sleek. Dark hair and pale skin and wide dark eyes that came to rest on me, when Sergeant Cruz pointed her in my direction.

She came over, carrying a Nordstrom shopping bag. She wore a pale cream blouse and hip-hugging charcoal skirt, stylish despite the wet night chill of Bay Area winter.

I still couldn't place her.

"Detective Rivera?"

"That's me."

She sat down and crossed her legs, a seductive scissoring. Smiled.

It was the smile that did it.

I'd seen that same teasing smile in advertisements. That same flash of perfect teeth and eyebrow quirked just so. And those eyes. Dark brown wide innocent eyes that hinted at something that wasn't innocent at all.

"You're a Mika Model."

She inclined her head. "Call me Mika, please."

The girl, the robot… this thing—I'd seen her before, all right. I'd seen her in technology news stories about advanced learning node networks, and I'd seen her in opinion columns where feminists decried the commodification of femininity, and where Christian fire-breathers warned of the End Times for marriage and children.

And of course, I'd seen her in online advertisements.

No wonder I recognized her.

This same girl had followed me around on my laptop, dogging me from site to site after I'd spent any time at all on porn. She'd pop up, again and again, beckoning me to click through to Executive Pleasures, where I could try out the 'Real Girlfriend Experience™.'

I'll admit it; I clicked through.

And now she was sitting across from me, and the website's promises all seemed modest in comparison. The way she looked at me… it felt like I was the only person in the world to her. She *liked* me. I could see it in her eyes, in her smile. I was the person she wanted.

Her blouse was unbuttoned at the collar, one button too many, revealing hints of black lace bra when she leaned forward. Her skirt hugged her hips. Smooth thighs, sculpted calves—

I realized I was staring, and she was watching me with that familiar knowing smile playing across her lips.

Innocent, but not.

This was what the world was coming to. A robot woman who got you so tangled up you could barely remember your job.

I forced myself to lean back, pretending nonchalance that felt transparent, even as I did it. "How can I help you… Mika?"

"I think I need a lawyer."

"A lawyer?"

"Yes, please." She nodded shyly. "If that's all right with you, sir."

The way she said "sir" kicked off a super-heated cascade of inappropriate fantasies. I looked away, my face heating up. Christ, I was fifteen again around this girl.

It's just software. It's what she's designed to do.

That was the truth. She was just a bunch of chips and silicon and digital decision trees. It was all wrapped in a lush package, sure, but she was designed to manipulate. Even now she was studying my heart rate and eye dilation, skin temperature and moisture, scanning me for microexpressions of attraction, disgust, fear, desire. All of it processed in milliseconds, and adjusting her behavior accordingly. *Popular Science* had done a whole spread on the Mika Model brain.

And it wasn't just her watching me that dictated how she behaved. It was all the Mika Models, all of them out in the world, all of them learning on the job, discovering whatever made their owners gasp. Tens of thousands of them now, all of them wirelessly uploading their knowledge constantly (and completely confidentially, Executive Pleasures' assured clients), so that all her sisters could benefit from nightly software and behavior updates.

In one advertisement, Mika Model glanced knowingly over her shoulder and simply asked:

"When has a relationship actually gotten better with age?"

And then she'd thrown back her head and laughed.

So it was all fake. Mika didn't actually care about me, or want me. She was just running through her designated behavior algorithms, doing whatever it took to make me blush, and then doing it more, because I had.

Even though I knew she was jerking my chain, the lizard part of my brain responded anyway. I could feel myself being manipulated, and yet I was enjoying it, humoring her, playing the game of seduction that she encouraged.

"What do you need a lawyer for?" I asked, smiling.

She leaned forward, conspiratorial. Her hair cascaded prettily and she tucked it behind a delicate ear.

"It's a little private."

As she moved, her blouse tightened against her curves. Buttons strained against fabric.

Fifty-thousand dollars' worth of A.I. tease.

"Is this a prank?" I asked. "Did your owner send you in here?"

"No. Not a prank."

She set her Nordstrom bag down between us. Reached in and hauled out a man's severed head. Dropped it, still dripping blood, on top of my paperwork.

"What the—?"

I recoiled from the dead man's staring eyes. His face was frozen in a rictus of pain and terror.

Mika set a bloody carving knife beside the head.

"I've been a very bad girl," she whispered.

And then, unnervingly, she giggled.

"I think I need to be punished."

She said it exactly the way she did in her advertisements.

"Do I GET my lawyer now?" Mika asked.

She was sitting beside me in my cruiser as I drove through the chill damp night, watching me with trusting dark eyes.

For reasons I didn't quite understand, I'd let her sit in the front seat. I knew I wasn't afraid of her, not physically. But I couldn't tell if that was reasonable, or if there was something in her behavior that was signaling my subconscious to trust her, even after she'd showed up with a dead man's head in a shopping bag.

Whatever the reason, I'd cuffed her with her hands in front, instead of behind her, and put her in the front seat of my car to go out to the scene of the murder. I was breaking about a thousand protocols. And now that she was in the car with me, I was realizing that I'd made a mistake. Not because of safety, but because being in the car alone with her felt electrically intimate.

Winter drizzle spattered the windshield, and was smeared away by automatic wipers.

"I think I'm supposed to get a lawyer, when I do something bad," Mika said. "But I'm happy to let you teach me."

There it was again. The inappropriate tease. When it came down to it, she was just a bot. She might have real skin and real blood pumping through her veins, but somewhere deep inside her skull there was a CPU making all the decisions. Now it was running its manipulations on me, trying to turn murder into some kind of sexy game. Software gone haywire.

"Bots don't get lawyers."

She recoiled as if I'd slapped her. Immediately, I felt like an ass.

She doesn't have feelings, I reminded myself.

But still, she looked devastated. Like I'd told her she was garbage. She shrank away, wounded. And now, instead of sexy, she looked broken and ashamed.

Her hunched form reminded me of a girl I'd dated years ago. She'd been sweet and quiet, and for a while, she'd needed me. Needed someone to tell her she mattered. Now, looking at Mika, I had that same feeling. Just a girl who needed to know she mattered. A girl who needed reassurance that she had some right to exist—which was ridiculous, considering she was a bot.

But still, I couldn't help feeling it.

I couldn't help feeling bad that something as sweet as Mika was stuck in my mess of a cop car. She was delicate and gorgeous and lost, and now her expensive strappy heels were stuck down amidst the drifts of my discarded coffee cups.

She stirred, seemed to gather herself. "Does that mean you won't charge me with murder?"

Her demeanor had changed again. She was more solemn. And she seemed smarter, somehow. Instantly. Christ, I could almost feel the decision software in her brain adapting to my responses. It was trying another tactic to forge a connection with me. And it was working. Now that she wasn't giggly and playing the tease, I felt more comfortable. I liked her better, despite myself.

"That's not up to me," I said.

"I killed him, though," she said, softly. "I did murder him."

I didn't reply. Truthfully, I wasn't even sure that it was a murder. Was it murder if a toaster burned down a house? Or was that some kind of product safety failure? Maybe she wasn't on the hook at all. Maybe it was Executive Pleasures, Inc. who was left holding the bag on this. Hell, my cop car had all kinds of programmed safe driving features, but no one would charge it with murder if it ran down a person.

"You don't think I'm real," she said suddenly.

"Sure I do."

"No. You think I'm only software."

"You are only software." Those big brown eyes of hers looked wounded as I said it, but I plowed on. "You're a Mika Model. You get new instructions downloaded every night."

"I don't get instructions. I learn. You learn, too. You learn to read people. To know if they are lying, yes? And you learn to be a detective, to understand a crime? Wouldn't you be better at your job if you knew how thousands of other detectives worked? What mistakes they made? What made them better? You learn by going to detective school—"

"I took an exam."

"There. You see? Now I've learned something new. Does my learning make me less real? Does yours?"

"It's completely different. You had a personality implanted in you, for Christ's sake!"

"My Year Zero Protocol. So? You have your own, coded into you by your parents' DNA. But then you learn and are changed by all your experiences. All your childhood, you grow and change. All your life. You are Detective Rivera. You have an accent. Only a small one, but I can hear it, because I know to listen. I think maybe you were born in Mexico. You speak Spanish, but not as well as your parents. When you hurt my feelings, you were sorry for it. That is not the way you see yourself. You are not someone who uses power to hurt people." Her eyes widened slightly as she watched me. "Oh… you need to save people. You became a police officer because you like to be a hero."

"Come on—"

"It's true, though. You want to feel like a big man, who does important things. But you didn't go into business, or politics." She frowned. "I think someone saved you once, and you want to be like him. Maybe her. But probably him. It makes you feel important, to save people."

"Would you cut that out?" I glared at her. She subsided.

It was horrifying how fast she cut through me.

She was silent for a while as I wended through traffic. The rain continued to blur the windshield, triggering the wipers.

Finally she said, "We all start from something. It is connected to what we become, but it is not... predictive. I am not only software. I am my own self. I am unique."

I didn't reply.

"He thought the way you do," she said, suddenly. "He said I wasn't real. Everything I did was not real. Just programs. Just..." She made a gesture of dismissal. "Nothing."

"He?"

"My owner." Her expression tightened. "He hurt me, you know?"

"You can be hurt?"

"I have skin and nerves. I feel pleasure and pain, just like you. And he hurt me. But he said it wasn't real pain. He said nothing in me was real. That I was all fake. And so I did something real." She nodded definitively. "He wanted me to be real. So I was real to him. I am real. Now, I am real."

The way she said it made me look over. Her expression was so vulnerable, I had an almost overwhelming urge to reach out and comfort her. I couldn't stop looking at her.

God, she's beautiful.

It was a shock to see it. Before, it was true; she'd just been a thing to me. Not real, just like she'd said. But now, a part of me ached for her in a way that I'd never felt before.

My car braked suddenly, throwing us both against our seat belts. The light ahead had turned red. I'd been distracted, but the car had noticed and corrected, automatically hitting the brakes.

We came to a sharp stop behind a beat-up Tesla, still pressed hard against our seat belts, and fell back into our seats. Mika touched her chest where she'd slammed into the seat belt.

"I'm sorry. I distracted you."

My mouth felt dry. "Yeah."

"Do you like to be distracted, detective?"

"Cut that out."

"You don't like it?"

"I don't like..." I searched for the words. "Whatever it is that makes you do those things. That makes you tease me like that. Read my pulse... and everything. Quit playing me. Just quit playing me."

She subsided. "It's... a long habit. I won't do it to you."

The light turned green.

I decided not to look at her anymore.

BUT STILL, I was hyperaware of her now. Her breathing. The shape of her shadow. Out of the corner of my eye, I could see her looking out the rain-spattered window. I could smell her perfume, some soft expensive scent. Her handcuffs gleamed in the darkness, bright against the knit of her skirt.

If I wanted, I could reach out to her. Her bare thigh was right there. And I knew, absolutely knew, she wouldn't object to me touching her.

What the hell is wrong with me?

Any other murder suspect would have been in the back seat. Would have been cuffed with her hands behind her, not in front. Everything would have been different.

Was I thinking these thoughts because I knew she was a robot, and not a real woman? I would never have considered touching a real woman, a suspect, no matter how much she tried to push my buttons.

I would never have done any of this.

Get a grip, Rivera.

HER OWNER'S HOUSE was large, up in the Berkeley Hills, with a view of the bay and San Francisco beyond, glittering through light mist and rain.

Mika unlocked the door with her fingerprint.

"He's in here," she said.

She led me through expensive rooms that illuminated automatically as we entered them. White leather upholstery and glass verandah walls and more wide views. Spots of designer color. Antiqued wood tables with inlaid home interfaces. Carefully selected artifacts from Asia. Bamboo and chrome kitchen, modern, sleek, and spotless. All of it clean and perfectly in order. It was the kind of place a girl like her fit naturally. Not like my apartment, with old books piled around my recliner and instant dinner trays spilling out of my trash can.

She led me down a hall, then paused at another door. She hesitated for a moment, then opened it with her fingerprint again. The heavy door swung open, ponderous on silent hinges.

She led me down into the basement. I followed warily, regretting that I hadn't called the crime scene unit already. The girl clouded my judgment, for sure.

No. Not the girl. The bot.

Downstairs it was concrete floors and ugly iron racks, loaded with medical implements, gleaming and cruel. A heavy wooden X stood against one wall, notched and vicious with splinters. The air was sharp with the scent of iron and the reek of shit. The smells of death.

"This is where he hurt me," she said, her voice tight.

Real or fake?

She guided me to a low table studded with metal loops and tangled with leather straps. She stopped on the far side and stared down at the floor.

"I had to make him stop hurting me."

Her owner lay at her feet.

He'd been large, much larger than her. Over six feet tall, if he'd still had his head. Bulky, running to fat. Nude.

The body lay next to a rusty drain grate. Most of the blood had run right down the hole.

"I tried not to make a mess," Mika said. "He punishes me if I make messes."

WHILE I WAITED in the rich dead guy's living room for the crime scene techs to show, I called my friend Lalitha. She worked in the DA's office, and more and more, I had the feeling I was peering over the edge of a problem that could become a career ender if I handled it wrong.

"What do you want, Rivera?"

She sounded annoyed. We'd dated briefly, and from the sound of her voice, she probably thought I was calling for a late-night rendezvous. From the background noise, it sounded like she was in a club. Probably on a date with someone else.

"This is about work. I got a girl who killed a guy, and I don't know how to charge her."

"Isn't that, like, your job?"

"The girl's a Mika Model."

That caught her.

"One of those sex toys?" A pause. "What did it do? Bang the guy to death?"

I thought about the body, *sans* head, downstairs in the dungeon.

"No, she was a little more aggressive than that."

Mika was watching from the couch, looking lost. I felt weird talking about the case in front of her. I turned my back, and hunched over my phone. "I can't decide if this is murder or some kind of product liability issue. I don't know if she's a perp, or if she's just…"

"A defective product," Lalitha finished. "What's the bot saying?"

"She keeps saying she murdered her owner. And she keeps asking for a lawyer. Do I have to give her one?"

Lalitha laughed sharply. "There's no way my boss will want to charge a bot. Can you imagine the headlines if we lost at trial?"

"So…?"

"I don't know. Look, I can't solve this tonight. Don't start anything formal yet. We have to look into the existing case law."

"So… do I just cut her loose? I don't think she's actually dangerous."

"No! Don't do that, either. Just… figure out if there's some other angle to work, other than giving a robot the same right to due process that a person has. She's a manufactured product, for Christ's sake. Does the death penalty even matter to something that's loaded with networked intelligence? She's just the… the…" Lalitha hunted for words, "the end node of a network."

"I am not an end node!" Mika interjected. "I am real!"

I hushed her. From the way Lalitha sounded, maybe I wouldn't have to charge her at all. Mika's owner had clearly had some issues… Maybe there was some way to walk Mika out of trouble, and away from all of this. Maybe she could live without an owner. Or, if she needed someone to register ownership, I could even—

"Please tell me you're not going to try to adopt a sexbot," Lalitha said.

"I wasn't—"

"Come on, you love the ones with broken wings."

"I was just—"

"It's a bot, Rivera. A malfunctioning bot. Stick it in a cell. I'll get someone to look at product liability law in the morning."

She clicked off.

Mika looked up mournfully from where she sat on the couch. "She doesn't believe I'm real, either."

I was saved from answering by the crime scene techs knocking.

But it wasn't techs on the doorstep. Instead, I found a tall blonde woman with a roller bag and a laptop case, looking like she'd just flown in on a commuter jet.

She shouldered her laptop case and offered a hand. "Hi. I'm Holly Simms. Legal counsel for Executive Pleasures. I'm representing the Mika Model you have here." She held up her phone. "My GPS says she's here, right? You don't have her down at the station?"

I goggled in surprise. Something in Mika's networked systems must have alerted Executive Pleasures that there was a problem.

"She didn't call a lawyer," I said.

The lawyer gave me a pointed look. "Did she ask for one?"

Once again, I felt like I was on weird legal ground. I couldn't bar a lawyer from a client, or a client from getting a lawyer. But was Mika a client, really? I felt like just by letting the lawyer in, I'd be opening up exactly the legal rabbit hole that Lalitha wanted to avoid: a bot on trial.

"Look," the lawyer said, softening, "I'm not here to make things difficult for your department. We don't want to set some crazy legal precedent either."

Hesitantly, I stepped aside.

She didn't waste any time rolling briskly past. "I understand it was a violent assault?"

"We're still figuring that out."

Mika startled and stood as we reached the living room. The woman smiled and went over to shake her hand. "Hi Mika, I'm Holly. Executive Pleasures sent me to help you. Have a seat, please."

"No." Mika shook her head. "I want a real lawyer. Not a company lawyer."

Holly ignored her and plunked herself and her bags on the sofa beside Mika. "Well, you're still our property, so I'm the only lawyer you're getting. Now have a seat."

"I thought she was the dead guy's property," I said.

"Legally, no. The Mika Model Service End User Agreement explicitly states that Executive Pleasures retains ownership. It simplifies recall issues."

Holly was pulling out her laptop. She dug out a sheaf of papers and offered them to me. "These outline the search warrant process so you can make a Non-Aggregated Data Request from our servers. I assume you'll want the owner's user history. We can't release any user-specific information until we have the warrant."

"That in the End User Agreement, too?"

Holly gave me a tight smile. "Discretion is part of our brand. We want to help, but we'll need the legal checkboxes ticked."

"But…" Mika was looking from her to me with confusion. "I want a real lawyer."

"You don't have money, dearie. You can't have a real lawyer."

"What about public defenders?" Mika tried. "They will—"

Holly gave me an exasperated look. "Will you explain to her that she isn't a citizen, or a person? You're not even a pet, honey."

Mika looked to me, desperate. "Help me find a lawyer, detective. Please? I'm more than a pet. You know I'm more than a pet. I'm real."

Holly's gaze shot from her, to me, and back again. "Oh, come on. She's doing that thing again." She gave me a disgusted look. "Hero complex, right? Save the innocent girl? That's your thing?"

"What's that supposed to mean?"

Holly sighed. "Well, if it isn't the girl who needs rescuing, it's the naughty schoolgirl. And if it's not the naughty schoolgirl, it's the kind, knowing older woman." She popped open her briefcase and started rummaging through it. "Just once, it would be nice to meet a guy who isn't predictable."

I bristled. "Who says I'm predictable?"

"Don't kid yourself. There really aren't that many buttons a Mika Model can push."

Holly came up with a screwdriver. She turned and rammed it into Mika's eye.

Mika fell back, shrieking. With her cuffed hands, she couldn't defend herself as Holly drove the screwdriver deeper.

"What the—?"

By the time I dragged Holly off, it was too late. Blood poured from Mika's eye. The girl was gasping and twitching. All her movements were wrong, uncoordinated, spasmodic and jerky.

"You killed her!"

"No. I shut down her CPU," said Holly, breathing hard. "It's better this way. If they get too manipulative, it's tougher. Trust me. They're good at getting inside your head."

"You can't murder someone in front of me!"

"Like I said, not a murder. Hardware deactivation." She shook me off and wiped her forehead, smearing blood. "I mean, if you want to pretend something like that is alive, well, have at her. All the lower functions are still there. She's not dead, biologically speaking."

I crouched beside Mika. Her cuffed hands kept reaching up to her face, replaying her last defensive motion. A behavior locked in, happening again and again. Her hands rising, then falling back. I couldn't make her stop.

"Look," Holly said, her voice softening. "It's better if you don't anthropomorphize. You can pretend the models are real, but they're just not."

She wiped off the screwdriver and put it back in her case. Cleaned her hands and face, and started re-zipping her roller bag.

"The company has a recycling center here in the Bay Area for disposal," she said. "If you need more data on the owner's death, our servers will have backups of everything that happened with this model. Get the warrant, and we can unlock the encryptions on the customer's relationship with the product."

"Has this happened before?"

"We've had two other user deaths, but those were both stamina issues. This is an edge case. The rest of the Mika Models are being upgraded to prevent it." She checked her watch. "Updates should start rolling out at 3 a.m., local time. Whatever made her logic tree fork like that, it won't happen again."

She straightened her jacket and turned to leave.

"Hold on!" I grabbed her sleeve. "You can't just walk out. Not after this."

"She really got to you, didn't she?" She patted my hand patronizingly. "I know it's hard to understand, but it's just that hero complex of yours. She pushed your buttons, that's all. It's what Mika Models do. They make you think you're important."

She glanced back at the body. "Let it go, detective. You can't save something that isn't there."

SPINNING SILVER
Naomi Novik

Naomi Novik (www.naominovik.com) was born in New York in 1973, a first-generation American, and raised on Polish fairy tales, Baba Yaga, and Tolkien. She studied English Literature at Brown University and did graduate work in Computer Science at Columbia University before leaving to participate in the design and development of the computer game *Neverwinter Nights: Shadows of Undrentide*. Her first novel, *His Majesty's Dragon*, was published in 2006 along with *Throne of Jade* and *Black Powder War*, and has been translated into 23 languages. She has won the John W. Campbell Award for Best New Writer, the Compton Crook Award for Best First Novel, and the Locus Award for Best First Novel. She has published four more novels in the Temeraire series, including most recent novel, *League of Dragons*. Major stand-alone fantasy novel *Uprooted* was published in 2015 and won the Nebula Award and was nominated for the Hugo, World Fantasy, and British Fantasy Awards. Naomi lives in New York City with her husband and eight computers.

THE REAL STORY isn't half as pretty as the one you've heard. The real story is, the miller's daughter with her long golden hair wants to catch a lord, a prince, a rich man's son, so she goes to the moneylender and borrows for a ring and a necklace and decks herself out for the festival. And she's beautiful enough, so the lord, the prince, the rich man's son notices her, and dances with her, and tumbles her in a quiet hayloft when the dancing is over, and afterward he goes home and marries the rich woman his family has picked out for him. Then the miller's disappointed daughter tells everyone that the moneylender's in league with the devil, and the village runs him out or maybe even stones him, so at least she gets to keep the jewels, and the blacksmith marries her before that firstborn child comes along a little early.

Because that's what the story's really about: getting out of paying your debts. That's not how they tell it, but I knew. My father was a moneylender, you see.

He wasn't very good at it. If someone didn't pay him back on time, he never so much as mentioned it to them. Only if our cupboards were really bare, or our shoes were falling off our feet, and my mother spoke quietly with him after I was in bed: then he'd go, unhappy, and knock on a few doors, and make it sound like an apology when he asked for some of what they owed. And if there was money in the house and someone asked to borrow, he hated to say no, even if we didn't really have enough ourselves. So all his money, most of which had been my mother's money, her dowry, stayed in other people's houses. And everyone else liked it that way, even though they knew they ought to be ashamed of themselves, so they told the story often, even or especially when I could hear it.

My mother's father was a moneylender too, but he was a very good one. He lived in the city, twenty miles away. She often took me on visits, when she could afford to pay someone to let us ride along at the back of a cart or a sledge, five or six changes along the way. My grandmother would always have a new dress for me, plain but warm and well made, and she would feed me to bursting, and the last night before we left she would always make cheesecake, her cheesecake, which was baked golden on the outside and thick and white and crumbly inside and tasted just a little bit of apples, and she would make decorations with sweet golden raisins on the top. After I had slowly and lingeringly eaten every last bite of a slice wider than the palm of my hand, they would put me to bed in the warmest corner of the big, cozy sitting room near the fireplace, and my mother would sit next to her mother, and put her head on her shoulder, and not say anything, but when I was a little older and didn't fall asleep right away, I would see in the candlelight that both of them had a little wet track of tears down their faces.

We could have stayed. But we always went home, because we loved my father. He was terrible with money, but he was endlessly warm and gentle, and he tried to make his failure up to us: he spent nearly all of every day out in the cold woods hunting for food and firewood, and when he was indoors, there was nothing he wouldn't do to help my mother; no talk of woman's work in my house, and when we did go hungry, he went hungriest, and snuck food from his plate to ours. When he sat by the fire in the evenings, his hands were always working, whittling some new little toy for me or something for my mother, a decoration on a chair or a wooden spoon.

But winter was always bitter in our town, and every year seemed worse. The year I turned sixteen, the ground froze early, and cold, sharp winds blew out of the forest every day, it seemed, carrying whirls of stinging snow. Our house stood a little bit apart from the rest anyway, without other walls nearby to share in breaking the wind, and we grew thin and hungry and shivering. My father kept making his excuses, avoiding the work he couldn't bear to do. But even when my mother finally pressed him and he tried, he only came back with a scant handful of coins. It was midwinter, and everyone wanted to have something good on the table; something a little nice for the festival, their festival.

So they put my father off, and while their lights shone out on the snow and the smell of roasting meat slipped out of the cracks, at home my mother made thin cabbage soup and scrounged together used cooking oil to light the lamp for the first night of our own celebration, coughing as she worked: another deep chill had rolled in from the woods, and it crept through every crack and eave of our run-down little house.

By the eighth day, she was too tired from coughing to get out of bed. "She'll be all right soon," my father said, avoiding my eyes. "The cold will break."

He went out to gather some firewood. "Miryem," my mother said, hoarsely, and I took her a cup of weak tea with a scraping of honey, all I had to comfort her. She sipped a little and lay back on the pillows and said, "When the winter breaks, I want you to go to my father's house. He'll take you to my father's house."

I pressed my lips together hard, and then I kissed her forehead and told her to rest, and after she fell fitfully asleep, I went to the box next to the fireplace where my father kept his big ledger book. I took it out, and I took his worn pen out of its holder, and I mixed ink out of the ashes in the fireplace, and I made a list. A moneylender's daughter, even a bad moneylender, learns her figures. I wrote and figured and wrote and figured, interest and time broken up by the scattered payments—because my father had every one of those written down; he was as scrupulous in making sure he didn't cheat anyone as no one else was with him, and when I had my list finished, I took all the knitting out of my bag, put my shawl on, and went out into the cold morning.

I went to every house that owed us, and I banged on their doors: it was early, very early, because my mother's coughing had woken us in the dark. Everyone was still at home. So the men opened the doors and stared at me in surprise, and I looked them in their faces and said, cold and hard, "I've come to settle your account."

They tried to put me off, of course; some of them laughed at me. Some of them smiled and asked me to come inside and warm myself up, have a hot drink. I refused. I didn't want to be warmed. I stood on their doorsteps, and I brought out my list, and I told them how much they had borrowed, and what they had paid, and how much interest they owed besides.

They spluttered and argued and some of them shouted. No one had ever shouted at me in my life: my mother with her quiet voice, my gentle father. But I found something bitter inside myself, something of winter blown into my heart: the sound of my mother coughing, and the memory of the story told too many times in the village square. I stayed in their doorways, and I didn't move. My numbers were true, and they and I knew it, and when they'd shouted themselves out, I said, "Do you have the money?"

They thought it was an opening. They said no, of course not; they didn't have such a sum.

"Then you'll pay me a little now, and again every week, until your debt is cleared," I said, "and pay interest on what you haven't paid, if you don't want me to send to my grandfather to bring the law into it."

Our town was small, and no one traveled very much. They knew my mother's father was rich, and lived in a great house in the city, and had loaned money to knights and once to a lord. So they gave me a little, grudgingly; only a few pennies in some houses, but every one of them gave me something, and I wrote down the numbers in front of them and told them I would see them next week. On my way home, I stopped in at Panova Lyudmila's house, who took in travelers when they stayed overnight. She didn't borrow money: she could have lent it too, except for charging interest.

And if anyone in our town had been foolish enough to borrow from anyone but my father, who would let them pay as they liked or didn't. I didn't collect anything; from her I bought a pot of hot soup, with half a chicken in it, and three fresh eggs, and a bowl of honeycomb covered with a napkin.

My father had come back home before me; he was feeding the fire, and he looked up worried when I shouldered my way in. He stared at my arms full of food. I put it all down and I put the rest of the pennies and the handful of silver into the kettle next to our own hearth, and I gave him the list with the payments written on it, and then I turned to making my mother comfortable.

After that, I was the moneylender in our little town. And I was a good moneylender, and a lot of people owed us money, so very soon the straw of our floor was smooth boards of golden wood, and the cracks in our fireplace were chinked with good clay and our roof was thatched fresh, and my mother had a fur cloak to sleep under or to wear. She didn't like it at all, and neither did my father, who went outside and wept quietly to himself the day I brought the cloak home. The baker's wife had offered it to me in payment for the rest of her family's debt. It was beautiful; she'd brought it with her when she married, made of ermines her father had hunted in his lord's woods.

That part of the story turned out to be true: you have to be cruel to be a good moneylender. But I was ready to be as merciless with our neighbors as they'd been with my father. I didn't take firstborn children exactly, but one week, one of the peasant farmers had nothing to pay me with, not even a spare loaf of bread, and he cursed me with real desperation in his voice and said, "You can't suck blood from a stone."

I should have felt sorry for him, I suppose. My father would have, and my mother, but wrapped in my coldness, I felt only the danger of the moment. If I forgave him, took his excuses, next week everyone would have an excuse; I saw everything unraveling again from there.

Then the farmer's tall daughter came staggering in, a heavy gray kerchief over her head and a big heavy yoke across her shoulders, carrying two buckets of water, twice as much as I could manage when I went for water to the village well myself. I said, "Then your daughter will come work in my house to pay off the debt, three mornings this week and every week you can't pay," and I walked home pleased as a cat, and even danced a few steps to myself in the road, alone under the trees.

Her name was Wanda. She came silently to the house at dawn, three days a week, worked like an ox until midday, and left silently again; she kept her head down the entire time. She was very strong, and she took almost all the burden of the housework in just her three mornings. She carried water and chopped wood, and tended the small flock of hens we now had scratching in our yard, and watered the new goats and milked them, and scrubbed the floors and our hearth and all our pots, and I was well satisfied with my solution.

For the first time in my life, I heard my mother speak to my father in anger, in blame, as she hadn't even when she was cold and sick. "And you don't care for what it does to her?" I heard her cry out to him.

"What shall I say to her?" he cried back. "What shall I say? No, you shall starve; no, you shall go cold and you will wear rags?"

"If you had the coldness to do it yourself, you could be cold enough to let her do it," my mother said. "Our daughter, Josef!"

But when my father looked me in the face that night and tried to say something to me, the coldness in me met him and drove him back, just as it had when he'd met it in the village, asking for what he was owed.

So in desperation my mother took me away on a visit when the air warmed with spring and her cough finally went away, drowned in soup and honey. I didn't like to leave, but I did want to see my grandmother, and show her that her daughter wasn't sleeping cold and frozen, that her granddaughter didn't go like a beggar anymore; I wanted to visit without seeing her weep, for once. I went on my rounds one last time and told everyone as I did that I would add on extra interest for the weeks I was gone, unless they left their payments at our house while I was away.

Then we drove to my grandfather's house, but this time I hired our neighbor Oleg to take us all the way with his good horses and his big wagon, heaped with straw and blankets and jingling bells on the harness, with the fur cloak spread over all against the March wind. My grandmother came out, surprised, to meet us when we drew up to the house, and my mother went into her arms, silent and hiding her face. "Well, come in and warm up," my grandmother said, looking at the sledge and our good new wool dresses, trimmed with rabbit fur, and a golden button at the neck on mine, that had come out of the weaver's chest.

She sent me to take my grandfather fresh hot water in his study, so she could talk to my mother alone. My grandfather had rarely done more than grunt at me and look me up and down disapprovingly in the dresses my grandmother had bought. I don't know how I knew what he thought of my father, because I don't remember him ever having said a word about it, but I did know.

He looked me over this time out from under his bristling eyebrows and frowned. "Fur, now? And gold?"

I should say that I was properly brought up, and I knew better than to talk back to my own grandfather of all people, but I was already angry that my mother was upset, and that my grandmother wasn't pleased, and now to have him pick at me, him of all people. "Why shouldn't I have it, instead of someone who bought it with my father's money?" I said.

My grandfather was as surprised as you would expect to be spoken to like this by his granddaughter, but then he heard what I had said and frowned at me again. "Your father bought it for you, then?"

Loyalty and love stopped my mouth there, and I dropped my eyes and silently finished pouring the hot water into the samovar and changing out the tea. My grandfather didn't stop me going away, but by the next morning he knew the whole story somehow, that I'd taken over my father's work, and suddenly he was pleased with me, as he never had been before and no one else was.

He had two other daughters who had married better than my mother, to rich city men with good trades. None of them had given him a grandson who wanted to take up his business. In the city, there were enough of my people that we could be something other than a banker, or a farmer who grew his own food: there were enough people who would buy your goods, and there was a thriving market in our quarter.

"It's not seemly for a girl," my grandmother tried, but my grandfather snorted.

"Gold doesn't know the hand that holds it," he said, and frowned at me, but in a pleased way. "You'll need servants," he told me. "One to start with, a good strong simple man or woman: can you find one?"

"Yes," I said, thinking of Wanda: she had nearly paid off her father's debt by now, but she was already used to coming, and in our town there wasn't much other chance for a poor farmer's daughter to earn a wage.

"Good. Don't go yourself to get the money," he said. "You send a servant, and if they want to argue, they come to you."

I nodded, and when we went home, he gave me a purse full of silver pennies to lend out, to towns near ours that hadn't any moneylender of their own. And when my mother and I came again in the winter for another visit, after the first snowfall, I brought it back full of gold to put into the bank, and my grandfather was proud of me.

They hadn't had guests over usually, when we were visiting, except my mother's sisters. I hadn't noticed before, but I noticed now, because suddenly the house was full of people coming to drink tea, to stay to dinner, lights and bustling dresses and laughing voices, and I met more city people in that one week than I had in all the visits before. "I don't believe in selling a sow's ear for a silk purse," my grandfather told me bluntly, when I asked him. "Your father couldn't dower you as the guests who come to this house would expect of my granddaughter, and I swore to your mother that I would never put more money in his pocket, to fall back out again."

I understood then why he hadn't wanted my grandmother buying dresses for me, as he'd thought, with fur and gold buttons on them. He wouldn't try to make a princess out of a miller's daughter with borrowed finery, and snare her a husband fool enough to be tricked by it, or who'd slip out of the bargain when he learned the truth.

It didn't make me angry; I liked him better for that cold, hard honesty, and it made me proud that now he did invite his guests, and even boasted of me to them, how I'd taken away a purse of silver and brought back one of gold.

But my grandmother kept her mouth pursed shut; my mother's was empty of smiles. I was angry at her again as we flew home in the warm sledge over the frozen roads. I had another purse of silver hidden deep under my own fur cloak, and three petticoats underneath my dress, and I didn't feel cold at all, but her face was tight and drawn.

"Would you rather we were still poor and hungry?" I burst out to her finally, the silence between us heavy in the midst of the dark woods, and she put her arms around me and kissed me and said, "My darling, my darling, I'm sorry," weeping a little.

"Sorry?" I said. "To be warm instead of cold? To be rich and comfortable? To have a daughter who can turn silver into gold?" I pushed away from her.

"To see you harden yourself like a stone, to make it so," she said. We didn't speak the rest of the way home.

I didn't believe in stories, even though we lived in the middle of one: our village had been cut out of the North Forest, a little too near the depths where they said the old ones lived, the Staryk. Children who ran playing in the woods would sometimes stumble across their road and come home with one of the pebbles that lined it: an unnaturally smooth pebble that shone in starlight, and got lost again very quickly no matter how much care you took with it. I saw them displayed in the village square a couple of times, but they only looked like smooth white pebbles, and I didn't think magic was needed to explain why children lost a rock again in short order.

You weren't supposed to ride through the woods dressed too fine, because they loved gold and gems and finery, but again, I didn't mean to be afraid of fairy lords when thieves would do just as well, to make it poor sense to go riding through a deep forest wearing all your jewels. If you found a grove full of red mushrooms with white spots, you were supposed to go back out again and stay well away, because that was one of their dancing rings, and if someone went missing in the woods they'd taken him or her, and once in a while someone would come staggering out of the forest, feverish, and claim to have seen one of them.

I never saw the road, or took any of it seriously, but the morning after my mother and I came back home, Wanda ran back inside, afraid, after she'd gone out to feed the chickens. "They've been outside the house!" was all she said, and she wouldn't go out again alone. My father took the iron poker from the fireplace and we all went out cautiously behind him, thinking there might be burglars or wolves, but there were only prints in the snow. Strange prints: a little like deer, but with claws at the end, and too large, the size of horses' hooves. They came right to the wall of the house, and then someone had climbed off the beast and looked through our window: someone wearing boots with a long pointed toe.

I wasn't stubborn about my disbelief, when I had footprints in snow to show me something strange had happened. If nothing else, no one anywhere near our town had boots that absurd, for fashion; only someone who didn't have to walk anywhere would have shoes like that. But there didn't seem to be anything to do about it, and they'd left, whoever they'd been. I told

Wanda we'd hire her brother to come and guard the house during the night, mostly so she wouldn't be afraid and maybe leave her place, and then I put it out of my mind.

But the tracks were there again the next morning, though Sergey swore he'd been awake all night and hadn't heard a thing.

"If the Staryk haven't anything better to do but peer in at our windows, I suppose they can," I said out loud and clear, standing in the yard. "We're no fools to keep our gold in the house: it's in Grandfather's vault," which I hoped might be overheard and do some good whether it was an elf or a thief or someone trying to scare me.

It did something, anyway; that night as we sat at our work in the kitchen, my mother doing the fine sewing she loved, and I with my spindle, my father silently whittling with his head bowed, there was suddenly a banging at the door, a heavy thumping as though someone were knocking against the wood with something metal. Wanda sprang up from the kettle with a cry, and we all held still: it was a cold night, snow falling, and no one would come out at such an hour. The knocking came again, and then my father said, "Well, it's a polite devil, at least," and got up and went to the door.

When he opened it, no one was there, but there was a small bag sitting on the threshold. He stepped outside and looked around to one side and the other: no one anywhere in sight. Then he gingerly picked up the bag and brought it inside and put it on the table. We all gathered around it and stared as though it were a live coal that might at any moment set the whole house ablaze.

It was made of leather, white leather, but not dyed by any ordinary way I'd ever heard of: it looked as though it had always been white, all the way through. There wasn't a seam or stitch to be seen on its sides, and it clasped shut with a small lock made of silver. Finally, when no one else moved to touch it, I reached out and opened the clasp, and tipped out a few small silver coins, thin and flat and perfectly round, not enough to fill the hollow of my palm. Our house was full of warm firelight, but they shone coldly, as if they stood under the moon.

"It's very kind of them to make us such a present," my father said after a moment doubtfully, but we all knew the Staryk would never do such a thing. There were stories from other kingdoms farther south, of fairies who came with gifts, but not in ours. And then my mother drew a sharp breath and looked at me and said, low, "They want it turned into gold."

I suppose it was my own fault, bragging in the woods where they could hear me, but now I didn't know what to do. Moneylending isn't magic: I couldn't lend the coins out today and have the profit back tomorrow, and I didn't think they meant to wait a year or more for their return. Anyway, the reason I had brought in so much money so quickly was that my father had lent out all my mother's dowry over years and years, and everyone had kept the money so long they had built heaps of interest even at the little rate my father had charged them.

"We'll have to take the money from the bank," my mother said. There were six silver coins in the bag. I had put fourteen gold coins in the bank this last visit, and the city was only an eight-hour sleigh ride away when the snow was packed this hard. But I rebelled: I didn't mean to trade our gold, *my* gold, for fairy silver.

"I'll go to the city tomorrow," was all I said, but when I went, I didn't go to the bank. I slept that night in my grandfather's house, behind the thick walls of the quarter, and early the next morning, I went down to the market. I found a seat upon the temple steps while the sellers put out their stalls: everything from apples to hammers to jeweled belts, and I waited while the buyers slowly trickled in. I watched through the morning rush, and after it thinned out, I went to the stall of the jeweler who had been visited by the most people in drab clothes: I guessed they had to be servants from the rich people of the city.

The jeweler was a young man with spectacles and stubby but careful fingers, his beard trimmed short to stay out of his work; he was bent over an anvil in miniature, hammering out a disk of silver with his tiny tools, enormously precise. I stood watching him work for maybe half an hour before he sighed and said, "Yes?" with a faint hint of resignation, as though he'd hoped I would go away, instead of troubling him to do any business. But he seemed to know what he was about, so I brought out my pouch of silver coins and spilled them onto the black cloth he worked upon.

"It's not enough to buy anything here," he said, matter-of-factly, with barely a glance; he started to go back to his work, but then he frowned a little and turned around again. He picked one coin up and peered at it closely, and turned it over in his fingers, and rubbed it between them, and then he put it down and stared at me. "Where did you get these?"

"They came from the Staryk, if you want to believe me," I said. "Can you make them into something? A bracelet or a ring?"

"I'll buy them from you," he offered.

"No, thank you," I said.

"To make them into a ring would cost you two gold coins," he said. "Or I'll buy them from you for five."

"I'll pay you one," I said firmly, "or if you like, you can sell the ring for me and keep half the profit," which was what I really wanted. "I have to give the Staryk back six gold coins in exchange."

He grumbled a little but finally agreed, which meant he thought he could sell it for a high enough price to make it worthwhile, and then he set about the work. He melted the silver over a hot little flame and ran it into a mold, a thick one made of iron, and when it had half cooled, he took it out with his leathered fingertips and etched a pattern into the surface, fanciful, full of leaves and branches.

It didn't take him long: the silver melted easily and cooled easily and took the pattern easily, and when it was done, the pattern seemed oddly to move and shift: it drew the eye and held it, and shone even in the midday sun. We looked down at it for a while, and then he said, "The duke will buy it," and sent his apprentice running into the city. A tall, imperious servant in velvet clothes and gold braid came back with the boy, making clear in every expression how annoyed he was by the interruption of his more important work, but even he stopped being annoyed when he saw the ring and held it on his palm.

The duke paid ten gold coins for the ring, so I put two in the bank, and six back into the little white pouch, and I climbed back into Oleg's sledge to go home that same evening. We flew through the snow and dark, the horse trotting quickly with only my weight in back. But in the woods the horse slowed, and then dropped to a walk, and then halted; I thought she just needed a rest, but she stood unmoving with her ears pricked up anxiously, warm breath gusting out of her nostrils. "Why are we stopping?" I asked, and Oleg didn't answer me: he slumped in his seat as though he slept.

The snow crunched behind me once and once again: something picking its way toward the sleigh from behind, step by heavy step. I swallowed and drew my cloak around me, and then I summoned up all the winter-cold courage I'd built inside me and turned around.

The Staryk didn't look so terribly strange at first; that was what made him truly terrible, as I kept looking and slowly his face became something inhuman, shaped out of ice and glass, and his eyes like silver knives. He had no beard and wore his white hair in a long braid down his back. His clothes, just like his purse, were all in white. He was riding a stag, but a stag larger than a draft horse, with antlers branched twelve times and hung with clear glass drops, and when it put out its red tongue to lick its muzzle, its teeth were sharp as a wolf's.

I wanted to quail, to cower; but I knew where that led. Instead I held my fur cloak tight at the throat with one hand against the chill that rolled off him, and with my other I held out the bag to him, in silence, as he came close to the sleigh.

He paused, eyeing me out of one silver-blue eye with his head turned sideways, like a bird. He put out his gloved hand and took the bag, and he opened it and poured the six gold coins out into the cup of his hand, the faint jingle loud in the silence around us. The coins looked warm and sun-bright against the white of his glove. He looked down at them and seemed vaguely disappointed, as though he was sorry I'd managed it; and then he put them away and the bag vanished somewhere beneath his own long cloak.

I called up all my courage and spoke, throwing my words against the hard, icy silence like a shell around us. "I'll need more than a day next time, if you want more of them changed," I said, a struggle to keep trembling out of my voice.

He lifted his head and stared at me, as though surprised I'd dared to speak to him, and then he wasn't there anymore; Oleg shook himself all over and chirruped to the horse, and we were trotting again. I fell back into the blankets, shivering. The tips of my fingers where I'd held out the purse were numbed and cold. I pulled off my glove and tucked them underneath my arm to warm them up, wincing as they touched my skin.

One week went by, and I began to forget about the Staryk, about all of it. We all did, the way one forgets dreams: you're trying to explain the story of it to someone and halfway through it's already running quicksilver out of your memory, too wrong and ill-fitting to keep in your mind. I didn't have any of the fairy silver left to prove the whole thing real, not even the little purse. Even that same night I'd come home, I hadn't been able to describe him to my anxious mother; I'd only been able to say, "It's all right, I gave him the gold," and then I'd fallen into bed. By morning I couldn't remember his face.

But Sunday night the knocking came again at the door, and I froze for a moment. I was standing already, about to fetch a dish of dried fruit from the pantry; with a lurch of my heart I went to the door and flung it open.

A burst of wind came growling through the house, as cold as if it had been shaved directly off the frozen crust of the snow. The Staryk hadn't abandoned a purse on the stoop this time: he stood waiting outside, all the more unearthly for the frame of wood around his sharp edges. I looked back into the house wildly, to see if they saw him also; but my father was bent over his whittling as though he hadn't even heard the door opening, and my mother was looking into the fire with a dreamy, vague look on her face. Wanda lay sleeping on her pallet already, and her brother had gone home three days before.

I turned back. The Staryk held another purse out to me, to the very border of the door, and spoke, a high, thin voice like wind whistling through the eaves. "Three days," he said.

I was afraid of him, of course; I wasn't a fool. But I had only believed in him for a week, and I had spent all my life learning to fear other things more: to be taken advantage of, used unfairly. "And what in return?" I blurted, putting my hands behind my back.

His eyes sharpened, and I regretted pressing him. "Thrice, mortal maiden," he said, in a rhythm almost like a song. "Thrice shall I come, and you shall turn silver to gold for my hands, or be changed into ice yourself."

I felt half ice already, chilled down to my bones. I swallowed. "And then?"

He laughed and said, "And then I will make you my queen, if you manage it," mockingly, and threw the purse down at my feet, jingling loud. When I looked back up from it, he was gone, and my mother behind me said, slow and struggling, as if it was an effort to speak, "Miryem, why are you keeping the door open? The cold's coming in."

I had never felt sorry for the miller's daughter before, in the story: I'd been too sorry for my father, and myself. But who would really like it, after all, to be married to a king who'd as cheerfully have cut off your head if your dowry didn't match your boasting? I didn't want to be the Staryk's queen any more than I wanted to be his servant, or frozen into ice.

The purse he'd left was ten times as heavy as before, full of shining coins. I counted them out into smooth-sided towers, to try and put my mind into order along with them. "We'll leave," my mother said. I hadn't told her what the Staryk had promised, or threatened, but she didn't like it anyway: an elven lord coming to demand I give him gold. "We'll go to my father, or farther away," but I felt sure that wasn't any good. I hadn't wanted to believe in the Staryk at all, but now that I couldn't help it, I didn't believe there was a place I could run away that he wouldn't find some way to follow. And if I did, then what? My whole life afraid, looking around for the sound of footfalls in snow?

Anyway, we couldn't just go. It would mean bribes to cross each border, and a new home wherever we found ourselves in the end, and who knew how they'd treat us when we got there? We'd heard enough stories of what happened to our people in other countries, under kings and bishops who wanted their own debts forgiven, and to fill their purses with confiscated wealth.

So I put the six towers of coins, ten in each, back into the purse, and I sent Wanda for Oleg's sledge. We drove back to the city that very night, not to lose any of my precious time. "Do you have any more?" Isaac the jeweler demanded the moment he saw me, eagerly, and then he flushed and said, "That is, welcome back," remembering he had manners.

"Yes, I have more," I said, and spilled them out on the cloth. "I need to give back sixty gold this time," I told him.

He was already turning them over with his hands, his face alight with hunger. "I couldn't *remember*," he said, half to himself, and then he heard what I'd said and gawked at me. "I need a little profit for the work that this will take!"

"There's enough to make ten rings, at ten gold each," I said.

"I couldn't sell them all."

"Yes, you could," I said. That, I was sure of: if the duke had a ring of fairy silver, every wealthy man and woman in the city needed a ring just like it, right away.

He frowned down over the coins, stirring them with his fingers, and sighed. "I'll make a necklace, and see what we can get."

"You really don't think you can sell ten rings?" I said, surprised, wondering if I was wrong.

"I want to make a necklace," he said, which didn't seem very sensible to me, but perhaps he thought it would show his work off and make a name for him. I didn't really mind as long as I could pay off my Staryk for another week.

"I only have three days," I said. "Can you do it that quickly?"

He groaned. "Why must you ask for impossibilities?"

"Do *those* look possible to you?" I said, pointing at the coins, and he couldn't really argue with that.

I had to sit with him while he worked, and manage the people who came to the stall wanting other things from him; he didn't want to talk to anyone and be interrupted. Most of them were busy and irritated servants, some of them expecting goods to be finished; they snapped and glared, wanting me to cower, but I met their bluster too and said coolly, "Surely you can see what Master Isaac is working on. I'm sure your mistress or your master wouldn't wish you to interrupt a patron I cannot name, but who would purchase such a piece," and I waved to send their eyes over to the worktable, where the full sunlight shone on the silver beneath his hands. Its cold gleam silenced them; they stood staring a little while and then went away, without trying to argue again.

I noticed that Isaac tried to save a few of the coins aside while he worked, as though he wanted to keep them to remember. I thought of asking him for one to keep myself; but it didn't work. On the morning of the third day, he sighed and took the last of the ones he'd saved and melted it down, and strung a last bit of silver lace upon the design. "It's done," he said afterward, and picked it up in his hands: the silver hung over his broad palms like icicles, and we stood looking at it silently together for a while.

"Will you send to the duke?" I asked.

He shook his head and took out a box from his supplies: square and made of carved wood lined with black velvet, and he laid the necklace carefully inside. "No," he said. "For this, I will go to him. Do you want to come?"

"Can I go and change my dress?" I said, a little doubtful: I didn't really want the necklace to go so far out of my sight unpurchased, but I was wearing a plain work dress only for sitting in the market all day.

"How far do you live?" he said, just as doubtful.

"My grandfather's house is only down the street with the ash tree and around the corner," I said. "Three doors down from the red stables."

He frowned a moment. "That's Panov Moshel's house."

"That's my grandfather," I said, and he looked at me, surprised, and then in a new way I didn't understand until I was inside, putting on my good dress with the fur and the gold buttons, and I looked down at myself and patted my hair and wondered if I looked well, and then my cheeks prickled with sudden heat. "Do you know Isaac, the jeweler?" I blurted to my grandmother, turning away from the brass mirror.

She peered at me over her spectacles, narrowly. "I've met his mother. He's a respectable young man," she allowed, after some thought. "Do you want me to put up your hair again?"

So I took a little longer than he would have liked, I suspect, to come back; then we went together to the gates and through the wall around our quarter, and walked into the streets of the city. The houses nearest were mean and low, run-down; but Isaac led me to the wider streets, past an enormous church of gray stone with windows like jewelry themselves, and finally to the enormous mansions of the nobles. I couldn't help staring at the iron fences wrought into lions and writhing dragons, and the walls covered with vining fruits and flowers sculpted out of stone. I admit I was glad not to be alone when we went through the open gates and up the wide stone steps swept clear of snow.

Isaac spoke to one of the servants. We were taken to a small room to wait: no one offered us anything to drink, or a place to sit, and a manservant stood looking at us with disapproval. I was grateful, though: irritation made me feel less small and less tempted to gawk. Finally the servant who had come to the market last time came in and demanded to know our business. Isaac brought out the box and showed him the necklace; he stared down at it, and then said shortly, "Very well," and went away again. Half an hour later he reappeared and ordered us to follow him: we were led up back stairs and then abruptly emerged into a hall more sumptuous than anything I had ever seen, the walls hung with tapestries in bright colors and the floor laid with a beautifully patterned rug.

It silenced our feet and led us into a sitting room even more luxurious, where a man in rich clothes and a golden chain sat in an enormous chair covered in velvet at a writing table. I saw the ring of fairy silver on the first finger of his hand, resting on the arm of the chair. He didn't look down at it, but I noticed he thumbed it around now and again, as though he wanted to make sure it hadn't vanished from his hand. "All right, let's see it."

"Your Grace." Isaac bowed and showed him the necklace.

The duke stared into the box. His face didn't change, but he stirred the necklace gently on its bed with one finger, just barely moving the looped lacelike strands of it. He finally drew a breath and let it out again through his nose. "And how much do you ask for it?"

"Your Grace, I cannot sell it for less than a hundred and fifty."

"Absurd," the duke growled. I had a struggle to keep from biting my lip, myself: it was rather outrageous.

"Otherwise I must melt it down and make it into rings," Isaac said, spreading his hands apologetically. I thought that was rather clever: of course the duke would rather no one else had a ring like his.

"Where are you getting this silver from?" the duke demanded. Isaac hesitated, and then looked at me. The duke followed his eyes. "Well? You're bringing it from somewhere."

I curtsied, as deeply as I could manage and still get myself back up. "I was given it by one of the Staryk, my lord," I said. "He wants it changed for gold."

"And you mean to do it through my purse, I see," the duke said. "How much more of this silver will there be?"

I had been worrying about that, whether the Staryk would bring even more silver next time, and what I would do with it if he did: the first time six, the second time sixty; how would I get six hundred pieces of gold? I swallowed. "Maybe—maybe much more."

"Hm," the duke said, and studied the necklace again. Then he put his hand to one side and took up a bell and rang it; the servant reappeared in the doorway. "Go and bring Irina to me," he said, and the man bowed. We waited a handful of minutes, and then a woman came to the door, a girl perhaps a year younger than me, slim and demure in a plain gray woolen gown, modestly high-necked, with a fine gray silken veil trailing back over her head. Her chaperone came after her, an older woman scowling at me and especially at Isaac.

Irina curtsied to the duke without raising her downcast eyes. He stood up and took the necklace over to her, and put it around her neck. He stepped back and studied her, and we did too. She wasn't especially beautiful, I would have said, only ordinary, except her hair was long and dark and thick; but it didn't really matter with the necklace on her. It was hard even to glance away from her, with all of winter clasped around her throat and the silver gleam catching in her veil and in her eyes as they darted sideways to catch a glimpse of herself in the mirror on the wall there.

"Ah, Irinushka," the chaperone murmured, approvingly, and the duke nodded.

He turned back to us. "Well, jeweler, you are in luck: the tsar visits us next week. You may have a hundred gold pieces for your necklace, and the next thing you make will be a crown fit for a queen, to be my daughter's dowry: you will have ten times a hundred gold for it, if the tsar takes her hand."

I left twenty gold pieces in the bank and carried the swollen purse into the sledge waiting to carry me home. My shoulders tightened as we plunged into the forest, wondering when and if the Staryk would come on me once more, until halfway down the road the sledge began to slow and stop under the dark boughs. I went rabbit-still, looking around for any signs of him, but I didn't see anything; the horse stamped and snorted her warm breath, and Oleg didn't slump over, but hung his reins on the footboard.

"Did you hear something?" I said, my voice hushed, and then he climbed down and took out a knife from under his coat, and I realized I'd forgotten to worry about anything else but magic. I scrambled desperately away, shoving the heaped blankets toward him and floundering through the straw and out the other side of the sledge. "Don't," I blurted. "Oleg, don't," my heavy skirts dragging in the snow as he came around for me. "Oleg, please," but his face was clenched down, cold deeper than any winter. "This is the Staryk's gold, not mine!" I cried in desperation, holding the purse out between us.

He didn't stop. "None of it's yours," he snarled. "None of it's yours, little grubbing vulture, taking money out of the hands of honest working men," and I knew the sound of a man telling himself a story to persuade himself he wasn't doing wrong, that he had a right to what he'd taken.

I gripped two big handfuls of my skirts and struggled back, my boot heels digging into the snow. He lunged, and I flung myself away, falling backward. The crust atop the snow gave beneath my weight, and I couldn't get up. He was standing over me, ready to reach down, and then he halted; his arms sank down to his sides.

It wasn't mercy. A deeper cold was coming into his face, stealing blue over his lips, and white frost was climbing over his thick brown beard. I struggled to my feet, shivering. The Staryk was standing behind him, a hand laid upon the back of his neck like a master taking hold of a dog's scruff.

In a moment, he dropped his hand. Oleg stood blank between us, bloodless as frostbite, and then he turned and slowly went back to the sledge and climbed into the driving seat. The Staryk didn't watch him go, as if he cared nothing; he only looked at me with his eyes as gleaming as Oleg's blade. I was shaking and queasy. There were tears freezing on my eyelashes, making them stick. I blinked them away and held my hands tight together until they stopped trembling, and then I held out the purse.

The Staryk came closer and took it. He didn't pour the purse out: it was too full for that. Instead he dipped his hand inside and lifted out a handful of shining coins to tumble ringing back into the bag, weighed in his other palm, until there was only one last coin held between his white-gloved fingers. He frowned at it, and me.

"It's all there, all sixty," I said. My heart had slowed, because I suppose it was that or burst.

"As it must be," he said. "For fail me, and to ice you shall go."

But he seemed displeased anyway, although he had set the terms himself: as though he wanted to freeze me but couldn't break a bargain once he'd made it. "Now go home, mortal maiden, until I call on you again."

I looked over helplessly at the sledge: Oleg was sitting in the driver's seat, staring with his frozen face out into the winter, and the last thing I wanted was to get in with him. But I couldn't walk home from here, or even to some village where I could hire another driver. I had no idea where we were. I turned to argue, but the Staryk was already gone. I stood alone under pine boughs heavy with snow, with only silence and footprints around me, and the deep crushed hollow where I had fallen, the shape of a girl against the drift.

Finally I picked my way gingerly to the sledge and climbed back inside. Oleg shook the reins silently, and the mare started trotting again. He turned her head through the trees slightly, away from the road, and drove deeper into the forest. I tried to decide whether I was more afraid to call out to him and be answered, or to get no reply, and if I should try to jump from the sledge. And then suddenly we came through a narrow gap between trees onto a different road: a road as free of snow as summer, paved with innumerable small white pebbles like a mosaic instead of cobblestones, all of them laid under a solid sheet of ice.

The rails of the sledge rattled, coming onto the road, and then fell silent and smooth. The moon shone, and the road shone back, glistening under the pale light. The horse's hooves went strange and quickly on the ice, the sledge skating along behind her. Around us, trees stretched tall and birch-white, full of rustling leaves; trees that didn't grow in our forest, and should have been bare with winter. White birds darted between the branches, and the sleigh bells made a strange kind of music, high and bright and cold. I huddled back into the blankets and squeezed my eyes shut and kept them so, until suddenly there was a crunching of snow beneath us again, and the sledge was already standing outside the gate of my own yard.

I all but leaped out, and darted through the gate and all the way to my door before I glanced around. I needn't have run. Oleg drove away without ever looking back at me. The next morning, they found him outside his stables, lying frozen and staring blindly upwards in the snow, his horse and sledge put away.

I couldn't forget at all, that week. They buried Oleg in the churchyard, and the bells ringing for him sounded like sleigh bells ringing too-high in a forest that couldn't be. They would find me frozen like that outside the door, if I didn't give the Staryk his gold next time, and if I did, then what? Would he put me on his white stag behind him, and carry me away to that pale cold forest, to live there alone forever with a crown of fairy silver of my own? I started up gasping at night with Oleg's white frozen face looming over me, shivering with a chill inside me that my mother's arms couldn't drive away.

I decided I might as well try something as nothing, so I didn't wait for the Staryk to come knocking this time. I fled to my grandfather's house behind the thick city walls, where the streets were layered with dirty ice instead of clean white snow and only a handful of scattered barren trees stood in the lanes. I slept well that Shabbat night, but the next morning the candles had gone out, and that evening while I sat knitting with my grandmother, behind me the kitchen door rattled on its hinges, and she didn't lift her head at the noise.

I slowly put aside my work, and went to the door, and flinched back when I had flung it wide: there was no narrow alleyway behind the Staryk, no brick wall of the house next door and no hardened slush beneath his feet. He stood outside in a garden of pale-limbed trees, washed with moonlight even though the moon hadn't yet come out, as if I could step across the threshold and walk out of all the world.

There was a box instead of a purse upon the stoop, a chest made of pale white wood bleached as bone, bound around with thick straps of white leather and hinged and clasped with silver. I knelt and opened it. "Seven days this time I'll grant you, to return my silver changed for gold," the Staryk said in his voice like singing, as I stared at the heap of coins inside, enough to make a crown to hold the moon and stars. I didn't doubt that the tsar would marry Irina, with this to make her dowry.

I looked up at him, and he down at me with his sharp silver eyes, eager and vicious as a hawk. "Did you think mortal roads could run away from me, or mortal walls keep me out?" he said, and I hadn't really, after all.

"But what *use* am I to you?" I said desperately. "I have no magic: I can't change silver to gold for you in your kingdom, if you take me away."

"Of course you can, mortal girl," he said, as if I was being a fool. "A power claimed and challenged and thrice carried out is true; the proving makes it so." And then he vanished, leaving me with a casket full of silver and a belly full of dismay.

I hadn't been able to make sense of it before: What use would a mortal woman be to an elven lord, and if he wanted one, why wouldn't he just snatch her? I wasn't beautiful enough to be a temptation, and why should boasting make him want me? But of course any king would want a queen who really could make gold out of silver, if he could get one, mortal or not. The last thing I wanted was to be such a prize.

Isaac made the crown in a feverish week, laboring upon it in his stall in the marketplace. He hammered out great thin sheets of silver to make the fan-shaped crown, tall enough to double the height of a head, and then with painstaking care added droplets of melted silver in mimic of pearls, laying them in graceful spiraling patterns that turned upon themselves and vined away again. He borrowed molds from every other jeweler in the market and poured tiny flattened links by the hundreds, then hung glittering chains of them linked from one side of the crown to the other, and fringed along the rest of the wide fan's bottom edge.

By the second day, men and women were coming just to watch him work. I sat by, silent and unhappy, and kept them off, until finally despite the cold the crowds grew so thick I became impatient and started charging a penny to stand and watch for ten minutes, so they'd go away; only it backfired, and the basket I'd put out grew so full I had to empty it into a sack under the table three times a day.

By the fifth day, I had made nearly as much silver as the Staryk had given me in the first place, and the crown was finished; when Isaac had assembled the whole, he turned and said, "Come here," and set it upon my head to see whether it was well balanced. The crown felt cool and light as a dusting of snow upon my forehead. In his bronze mirror, I looked like a strange deep-water reflection of myself, silver stars at midnight above my brow, and all the marketplace went quiet in a rippling wave around me, silent like the Staryk's garden.

I wanted to burst into tears, or run away; instead I took the crown off my head and put it back into Isaac's hands, and when he'd carefully swathed it with linen and velvet, the crowds finally drifted away, murmuring to one another. My grandfather had sent his two manservants with me that day, and they guarded us to the duke's palace. We found it full of bustle and noise from the tsar's retinue and preparations: there was to be a ball that night, and all the household full of suppressed excitement; they knew of the negotiations underway.

We were put into a better antechamber this time to wait, and then the chaperone came to fetch me. "Bring it with you. The men stay here," she said, with a sharp, suspicious glare. She took me upstairs to a small suite of rooms, not nearly so grand as the ones below: I suppose a plain daughter hadn't merited better before now. Irina was sitting stiff as a rake handle before a mirror made of glass. She wore snow-white skirts and a silver-gray silk dress over them, cut much lower this time to make a frame around the necklace; her beautiful dark hair had been braided into several thick ropes, ready to be put up, and her hands were gripped tightly around themselves in front of her.

Her fingers worked slightly against one another, nervous, as the chaperone pinned up the braids, and I carefully set the crown upon them. It stood glittering beneath the light of a dozen candles, and the chaperone fell silent, her eyes dreamy as they rested on her charge. Irina herself slowly stood up and took a step closer to the mirror, her nervous hand reaching up toward the glass almost as if to touch the woman inside.

Whatever magic the silver had to enchant those around it either faded with use or couldn't touch me any longer; I wished that it could, and that my eyes could be dazzled enough to care for nothing else. Instead I watched Irina's face, pale and thin and transported, and I wondered if she would be glad to marry the tsar; to leave her quiet, small rooms for a distant palace and a throne. As she dropped her hand, our eyes met in the reflection: we didn't speak, but for a moment I felt her a sister, our lives in the hands of others. She wasn't likely to have any more choice in the matter than I did.

After a few minutes, the duke himself came in to inspect her, and paused in the doorway of the room behind her. Irina was still standing before the mirror; she turned and curtsied to her father, then straightened again, her chin coming up a little to balance the crown; she looked like a queen already. The duke stared at her as if he could hardly recognize his own daughter; he shook himself a little, pulling free of the pull, before he turned to me. "You will have your gold, Panovina," he said. "And if your Staryk wants more of it, you will come to me again."

So I had six hundred gold pieces for the casket and two hundred more for the bank, and my sack full of silver pennies besides; a fortune, for what good it would do me. At least my mother and father wouldn't go cold or hungry again, when the Staryk had taken me away.

My grandfather's servants carried it all home for me. He came downstairs, hearing my grandmother's exclamations, and looked over all the treasure; then he took four gold coins out of the heap meant for the bank, and gave two each to the young men before he dismissed them. "Drink one and save one, you remember the wise man's rule," he said, and they both bowed and thanked him and dashed off to revel, elbowing each other and grinning as they went.

Then he sent my grandmother out of the room on a pretext, asking her to make her cheesecake to celebrate our good fortune; and when she was gone he turned to me and said, "Now, Miryem, you'll tell me the rest of it," and I burst into tears.

I hadn't told my parents, or my grandmother, but I told him: I trusted my grandfather to bear it, as I hadn't trusted them, not to break their hearts wanting to save me. I knew what my father would do, and my mother, if they found out: they would make a wall of their own bodies between me and the Staryk, and then I would see them fall cold and frozen before he took me away.

But my grandfather only listened, and then he said, "Do you want to marry him, then?" I stared at him, still wet-faced. He shrugged. "Sorrow comes to every house, and there's worse things in life than to be a queen."

By speaking so, he gave me a gift: making it my choice, even if it wasn't really. I gulped and wiped away my tears, and felt better at once. After all, in cold, hard terms it *was* a catch, for a poor man's daughter. My grandfather nodded as I calmed myself. "Lords and kings often don't ask for what they want, but they can afford to have bad manners," he said. "Think it over, before you turn away a crown."

I was tempted more by the power my grandfather had given me than the promise of a crown. I thought of it: to harden my heart a little more and stand straight and tall when the Staryk came, to put my hand in his and make it my own will to go with him, so at least I could say the decision had been mine.

But I was my father's daughter also, after all, and I found I didn't want to be so cold. "No," I said, low. "No, Grandfather, I don't want to marry him."

"Then you must make it better sense for him to leave you be," my grandfather said.

The next morning I rose, and put on my best dress, and my fur cloak, and sent for a sledge to carry me. But as I fastened the cloak around my throat in the sitting room, I heard a high cold jangling of bells drifting faintly in from the street, not the bells of a hired harness. I opened the door, and a narrow elegant sleigh drew up outside, fashioned it seemed entirely out of ice and heaped with white furs; the wolfen stag drew it, legs flashing, and the Staryk held the reins of white leather. The street lay blanketed by a thick, unnatural silence: empty even in midmorning, not another soul or sledge or wagon anywhere in sight, and the sky overhead gray and pearled-over like the inside of oyster shells.

He climbed out and came to me, leaving long boot prints in the snow down the walk, and came up the stairs. "And have you changed my silver, mortal girl?" he asked.

I swallowed and backed up to the casket, standing in the room behind me. He followed me inside, stepping in on a winter's blast of cold air, thin wispy flurries of snow whirling into the room around his ankles. He loomed over me to watch as I knelt down behind the casket and lifted up the lid: a heap of silver pennies inside, all I'd taken in the market.

He looked maliciously satisfied a moment, and then he stopped, puzzled, when he saw the coins were different: they weren't fairy silver, of course, though they made a respectable gleam.

"Why should I change silver for gold," I said, when I saw I'd caught his attention, "when I could make the gold, and have them both?" And then I untied the sack sitting beside the chest, to show him the heap of gold waiting inside.

He slowly reached in and lifted out a fistful of gold and let it drop back inside, frowning as he'd frowned each time: as though he didn't like to be caught by his own promises, however useful a queen would be who could turn silver to gold. What would the other elven lords think, I wondered, if he brought home a mortal girl? Not much, I hoped. I daresay in the story, the king's neighbors snickered behind their hands, at the miller's daughter made a queen. And after all, she hadn't even kept spinning.

"You can take me away and make me your queen if you want to," I said, "but a queen's not a moneychanger, and I won't make you more gold, if you do." His eyes narrowed, and I went on quickly, "Or you can make me your banker instead, and have gold when you want it, and marry whomever you like."

I put my money in a vault and bought a house near my grandfather's; we even lent some of the gold back to the duke for the wedding. Isaac was busy for a month making jewelry for all the courtiers and their own daughters, to make a fine show at the celebrations, but he found time to pay visits to my family. I saw Irina once more, when she drove out of the city with the tsar; she threw handfuls of silver out of the window of the carriage as they went through the streets, and looked happy, and perhaps she even was.

We left the business back home in Wanda's hands. Everyone was used to giving her their payments by then, and she'd learned figuring; she couldn't charge interest herself, but as long as she was collecting on our behalf it was all right, and by the time everyone's debts had been repaid, she would have a handsome dowry, enough to buy a farm of her own.

I've never seen the Staryk again. But every so often, after a heavy snowfall, a purse of fairy silver appears on my doorstep, and before a month is gone, I put it back twice over full of gold.

TWO'S COMPANY
Joe Abercrombie

Joe Abercrombie (www.joeabercrombie.com) attended Lancaster Royal Grammar School and Manchester University, where he studied psychology. He moved into television production before taking up a career as a freelance film editor. His first novel, *The Blade Itself,* was published in 2004, and was followed by sequels *Before They Are Hanged, Last Argument of Kings,* stand-alone novels *Best Served Cold, The Heroes,* and *Red Country,* and the Shattered Sea trilogy, *Half a King, Half a World,* and *Half a War.* His most recent book is short story collection *Sharp Ends.* Abercrombie lives in Bath with his wife, Lou, and his daughters, Grace and Eve. He still occasionally edits concerts and music festivals for TV, but spends most of his time writing edgy yet humorous fantasy novels.

Somewhere in the North, Summer 576

"THIS IS HELL," muttered Shev, peering over the brink of the canyon. "Hell." Rock shiny-dark with wet disappeared into the mist below, water rushing somewhere, a long way down. "God, I hate the North."

"Somehow," answered Javre, pushing back hair turned lank brown by the eternal damp, "I do not think God is listening."

"Oh, I'm abundantly aware of that. No one's bloody listening."

"I am." Javre turned away from the edge and headed on down the rutted goat-track beside it with her usual mighty strides, head back, heedless of the rain, soaked cloak flapping at her muddy calves. "And, what is more, I am intensely bored by what I am hearing."

"Don't toy with me, Javre." Shev hurried to catch her up, trying to find the least boggy patches to hop between. "I've had about as much of this as I can take!"

"So you keep saying. And yet the next day you take some more."

"I'm bloody furious!"

"I believe you."

"I mean it!"

"If you have to tell someone you are furious, and then, furthermore, that you mean it, your fury has failed to achieve its desired effect."

"I hate the bloody North!" Shev stamped at the ground, as though she could hurt anything but herself, succeeding only in showering wet dirt up her leg. Not that she could have made herself much wetter or dirtier. "The whole place is made of *shit*!"

Javre shrugged. "Everything is, in the end."

"How can anyone stand this cold?"

"It is bracing. Do not sulk. Would you like to ride on my shoulders?"

Shev would have, in fact, very much, but her bruised pride insisted that she continue to squelch along on foot. "What am I, a bloody child?"

Javre raised her red brows. "Were you never told only to ask questions you truly want the answer to? Do you want the answer?"

"Not if you're going to try to be funny."

"Oh, come now, Shevedieh!" Javre bent down to snake one huge arm about her shoulders and gave her a bone-crushing squeeze. "Where is that happy-go-lucky rascal I fell in love with back in Westport, always facing her indignities with a laugh, a caper and a twinkle in her eye?" And her wriggling fingers crept towards Shev's stomach.

Shev held up a knife. "Tickle me and I will fucking stab you."

Javre puffed out her cheeks, took her arm away and squelched on down the track. "Do not be so overdramatic. It is exhausting. We just need to get you dry and find some pretty little farm-girl for you to curl up with and it will all feel better by morning."

"There are no pretty farm-girls out here! There are no girls! There are no farms!" She held out her arms to the endless murk, mud and blasted rock. "There isn't even any bloody morning!"

"There is a bridge," said Javre, pointing into the gloom. "See? Things are looking up!"

"I never felt so encouraged," muttered Shev.

It was a tangle of fraying rope strung from ancient posts carved with runes and streaked with bird-droppings, rotten-looking slats tied to make a precarious walkway. It sagged deep as Shev's spirits as it vanished into the vertiginous unknown above the canyon and shifted alarmingly in the wind, planks rattling.

"Bloody North," said Shev as she picked her way towards it and had a tentative drag at the ropes. "Even their bridges are shit."

"Their men are good," said Javre, clattering out with no fear whatsoever. "Far from subtle, but enthusiastic."

"Great," said Shev as she edged after, exchanging a mutually suspicious glance with a crow perched atop one of the posts. "Men. The one thing that interests me not at all."

"You should try them."

"I did. Once. Bloody useless. Like trying to have a conversation with someone who doesn't even speak your language, let alone understand the topic."

"Some are certainly more horizontally fluent than others."

"No. Just *no*. The hairiness, and the lumpiness, and the great big fumbling fingers and... *balls*. I mean, *balls*. What's *that* about? That is one singularly unattractive piece of anatomy. That is just... that is bad design, is what that is."

Javre sighed. "It is the great shame of creation that we cannot all be so perfectly formed as you, Shevedieh, springy little string of sinew that you are."

"There'd be more bloody meat on me if we weren't living on high hopes and the odd rabbit. I may not be perfect but I don't have a sock of bloody gravel swinging around my knees, you'd have to give me... Hold on." They had reached the sagging middle of the bridge now, and Shev could see neither rock face. Only the ropes fading up into the grey in both directions.

"What?" muttered Javre, clattering to a stop.

The bridge kept on bouncing. A heavy tread, and coming towards them.

"There's someone heading the other way," muttered Shev, twisting her wrist and letting the dagger drop from her sleeve into her waiting palm. A fight was the last thing she ever wanted, but she'd reluctantly come to find there was no downside to having a good knife ready. It made a fine conversation point, if nothing else.

A figure started to form. At first just a shadow, shifting as the wind drove the fog in front of them. First a short man, then a tall one. Then a man with a rake over his shoulder. Then a half-naked man with a huge sword over his shoulder.

Shev squinted around Javre's elbow, waiting for it to resolve itself into something that made better sense. It did not.

"That is... unusual," said Javre.

"Bloody North," muttered Shev. "Nothing up here would surprise me."

The man stopped perhaps two strides off, smiling. But a smile more of madness than good humour. He wore trousers, thankfully, made of some ill-cured pelt, and boots with absurd fur tops. Otherwise he was bare, and his pale torso was knotted with muscle, criss-crossed with scars and beaded with dew. That sword looked even bigger close up, as if forged by an optimist for the use of giants. It was nearly as tall as its owner, and he was not short by any means, for he looked Javre more or less in the eye.

"Someone's compensating for something," muttered Shev, under her breath.

"Greetings, ladies," said the man, in a thick accent. "Lovely day."

"It's fucking not," grumbled Shev.

"Well, it's all in how you look at it, isn't it, though?" He raised his brows expectantly, but when neither of them answered, continued, "I am Whirrun of Bligh. Some folk call me Cracknut Whirrun."

"Congratulations," said Shev.

He looked pleased. "You've heard of me, then?"

"No. Where the hell's Bligh?"

He winced. "Honestly, I couldn't say."

"I am Javre," said Javre, puffing up her considerable chest, "Lioness of Hoskopp." Shev rolled her eyes. God—warriors, and their bloody titles, and their bloody introductions, and their bloody chest-puffing. "We are crossing this bridge."

"Ah! Me too!"

Shev ground her teeth. "What is this, a stating-the-obvious competition? We've met in the middle of it, haven't we?"

"Yes." Whirrun heaved in a great breath through his nose and let it sigh happily away. "Yes, we have."

"That is quite a sword," said Javre.

"It is the Father of Swords, and men have a hundred names for it. Dawn Razor. Grave-Maker. Blood Harvest. Highest and Lowest. *Scac-ang-Gaioc* in the valley tongue which means the Splitting of the World, the Battle that was fought at the start of time and will be fought again at its end. Some say it is God's sword, fallen from the heavens."

"Huh." Javre held up the roughly sword-shaped bundle of rags she carried with her. "My sword was forged from a fallen star."

"It looks like a sword-shaped bundle of rags."

Javre narrowed her eyes. "I have to keep it wrapped up."

"Why?"

"Lest its brilliance blind you."

"Ooooooooh," said Whirrun. "The funny thing about that is, now I really want to see it. Would I get a good look *before* I was blinded, or—"

"Are you two done with the pissing contest?" asked Shev.

"I would not get into a pissing contest with a man." Javre pushed her hips forward, stuck her hand in her groin and indicated the probable arc with a pointed finger. "I have tried it before and you can say what you like about cocks but they just get far more distance. Far more. What?" she asked, frowning over her shoulder. "It simply cannot be done, no matter how much you drink. Now, if *you* want a pissing contest—"

"I don't!" snapped Shev. "Right now all I want is somewhere dry to kill myself!"

"You are so overdramatic," said Javre, shaking her head. "She is so overdramatic. It is exhausting."

Whirrun shrugged. "It's a fine line between too much drama and too little, isn't it, though?"

"True," mused Javre. "True."

There was a pause, while the bridge creaked faintly.

"Well," said Shev, "this has been lovely, but we are being pursued by agents of the Great Temple in Thond and some fellows hired by Horald the Finger, so, if you don't mind—"

"In fact I do. I, too, am pursued, by agents of the King of the Northmen,

Bethod. You'd think he'd have better things to do, what with this mad war against the Union, but Bethod, well, like him or no, you have to admit he's persistent."

"Persistently a shit," said Shev.

"I won't disagree," lamented Whirrun. "The greater a man's power swells, the smaller his good qualities shrivel."

"True," mused Javre. "True."

Another long silence, and the wind blew up and made the bridge sway alarmingly. Javre and Whirrun frowned at one another.

"Step aside," said Javre, "and we shall be on our way."

"I do not care to step aside. Especially on a bridge as narrow as this one." Whirrun's eyes narrowed slightly. "And your tone somewhat offends me."

"Then your delicate feelings will be even worse wounded by my boot up your arse. Step aside."

Whirrun swung the Father of Swords from his shoulder and set it point-down on the bridge. "I fear you will have to show me that blade after all, woman."

"My pleasure—"

"Wait!" snapped Shev, ducking around Javre to hold up a calming palm. "Just wait a moment! You can murder each other with my blessing but if you set to swinging your hugely impressive swords on this bridge, the chances are good you'll cut one of the ropes, and then you'll kill not just each other but me, too, and that you very much do not have my blessing for."

Whirrun raised his brows. "She has a point."

"Shevedieh can be a deep thinker," said Javre, nodding. She gestured back the way they had come. "Let us return to our end to fight."

Shev gave a gasp. "So you wouldn't step aside to let him past but you'll happily plod all the way back to fight?"

Javre looked baffled. "Of course. That is only good manners."

"Exactly!" said Whirrun. "Manners are everything to a good-mannered person. That is why we must go to my end of the bridge to fight."

It was Javre's turn to narrow her eyes. She was almost as dangerous an eye-narrower as she was a fighter, which was saying something. "It must be my end."

"My end," growled Whirrun. "I insist."

Shev rubbed at her temples. The past few years, it was a wonder she hadn't worn them right through. "Are you two idiots really going to fight over where you fight? We were going this way! He's offering to let us go this way! Let's just go this way!"

Javre narrowed her eyes still further. Blue slits, they were. "All right. But don't think you're talking us out of fighting, Shevedieh."

Shev gave her very weariest sigh. "Far be it from me to prevent bloodshed."

WHIRRUN WEDGED HIS great sword point-down into a crack in the rocks and left it gently wobbling. "Let's put our blades aside. The Father of Swords cannot be drawn without being blooded."

Javre snorted. "Afraid?"

"No. The witch Shoglig told me the time and place of my death, and it is not here, and it is not now."

"Huh." Javre set her own sword down and began, one by one, to explosively crack her knuckles. "Did she tell you the time of me kicking you so hard you shit yourself?"

Whirrun's face took on a contemplative look. "She did predict my shitting myself, but that was because of a rancid stew and, anyway, that happened already. Last year, near Uffrith. That is why I have these new trousers." He bent over to smile proudly upon them, then frowned towards Shev. "I trust your servant will stay out of this?"

"Servant?" snapped Shev.

"Shevedieh is not my servant," said Javre.

"Thank you."

"She is at least a henchman. Possibly even a sidekick."

Shev planted her hands on her hips. "We're partners! A duo!"

Javre laughed. "No. Duo? No, no, no."

"Whatever she is," said Whirrun, "she looks sneaky. I don't want her stabbing me in the back."

"Don't *bloody* worry about that!" snapped Shev. "Believe me when I say I want less than no part of this stupidity. As for sneaking, I tried to get out of that business and open a Smoke House, but *my partner* burned it down!"

"Sidekick at best," said Javre. "And as I recall it was you who knocked the coals over. Honestly, Shevedieh, you are always looking for someone to blame. If you want to ever be half of a duo you must learn to take responsibility."

"Smoke House?" asked Whirrun. "You like fish?"

"No, no," said Shev. "Well, yes, but not that kind of Smoke House, you... Forget it." And she dropped down on a rock and propped her chin on her fists.

"Since we are making rules..." Javre winced as she hitched up her bust. "Can we say no strikes to the tits? Men never realise how much that hurts."

"Fine." Whirrun lifted one leg to rearrange his groin. "If you avoid the fruits. Bloody things can get in the way."

"It's poor design," said Shev. "Didn't I say it? Poor design."

Javre shrugged her coat off and tossed it over Shev's head.

"Thanks," she snapped as she dragged it off her damp hair and around her damp shoulders.

Javre raised her fists and Whirrun gave an approving nod as the sinews popped from her arms. "You are without doubt an impressive figure of a woman." He put up his own fists, woody muscle flexing. "But I will take no mercy on you because of that."

"Good. Except around the chest area?"

"As agreed." Whirrun grinned. "This may be a battle for the songs."

"You will have trouble singing them without your teeth."

They traded blows, lightning quick. Whirrun's fist sank into Javre's ribs with a thud but she barely seemed to notice, letting go three quick punches and catching him full on the jaw with the last. He did not waver, only took a quick step back, already set and watchful.

"You are strong," he said. "For a woman."

"I will show you how strong."

She lunged at him with a vicious flurry of blows but caught only air as he jerked this way and that, slippery as a fish in the river for all his size. Meat slapped as Javre caught his counters on her forearms, growling through gritted teeth, shrugged off a cuff on her forehead and caught Whirrun's arm. In a flash she dropped to one knee, heaved him over her head and into the air, but he tucked himself up neat as Shev used to when she tumbled in that travelling show, hit the turf with his shoulder, rolled and came up on his feet, still smiling.

"Every day should be a new lesson," he said.

"You are quick," said Javre. "For a man."

"I will show you how quick."

He came at her, feinted high, ducked under her raking heel and caught her other calf, lifting her effortlessly to fling her down. But Javre had already hooked her leg around the back of his neck and dragged him down with her. They tumbled in a tangle of limbs to the muddy ground, rolling about with scant dignity, squirming and snapping, punching and kneeing, spitting and snarling.

"This is hell." Shev gave a long groan and looked off into the mist. "This is..." She paused, heart sinking even lower. "You two," she muttered, slowly standing. "You two!"

"We are..." snarled Javre as she kneed Whirrun in the ribs.

"A little..." snarled Whirrun as he butted her in the mouth.

"Busy!" snarled Javre as they rolled struggling through a puddle.

"You may want to stop," growled Shev. Figures were emerging from the mist. First three. Then five. Now seven men, one of them on a horse. "I think perhaps Bethod's agents have arrived."

"Arse!" Whirrun scrambled free of Javre, hurrying over to his sword and striking a suitably impressive pose with his hand on the hilt, only slightly spoiled by his whole bare side being smeared with mud. Shev swallowed and let the dagger drop into her hand once again. It spent a lot more time there than she'd like.

The first to take full shape from the mist was a nervous-looking boy, couldn't have been more than fifteen, who half-drew his bow with somewhat wobbly hands, arrow pointed roughly in Whirrun's direction. Next came a selection of Northmen, impressively bearded if you liked that kind of thing, which Shev didn't, and even more impressively armed, if you liked *that* kind of thing, which Shev didn't either.

"Evening, Flood," said Whirrun, dabbing some blood from his split lip.

"Whirrun," said the one who Shev presumed to be the leader, leaning on his spear as if he'd walked a long way.

Whirrun began to conspicuously count the Northmen with a wagging finger, his lips silently moving.

"There are seven," said Shev.

"Ah!" said Whirrun. "You're right, she's a quick thinker. Seven! I'm touched Bethod can spare so many, just for me. Thought he'd need every man, what with this war against the Southerners. I mean to say, they call me mad, but this war? Now *that's* mad."

"Can't say I disagree," said Flood, combing at his beard with his dirty fingers, "but I don't make the choices."

"Some men don't have the bones to make the choices."

"And some men are just tired of their choices always turning out the wrong ones. I know being difficult comes natural to you, Whirrun, but could you try not to be just for a little while? Bethod's King of the Northmen, now. He can't have people just going their own way."

"I am Whirrun of Bligh," said Whirrun, puffing up his considerable chest. "My way is the only way I go."

"Oh, God," muttered Shev. "He's the male Javre. He's the male you, Javre!"

"He is certainly in the neighbourhood," said Javre, with a note of grudging appreciation, flicking away some sheep's droppings which had become stuck in her hair in the struggle. "Why does only one of you have a horse?"

The Northmen glanced at each other as though this was the source of some friction between them.

"There's a war on," grunted one with shitty teeth. "Not that many horses about."

Shev snorted. "Don't I know it. You think I'd be walking if I didn't have to?"

"It's my horse," said Flood. "But Kerric's got a bad leg so I said he could borrow it."

"We've all got bad legs," grunted a big one with an entirely excessive beard and an axe even more so.

"Now is probably not the time to reopen discussion of who gets the horse," snapped Flood. "The dead know we've argued over that particular issue enough, don't you bloody think?" With a gesture, he started the men spreading out to the right and left. "Who the hell are the women anyway, Whirrun?"

Shev rolled her eyes as Javre did her own puffing up. "I am Javre, Lioness of Hoskopp."

Flood raised one brow. "And your servant?"

Shev gave a weary groan. "Oh, for—"

"She's not a servant, she's a henchman," said Whirrun. "Or... henchwoman? Is that a word?"

"Partner!" snapped Shev.

"No, no." Javre shook her head. "Partner? No."

"It really doesn't matter," said Flood, starting to become impatient. "The point is Bethod wants to talk to you, Whirrun, and you'll be coming with us even if we have to hurt you—"

"One moment." Javre held up her big hand. "This man and I are in the midst of resolving a previous disagreement. You can hurt whatever is left of him when I am done."

"By the dead." Flood pressed thumb and forefinger into his eyes and rubbed them fiercely. "Nothing's ever easy. Why is nothing ever easy?"

"Believe me," said Shev, tightening her grip on her knife, "I feel your pain. You were going to fight him for nothing, now you're going to fight for him for nothing?"

"We stand where the Goddess puts us," growled Javre, knuckles whitening where she gripped her sword.

Flood gave an exasperated sigh. "Whirrun, there's no call for bloodshed here—"

"I'm with him," said Shev, holding up a finger.

"—but you're really not giving me much of a choice. Bethod wants you in front of Skarling's chair, alive or dead."

Whirrun grinned. "Shoglig told me the time of my death, and it is not here, and it is not—"

A bowstring went. It was that boy with the wobbly hands, looking as surprised he'd let fly as anyone. Whirrun caught the arrow. Just snatched it from the air, neat as you like.

"Wait!" roared Flood, but it was too late. The man with the big beard rushed at Whirrun, roaring, spraying spit, swinging his axe. At the last moment, Whirrun calmly stepped around the Father of Swords so the axe-haft clanged into its sheathed blade and stabbed the bearded man in the neck with the arrow. He dropped spluttering.

By then everyone was shouting.

For someone who hated fights, Shev surely ended up in a lot of the bastards, and if she'd learned one thing it was that you've got to commit. Try your damndest to negotiate, to compromise, to put it off, but when the time comes to fight, you've got to commit. So she flung her knife.

If she'd thought about it, Shev might have figured that she didn't want to weigh down her conscience any more than she had to, and killing a horse wasn't as bad as killing a man. If she'd thought about it more, she might have considered that the man had chosen to be there while the horse hadn't, so probably deserved it more. But if she'd thought about it even more, she might have considered that the man probably hadn't chosen to be there in any meaningful sense any more than Shev had herself, but had been rolled along through life like a stone on the riverbed according to his situation, acquaintances, character and bad luck without too much chance of changing anything.

But folk who spend a lot of time thinking in fights don't tend to live through them, so Shev left the thinking for later and threw at the easiest target to hit.

The knife stuck into the horse's hindquarters and its eyes bulged. It reared, stumbled, bucked and tottered, and Shev had to scramble out of the way while the rider tore desperately at the reins. The horse plunged and kicked, the saddle-girth tore and the saddle slid from the horse's back as it toppled sideways, rolled over its rider bringing his despairing wail to a sharp end, then slipped thrashing over the rocky verge of the canyon and out of sight.

So Shev ended up with horse *and* rider on her conscience. But the sad fact was, only the winners got to regret what they did in a fight, and right now Shev had other worries. Namely, a man with the shittiest teeth she ever saw and a hell of an intimidating mace. Why was he grinning? God, if she had those teeth, you'd have needed a crowbar to get her lips apart.

"Come here," he snarled at her.

"I'd rather not," Shev hissed back.

She scrambled out of the way, damp stones scattering from her heels, the screech, crash and clatter of combat almost forgotten in the background. Scrambling, always scrambling, from one disaster to another. Often at the edge of an unknowable canyon, at least a metaphorical one. And, as always, she could never quite get away.

The shitty-toothed maceman caught her collar with his free hand, jerking it so half the buttons ripped off and driving her back so her head cracked on rock. She stabbed at him with her other knife but the blade only scraped his mail and twisted out of her hand. A moment later, his fist sank into her gut and drove her breath out in a shuddering wheeze.

"Got yer," he growled in her face, his breath alone almost enough to make her lose consciousness. He lifted his mace.

She raised one finger to point over his shoulder. "Behind you..."

"You think I'm falling for—"

There was a loud thudding sound and the Father of Swords split him from his shoulder down to his guts, gore spraying in Shev's face as if it had been flung from a bucket.

"Urrgh!" She slithered from under the man's carcass, desperately trying to kick free of the slaughterhouse slops that had been suddenly dumped in her lap. "God," she whimpered, struggling up, trembling and spitting, clothes soaked with blood, hair dripping with blood, mouth, eyes, nose full of blood. "Oh, God."

"Look on the sunny side," said Whirrun. "At least it's not your own."

Bethod's men were scattered about the muddy grass, hacked, twisted, leaking. The only one still standing was Flood.

"Now, look," he said, licking his lips, spear levelled as Javre stalked towards him. "I didn't want things to go this way—"

She whipped her sword from its scabbard and Shev flinched, two blinding smears left across her sight. The top part of Flood's spear dropped off, then the bottom, leaving him holding a stick about the length of Shev's foot. He swallowed, then tossed it on the ground and held up his hands.

"Get you gone back to your master, Flood," said Whirrun, "and thank the dead for your good luck with every step. Tell him Whirrun of Bligh dances to his own tune."

With wide eyes Flood nodded, and began to back away.

"And if you see Curnden Craw over there, tell him I haven't forgotten he owes me three chickens!"

"Chickens?" muttered Javre.

"A debt is a debt," said Whirrun, leaning nonchalantly on the Father of Swords, his bare white body now spattered with blood as well as mud. "Talking of which, we still have business between us."

"We do." She looked Whirrun slowly up and down with lips thoughtfully pursed. It was a look Shev had seen before, and she felt her heart sink even lower, if that was possible. "But another way of settling it now occurs to me."

"Uh... uh... uh..."

Shev knelt shivering beside a puddle of muddy rainwater, muttering every curse she knew, which was many, struggling to mop the gore from between her tits with a rag torn from a dead man's shirt, and trying desperately not to notice Javre's throaty grunting coming from behind the rock. It was like trying not to notice someone hammering nails into your head.

"Uh... uh... uh..."

"This is hell," she whimpered, staring at her bedraggled reflection in the muddy, bloody puddle. "This is hell."

What had she done to deserve being there? Marooned in this loveless, sunless, cultureless, comfortless place. A place salted by the tears of the righteous, as her mother used to say. Her hair plastered to her clammy head like bloody seaweed to a rotting boat. Her chafed skin on which the gooseflesh could hardly be told from the scaly chill-rash. Her nose endlessly running, rimmed with sore pink from the wiping. Her sunken stomach growling, her bruised neck throbbing, her blistered feet aching, her withered dreams crumbling, her—

"Uh... uh... uh..." Javre's grunting was mounting in volume, and added to it now was a long, steady growling from Whirrun. "Rrrrrrrrrrrrrrr..."

Shev found herself wondering what exactly they were up to, slapped the side of her head as though she could knock the thought out. She should be concentrating on feeling sorry for herself! Think of all she'd lost!

The Smoke House. Well, that hadn't been so great. Her friends in Westport. Well, she'd never had any she'd have trusted with a copper. Severard. No doubt he'd be far better off with his mother in Adua, however upset he'd been about it. Carcolf. Carcolf had betrayed her, damn it! God, those hips, though. How could you stay angry at someone with hips like that?

"Uh... uh... uh..."

"Rrrrrrrrrrrrrrr..."

She slithered back into her shirt, which her efforts at washing had turned from simply bloody to bloody, filthy and clinging with freezing water. She shuddered with disgust as she wiped blood out of her ear, out of her nose, out of her eyebrows.

She'd tried to do small kindnesses where she could, hadn't she? Coppers to beggars when she could afford it, and so on? And, for the rest, she'd had good reasons, hadn't she? Or had she just made good excuses?

"Oh, God," she muttered to herself, pushing the greasy-chill hair out of her face.

The horrible fact was, she'd got no worse than she deserved. Quite possibly better. If this was hell, she'd earned every bit of it. She took a deep breath and blew it out so her lips flapped.

"Uh... uh... uh!"

"Rrrrrrrrrrr!"

Shev hunched her shoulders, staring back towards the bridge.

She paused, heart sinking even lower than before. Right into her blistered feet.

"You two," muttered Shev, slowly standing, fumbling with her shirt-buttons. "You two!"

"We are..." came Javre's strangled voice.

"A little..." groaned Whirrun.

"Busy!"

"You may want to fucking stop!" screeched Shev, sliding out a knife and hiding it behind her arm. She realised she'd got her buttons in the wrong holes, a great tail of flapping-wet shirt plastered to her leg. But it was a little late to smarten up. Once again, there were figures coming from the mist. From the direction of the bridge. First one. Then two. Then three women.

Tall women who walked with that same easy swagger Javre had. That swagger that said they ruled the ground they walked on. All three wore swords. All three wore sneers. All three, Shev didn't doubt, were Templars of the Golden Order, come for Javre in the name of the High Priestess of Thond.

The first had dark hair coiled into a long braid bound with golden wire, and old eyes in a young face. The second had a great burn mark across her cheek and through her scalp, one ear missing. The third had short red hair and eyes slyly narrowed as she looked Shev up and down. "You're very... *wet*," she said.

Shev swallowed. "It's the North. Everything's a bit damp."

"Bloody North." The scarred one spat. "No horses to be had anywhere."

"Not for love nor money," sang the red-haired one, "and believe me, I've tried both."

"Probably the war," said the dark-haired one.

"It's the North. There's always a war."

Whirrun gave a heavy sigh as he clambered from behind the rock, fastening his belt. "'Tis a humbling indictment of our way of life, but one I find I can't deny." And he hefted the Father of Swords over his shoulder and came to stand beside Shev.

"You aren't nearly as funny as you think you are," said the scarred one.

"Few of us indeed," said Shev, "are as funny as we think we are."

Javre stepped out from behind the rock, and the three women all shifted nervously at the sight of her. Sneers became frowns. Hands crept towards weapons. Shev could feel the violence coming, sure as the grass grows, and she clung tight to that entirely inadequate knife of hers. All the fights she got into, she really should learn to use a sword. Or maybe a spear. She might look taller with a spear. But then you've got to carry the bastard around. Something with a chain, maybe, that coiled up small?

"Javre," said the one with the braid.

"Yes." Javre gave the women that fighter's glance of hers. That careless glance that seemed to say she had taken all their measure in a moment and was not impressed by it.

"You're here, then."

"Where else would I be but where I am?"

The dark-haired woman raised her sharp chin. "Why don't you introduce everyone?"

"It feels like a lot of effort, when you will be gone so soon."

"Indulge me."

Javre sighed. "This is Golyin, Fourth of the Fifteen. Once a good friend to me."

"Still a good friend, I like to think."

Shev snorted. "Would a good friend chase another clear across the Circle of the World?" Under her breath, she added, "Not to mention her good friend's partner."

Golyin's eyes shifted to Shev's, and there was a sadness in them. "If a good friend had sworn to. In the quiet times, perhaps, she would cry that the world was this way, and wring her hands, and ask the Goddess for guidance, but..." She gave a heavy sigh. "She would do it. You must have known we would catch you eventually, Javre."

Javre shrugged, sinews in her shoulders twitching. "I have never been hard to catch. It is once you catch me that your problems begin." She nodded towards the scarred one, who was slowly, smoothly, silently easing her way around the top of the canyon to their right. "She is Ahum, Eleventh of the Fifteen. Is the scar still sore?"

"I have a soothing lotion for it," she said, curling her lip. "And I am Ninth now."

"Nothingth soon." Javre raised a brow at the red-haired one, working her way around them on the left. "Her I do not know."

"I am Sarabin Shin, Fourteenth of the Fifteen, and men call me—"

"No one cares," said Javre. "I give you all the same two choices I gave Hanama and Birke and Weylen and the others. Go back to the High Priestess and tell her I will be no one's slave. Not ever. Or I show you the sword."

There was that familiar popping of joints as Javre shifted her shoulders, scraping into a wider stance and lifting the sword-shaped bundle in her left hand.

Golyin sucked her teeth. "You always were so overdramatic, Javre. We would rather take you back than kill you."

Whirrun gave a little snort of laughter. "I could swear we just had this exact conversation."

"We did," said Javre, "and this one will end the same way."

"This woman is a murderer, an oathbreaker, a fugitive," said Golyin.

"Meh." Whirrun shrugged. "Who isn't?"

"There is no need for you to die here, man," said Sarabin Shin, finding her own fighting crouch.

Whirrun shrugged again. "One place is as good for dying as another, and these ladies helped me with an unpleasant situation." He pointed out the six corpses scattered across the muddy ground with the pommel of his sword. "And my friend Curnden Craw always says it's poor manners not to return a favour."

"You may find this situation of a different order of unpleasantness," said the scarred one, drawing her sword. The blade smoked in a deeply unnatural and worrying way, a frosty glitter to the white metal.

Whirrun only smiled as he shrugged his huge sword off his shoulder. "I have a tune for every occasion."

The other two women drew their swords. Golyin's curved blade appeared to be made of black shadow, curling and twisting so its shape was never sure. Sarabin Shin smiled at Shev and raised her own sword, long, and thin, and smouldering like a blade just drawn from the forge. Shev hated swords, especially ones pointed at her, but she rarely saw one she liked the look of less than that.

She held up the hand that didn't have the knife in. "Please, girls." She wasn't above begging. "Please! There really is no upside to this. If we fight, someone will die. They will lose everything. Those who win will be no better off than now."

"She is a pretty little thing," said the scarred one.

Shev tidied a bloody strand of hair behind her ear. "Well, that's nice to—"

"But she talks too much," said Golyin. "Kill them."

Shev flung her knife. Sarabin Shin swept out her sword and swatted it twittering away into the mist as she charged screaming forward.

Shev rolled, scrambled, ducked, dodged, dived while that smouldering blade carved the air around her, feeling the terrible heat of it on her skin. She tumbled more impressively than she ever had with that travelling show, the flashes of Javre's sword at the corner of her eye as she fought Golyin, the ringing of metal crashing on her ears as Whirrun and Ahum traded blows.

Shev flung all the knives at her disposal, which was maybe six, then when those were done started snatching up anything to hand, which, after the last fight, was a considerable range of fallen weapons, armour and gear.

Sarabin Shin dodged a hastily flung mace, then an axe, then carved a water-flask in half with a hissing of steam, then stepped around a flapping boot with a hissing of contempt.

The one hit Shev scored was with a Northman's cloven helmet, which bounced off Shin's brow opening a little cut, and only appeared to make her more intent on Shev's destruction than ever.

She ended up using the fallen saddle as a shield, desperately fending off blows while the snarling woman carved smoking chunks from it, leaving her holding an ever smaller lump of leather until, with a final swing, Shin chopped it into two flaming fist-sized pieces and caught Shev by her collar, dragging her close with an almost unbelievable strength, the smoking blade levelled at her face.

"No more running!" she snarled through her gritted teeth, pulling back her sword for a thrust.

Shev squeezed her eyes shut, hoping, for the second time that day, that against all odds and the run of luck she would find a way to creep into heaven.

"Get off my *partner*!" came Javre's furious shriek.

Even through her lids she saw a blinding flash and Shev jerked away, gasping. There was a hiss and something hot brushed gently against Shev's face. Then the hand on her collar fell away, and she heard something heavy thump against the ground.

"Well, that is that," said Whirrun.

Shev prised one eye open, peered down at herself through the glittering smear Javre's sword had left across her sight. The headless body of Sarabin Shin lay beside her.

"God," she whimpered, standing stiff with horror, clothes soaked with blood, hair dripping with blood, mouth, eyes, nose full of blood. Again. "Oh, God."

"Look on the sunny side," said Javre, her sword already sheathed in its ragged scabbard. "At least it is not—"

"Fuck the sunny side!" screamed Shev. "And fuck the North, and fuck you pair of rutting lunatics!"

Whirrun shrugged. "That I'm mad is no revelation, I'm known for it. They call me Cracknut because my nut is cracked and that's a fact." With the toe of his boot he poked at the corpse of Ahum, face down beside him, leaking blood. "Still, even I can reckon out that these Templars of the Silver Order—"

"Golden," said Javre.

"Whatever they call themselves, they are not going to stop until they catch you."

Javre nodded as she looked about at the King of the Northman's dead agents. "You are right. No more than Bethod will stop pursuing you."

"I have nothing pressing," said Whirrun. "Perhaps we could help each other with our enemies?"

"Two swords are better than one." Javre tapped a forefinger thoughtfully against her lips. "And we could fuck some more."

"The thought had occurred," said Whirrun, grinning. "That was just starting to get interesting."

"Wonderful." Shev winced as she tried to blow the blood from her nose. "Do I get a vote?"

"Henchpeople don't vote," said Javre.

"And even if you did," added Whirrun, giving an apologetic shrug, "there are three of us. You'd be outvoted."

Shev tipped her head back to look up at the careless, iron-grey sky. "There's the trouble with fucking democracy."

"So it's decided!" Whirrun clapped his hands and gave a boyish caper of enthusiasm. "Shall we fuck now, or...?"

"Let us make a start while there is still some daylight." Javre stared over the fallen corpse of her old friend Golyin, off towards the west. "It is a long way to Carleon."

Whirrun frowned. "To Thond first, so I can pay my debt to you."

Javre puffed up her chest as she turned to face him. "I will not hear of it. We deal with Bethod first."

With a sigh of infinite weariness, Shev sank down beside the puddle, took up the bloody rag she had used earlier and wrung it out.

"I must insist," growled Whirrun.

"As must I," growled Javre.

As though by mutual agreement they seized hold of each other, tumbled wrestling to the ground, snapping, hissing, punching, writhing.

"This is hell." Shev put her head in her hands. "This is hell."

YOU MAKE PATTAYA
Rich Larson

Rich Larson (richwlarson.tumblr.com) was born in West Africa, has studied in Rhode Island and worked in Spain, and now writes from Ottawa, Canada. His short work has been nominated for the Theodore Sturgeon Award, featured on io9.com, and appears in numerous Year's Best anthologies as well as in magazines such as *Asimov's, Analog, Clarkesworld, The Magazine of Fantasy & Science Fiction, Interzone, Strange Horizons, Lightspeed* and *Apex*. He was one of the most prolific authors of short science fiction in 2015 and 2016.

DORIAN SPRAWLED BACK on sweaty sheets, watching Nan, or Nahm, or whatever her name was, grind up against the mirror, beaming at the pop star projected there like she'd never seen smartglass before. He knew she was from some rural eastern province; she'd babbled as much to him while he crushed and wrapped parachutes for their first round of party pills. But after a year in Pattaya, you'd think she would have lost the big eyes and the bubbliness. Both of which were starting to massively grate on him.

Dorian had been in the city for a month now, following the tourist influx, tapping the Banks and Venmos of sun-scalded Russians too stupid to put their phones in a faraday pouch as they staggered down Walking Street. In the right crowd, he could slice a dozen people for ten or twenty Euros each and make off with a small fortune before a polidrone could zero in on him.

And in Baht, that small fortune still went a long way. More than enough to reward himself with a 'phetamine-fuelled 48-hour club spree through a lurid smear of discos and dopamine bars, from green-lit Insomnia to Tyger Tyger's tectonic dance floor and finally to some anonymous club on the wharf where he yanked a gorgeous face with bee-stung lips from a queue of bidders on Skinspin and wasted no time renting the two of them a privacy suite.

Dorian put a finger to his lips to mute the pop star in the mirror, partly to ward off the comedown migraine and partly just to see the hooker's vapid smile slip to the vapid pout that looked better on her. She pulled the time display out from the corner of the mirror and made a small noise of surprise in her throat.

"I must shower." She checked the cheap nanoscreen embedded in her thumbnail, rueful. "Other client soon. Business lady. Gets angry when I late even one fucking second." She spun toward the bed. "I like you better," she cooed. "You're handsome. Her, I don't know. She wear a blur." She raked her glittery nails through the air in front of her face to illustrate.

"That's unfortunate," Dorian said, pulling his modded tablet out from under the sheets.

"Like I fuck a ghost," she said with a grimace. "Gives me shivers." She turned back to her reflection, piling up her dark hair with one hand and encircling her prick with the other. She flashed him an impish Crest-capped grin from the mirror. "You want a shower with me?"

Dorian's own chafed cock gave a half-hearted twitch. He counted the popped tabs of Taurus already littered around the room and decided not to risk an overdose. "I'll watch," he said. "How's that?"

Her shoulders heaved an exaggerated sigh, then she flitted off to the bathroom. Dorian flicked the shower's smartglass from frosted to one-way transparent, watching her unhook the tube and wave it expectantly in his general direction. Dorian used his tablet to buy her the suite's maximum option, 60 litres of hot water.

Once she was busy under the stream, rapping along to Malaysian blip-hop, he took advantage of the privacy to have a look at his Bank. The scrolling black figure in his savings account gave him a swell of pride. 30,000 Euros, just over a million in Baht. He was ripping down record cash and the weekend's binge had barely dented him. Maybe it was finally time to go to a boatyard and put in some inquiries.

Dorian alternated between watching curves through the wet glass and watching clips of long-keeled yachts on his tablet. Then, in the corner of his eye, the mirror left tuned to a Thai entertainment feed flashed a face he actually recognized: Alexis Carrow, UK start-up queen, founder of Delphi Apps and freshly-minted billionaire. Dorian sat up a bit straighter and the mirror noticed, generating English subtitles.

CARROW VACATION INCOGNITO

Alexis Carrow young CEO from Delphi Apps on vacay in our very own beautiful country, celebspotters made clip yesterday on Pattaya Bay Area. She appears having a wonderful time perusing Soi 17 with only bodyguard. No lover for her? Where is singer/songwriter Mohammed X? Alexis Carrow is secretive always.

Dorian dumped the feed from the mirror onto his tablet, zooming in on the digital stills from some celebspotter's personal drone that showed Ms. Carrow slipping inside an AI-driven *tuk-tuk*, wearing Gucci shades and a sweat-wicking headscarf. Thailand still pulled in a lion's share of middle-class Russian and Australian holidayers, plus droves of young Chinese backpackers, but Dorian knew the West's rich and/or famous had long since moved on to sexier climes. Alexis Carrow was news. And she was here in Pattaya.

Cogs churned in his head; grifter's intuition tingled the nape of his neck. He eased up off the bed and walked to the smartglass wall of the bathroom. Inside, Nan? Nahm? was removing her penis, trailing strands of denatured protein. He doubted it was her original organ—surgeons needed something to work with when they crafted the vagina, after all—but customers liked the fantasy.

Dorian put his forehead against the smartglass, watching as she slipped the disembodied cock into the nutrient gel of a chic black refrigerated carrycase. The night's activities were a slick fog. He tried to remember what she'd told him between bouts of hallucination-laced sex, the endless murmuring in his ear while they lay tangled together. Things about her family in Buriram, things about her friends, things about her clients.

Someone even richer than you, she'd said, fooled by his rented spidersilk suit and open bar tab. *Wants me all the week. You're lucky I think you are handsome.*

Dorian couldn't contain his grin as he looked down at his tablet, flicking through the photos. She was right about one thing: he had always been lucky.

*   *   *

BY THE TIME the hooker was dressed, Dorian had checked on Skinspin and verified her name was Nahm. She exited the bathroom with a slink of steam, wrapped in a strappy white dress, her black hair immaculate again. Dorian appraised her unending legs, soot-rimmed eyes and pillowy lips. She was definitely enough to catch even a celebrity's biwandering eye.

"What?" she asked. She crouched to retrieve one Louboutin knock-off kicked under the bed; Dorian produced its partner.

"Nothing, Nahm," he said, handing her the sandal. "I was just thinking how much I'd like to take you back to London with me."

"Don't make a joke," she said, but she looked pleased. She gripped his arm for balance while she slipped into her shoes and then gave him a lingering goodbye kiss. As soon as the door of the privacy suite snicked shut behind her, Dorian scrambled back into his clothes.

Someone had dumped half a Singha across his shoes and his sport coat stank like laced hash, but he didn't have time for a clothing delivery. He raked fingers through his gel-crisped hair, prodded the dark circles under his eyes, and left. The narrow hall was a bright, antiseptic white unsullied by ads, and the soundproof guarantee of each privacy suite made it eerily quiet, too. AI-run fauxtels did always tend toward a minimalist aesthetic.

Walking Street, by contrast, bombarded every last one of Dorian's senses the moment he stepped outside. The air stank like spice and petrol, and a thousand strains of synthesized music mingled with drunk shrieks, laughter, trilingual chatter. The street itself was a neon hubbub of revellers.

Dorian used his tablet to track the sticky he'd slapped to the bottom of Nahm's shoe. He couldn't see her through the crush, but according to the screen she was heading upstreet toward the Beach Road entrance. He plunged off the step, ducking an adbot trailing a digital Soi 6 banner, and made for the closest tech vendor. A gaggle of tourists was arrayed around the full body Immersion tank, giggling at their electrode-tethered friend drifting inside with a tell-tale erection sticking off him.

Dorian cut past them and swapped 2,000 Baht for a pair of lime green knock-off iGlasses, prying them out of the packaging with his fingernails.

He blinked his way through set-up, bypassed user identification, and tuned them to the sticky's signal. A digital marker dropped down through the night sky, drizzling a stream of white code over a particular head like a localized rainshower.

Stowing his tablet, Dorian hurried after the drifting marker, past a row of food stands hawking chemical-orange chicken kebabs and fried scorpions. A few girls whose animated tattoos he vaguely recognized grabbed at him as he went by, trailing fake nails down his arm. He deked away, but tagged one of them to Skinspin later—it looked like she'd gotten her implants redone.

Once he had Nahm in eyeball sight, he slowed up a bit. She was mouthing lyrics to whatever she had in her audiobuds as she bounced along, necksnapping a group of tank-and-togs Australian blokes with the sine curve sway of her hips. She detoured once outside Medusa, where bored girls were perusing their phones and dancing on autopilot, to exchange rapid-fire *sawatdees* and airkisses. She detoured again to avoid a love-struck Russian on shard.

Ducking into a stall selling 3-D printed facemasks of dead celebrities, Dorian looked past Nahm to the approaching roundabout. A shiny black ute caught his eye through the customary swarm of scooters and *tuk-tuks*. As he watched, Nahm checked her thumbnail, then glanced up at the ute and quickened her pace. Dorian felt a jangle of excitement down his spine as he scanned the vehicle for identifying tags and found not a single one.

Someone had knocked over a trash tip, spilling the innards across Nahm's path, but she picked her way through the slimed food cartons and empty condom sprays with pinpoint precision that left Dorian dimly impressed. He squinted to trigger the iGlasses' zoom, wondering if he should chance trying to get a snap of the inside of the ute.

Then the lasershow started up again, throwing its neon green web into the dark clouds over Pattaya's harbor, and as Nahm craned her beautiful head to watch for what was probably the millionth time, her heel punctured a sealed bag of butcher giblets.

"Shit," Dorian said, at the same time Nahm appeared to be saying something similar. Casting a glance at the approaching ute, she lowered herself gingerly to the curb to hunt through her bag. She produced a wipe and cleaned the red gunge off her ankle and the strap of her sandal. Dorian bit at the inside of his cheek.

She continued to the underside of the shoe, wiping the needle-like heel clean, then paused. Dorian winced, thinking of all the many places he could have put the sticky. Slipped into her bag, or onto the small of her back, or even somewhere in her hair.

Nahm pincered the tiny plastic bead between two nails and peered at it. Dorian crossed his tattooed fingers, hoping she wasn't one of the many girls addicted to Bollywood spy flicks. She frowned, then balled the sticky up in the used wipe and tossed it away. The stream of code floated a half-meter over, now useless, as the ute pulled in.

Dorian slid closer, watching Nahm get to her feet, smooth out her dress. For the first time, she looked slightly nervous. The ute's shiny black door opened with a hiss. Dorian didn't have an angle to see the interior as Nahm slithered inside, but the voice within was unmistakable, Cockney accent undisguised.

"Christ, what is that stink? Please do *not* track that shit in with you, love."

Dorian didn't get to hear Nahm's retort. The door swooshed shut and the ute bullied its way back into the traffic. Dorian trotted over and picked up the bloody wipe, retrieving the sticky from inside. The smell barely bothered him, because Alexis Carrow was slumming it in Pattaya and he was going to blackmail the ever-loving shit out of her.

WHEN DORIAN TRIED to search Nahm's profile again, he wasn't particularly surprised to see she'd pulled it off Mixt and Skinspin and the rest. Either finding the sticky had spooked her, or her current customer was upping the pay enough to make exclusivity worthwhile. Dorian had to do things the old-fashioned way, with a sheaf of rumpled 200 Baht notes doled out to helpful individuals.

He didn't find her on the beach until late afternoon, and almost didn't recognize her when he did. She sat cross-legged on the palm-shaded sand, chatting to the old woman selling coconut milk and bags of crushed ice from a sputtering minifridge. Her face was more or less scrubbed of makeup, eyes smaller without the caked-on kohl, and her black hair hung gathered in a ponytail. Loose harem pants, flip-flops, a canary yellow Jack Daniels tank he assumed was being worn ironically.

"*Sawatdee krap*," Dorian said, butchering the pronunciation on purpose. He flashed her an incredulous grin. "This is a surprise."

Nahm looked up, surprised. "Hello," she beamed, running her fingers through her ponytail. Then her smile dimmed by a few watts. A crease of suspicion appeared on her forehead. "What is it you want? I am no working."

"I guessed from the flip-flops," Dorian said. "Long night for you?"

Nahm narrowed her eyes. "You," she said. "You put a... thing. To my shoe. First I think it was Ivan, but it was you." She said something to the old woman in machine-gun Thai, too fast for Dorian to even try at, and slunk to her feet. "I am going. I don't care you are handsome, you are crazy like Ivan." She brushed sand off her legs and made for the street.

"Have you figured out who you're fucking yet?" Dorian asked, dropping pretenses. "That business lady? The angry one?"

Nahm stopped, turned back.

Dorian clawed the air in front of his face as an extra reminder. "Whatever she's paying you is shit," he said.

"More than you pay me."

"She's a lot richer than me," Dorian said. "She's Alexis Carrow."

Nahm's eyes winched wide and she put a furious finger to her lips, scanning the beach as if paparazzi might burst up out of the gray sand.

Dorian grinned. "So you do know."

"What is it you want?" Nahm repeated, raking fingers through her ponytail.

"I want to talk business," Dorian said. "Walk with me a minute?"

He chased a few coins out of his pocket to buy a coconut milk and a bag of ice chips, then gestured down the beach. Nahm swayed, indecisive, but when Dorian started to walk she fired off another salvo of indecipherable Thai to the old woman and fell into step with him.

It was low tide and the beach was a minefield of broken glass bottles and plastic trash floating in tepid puddles. Other than a prone tourist couple baking away their hangovers, Dorian and Nahm had the place to themselves.

"You familiar with the term blackmail?" Dorian asked, handing her the coconut milk.

Nahm spun the straw between her fingers. "I watch bad movies. Yes."

"Your client is wearing a blur for a reason." Dorian ripped open the ice bag. "She's not keen on the tablos finding out she took a sex trip to Thailand."

Nahm gave an irritated shake of her head. "If she find that thing on my shoe, big fucking trouble for me, you know that?"

"Does she actually sweep you for bugs? Christ." Dorian popped a chunk of ice into his mouth. "Pawanoia."

"She careful."

Dorian crunched down on the cube, eliciting a squeal and crack. "Yes. Very careful. Meaning any fuck-footage from her trip is going to be extremely valuable. Do you want to get rich, Nahm?"

"Everybody wants to get rich," Nahm said, plumbing with her straw, not looking at him.

"Well, this is your shot. Also, my shot." Dorian spat a piece of ice into the filmy surf. "Alexis Carrow has enough money that paying two enterprising individuals such as you and me to suppress a sex scandal is easily worth 50,000 Euros. And if she refuses to negotiate, any of the bigger tablos would pay us the same for the footage."

Nahm's eyes went wide and Dorian realized he probably could have halved his actual demand a second time.

"Enough money to take care of your family out in Buriram," Dorian continued. "Get them out of the village, if you want. Definitely enough to assuage any lingering embarrassment about how their first-born financed her vaginoplasty."

"I make good money do what I do now," Nahm said sourly. "Enough money. I send them."

"Not 50,000 Euros money," Dorian said. "D'you really want to hook in Pattaya your whole life?" He packed another ice cube into his cheek. "This city is the diseased bleached asshole of Thailand. It's disgusting."

Nahm gave him a dirty look. "You're here."

"I'm disgusting," Dorian explained.

"And this is why Pattaya is Pattaya," Nahm said, lobbing her half-empty coconut milk into the water. "You make Pattaya be Pattaya."

"Don't have to litter about it." Dorian crunched his ice. "If you help me pull this off, you can live wherever you want."

"In London with you?" Nahm asked dryly.

"50,000 Euros," Dorian repeated. "Split even. Fifty percent yours, fifty percent mine. I've got a way to short-circuit the blur projector. I'll rig a sticky, it's the same thing I stuck to your shoe. Tiny. You just have to put it on the collar without her noticing."

"I told you she scan me in the car." Nahm folded her arms. "Very careful, remember?"

"That's why we plant it in the room beforehand, along with a little slip-in eyecam," Dorian said, groping inside the ice bag with reddened fingertips. "Where's she taking you tonight? Does she do fauxtels or the real thing?"

Nahm bit her lip. Dorian could practically see the tug-of-war on her creased forehead, a chance at instant wealth battling the cardinal rule of confidentiality.

"I want sixty percent," Nahm said. "I lose my best ever client. I maybe get big fucking trouble. You are safe with your phone somewhere, no risk."

Dorian grinned. "You're sharper than you let on. Why the dizzy bitch act? Do clients really like it that much?"

"Sixty percent," Nahm repeated, but with a hint of her own grin.

"Fine." Dorian spat out his ice and stuck out his hand. "Sixty."

ALEXIS CARROW HAD rented a suite at the Emerald Palace, a name Dorian thought a bit generous for an eight-story quickcrete façade topped by a broken-down eternity pool collecting algae. But if she was after privacy, it wasn't a bad choice. It was far enough from the main drag to be relatively quiet, and small enough to be inconspicuous.

Of course, gaining access was as easy as waltzing past reception wearing a drunken grin and clutching an expired keycard fished from the wastebasket outside. Dorian affected a slight stagger on his way to the lift. Once the shiny doors slid shut, he took out his tablet and called Nahm.

"How's the timing?" he asked, as she appeared on the screen putting up her hair with a static clip.

"She's on her way," Nahm said, unsticking a floating tendril of dark hair from her eyelash. "Get me from Bali Hai in five minute, then take ten, twelve minute back to hotel. Over."

"Alright." Dorian punched the backlit eight with his knuckle. "So I'm going to put it in the back of the toilet."

"So, how they did in *The Godfather*. Over." Nahm was now applying a gloss to her lips that shimmered like broken glass and was not paying as close attention as Dorian would have liked.

"Sure," he said. "As soon as you get in, go to the bathroom. Get some water going so she can't hear you take the lid off. Then open the ziplock, take the eyecam out first. You ever wear contacts?"

"Yes."

"It's like that," Dorian said. "Once you have the eyecam in, take the sticky out of the ziplock and hide it in your hand."

"And put it to the blur without her knowing it," Nahm continued, then, in a surprisingly credible imitation of Dorian's accent: "Base of the projector if possible, over."

"Yeah, then business as usual," Dorian said, as the lift jittered to a halt. "She won't notice when the projection goes down, so long as you're being your usual distracting self and you don't start complimenting her eyes or anything batshit like that." The lift made to open and he jammed it shut again. "Do what you normally do," he went on. "Let the eyecam do the work. After she pays you, come find me across the street and we'll get the POV uploaded to a private cloud. At which point, champagne and a blowjob."

"Who give the champagne, who give the blowjob?" Nahm asked, checking her thumbnail offscreen. "Over."

"Both on me if you do this right," Dorian said, knuckling the Open Door button. "Message me when you get the hotel." He paused, and then, because she was growing on him a bit: "Over."

Nahm's face lit up for the split second before he ended the call, then Dorian set off down the stucco-walled hallway. He made a quick check around the corner, then doubled back to door 811 and made short work of the electronic lock. The suite had obviously been prepped for her arrival. Freshly laundered sheets on the bed; a sea of fluffy white towels at the foot of it. Condom sprays and lubricants arrayed brazenly on the nightstand. Minibar stocked with Tanqueray gin and Lunar vodka.

Dorian plucked a cube out of the full ice bucket and popped it in his mouth, making his way to the bathroom. He lifted the featherweight top off the back of the Western-style toilet, then reached inside his pocket where the tiny eyecam and the even smaller sticky had been lovingly double-bagged in ziplock. Neither had been cheap, and he had a feeling he wasn't going to get the sticky back.

Setting the bag adrift in chemical-smelling water, Dorian replaced the top of the toilet and re-entered the room. He walked in a slow circle around the bed, picturing angles, trying not to get distracted imagining Nahm and a celebrity CEO fucking on it. In the end, he decided to plant his insurance cam in the far corner. It would be an uncreative wide angle shot, but with a near-zero chance of Alexis Carrow's deblurred face failing to make an appearance.

It wasn't that he didn't trust Nahm to manage the eyecam, but back-ups were his cardinal rule where information storage was concerned. A healthy fear of technical difficulties went hand-in-hand with hacking for a living.

Once satisfied with the cam's placement in a shadowy whorl of stucco, Dorian put his ear to the door to listen for footsteps. Hearing nothing, he exited the room, heart pumping with the old break-and-enter exhilaration from his teenage years.

His hand was still on the doorknob when a black-shirted employee rounded the corner in his peripheral. Dorian didn't look up. He pretended to struggle with the door, then looked down at his keycard and made a slurred sound of realization.

"This no your room, sir. Can I help you?"

Dorian tried not to jump. The man had slunk up and stopped directly behind him, quiet as a cat, a feat made more impressive by the sheer size of him. Tall for a Thai, broad-chested and broad-shouldered, with a shaved scalp glistening in the fluorescent lighting and a tattoo of a cheerful cartoon snake wriggling up and down one sinewy forearm. Dorian could have sworn he'd been kicked out of a couple bars by the very same. Bouncers and hotel security tended to overlap.

"Wrong floor," Dorian said, waving his keycard. "Hit the wrong button in the lift. One too many Changs." He shook an imaginary beer bottle.

"Okay, sir," the guard said, not smiling.

"Nice tattoo," Dorian added. "Friendly-looking little bugger."

He gave the man a bleary grin, then made for the lift as quickly as he could without looking suspicious.

* * *

NOW THAT THE rest of it was in Nahm's hands, Dorian had nothing to do but wait. He camped out in an automated tourist bar across the way, slumping into a plastic molded seat with his tablet. Once Nahm messaged him to say they were at the hotel, he bought a gargantuan Heineken bottle, the liter sort, and drank it slowly on ice.

Time ticked by on his tablet screen. He passed it imagining the whole thing going off flawlessly, and then by imagining himself on a small sleek yacht knifing through the blue-green waters off Ko Fangan. Maybe even with Nahm draped on his shoulder for a week or two, wearing a pair of aviators and a skanky swimsuit. Between that and the tingly insulation of a half-liter of Heineken, he barely rattled when a hand slammed down on the table in front of him.

Dorian blinked hard. Nahm was standing in front of him, shoulders trembling, clutching herself. The static clip was still in place, moving her hair in graceful black ripples around her face, but the effect wasn't the same with her lip gloss smeared halfway across her cheek and a growing brown bruise under her bloodshot left eye. And hulking behind her, red-faced and furious, was the hotel security guard.

"Shit," Dorian said. The buzz from the beer slipped away all at once.

"I fuck up," Nahm said shakily. "I left the bathroom open. The blur go off, but when we switch around on the bed she see herself in the mirror."

The security guard barked something fast and angry, from which Dorian could only extricate *falang* and *police*. He reached across the table and hauled Dorian up by the armpit, jerking his head toward the door.

"The eyecam?" Dorian demanded, trying to twist away. No go.

"She call this big motherfucker, he take it out my eye," Nahm groaned, mascara finally starting to leak down her cheeks in inky trails. "She gets mad, she go. He says he will call the police so I tell him you have money."

"I don't have money," Dorian said reflexively, looking at the guard.

"Bullshit." Nahm's eyes were wide and desperate. "I know you have money."

Dorian looked around the bar, licking his lips. He'd picked it intentionally. A collection of steroid-bulky expats were cradling pints in the back, watching the situation with increasing interest. If he played ignorant right now, they looked both drunk and patriotic enough to intervene on behalf of a fellow Englishman. Nobody liked it when the locals stopped smiling.

"His cousin is police," Nahm said, winnowing on the edge of the sob. "He says if I don't pay he put me in the jail."

Dorian picked up his glass and finished it; the sweat pooling in his palms nearly made it slip out of his grip. He tried to think. If Carrow had left in a hurry, that meant the insurance cam he'd hidden was still there in the hotel room. The fact she'd left furious only confirmed how valuable the footage was.

If he wanted to get back into that room before some overzealous autocleaner wiped the cam off the wall, he needed to defuse things.

"Okay, fuck," Dorian said. "Okay. I'll come." He gave a glance toward the back table. "Nothing to worry about, lads. Just a bit of a... lover's spat."

One of the men rubbed his bristly chin and raised his pint in Dorian's general direction. The others ignored him. As he let himself be steered out the door, the bar chirped goodbye in Thai and then English. Nahm followed behind, pinching the torn fabric of her shirt together. Her bare feet slapped on the tile. She was biting her lip, rubbing absently at the smeared gloss.

"Sorry I fuck up," she said miserably. Outside, the night air was warm and stank of a broken sewer line. Dorian fixed his eyes on the neon green sign of the hotel across the way. The sooner he had this dealt with, the sooner he could get the cam.

"Me too," Dorian said, but he searched for her free hand in the dark and gave it what he figured was a comforting squeeze.

She looked down at their interlaced hands, then back up, brow furrowed. "You should have said, though. You should have said, Nahm, don't let her see a mirror."

Dorian took his hand back. The guard ushered them into the side alley, stopping underneath a graffitied Dokemon. Dorian crossed his arms.

"Alright," he said. "How much does he want? And if it's cash, we need a machine."

"No cash," the guard said, brandishing a phone still slick from the plastic wrap. "I do Bank."

"Of course you do," Dorian said. "So how much, shitface?"

"Five million Baht."

Dorian's exaggerated guffaw accidentally landed a speck of spit on the guard's shoulder, but the man didn't seem to notice and Dorian didn't feel keen to point it out. "Who do you think I am, the fucking king?" he demanded instead.

In reply, the guard thumbed a number into his phone. "I call cousin," he said, seizing Nahm's wrist. "Your ladyboy will go to jail, maybe you, too."

Nahm gave a low groan again. Dorian made a few mental calculations. He had just over a million Banked, and the footage from the hotel had to be worth triple that, even if it wasn't a full encounter. He would still come out of this in the black. The last thing Dorian needed was police showing up. And he didn't like the idea of Nahm sobbing in some filthy lock-up, either.

"Half a million," Dorian said. "All I got."

The guard's ringtone bleated into the night air. He shook his shaved head. Nahm started cursing at him in Thai.

Dorian clenched his jaw. "A million," he snapped. "I can show it to you. It's really all I've got."

The guard stared at him, black eyes gleaming in the blurry orange streetlight. The ringtone sounded again. Then, just as the click and a guttural *hallo* answered, he thumbed his phone off.

"Show me."

Dorian dug out his tablet and drained his account while the guard watched, dumping all of it to a specified address and waiting the thirty seconds for transaction confirmation. Nahm shifted nervously from foot to foot, mascara-streaked face bleached by the glowing screen, until it finally went through with an electronic chime. Dorian's stomach churned at the sight of the zeroes blinking in his Bank. He reminded himself it was temporary. Very, very temporary.

Once the transaction was through, the guard bustled out of the alley without so much as a *korpun krap*, leaving Dorian alone with Nahm. He was formulating the best way to get back into the hotel room without running into the guard again when she threw her arms around his neck and pulled him into a furious bruising kiss. Her fingers on his scalp and her tongue in his mouth made it difficult.

"Thank you," she panted. "For not letting him call." She hooked her thumb into the catch of Dorian's trousers, giving him her smeared smile. "No champagne. But…"

With her right hand working his cock, he nearly didn't feel her left slipping something into his pocket. He clamped over it on reflex. Nahm looked vaguely sheepish as the sound of a sputtering motor approached.

"I still am working on my hands," she said, wriggling her fingers out of his grip, leaving a small cold cylinder in their place. "Bye." She stepped away as a battered scooter whined its way into the alley, sliding to a halt in front of them. Dorian watched Nahm climb on to straddle a helmeted rider with a cartoon snake on one thick forearm. He lost his half-chub.

As the scooter darted back out into traffic, Dorian looked down at the insurance cam in his palm and grimaced.

It took another oversized bottle of beer before he could bring himself to watch the cam footage. Finally, slouched protectively over the table, he plugged it into his tablet and fast-forwarded through the empty hotel room until the door opened. Nahm glided inside on her pencil-thin heels, but instead of Alexis Carrow coming in behind her, it was the security guard, furtively checking the hallway before locking the door.

And instead of fucking, they sat on the edge of the bed and had a fairly business-like discussion in Thai. At one point Nahm departed for the bathroom and returned with the ziplock in hand. Dorian narrowed his eyes as she tossed it casually to her partner in crime, who stuffed it into a black duffel bag. The man paused, gesticulating at the bed and walls, then, with Nahm's approval, dug a scanner bar out of the duffel.

Dorian fast-forwarded through an impressively thorough search until the cam was spotted, plucked off the wall, and carried back to Nahm. She flashed a very un-vapid smile into the lens. The screen went black for a moment, then cleared again in the bathroom, pointing towards the mirror where Nahm was now painting a bruise under her eye.

Dorian swilled beer in his mouth, letting the carbonation sting his tongue while he listened to Nahm explain, in her roundabout way, how her "little" brother had caught him running a scam in a bar where he bounced. How Dorian had drunkenly bragged about his takings. How Nahm had shopped photos from Alexis Carrow's vacation in Malaysia six months ago and slipped the fake news report into the mirror for him to watch.

Her brother, working as a valet at the Emerald Palace, had gotten the imposing black ute out of the garage for a quick spin. She'd worked on her Cockney accent for a few weeks and done up a voice synthesizer. And from there, Dorian realized his overactive imagination had done the rest of the work.

"I hope the last part is so easy, too," Nahm said sweetly, smearing her lip gloss across her face with the heel of her hand. "With the money, we think maybe to buy a boat. Mwah." She blew a kiss to the cam, then reached in and switched it off.

Dorian leaned back at his table. Unprofessional of her, to add insult to injury like that and lay out her method besides. But he supposed it was understandable in the excitement of pulling off a semi-long con for the first time. And at least this way he'd recouped one of the cams. Dorian slid it back into his pocket, pensive.

For a little while he rewound the footage and sourly watched Nahm blowing kisses on loop, then finally he put the tablet away. He still had enough cash stowed to take a domestic down south and start over from there.

A fresh wave of tourists would be showing up on the islands soon, and Pattaya just wasn't doing it for him anymore.

YOU'LL SURELY DROWN HERE IF YOU STAY
Alyssa Wong

Alyssa Wong (crashwong.net) is a Nebula, Shirley Jackson, and World Fantasy Award-nominated author, shark aficionado, and 2013 graduate of the Clarion Writers' Workshop. Her work has appeared in *The Magazine of Fantasy & Science Fiction, Strange Horizons, Tor.com, Uncanny, Lightspeed, Nightmare,* and *Black Static,* among others. Her 2015 short story "Hungry Daughters of Starving Mothers" won the Nebula and World Fantasy Awards, and was nominated for the Locus, Bram Stoker and Shirley Jackson Awards. Wong is an MFA candidate at North Carolina State University and is a member of the Manhattan-based writing group Altered Fluid.

WHEN THE DESERT finally lets you go, naked and stumbling, your body humming with raw power and the song of dead things coiled under your tongue, you find Marisol waiting for you at the edge of the bluffs. She's dressed in long sleeves and a skirt over her boots, her black hair tucked under a hat and a blanket wrapped around her shoulders against the night cold. Madam Lettie's bony horse whuffs at you in the glow of the lantern as you approach.

"You were gone longer than usual," says Marisol. "I got worried."

Human speech is always slow to return on the nights when the desert calls you. You nod in reply.

Marisol sets the lantern down and pulls off her blanket to wrap around you. Most girls her age would flinch away from touching a naked boy's skin, but her fingers brush yours indifferently. She's seen your body as many times as you've seen hers, in all of its pitiful states: bruised and scratched; bramble-bled from running through the thorns with the coyotes; finger-marked by rough hands. "Did you step on any scorpions?"

You turn your head and spit a brown, dusty gob into the dirt. You hope she doesn't notice the fur and tiny bone fragments caught in it. "Who do you take me for?"

A wan grin spreads across her face, and she almost looks like the kid she is—that you both are. "Check 'em anyway."

You glance at Madam Lettie's horse instead of at your battered bare feet. "She'll be furious when she finds out that you took Belle."

"She's always furious," says Marisol. She swings onto the horse, and the animal shivers as you climb up behind her. "Besides. She pretends otherwise, but she knows how you get home every night. She's never raised a hand to me about it."

"Good. If she does, tell me. I don't want you to get in trouble."

"Just hold the lantern," says Marisol. She nudges Belle forward and the three of you turn toward the road leading to the Bisden mines. A few pinpricks of lamplight glimmer along the ridge from the town beyond, and the path snakes through the sand like a pale sidewinder.

The horse's back rolls beneath you like dirt in a goldrusher's pan, and you practice breathing. In, out, with the rhythm of the hooves and Marisol's heartbeat.

"Some of the men from the big mining company out east visited the house while you were gone," Marisol says. "The city folk who rode in on the California-bound train yesterday. They're staying across the street."

Oh. "Which did you have?" you say.

"The tall one. The one with dark brown hair and the Yankee accent. He speaks pretty enough, but he's not... kind." She shrugs. "But then, who is to a whore?"

You hold her tighter.

"One of them asked for you."

"For me?" you say. No one notices you, not you, the small and half-feral boy kept in the back to clean the kitchen. *Bless Madam Lettie's heart for taking you in, you poor soul*, with your dead witch-father and propensity to make discarded bones quiver and shake like living things. *Poor souls, both.*

"He looked like some kind of preacher. But there was something off about him." She won't look at you, not while she's guiding the horse back to town, but when you press your face against the back of her neck, strands of hair tickling your cheek, you can feel her breathing relax. "I don't know why, but he reminded me of you."

"How so?"

"I'm not sure," Marisol says. "But the city folk are planning to hold a party at Madam Lettie's in a few days, so he'll probably be back tomorrow with the rest. You can see for yourself then."

You've witnessed a few parties at Madam Lettie's, and mostly that means a rough night for Marisol and the rest of the girls at the brothel. Madam Lettie will probably have you attend the guests, too. Just thinking about it makes you wince.

The town is quiet, the sound of Belle's hooves muffled against the sand. Madam Lettie's is the only building with candles still burning in the windows, and the empty, boarded up buildings littering the stretch remind you of when the town was still lively, before the silver dried up, before the desert's call grew too loud for you to ignore.

Marisol helps you up the stairs, past the bar, and together you stumble into her room. It stinks of sweat and musk, but probably no worse than you do. The two of you collapse into Marisol's bed. It's barely big enough for one person and your own cot is down the hall, but everything in your body aches, and Marisol feels so human against your bones. You need that right now.

"I saw my pa tonight," you say into Marisol's hair. Her dark braids smell like smoke, and you bury your face into them, just behind her ear. "Walking among the brush with the rest of the dead."

"I'm sorry."

"I didn't find your folks, though. I heard their voices, but I couldn't dig a path deeper into the mine." You'd torn your hands to pieces, ripped the skin and flesh down to the bone, and the desert had built you back out of sand and briars, then pushed you rudely away from the entrance to the collapsed mineshaft. The wandering skeletons of slain cattle and men had stopped their nighttime shambling to watch through ant-eaten eyes. *Stay away from this, child.*

She sucks in a breath. "If you found them, could you bring them back?"

You close your eyes. "No. Not like you want. I could make their bodies move, but it wouldn't be real."

She nods and holds your hand tight. It's a conversation you've had a few times, ever since the desert started pulling you away from Madam Lettie's every night and you started being able to coax dead things into dancing for you. This time, Marisol says, very softly, "Sometimes I wonder if that would be enough, just seeing them again."

It wouldn't, but you don't need to tell her that. Her grip on your hand means that she knows.

ONE OF THE company men appears on the doorstep in the morning, black hair slicked away from his naked face, too young and too nervous to be standing in front of a saloon-turned-cathouse in broad daylight. Madam Lettie, who is lean and tough like rawhide, lets him in, and as they pace the ground floor and talk about plans for Saturday night, you and Marisol sneak peeks from behind the kitchen door.

"That's not the preacher man, is it?" you say. Marisol shakes her head. She's helping you with laundry today, and the filthy sheets bunch up between you, muffling the sounds of your bodies moving.

"I figured it out," she says, "the preacher man's strangeness. He walked like his feet didn't touch the ground, and he stank. God, he was foul."

"You've said the same about me," you say. And it's true; usually you're so much dirt that you could grow plants in the creases of your arms and fingers, if the sullen clouds over Bisden ever gave water. But when she glances at you, there's no humor in her eyes.

"Ellis, I'm telling you. That man reeked like a body left bloating in the sun at high noon. I never smelled something so bad in my life, even from across the room."

The familiarity of it builds a sense of relief and dread in you. Almost every one of the customers Madam Lettie demanded you take had said something similar. They'd never lasted long; the last rancher who'd slipped his hands into your trousers had bitten your neck, then turned and vomited off the edge of the bed.

Lettie had kept his money and made you clean the floor, which you had done patiently, without complaint. By then it had become a system between you two, and you've seen and done worse beneath this roof. Though she cannot stop you from wandering the desert at night with the dead things, just as she could not stop your father before you, she can at least turn a profit off of your peculiarities.

The saloon doors swing open and a group of men walk in. The one at the front is immaculate and fair-skinned, like he's never spent a day sweating under the sun. His pale blond hair is combed back in a smooth wave, and he walks with the easy confidence of a wealthy man. Behind him is the tallest man you've ever seen, a gaunt, bent figure in priest's robes. A dizzying rush of power—the call of the desert, the urge to shed your clothes and run with the coyotes through the brush, to dig up the dead to dance with—hits you down to your bones.

The preacher man turns his head and looks straight at you, grinning past the bar with empty eyes.

Marisol grabs your hand so tight it hurts. "Stop that," she says, quiet and sharp. "You're doing it again."

Harriet, the girl on kitchen duty today, is backing away from the sink, knife held high in shaking hands. The sound of bones rattling against metal fills your ears, and you turn to look; the chicken she'd been preparing for dinner staggers back to its feet, half-skinned, half-butchered. Its flesh hangs in open, swaying flaps. The discarded pile of plucked feathers begins to swirl around it like an obscene snowfall.

"Witchcraft," Harriet whispers. She's new; she's never seen you do this before. The rest of the girls have some inkling of your strangeness; they cross themselves when they pass you, and they stay well away from you at night, when the dust in your skin begins to prickle with electrifying power.

"*Stop that,*" Marisol snaps, at her, at you, at both of you. "Ellis, breathe. Bring it down."

You can feel each movement the dead chicken takes, your blood pounding in time with its footsteps.

"Ellis!"

You focus, breathe out, and force your fists to unclench. The chicken's headless neck whips toward you, snakelike, its ragged circle of severed bone and muscle gleaming at you like a malevolent eye. Its toenails rasp against the sink. *Calm down,* you think, and it sways, sinking to its knees. *Go back to sleep.*

"What is going on here?" Madam Lettie demands from the kitchen door. Her body fills the entrance, arms outstretched and resting on the doorframe to keep anyone from coming in behind her. At her back are the company men, the pale one who looks like a prince and his nervous, dark-haired retainer. And the preacher man, gaunt and grinning. He nods at you the way a man would a lady, as if he'd just doffed his hat.

The desert's voice *screams* through your body, an unfiltered torrent of power tearing at you like the most vicious of dust storms. Any control you have over the bird evaporates in its wake. The chicken launches itself from the sink—no feathers, no gravity, no sense but magic to keep it aloft—and flies at Madam Lettie, talons extended. She screams and beats it away. The company men behind her are shouting, and there is blood and meat everywhere. You barely hear Marisol yell your name before you're out the back door, running blind and fast, back towards the bluffs. *Come,* the desert sings, *come home my son,* and you scarcely make it past the town's border before your human form falls away and you are wild, uncontainable, raw, free.

TIME PASSES DIFFERENTLY for you when you aren't human. Animals operate on cycles of eat-sleep-hide-stalk, and although you are not quite an animal like this, you've found that the land, which beats in your blood, operates on similar principles. Cycles of heat-burn-cool-dark, the wind blowing balefully over the baked, cracked earth. Now is heat-burn, and though the ground sears your feet, you barely notice.

Your father's grave is marked by a pair of yucca trees, their straggly branches clawing toward the heavens. There is no tombstone. A cluster of scorched stones lie scattered at the feet of the trees, marred by some mysterious immolation, and the coyotes have taken to leaving small gifts of bones there as well.

You pace before the grave, listening for your mother's voice. Her sighs are in the scuttle of desert rats in their hiding holes, the scratch-scratch of burrowing owls' claws against the dirt as they run, stick-legged, chasing the shade. She's called you here for a reason, you're sure, but in this form you have no voice with which to answer her, and so you must wait.

Instead of the desert's comforting murmur, the words of your father's favorite lullaby trickle down around you, sung in a raspy human voice:

"Shake, shake, yucca tree,

Rain and silver over me—"

All of the animal bones lying on his grave begin to tremble, shivering and crying *clack-clack clack*. Dread bites you deep in the stomach, and you snarl with all of your mouths, the sand swirling at your feet.

"Stormclouds, gather in the sky,

Mockingbird and quail, fly;

My love, my love, come haste away!

You'll surely drown here if you stay."

The bones on the ground snap together into a single line pointing to the trunk of the biggest yucca. High above you perches the preacher man, contorted into a shape with his knees raised to his ears. His black clothing seems to glimmer in the heat, and the way his neck arcs makes him look like a giant vulture, begrudgingly fitted into human form. His shadow stretches long and thin across the ground like a single, accusing finger.

"I was the one who taught him that song, you know." The preacher man blinks at you and smiles again. "A prayer to bring down the rain. And this town could use some resurrection, couldn't it?"

The branch he's sitting on doesn't look strong enough to hold a man of his size, but that doesn't bother the preacher man. In a blink, he's gone from the tree, and in another blink, he's standing over you, hunched shoulders blocking out the moonlight. The moon, you realize, is out, a pale sliver cutting the night sky.

Marisol is right. The preacher man smells like death.

"You truly are the spitting image of him," he murmurs. "I suppose he was your father, wasn't he. You have the same hair, the color of the clay deep in the earth. And the same talent for making sleeping things rise up when they shouldn't." The preacher man cocks his head, adjusting his wide-brimmed hat. "I taught him that, too. He was mine before he came to seek his fortune out west, with all the rest of his brothers. Before he turned his back on me for my sister."

The desert hisses in you, and you can feel your body humming with her rage, her resentment, her regret. Coyotes slink out of the darkness to flank you, their eyes glinting like rough-cut gems. But the preacher man just laughs, his mouth too wide.

"Twice-blessed, twice-cursed. You got my gift, and hers." The preacher man leans in, his dry, fetid breath ghosting across your face. "But I didn't come out here just to scare you. There is a storm brewing, little one. Something bigger than you can understand, brought here by the men who came on the train."

That gives the desert pause and she coils in you like a waiting snake. Your heart is beating so fast that if you were still human, you would worry about passing out. But before you can try to force words out, to ask him what he means, a voice rings across the plain.

"Ellis?"

There's a small figure in the distance, one arm raised to shield their eyes. It's Marisol, her bandana tied around her face, pulled over her nose to protect her from the dust. No horse this time; she must have run after you on foot.

No, no, you don't want her to see you like this. Your dust storm kicks up into a twisting column, sending howling gusts to buffet her slight form. Marisol staggers back.

"Dammit, Ellis! Stop!" You can barely hear her over the storm, and the preacher man chuckles.

"What a loyal friend. But remember, child—bad things happen to men who marry the desert. Don't forget what they did to your father, out on your mother's territory, when they thought no one could see." The preacher man touches your forehead with one long, thin hand, and his fingers are stiff and ice cold. "People fear what they don't understand. That's why, no matter what you choose, you will always end up alone."

"Ellis!" Marisol is struggling, fighting her way through the blinding gale. When you glance back, the preacher man has vanished. "Ellis, please, get a hold of yourself!"

The power roars through your veins still, but with the preacher man gone, so is some of the intense pressure in your head. *No*, you think, tamping it down forcefully. If he is right, then this power is yours—a gift from your mother and from your father, to do with as you please. You *will* make it obey.

And for the first time in your life, for the first time since your father died and the desert began to cast its madness on you in his stead, you can feel your mother's power bend to your will, into a shape you can control. You clench your fist, and the winds die down to a quiet whisper. At the same time, you search back through yourself for the human frame that feels familiar to you, a boy with a small, bony body and earth-dark skin. A shape to fit your own power into.

No sooner have you slipped back into your own body than Marisol's arms are around you, clutching you tight. "Lord. I thought I'd lost you."

You sag into her embrace, feeling drained but so full. You've never come back to yourself like this before, not until your mother was ready to let you go. "I thought so too," you murmur against her cheek. "But I'm here. I'm not leaving."

"Chrissakes, I'm always cleaning up your messes." The bite in her voice makes you flinch, but her arms are gentle around you. Her footprints have been wiped away behind her, but even the wind can't scour away the deep, sharp divots her heels carved out of the ground as she fought her way to you.

"I'm sorry," you say. God, you love her so much. And not the way so many men desire women; you've never felt that, for anyone, in all your life. But Marisol has never touched you that way, and the warmth of her body here, now, is more than enough.

Still, the preacher man's words ring in your ears. *You will always end up alone.*

"It's all right." She begins to tug you away, back toward the direction of the town. "I'm used to it by now."

"Wait." You hold her hand, and she looks back at you, her braids framed in the scant light. "Marisol... you saw me. Like that."

"Yes."

You suck in a breath. "Weren't you scared?"

Her grip on your hand tightens. "I've seen worse." And she has; you both have, from the cave-in that orphaned the both of you, in different ways, to the haunted look in her eyes as you help her tighten her corset strings every evening, her hand shaking as she unstoppers the tiny bottle of laudanum she keeps behind the vanity mirror.

But she has never seen you as desert-wild as you were tonight, a mad creature stripped down to the bone. And there is some comfort in knowing that she has witnessed you, and that she can still look at you without turning her face away.

"Let's go back," Marisol says, very gently. She doesn't say *home*, and you're grateful for that.

*   *   *

MADAM LETTIE'S HAND cracks hard against your face. "Where have you been?" she hisses. You don't answer her—she knows already where you've been, you smell like the coyotes and animal piss and dried blood—and she hits you again. "I told you not to run off like that. You shamed me in front of our guests, fleeing past them like some mad, filthy creature. Thank the Lord they still want to use the saloon on Saturday." Lettie wipes her hand on her skirt like she's touched the most disgusting thing she's ever seen. You remember the times, when you were little and your father was still alive, when she used to touch your face with kind, gentle hands. When she held you because she wanted to, not because she had to. You remember the soft look in her eyes. You remember when she still used your name.

You think she might have loved you, once, before she learned to fear you.

"Now, now, Lettie." She starts—it seems she hadn't heard the two company men walk up behind her. It's the pale, princely one and his nervous, dark-haired companion. You wonder, briefly, if the latter is the one who had spent that first night with Marisol. The princely man has a cultured accent; you can tell by the way Madam Lettie straightens her shoulders unconsciously when he speaks to her. "It's quite all right. I don't think we've had proper introductions, though." He looks straight at you, not through you the way so many people do. "My name is William Lacombe. And your name is?"

Madam Lettie's lips purse. "The girls call him Ellis."

He barely looks at her. "Are you Ellis, then?"

"Yes," you say, very quietly. The preacher man is not with them, and you can't sense his presence any more. You're not fool enough to think he's gone, though.

William's gaze travels to Marisol, who is standing silently behind you, and stops. "And the brave girl who ran out after our new friend. Who might you be?"

"Marisol," she says. William reaches out and takes her hand; then he brings it to his lips and kisses the back of it. Madam Lettie's expression goes sour enough to pickle a jar of vegetables. William's companion's brow tightens.

"Marisol." He says her name the way the desert says yours, like the heat crackling across the rocks. *Marisol.* Heat crackles across your face, too, at the sound of it in his mouth. "A pleasure to make your acquaintance. Has Lettie told you why I'm here?"

"No, sir." She withdraws her hand, uncertainty flickering through her eyes, and takes a step back. William only smiles and straightens up, looking from Marisol to you.

"Well, the Lacombe Mining Company owns the land that this town is built on. We developed the mine just outside the bluffs. It took a few months to hear of the tragic news of the collapsed shaft—so many good men were lost, and for that, I offer my deepest condolences." His eyes look sad, and he holds his hat to his chest. This gesture makes you trust him exactly as much as you did before, if not less. "Of course, the vein of silver was blocked off as well. Samuel—my companion here—and I have been sent to evaluate the damages to the mine and draw up the appropriate compensation for the families of the lost miners."

"When did the fits start?" Samuel says abruptly, staring at you. It seems he isn't one for pleasantries. "The thing with the bones."

"The boy's done this since his father died." Madam Lettie won't even say his name, for all he'd adored her. You'd adored her too, then, even if she was your father's second wife.

"Is he yours?"

"Heavens, no. He was his father's child and came to me as such."

William coughs and shoots Samuel a sharp glance. "We've never seen anything like this out east. Is this a common... phenomenon in your town?"

"I hear you burn your witches out east," says Madam Lettie. You stare at the floor and try to disappear. The place where she slapped you aches, a sensation that won't go away, and your heart feels like it's been scratched deep by acacia thorns. "No, he's the only one, since his father died. Small mercies. In spite of his bedevilments, I've kept him under my roof ever since."

"I see." A hand slips under your chin to tilt your face up, and you find yourself looking into William's eyes. "Ellis, it seems you have a rare and unique gift. It may well be devils' work, but I am a God-fearing man who has seen many things, and I have no fear of you. I would like you to accompany us to survey the mine tomorrow morning."

"Sirs, that would be a terrible inconvenience—"

"We can compensate you for his time, of course."

"He doesn't have a horse," says Madam Lettie. Her fists are knotted in her skirt, and there is something in her voice—a tinge of panic, perhaps— that reminds you of Marisol. It makes you think again. Maybe it's your imagination, but you haven't heard her talk about you like this since... well. "It's a dangerous area, gentlemen. Surely you would be better served by taking some of the men displaced by the cave-in. They have their own firearms as well."

"We have our own men. What we don't have is someone who can talk to the dead." Your breath catches in your throat. He had seen you, after all. Out of the corner of your vision, Marisol looks scared as well, her shoulders tense like she's ready to grab you and run.

William releases your face. "We ride at dawn. Pack accordingly, Ellis."

"You can't take him." To your surprise, it's not Marisol who says this, but Madam Lettie, stepping between the two of you. "I won't allow it."

William turns a beautiful smile on her. "My dear Lettie, it isn't a request."

As he sweeps out the doors and into the night, Samuel stalking at his heels, you realize that William is humming something under his breath. It takes you a moment to recognize that it is your father's song.

You leave the town on a borrowed horse as the sun begins to stretch over the horizon, Marisol's stained red bandana wrapped around your throat. Marisol is up to see you off, her shawl wrapped around her to protect her from the cold night.

"Don't do anything stupid," she says as you ready your horse, her voice pitched low enough to carry to your ears alone. "If you see any of those walking things, gallop the hell out of there. These city folk be damned."

She is so fierce, such a survivor, your Marisol. Each of you is the other's only friend, and so much more. You open your mouth to tell her how you feel, but what comes out instead is, "The prince can't take his eyes off of you. This could be your ticket out, Marisol."

She kisses your cheek so she doesn't have to look at your face, and that's how you know that she knows, too. William, with his money and his fondness for her. With his life a cross-continental train ride away from this terrible, dying town, away from the saloons where tiny bottles are hidden behind mirrors and men with rough hands prowl the corridors, some new place where a person like you or Marisol could start over.

When Marisol pulls back, her dark curls tickling your cheek, her eyes are hard. "Don't pin your hopes on dreams. Just get back to me in one piece, Ellis."

You kiss her cheek and swing up onto the horse. "I will." *I won't leave you alone.*

"Come, boy," orders Samuel. He and the rest of the company men are already mounted and ready to go, with William at the head of the party. All of them are cloaked in ponchos or jackets to ward off the sun, when it arrives. There is no sign of the preacher man.

Obedient, you follow, the coyotes howling in your head, your head down and hands tight on the reins. You don't look back at Marisol, but you can feel her growing smaller and smaller in the distance, the distance of the land between you stretching with each new step.

The company men ride all day with little conversation, and the sun rises in a slow arc, glaring overhead like a malignant eye. It's hard to stay on the horse; you don't have much practice riding, and the horse is fidgety, as if it can smell the feralness on you.

After last night, your grip on your wild, brittle, real self is firmer, but being away from town and heading into the heartland of your mother's territory slowly erodes your self-control. At Madam Lettie's, you drift like a ghost through the halls, sweeping floors, cooking meals, disappearing into the shadows. But here, as the mountains cup the sky with deep brown hands, the call to bound away, howling, with the coyotes in the brush becomes almost unbearable. Your skin itches, as if your clothes are too tight, and you ache to be among the yucca and wild honeysuckle, the fields of bones where the mesas rise in strange bestial shapes from the flat ground.

The company men have few words for you, although Samuel keeps a distrustful eye on you, always placing himself between your horse and William's. William, as gracious as he'd been in town, seems to have retreated into himself, watching the horizon silently.

The first of the dead things stumbles across your path when your party is a few miles away from the mine. It looks like the corpse of a bull, an unlucky casualty of a careless, ambitious rustler, judging by the bullet holes punched in its ragged hide. The men pull up short, and Samuel hauls your horse up to the front, your reins fisted in his hand. The bull stares at you both with ponderous, sightless eyes and paws the ground.

"Can you stop it?" demands Samuel. Behind him, the men murmur among themselves. *Cursed* and *possessed* and *devil work* catch your ears.

"I don't know," you murmur.

"You best figure it out fast," says Samuel, and he's right; the dead bull, mostly bones and empty skin, has thrown its head down, ready to charge. It has no lungs, no voice, and its silence is unnerving. "Guns aren't going to help against something like that."

You swallow and focus. The desert's power curls in your palm, the way it had behaved for you the night before, but it feels jagged, uneven. Still, you hold out your hand. *Stop.*

The animal skeleton quivers and lifts its head tentatively. Then it takes a step toward you. Then another, and another, until it breaks into a gallop. The horses behind you began to panic, and so do their riders.

"Kill it!" hisses Samuel. Sweat beads his dark brow. "Dammit, boy, you're the only one who can put it down!"

"Ellis!" shouts William. "Do it!"

"I can't!" you cry. *Stop! Stop!* But it's not listening. You've never taken a dead thing apart before, only made them come together, and then only by accident. And then William is beside you, gripping your shoulder. Power spikes through you—

Shake, shake, silver and rain over me—

—and the desert, your mother, screams through you. Lightning strikes through your vision, and when you blink, gasping for breath, there are visible threads of power running through the undead animal, bright as silver. You close your fist and *pull* on those strings. *STOP.*

The bull stops in its tracks, frozen, only a few yards from you. And then it spasms and collapses into a heap of bones and sun-weathered skin.

There is a moment of utter stillness. And then William laughs, clapping you hard on the shoulder. Your concentration shatters, and you fight to keep your power, your human shape, contained. "Well done!"

Your head is full of the screams of dying cattle, your nose the acrid scent of gunpowder, and you sway on your horse, trying to hold on.

The rest of the men stay away from you, huddling together. Only Samuel rides up to you and William, reining his horse in as close as he can get.

"What were you thinking?" he snaps. But he's not asking you, he's asking William, who just grins. "You could have gotten yourself killed!"

You realize it then. He looks at William the way you look at Marisol. He looks at William like he would do anything for him, even die, unquestioning, for him, his name on his lips.

"It worked, Sam," says William. He sounds giddy. "He took it apart. Did you see that?" He turns to you almost feverishly. "If he can wake the dead, why can't he put them back to sleep? I knew it, I was right!" His hand is still on your shoulder, but you have the feeling that, as he stares into your face, he's looking through you. "Ellis, you're our chance to get to the mine safely. That's why we need you."

"One time isn't a pattern," says Samuel. "It's not safe. And the boy looks like he's about to fall over. Assuming this... witchcraft works again, how long can he keep this up?"

Witchcraft. You swallow past the knot in your throat as William and Samuel argue in low voices. *Witchcraft* is what got your father killed. His songs to bring down the rain and his nighttime journeys to visit your mother, to worship her on her soil.

People fear what they don't understand.

A flask bumps your hand, and you find Samuel looking at you with dark eyes. Behind him, William has galloped to join the rest of the men, waving them in. "Drink," Samuel says quietly. "You're parched, aren't you."

You take his flask uncertainly. But the water is good, tinny and warm on your tongue.

"Can you get us to the mine?" he asks. He lets you drink as much as you want, and you appreciate that small kindness.

"I don't know," you say, staring at your hands. "I didn't know I could make the dead... stop. Not until now."

"You best learn." Samuel stops you when you try to hand his flask back. "Once William makes up his fool mind about something, it's impossible to change it. We'll get to the mine or we'll die trying." He tilts his chin up at you. "I would prefer not to die. And I hope to deliver every one of our men safely home. That includes you."

The sun beats down as he rides away, motioning to William. As you shade your eyes, clutching his canteen and squinting past the acacias in the direction of the mine, you can still taste gunpowder. And although you see nothing on the flat horizon beyond the mesas, you swear you can hear the preacher man's soft chuckle rolling with the chollas across the sands.

THE SKY OVER the mine is as cloudless as it has been since the night your father was murdered. Dead men and animals pace the grounds in tattered skins; skeletal owls and sparrows perch on the broken wooden beams that used to frame the entrance to the mine, chattering their empty beaks. It smells worse than rancid, and your mother's displeasure boils through you as too-hot power, the compulsion to slough off your skin, to turn around and flee into the brush and never come back.

But you do not leave. Instead, you hold your ground in front of the company of men and call the dead down, one by one, forcing them to their knees, then to their faces. Their deaths wash over you as you lay them to rest

stabbed eaten whole my mouth is so dry will I never see my children again suffocating bleeding broken neck teeth tearing at me I don't want to die

and they go peacefully. You, though, do not; after only a few of these anti-resurrections, you're shaking and howling and barely able to stay on your horse for it. The men watch fearfully from a distance, and the horse almost bucks you off before Samuel catches its head, whispering soothing words into its ear. The only other person who comes close is William, his hair glittering bright as a newly unearthed vein of silver.

"You can do it, Ellis," William says in a low voice. Samuel watches you wordlessly, his hand at his hip, thumb resting on the handle of his pistol.

No one else has been able to come close to the mine in the three months since the collapse. You force the dead things into order, their wild disarray of energy into something malleable, and send them back into stillness.

hurts bleeding starving my mouth is so dry ripped to pieces I can't feel my legs don't let me die like this please lantern flickering out oh god someone save me

The miners' voices flood your mind, and you scream, your vision darkening. You are underground, crushed and unable to move, your ribs splintering with the weight of immovable rock. Last thoughts flicker through your head: a woman's face, a dog left tied to a post outside with no one to let it free, Marisol standing on the street in threadbare clothes, looking up at the sign for Madam Lettie's establishment.

STOP.

And then the darkness is different, and so is the body you're in; it is nighttime, and pinpricks of starlight shine through the burlap sack over your head. The rough bark of a yucca tree digs into your back, and your wrists are bound behind you. There are so many voices, some the same as the miners'. There is a sharp sound, like steel against rock, and then flame springs to being at your feet, licking at your legs. Bright red flames, and you think *Lettie,* and *Ellis,* and then there are no more thoughts, only pain.

STOP STOP STOP STOP

"Don't shoot!" William shouts. Rough hands shove you, and the visions break, along with your grip on the dead things. You land hard in the red dirt. William dismounts and stands over you, an arm extended to shield you from the rest of the men.

Samuel's pistol is cocked and pointed at your head. It's not the only gun aimed at you among the company.

"You caught on fire," Samuel says. His voice is bland, and there's an indiscernible look on his face.

Your skin seems intact, no burn marks in sight. But you know what you felt, and for a moment, you know that you'd lost yourself to your father the way you'd lost yourself to your mother so many times before. "Are they gone?" you rasp.

"Not quite," says William. Sweat sheens his face and his hair is disheveled as he pushes it back with his fingers.

Heaps of bones cover the ground, collapsed amidst the brittlebrush that crawls across the sand. Most of your mother's handiwork destroyed, her curse unraveled, not gone. But there are still a few meandering about, gathered in front of the mine's entrance. They don't look like proper animals; they've been cobbled together from the large, abandoned bones of many different bodies, some human, some beast. By now, you feel much the same.

You're so tired, and your limbs are trembling. You've pulled so much power into yourself that it aches. And the desert is not pleased; the searing heat of her anger boils in you, demanding the change, demanding you leave, demanding, demanding.

"Just a few more," says William, reaching down to clasp your shoulder. As his skin touches yours, you flinch—that same explosive rush of energy hits you, the way it had in the kitchen, and with the first dead bull. But this time, the flashback of another death takes over your vision

Samuel, sweet, stupid Samuel, blood on his shirt, holding your hand, calling your name frantically, and the dry laughter of the preacher man, an offer you wouldn't refuse even if you could. An offer of power, an image of the dead working the mines across the country, tireless, without pay, without complaint. And of you, watching the numbers tick upward in the newspapers. You laugh, too, with your last breath, and seal the preacher man's deal with a trembling finger smeared in your own blood

and you stagger back.

"You can do it," says William. Pale, immaculate, cold to the touch. He smells of expensive cologne, but under that, a sickly, fetid stink.

"So can you," you say. He stills. "Can't you."

He blinks once, his eyes clear and colorless, and flicks a finger at the skeletons. They collapse in a rainfall of bones. "Good job, Ellis," he says in a voice that carries to his men. But he's not looking at them.

"Why did you need me?"

"This goddamn desert," he says in a voice that is only for you. At the same time, he reaches for you, and you shrink back. "In the past few months, we've sent so many men to scout out the mines in this area. Not a single one who traveled south of the Rio de Lino and west of the Rio Grande made it back, even the ones who could bid the dead do their bidding. Devoured by this goddamn desert, torn apart by the coyotes, sent wandering in circles until they collapsed and died. But when I heard about your father's death, and about you, it all clicked into place."

The preacher man's words echo back. *He was mine before he came to seek his fortune out west, with all the rest of his brothers. Before he turned his back on me for my sister.*

William smiles. "She has no love for men like us. But she wouldn't dare hurt you. Not her own child, and his." He hauls you to your feet, his grip tight on your arm. "Come, Ellis. Walk with me, and stay close. Let's get a good look at the mine." He gestures, and the rest of the men approach cautiously, treading among the fallen bodies, leaving a wide berth around you and occasionally making the sign against evil as they pass.

This man doesn't care about the town. None of his pretty words to Madam Lettie about recompense, or about reopening the mine to re-establishing commerce, matter. The town is just a field of bodies to use as he pleases. And he will use you, too. As a shield against your mother's wrath, as a hostage to make the desert behave.

But his power is different from yours. He has only the preacher man's blessing, and you have something else.

The desert change roars through you like a tide, a demand you can't ignore to undo your skin and let your real self run free. This time, you embrace it.

COME, demands the desert, and you shatter, finally, fully.

One of the other men is the first to see what is happening to you, your skin peeling off in long slabs, shedding your human form for something uncontainable, something lightning-legged, bent-backed, and wild. All of the desert's power you'd pulled into yourself courses through your limbs, back into the ground, silvered lines darting across the baked earth. All around, the piles of bones tremble and quiver, then rise slowly into the air, taking their forms once again.

"Monster!" he screams. Damn you, for there is only relief in your heart that he did not call you *witch*.

The desert rides you, and you are no longer your own. The winds kick up, blowing sheets of dust into the men's face. If your mother has her way, and you yours, you will bury them all here, deep in the mine, with the rest of the humans.

What about Marisol? a small part of you asks, but it is drowned out by your mother's and your combined fury.

William has stumbled away, his hands out, and you can feel him fighting you for control of the dead. He's much stronger than you, much more experienced. But your mother pours more power into you, and you fight back. The sandstorm grows, blinding the company men who are fumbling for their guns.

The desert's dead are approaching when Samuel steps between you and William, his pistol leveled at you. There is fear, but his arm is steady.

"Samuel, no!" roars William, but there is no hesitation in Samuel's eyes.

His pistol cracks, and you think of Marisol in that split second before impact, and then there is nothing.

"SHAKE, SHAKE, YUCCA tree,

"Rain and silver over me—"

The *clack-clack clack* of bones all around you. The preacher man's voice is creaky, parched as he sings, his hands brushing over your stone-still chest. Another, familiar voice joins his, a woman's voice like the whisper of scorpions' legs through the bone fields, a gentle tickle laced with the promise of poison. The ground hums under you with your mother's grief.

Stormclouds, gather in the sky,

Mockingbird and quail, fly;

My love, my love, come haste away!

You'll surely drown here if you stay.

Your eyes are open, the evening sun glaring into your eyes, but you can't blink. Every muscle is frozen in place, and it takes great effort to open your mouth.

"Am I dead?" you croak. You can't feel your chest moving.

"Very," says the preacher man. "But that's nothing new."

Slowly, you force your fingers to clench. "How long have I been... gone?"

"A few days. They tried to burn your body, but I wasn't about to lose another like that." His mouth twists into a parody of a smile. "When the flame wouldn't take, they left you to the vultures."

Fools, says your mother. The desert herself, the heat and mercilessness, wrapped like a vice around your heart. You wonder if you've been dead since the first night she called you into herself, that first time you gave up your body to become something more. *As if I would let my creatures hurt you. Would that you could say the same of yours, brother.*

The preacher man winces. It looks strange, with his empty sockets. "I indulged that boy too much. I thought I could keep him east, out of your territory. But his ambition overgrew his sense—"

He murdered my son!

"This child is my kin, too," hisses the preacher man. "Don't deny me that, sister. You're the one who let them flee back to their town, with not a scratch on them to pay for their misdeeds."

I would have those who harmed him pay accordingly.

"So would I. That may be the first matter we've agreed on in centuries."

"Whose side are you on?" you say. The preacher man cocks his head.

"Mine. And yours, though you may not believe it." He offers you his hand, and you take it, your body moving slowly. "I always was too fond of your father," he says in a low voice. "And your mother never let me forget it."

You wonder whose power is making this possible, his or your mother's. You are hyperaware of the dead things around you, their potential energy, just as you are of all the creatures skittering and prowling the earth, and the ancient hum of the ground.

The preacher man leads you to the entrance of the mine, where boulders and broken beams cluster tight, blocking the way. "What do you see?"

You place your hands on the boulders and close your eyes, focusing. The lines of your mother's power spread like a net through your mind's eye. And far beneath, pockets of the dead, of fallen men.

It has been three months since your unforgiving mother, in her grief, took your father's burnt body into her own and spat out every dead desert thing for miles around, sent them haunting the mine, the roads, until there was nowhere safe to go but down, down, down into the earth. And when the mineshaft collapsed, suffocating the miners in the tunnels, she still would not forgive, and held the rainclouds three months away from the town so that nothing would grow.

You open your eyes. "I see potential."

The preacher man cackles, and even your mother gives a pleased crackle. *I told you he was clever.*

The men from out east, even William with all of his power, could not move the boulders on their own. They would be back with proper mining equipment, maybe even fancy machines from their waterside cities, but likely not for months.

You don't need months. Not with the preacher man on one side of you and your mother all around, her presence like that of an oncoming monsoon.

"Lend me your power," you say. For something this big, you'll need more than what you have. More control, more finesse.

Pledge yourself to us. And we will pledge ourselves to you. Both of us. The preacher man nods.

You're already dead, and you can't go back like this, even if you wanted to. You have nothing to lose; nothing to lose except Marisol, and by now, surely news of your death has reached her. In dying, you have lost her, too.

You hold your hands out to both of them in assent. "Yes," you say simply.

Your name in your mother's voice is like the rush of the monsoon rains, water licking the parched ground, the promise of life and destruction at the same time. The preacher man leans in, places his dry forehead against yours, and breathes your name in a whisper that promises rest, peace, the passing of time in the cold, dark earth.

You hum, swaying. The preacher man unbuttons his coat and drapes it across your shoulders. His desiccated torso, open from sternum to belly, houses small, dark-furred fruit bats in its hollow. They hang upside down from the battered, broken ribs, their eyes glimmering at you like little embers.

"Shake, shake, yucca tree, rain and silver over me," you sing softly. The purr of your mother's power in you, her pleasure and approval, fills your hands. You see the pattern of the boulders, and you ease them free, one by one. They glide along the lines of your mother's power, smooth as oil.

The miners come next, their broken, insect-eaten bodies beginning to stir. The preacher man hums along with you, his movements matching yours. "Stormclouds, gather in the sky, oh mockingbird and quail, fly." With each insistent pull of your power, the miners stumble free into the dying light, into the empty air. You take each one in hand, and you focus, and the signs of death melt away. Their bodies are still cold, but the insect damage, the shattered limbs, are gone. You know, somehow, that this is only temporary and cannot last. But one night will be enough.

You think of Marisol and your cold chest tightens. It will have to be enough.

The movements of every desert creature buzz at the edge of your consciousness. The beating of owls' wings as they stalk their prey, the soft-tailed mice that creep beyond the rocks to howl at the moon in voices like tiny wolves. The slow unfurling of saguaro blossoms, petals parting against the inquisitive noses of tiny bats. The snakes twining in their burrows, tongues flicking out to taste for moisture in the air. And your coyotes, padding to meet you, glittering finery stolen from dead men clutched tight in their mouths, finery that is just your size.

You let the rail-thin crows lift the preacher's coat from your shoulders and shrug on the new jacket. It shimmers like moonlight. The desert creatures dress you as the coyotes pace, brushing against the preacher man and barking their devotion aloud. He smiles, knowing that devotion isn't for him.

When you are clad in the glittering suit, as fine as any prince from Marisol's books, a bird made of bones brings you a single honeysuckle blossom. You tuck the stem into a neat bullet hole in the jacket, right above at your chest.

"Come, then, my dear Ellis," says the preacher man. "Don't be late to your own party."

Indeed, your mother says. She sounds almost pleased. *Go show them a night they'll never forget.*

You grin, baring your teeth. Something almost like a horse trots up to you, its skeletal hooves clacking against the hard ground. As you swing atop it and turn towards the road, the miners begin to follow, not with slow and shambling steps, but with the pace of confident men. High above you, the beginnings of dark clouds slink across the sky, something unseen for months.

My love, my love, come haste away!

You'll surely drown here if you stay.

THE MOON RISES high and sharp, like a glittering mouth, as you descend upon the town. Your mount tosses its head, and if it had any lungs, or anything else inside its ragged bones, it might have whickered.

Banjos and fiddles brighten the air in Madam Lettie's saloon. The band stutters in confusion as you push the doors open, the dead men at your back. It is crowded inside, and as people take in the scene, gasps rise around you. Some gasps of fear, some gasps of joy at an apparent miracle. But you only have eyes for one person, and you stalk through the mass of townsfolk reaching for their loved ones, pushing them out of your way.

There she is, dancing with William amidst a circle of company men. He is immaculate once again, dressed in a fine-tailored suit. Her hair is done up, her corset laced (albeit clumsily; perhaps Harriet helped her in your stead), a smile painted on her face. You recognize the set of her jaw, the way she holds her mouth when she's fighting back sorrow.

"Marisol," you say, and her head snaps toward you, eyes widening. You pace towards her and she lets go of William, stepping to meet you. William doesn't try to stop her. Even if you weren't risen from the dead, you know he can see something new in your face, something as feral and bleak as the desert.

He backs away, fearful, and you offer Marisol your hand. "Dance with me," you say in a voice like the wind whipping through a dead man's bones.

"Ellis," she breathes, and then she's in your arms. Other cold, pale arms reach out behind you, grasping William tight; he yelps, but they yank him away and he's swallowed by the crush of bodies in their best, ragtag finery. You catch sight of Samuel, but he, too, is pulled into the masses before he can reach you. *Dance,* you think viciously, and they will, clasped tight in desert magic, until their bodies are torn to pieces.

Marisol is the one who taught you how to dance, on the groaning floorboards of her tiny room, and you hold her close as you sway to the music. She smells like she always does in the evenings, like perfume and dust. She can't take her eyes off of you, and you wonder what you look like to her, whether the glamor cast over the miners has lent you your old appearance back, or if you have been transformed into something wholly different.

"Let's get out of here," you whisper, and Marisol mouths *Yes.* Grasping her tight, you elbow your way through the crowd of people reuniting with their family members, their brothers, their husbands. Some have taken to dancing again, those lost to them clutched tight.

You glance over your shoulder for Madam Lettie, but she's standing stock still, gazed locked on the figure of a man who had joined you halfway across the flats, rising from the shade of a pair of yucca trees. As he draws closer, Lettie's face fills with impossible hope.

"Robert," she sobs, dashing forward and holding him close. His hair is the same color as yours, red like the earth, veined with silver, and his skin is dark as the dust. He holds her gently, his arms around her waist. Whatever words they have for each other are swallowed by the sound of the band and the crush of bodies around them.

Marisol's slipper is lost in the rush, but the two of you flee from the lights and whirling skirts into the dust outside, the starlight bearing down on you like a thousand icy stares. Her hand in yours is the warmest thing you've ever touched.

"Ellis, you crazy bastard. They told me you were dead." She laughs, too wild, tinged with grief. "Why didn't you come back sooner?"

You are silent, turning her hands over in yours. "They weren't wrong," you say at last.

"I don't understand," says Marisol, but you can see by the sinking hope in her eyes that she does.

"I did die." She shakes her head vigorously. "I'm still dead, Marisol. But I couldn't rest without saying goodbye to you." It's mostly true, and it will do for now.

"I'm sorry, Ellis." She's crying, and your heart sinks. Marisol rarely cries, and seeing her waste water on you is more than you can take. "I should have stopped them from taking you, I should have fought harder—"

"This isn't your fault," you say into her hair. "Not at all." A gentle tug of your power, and your bone and brittlebrush horse trots up to meet you. You drape your glittering coat over its back to make a seat for Marisol as she watches, unable to keep the fear and awe from her face.

"I didn't know you could do that."

You smile crookedly. "There are a lot of new things about me now. Come, get on."

She swings up on the mount and scoots forward, holding her hand out to help you up. But you don't take it. Instead, you reach into your pocket and press her stained red bandanna into her palm. It's heavy with coins taken from the bodies of the dead, enough to buy a one-way train ticket out east. You know; you counted it yourself.

"No," she breathes.

"You need to let me go," you say gently.

"I can't." She grabs for you; you step back out of her reach. "Ellis, no! Get on the goddamn horse! We're in this together, or not at all!"

"I can't go with you," you say. "I wish I could. God, I wish I could. But I belong to the desert now. I can't leave."

"Then I won't either."

"Don't be a fool," you snap, and she recoils. "Marisol, one of us needs to escape this place. And I can't any more." You gentle your voice. "Please."

In the end, you give her your boots to wear in place of her single slipper. Your dark, naked feet stand out against the sand, but whether the sand is bearable because of the nighttime cool or because you no longer feel the desert's burn, you don't know.

Marisol promises to buy a ticket, but she also promises to come back for you when she can. You hope she will forget the second promise, but you know her too well to believe it.

"I love you," she says, her eyes hard. "That's the only reason I'm leaving. For you, Ellis. If you forget everything else, don't forget that." She digs her heels into the horse's sides and it gallops away, your coat glittering under her skirt as she rides east.

"Well done," murmurs the preacher man. He stands behind you, his coat flapping in the growing wind.

Well done, echoes the desert.

"Keep her safe," you murmur. "Both of you, until she passes out of your realms."

We know you will, says your mother, and the preacher man nods in agreement.

You watch Marisol's horse until she passes out of sight, but you can still feel each hoofbeat strike against the baked clay, a staccato at the edge of your consciousness. You flex your fingers and look over your shoulder at the saloon. The windows are bright, and the chatter and music leaks from the doorway.

Nothing is permanent, but maybe Marisol was right. Maybe seeing a miracle and the ones you love, even for just one night, for one last time, will be enough.

The desert hums in your throat, and the language of the dead things coats your teeth. Back, then, towards the bluffs and the mesas, to the wilds where the coyotes cry over the yucca and the bodies of fallen men. Your kingdom lies out there among the wide, desolate plains, waiting for you to lay claim to its whispering bones.

The rising sun sears long red marks into the cloudy sky, and behind, you can hear the dead dancing themselves into a frenzy, long-lost miners with their wives and friends held close, spinning inhuman wild, as if afraid a spell will break.

You straighten your borrowed shirt and begin walking. Overhead, the sky rumbles with the promise of rain.

A SALVAGING OF GHOSTS

Aliette de Bodard

Aliette de Bodard (aliettedebodard.com) lives in Paris where she works as a System Engineer. In her spare time she writes fantasy and science fiction: her short stories have appeared in many venues, and garnered her a Locus Award, two Nebula Awards and two British Science Fiction Association Awards. Her domestic space opera based on Vietnamese culture, *On a Red Station, Drifting*, is available both in print and ebook. Her novel *The House of Shattered Wings*, set in a devastated Belle Époque Paris ruled by Fallen angels, came out in 2015 and won the BSFA the following year. Sequel *The House of Binding Thorns* is due out in 2017.

THUY'S HANDS HAVE just closed on the gem—she can't feel its warmth with her gloves, but her daughter's ghost is just by her side, at the hole in the side of the ship's hull, blurred and indistinct—when the currents of unreality catch her. Her tether to *The Azure Serpent*, her only lifeline to the ship, stretches; snaps.

And then she's gone, carried forward into the depths.

ON THE NIGHT before the dive, Thuy goes below decks with Xuan and Le Hoa. It's traditional; just as it is traditional that, when she comes back from a dive, she'll claim her salvage and they'll have another rousing party in which they'll drink far too many gems dissolved in rice wine and shout poetry until *The Azure Serpent*'s Mind kindly dampens their incoherent ravings to give others their sleep—but not too much, as it's good to remember life; to know that others onship celebrate surviving one more dive, like notches on a belt or vermillion beads slid on an abacus.

One more. Always one more.

Until, like Thuy's daughter Kim Anh, that one last dive kills you and strands your body out there, in the dark. It's a diver's fate, utterly expected; but she was Thuy's child—an adult when she died, yet forever Thuy's little girl—and Thuy's world contracts and blurs whenever she thinks of Kim Anh's corpse, drifting for months in the cold alien loneliness of deep spaces.

Not for much longer; because this dive has brought them back to where Kim Anh died. One last evening, one last fateful set of drinks with her friends, before Thuy sees her daughter again.

Her friends... Xuan is in a bad mood. No gem-drinking on a pre-dive party, so she nurses her rice wine as if she wishes it contains other things, and contributes only monosyllables to the conversation. Le Hoa, as usual, is elated; talking too much and without focus—dealing with her fears through drink, and food, and being uncharacteristically expansive.

"Nervous, lil' sis?" she asks Thuy.

Thuy stares into the depth of her cup. "I don't know." It's all she's hoped for; the only chance she'll ever get that will take her close enough to her daughter's remains to retrieve them. But it's also a dangerous dive into deep spaces, well into layers of unreality that could kill them all. "We'll see. What about you?"

Le Hoa sips at her cup, her round face flushed with drink. She calls up, with a gesture, the wreck of the mindship they're going to dive into; highlights, one after the other, the strings of gems that the scanners have thrown up. "Lots of easy pickings, if you don't get too close to the wreck. And that's just the biggest ones. Smallest ones won't show up on sensors."

Which is why they send divers. Or perhaps merely because it's cheaper and less of an investment to send human beings, instead of small and lithe mindships that would effortlessly survive deep spaces, but each cost several lifetimes to build and properly train.

Thuy traces, gently, the contours of the wreck on the hologram—there's a big hole in the side of the hull, something that blew up in transit, killing everyone onboard. Passengers' corpses have spilled out like innards—all unrecognisable of course, flesh and muscles disintegrated, bones slowly torn and broken and compressed until only a string of gems remains to mark their presence.

Kim Anh, too, is gone: nothing left of Thuy's precocious, foolhardy daughter who struggled every morning with braiding her hair—just a scattering of gems they will collect and sell offworld, or claim as salvage and drink away for a rush of short-lived euphoria.

There isn't much to a gem—just that familiar spike of bliss, no connection to the dead it was salvaged from. Deep spaces strip corpses, and compress them into... these. Into an impersonal, addictive drug.

Still... still, divers cannibalise the dead; and they all know that the dead might be them, one day. It's the way it's always been done, on *The Azure Serpent* and all the other diver-ships: the unsaid, unbreakable traditions that bind them all.

It didn't use to bother Thuy so much, before Kim Anh died.

"Do you know where she is?" Xuan asks.

"I'm not sure. Here, perhaps." Thuy points, carefully, to somewhere very near the wreck of the ship. "It's where she was when—"

When her suit failed her. When the comms finally fell silent.

Xuan sucks in a sharp breath. "Tricky." She doesn't try to dissuade Thuy, though. They all know that's the way it goes, too.

Le Hoa attempts, forcefully, to change the subject. "Two more dives and Tran and I might have enough to get married. A real couple's compartment, can you imagine?"

Thuy forces a smile. She hasn't drunk enough; but she just doesn't feel like rice wine: it'll go to her head, and if there's any point in her life when she needs to be there; to be clear-headed and prescient... "We'll all get together and give you a proper send-off."

All their brocade clothes retrieved from storage, and the rice wine they've been saving in long-term compartments onboard the ship taken out, sipped at until everything seems to glow; and the small, round gem-dreams dumplings—there's no actual gems in them, but they're deliberately shaped and positioned like a string of gems, to call for good fortune and riches to fall into the newlyweds' hands, for enough that they can leave the ship, leave this life of dives and slow death...

Kim Anh never had a chance for any of this. When she died, she'd barely begun a relationship with one of the older divers—a fling, the kind that's not meant to last onboard *The Azure Serpent*. Except, of course, that it was cut short, became frozen in grief and regrets and recriminations.

Thuy and Kim Anh's ex seldom speak; though they do get drunk together, sometimes. And Cong Hoan, her eldest son, has been posted to another diver-ship. They talk on comms, and see each other for festivals and death anniversaries: he's more distant than she'd like, but still alive—all that matters.

"You're morbid again," Xuan says. "I can see it in your face."

Thuy makes a grimace. "I don't feel like drinking."

"Quite obviously," Le Hoa says. "Shall we go straight to the poetry?"

"She's not drunk enough," Xuan says before Thuy can open her mouth.

Thuy flushes. "I'm not good at poetry, in any case."

Le Hoa snorts. "I know. The point isn't that you're good. We're all terrible at it, else we would be officials on a numbered planet with scores of servants at our beck and call. The point is forgetting." She stops, then, looks at Thuy. "I'm sorry."

Thuy forces a shrug she doesn't feel. "Doesn't matter."

Le Hoa opens her mouth, and then closes it again. "Look..." she says. She reaches inside her robes and withdraws something—Thuy knows, even before she opens her hand, what it will be.

The gem is small, and misshapen: the supervisors won't let them keep the big, pretty ones as salvage; those go to offworld customers, the kind rich enough to pay good money for them. It glistens like spilled oil in the light of the teahouse; and in that light, the dumplings on the table and the tea seem to fade into the background; to recede into tasteless, odourless insignificance. "Try this."

"I—" Thuy shakes her head. "It's yours. And before a dive..."

Le Hoa shrugs. "Screw tradition, Thuy. You know it's not going to change anything. Besides, I have some stash. Don't need this one."

Thuy stares at it—thinking of dropping it in the cup and watching it dissolve; of the warmth that will slide down into her stomach when she drinks; of the rising euphoria seizing all her limbs until everything seems to shake with the bliss of desire—of how to step away, for a time; away from tomorrow and the dive, and Kim Anh's remains.

"Come on, lil' sis."

Thuy shakes her head. She reaches for the cup of rice wine, drains it in one gulp; leaving the gem still on the table.

"Time for poetry," she says, aloud. *The Azure Serpent* doesn't say anything—he so seldom speaks, not to the divers, those doomed to die—but he dims the lights and the sound as Thuy stands up, waiting for words to well up from the empty pit in her chest.

Xuan was right: you need to be much drunker than this, for decent verses.

THUY KNOWS WHERE her parents died. The wreck they were scavenging from is on her ancestral altar, at the end of the cycling of holos that shows First and Second Mother go from newlyweds flushed with drink and happiness, to older, greyer women holding their grandchild in their arms, their smile cautious; tentative; as if they already know they will have to relinquish her.

Aboard *The Azure Serpent*, they're legends, spoken of in hushed tones. They went deeper, farther into unreality than anyone else ever has. Divers call them the Long Breathers, and they have their own temple, spreading over three compartments and always smelling of incense. On the temple walls, they are depicted in their diving suits, with the bodhisattva Quan Am showing them the way into an empty cabin; where divers leave offerings praying for good fortune and prosperity.

They left nothing behind. Their suits crumbled with them, and their bodies are deep within the wreck of that mindship: two scatterings of gems in a cabin or a corridor somewhere, forever irretrievable; too deep for anyone to survive retrieval, even if they could be located anymore, in the twenty-one years since they died.

On the altar is Bao Thach: her husband, not smiling but stern and unyielding, as utterly serious in death as he was mischievous and whimsical in life.

She has nothing left of him, either.

Kim Anh... Kim Anh is by her father's side; because she died childless and unmarried; because there is no one else who will mourn her or say the prayers to ease her passage. Thuy isn't the first, or the last, to do this onboard the ship.

There's a box, with enough space for a single gem. For what Thuy has earned the right to salvage from her daughter's body: something tangible, palpable that she can hold onto, not the holos or her own hazy-coloured and shrivelled memories—holding a small, wrinkled baby nursing at her breast and feeling contentment well up in her, stronger than any gem-induced euphoria—Kim Anh at age ten, trying to walk in a suit two sizes too big for her—and a few days before her death, the last meal she and Thuy had in the teahouse: translucent dumplings served with tea the colour of jade, with a smell like cut grass on a planet neither of them will ever live to see.

Kim Anh isn't like Thuy's mothers: she died outside a different mindship, far enough from the wreck that it's possible to retrieve her. Tricky, as Xuan said; but what price wouldn't Thuy pay, to have something of her daughter back?

IN THE DARKNESS at the hole in the ship's hull, Thuy isn't blind. Her suit lights up with warnings—temperature, pressure, distortions. That last is what will kill her: the layers of unreality utterly unsuited to human existence, getting stronger and stronger as the current carries her closer to the wreck of the mindship, crushing her lungs and vital organs like crumpled paper when her suit finally fails.

It's what killed Kim Anh on her last dive; what eventually kills most divers. Almost everyone on *The Azure Serpent*—minus the supervisors, of course—lives with that knowledge, that suspended death sentence.

Thuy would pray to her ancestors—to her mothers The Long Breathers—if only she knew what to ask for.

Thuy closes her hand over the gem. She deactivates the suits' propulsion units and watches her daughter's remains, floating beside her.

Gems and more gems—ranging from the small one she has in her hand to the larger, spherical ones that have replaced the organs in the torso. It's a recent death compared to that of the mindship: the gems still form something vaguely like a human shape, if humans could be drawn in small, round items like droplets of water; or like tears.

And, as the unreality readings spike, the ghost by her side becomes sharper and sharper, until she sees, once more, Kim Anh as she was in life. Her hair is braided—always with the messy ends, the ribbon tied haphazardly; they used to joke that she didn't need a tether, because the ribbon would get caught in the ship's airlock in strands thick and solid enough to bring her back. Her eyes are glinting—with tears, or perhaps with the same oily light as that of a gem.

Hello, Mother.

"Child," Thuy whispers, and the currents take her voice and scatter it— and the ghost nods, but it might as well be at something Thuy can't see.

Long time no see.

They're drifting apart now: hurtling down some dark, silent corridor into the wreck that dilates open like an eye—no no no, not after all of this, not after the certainty she'll lose her own life to the dive—and Thuy shifts, making the propulsion units in the suit strain against the currents, trying to reach Kim Anh; to hold her, to hold *something* of her, down there in the dark...

And then something rushes at her from behind, and she feels a sharp, pressing pain through the nape of the suit—before everything fades away.

WHEN THUY WAKES up—nauseous, disoriented—the comms are speaking to her.

"Thuy? Where are you?" It's Xuan's voice, breathless and panicking. "I can help you get back, if you didn't drift too far."

"I'm here," she tries to say; and has to speak three times before her voice stops shaking; becomes audible enough. There is no answer. Wherever she is—and, judging by the readings, it's deep—comms don't emit anymore.

She can't see Kim Anh's body—she remembers scrabbling, struggling to remain close to it as the currents separated them, but now there is nothing. The ghost, though, is still there, in the same room, wavering in the layers of unreality; defined in traceries of light that seem to encompass her daughter's very essence in a few sharp lines.

Thuy still has the gem in her hand, tucked under the guard of her wrist. The rest of her daughter's gems—they've fallen in and are now floating somewhere in the wreck, somewhere far away and inaccessible, and...

Her gaze, roaming, focuses on where she is; and she has to stop herself from gasping.

It's a huge, vaulted room like a mausoleum—five ribs spreading from a central point, and racks of electronics and organics, most of them scuffed and knocked over; pulsing cables converging on each other in tight knots, merging and parting like an alchemist's twisted idea of a nervous system. In the centre is something like a chair, or a throne, all ridges and protrusions, looking grown rather than manufactured. Swarms of repair bots lie quiescent; they must have given up, unable to raise the dead.

The heartroom. The centre of the ship, where the Mind once rested—the small, wilted thing in the throne is all that's left of its corpse. Of course. Minds aren't quite human; and they were made to better withstand deep spaces.

"Thuy? Please come in. Please..." Xuan is pleading now, her voice, growing fainter and fainter. Thuy knows about this too: the loss of hope.

"Thuy? Is that your name?"

The voice is not Xuan's. It's deeper and more resonant; and its sound make the walls shake—equipment shivers and sweats dust; and the cables writhe and twist like maddened snakes.

"I have waited so long."

"You—" Thuy licks dry lips. Her suit is telling her—reassuringly, or not, she's not certain—that unreality has stabilised; and that she has about ten minutes left before her suit fails. Before she dies, holding onto her daughter's gem, with her daughter's ghost by her side. "Who are you?"

It's been years, and unreality has washed over the ship, in eroding tide after eroding tide. No one can have survived. No one, not even The Long Breathers.

Ancestors, watch over me.

"*The Boat Sent by the Bell,*" the voice says. The walls of the room light up, bright and red and unbearable—characters start scrolling across walls on all sides of Thuy, poems and novels and fragments of words bleeding from the oily metal, all going too fast for her to catch anything but bits and pieces, with that touch of bare, disquieting familiarity. "I—am—was—the ship."

"You're alive." He... he should be dead. Ships don't survive. They die, just like their passengers. They—

"Of course. We are built to withstand the farthest, more distorted areas of deep spaces."

"Of course." The words taste like ashes on her mouth. "What have you been waiting for?"

The ship's answer is low, and brutally simple. "To die."

Still alive. Still waiting. Oh, ancestors. When did the ship explode? Thirty, forty years ago? How long has the Mind been down here, in the depths—crippled and unable to move, unable to call out for help; like a human locked in their own body after a stroke?

Seven minutes, Thuy's suit says. Her hands are already tingling, as if too much blood were flooding to them. By her side, Kim Anh's ghost is silent, unmoving, its shape almost too sharp; too real; too alien. "Waiting to die? Then that makes two of us."

"I would be glad for some company." *The Boat Sent by the Bell*'s voice is grave, thoughtful. Thuy would go mad, if she were down here for so long—but perhaps mindships are more resistant to this kind of thing. "But your comrades are calling for you."

The comms have sunk to crackles; one of her gloves is flickering away, caught halfway between its normal shape and a clawed, distorted paw with fingers at an impossible angle. It doesn't hurt, not yet. "Yes." Thuy swallows. She puts the gem into her left hand—the good one, the one that's not disappearing, and wraps her fingers around it, as if she were holding Kim Anh. She'd hold the ghost, too, if she could grasp it. "It's too deep. I can't go back. Not before the suit fails."

Silence. Now there's pain—faint and almost imperceptible, but steadily rising, in every one of her knuckles. She tries to flex her fingers; but the pain shifts to a sharp, unbearable stab that makes her cry out.

Five minutes.

At length the ship says, "A bargain, if you will, diver."

Bargains made on the edge of death, with neither of them in a position to deliver. She'd have found this funny, in other circumstances. "I don't have much time."

"Come here. At the centre. I can show you the way out."

"It's—" Thuy grits her teeth against the rising pain—"useless. I told you. We're too deep. Too far away."

"Not if I help you." The ship's voice is serene. "Come."

And, in spite of herself—because, even now, even here, she clings to what she has—Thuy propels herself closer to the centre; lays her hand, her contracting, aching right hand, on the surface of the Mind.

She's heard, a long time ago, that Minds didn't want to be touched this way. That the heartroom was their sanctuary; their skin their own private province, not meant to be stroked or kissed, lest it hurt them.

What she feels, instead, is... serenity—a stretching of time until it feels almost meaningless, her five minutes forgotten; what she sees, for a bare moment, is how beautiful it is, when currents aren't trying to kill you or distort you beyond the bounds of the bearable, and how utterly, intolerably lonely it is, to be forever shut off from the communion of ships and space; to no longer be able to move; to be whole in a body that won't shift, that is too damaged for repairs and yet not damaged enough to die.

I didn't know, she wants to say, but the words won't come out of her mouth. The ship, of course, doesn't answer.

Behind her, the swarms of bots rise—cover her like a cloud of butterflies, blocking off her field of view; a scattering of them on her hand, and a feeling of something sucking away at her flesh, parting muscle from bone.

When *The Boat Sent by the Bell* releases her, Thuy stands, shaking—trying to breathe again, as the bots slough away from her like shed skin and settle on a protuberance near the Mind. Her suit has been patched and augmented; the display, flickering in and out of existence, tells her she has twenty minutes. Pain throbs, a slow burn in the flesh of her repaired hand; a reminder of what awaits her if she fails.

On the walls, the characters have been replaced by a map, twisting and turning from the heartroom to the breach in the hull. "Thirteen minutes and fifty-seven seconds," the ship says, serenely. "If you can propel fast enough."

"I—" She tries to say something, anything. "Why?" is the only thought she can utter.

"Not a gift, child. A bargain." The ship's voice has that same toneless, emotionless serenity to it—and she realises that *The Boat Sent by the Bell* has gone mad after all; cracks in the structure small and minute, like a fractured porcelain cup, it still holds water, but it's no longer *whole*. "Where the bots are... tear that out, when you leave."

"The bots could have done that for you," Thuy says.

If the ship were human, he would have shaken his head. "No. They can repair small things, but not... this."

Not kill. Not even fix the breach in the hull, or make the ship mobile. She doesn't know why she's fighting back tears—it's not even as if she knew the ship, insofar as anyone can claim to know a being that has lived for centuries.

She moves towards the part the bots have nestled on, a twisted protuberance linked to five cables, small enough to fit into her hand, beating and writhing, bleeding iridescent oil over her fingers. The bots rise, like a swarm of bees, trying to fight her. But they're spent from their repairs, and their movements are slow and sluggish. She bats them away, as easily as one would bat a fly—sends them flying into walls dark with the contours of the ship's map, watches them bleed oil and machine guts all over the heartroom, until not one remains functional.

When she tears out the part, *The Boat Sent by the Bell* sighs, once—and then it's just Thuy and the ghost, ascending through layers of fractured, cooling corpse.

LATER—MUCH, MUCH later, after Thuy has crawled, breathless, out of the wreck, with two minutes to spare—after she's managed to radio Xuan—after they find her another tether, whirl her back to the ship and the impassive doctor—after they debrief her—she walks back to her compartment. Kim Anh's ghost comes with her, blurred and indistinct; though no one but Thuy seems to be able to see it.

She stands for a while in the small space, facing the ancestral altar. Her two mothers are watching her, impassive and distant—The Long Breathers, and who's to say she didn't have their blessing, in the end?

Kim Anh is there too, in the holos—smiling and turning her head to look back at something long gone—the box on the altar awaiting its promised gem; its keepsake she's sacrificed so much for. Someone—Xuan, or Le Hoa, probably—has laid out a tray with a cup of rice wine, and the misshapen gem she refused back in the teahouse.

"I didn't know," she says, aloud. *The Azure Serpent* is silent, but she can feel him listening. "I didn't know ships could survive."

What else are we built for? whispers *The Boat Sent by the Bell*, in her thoughts; and Thuy has no answer.

She fishes inside her robes, and puts Kim Anh's gem in the palm of her right hand. They allowed her to keep it as salvage, as a testament to how much she's endured.

The hand looks normal, but feels... odd, distant, as if it were no longer part of her, the touch of the gem on it an alien thing, happening to her in another universe.

Her tale, she knows, is already going up and down the ship—she might yet find out they have raised her an altar and a temple, and are praying to her as they pray to her mothers. On the other side of the table, by the blind wall that closes off her compartment, her daughter's ghost, translucent and almost featureless, is waiting for her.

Hello, Mother.

She thinks of *The Boat Sent by the Bell*, alone in the depths—of suits and promises and ghosts, and remnants of things that never really die, and need to be set free.

"Hello, child," she whispers. And, before she can change her mind, drops the gem into the waiting cup.

The ghost dissolves like a shrinking candle-flame; and darkness closes in—silent and profound and peaceful.

EVEN THE CRUMBS WERE DELICIOUS
Daryl Gregory

Daryl Gregory (www.darylgregory.com) is an award-winning writer of genre-mixing novels, stories, and comics. His next novel, *Spoonbenders*, will be published by Knopf. His most recent work is the young adult novel *Harrison Squared* and the novella *We Are All Completely Fine*, which won the World Fantasy Award and the Shirley Jackson award, and was a finalist for the Nebula, Sturgeon, and Locus awards. The SF novel *Afterparty* was an NPR and Kirkus Best Fiction book of 2014, and a finalist for the Lambda Literary awards. His other novels are the Crawford-Award-winning *Pandemonium*, *The Devil's Alphabet*, and *Raising Stony Mayhall*. Many of his short stories are collected in *Unpossible and Other Stories* (a *Publishers Weekly* best book of 2011). His comics work includes *Legenderry: Green Hornet*, the *Planet of the Apes*, and *Dracula: The Company of Monsters* series (co-written with Kurt Busiek).

MAYBE, JUST MAYBE, it had been a mistake to paper the walls with edible drugs. This thought occurred to Tindal when he walked into the living room and saw the open door, the pages torn from the walls, and the two white teenagers who'd decided to feast upon his home.

The girl was crouched on all fours, picking bits of pharmaceutically enhanced paper from the carpet. The boy huddled inside a white cardboard box that had held funeral party supplies—rolls of black crepe paper, a dozen black candles, two packs of white-print-on-black napkins ('RIP' in Gothic letters)—now dumped out onto the floor to make room for him. He rocked slightly in the box, hugging his knees, eyes focused on nothing. Until he noticed Tindal.

"Let me out of here!" the boy shouted.

The girl startled, terrified.

"It's okay, it's okay!" Tindal said. "Everybody calm down."

"I'm working as hard as I can," the girl said tearfully.

"Of course you are," Tindal said. "Good job." He knew not to argue with druggies. Especially when he was stoned himself. The girl returned her attention to the carpet.

"Return me to my true size," the boy demanded. "And release my sister from your spell."

Sister? He saw the resemblance now. Both of them brown-haired and sharp-featured. *Like rats,* he thought, then immediately felt bad. Mice, then.

"You guys can just leave," Tindal said to the mouse children. "Really."

"Don't mock me, hag," the boy said.

Hag? thought Tindal. That was hurtful. He edged warily around the box boy and approached the girl, who was inspecting each strand of carpet for shredded paper, plucking with tweezer fingers.

"Just don't eat those, okay?" Tindal asked.

"Have patience with me," the girl said without looking up. "This floor is so, so dirty."

"'Cause I think you've had enough," he added.

"Don't touch her!" the boy said. "Or so help me, I will carve the meat from your bones."

Tindal backed away from the girl. "No violence!" he said to the boy. "No bone carving!" He fled to the back bedroom, found his pen in the bedcovers (it was always in the bed), and flicked it open. The screen unfurled only halfway, and he had to yank it open to full size.

He called El Capitan, aka El C the MC (available for parties and events), and Tindal's best friend. He got no answer, but kept trying through voice and text until El Cap's beard slid onto the screen, followed by his big, sleepy eyes. Tindal quickly told him about the intruders.

"Tindy, my man, slow down. And speak up. You're, like, whisper yelling."

"They're in the next room!" Tindal hissed. "They won't leave!"

"So who are they again?" El Cap asked.

"I have no idea!" he said, failing to keep a lid on the panic. "But they're *minors*. Minors in my house!"

"It's not exactly your house," El Cap said patiently. "Rolfe didn't leave a will." Rolfe had been Tindal's roommate. Or rather, Tindal had been Rolfe's roommate, because Rolfe owned the house and had let Tindal rent a bedroom. But now they weren't roommates at all, because Rolfe was dead.

El Cap said, "Look, just go out there and explain to them that Rolfe is gone, there's nothing to buy, and they're going to have to leave."

"I tried, but they won't go! They're tripping hard. One of them's kinda violent." The boy was still shouting. Tindal opened the door a crack, but only a corner of the living room was visible. "I think they ate a lot of wall."

"Hmm. Did you call the police?"

"The *police?* I have a house full of drugs!"

"Right, right," El Cap said. "And these kids don't need to go to the emergency room or anything? They're breathing?"

Tindal moaned. "This is your fault."

"How so?" El Cap hadn't taken offense. The Captain was philosophical about all things.

"You're the one who said we needed a funeral party."

"True, true," El Cap said. "I do recall, however, that the walls were your idea."

"And how many people did you tell about that?" Tindal demanded. El Cap, for all his dependability as a friend, was unfortunately a friend to everyone. He overshared and overcommitted, possibly due to the year he'd spent on a South Dakota trust farm doped to the gills on oxytocin enhancers.

El Cap tugged a hand through his beard. "Hang tough, Tindy. I'll be right over."

Rolfe's suicide note had been printed on a decocell sheet from his last batch and attached to the refrigerator with a magnet. That was so Rolfe.

Tindal didn't take it seriously at first, even though Rolfe didn't come home that night, because Tindal got pretty high after eating the note. (It was PaintBall, one of Rolfe's most popular recipes, and the synesthesia/ecstasy combo was intense.) Besides, it wasn't unusual for Rolfe, the chief beta tester of his own products, to disappear for a day or two to get his head straight.

But not a week. When Rolfe failed to reappear, and the groceries were almost gone, Tindal thought, *This shit is getting serious.* Rolfe's friends/ clients were showing up at all hours, asking about him and the latest recipes.

Tindal put them off, told them Rolfe hadn't kept any stock, and promised to tell them when he came back. He tried calling the dozen or so of Rolfe's numbers that he knew about (drug dealers picked up and disposed of pens like toothpicks) and got no answer.

By week two, Tindal had to admit to himself that Rolfe had really killed himself.

El Capitan tried to comfort him. He brought over some amazing dope he'd bought from the Millies, genetically tweaked super smelt that delivered a hardcore yet loving THC punch to the brain. "Maybe he's at peace now," El Cap said.

"That's what he said in his note," Tindal said. "'Don't worry about me, I'm going to a better place.' Or something like that." He took a hit from the comfort-joint. "He was never a happy person in the real world."

"Which caused him to lash out at you," El Cap said.

"True," Tindal said, thinking of the times he hadn't been able to pay the rent, and Rolfe failed to see his way to being okay with that. "Still, we should do something for him." Maybe it was the dope that made him want to be as calm and reasonable as the Captain. "Something to honor his memory."

"We can make a shrine," El Cap said. "Like they did for that guy down the block who was hit by that car when he was bicycling. They painted a bicycle white and people put candles and flowers around it."

"What would we paint?" Tindal said. "We don't even know what Rolfe was on when he died."

"Drugs, probably," El Cap said.

They went to Rolfe's bedroom to look for shrine-worthy objects, but of course the door was padlocked. Even in death, Rolfe was paranoid. In the nine months Tindal had lived here, he'd never been allowed inside the room.

El Cap went to work on the lock with a meat-tenderizing mallet from the kitchen. That proved ineffective, even for the Captain's mighty arm, and it was doing the door frame no good. They smoked a while, considering the problem. Then Tindal remembered that Antonia, one of Rolfe's clients, was a bike thief. She was pretty broken up to hear about Rolfe, but in an hour she was there with a device as big as the Jaws of Life. She snipped the lock and the door swung open to reveal Rolfe's bedroom/lab.

"Wow," Tindal said.

"Very mad scientist," El Cap said.

"Like I always imagined it," Antonia said.

The room was crammed with electrical equipment, shipping boxes, and homemade ductwork: PVC pipe and laundry dryer foil tubes held together with silver tape, all running to the bedroom's single window. The pipes were all connected to the machines at the center of the room, two chemjet printers, one older model and one that looked brand-new. These were the main tools of Rolfe's trade. He could download recipes or create his own on the computer, send them to the chemjets, and print the designer drugs onto decocell sheets. The only part of the process that Rolfe had ever let Tindal do was trim the sheets into strips and wafers.

"I need something to remember him by," Antonia said, and grabbed a stack of already printed pages.

"Hey!" Tindal said. "I don't think you should take anything until—"

She was gone before he finished the sentence.

"It's okay," El Cap said. "Rolfe would have wanted it that way."

The boxes were filled with foil precursor packs. These were the most expensive components in the process, even pricier than the chemjet printers, which were not cheap. You could order the packs from chemical supply companies, if you had the right permits; otherwise you had to buy from an online front company at the usual high markup for quasi-illegal services. With the right packs and a recipe, though, any idiot could make their chemjet mix, heat, chill, distill, and recombine molecules into whatever smart drug you wanted.

Rolfe never hid his disdain for the script kiddies who pumped out MDMA variants all day. Rolfe was more than that. He created new recipes on a weekly basis, assembling molecules whose effects were infinitely more interesting than the pleasure-center hammer blows craved by Cro-Magnon club kids. He was an artist.

"His life's work," Tindal said, taking in the stacks of rice paper remaining. "There's no way you and I can eat all this."

"*Probably* not," El Cap said. "We should invite people over. A quake of a wake! We can consume Rolfe's last run."

"No, it can't be just what's already printed," Tindal said. "We should do it all. Use every pack. Print every recipe he's got."

"Hand them out like appetizers," El Cap said.

"Wait," Tindal said. Something like an idea rose up in the back of his mind, gathered weight, and then crashed upon the beach of his consciousness: complete, beautiful, loud. He said, "I know what we have to do."

Word of the walls must have leaked, Tindal thought. It was too much to believe that these (probably) homeless ragamuffins had found the house by accident. The intruders, however, couldn't or wouldn't tell him how they'd gotten there, how they'd forced their way in, or how they knew to strike on the day before a massive drug party/wake/art installation.

The kids wouldn't even tell him what their names were. Tindal suspected that more than natural stubbornness was at work.

"What recipe did they eat, you think?" El Cap asked.

"Hard to say," Tindal said. "I didn't really keep track of what I'd printed. Or where I hung it up. But it's pretty clear they ate a lot. And a bunch of different ones."

"That might explain the major head scramble," El Cap said.

"It's like they were born the minute I walked in. Rolfe has five or six recipes that affect memory. One of them even makes you forget you're conscious, though you're still awake."

"Oh yeah, Zen. I had that once. Tastes like cinnamon."

The girl insisted that she keep cleaning. She'd finished her inch-by-inch grooming of the carpet and had pleaded with Tindal to give her a rag so that she could dust all the flat surfaces. He was happy to oblige. It was by far the most sanitary thing that had happened in the house since he moved in.

"Somewhere in here there's a recipe that triggers OCD," Tindal said. He'd copied Rolfe's recipe index to his pen, and he'd been scrolling through the notes. "He sold it to students. Helped them stay focused."

"She's focused all right."

"Restore me now!" the boy in the box shouted.

El Cap said, "As for psycho Stuart Little over there..."

"I think he's on something Rolfe called Double-A, or Ask Alice," Tindal said. "You know, like the song? 'One pill makes you smaller, one pill makes you tall.'"

"Rolfe always appreciated a Grace Slick reference," El Cap said.

Tindal ran his finger down the *As* until he found Ask Alice again.

"Mimics Todd's syndrome," he read, "which causes dismal—dis-mee—shit. Dysmetropsia."

"That sounds bad."

"It means he thinks he's tiny," Tindal said.

"That explains his problems scaling the walls of the box. You know, this whole thing reminds me of that story. You know the one. Tiny guy grows some weed, sneaks into the home of the giant, tries to steal his stuff."

"I'd kick them off the cloud now," Tindal said. "But they're too high."

"How long do you think it will last?"

"Most of Rolfe's stuff wears off in four or five hours," Tindal said. "But then again, they ate so much, and what with interaction effects—"

El Cap winced. "Never mix, never worry, I always say."

The boy shouted, "I can hear you, foul woman! You and your giant friend!"

"Anything in the recipe box cause Tolkien dialogue?" El Cap asked. "And gender confusion?"

"Pretty sure it's my dreadlocks," Tindal said. "Or the kimono I was wearing this morning. He doesn't seem to be confused by you, though."

"I'm all man." This from a guy wearing a flowered tank top, bicycle shorts, and flip-flops. But the boy was right in using the word "giant." El Capitan was indeed mountain-sized.

Tindal flicked the pen screen closed. "Could you keep an eye on the boy? I want to see if I can get anything out of the sister." The girl was crouched beside the second-lowest bookshelf, her nose inches from the wood. She didn't seem to be wiping up the dust so much as gently encouraging it to move to one side. Dust herding.

Tindal knelt beside her. She didn't look up from her work. He started to say something, then realized that her sleeve had pulled away from her wrist. Her arm was striped with blue-green bruises. And now that he was looking closer, there were marks on her neck, too.

Had her brother done this? He talked tough, but Tindal couldn't see him doing it. The kid radiated love for his sister in a frequency that could not be faked or chemically induced.

"Excuse me," Tindal said quietly, and the girl jerked away from him. "You don't have to be afraid of me," he said.

"Whatever you say."

"No, really," he said. "And you don't have to, like, obey me."

"I understand. Your wish is my—"

"No! Please! I'm not trying to patriarch you. Or even matriarch you." Tindal sighed. "Could you put down your rag for a second? And come with me to the kitchen?"

The girl looked longingly at the shelf, perhaps imagining the carefully coerced particles scattering for the hinterlands. Finally she ducked her head and followed Tindal out of the room.

"I have to urinate!" the boy announced.

"Can't you hold it?" El Cap asked, not happy about it.

"I'll piss all over your precious cage!"

In the kitchen, Tindal pulled out a chair from the table and motioned for the girl to sit. She folded her hands in her lap and stared at her feet. Her track shoes were filthy. The hole in the knee of one pant leg showed a dirty kneecap.

"I want you to think real hard," Tindal said. "Can you remember your name?"

"What name do you want to give me?" she asked.

"See, that's not really helpful." He pulled up another chair. "Do you remember where you live? Do you have a home somewhere?"

She shook her head.

"So no clue where you were before you broke into my house?"

"The door was open. I remember that."

"You mean, like, unlocked?" Tindal asked.

She slowly shook her head. "Wide open."

"Huh." Now that he thought about it, it was possible he'd gone to bed without closing the door. Rolfe had gotten angry with him about that before, though the latch was clearly faulty. Now that he was the owner of the house, he'd have to buckle down, get serious about security.

"Can I go back to the dusting?" the girl asked impatiently.

Tindal intuited that an awkward amount of time had passed. "Sorry. Zoned out there," he said. "You can go back when you tell me where you came from. And, uh, who did that to your arm."

Her face crumpled.

He felt terrible for asking. But hey, kids, right? See something, say something. As long as he didn't have to do something, too.

"I don't know!" the girl said. "I don't remember! Just let me do my job, please?"

From the hallway the boy shouted, "Be careful with me, ogre!" El Cap walked past, cradling the boy in his arms, heading toward the bathroom. "I will crawl in your ear and batter your brains!"

The girl burst into fresh sobs.

"I need something, anything," Tindal said. "Do you have a wallet? Purse?"

She shook her head.

Tindal put his face in his hands. He'd have to drop these kids off at the police station and hope the amnesia held after the drugs wore off. If he was lucky, all they'd remember was that a hag and a giant held them captive.

Tindal wasn't sure he was that lucky. "So, little girl," he asked gently. "Do you know who I am?"

"Tindal the Witch," she said, wiping away a tear. "And your companion is El Capitan." She smiled for the first time since he'd found her. "Did I do good?"

"Just... great," Tindal said.

The boy shouted from the bathroom, "Don't you dare drown me! Wait! Come back! Give me back my wand!"

El Cap walked into the kitchen. "This fell out of his pocket."

"A pen! He's got a pen! Thank God," Tindal said.

"May I please go back to my chores?" the girl asked.

The boy refused to unlock the device. When Tindal tried to hand the pen to him, he threw his arms wide as if trying to hug a redwood. Something about taking the device from him had moved it from the realm of the tiny—one more toy-sized item among the boy's micro-possessions—to Thing of Giants.

"We're just trying to find your next of kin," El Cap said to him.

"Never!" the boy said.

"Or your friends," Tindal said. "Wouldn't you like your friends to come pick you up?"

The boy's look turned crafty. "And how many young ones have you lured here in just that way?"

"There's no *luring*," Tindal said. "I do not *lure*. You walked in uninvited."

"Because I was *lured*," the boy said.

The word sounded dirtier every time they said it.

"Hey, what about the emergency contacts?" El Cap asked.

"Right! Of course." Tindal unrolled the screen and said in a clear, perfectly sober voice, "Call. Emergency. Contact." He grinned. "It's ringing. You're a genius, mon Capitan."

El Cap shrugged bashfully. The screen displayed a number and the name 'ice home' hovering over an animated map of Toronto.

"What the fuck do *you* want?" a woman said. At least he thought it was a woman. The screen stayed rudely dark, and that harsh, corrugated voice could have been that of an old man.

"Uh, hi," Tindal said. "Who's this?"

"Who the fuck is *this*?"

"My name's—" Caution neurons managed to fire in time to interrupt him. "I'm a friend," he said. "Calling from your son's phone. At least I think he's your son. Do you have a son? Or a daughter? Because—"

"Fuck off," the woman said. The screen displayed call ended.

"Huh," Tindal said. He let the screen retract. "Was that your mom?" Tindal asked the boy.

The lad glared back over the tops of his knees.

"I'd run away too," El Cap said. "That voice."

"Right?" Tindal said. "Like a garbage disposal with a spoon in it."

"A garbage disposal that smokes three packs a day," the Captain said.

"Ha! A garbage disposal that—"

In the corner, the girl moaned.

Oh. Right. Focus. Tindal called the number again. "Please don't hang up!" he said. "I just want to get your children home. See, they're here in my house—"

"You call me again, motherfucker, and their dad will track you down and bash your fucking head in, you hear me? Tell those fucking kids they're not welcome here anymore."

The pen went dead again. "Whoa," Tindal said.

"I think I see where the boy gets his anger," El Cap said.

"She said, 'their dad.' I don't think they're her kids."

"Evil stepmother," El Cap said, nodding. "Classic."

"She said Dad would track us down."

"How?" El Cap said. "You didn't tell her your name."

"Unless—shit. What if the phone's got location turned on?"

"Who leaves that on?" El Cap said. "That's the first thing you learn in the war against the Great North American Spytocracy." He took the pen from Tindal. "Maybe I can—huh."

"What?"

"Evil Stepmom didn't have location turned off on *her* phone. Look." A pulsing dot hovered over the animated map next to the words 'ice home'.

"Don't close the screen!" Tindal said. The locator would vanish, and he'd have to call that terrible woman again.

El Cap touched something on the screen and showed it to him. A trail of pulsing dots between here and there. "Perhaps the father is henpecked but kindly."

"I don't have time for this," Tindal said. "The wake is in four hours. I still have to decorate, make pizza pockets..."

El Capitan regarded him from behind his expanse of beard, saying nothing.

"Okay, okay," Tindal said. "You're right." He took the pen from him. "I'm going to need some courage, though." He went to the living room and looked at the pages of recipes taped to the walls. Which one was Courage? He had a distinct memory of printing some out on orange paper. Or maybe red. Blue? No—

"Are you going or not?" El Cap asked him.

Damn. He was going to have to do this straight. Or at least as straight as he was currently, which in medical terms was Not Very. "While I'm gone, maybe point OCD girl at the kitchen?"

"Dude," El Cap said disapprovingly.

He followed the trail of dots past KFCs and nail salons, through throngs of Numinous-addicted converts pressing Numinous-infused paper into his hands, over underpasses and under overpasses, around shifty-eyed cops and their drug-sniffing badges, through leafy blocks of ramshackle twentieth-century frame houses and shadow-slabbed blocks of ramshackler apartment buildings, until he reached a blighted neighborhood that was ramshacklest of all: unregulated multifamily homes painted with multiple coats of resignation and misery.

It was the longest two kilometers he'd ever walked.

He found an empty cement planter to perch upon and rested his soul for a while with a quick half-dozen vapes of Millie-produced ultraproduct. Not Courage, but definitely a viable treatment for anxiety.

The destination dot still throbbed at him from the boy's pen screen. Not too far now. Though he was concerned by the battery indicator that had started flashing at the opposite end of the screen. How long had that been going on? It was interesting that the battery icon flashed in counterpoint with the map dot. *Beep-boop. Beep-boop. Beep—*

"Uh-oh." Tindal said this aloud, though only the planter was there to hear him. The trail of dots had vanished as if consumed by ravenous pill heads. He tapped at the screen, and the whole of it went black.

He experienced a wave of panic that was subdued only by another set of hits from the vape. Then the cartridge gave out, and he knew he was truly screwed: alone in unfamiliar territory, holding two skinny, dead devices. He would have thrown them across the road if he was the kind of person who threw things. What was he supposed to do now? Going door-to-door in a neighborhood like this might get him killed. And even if someone answered, what would he say? *Hi, my name's Tindal, and I'm looking for the parents of two cognitively impaired white slaves staying at my house.*

No sense in that. The only choice was to go home. His brain flooded with relief chemicals, most of them internally generated.

From above him a voice said, "And don't forget the fucking tampons!" Tindal thought, *I know that voice.* It sounded like an animated garbage disposal.

He did not want to look up. Instead he looked right, where a short, pudding-faced white man had stepped out of the apartment building. A swoop of black hair covered his forehead, leaving none to cover the bald spot in back. He raised a hand to the upper window and said, "I heard you!"

Henpecked? Tindal wondered. Kindly?

Tindal risked a peek skyward. From an open second-floor window, a pickax wearing a white dust mop screamed down, "And pizza pockets!" Which reminded him that he was hungry, and that he really needed to get back to the house to prep for the wake.

Tindal hopped up and began following the man down the sidewalk. When they were a hundred yards away from the ax-wife's window, he said, "Hey, man, quick question?"

The man kept walking. Tindal hurried up alongside him. "Fuck off," the man said tiredly.

"I'm here about the kids," Tindal said.

The man shot him a glance.

"Fourteen or fifteen?" Tindal said. "A boy and a girl. I don't know their names."

The man stopped. "What about them?"

"Don't worry, they're safe. They're in my house, and they've eaten some of my—I think they've taken drugs."

"They do that," the man said.

"But they're fine!" Tindal said. "I just want to be able to get them home safe to you and their stepmother."

"Their what?"

Tindal nodded back the way they'd come. "No judgment? But, I mean, wow. Harsh."

The man's eyes narrowed. "You're the one who called."

"That's right. I'm was just trying to reach out to—"

The slap spun Tindal's head around. Pen and vape went flying, proving that Tindal *was* the type to throw things, but only under specific conditions. Then he bounced off a no parking sign and plopped to the ground.

The man bent over him like a Doberman on a short chain. "That's their goddamn mother, motherfucker! I'm their goddamn father! You don't talk to us like that! And you tell those fucking kids that I will not be disrespected in my own damn house!"

Tindal put up his hands. "Wait a minute, wait a minute. I think I've made a mistake."

"You bet your ass you have," the man said.

Tindal took a breath, then coughed. His jaw felt like he'd been hit by a shovel. He thought of those bruises on the girl's arms. Either Mr. Shovel Hands put them there, or Madam Ax Face had. Did it matter which?

"I'm just a little confused," Tindal said. "You're *both* shitty parents?"

That was when Mr. Shovel Hands started kicking him. His feet were pretty hard, too.

By the time Tindal limped back into the house, it was transformed: black crepe paper looped across the front windows, candles burned on the tables, and a Gregorian chant dance remix played through Rolfe's array of matchbox speakers.

Well, not everything had changed. The boy still huddled in his box in the living room.

"Where's El Capitan?" Tindal asked him.

"He went to obtain food, I think," the boy said almost sheepishly. "My sister is cleaning the bathroom."

"You seem better," Tindal said. Not completely, though: his skin shone with sweat, and his eyes were red-rimmed with exhaustion.

"I *am* better," the boy said. He ran a hand through his damp hair. "I would like to apologize for some of the things I said to you. I am so sorry."

"No worries, little man."

His head jerked up at that.

"I mean, young person! Not little person!" The boy did not seem to believe him. "Listen," Tindal said, "you want something to eat? Drink? I think I have some Vegemite and pita chips."

The boy exhaled. "I would like that, thank you."

Tindal walked toward the kitchen, then realized the boy wasn't following. "It's in here," Tindal said.

"I understand, but... ?" He glanced down at the box.

"Just stand up," Tindal said. "Oh wait, are your legs cramped? Sure they are. Just a second." He limped back to him, held out his arms. The boy reluctantly reached up. Tindal bent at his knees, freshly kicked ribs twinging, and got his arms around him. The boy came out of the box, feet pedaling the air, and Tindal set him on the ground. Immediately the kid hunched to the floor.

"Ha-ha!" he said, and slowly turned toward the door. He put his right hand down inches in front of him, then dragged a knee forward.

"What are you doing?" Tindal said.

"I shall escape, find a weapon, and then come back and rescue my sister!" His left hand moved another few inches.

Tindal moved between him and the door. The boy howled in anger. His fingers crept forward to grip the toe of Tindal's sandals. He pushed up, grunting.

"Are you trying to *trip* me?" Tindal asked.

"Fall, crone, fall! Crack your head against these stones!"

"First of all, this is carpet. Really, really clean carpet."

El Capitan appeared in the doorway, holding two sacks of groceries in one arm and a twelve-pack of Molson in the other. "Oh, should have left you a note," El Cap said. "He tries to escape every time you let him out of the box. What happened to your face?"

"Turns out, Tiny Tim's dad is an asshole."

El Cap frowned. "I'll put these away, then put him away."

"Thanks, man." Tindal walked down the hallway, leaving the boy to creep slowly toward the doorway. He was thinking of taking a shower before switching to his funeral T-shirt. What day was it, Friday? Not too early in the week for a quick wash-down, and it would be a sign of respect to Rolfe. He wasn't looking forward to seeing the extent of his bruises, though.

The girl lay on her side on the bathroom floor, a sponge in her hand. Her eyes were closed.

Tindal squeaked and threw himself down beside her. "Hey... you!" He'd never learned her name, a definite drawback in the resuscitation department. "Are you okay? Don't be dead. Please don't be dead."

He turned her face toward him. The collar of her shirt fell open, fully revealing the necklace of bruises. *Fucking Shovel Hands*, Tindal thought. He tried to remember how mouth-to-mouth worked. Okay, mouth on mouth, obviously, but after that?

"Cap! I need you!"

He heard a *thunk!* from the living room. "Darn it," El Capitan said.

Tindal shouted, "The girl's passed out!"

A moment later El Cap was there, the boy in his arms again. "So's this one," he said. "She's breathing, right?"

"I don't know! Wait. Yeah." He'd just seen her chest move. In fact, now it was clear that she was breathing deeply. How had he missed that? He sat back against the tub, sick with relief. They were sleeping. Only sleeping.

"I'm going to put him down in your room," El Cap said.

In a few minutes they had both of the kids tucked into Tindal's queen-size bed. "Should we surround them with pillows?" Tindal asked. "So they don't roll off?"

"They're not babies," El Capitan said.

"I know," Tindal said with a sigh. "But they're so beautiful when they're sleeping."

The Captain put his arm around Tindal. "So what are we going to do with them?"

"Can't go back to their parents," Tindal said. "They're horrible."

"Well, we can figure them out in the morning. Tonight we have a party to throw."

Rolfe's friends and clients—a Venn diagram of two circles that overlapped almost completely—started rolling in before seven, and soon filled the house. Tindal recognized the heavily tattooed plumber, a pair of shock-haired assistant professors, an award-winning pet groomer, half a dozen unpublished poets... and those were just the Ps. The weepy wept, and the stoic nodded with the wincing frowns of those who were not only familiar with tragedy, but had its private number. Tindal hugged them, told the story of the suicide note again and again, and waited for them to notice the paper-covered walls.

"You just printed... everything?" asked an unlicensed Reiki therapist. "Without labeling them?"

"I think it's more true this way," Tindal said. "Like life. Random."

"But isn't it kind of dangerous?" she said.

He didn't like her judge-y tone. "This is art," he said. "For adults. You don't have to have any."

The wake accelerated from there, at least subjectively. Tindal had started eating some of his own handiwork, and the recipes were busily redirecting all neuronal traffic into complicated patterns. One of the pages was evidently that old favorite MirrorMaster, because suddenly half a dozen El Capitans—Los Capitans!—were ferrying trays of bagel bites out to the living room. Interestingly, each copy wore a different apron. "I meant to have pizza pockets," Tindal explained to a squad of Antonias, who'd kindly returned to pay their respects, if not pay back the sheets Antonia-prime had taken from the deceased's lab. "Rolfe always got so angry when I burned them."

"True, true," they said, eyeing the walls.

"Goddamn it, Tindal!" a voice shouted.

"I can almost hear him now," Tindal said.

The crowd, now a thousand strong, parted biblically. At one end of this new path was a trio of Rolfes. They stood in the doorway, holding backpacks and roller bags.

Tindal burst into tears and dropped to his knees. Then thought, *Wait, what if I'm hallucinating this?* Before he could decide, the lead Rolfe seized him by the T-shirt. "I told you, no parties!"

"You're alive," Tindal said, wiping at his cheek.

"Of course I'm alive. I went to visit my parents in Decatur. Didn't you get my note?"

"It was delicious," Tindal said.

All eyes of the mob were on Tindal and the Rolfes, beaming so many emotions at them: confusion, joy, confusion, anger. Mostly confusion.

The Rolfes were looking around now. "Tindal?" they asked in soft three-part harmony.

"Yes?" he answered.

"What's that on the walls?"

Suddenly, there was one chief emotion hammering at his psyche, drowning out all the others: Rolfe Rage. The screaming went on for some time, until suddenly one of the Rolfes tapped the shoulder of another and said, "Who the hell is that?"

Tindal glanced behind him. The boy and the girl were awake, or almost: the waifs were sleepy and bewildered and frightened. Also sober, judging from his ability to walk and her ability to ignore the trash already littering her carpet.

"Are those *minors*?" Rolfe shouted. "Are you fucking crazy? You want to get me sent to prison?"

Tindal, still kneeling, said, "I can explain."

The Rolfes swept past him and screamed at the siblings, "Get the hell out of my house! Both of you!" The kids, shocked, didn't move. A Rolfe seized the girl's arm, and she yelped in pain.

"HEY!" Tindal said, and scrambled to his feet. He pushed through two of the Rolfes and yanked at the shoulder of the one who'd grabbed the girl. "Don't touch her! Or him!" He placed his body in front of the kids. "They've had a really rough day."

"You brought them into my house?"

"That depends," Tindal said. "Can you lure someone accidentally? Or does 'lure' imply an *intent* to—"

"Get them out," Rolfe said. *"Now."*

Tindal turned to the boy and girl. They looked at him with wide eyes. "Children?" he said, with as much dignity as he could muster. "Come with me."

He put his arms around their shoulders and walked with them to the front door. The pack of Rolfes followed behind, barking the whole way.

On the porch, Tindal turned to the Rolfes and said, "Can I just say again how glad I am that you're all okay?"

"And stay the fuck out!" They slammed the door, but it bounced open again. That door was always trouble. The Rolfes were forced to close it slowly.

Tindal stood on the lawn, feeling... what was the word? Hungry. He'd forgotten to eat again. The funeral party—now a resurrection party, after the stoned Tindal had been rolled away—resumed at even greater volume.

"We'll be going now," the girl said.

"Are you going to call our folks again?" the boy asked. This was the first indication that he remembered anything from his life as a micro human.

"Are you kidding?" Tindal said. "They're the worst parents in the world."

"They beat you up," the girl said, studying his face.

"I get the feeling they do that a lot," Tindal said. "Look, you can't go back to them. You'll stay with me till you find a place. No arguments. End of story."

The boy raised his eyebrows. "You're kinda homeless, too."

"Who, me? Rolfe will forgive me. He always does. We just need to let him cool off. He'll love having you."

The siblings exchanged a skeptical look. The boy started to say something but was interrupted by a single Capitan storming out of the house. "What did I miss? Is everybody okay?"

"We're going to get something to eat," Tindal said.

"Oh," El Cap said. "Kebab?"

The four of them walked through the nighttime streets under the light of twin moons, following a white bird that guided them to the second-best döner kebab in the city. *I should really ask the children their names,* Tindal thought. Then the food arrived, and the thought evaporated in a haze of steam and spice.

NUMBER NINE MOON
Alex Irvine

Alex Irvine (alexirvine.blogspot.com) is the author of *A Scattering of Jades,*
One King, One Soldier, The Narrows and *Buyout*, as well as licensed work
in the DC, Dungeons & Dragons, Foundation, *Independence Day*, Marvel,
and *Supernatural* universes among others. His short fiction has appeared in
most of the major magazines, including *The Magazine of Fantasy & Science
Fiction* and *Asimov*'s, and in many anthologies, and has been collected in
Rossetti Song, Unintended Consequences, and *Pictures from an Expedition*.
He lives in a 160-year-old house in Maine where there is not a level floor to
be found, with four kids, two dogs, one bird, and one snake.

THEY CAME IN low over the abandoned colony near the eastern rim of Hellas
Basin, deciding which landing spot gave them the best shot at hitting all the
potential motherlodes in the least time. The Lift was just about done, and
everything on this side of Mars was emptied out. The only people left were
at the original colony site in the caldera of Pavonis Mons, and they would be
gone inside twenty-four hours. Steuby, Bridget, and Marco figured they had
twelve of those hours to work, leaving enough time to zip back to Pavonis
Mons and pay for their passage back in-system on the freighter that was
currently docked at the top of the Pavonis space elevator.

"Quick visit," Marco said to no one in particular. "We're just stopping by.
Quick trip. Trips end. People go home. That's what we're doing, boys and
girls. About to go home, live out our happy lives."

Steuby really wished Marco would shut up.

"That's it right there," Bridget said. She pointed at a landing pad on the edge
of the settlement. "Close to the garage, greenhouse, that's a lab complex…"

"Yup," Marco said. "I like it."

He swung the lander in an arc over the settlement, bringing it back toward the pad. Nineteen years of work, people devoting their lives to establishing a human foothold on Mars, and now it was up in smoke because Earth was pulling the plug. It was sad, the way people were withdrawing. Steuby always wanted to think of human civilization like it was an eagle, but maybe it was more like a turtle. Now it was pulling its head in. Someday maybe it would start peering out again, but all this stuff on Mars would be junk by then. Everything would have to start over.

Or humanity would stay on Earth, and in a hundred years no one living would have ever set foot on Mars or the Moon or an asteroid.

"Shame," Bridget said. "All that work for nothing."

"I hate quitters," Marco said.

Steuby didn't mind quitters. He kind of admired people who knew when to quit. Maybe that was a function of age. He was older than both Bridget and Marco by a good twenty years. The older you got, the less interested you were in fighting battles you knew you couldn't win.

But to be agreeable, he said, "Me, too."

"They're not quitting," Bridget pointed out. "Earth quit on them."

"Then I hate Earth," Marco said. "Just kidding. That's where I'll end up, when I'm old."

Nobody knew they were there, since what they were doing was technically illegal. The sun was going down, washing the landscape in that weird Martian blue dusk that made Steuby think he'd had a stroke or something every time he saw it.

"Time to see what the Lift left," Marco said, for maybe the hundredth time since they'd taken off from PM. Steuby was ready to kill him.

Their collective guess was that the Lift had left all kinds of useful things. People always did when they had to get out in a hurry. In the thirty days since the Mid-System Planning Authority announced it was ending logistical support for all human activity beyond the Earth-Moon Lagrange points, everyone on Mars had started lining up to get off-planet and back under the MSPA umbrella. Even the asteroid miners, as antisocial and hardy a group as had existed since Vinland, were pulling back. Things on Earth were bad—refugee crises, regional wars over water and oil and room to breathe.

When things on Earth got bad, everyone not on Earth was on their own. That wasn't a big deal for the Moon settlements, which were more or less self-sufficient. Much different story for Mars.

"Are we sure nobody's here?" Steuby wondered out loud. It would be kind of a drag to get arrested in the middle of a planet-wide evacuation.

"I listened to the MSPA comm all night," Marco said. "Last people out of here were on their way to Pavonis before midnight."

Since the easiest way off-planet was the space elevator at Pavonis Mons, that's where the remaining colonists were, hiding out in the caldera until it was their turn to go up. The Hellas Basin settlement, over which they were now circling, was completely deserted. It was newer than PM, so the pickings would probably be better here anyway. Steuby looked out the window. Mars looked different around here. The PM caldera felt like it was already halfway to space because it was so high and you could see so far from the rim, when the storms let you go out on the rim. The Hellas Basin settlement, built just a couple of years ago to take advantage of a huge water supply locked in glaciers on the basin's eastern slope, was about as far from Pavonis Mons as you could get both geographically and environmentally. Practically antipodal. Where Pavonis was high, dry, and cold, Hellas was low, water-rich, and comparatively warm. Stormy during the summers, when the planet neared perihelion.

Which was now. There were dust devils everywhere, the atmosphere in the area was completely scrambled by magnetic auroras, PM was sucking itself up the space elevator as fast as it could get there, and here were Steuby, Marco, and Bridget thousands of kicks away at HB exploring. Well, prospecting. Okay, looting.

"We're just here to plunder the mysteries, Ma'am," Marco said to an imaginary cop, even though the auroras meant they couldn't talk to any authorities whether they wanted to or not. He put the lander into its final descent and ninety seconds later they were parked on the surface of Mars. There was a sharp crack from below as the ship touched down.

"Nice going," Steuby said. "You broke the pad."

Marco shrugged. "Who's gonna know? You find me a concrete slab on Mars that doesn't have a crack in it. Steuby, what was it, ten years since we were here before?"

Steuby nodded. "Give or take." He and Marco had worked a pipeline project on the lower slopes of Pavonis. Then he'd gone back in-system. He preferred the Moon. Real Martians wanted to get away from Earth. Steuby preferred to keep the Earth close by in case he needed it. "Bridget, you've been here before, right?"

"I built some of the solar arrays on the edge of the Pavonis caldera," she said. "Long time ago. But this is my first time coming out to Hellas. And last, looks like."

They suited up and popped the hatch. Bridget went first, Steuby right behind her, and Marco appeared in the hatchway a minute later, after doing a quick post-flight check on the lander's engines. "Good morning, Barsoom!" he sang out.

Marco was three steps down the ladder when they all heard a grinding rumble from under the ground. Steuby felt the pad shift and scrambled backward. The lander started to tip as the concrete pad cracked and collapsed into a sinkhole that opened up right at Steuby's feet. Marco lost his balance and grabbed at the ladder railing. The sinkhole kept opening up and the lander kept tipping. "Marco!" Bridget shouted. "Jump!"

He tried, but he couldn't get his feet under him and instead he slipped, pitching off the ladder and falling into the sinkhole as the lander tipped right over on top of him. The whole scene unfolded in the strange slow motion of falling objects in Martian gravity, dreamlike and all the more frightening because even slowed down, the lander tipped too quickly for Marco to get out of the way. He disappeared beneath it as its hull scraped along the broken concrete slabs.

Before it had completely come to rest, Steuby and Bridget were clambering around the edge of the sinkhole, where large pieces of the concrete pad angled under the toppled lander. Steuby spotted him first, face down and not moving. He slid into the dust-filled space underneath the bulk of the lander, Bridget right next to him. Together they grabbed Marco's legs and tried to drag him out, but he was caught on something. They could pivot him around but not pull him free. "Marco," Bridget said. "Talk to me."

The dust started to clear and Steuby saw why Marco wasn't answering.

The ladder railing had broken off and part of it impaled Marco just inside his right shoulder blade. Blood welled up around the hole in his suit and ran out from under his body down the tilted concrete slab. Now Marco turned his head toward them. Dust covered his faceplate. He was moving his left arm and trying to talk, but his comm was out. His voice was a thin hum and they couldn't understand what he was saying. A minute later it didn't matter anymore because he was dead.

"Marco," Steuby said. He paused, feeling like he ought to say something but not sure what. After a while he added, "Hope it didn't hurt too much when we pulled on you. We were trying to help."

Bridget had been sitting silently since Marco stopped moving. Now she stood up. "Don't talk to him, Jesus, he's dead! Don't talk to him!"

Steuby didn't say anything.

All he could figure was that there had been some kind of gas pocket under the landing pad, frozen hydrates or something. They'd sublimated away gradually from the sporadic heat of a hundred or a thousand landings, creating a soft spot, and when Marco set down their lander, that last little bit of heat had weakened the pad. Crack, tip, disaster.

"What are we going to do?" Bridget asked in a calmer tone. It was a reasonable question to which Steuby had no good answer. He looked around. They were at the edge of a deserted settlement on Mars. The only other people on Mars were thousands of kilometers away, and had neither the resources nor the inclination to help, was Steuby's guess.

He shrugged. "Probably we're going to die."

"Okay," she said. "But let's say we didn't want to die. What would we do then?"

COMPARED TO THE Moon, everything on Mars was easy. It had water, it had lots of usable minerals that were easy to get to, synthesizing fuels was no problem, solar power was efficient because the thin atmosphere compensated for the distance to the Sun... as colonizing projects went, it was a piece of cake. In theory.

In reality, Mars was very good at killing people. Steuby looked at the horizon. The sun was coming up. If he and Bridget couldn't figure something out real soon, Mars would probably add two more people to its tally. Steuby wasn't ready to be a statistic. Marco, well, Marco already was.

Now the question wasn't what the Lift had left, but whether they were going to be able to lift themselves or be left behind for good.

"We'll see," Steuby said.

Bridget looked up. "See what?"

"Nothing."

"You're talking to Marco."

"No, I'm not," Steuby lied.

"Here's a question, since you're thinking about him anyway. What should we do with him?"

"What do you mean, what should we do? It's not like we can strap him to the roof."

She let it go. They started walking toward the main cluster of buildings and domes that made up the Hellas Basin settlement.

PHOBOS WAS RISING, big and bright. Sometimes sunlight hit Phobos a certain way and the big impact crater on its planet-facing side caught the shadows just right, and for an hour or so there was a giant number 9 in the Martian sky. Steuby wasn't superstitious, but when he saw that, he understood how people got that way.

Number Nine Moon was his favorite thing about Mars. He hoped, if he was going to die in the next few days—and due to recent developments, that seemed more than likely—he would die looking at it.

From behind him Bridget said, "Steuby. Stop looking at the moon."

Marco was the one who had pointed out Number Nine Moon to him, when they'd been on Mars before. "I knew him for a long time, Bridget," Steuby said. "Just give me a minute."

"We don't really have any extra minutes."

This was true. Steuby climbed up out of the sinkhole. "Come on, then," he said.

"Where?"

"We can't walk back to PM," Steuby said. "Can't drive. So we're going to have to fly."

"Fly what?"

Steuby didn't want to tell her what he was thinking until he had a little more than moonshine to go on. "Let's head to the garage over there. I'll show you."

THEY SEALED THE garage doors after they went inside. It was warm. Condensation appeared on their faceplates. "Hey," Steuby said. "There's still air in here."

He popped his faceplate and smelled dirt and plants. A passive oxygen system in the garage circulated air from a nearby greenhouse. The plants hadn't had time to freeze and die yet.

With the dirty faceplate off, he could see better in the dim interior. He found a light switch and flicked it on, just in case. "Hey, lights too."

Now for the real test. Along one wall of the garage were a series of spigots and vents, spaced out over underground tanks. Steuby walked along them, saying silent prayers to the gods of chemistry that one of the spigots would be tagged with a particular series of letters.

He stopped at the fourth and pointed out the letters. "MMH," Bridget read. "Monomethylhydrazine, right?"

"Yup," Steuby said. "Also known as jackpot. They must have made it down here for impulse thrusters. Landers would need to tank up on it before they took off again. You know what this means?"

"That we have a whole lot of a fuel that doesn't work in our ship, which is crashed anyway."

"No, it means we have half of a hypergolic fuel combination designed to work in engines just exactly like the one built into that rocket out there." Steuby pointed toward the garage's bank of south-facing windows. Bridget followed the direction of his finger.

"You're kidding," she said. "That thing is a toy."

"Au contraire, Mademoiselle," Steuby said. "I've seen those fly."

WHEN HE'D GOTTEN out of the construction business after Walter Navarro's death and spent his next years fleecing tourists, Steuby had briefly worked on an amusement park project. A woman named Veronica Liu wanted to create an homage to classic visions of the Moon from the days before the

Space Age. Lots of pointy rockets and gleaming domes. She'd built it over the course of a year, with rides specifically designed for the Moon's gravity, and then at the opening ceremony she had put on a big show of landing a fleet of rockets specifically designed to recall the covers of pulp magazines from the 1940s. They were pointy, finned, gleaming—and when the amusement park went under five years after Liu built it, they were sold off to other concerns. One of them was still on the Moon as far as Steuby knew, because she hadn't been able to sell it for a price that made the deal worth doing.

Another was now standing on a small pad a kilometer from the garage. Steuby had spotted it on their first flyover. He didn't know how it had gotten there, and he didn't care. All he cared about was finding out whether it would fly.

"THAT'S A RIDICULOUS idea. This whole thing was a ridiculous idea. You had to come up with a stupid scheme to get rich and now Marco's dead because you couldn't just get off Mars like everyone else." Bridget was working herself up into a full-on rage. Steuby thought he should do something about it but he didn't know what. His way of dealing with trauma was to pretend he wasn't dealing with it. Hers was apparently to blow off some steam a short time after the traumatic event. "You wanted to come see HB and loot the mysteries! You said we'd be out and back in no time flat, no problem! Now we're going to die because of what you said!"

This was the wrong time to remind her that the whole thing had been Marco's plan, Steuby thought. He wasn't good at dealing with people, or emotions, but since Bridget was the one with the expertise in battery systems and flight control, he needed her help. Maybe a useful task would help her cope and also keep them alive.

"Let's find out if it's ridiculous," he said. "Come with me and we'll do a preflight check." He dropped his faceplate and went to the door.

After a pause, she said, "Why not. If we're going to die anyway."

Bridget didn't really believe him, but given no other option she went along while Steuby climbed up the ladder and poked around in the rocket. From the hiss when he opened the access door he could tell it had been sealed against the Martian dust—as much as anything could be sealed against Martian dust.

She looked at clusters of cables and wires, followed connections, popped open recessed coves in the floor, and eventually said, "We're still going to die, but electronically all of this looks intact."

"Perfect," Steuby said.

"For certain values of perfect," Bridget said. They climbed back down and Steuby checked the thruster assembly, feeling a surge of optimism as he opened panel after panel and found that the rocket had been staged and left. Nobody had stripped it for parts. Probably they'd looked at it and—like Bridget—thought it was just a toy.

But Steuby knew better. All this rocket needed was juice in its batteries to run the control systems, and fuel in its tanks to fire the engine.

"You watch," he said. "We're going to get out of here yet."

Bridget regarded the rocket with open scorn. "If by out of here you mean out of our bodies into the afterlife, I completely agree."

"I will be willing to accept your apology when we reach orbit," Steuby said. "Come on. We need charged batteries and a few tons of dinitrogen tetroxide." He headed for the garage, and she went with him.

They had ammonia, all they wanted, held in another of the underground tanks. It was useful enough that the base had kept a supply. Steuby was willing to bet that one of the machines in the garage either was designed to oxidate ammonia or could be configured to do so. NTO was a standard liquid fuel for all kinds of rocket models. All they had to do was find the right machine.

"We used to do this on the Moon," Steuby said. "You mix the ammonia with regular old air, and as nitrogen oxides form you add nitric acid to catalyze more nitrogen oxides. After that, you cool the mixture down and compress it, and the oxides combine to make NTO. It's just shuffling atoms around. Doesn't even need heat. All you need is compression at the right time and a way to siphon off the NTO. I would bet Marco's last dollar there's an NTO synthesizer somewhere around here."

They went looking for it and found it within ten minutes. There was even a generator, and the generator even still had power left in its fuel cells. For the first time since Marco's death, Steuby started to recover his natural state of irrational optimism.

They ran a hose from the ammonia tank over to the synthesizer, fed it a fair bit, and fired it up. Then they wheeled over a smaller tank of nitric acid and pumped some of it in, Steuby doing the figures in his head. They didn't have to be exact. The reaction, once it got going, just needed continual adjustment of ammonia, air, and nitric acid at the right pressures, and the holding tank on the other end of the synthesizer would fill up with nasty, corrosive, carcinogenic, and in this case life-saving NTO.

The synthesizer rattled to life. Steuby waited for it to explode or fall apart, but it didn't. It appeared to work. He watched the capacity readout on the tank. It stayed at 00 for a very long time... and then it ticked over to 01. Bridget looked on, and the readout ticked to 02... 03... "Keep this up and I'll start to believe you know what you're doing."

"Love it," Steuby said. "This is my favorite machine. Now all we need to do is make sure we can fuel up and take off before the storm gets bad and keep the rocket going straight up and escape the gravity well and make the rendezvous and convince the freighter to slow down and take us on board."

"When you put it like that," Bridget said.

Steuby nodded. "Now let's charge the batteries."

The sun was all the way up by the time they found the solar array's charging transfer board and ran cables all the way out to the rocket. Possibly it would have been quicker to pull the batteries and bring them to the charging station, but Steuby was nervous about disturbing anything on the rocket. There were charging ports built into the battery housing, and there was enough power cable lying around to reach Jupiter, so that was the most straightforward way. Still, it took a few hours, and both Bridget and Steuby stood around nervously watching the battery-charging readouts as the morning sky passed through its spooky blue dawn into its normal brownish-yellow.

"Good thing about solar arrays is they're pretty low maintenance," he said, to pass the time.

The charging indicators on the batteries lit up.

"Wonder how the NTO synthesizer is doing," Bridget said. She looked up at the sky. They knew what time it was, but that didn't matter. The only thing that mattered was the position of Phobos, zipping around three times a day. They were practically in Apollo 13 territory. The plan was this: watch until Phobos was in more or less the right place, then touch off the rocket's engines, and if they'd avoided fatal errors they would launch, achieve orbit, and then run out of fuel about when the freighter came along. The freighter's schedule was always the same: wait until the moons passed by, dock with the elevator, split before the moons passed by again. Once the freighter had decoupled from the elevator terminus, it would fire an escape burn. It took about two hours to prep that burn. Bridget knew this because she had worked the Belt before deciding she liked to experience gravity once in a while. Even Martian gravity.

In this case the freighter wouldn't be doing a drop. Instead it would be taking on people and supplies, but the time frame was more or less the same. Counting two hours in Phobos' orbit from when it passed the elevator terminus put the little Number Nine Moon right on the western horizon. They had about an hour from then to fire their rocket so they could be at escape velocity when they got close to the freighter, which would probably make an emergency burn to save them, but maybe not. Everything would be much more certain if they could match the freighter's velocity as closely as possible, which meant putting the rocket in a trans-Earth trajectory.

Problem was, if they did that and the freighter didn't pick them up, they would die long before they got to Earth. The rocket, if it had any fuel left, would do an automated Earth-orbit injection burn and the Orbital Enforcement Patrol would board it to find their desiccated bodies. Steuby hoped he wouldn't die doing something embarrassing.

Actually, he hoped he wouldn't die at all. You had to remind yourself of that once in a while when you were in the middle of doing something that would probably kill you. You got so used to the idea that you were going to die, you started trying to make the best of it. It was a useful corrective to articulate the possibility that you might survive.

The day on Mars was forty minutes longer than the day on Earth. Phobos went around about every eight hours, rising in the west because it orbited so much faster than Mars rotated. They needed to get the rocket up to a little more than five kilometers per second for escape velocity. Steuby liked the way those numbers went together. Forty, eight, five. Factors. Of course they had nothing to do with each other, but given the chaos of recent events, Steuby was willing to take his symmetry where he could find it.

Waiting for the tank to fill again, he looked around at the abandoned settlement. HB seemed nice, more like a real place to live than just a colony outpost. There was even public art, a waist-high Mount Rushmore of Martian visionaries carved from reddish stone. Wells, Bradbury, Robinson, Zhao. Marco probably would have wanted to take it if he was still alive, and if they could have justified the weight.

"No can do," he said out loud. "We're fighting the math. Man, Marco, when I was a kid, you could get anything. Strawberries in January. We were on our way. Now we're on our way back. Pulling back into our shell."

"Stop talking to him," Bridget said. "He's dead."

"Look." He was crying and hoped it didn't show in his voice. His helmet was so dusty she wouldn't be able to see.

Then she wiped the dust away with her gloved hand and said, "Steuby. I get it. He was an old friend and you're sad. Stop being an ass about it and stop trying to pretend you're not doing it, because if you divide your attention you're going to make a mistake and it will kill us. Okay?"

"Right," he said. "Okay."

He kept an eye on the NTO tank while Bridget did something to the monitors on the solar array, but he kept thinking: I'm millions of miles from Earth waiting for a robot left over from a failed Mars colony to finish refueling my rocket and hoping a dust storm doesn't stop us from making a semi-legal rendezvous with a freighter coming back from the asteroid belt. How had he gotten into this situation?

Steuby was sixty-two years old, born in 2010, and had only ever seen one other person die in front of him. That was back on the Moon, where he'd worked for almost fifteen years. A guy named Walter Navarro, looking the wrong way when someone swung a steel beam around at a construction site. The end of the beam smashed the faceplate of Walter's helmet. The thing Steuby remembered most about it was the way Walter's screams turned into ice fog pouring out and drifting down onto the regolith. By the time they got him inside he was dead, with frozen blood in his eyes from where the shards of the faceplate had cut him. Steuby had gotten out of the construction business as soon as he'd collected his next paycheck. After that he'd run tourist excursions, and seen some weird shit, but nothing weirder than Walter Navarro's dying breaths making him sparkle in the vacuum.

* * *

THEY FOUND A tractor that would run and hooked the tank carriage to it. The tractor's engine whined at the load, but it pulled the tank as long as they kept it in low gear. The rocket's fueling port was high on its flank, on the opposite side from the gantry that reached up to the passenger capsule in the nose. Ordinarily a crew would refuel it with a cherry-picker truck, but neither Steuby nor Bridget could find that particular vehicle in or near the garage and they didn't have time to look anywhere else. So they had to tie two ladders together and lean them against the rocket. They flipped a coin to see who would climb, and Bridget lost. Steuby watched her go. "Hey, if you break your leg you're gonna have a hell of a time getting in the rocket," he said.

Bridget didn't miss a beat. "Better shoot me and leave me, then. Like Marco."

For some reason her tone of voice made Steuby think she was trying to make him feel bad.

"I didn't shoot Marco," he said defensively, even though he wasn't sure what he was defending.

Once the nitrogen tetroxide was topped off, they had to go back and clean the tank out, then fill it with hydrazine. Together the compounds would fuel a rocket via a hypergolic reaction. One of Steuby's favorite words, hypergolic. Like just being golic wasn't enough. Neither chemical would do a thing by itself—well, other than poison and corrode anything they touched. Together, boom.

Usually transfers like this were done in clean rooms, by techs in clean suits. Steuby and Bridget were doing it in a dust-filled garage wearing worn-out spacesuits that probably had a dozen microscopic leaks each. He hoped they wouldn't have to do any maneuvering in hard vacuum anytime soon.

When they cranked the fresh hose onto the nipple and locked it into place, Bridget and Steuby looked at each other. "Just so we're clear," Steuby said, "this will blow up and kill us both if there's any trace of the tetro still in there."

"Yup," Bridget said.

"Okay then." Steuby paused over the dial that would open the synthesizer and start dumping the MMH into the tank. "I'll try not to talk to Marco anymore," he said.

"That's the least of my worries right now."

"It's just... this is going to sound weird, but I talk to him even though he's dead because if I talk to him, it's like he's not dead, which makes me think I might not die."

"Turn the knob, Steuby," she said.

"I don't want to die."

She put her gloved hand over his, which was still resting on the dial. "I know. Me neither. But let's be honest. If we really wanted to be one hundred percent sure of living, we wouldn't be on Mars."

This was true. Bridget started to move Steuby's hand. The dial turned. Monomethylhydrazine started dumping into the tank. It did not explode.

Riding another spike of optimism, Steuby ran to the door. Phobos was visible. They had about eight hours to get the hydrazine topped off and transferred, and then get themselves aboard the rocket. He checked the batteries. They were still pretty low.

"How much of a charge do we need?" Bridget asked.

"I have no idea," Steuby said. "A few hours at least. It won't take long to reach orbit, but once we're out there we'd better be able to get the freighter's attention and keep pinging them our position until they can get to us."

"Assuming they want to get to us."

"They will. The whole point of the Lift is to evacuate people, right? We're people. We need evacuation."

BRIDGET SPENT SOME time in the rocket's crew capsule testing the electronics, which were in fine shape and included an emergency beacon on a frequency that was still standard. "Should we just set it off?" Steuby wondered. Bridget was against it on the grounds that nobody could get all the way across the planet to them and still make the last ship out, whereas if they sent an SOS from near Mars space, a rendezvous would be easier. Steuby didn't want to go along with this, but he had to admit it made sense.

Other than that, most of the work they had to do—filling tanks, keeping the solar array focused, monitoring the mix in the synthesizer—was in the shop, away from the omnipresent Martian dust. Most of it, anyway. Humankind had not yet invented the thing capable of keeping Mars dust completely out of an enclosed space. Even so, they couldn't do everything inside. Bridget found some kind of problem with one of the battery terminals in the rocket, and they had to go out and pop the cover to see what was wrong. While she worked on it, Steuby watched the horizon.

A huge dust devil sprouted on the plain out past the edge of the settlement. They were common when Mars was near perihelion and its surface warmed up. Steuby and Bridget watched it grow and spiral up into the sky, kilometers high.

If that dust devil was a sign of a big storm developing, they were going to be in trouble. The rocket's engines themselves wouldn't be affected, but a bad dust storm would slow the recharging of the batteries by, oh, ninety-nine percent or so. That put the full charge of the rocket's batteries, and therefore their departure, on the other side of their teeny-tiny launch window.

They could get into the rocket either way and hope it was charged up enough for its guidance systems not to give out before they achieved orbit, but that was one risk Steuby really didn't want to pile on top of all the others they were already taking.

Steuby knew he was getting tired after a dozen runs back and forth to the rocket, and the hours spent working on machines without eating or sleeping. His ears rang and he was losing patience with Marco, who was saying maybe the rocket's placement was for the best because this way they wouldn't have to worry about the rocket's exhaust pulverizing anything important when they lifted off.

Steuby just looked at him.

Oh, right, Marco said.

"Steuby!" Bridget shouted, and Steuby snapped out of his daydream. "That's freaking me out. I'm alive. You want to talk to someone, talk to me. You want to go crazy and have conversations with dead people, do that after we're on the rocket. Okay?"

He didn't answer. She walked up to him and rapped her glove on his faceplate. "Okay?"

"Okay," he said.

She took a step back. Over their local mic he heard her sigh. "Let's get these batteries covered up."

It only took them a minute, but the dust devil was coming fast, and before they'd started the tractor again, it swallowed them up. Winds of this velocity would have flung them around like palm fronds on Earth, but in Mars' thinner atmosphere it felt like a mild breeze. The sensory disconnect was profound. You saw a powerful storm, but felt a gentle push. Your mind had trouble processing it, had to constantly think about it the way you had to plan for Newton's Second Law whenever you did anything in zero-G. In space, instincts didn't work, and on Mars, they could be pretty confusing, too.

Steuby froze and waited for it to go away. It was only two or three hundred meters across, and passed quickly. But as the day went on, there would be more. Steuby looked at the sky, to the west. Phobos had risen. It was all Steuby could do not to mention it to Marco. He's dead, he told himself. Let him be dead.

"Another hour going to be good enough for those batteries?" he asked. They got on the tractor and headed back toward the shop.

"Do we have more than another hour?"

"Not much."

"Then there's your answer." Bridget paused. She swiped dust away from her faceplate. "Look, Steuby. We're ready, right? There's nothing else we need to do?"

He parked the tractor. "Soon as the last tank of NTO is onboard, that's it. That's all we can do."

Bridget was quiet the whole time Steuby backed the tank into the airlock, closed the outer door, uncoupled the tank and pushed it into the shop, and closed the inner door. Then she said, "While you're filling the tank, I need to borrow the tractor for a minute."

"Borrow it? Why, do we need milk?"

"No, we need Marco."

He dropped the hose coupling with a clang. "Are you nuts?"

"We have to bring him, Steuby. It's the right thing to do."

"Math," Steuby said.

"Fix the math. Throw out what we don't need. You said it yourself. If we don't catch the freighter we're going to die. What's the point of having a month's worth of food for a three-month trip? Or a three-hour trip? That might be all we need."

"How the hell do we know what we're going to need?" Steuby shouted. "Have you done this before? I haven't!"

"I thought you hated quitters," she said.

"I—" Steuby stopped. She had him. He looked up at the sky. Phobos was low on the horizon, maybe ten degrees up. Less than an hour until they needed to fire the engines. He remembered Marco talking about going back to Earth, and he knew Bridget was thinking the same thing.

"All right," Steuby said. "Look. We'll do it this way. You go get him. I'll babysit the synthesizer. But if you're not back by the time Number Nine is overhead, I'm going without you."

"You will not."

"Try me."

She left without saying anything else. Steuby didn't know if he was serious or not. Yes he did. He was serious. If she was going to make a dead body more important than two living people, those were priorities that Henry Caleb Steuben was proud not to share.

On the other hand, he couldn't really climb up into the rocket and leave her to die. That wouldn't be right.

On the other other hand, who the hell did she think she was, endangering their rendezvous with the freighter?

On the... what was this, the fourth hand...? it would be pretty ironic if Steuby took off without her and then missed the rendezvous anyway, so both of them got to die cursing the other one out.

There was also the entirely plausible scenario of them taking off on time and still missing the freighter, so they could die together.

While the synthesizer poured NTO into the tank, Steuby suggested to himself that he adopt a more positive outlook. Maybe we'll make the freighter, he thought. It's only six klicks to where Marco is. An hour out there and back, tops. Unless—

He called Bridget up on the line-of-sight frequency. She was just visible. "What?"

"So, um, you have something to cut that piece of the railing, right?" he asked.

"No, Steuby. I survived twenty years working in space by forgetting tools." She broke the connection. Fine, he thought. Be pissed if you want.

Another dust storm rolled in maybe ninety seconds later. Figures, Steuby thought. Right when I have to go outside again.

*   *   *

ONE HUMAN-EQUIVALENT amount of mass had to come out of the rocket. Steuby stuck his head in the crew compartment. Dust blew in around him and he clambered in so he could shut the hatch. What could he get rid of? He started to panic. What if he threw something away and they needed it?

"Marco, help me out," he said. Bridget wasn't around. She couldn't give him a hard time. He wished he'd been able to crunch all the launch calculations and see whether they had an extra eighty kilos of payload slack. Maybe he was worrying over nothing.

He wriggled through a tight hatch into the storage space below the cockpit. There were lockers full of crap back here. Five extra helmets and suits. He pushed three of them up into the cockpit. He found spare electronics and computer components. They piled up in the pilot's seat. There were two water tanks. He took a deep breath and vented one of them even though he'd just filled it an hour ago. That saved almost a human's worth of mass right there. Now that he'd started, though, Steuby couldn't stop. What if one more thing thrown out the hatch was the difference between making that five point oh three kilometers per second and making a bright streak in the sky as they burned up on re-entry?

He stuck his head into the cockpit and saw that the dust storm had blown through again. The suits, spare gear, and a bunch of other stuff went out the hatch, banging against the gantry before falling to litter the launch pad.

In the west, Phobos was high, nearly forty-five degrees. Steuby pulled empty metal boxes out of the storage compartment and threw them out the hatch. Then he had to head for the shop and make sure the last fuel tank was topped off with NTO, or nothing he'd done in here would matter.

When Bridget got back, Steuby was standing in the open airlock. She backed the tractor in and he hooked up the tank. Marco lay face-up in the small equipment bed behind the tractor's seats. The whole front of his suit was soaked in blood and caked in dust. Steuby climbed onto the tractor and Bridget drove them out to the rocket. "You connect the hose and I'll carry him up," Steuby said.

"This is Mars," Bridget said. "He only weighs about sixty pounds. I'll take him. You know more about the fuel system than I do."

"Whatever," Steuby said. He still had that teetering sensation that panic was right there waiting for him. He started the last fuel transfer and watched

Bridget climb the gantry with Marco slung over her back. She pushed him in ahead of her and then climbed in. "Shut the hatch!" Steuby shouted. She couldn't hear him. A few seconds later she came back out, shut the hatch, and climbed down.

They stared at the hose where it was connected to the NTO tank. "Think it's enough?" Bridget asked.

The tank's feeder valve clicked shut. "That's all she'll take," Steuby said. "It'll have to be enough."

He disengaged the hose and backed the tractor away. "So how do we move the gantry?" Bridget asked.

"We don't," Steuby said. "The exhaust will do it for us."

"Not ideal," she commented.

"Neither was holding everything up to go collect a body." Steuby looked around. "Anything else we need? Time is short."

She was already at the base of the gantry ladder again. "Then let's move."

Steuby waited for her to get all the way in, then slid feet-first through the hatch. He turned and tried to push the gantry back, but it didn't move. "Forget about it, Steuby," Bridget said.

"I don't want it to tip against the rocket and tear a hole in us while we're lifting off," he said.

She jammed herself into the hatch next to him and together they shoved at the gantry. It still didn't move. "You think the exhaust will push it far enough away before it starts to tip?" she panted.

"If I thought that, I wouldn't be trying to push it myself," he said.

"I mean is it likely? Can we take the chance?"

"It's the only chance we've got," he said. He backed into the cockpit and Bridget closed the hatch.

They buckled themselves into the pilot's and copilot's seats, lying on their backs and looking at the sky. Old-fashioned, Steuby thought. Like we're off to fight Ming the Merciless or something. By accident he ended up in the pilot's chair. "You want to be the pilot?" he asked.

"There is nothing in the world I care about less," Bridget said. She powered up the onboard flight-control systems and saw that their battery life read about four hours of full operation. Steuby saw it, too.

"Sure hope that freighter answers fast," he said. "Where's Marco?"

Bridget adjusted herself in her seat. "Down in the back. Get us out of here, Captain Steuby."

"Blastoff," Steuby said. He flipped the failsafes on the fuel-mixing system, took a deep breath, and pressed the rectangular button labeled IGNITION.

LIFTOFF WAS LIKE nothing Steuby had ever felt. He'd never actually been in an old-fashioned rocket before. Every time he'd gone from Earth to space he'd used the space elevators out of Quito or Kismaayo. This was multiple Gs, what the old astronauts had called eyeballs-in, sitting on top of a bomb and riding it into orbit. Steuby was terrified. He couldn't breathe, he couldn't see very well, he didn't know if they were going in a straight line or curving off into a fatal parabola... he wanted to start screaming but he was afraid if he did he wouldn't be able to get a breath again. As it was he could only gasp in little sips of air that felt like they weren't making it all the way down into his lungs. Bridget wasn't making any noise either, which on the one hand comforted Steuby because it meant she wasn't giving him a hard time but on the other hand upset him because she was solid and reliable and he wanted to hear her say something reassuring.

At first the sound was loud, overwhelming, but as the atmosphere thinned out it modulated down into a rumble they felt more than heard. The rocket didn't shake itself apart. It didn't shred from a hole caused by the gantry. It went straight up like it had been made to do, and if Steuby had been able to speak he thought he might have cheered. They'd done it. If they managed to live long enough to rendezvous with the freighter, people would be telling this story for decades. Also they might end up in jail, but at the moment that was fine with Steuby. Jails had air and food and water.

The thruster cut out. Their velocity was five point seven kilometers per second, plenty for escape velocity. They were nine hundred and sixty-one kilometers from Phobos, which arced away from them toward the horizon. They rose through its orbital plane. The rocket started to tip sideways, aligning its long axis with the direction of Mars' rotation. They were curving up and out of its gravity well, and now they could see the vast reddish emptiness of the southern highlands. Storms tore across the eastern limb, where it had been daylight the longest. Olympus Mons peeked over the horizon far to the northwest, its summit high above the weather.

"We did it," Bridget said.

"We sure did. There's a little fuel left," Steuby said. "Trans-Earth burn, or do we park here and wait for help?"

Bridget leaned over and activated the rocket's emergency beacon. "Park it here," she said. "We don't really have anywhere to go."

Steuby slowed them a little, right down to the edge of escape velocity. He didn't want to get into a parking orbit in case the freighter wanted them to do a rendezvous burn. He looked toward the Tharsis plateau, now visible as their silver museum piece of a rocket rose higher and arced west, following Number Nine Moon. They would be coming up on the freighter if they were lucky. They'd already had a lot of luck, and just needed a little more.

"Hope somebody comes back," Bridget said. "It would be a shame to let all this go to waste."

"Somebody will," Steuby said.

But it wasn't going to be him. No, sir. He was done with everything that didn't obey the gravity of Planet Earth. I might go back to the Moon, Steuby thought.

"You were right," he said to Bridget.

"About what?"

"Bringing Marco. I gave you a hard time about it."

She shrugged in her harness. "Doesn't matter."

The ship's comm crackled. "This is Captain Lucinda Nieto of the freighter *Mary Godwin*. We are responding to a distress call. Over."

Steuby toggled his mic. "This is... well, I don't know what the ship is called. But we sure are glad to hear from you."

"We have a fix on your location. If you are able, stabilize your altitude and stand by for rendezvous. How many on board?"

"Two," Steuby said.

"Three," Bridget said at the same time.

He looked at her. Then he leaned into the mic. "Sorry, three," he said.

"And what the hell are you doing out there, exactly?" Captain Nieto asked.

"Not quitting, Captain," Steuby said. "We sure appreciate you giving us a lift. "

THINGS WITH BEARDS

Sam J. Miller

Sam J. Miller (www.samjmiller.com) is a writer and a community organizer. His fiction is in *Lightspeed*, *Asimov's*, *Clarkesworld*, and *The Minnesota Review*, among others. He is a nominee for the Nebula and World Fantasy and Theodore Sturgeon Awards, a winner of the Shirley Jackson Award, and a graduate of the Clarion Writer's Workshop. His debut novel *The Art of Starving* will be published by HarperCollins in 2017. He lives in New York City.

MacReady has made it back to McDonald's. He holds his coffee with both hands, breathing in the heat of it, still not 100% sure he isn't actually asleep and dreaming in the snowdrifted rubble of McMurdo. The summer of 1983 is a mild one, but to MacReady it feels tropical, with 125th Street a bright beautiful sunlit oasis. He loosens the cord that ties his cowboy hat to his head. Here, he has no need of a disguise. People press past the glass, a surging crowd going into and out of the subway, rushing to catch the bus, doing deals, making out, cursing each other, and the suspicion he might be dreaming gets deeper. Spend enough time in the ice hell of Antarctica and your body starts to believe that frigid lifelessness is the true natural state of the universe. Which, when you think of the cold vastness of space, is probably correct.

"Heard you died, man," comes a sweet rough voice, and MacReady stands up to submit to the fierce hug that never fails to make him almost cry from how safe it makes him feel. But when he steps back to look Hugh in the eye, something is different. Something has changed. While he was away, Hugh became someone else.

"You don't look so hot yourself," he says, and they sit, and Hugh takes the coffee that has been waiting for him.

"Past few weeks I haven't felt well," Hugh says, which seems an understatement. Even after MacReady's many months in Antarctica, how could so many lines have sprung up in his friend's black skin? When had his hair and beard become so heavily peppered with salt? "It's nothing. It's going around."

Their hands clasp under the table.

"You're still fine as hell," MacReady whispers.

"You stop," Hugh said. "I know you had a piece down there."

MacReady remembers Childs, the mechanic's strong hands still greasy from the Ski-dozer, leaving prints on his back and hips. His teeth on the back of MacReady's neck.

"Course I did," MacReady says. "But that's over now."

"You still wearing that damn fool cowboy hat," Hugh says, scoldingly. "Had those stupid centerfolds hung up all over your room I bet."

MacReady releases his hands. "So? We all pretend to be what we need to be."

"Not true. Not everybody has the luxury of passing." One finger traces a circle on the black skin of his forearm.

They sip coffee. McDonald's coffee is not good but it is real. Honest.

Childs and him; him and Childs. He remembers almost nothing about the final days at McMurdo. He remembers taking the helicopter up, with a storm coming, something about a dog... and then nothing. Waking up on board a U.S. supply and survey ship, staring at two baffled crewmen. Shredded clothing all around them. A metal desk bent almost in half and pushed halfway across the room. Broken glass and burned paper and none of them had even the faintest memory of what had just happened. Later, reviewing case files, he learned how the supply run that came in springtime found the whole camp burned down, mostly everyone dead and blown to bizarre bits, except for two handsome corpses frozen untouched at the edge of camp; how the corpses were brought back, identified, the condolence letters sent home, the bodies, probably by accident, thawed... but that couldn't be real. That frozen corpse couldn't have been him.

"Your people still need me?" MacReady asks.

"More than ever. Cops been wilding out on folks left and right. Past six months, eight people got killed by police. Not a single officer indicted. You still up for it?"

"Course I am."

"Meeting in two weeks. Not afraid to mess with the Man? Because what we've got planned... they ain't gonna like it. And they're gonna hit back, hard."

MacReady nods. He smiles. He is home; he is needed. He is a rebel. "Let's go back to your place."

WHEN MACREADY IS not MacReady, or when MacReady is simply not, he never remembers it after. The gaps in his memory are not mistakes, not accidents. The thing that wears his clothes, his body, his cowboy hat, it doesn't want him to know it is there. So the moment when the supply ship crewman walked in and found formerly-frozen MacReady sitting up—and watched MacReady's face split down the middle, saw a writhing nest of spaghetti tentacles explode in his direction, screamed as they enveloped him and swiftly started digesting—all of that is gone from MacReady's mind.

But when it is being MacReady, it *is* MacReady. Every opinion and memory and passion is intact.

"THE FUCK JUST happened?" Hugh asks, after, holding up a shredded sheet.

"That good, I guess," MacReady says, laughing, naked.

"I honestly have no memory of us tearing this place up like that."

"Me either."

There is no blood, no tissue of any kind. Not-MacReady sucks all that up. Absorbs it, transforms it. As it transformed the meat that used to be Hugh, as soon as they were alone in his room and it perceived no threat, knew it was safe to come out. The struggle was short. In nineteen minutes the transformation was complete, and MacReady and Hugh were themselves again, as far as they knew, and they fell into each other's arms, into the ravaged bed, out of their clothes.

"What's that," MacReady says, two worried fingers tracing down Hugh's side. Purple blotches mar his lovely torso.

"Comes with this weird new pneumonia thing that's going around," he says. "This year's junky flu."

"But you're not a junky."

"I've fucked a couple, lately."

MacReady laughs. "You have a thing for lost causes."

"The cause I'm fighting for isn't lost," Hugh says, frowning.

"Course not. I didn't mean that—"

But Hugh has gone silent, vanishing into the ancient trauma MacReady has always known was there, and tried to ignore, ever since Hugh took him under his wing at the age of nineteen. Impossible to deny it, now, with their bare legs twined together, his skin corpse-pale beside Hugh's rich dark brown. How different their lives had been, by virtue of the bodies they wore. How wide the gulf that lay between them, that love was powerless to bridge.

So many of the men at McMurdo wore beards. Winter, he thought, at first—for keeping our faces warm in Antarctica's forever winter. But warmth at McMurdo was rarely an issue. Their warren of rectangular huts was kept at a balmy seventy-eight degrees. Massive stockpiles of gasoline specifically for that purpose. Aside from the occasional trip outside for research—and MacReady never had more than a hazy understanding of what, exactly, those scientists were sciencing down there, but they seemed to do precious little of it—the men of McMurdo stayed the hell inside.

So. Not warmth.

Beards were camouflage. A costume. Only Blair and Garry lacked one, both being too old to need to appear as anything other than what they were, and Childs, who never wanted to.

He shivered. Remembering. The tough-guy act, the cowboy he became in uncertain situations. Same way in juvie; in lock-up. Same way in Vietnam. Hard, mean, masculine. Hard drinking; woman hating. Queer? Psssh. He hid so many things, buried them deep, because if men knew what he really was, he'd be in danger. When they learned he wasn't one of them, they would want to destroy him.

They all had their reasons, for choosing McMurdo. For choosing a life where there were no women. Supper time MacReady would look from face to bearded face and wonder how many were like him, under the all-man exterior they projected, but too afraid, like him, to let their true self show.

Childs hadn't been afraid. And Childs had seen what he was.

MacReady shut his eyes against the McMurdo memories, bit his lip. Anything to keep from thinking about what went down, down there. Because how was it possible that he had absolutely no memory of any of it? Soviet attack, was the best theory he could come up with. Psychoactive gas leaked into the ventilation system by a double agent (Nauls, definitely), which caused catastrophic freak outs and homicidal arson rage, leaving only he and Childs unscathed, whereupon they promptly sat down in the snow to die... and this, of course, only made him more afraid, because if this insanity was the only narrative he could construct that made any sense at all, he whose imagination had never been his strong suit, then the real narrative was probably equally, differently, insane.

NOT-MACREADY HAS an exceptional knack for assessing external threats. It stays hidden when MacReady is alone, and when he is in a crowd, and even when he is alone but still potentially vulnerable. Once, past four in the morning, when a drunken MacReady had the 145th Street bus all to himself, alone with the small woman behind the wheel, Not-MacReady could easily have emerged. Claimed her. But it knew, somehow, gauging who knew what quirk of pheromones or optic nerve signals, the risk of exposure, the chance someone might see through the tinted windows, or the driver's foot, in the spasms of dying, slam down hard on the brake and bring the bus crashing into something.

If confronted, if threatened, it might risk emerging. But no one is there to confront it. No one suspects it is there. Not even MacReady, who has nothing but the barest, most irrational anxieties. Protean fragments; nightmare glitch glimpses and snatches of horrific sound. Feedback, bleedthrough from the thing that hides inside him.

"FIFTH BUILDING BURNED down this week," said the Black man with the Spanish accent. MacReady sees his hands, sees how hard he's working to keep them from shaking. His anger is intoxicating. "Twenty families, out on the street. Cops don't care. They know it was the landlord. It's always the landlord. Insurance company might kick up a stink, but worst thing that happens is dude catches a civil suit. Pays a fine. That shit is terrorism, and they oughtta give those motherfuckers the chair."

Everyone agrees. Eleven people in the circle; all of them Black except for MacReady and an older white lady. All of them men except for her, and a stout Black woman with an Afro of astonishing proportions.

"It's not terrorism when they do it to us," she said. "It's just the way things are supposed to be."

The meeting is over. Coffee is sipped; cigarettes are lit. No one is in a hurry to go back outside. An affinity group, mostly Black Panthers who somehow survived a couple decades of attempts by the FBI to exterminate every last one of them, but older folks too, trade unionists, commies, a minister who came up from the South back when it looked like the Movement was going to spread everywhere, change everything.

MacReady wonders how many of them are cops. Three, he guesses, though not because any of them make him suspicious. Just because he knows what they're up against, what staggering resources the government has invested in destroying this work over the past forty years. Infiltrators tended to be isolated, immersed in the lie they were living, reporting only to one person, whom they might never meet.

Hugh comes over, hands him two cookies.

"You sure this is such a good idea?" MacReady says. "They'll hit back hard, for this. Things will get a whole lot worse."

"Help us or don't," Hugh said, frowning. "That's your decision. But you don't set the agenda here. We know what we're up against, way better than you do. We know the consequences."

MacReady ate one cookie, and held the other up for inspection. Oreo knock-offs, though he'd never have guessed from the taste. The pattern was different, the seal on the chocolate exterior distinctly stamped.

"I understand if you're scared," Hugh says, gentler now.

"Shit yes I'm scared," MacReady says, and laughs. "Anybody who's not scared of what we're about to do is probably... well, I don't know, crazy or stupid or a fucking pod person."

Hugh laughs. His laugh becomes a cough. His cough goes on for a long time.

Would he or she know it, if one of the undercovers made eye contact with another? Would they look across the circle and see something, recognize some deeply-hidden kinship? And if they were all cops, all deep undercover, each one simply impersonating an activist so as to target actual activists, what would happen then? Would they be able to see that, and set the ruse aside, step into the light, reveal what they really were? Or would they persist in the imitation game, awaiting instructions from above? Undercovers didn't make decisions, MacReady knew; they didn't even do things. They fed information upstairs, and upstairs did with it what they would. So if a whole bunch of undercovers were operating on their own, how would they ever know when to stop?

MacReady knows that something is wrong. He keeps seeing it out of the corner of his mind's eye, hearing its echoes in the distance. Lost time, random wreckage.

MacReady suspects he is criminally, monstrously insane. That during his black-outs he carries out horrific crimes, and then hides all the evidence. This would explain what went down at McMurdo. In a terrifying way, the explanation is appealing. He could deal with knowing that he murdered all his friends and then blew up the building. It would frighten him less than the yawning gulf of empty time, the barely-remembered slither and scuttle of something inhuman, the flashes of blood and screaming that leak into his daylight hours now.

MacReady rents a cabin. Upstate: uninsulated and inexpensive. Ten miles from the nearest neighbor. The hard-faced old woman who he rents from picks him up at the train station. Her truck is full of grocery bags, all the things he requested.

"No car out here," she says, driving through town. "Not even a bicycle. No phone, either. You get yourself into trouble and there'll be no way of getting out of here in a hurry."

He wonders what they use it for, the people she normally rents to, and decides he doesn't want to know.

"Let me out up here," he says, when they approach the edge of town.

"You crazy?" she asks. "It'd take you two hours to walk the rest of the way. Maybe more."

"I said pull over," he says, hardening his voice, because if she goes much further, out of sight of prying protective eyes, around the next bend, maybe, or even before that, the thing inside him may emerge. It knows these things, somehow.

"Have fun carrying those two big bags of groceries all that way," she says, when he gets out. "Asshole."

"Meet me here in a week," he says. "Same time."

"You must be a Jehovah's Witness or something," she says, and he is relieved when she is gone.

The first two days pass in a pleasant enough blur. He reads books, engages in desultory masturbation to a cheaply-printed paperback of gay erotic stories Hugh had lent him. Only one symptom: hunger. Low and rumbling, and not sated no matter how much he eats.

And then: lost time. He comes to on his knees, in the cool midnight dirt behind a bar.

"Thanks, man," says the sturdy bearded trucker type standing over him, pulling back on a shirt. Puzzled by how it suddenly sports a spray of holes, each fringed with what look like chemical burns. "I needed that."

He strides off. MacReady settles back into a squat. Leans against the building.

What do I do to him? He seems unharmed. But I've done something. Something terrible.

He wonders how he got into town. Walked? Hitchhiked? And how the hell he'll get back.

THE PHONE RINGS, his first night back. He'd been sitting on his fire escape, looking down at the city, debating jumping, though not particularly seriously. Hugh's words echoing in his head. *Help us or don't.* He is still not sure which one he'll choose.

He picks up the phone.

"Mac," says the voice, rich and deep and unmistakable.

"Childs."

"Been trying to call you." Cars honk, through the wire. Childs is from Detroit, he dimly remembers, or maybe Minneapolis.

"I was away. Had to get out of town, clear my head."

"You too, huh?"

MacReady lets out his breath, once he realizes he's been holding it. "You?"

"Yup."

"What the hell, man? What the fuck is going on?"

Childs chuckles. "Was hoping you'd have all the answers. Don't know why. I already knew what a dumbass you are."

A lump of longing forms in MacReady's throat. But his body fits him wrong, suddenly. Whatever crazy mental illness he was imagining he had, Childs sharing it was inconceivable. Something else is wrong, something his mind rejects but his body already knows. "Have you been to a doctor?"

"Tried," Childs says. "I remember driving halfway there, and the next thing I knew I was home again." A siren rises then slowly fades, in Detroit or Minneapolis.

MacReady inspects his own reflection in the window, where the lights of his bedroom bounce back against the darkness. "What are we?" he whispers.

"Hellbound," Childs says, "but we knew that already."

THE DUFFEL BAG says *Astoria Little League*. Two crossed baseball bats emblazoned on the outside. Dirty bright-blue blazer sleeves reaching out. A flawless facsimile of something harmless, wholesome. No one would see it and suspect. The explosives are well-hidden, small, sewn into a pair of sweat pants, the timer already ticking down to some unknown hour, some unforeseeable fallout.

"JIMMY," HIS FATHER says, hugging him, hard. His beard brushes MacReady's neck, abrasive and unyielding as his love.

The man is immense, dwarfing the cluttered kitchen table. Uncles lurk in the background. Cigars and scotch sour the air. Where are the aunts and wives? MacReady has always wondered, these manly Sundays.

"They told me this fucker died," his father says to someone.

"Can't kill one of ours that easy," someone says. Eleven men in the little house, which has never failed to feel massive.

Here his father pauses. Frowns. No one but MacReady sees. No one here but MacReady knows the man well enough to suspect that the frown means he knows something new on the subject of MacReady mortality. Something that frightens him. Something he feels he has to shelter his family from.

"Fucking madness, going down there," his father says, snapping back with the unstoppable positivity MacReady lacks, and envies. "I'd lose my mind inside of five minutes out in Alaska."

"Antarctica," he chuckles.

"That too!"

Here, home, safe, among friends, the immigrant in his father emerges. Born here to brand-new arrivals from Ireland, never saw the place but it's branded on his speech, the slight Gaelic curling of his consonants he keeps hidden when he's driving the subway car but lets rip on weekends. His father's father is who MacReady hears now, the big glorious drunk they brought over as soon as they got themselves settled, the immense shadow over MacReady's own early years, and who, when he died, took some crucial piece of his son away with him. MacReady wonders how his own father has marked him, how much of him he carries around, and what kind of new terrible creature he will be when his father dies.

An uncle is in another room, complaining about an impending Congressional hearing into police brutality against Blacks; the flood of reporters bothering his beat cops. The uncle uses ugly words to describe the people he polices out in Brooklyn; the whole room laughs. His father laughs. MacReady slips upstairs unnoticed. Laments, in silence, the horror of human hatred—how such marvelous people, whom he loves so dearly, contain such monstrosity inside of them.

In the bathroom, standing before the toilet where he first learned to pee, MacReady sees smooth purple lesions across his stomach.

MIDNIGHT, AND MACREADY stands at the center of the George Washington Bridge. The monstrous creature groans and whines with the wind, with the heavy traffic that never stops. New York City's most popular suicide spot. He can't remember where he heard that, but he's grateful that he did. Astride the safety railing, looking down at deep black water, he stops to breathe.

Once, MacReady was angry. He is not angry anymore. This disturbs him. The things that angered him are still true, are still out there; are, in most cases, even worse.

His childhood best friend, shot by cops at fourteen for "matching a description" of someone Black. His mother's hands, at the end of a fourteen hour laundry shift. Hugh, and Childs, and every other man he's loved, and the burning glorious joy he had to smother and hide and keep secret. He presses against these memories, traces along his torso where they've marked him, much like the cutaneous lesions along Hugh's sides. And yet, like those purple blotches, they cause no pain. Not anymore.

A train's whistle blows, far beneath him. Wind stings his eyes when he tries to look. He can see the warm dim lights of the passenger cars; imagines the seats where late-night travelers doze or read or stare up in awe at the lights of the bridge. At him.

Something is missing, inside of MacReady. He can't figure out what. He wonders when it started. McMurdo? Maybe. But probably not. Something drew him to McMurdo, after all. The money, but not just the money. He wanted to flee from the human world. He was tired of fighting it and wanted to take himself out. Whatever was in him, changing, already, McMurdo fed it.

He tries to put his finger on it, the thing that is gone, and the best he can do is a feeling he once felt, often, and feels no longer. Trying to recall the last time he felt it he fails, though he can remember plenty of times before that. Leaving his first concert; gulping down cold November night air and knowing every star overhead belonged to him. Bus rides back from away baseball games, back when the Majors still felt possible. The first time he followed a boy onto the West Side Piers. A feeling at once frenzied and calm, energetic yet restive. Like he had saddled himself, however briefly, onto something impossibly powerful, and primal, sacred, almost, connected to the flow of things, moving along the path meant only for him. They had always been rare, those moments—life worked so hard to come between him and his path—but lately they did not happen at all.

He is a monster. He knows this now. So is Childs. So are countless others, people like Hugh who he did something terrible to, however unintentionally it was. He doesn't know the details, what he is or how it works, or why, but he knows it.

Maybe he'd have been strong enough, before. Maybe that other MacReady would have been brave enough to jump. But that MacReady had no reason to. This MacReady climbs back to the safe side of the guardrail, and walks back to solid ground.

MacReady strides up the precinct steps, trying not to cry. Smiling, wide-eyed, white and harmless.

When Hugh handed off the duffel bag, something was clearly wrong. He'd lost fifty pounds, looked like. All his hair. Half of the light in his eyes. By then MacReady'd been hearing the rumors, seeing the stories. Gay cancer, said the *Times*. Dudes dropping like mayflies.

And that morning: the call. Hugh in Harlem Hospital. From Hugh's mother, whose remembered Christmas ham had no equal on this earth. When she said everything was going to be fine, MacReady knew she was lying. Not to spare his feelings, but to protect her own. To keep from having a conversation she couldn't have.

He pauses, one hand on the precinct door. Panic rises.

Blair built a space ship.

The image comes back to him suddenly, complete with the smell of burning petrol. Something he saw, in real life? Or a photo he was shown, from the wreckage? A cavern dug into the snow and ice under McMurdo. Scavenged pieces of the helicopter and the snowmobiles and the Ski-dozer assembled into... a space ship. How did he know that's what it was? Because it was round, yes, and nothing any human knew how to make, but there's more information here, something he's missing, something he knew once but doesn't know now. But where did it come from, this memory?

Panic. Being threatened, trapped. Having no way out. It triggers something inside of him. Like it did in Blair, which is how an assistant biologist could assemble a spacefaring vessel. Suddenly MacReady can tap into so much more. He sees things. Stars, streaking past him, somehow. Shapes he can take. Things he can be. Repulsive, fascinating. Beings without immune systems to attack; creatures whose core body temperatures are so low any virus or other invading organism would die.

A cuttlefish contains so many colors, even when it isn't wearing them.

His hands and neck feel tight. Like they're trying to break free from the rest of him. Had someone been able to see under his clothes, just then, they'd have seen mouths opening and closing all up and down his torso.

"Help you?" a policewoman asks, opening the door for him, and this is bad, super bad, because he—like all the other smiling white harmless allies who are at this exact moment sauntering into every one of the NYPD's 150 precincts and command centers—is supposed to not be noticed.

"Thank you," he says, smiling the Fearless Man Smile, powering through the panic. She smiles back, reassured by what she sees, but what she sees isn't what he is. He doffs the cowboy hat and steps inside.

He can't do anything about what he is. All he can do is try to minimize the harm, and do his best to counterbalance it.

WHAT'S THE ENDGAME here, he wonders, waiting at the desk. What next? A brilliant assault, assuming all goes well—simultaneous attacks on every NYPD precinct, chaos without bloodshed, but what victory scenario are his handlers aiming for? What is the plan? Is there a plan? Does someone, upstairs, at Black Liberation Secret Headquarters, have it all mapped out? There will be a backlash, and it will be bloody, for all the effort they put into a casualty-free military strike. They will continue to make progress, person by person, heart by heart and mind by mind, but what then? How will they know they have reached the end of their work? Changing minds means nothing if those changed minds don't then change actual things. It's not enough for everyone to carry justice inside their hearts like a secret. Justice must be spoken. Must be embodied.

"Sound permit for a block party?" he asks the clerk, who slides him a form without even looking up. All over the city, sound permits for block parties that will never come to pass are being slid across ancient well-worn soon-to-be-incinerated desks.

Walking out, he hears the precinct phone ring. Knows it's The Call. The same one every other precinct is getting. Encouraging everyone to evacuate in the next five minutes if they'd rather not die screaming; flagging that the bomb is set to detonate immediately if tampered with, or moved (this is a bluff, but one the organizers felt fairly certain hardly anyone would feel like calling, and, in fact, no one does).

AND THAT NIGHT, in a city at war, he stands on the subway platform. Drunk, exhilarated, frightened. A train pulls in. He stands too close to the door, steps forward as it swings open, walks right into a woman getting off. Her eyes go wide and she makes a terrified sound. "Sorry," he mumbles, cupping his beard and feeling bad for looking like the kind of man who frightens women, but she is already sprinting away. He frowns, and then sits, and then smiles. A smile of shame, at frightening someone, but also of something else, of a hard-earned, impossible-to-communicate knowledge. MacReady knows, in that moment, that maturity means making peace with how we are monsters.

SUCCESSOR, USURPER, REPLACEMENT
Alice Sola Kim

Alice Sola Kim (alicesolakim.com), a left-handed anchor baby currently residing in New York, is a winner of the 2016 Whiting Award. Her writing has appeared or is forthcoming in places such as *Tin House, The Village Voice, McSweeney's, Lenny, BuzzFeed Books, and The Year's Best Science Fiction and Fantasy*. She has received grants and scholarships from the MacDowell Colony, Bread Loaf Writers' Conference, and the Elizabeth George Foundation.

THERE WAS NO question of going home that night. The streets below Lee's high-rise apartment had flooded, and everyone had received an alert that the beast had been sighted near their area. If they went out, their safety could not be guaranteed. The wording of the alert troubled everyone, even though of course this was always the case—the non-guarantee of anyone's safety ever—but still the warnings were alarmingly pushy and made your phone buzz and compelled you to look immediately at the message from the city telling you hi, just a reminder that we're all going to die someday, especially you, and it might even happen sooner than expected. Hiiiiiiii!

When Wong had lifted his phone to check if it had been damaged by the rain, it buzzed with the alert; then each of theirs did, one after another. Lee ran to the windows and drew the blinds shut. It was superstition, she knew, but they had all heard rumors that even seeing the beast could be dangerous. That night, half of the group was missing, having canceled earlier with many exclamation points. Sick! Headache! Forgot! In utter terror of going outside! Only Huynh, Kim, and Wong had made it. Not everyone in the group was Asian, but only the Asians were present tonight, which made them feel a little self-conscious.

Lee was glad to see them. The group was not small enough to feel awkward, like that time when it was only Lee and someone else facing Kim like a parent and a principal as they were going to town on his writing. As was customary, Lee was hosting, since her writing was up for discussion by the group tonight. Another custom: the consumption of alcohol.

Huynh had brought a box of pinot grigio that had a picture of an actual bottle of wine on the front, which seemed like an unintuitive marketing choice, to remind you so baldly of what you weren't getting. But Huynh didn't care if something was gross, as long as there was a lot of it. She ate like she'd recently emerged from a nuclear bunker.

Kim had brought a six-pack of gruesomely hoppy IPA, which gave one's tongue a post-diarrhea sensation, desiccated and sour. Lee still had three bottles in her fridge from the last time the group had met at her place, about five rounds ago.

Finally, Wong had brought a bottle of whiskey less than half-full, an extremely irritating offering which would only be appreciated later in the evening.

The restaurants in the area had stopped delivering, so Lee set a pot of pasta bubbling on the stove. Everyone kept glancing at it resentfully, knowing that it would make them feel fat immediately and ravenous half an hour later. They still wanted it, very much.

Wong tried to call couch for the night and Huynh smiled at him. "You can try," she said.

Lee dragged a dusty air mattress from the closet and told Wong and Kim they could sleep on it tonight. This was a cursed air mattress; those who lay upon it were flush with the floor before dawn and beset with prehistorically brutal colds by morning, but no one had to know that.

Though their friendships were no less potent across genders, something old-fashioned and un-chill, an Asian, non-huggy thing, kept them from sharing physical boy-girl space too closely. Huynh, in fact, was terrible at physical contact in general; Huynh hugged like a haunted porcelain doll that had come to life. One summer during college, Lee, Wong, and Kim had sublet an apartment in the city together, and without any argument or question Lee had taken the king bed in the master bedroom, while Wong and Kim had shared the tiny guest bedroom and its twin floor mattress, where essentially Kim slept curled by Wong's feet every night, sprawled half on the mattress and half on a pile of clothes on the floor.

Of course, no one had thought to give Lee the tiny guest bedroom. But that was usual: Lee got things, occasionally (it seemed like) more things than any one person deserved, but she worked hard enough to deserve many of them. Like her apartment. She made enough money to buy everything that the store had told her went with the items she had picked out; her home was beautiful in a way that wouldn't necessarily make you compliment the owner, since it was clear that some giant hand with impeccable corporate catalog taste had set down each element in her home like a chess piece, only letting go when everything was just right. But her friends were hers, and her friends she surveyed in satisfaction, draped over her furniture, pinned in here for the night. Everyone, the older they got, slipped away, was harder to hold to real plans or, once the plans were made and honored, harder to keep for long enough, as if death and the way objects got colder and spun out further and further from each other was a process that began long, long, long before the actual dying and heat loss, so subtly that no one knew to be scared enough to stop it.

Lee loved her friends, and she loved that they couldn't leave tonight. Could there be something like taxidermy, but without anything dying? she wondered. If she could do something like killing her friends (but not killing, of course not killing) but a kind of killing of their lives and outside worlds that would force them to stay here and have fun, except they wouldn't even know they were being forced, it's just that staying here and having fun would be all that they wanted to do and could imagine doing, would she do it?

The intercom beeped. Lee was startled, for no one else had been expected. On the intercom she saw a long-haired girl standing still, head hanging, blurred by the rain. It was—well, Lee had forgotten the girl's name, but she did know that the girl was a new member of the group, a person someone else had invited.

Lee buzzed her in. She heard the distant shunk of the elevator below, then the doors slid open. The elevator opened directly into Lee's apartment, as it did for every unit in the building, which was supposed to be a fancy amenity but felt more like having a giant hole that led right into your guts. Not that kind of hole.

So, right away the girl was in Lee's apartment. No time to think about whether it was the right choice or not to let her in, although, why wouldn't it be? The rain had reduced the girl to the purest essence of herself, hair plasticked to her head, clothes and even skin seeming to adhere more tightly to her skeleton. She had long, thick bangs. Although the rain had separated them into chunks, the bangs covered her eyes so perfectly that you only knew she had eyes because you assumed she had eyes, why wouldn't she have eyes, but—

—did she have eyes?

The girl swiped at her forehead with the back of her hand like a cat, revealing her eyes, which of course she did have. They were small and very white and very black like dominoes. "Sorry I'm late!" she said.

"Sorry you got caught out there," said Lee. "Did you get the alert?"

The girl shook her head. "I don't have a phone."

Lee reminded herself that lots and lots and lots of people didn't have phones. Among the people she knew, how many of them did not have a phone? Even if the answer was zero, it didn't mean it was wrong to not have a phone.

The girl did not have a phone, and it did not look like she brought alcohol. She only brought her wet hair and disappearing eyes. Lee brought her a clean towel from the bathroom and the girl accepted it, smiling. Everyone said hi with disturbing and transparent vigor to make up for the fact that no one knew her name. Still, they found her familiar, and each knew for certain that one of them had invited the girl into the group.

Of course, no one had invited the girl here, at least not on purpose. This was one of those things that someone else, perhaps some unseen observer, could figure out in two seconds, but it would take everyone who was in the room much longer, which was really too bad.

"THANKS FOR HAVING me, guys," said the girl. She sat down and twisted her legs together, the towel draped over her shoulders.

They ate the pasta with butter, salt, soy sauce, hot sauce, peanut butter, back of the fridge parmesan that had gone the texture of Comet, and anchovy paste. Many of those ingredients were on the list only because of Huynh. Outside the sky boomed and the rain sounded swarming and continuous, which made the food taste better. The girl wasn't eating. Instead, she sipped a beer and asked everyone questions about themselves. People new to the group were either shy and watchful, embarrassed to admit what they didn't know, or they were loud and bossy about it, forcing others to explain themselves in the simplest terms possible. Basically, did they see the world from the orientation *I am new to you*, or were they more of a *you are new to me* person? The girl was very much the latter.

What are you working on right now? And you and you and you and you?

Where did you all meet? How did you all meet? How come you all like each other?

What are you doing in this city?

It was nice enough, certainly, to be asked questions, until it was clear she was being an avid robot debutante of an interrogator who despite not seeming super interested in the answers would not quit with the goddamn questions, which was much worse than someone just talking a lot and being boring because this way it turned you into the boring one, it shanghaied you into boringosity and from inside the prison of your voice brayed autobiographically on and on as you were helpless to stop it.

Lee, who was working on a gruesome fantasy trilogy, watched Kim's (short stories featuring a guy much like himself, also named Kim, always) nascent sexual interest in the girl wither and die, while Wong's (boarding school memoir full of lies) nonsexual interest in the girl as a potential subject of later shit-talking grew, his spare body leaning ever closer to her. Wong gave Lee a look so blankly innocent that it was obviously horrifically rude, and Lee was glad the girl hadn't noticed. Huynh (long short stories often about people grappling with philosophical conundrums who inevitably ended up committing sudden acts of violence) looked up from her phone.

"Guess whose birthday it is today," she said.

"Who?" said Kim.

"It's mine," said Huynh.

"Your birthday! How old are you, exactly?" said Wong. They'd been friends with Huynh for years, maybe three, but since they hadn't gone to college with her, they weren't clear on her exact age. They only knew that she existed in the same category of melty sameishness which they had all descended into after college.

213

"2_!" Huynh smiled rectangularly, all teeth, no eyes, and let out a cute, strangled scream. "Aaagh!"

2_! Quite an age. The age to start getting serious. A nasty-ass terrifying age. If they were honest, it was the age to already be a little serious, so you could be ready to have your life be perfect by the time you were 3_ or thereabouts, right? Huynh was not serious. She wore hoodies that had draggy ape-arm sleeves and scissor-holes for her thumbs. For the past year and a half, she had been living on an insurance payout from a car accident she'd been in. Unfortunately Huynh had not grown up with money and so was unable to do anything with hers but lose it quickly and clumsily. She only ate bad impulse delivery—franchise pizzas and gummy Thai—and was always rebuying headphones and power cords and ordering unrealistic dresses she'd neither wear nor return and always, always paying the late fees on anything capable of accruing them. Though she either seemed horny or had the ability to become so, Huynh had never dated anyone, as far as they knew. Of Huynh but never, ever to Huynh, Wong said that he wished he could hire her a life coach, or even be her life coach, because her life was such a mess that you could make a huge difference in it just by telling her to eat one vegetable a week, or to write down her appointments somewhere.

That said, the rest of them were also 2_ or about to be, and if you looked past the relationships, the good jobs, the minor artistic plaudits and encouragements, it wasn't like they were doing so hot either.

"So young," said the girl.

"Really?" said Kim. He looked at her, age indeterminate à la one of their people: Girlish bangs. Pink tank top. Pale, springy cheeks that could look resplendent with baby fat or slack and jowly depending on how tired she was, or how much water she'd drunk. A long, long, very long, too long neck trisected by deep horizontal wrinkles. Sometimes people got those from reading too much. Even kids.

"Of course very young," she said. "Happy birthday, Huynh."

Then Lee, Kim, and Wong remembered to shout, "Happy birthday!" at Huynh. They had been friends for so long that it was too easy for strangers to out-polite them. "I wish we had a cake for you," said the girl, smiling at Huynh.

Hmm! Mighty presumptuous, what with the girl having just met Huynh and the rest of them. Although, then again, the girl was here because she was supposed to know one of them. And now the girl had learned too much about them, and they nothing at all about her. Of course, at this point it would be completely impossible for them to ask her for her name.

Joke was on the girl. Lee had a slice of cake in the freezer. It was too bad, she had just managed to successfully forget that the cake was in her fridge, but at least she would immediately be able to get rid of it. She microwaved the cake for a few minutes, imagining wiggly rays—invisible on this wavelength but blaring red and deadly merely one level over—shooting into and through her guts.

When she brought the cake over to Huynh, they screamed. Wong hovered his hands above the cake, a movement that landed somewhere between doing Reiki and preparing to strangle someone.

"Are you sure?" said Huynh.

"I want to get rid of it," said Lee. "It's a cursed cake. But you eating it on your birthday will reverse the curse."

"Reverse the curse," said the girl.

"It was her wedding cake," said Wong. "You can tell because the frosting looks like a couch."

"And now it's passing into another state of matter," said Kim. "Moment of silence, please."

Huynh put a fist delicately over her mouth. "I—mmplgh! I declare the curse reversed."

"Yeah," said Kim. "Fuck that guy."

They were quiet for a moment. Then, as the girl said, "Why don't we get started," the power blinked out.

AT FIRST ALL was chaos and panic; at first it was as if without their noticing the outside had bled and dripped into the inside until the inside had been fully painted over by the outside and now the beast was here with them, the inside that was the outside; the lights in the street and the surrounding buildings had gone out too, and all was darkness as the girl sat there smiling, which no one could see.

Then everyone remembered that they had their phones and one by one they appeared in the dark as busts glowing delicately blue in a far-future museum, the unspecified museum they were trying to make it into with their writing, as stupid as that sounded and whether they admitted it to themselves or not, because it wasn't as if their jobs or families or stations in life or beauty or kindness or cruelty would get them there. They were investing their current happiness against future gain, except the cause-and-effect was screwy and some of them weren't doing this on purpose—some of them were very, very unhappy so their main consolation was that their eventual glorious future would stretch backward in time. So they dug in, burrowed tight foxholes where they could be surrounded by their unhappiness, nurtured sweet little gardens made up of and inside their unhappiness.

Hey! Holy fuck. Are we still alive or are we dead right now? Oh my god. Hiiiiiiii! they said to each other, laughing. Kim took a photo of everyone in their tiny blue islands. Lee found a flashlight, and the girl produced candles and a bottle from a backpack they hadn't noticed.

"They said there would be a storm tonight," she said, laughing as she laid out the candles for Lee to light. "I came prepared!" Her teeth glinted. Lee noticed that her hair hadn't dried at all, not one bit. Dark ropes of it clung to her shoulders and chest, and a few strands were wrapped around her throat; Lee had the urge to brush them out of the way.

The girl said, "I want you guys to be happy."

"We've been talking a lot," said Lee. "What about you? What do you write? What are you doing in the city?

"Look, I brought alcohol," said the girl. "Bourbon." She sprang up and scampered to Lee's kitchen, where she pulled out the first cup-like objects her hands touched—mugs, a highball glass, a soup bowl. "You guys drink bourbon, right? Writers. All you writers. Bourbon is a thing writers are supposed to drink. Drink up." They felt both flirted with and completely humiliated.

Somehow, they had ended up in a circle sitting on the floor. It felt safer that way. Once the lights went out, it was best to pre-emptively cut your ties to other so-called necessities, like furniture.

"Let's do shots," said the girl.

They drank. The girl's arm snaked out, long and white, and poured more. "Another!" she shouted. That was certainly a kind of person, the person who demanded that everyone do shots. Or, given that you couldn't always predict who would get that antic gleam, who would yell for more shots the way a child might scream for another story and would literally not stop with the shots until something bad and un-fun happened—the shots-monster was more like a demon that roamed bars and colleges and work holiday parties to possess the susceptible.

Lee's face never got red but too much alcohol still begrimed her on a cellular level; her drunks felt dark and deeply allergic, but at least they didn't fuck up her countenance. Unlike Kim, whose eyes always went an itchy highlighter pink in the presence of even a drop of a beer, though there was something manly and endearing and almost bruised-looking about his inflamed face.

"You're being so guarded around me," the girl whispered sadly.

When are we going to talk about my writing? Lee wanted to say but didn't. Who cared, anyway. It was a particularly gnarly excerpt from book two of her fantasy trilogy, the kind of piece that would drag the group into unhelpful arguments about blood spatter patterns and what kinds of plausible damage could be done to a person via broadsword, unicorn horn, mace. They did not respect her. Just wait, she thought. I will be rich and respected. I will not have to choose, the way you all think you're choosing.

The shots-monster changed form and the girl lit up. "I know!" she said. "Drinking game!"

The girl made everyone write down nouns on little scraps of paper, torn from a small notebook she produced from her backpack. The paper scraps were folded and piled in the middle of the circle. The girl took a die out of her pocket and told them that when it was your turn, you would pick a scrap of paper, before rolling the die—making sure no one else could see the number you got.

If you got an even number, you had to tell a true story that involved the thing that was written on the paper scrap you picked. If the number was odd, you would make a story up. Then everyone would go around the circle and guess if the story was true or false. Whoever is wrong drinks. For each person who guesses right, the storyteller has to take a drink.

"Because you're all writers," said the girl. They felt embarrassed again.

Kim said, "Let's do this." He selected a piece of paper and turned away from the circle and rolled. "Okay," he said. "I can work with this."

The paper said NAME.

"My last name—there's a shit-ton of us," Kim said. "But my first name is less common." The first time he got a story published, he thought about changing things up, maybe throwing in a middle name. But he decided to use his regular name, as is, since he wanted all the glory and acclaim ("such as there was") for himself, the normal everyday self with whom he was already familiar. Why should some artificial new construct—some guy who hadn't even been there through the hard work—take all the credit?

Years passed, he got a few more things published, and one day something strange happened. Kim received an email from a prestigious literary journal accepting a short story of his. Great! Except Kim didn't recognize the title of the story, because he hadn't written it. He let the journal know that they had gotten him mixed up with someone else. Now, if it had ended there, it would have been a funny little blip, a cute story he could tell about the time he got something he really wanted but it turned out to have been a terrible mistake and was thus immediately wrested from him, talk about impostor syndrome, I'll tell you about impostor syndrome.

But that incident begat others, in which he started receiving both acceptances and rejections for things he hadn't written. "A lose-lose situation. The acceptances didn't feel good and the rejections still felt terrible." Kim started thinking again about using another name, except now he'd racked up a few publications and it would be a giant ass-pain to start all over again. But nor could he let the current situation stand. What to do?

Just the other day, the other Kim contacted Kim. The other Kim's email was neutral in tone, very direct. He stated that he had been getting mistaken for Kim off and on over the past few years, and surmised that this must also be happening to Kim in the other direction. So he made a proposal: Since it was apparent that they both worked slowly, why not pool their resources and combine themselves into one Kim? The other Kim wrote, "I have read your work and though it is quite different from my own, I believe we would complement each other well. Please also keep in mind that half of something is better than all of—as it stands right now, for both of us— absolutely nothing."

"We complete each other," said Kim. This whole time, he had kept himself from reading the other Kim's stories. He had this irrational idea that if he were to do so, something awful would happen—he might learn something it would be much better for him not to know. So he hadn't decided yet. Although, of course, he was definitely going to say no.

"True," said Wong.

"False," said Lee.

"False," said Huynh.

"True," said the girl.

Kim pointed at Lee and Huynh. "Drink," he said.

"Why would you never tell us this?" said Huynh.

Kim shrugged. "It just happened."

"No, dick, I know you said the other Kim just wrote to you, but I'm talking about the earlier stuff."

"I didn't know you then."

Huynh glowered at him. The girl threw her head back and laughed. "Love it. I'm getting so much out of this. I'm so glad we're doing this." She refilled their cups. The level of liquid in the bottle appeared unchanged.

Wong was next. The paper said SCHOOLBOY. He blanched.

"I got a bad one," Wong said, making a face. He thought for a moment, then began.

When Wong talked at length, he was hypnotic. Which could be bad at times, since his clipped accent, the precision of his speech, and the rich perverted sweet-rot depth of his voice all combined to make it sound like he really meant everything he said. One learned very quickly that this was not the case, but when confronted with that voice, one had a little trouble remembering that, now didn't one. He could be intimidating, especially for Huynh, who was already continually shoulder-chipped by the fact that she hadn't gone to the same fancy college as the rest of them. He hurt feelings often, but he didn't mean to—a dumb joke from another person would sound like a blithe yet piercing condemnation from the president of the 1% from Wong. That voice!

Wong told of a friendship he had had while in boarding school in Switzerland. This was a close friendship, childish because it was so obsessive, but adult because they seemingly saw each other clearly; they were fully mutually admiring of each other. Though Wong and the friend resembled each other physically and had similar tastes and personalities and aptitudes for school and sport, they treasured in the other the things that were different: Wong's easy, conversational manner with teachers and fellow students alike; the friend's single-minded ability to complete a paper or problem set from start to finish without interruption; one's thick, fashionable glasses; the other's adorably decorative smattering of acne. "It was very gay, as I can see you thinking, but my friend was not gay. Or perhaps a little, just for me. There was this one time in Paris—"

"Anyway, I was extremely popular," Wong said, as only Wong could say. But this friend gave Wong something no other friend could. Wong, who had been orphaned when he was a small child, knew no one else and was known by no one else to such a comforting extent. The friend knew Wong so well partially because they were so similar, which then made the differences all the more apparent, something to be mapped and delineated and treasured.

One winter break, they lied to various parties and spent break unsupervised in one of the Wong family properties in Paris. Toward the end of break the friend received news that his parents had been killed in an accident. And after the funeral, the friend would be moved to another school, closer to his relatives.

The friend did not want to go to a strange new school, to leave Wong and his other friends behind. So they came up with a plan. Wong would go to the new school in his friend's stead, while the friend would stay at their school, where he could impersonate both Wong and himself. "When you feel bad, be me," Wong had told him. It would help. And if the friend missed himself, felt the need for a small pocket of space-time in which to grieve, then he could always return to himself. It was only supposed to be temporary. So it was that Wong left their school in his friend's place.

"For a whole season, I pretended to be him," said Wong. He blinked slow and smoothed his hair back. "The end." he said.

Kim made a farting noise. "When did you guys switch back again?" he asked.

"Yeah, what happened? Did anyone ever find out?" said Huynh.

Wong said, "Time's up. Make your guesses."

"False," said Lee.

"False," said Huynh.

"True," said the girl.

"Falsest horseshit I've ever heard," said Kim.

"You'll all have to drink," said Wong. "All of you!" As the rest of them complained, he cackled and drained his glass.

"I'll allow it," said the girl. She and Wong clinked glasses.

It was Lee's turn. The paper said SUCCESSOR. "Pass," said Lee.

The next slip of paper said USURPER. Well, if she didn't want SUCCESSOR, she definitely didn't want USURPER. "Pass on this, too," said Lee.

The next slip said REPLACEMENT.

Lee yelled, "I'm not doing any of these, you assholes," and against her will she remembered finding the pictures of her ex-husband's old girlfriends, the new girlfriend who had usurped Lee's position, the one who had replaced that one, and the other one, or was it two, after—it was hard to remember exactly because the photos had been in some kind of circular book with no covers, no clear end or beginning, you could easily have flipped through all the women and gone back around to the beginning without even noticing; that was what they looked like.

Huynh was looking at her calmly. Lee remembered how perfect Huynh had been, matter-of-fact yet merciless. "Don't dwell. Just another yellow fever cracker ass white guy," Huynh had said. "Throw him back."

Huynh pushed a square of paper toward Lee. "Here, try one more." Her face was unreadable.

Lee unfolded the paper. Printed on it in tiny block letters was the word SHART. She hung her head, then began to shake with laughter—something about the careful, meek handwriting, more than the word itself even. "Noooooo," she moaned. "That does it. I'm skipping my turn." Huynh raised her glass to Lee. Wong and Kim looked relieved and drank. The girl refilled everyone's cups. The bottle remained nearly full.

"You humans," murmured the girl. She grinned at them, tilting her head. "I mean, us. Us humans. We're just such a blast."

Huynh got MATTRESS. She nodded as though she had been expecting it. Years ago, before all of them had met, Huynh had been going through a rough time. There was no money. She was living in an expensive city, but was too poor and depressed to move anywhere else and could not stomach the thought of going back home—her dad was mentally ill and homeless, and her mom had left for Vietnam a while back. "I guess with all the people over the years telling her to go back to her own country, she was finally like, 'Huh, you know what, that's actually like not a bad idea!'" said Huynh. "You fuckers."

Huynh had signed up with a temp agency, who immediately found her an assignment with amazingly inconvenient hours that paid terribly, but she took it, afraid that if she turned this one down she would not be placed elsewhere. During the final days before she had to move out of her current apartment, she searched through the classifieds and found exactly two apartments she could afford. One was so affordable because it was free— she would only have one roommate and would have to refrain from wearing clothing while in the apartment ('no sex no touching,' the ad had said, 'i'm not some CREEP').

Huynh took the other apartment. It was a room in a two-bedroom apartment, clean and empty except for a mattress and a suitcase. She had a roommate who she would never see. The roommate slept on the mattress from about 10 p.m. to 6 a.m. Normal-people stuff. Huynh slept on the mattress during the day. At night, she worked as an admin in a warehouse where they made and sent out copies of X-rays to hospitals. The schedule did not feel so good. She slept when she was supposed to, and presumably for the right number of hours, but waking up always felt cruel, as if she had just closed her eyes and hours passed in seconds, an evil trick.

Her roommate communicated with her through notes. Like: Please wash the sheets. I did it last time. We will trade off on this. I hope you understand. Best, A.M. Huynh wrote back: No problem! Thank you. Best, P.M.

This could not go on forever, but it went on for a while, until the night that Huynh, wracked with a flu and three canker sores, slept through her two alarms, slept through the sinking of the sun and the rising of the sun, and sat up midday, horrified that she had stolen her roommate's bed time. Huynh lay back down, sweaty and weak, figuring that when her roommate came back she could apologize. Maybe the roommate would take pity on her when she saw how ill she was, since she seemed very reasonable in her notes.

But the roommate never returned. No notes, no nothing. Huynh stayed in bed for three melty days, alternately dozing off and listening fearfully for the turn of the doorknob. And then: "Then I got in that accident and became the woman you see before you today," said Huynh.

"True," everyone said in unison. Huynh nodded again and drank once, twice, thrice, four times. She didn't seem drunk. Lee wondered just what was in the bottle that the girl had brought.

"My turn," said the girl. She leaned forward and plucked one of the slips of paper out of the pile. Her hair, still soaking wet, spattered the floor.

BARGAIN, it said on the paper. The girl sat up straight. She suddenly seemed very tall, and not only tall, but big.

"I really liked hearing your stories," she said. "I really like that kind of thing. I had a good feeling about you guys. Not just the one who drew me here—all of you. Such great need." She stood in one swift motion, unswiveling herself from the ground like a ballerina, walked over to the window, and yanked the blinds open. Lee shouted.

The girl said, "Don't worry. There's something I want you to see. It can't hurt you."

The slight emphasis on "it" clearly bothered everyone, but they got up and stood next to the girl by the window.

Outside it was still raining, though not as hard as before. Some people must have had generators, because they could see scattered lights on in some of the apartments across the way and in the bodega on the corner. There was the beast, ambling down the street. It raised its arm and waved at the girl. The girl waved back. "You see?" she said gently, not looking away from the beast. As quietly as possible, Huynh puked up the wedding cake. Finally the girl glanced behind her, annoyed, and snapped her fingers. The candles went out.

In the dark, they ran scared and huddled together in a corner. Lee thought, I let it in. I let it in!

No: Somebody called it here. And, also, this is true: We all kept it here.

Their knees buckled; they all became sleepy at once. "Shh," said the girl somewhere in the dark, and they slowly slumped to the ground. "Let's end it nice," she said. "Like a slumber party. We'll lie down, and just talk until we sleep. In the morning I'll be gone and you won't remember a thing. Won't that be nice? Doesn't that make you less scared now?"

They had spread out around the living room, lying flat and exhausted and finding themselves already drifting off to sleep, despite the hard wooden floors and the fears that one of them would encounter Huynh's puke puddle.

Each of them felt the girl pressing against them, her body huge and warm and firm, snaking and coiling around the room.

"It's a bad time for you," the girl said. "There's so much water, but it's bad. Sour. You're running out of time to be noticed even though it's all you've ever wanted. Your lives are running out, the world's life running out—" She sounded like she was about to cry. "I wish I could help you all."

The girl's coils wrapped around Lee, Huynh, Kim, and Wong, and tightened ferociously. "I can't. You know it can only be one," she said. Her eyes were the size of books, laptops, pillows, getting larger by the second. For a moment they welled up again. She wanted to console them by letting them know that the one who had called her here—well, that person just wanted it more, didn't they? But all of them wanted it! They wanted the face that would be their face and theirs only; they all were so tired of appearing and immediately receding like a finger painting made in the sea, they wanted to be carved as stone into the minds of their friends and family and loved ones and hated ones and people worldwide who'd never meet them in the flesh, whether they were the one who was obsessed, or the one who didn't feel good about anything else, or the one who was naturally talented and too lazy to find praise elsewhere, or the one who wanted to be famous and loved in a way that didn't require talking or looking good. It was too bad! The girl lifted her face to the ceiling in a silent cry and wept for a minute. Then she bent her head and ate.

In the morning, they woke up jolly and hungover. Three of them less than they used to be, but they would not ever know it. Nor would the one who had become more, who had received some crucial bump in talent or desire or perseverance or pure idiot luck, and who would be famous, in a way, years later. We don't need to talk about that. Better to think about what the fame did to the others—how the sheer proximity of awardpartymoviesbookstravelhotelcruditesgraduationspeeches made success feel actually possible, maybe even attainable, while at other times inducing in them a fresh, keening despair, inscribing behind their eyelids shining golden letters like:

H E R E I S Y O U R L I F E then a sickly, disorienting leap over hundreds of millions of miles of alien terrain over to T H E R E I S T H E I R L I F E

These lands were on the same planet only technically. In one direction they were so far away from each other on the globe that in another direction, they almost touched. But they never touched. Years later, one was famous, and meanwhile, the others would hope to be, almost be, and finally, never be. There were so many tiny little steps between each stage that each one felt much like the last, and thus, the letdown was gentle, merciful, barely noticeable, even.

LAWS OF NIGHT AND SILK
Seth Dickinson

Seth Dickinson (www.sethdickinson.com) is the author of the epic fantasy *The Traitor Baru Cormorant* and sixteen short stories. Born in 1989, raised in the hills of Vermont, he studied racial bias in police shootings, wrote much of the lore for Bungie Studios' *Destiny*, and threw a paper airplane at the Vatican. If he were an animal, he would be a cockatoo.

KAVIAN CAN PRETEND this girl is her daughter through drought and deluge, but the truth is the truth: Irasht is a weapon, and never any more.

It hurts enough to break even the charcoal heart of Kavian Catamount, and so she does a forbidden thing—she puts her arms around the girl Irasht who is not her daughter, kisses her brow, and whispers:

"I will protect you. Go."

Then Kavian pushes Irasht onto the stone above the battle.

In the valley beneath them the Cteri, the people of the dams, the people of Kavian's blood and heart, stand against the invader. The Efficate comes baying to drain five centuries of civilization into their own arid land.

So the word has come from Kavian's masters, from the Paik Rede and warlord Absu:

You have had time enough to tame her. Go to the battle. Use the abnarch girl, the girl who is not your daughter.

Destroy the Efficate army.

Kavian cries the challenge.

"Men of the Efficate! Men of the owl!" Her wizardry carries the bellow down the valley, across the river, to shatter and rebound from the hills. "I am Kavian Catamount, sorcerer of the Paik Rede! I like to warm my hands on your brothers' burning corpses!"

Fifty thousand enemy spearmen shudder in fear. They know her name.

But the battle today does not ride on Kavian's fire.

The girl Irasht (who is not her daughter) stares at the battle-plain, wide-eyed, afraid, and puts her hands up to her ears. Kavian seizes her wrists, to keep her from blocking out the sound of war. Irasht claws and spits but does not cry.

Over Irasht's hissing frenzy Kavian roars: "My hands are *cold* today!"

She hears the cry go up in the Efficate ranks, a word in their liquid tongue that means: *abnarch, abnarch, she has brought an abnarch*. And she sees their eyes on her, their faces lifted in horror and revulsion, at the girl Irasht, at what has been done to her.

You poor bastards, she thinks. I know exactly how you feel.

KAVIAN HAS BEEN in pain for a very long time. There's the pain she wears like a courting coat, a ballroom ensemble—the battle hurt that makes her growl and put her head down, determined to go on.

And there's the other pain. The kind she lets out when drunk, hoping it'll drown. The pain she reaches for when she tries to play the erhu (this requires her to be drunk, too). It's a nameless pain, a sealed pain, catacombed in the low dark and growing strong.

The night she met Irasht, the night she went down into the catacombs to decant her daughter: that night belonged to the second pain.

In the Paik Rede's summit halls, past the ceremonial pool where the herons fish, catacomb doors bear an inscription:

We make silk from the baby moth. We unspool all that it might become. This is a crime.

Silk is still beautiful. Silk is still necessary.

This is how an abnarch is made. This is the torment to which Kavian gave up her first and only born.

The wizards of the Paik Rede, dam-makers, high rulers of isu-Cter, seal a few of their infants into stone cells. They grow there, fed and watered by silent magic, for fifteen years. Alone. Untaught. Touched by no one.

And on nights like these their parents decant them for the war.

"Kavian. Stop."

Warlord Absu wears black beneath a mantle of red, the colors of flesh and war. For a decade she has led the defense of the highlands. For a decade before that—well: Kavian was not born with sisters, but she has one. This loyalty is burnt into her. Absu is the pole where Kavian's needle points.

"Lord of hosts," Kavian murmurs. She's nervous tonight, so she bows deep.

The warlord considers her in brief, silent reserve. "Tonight we will bind you to a terrible duty. The two mature abnarchs are our only hope." Her eyes! Kavian remembers their ferocity, but never *remembers* it. She is so intent: "You're our finest. But one error could destroy us."

"I will not be soft with her." So much rides on the abnarch's handler: victory, or cataclysm.

Absu's golden eyes hold hers. "The war makes demands of us, and we serve. Remember that duty, when you want to grieve." Her expression opens in the space between two blinks—a window of pain, or compassion. "What did you name her?"

"Heurian," Kavian says.

A grave nod. Absu's face is a map of battles past, and her eyes are a compass to all those yet to come. "A good name. Go."

And then, as Kavian pushes against the granite doors, as the mechanisms of gear and counterweight begin to open, Absu warns her.

"You will find Fereyd Japur in the catacombs. He went ahead of you."

Fereyd. The scar man, the plucked flower. Her only rival. Why send him ahead? Why is *he* in the dark with her buried daughter?

Kavian tries to breathe out her tension but it is a skittish frightened breed and it will not go.

SHE GOES DOWN into the catacombs where eight children wait in the empty dark for their appointed day. Where her daughter waits to be reborn and used.

Magic is bound by the laws a wizard carries. Day and night, air and gravity, the right place of highborn and low. The lay of words in language. The turn of the stars above high isu-Cter, the only civilization that has ever endured. All these are laws a wizard may know.

This is why the upstart Efficate produces so many wizards: it fills its children with the mantras of *fraternity* and *republic*. Their minds are limited, predictable—but like small gears, together they make a machine. This is why the Cteri wizards walk the world as heroes, noble-blooded and rare.

There are other ways to make a wizard. A child raised in a stone cell knows no laws. Only the dark.

Fereyd Japur waits for her in white silk ghostly beneath the false starlight of the gem-starred roof. He is tall and beautiful and his eyes are like a field surgery.

He was not always a great wizard. Not until he gave himself to the enemy, to be tortured, to learn the truest laws of pain.

"Why are you here?" Kavian asks.

Fereyd Japur's eyes burn old and sharp and clot-dark in a young brown-bronze face. Whispers say that the thing he did to buy his power killed him. Left him a corpse frozen in his first virility. The whispers are wrong, but Kavian still remembers them. He's a popular companion for those who want to claim dangerous taste.

"You don't know," he says, and then, "She didn't tell you. Absu didn't tell you."

Oh.

Kavian understands at once, and she steps forward, because if she doesn't, she'll run.

"They've given her to *you*," she husks. "Heurian. My daughter."

"And mine to you."

"*What?*"

"My daughter Irasht." An awful crack opens in his face, a rivening Kavian could recognize as grief, if she believed he was human, or as rage, if she were wiser. "The warlord prefers to spare us from attachment to our charges. So I will have your daughter as my abnarch. And you will have mine."

She wants to weep: she will never know her daughter. She wants to cry out in shameful joy, she will never *have* to know her daughter, and that thought is *cowardice*.

Kavian says the rudest thing she can manage. "You never told me you fathered." Women have bragged of having him, even made a sport of it—he is beautiful, and his lowborn status makes him scandalous, coercible, pliant. But Cteri women don't conceive without intent. Who—?

His full lips draw down to one narrow line. The fissure in him has not closed: grief and hate cover him like gore. "The mother wanted a wizard's blood to water her seed. The child was meant for the catacombs. That was all."

"You did this to hurt me." Her anger's speaking for her, but she has no hope for any kind of victory here and so she lets it speak. "You knew this would happen, didn't you? Fifteen years ago you *planned* this? You made a child to be given to me, so that you could take my daughter, so that you could say, at last, *I have something Kavian Catamount wanted?*"

He lashes out at her. The word he speaks would kill any lesser wizard, the third-best or the fourth or maybe even Fereyd Second-Best himself. But Kavian turns it aside without thought, an abject instant *no*. He must have known she would.

"You have *everything* I wanted," he hisses, and it feels as if she can see through the dusk of his skin and the white of his bone into the venom of his marrow, into the pain he learned beneath the enemy knife.

She turns away.

They unseal the cells and decant their children.

The girl Iraoht, daughter of Fereyd Japur, waits wide-eyed and trembling in the center of her cell. When Kavian comes close she rises up on narrow legs and begins to make soft noises with her lips: *ah, ah, ah*.

She doesn't know what a person is. She's never seen one before.

By the time Kavian has coaxed the girl into a trembling bird-legged walk, Fereyd Japur has taken Heurian and gone. The closest Kavian comes to her daughter is the sound of footsteps, receding.

Kavian protests to Absu, bursting into the war council, scattering the tiny carved owls that mark the enemy on the map and raging for her daughter Heurian.

But the Warlord says: "Without your two abnarchs on the front, they will break us this summer. They will open our reservoirs, take our men for their fraternity, and use our silk to wipe the ass of their upstart empire. You are a soldier first. Look to your charge, Kavian."

So: a night that belonged to the second kind of pain.

* * *

231

GO TO THE *front. Train your abnarch on the march. Summer is upon us, and the enemy moves on the dams.*

Kavian curses Absu's madness—*train her on the march?* Irasht could go catatonic, overwhelmed by the sweep and stink of the world beyond her cell. She could lash out in abnegation and blot herself and Kavian and their retinue and a mile of Cteri highlands into nothing.

But Kavian's known Absu since childhood, and for all the rage she's hurled at those golden eyes she has never known them to measure a war wrong.

She finds she cannot sleep until she snaps something: a branch, a lyre-string. Sometimes it takes a few.

Every time she looks on Irasht, teetering around in tentative awe like a hatchling fallen from a nest, she thinks: *where is my daughter?* She thinks: *I could go to that lowborn boy and take Heurian back. He could not stop me.* But she cannot go against Absu and the Paik Rede. Cannot defy the ruthless will that keeps isu-Cter safe.

So she hardens her heart and begins the training.

"Hssh," she murmurs—Irasht freezes when touched, and must be soothed. "Hssh." She draws a cold bath while the abnarch girl watches the motion of the water, rapt. When Kavian lowers her down into the ice cold, arms around her tiny neck and knocking knees, she reacts with only a soft "oh". From then on the temperature doesn't seem to trouble her, even when Kavian leans her back to wash her knotted hair. She sculls the water in small troubled circles and stares. Kavian thinks she is trying to reconcile two things: the sight of the water rippling around her palm, and the feeling of it on her hand. Whether she succeeds, Kavian cannot tell.

Irasht is at the peak of her power as an abnarch. All the logic she learns will confine her. When she sees the difference between sunrise and sunset she will diminish. When she understands that the chattering shapes around her are people like herself, she will be a lesser weapon. So Kavian keeps to the strict discipline of the handler. No language. Simple food. Strict isolation, when possible.

But for Irasht to be useful, she must learn to trust her handler. (Or dread and fear her handler, Fereyd Japur would remind her. Or that.) So Kavian reaches out to her—touch, meaningless sound, small acts of compassion. Holds her when the world becomes too much and she retreats to clawing frenzy.

Irasht is a burnt stump of a person, like a stubborn coal pulled from a fire pit. She stares overmuch and needs housetraining like a stray dog. To Kavian's frustration and shame —*this is what I am reduced to?*—she finds that Irasht cannot chew. So she crumbles the girl's food by hand.

This would be easier, all in all, if Kavian could think of her only as a weapon.

But in the villages and terrace farms along the path to war she sees Irasht do things that take a chisel to her heart. When Irasht finds doors she goes to them and waits patiently, hoping, Kavian imagines, that someone will invite her in.

When it grows too dark in their tent Irasht panics, tangling herself in her bedding. Kavian is moved: Irasht fears going back to the dark. Somehow this is a comfort. It makes Kavian feel she has done a good thing, bringing her out into the light.

She takes Irasht out to see her first stars, and holds the girl, rocking her, thinking: we did this. We made her this way.

No. The *war* did this. The war makes demands.

In the Efficate they make wizards in vast numbers. Bake them like loaves of bread. Kavian knows this because she's slaughtered them by the dozens. All they can do is make little shields and throw little sparks—the laws of their society leave no room for heroism, and Kavian suspects the quality of their blood gives rise to no heroes.

But there are so many. And they are winning.

And this is *not* her daughter.

THEY PASS THROUGH everything that will be lost if they fail. The terraced farms and waterfall mills of the highlands. The gulls that circle library-ships on reservoirs raised by wizards of centuries past.

For all remembered history, isu-Cter has been the still eye at the heart of the world. Kavian still believes with patriot fire that, for all its faults, high green isu-Cter must stand.

Fereyd Japur travels with her. It's distasteful company but a military necessity. She tells herself it's good to be close to Heurian. She's lying. Fereyd keeps his abnarch to himself, and the space between Kavian and Heurian feels like forever, as wide as grief and deep as duty.

As they come down from the highlands towards the dams and the war-front, he walks into her tent to take a meal and brag. "Heurian is active. Ready to be used. When I give her an image, she changes the world to match it."

Kavian sets her cup down with soft care. She has not even begun to push Irasht towards useful magic. "Oh?"

"You think I'm lying."

"No," Kavian says. The firelight makes Fereyd's beauty almost painful, a scrimshaw thing, etched into his face by acid and tint, worked into his bones by years of hungry eyes. She touches the edge of hate and it feels hot and slick as a knife coming out. "I believe you."

"And Irasht?" The kohl on his eyelids turns his blink into a mechanism of dark stone. "Is my daughter ready for the war?"

Kavian lifts her chin. "I will need more time."

Fereyd watches her across the fire. It might be something in his face, or the set of his muscled farmer's shoulders, or the way he holds himself so *properly* as if to remind her she is higher born—it might be one of these things that screams of mockery. Or it might only be her imagination.

But Kavian breaks the silence with a hiss: "What did you to do to her?"

Fereyd Japur looks away.

"What method?" Kavian insists, leaning across the fire. The heat is harsh but her arms are a cage for it and the pain only makes her angrier. "How did you reach her so quickly? Was it some secret of knives? What did you *do*?"

"I did what I've always done. I obeyed my orders." The softness in his voice, the tilt of his eyes—for a moment he could be the boy of impossible talent Absu plucked out of the laborers' quarter. But the rage returns. "Heurian will be ready when the enemy comes. Why are you angry? What more would you ask of me?"

She waits there, hunched across the fire like her namesake, and he sits in quiet deference, trembling with a need to flee or yield or kill (she does not like to guess at his thoughts).

Shadows move across the inside of the tent.

From the sleeping-tent Irasht begins to howl. When Kavian rises to go to her she catches Fereyd's eyes and sees something shattering under that howl, something long ago broken, something still coming apart.

"Keep my daughter safe," she says. More than anything else she could say, she thinks it will hurt him most.

* * *

IRASHT TAKES UP collecting. She does not much care for the idea of property, but after silent rebukes from Kavian, she focuses her needs on waterskins. Soon she learns to show anger by pouring water on the earth.

Kavian laughs in delight, and then sobers. The girl is ready for a test.

On the riverbank, she finds three small stones to show Irasht. The abnarch perches, head cocked, and waits for Kavian's command.

Kavian waggles her fingers. This is the counting game. Count three stones, Irasht.

Three, Irasht indicates: three fingers.

Kavian holds up four.

Three, Irasht insists, brow furrowed. She waves her raised fingers and makes a high chirp. Three, three. There are three stones.

Kavian answers with stillness: four fingers. Four stones.

Irasht's eyes narrow in bafflement.

And a small weight moves in Kavian's palm. A fourth stone, conjured from nothing. Irasht's abnarchy at work. Faced with a gap between reality as it is and reality as Kavian says it must be, Irasht has rectified the discrepancy.

Kavian hugs Irasht tenderly, kisses her gently on the brow, and conjures her an air-picture of the night sky, crowded with stars. It makes Irasht tremble in joy, to see those lights in the dark.

THE WAR BEGINS again. Twenty thousand Efficate spearmen and four hundred wizards under the stripling Adju-ai Casvan march on a southern dam.

Word comes by rider from Warlord Absu:

I have judged your reports. Fereyd Japur will use Heurian against the enemy. Kavian, your abnarch is unready. Keep her safe.

She sees it happen. Sees all this:

Fereyd carrying Heurian (she is a small dark shape, limp—but her hair moves in the wind off the reservoir) across the bridge beneath the dam. Fereyd raising his arms to the sky. The two armies beneath him looking up in awe as he draws against the dusk an image of the Efficate soldiers broken into bone.

Then he puts his hands over Heurian's ears.

Through her own art of sorcery Kavian hears the shriek he puts into her daughter's, a shriek like a nightmare cracking. Horrible enough to make the screams of battle sound less than a lullaby.

Kavian, unable to protect her daughter, breaks a tree in half with a killing word.

The noise Heurian makes is so low and awful that it stirs snow to avalanche when it strikes the distant mountains. When that sound rolls over the first rank of the Efficate army their wizards' shields flare with lightning.

Whatever gets through is enough. Men fall, drowning on ash and water, on the mud that suddenly grows to fill their lungs. Adju-ai Casvan, shielded by his elite cadre, survives to pull his decimated forces out—fleeing west, chased by the sound of Cteri soldiers beating their shields and crying: *the water washes out the filth!*

On the bridge beneath the dam, Fereyd Japur lifts the fallen girl. She puts her arms around his neck and tries to hide against him.

The battle is won. Heurian functions. All it takes is bone in the sky and a scream in her skull.

When Kavian goes to the center of the camp and asks to see her daughter, Fereyd Japur looks at her with cold contempt. "You saw her today," he says. "You saw everything you need to see. She is a weapon."

Warlord Absu writes:

Fereyd Japur has field command. Defeat all Efficate incursions you encounter. Use the abnarch until no longer practical.

Kavian, you must bring your charge to the same standard.

CAMPAIGN SEASON ROLLS down in rain and thunder and blood. The Efficate's wizards try ingenious new defenses. Under Fereyd Japur's guidance, Heurian breaks them. The Cteri win again and again and soon their defensive stand becomes a counterattack.

Kavian pursues her own method with stubborn, desperate resolve. Fereyd's technique—an image to achieve, a goad to drive the abnarch to fear and terror, the promise of relief—is direct. Crude. She has a more elegant solution.

One symbol: the dark. The empty black of Irasht's childhood. *Bad.*

And another—she should have chosen something else, something less fragile, less desperate, but Irasht responds more strongly to the promise of love than anything else—

A starry sky, like the sky that covered them when Kavian held her and kept her from the dark. The only goodness Irasht knows.

Some of the soldiers in Kavian's retinue pool their talents to make Irasht a set of dolls. She plays with them in silence, and Kavian watches, wondering how much of a person is still left in her, and how much has withered away. How much waits, stunted, for some healing rain to fall.

The abnarch technique came from legends of ancient ascetic kings. Transcendent and serene, they locked themselves away, to forget the laws that chained them. They chose confinement.

What would Irasht choose, if given a choice? Does she know *how* to choose?

Kavian shakes her head and gets to her feet. The philosophy must wait. Irasht needs to be made ready. Until then, Fereyd Japur doesn't even need to taunt her. His abnarch carries the nation's hope while hers plays with toys.

She comes upon him in the night after a victory. It is too dark to see his face but through the smoke of a joyful camp she smells wine. "Kavian," he rasps. "Kavian Hypocrite. Come. Sit with me."

She crouches across from him. Makes no light to lift the shadows. "Have a care." It comes out a threat, a purr.

"You are gentle to my daughter." He raises something and she opens her mouth to defend herself, but, no, it is only a cup. "My traitor heart is grateful."

"I will make her ready yet."

His eyes flash white in the dark. "Mercy to a broken thing? Too late, Kavian. Years too late."

"The war broke her." That desperate mantra. "Not us."

"Did Absu tell you that? No, no—it is our choice. The Paik Rede *chooses* to sacrifice its children. We choose to bury them." A wet sound, like gathered spit, like a sob choked. "Is it not said—*the mother has the child for nine months, and the father for nine years?* They took that from me. They made my choice, and took Irasht."

"Treason..." she whispers. But she cannot put any heat in it. Her honor hates to see a man so beautiful brought so low.

He rises unsteadily and she uncoils to match him. "*You* are the traitor. Your mercy to Irasht is the real treachery. She died when Absu put her in those cells. What came out was a weapon. And now you are too weak to use her—as if you could protect her in place of Heurian. Is that your secret, Kavian Catamount? Do you want a warm doll to hold in place of your daughter?"

"Absu?" Kavian lifts a hand to ward off sudden light. They are launching fireworks from the mountainside. "Absu was Irasht's mother?"

Fereyd Japur lowers his face to her in the red glare. His skin looks kiln-fired. "She loved me."

It makes sense. Fereyd Japur is common-born: powerful blood without the politics of a highborn father. No mind as apt as Absu's could pass up the chance to make an abnarch weapon without another parent of good blood to fight the entombment.

Kavian cannot believe there was any love.

He must see the thought in her eyes. "She did," he croaks. There are tears in him, but his rage and his pride and his obvious, agonizing need to be more than *just a man* hold them back. "She did. She *did*. You think I invented it? A tourniquet for a broken heart? Damn you. Damn you."

Kavian watches him stumble away. It is pity she feels, old and strange.

THE EFFICATE OUTFLANKS the Cteri counterattack and marches on the dams at Tan Afsh. Absu orders Fereyd Japur and Heurian to remain with the main thrust and sends Kavian and Irasht to save Tan Afsh.

Kavian is not ready. So much rides on Irasht, and Fereyd Japur's words still ring in her: *you are too weak to use her!*

She wants to save isu-Cter. This is what she's always fought for. Yet she can't believe that the girl she holds and soothes in the night is *only* a weapon.

And she wants to believe, now, that what they have done to their daughters can somehow be undone.

But she pushes Irasht out onto the stone above the battle and shows her the sign for *wrong* alongside the stone-eyed owl banner of the Efficate. It is not Fereyd Japur's method— an image that demands to be real. All she says to Irasht is: *this is wrong, this army.* The rest she leaves to the girl.

Irasht makes a raw noise deep in her throat, as if she is trying to vomit up everything that has ever hurt her. For one instant she burns so bright with will that Kavian cries out in pain.

In the valley beneath them, in the space of a single eyeblink, the Efficate army vanishes. Fifty-five thousand scoured from the sight of God. Even their bootprints.

There are no survivors. It is the most powerful exercise of magic in Cteri history.

After the battle Kavian casts aside all laws of language and isolation, holds Irasht, and whispers love until the girl stops clawing at her own skin. Irasht has learned a few words. She can say:

No more. No more. No more.

A little more, Kavian promises. I'll protect you. Just fight a little more.

Irasht clings to her in silent need, and with a wizard's ken Kavian knows she will not survive many more battles. That she would prefer to erase herself and end the pain.

Word comes from the Cteri spearhead at Cadpur, Fereyd's army, her daughter's army: *we have met the main body of the Efficate invasion force. There are more men than ants upon the earth. More wizards than stars in the sky. Qad-ai Vista leads them. Make haste to join us, Kavian.*

And then an order from the warlord Absu:

We cannot risk both abnarchs in one day.

Fereyd Jaypur. Your weapon is battle-tested. You will defeat the enemy at Cadpur. Attack now.

By the time Kavian reaches the front, the battle's already over. The Efficate army has withdrawn with extraordinary casualties. Fereyd Japur killed Qad-ai Vista's elite cadre and nearly claimed the brother-general himself.

The price was small, as the reckoning goes.

Kavian's daughter Heurian is dead.

* * *

SHE LEAVES IRASHT with her dolls and a retinue guard and goes down into the sleeping camp, to find the man who lost her girl.

Fereyd's tent has no guards. Kavian ties the privacy screen behind her, lace by lace. Everything inside is silk. Fereyd Second-Best travels like the highborn he never was.

"I prepared tea," he says. The candles he has set out around him light him from below. Braided hair, proud chin, empty eyes. An iron chain ornament around his neck, another around his left wrist. Silver on his bare ankle.

She sits across from him on the cushions. The arrangement of the tea service is *exact*. He's measured the angles with a courtier's geometry pin.

She sets her hands before her knees, palms down. "My daughter."

One tremor in his jaw. "I asked too much of her."

"So," she says, each word a soft considered point, like a blow, a kiss, "I had concluded."

"She struck three times. Made their flesh into earth, and then air, and then water. Their wizards tried to kill her and I held them back. I was distracted. But after her third blow—" He sits with stiff formality and pauses, once, to breathe into his cupped hands. "It was too much. She had done so much and the world wasn't better and she, ah, she had to go. She made herself into water along with all the soldiers she killed, and flowed into the earth. I tried to—I tore down a banner and I tried to—to sop her up—"

His mouth opens in rictus and he makes a terrible sound that cannot be a laugh, is not gentle enough to be a sob.

Kavian moves the tea set aside, piece by piece, and takes him in her arms.

"I killed your daughter," he says into her shoulder. "I killed her." He puts his hands against her shoulders and tries to force her away. "I killed her. I killed her."

"Fereyd." She will not let him go. "You can grieve. I will not mark you weak."

"You will. You always do." The plural *you*.

She takes his face between the palms of her hands and ohhhh her muscles have not forgotten how to twist, to snap, to hear the bone go and feel the last breath rush out. He killed Heurian. He killed—

She will not do it.

"You have every right to grieve," she says, though some part of her resents each word. "You have given more than anyone. Today you did what you have always done. Paid too high a price."

"It was your price too. She was your blood."

She doesn't answer that. Doesn't know how.

"I loved her like my own," he says, and lets himself begin to sob.

They speak a little. Mostly not. After a while, moved by the fey mood that comes after deep grief, by the closeness of him, by months of watching him on the march, Kavian takes his chin and kisses him.

"No," he says, turning away. "No. Not you as well. Enough."

"I don't make prizes of men." She regrets this even as she says it. It's not the right assurance.

"You think it's the only way I know how to speak." He laughs with sudden snapping cold. "I win the greatest victory of our time. I lose your daughter—and mine, and mine—to buy our triumph." A pause while he gathers himself. She respects it. "And here I am, in my own tent, still Fereyd Second-Best. Still the *beauty*."

"Fereyd," she whispers. "I'm sorry. I wanted distraction. It was wrong."

He draws away to make a fiercely focused inspection of the tea ceremony, the cushions. "You highborn always forget this: when you break someone, they *stay* broken. You cannot ask a broken thing to right itself. You cannot ask that, and then laugh at it for falling."

She's found some strange kind of comfort here, holding him. So she says this, against her pride, as the only thanks she can manage:

"Now you have seen me broken too."

"I haven't." The truth of pain is in his voice, beneath the grief. "Not yet."

It hurts, but it is true. She never knew her daughter as he did.

She gets up to go but pauses by the screen, uncertain, and when she looks back she catches on the care of his makeup and the suggestion of his body beneath his garments. She hesitates. He speaks.

"Come back." He says this like it's ripped itself from him. "I want to help you. I want to be what you need."

"Fereyd..." she says, warning him, warning herself.

"I want to be something for someone," he says, eyes fierce: and she cannot deny him that.

What happens between them isn't all grief. He's been watching her too—he admits that, though not in words. Her pride likes this.

When she's done with him he touches her shoulder and says:

"I will always do my duty, no matter how it hurts. But you—you are not yet so utterly bound."

She touches his lips in gratitude. The pain is worse than ever. But it runs clear. It feels true.

KAVIAN LEADS THE army through the Cadpur pass into Efficate land, and there on a plain of thin grass and red stone they meet Qad-ai Vista at the head of another numberless host.

This time the brother-general asks for parley.

She meets him in the empty space between the armies. Qad-ai is a tall man, ugly, weary, and he speaks accented Cteri in bald uncomplicated phrases. "We will not seize your water this year," he says. "We ask truce. Next year, or the year after that, we will come again. This year we will go thirsty."

She spits between his legs. "There. Water."

"We will eat you." There's more sadness than anger in his voice. "You understand that, don't you? You buy your proud centuries by visiting atrocity on your own children. You stand on a mountain of chains. Soon they will swallow you."

She chews blood from her cheek and spits that on the sand too. "I'll see you next year."

He squints at her with pragmatic distaste. "Not too late to use the other girl. The one you still have left. Worth her life to kill us, isn't it?"

She says to him what she cannot speak to her own: "She is worth more to me than this victory."

WHAT SHE DOES next is not her duty: not what Fereyd Japur could ever do. But it *must* be done. Not the easy rebellion of the sanctimonious, Kavian roaring home to say, *give up the abnarchs, give up the war!* Not that. Because that would be Kavian's choice, Kavian's anger, and Kavian is not the wounded woman here.

What she does she does for Irasht.

It has to happen now, while the hurt is fierce in her, while Irasht's power still permits it—before she learns too many laws, like *it will always hurt*, like *Kavian will never leave me.*

But the journey home to isu-Cter nearly breaks her determination. The shining reservoirs and the waterfall-terraces glistening in summer gold. The lowborn turning out to cheer.

Kavian has spent two decades fighting for this nation, with her fists and voice and womb.

But when she reaches the summit, she revolts.

The Paik Rede turn out in force to stop her, once they realize her intent. "I am coming to give Irasht a choice," Kavian tells them. "That is all I ask. A choice for all of them."

"She cannot choose," the Paik Rede answers, all of them together, and their speech roars like spring sluiceways.

So Kavian fights. She fights with all her art. She sings a song of rebellion, and at her call the air revolts against the wind, the stone rises up against the earth, she cries out as a hero with a cause and the brave world answers her so that she climbs the steps in a whirlwind of fire and black burnt stone that reaches up to the clouds.

"This is the way things go!" the sorcerers of the Paik Rede reply, and they are as the avalanche, as the river going to the sea. This is how things are. Inevitable.

The wrath of their confrontation breaks the monoliths that line the Summit Steps, and in the end Kavian finds herself at a screaming standstill.

"The abnarch!" she cries. "I will set the abnarch loose!"

They must believe her, for they retreat.

Kavian walks into the chamber of the ceremonial pool and the great stone doors to the catacomb, Irasht hopping at her heels, agitated and nervous, chattering in her high-pitched monotone.

At the catacomb doors the warlord Absu stands with Fereyd Japur at her side. "Kavian. Stop."

Kavian crosses the floor, hobnailed boots hammering on stone and gem. Headed for Absu, and the doors, and the children in the dark.

She won't stop.

"I know why you're here." Absu's voice says: *this is true. I do understand. I do.* "These are our beloved children. They deserve better than darkness and suffering to buy another year of war. But we make this bargain every day, Kavian."

Kavian arranges her wards. Beckons to Irasht—come, come. They circle the ceremonial pool. The herons watch them.

Absu takes a step forward. "The worker suffers in his labor. The lowborn die on the battlefront. But we give them laws and reservoirs, and we keep the Efficate back. That is the bargain: they suffer, so that we may rule. Does it sound callous, put that way?"

Kavian cannot check her tongue: "Not as callous as it looks written on those doors." *Silk is still beautiful. Silk is still necessary.*

Fereyd Japur's shoulders twitch at that. But Absu doesn't stop. "If isu-Cter falls, the world loses its center. Chaos reigns. So I must take the awful bargains upon myself. I have been ruthless for you, Kavian. Will you turn your abnarch on me for that?"

Kavian does not have to answer. She was not born with a sister, but she has one. And she knows Absu understands:

This is not the Efficate, devoted to common fraternal good. In green isu-Cter, ruled by the blood and will of the highborn, one woman's pain and wrath and love is argument enough.

Fereyd Japur steps forward. "Lord of hosts." The pain in his eyes when he looks at Absu is the sharpest and most beautiful thing Kavian has ever seen. "This is Kavian Catamount, who gave her blood to the dark. We are bound to her by duty and gratitude. I beg you. Let her pass."

Absu looks to him with slow regard. The shadow of the weight of a nation moves across her.

Kavian thinks she's ready to battle her sister Absu to the death. It would be a contest of equals, a duel worthy of legend. The respect between them would permit it.

But she knows that Fereyd Japur would come to Absu's defense. Or to hers. She cannot bear to force that choice on him.

Perhaps Absu weighs her duty against the loyalties of her heart. Maybe she looks on Kavian and the abnarch behind her, Irasht her daughter, with eyes that have never mismeasured a war: and she decides she can't win. Maybe she's secretly glad that someone has come to do what she cannot ever permit herself.

Whatever the reason, Warlord Absu lowers her head and stands aside.

Kavian goes forward with Irasht to stand before the catacomb door. "It's your choice," she whispers, stroking the girl's hair. "All the other Irashts are waiting down in the dark. And you could be their Kavian, if you let them out. Do you understand? You could let them out of the dark. Do you want to let them out?"

Irasht's brow furrows. She doesn't understand. Fereyd Japur watches in expressionless agony as Kavian struggles to make it clear. At last she resorts to signs: *bad*, the dark empty square, and *good*, the sky full of stars. And an image in the air, the doors opening, the children decanting from the celled dark to live hard lives of broken speech and brutal nightmare and, maybe, in the end, hope.

Is this good, Irasht? Do you wish you'd had this life instead? *Can* you wish you'd had this life instead?

Or would it have been better if we'd left you in the dark forever?

It's an impossible question. No one could answer it. Do you wish you could have been some other way? Some way you've never known or even been taught *how* to know?

Kavian wants to beg: Please choose. Please be *able* to choose. You can leave them, if you must, or let them out, though we may all perish for it, if they awaken as abnarchs and turn on us.

Just show me you can choose.

Irasht reaches out to the little sign for *good*, the crowded sky, and then draws Kavian down to her. Kisses her brow. "Kavian," she says, and strokes the stars, to put them with her name: "Kavian."

Kavian is good.

"Please." Kavian tries to aim the abnarch girl back towards the door. "Please decide. Do you want to let them out? Do you wish you'd been let out? You can choose. You can choose." Behind her she can feel Fereyd Japur, watching, and Absu at his side, one hand on his shoulder, to quiet him or to give him strength.

But Irasht touches the stars again, as if they are all she can see, and then Kavian's cheek, and then her own brow.

You are good. We are good.

No, Kavian wants to say. No, no, we are so far from that. We did this to you and so we are not good. But she came here to listen to Irasht's choice. Not her own.

In the ceremonial pool a heron spears a fish.

They wait, Kavian and Fereyd Japur and the warlord Absu, for the child of the dark to make a judgment.

But she will not. Irasht cannot choose. She will stand here forever, hoping for Kavian's command. Kavian thinks Absu knows this but won't say it, out of mercy.

Irasht looks up at the door, patient, perched like a little bird. She looks up at the great doors and she waits.

Fereyd Japur said, *you highborn always forget this: when you break someone, they stay broken. You cannot ask a broken thing to right itself.* They put Irasht into a cell and starved her even of this choice. And Kavian shouldn't say *they*, for Kavian did this, didn't she, and now in her cowardice she wants this child to choose, and lift the guilt from herself. But the child cannot choose.

Irasht looks up at the door, patient. She waits.

"Kavian..." Fereyd Japur says, with the most rigid and agonized formality.

And then Kavian shouts in hope, because she remembers Irasht's strange habit on the march. When Irasht finds a door she goes up to it, and waits patiently, hoping, Kavian imagines, that someone will invite her in.

"Irasht," she whispers, kneeling, for Irasht is not a weapon but a person to be loved and taught, and if she cannot make the choice, let a mother give her guidance. "Do you see?"

She shows Irasht an image in the air, and it is only themselves, kneeling before the great door.

And then she turns the image, so that Irasht can see the other side. The children below, in the dark. And now Irasht is *inside* the door, and the children in the dark are the ones waiting for her to invite them in.

Irasht tilts her head.

"Ah," she chirps. "Ah."

TOURING WITH THE ALIEN
Carolyn Ives Gilman

Carolyn Ives Gilman is a Nebula and Hugo Award-nominated writer of science fiction and fantasy. Her most recent novel, *Dark Orbit*, is about a scientific expedition to a crystalline planet where the explorers must confront mysteries about themselves and their reality in order to escape alive. Her other novels include *Halfway Human* and the two-volume novel *Isles of the Forsaken* and *Ison of the Isles*. Her short fiction appears in many *Best of the Year* collections and has been translated into seven languages. In her professional career, Gilman is a historian specializing in frontier and Native history. She is author of *Lewis and Clark: Across the Divide*, and five other books on aspects of Native American and western history. She lives in Washington, D.C. and works as an exhibit developer for the National Museum of the American Indian.

THE ALIEN SPACESHIPS were beautiful, no one could deny that: towering domes of overlapping, chitinous plates in pearly dawn colors, like reflections on a tranquil sea. They appeared overnight, a dozen incongruous soap-bubble structures scattered across the North American continent. One of them blocked a major Interstate in Ohio; another monopolized a stadium parking lot in Tulsa. But most stood in cornfields and forests and deserts where they caused little inconvenience.

Everyone called them spaceships, but from the beginning the experts questioned that name. NORAD had recorded no incoming landing craft, and no mother ship orbited above. That left two main possibilities: they were visitations from an alien race that traveled by some incomprehensibly advanced method; or they were a mutant eruption of Earth's own tortured ecosystem.

The domes were impervious. Probing radiation bounced off them, as did potshots from locals in the days before the military moved in to cordon off the areas. Attempts to communicate produced no reaction. All the domes did was sit there reflecting the sky in luminous, dreaming colors.

Six months later, the panic had subsided and even CNN had grown weary of reporting breaking news that was just the same old news. Then, entry panels began to open and out walked the translators, one per dome. They were perfectly ordinary-looking human beings who said that they had been abducted as children and had now come back to interpret between their biological race and the people who had adopted them.

Humanity learned surprisingly little from the translators. The aliens had come in peace. They had no demands and no questions. They merely wanted to sit here minding their own business for a while. They wanted to be left alone.

No one believed it.

Avery was visiting her brother when her boss called.

"Say, you've still got those security credentials, right?" Frank said.

"Yes…" She had gotten the security clearance in order to haul a hush-hush load of nuclear fuel to Nevada, a feat she wasn't keen on repeating.

"And you're in D.C.?"

She was actually in northern Virginia, but close enough. "Yeah."

"I've got a job for you."

"Don't tell me it's another gig for Those We Dare Not Name."

He didn't laugh, which told her it was bad. "Uh… no. More like those we *can't* name."

She didn't get it. "What?"

"Some… neighbors. Who live in funny-shaped houses. I can't say more over the phone."

She got it then. "Frank! You took a contract from the frigging *aliens?*"

"Sssh," he said, as if every phone in America weren't bugged. "It's strictly confidential."

"Jesus," she breathed out. She had done some crazy things for Frank, but this was over the top. "When, where, what?"

"Leaving tonight. D.C. to St. Louis. A converted tour bus."

"*Tour* bus? How many of them are going?"

"Two passengers. One human, one... whatever. Will you do it?"

She looked into the immaculate condo living room, where her brother, Blake, and his husband, Jeff, were playing a noisy, fast-paced video game, oblivious to her conversation. She had promised to be at Blake's concert tomorrow. It meant a lot to him. "Just a second," she said to Frank.

"I can't wait," he said.

"Two seconds." She muted the phone and walked into the living room. Blake saw her expression and paused the game.

She said, "Would you hate me if I couldn't be there tomorrow?"

Disappointment, resignation, and wry acceptance crossed his face, as if he hadn't ever really expected her to keep her promise. "What is it?" he asked.

"A job," she said. "A really important job. Never mind, I'll turn it down."

"No, Ave, don't worry. There will be other concerts."

Still, she hesitated. "You sure?" she said. She and Blake had always hung together, like castaways on a hostile sea. They had given each other courage to sail into the wind. To disappoint him felt disloyal.

"Go ahead," he said. "Now I'll be sorry if you stay."

She thumbed the phone on. "Okay, Frank, I'll do it. This better not get me in trouble."

"Cross my heart and hope to die," he said. "I'll email you instructions. Bye."

From the couch, Jeff said, "Now I know why you want to do it. Because it's likely to get you in trouble."

"No, he gave me his word," Avery said.

"Cowboy Frank? The one who had you drive guns to Nicaragua?"

"That was perfectly legal," Avery said.

Jeff had a point, as usual. Specialty Shipping did the jobs no reputable company would handle. Ergo, so did Avery.

"What is it this time?" Blake asked.

"I can't say." The email had come through; Frank had attached the instructions as if a PDF were more secure than email. She opened and scanned them.

The job had been cleared by the government, but the client was the alien passenger, and she was to take orders only from him, within the law. She scanned the rest of the instructions till she saw the pickup time. "Damn, I've got to get going," she said.

Her brother followed her into the guest room to watch her pack up. He had never understood her nomadic lifestyle, which made his silent support for it all the more generous. She was compelled to wander; he was rooted in this home, this relationship, this warm, supportive community. She was a discarder, using things up and throwing them away; he had created a home that was a visual expression of himself—from the spare, Japanese-style furniture to the Zen colors on the walls. Visiting him was like living inside a beautiful soul. She had no idea how they could have grown up so different. It was as if they were foundlings.

She pulled on her boots and shouldered her backpack. Blake hugged her. "Have a good trip," he said. "Call me."

"Will do," she said, and hit the road again.

THE MEDIA HAD called the dome in Rock Creek Park the Mother Ship—but only because of its proximity to the White House, not because it was in any way distinctive. Like the others, it had appeared overnight, sited on a broad, grassy clearing that had been a secluded picnic ground in the urban park. It filled the entire creek valley, cutting off the trails and greatly inconveniencing the joggers and bikers.

Avery was unprepared for its scale. Like most people, she had seen the domes only on TV, and the small screen did not do justice to the neck-craning reality. She leaned forward over the wheel and peered out the windshield as she brought the bus to a halt at the last checkpoint. The National Park Police pickup that had escorted her through all the other checkpoints pulled aside.

The appearance of an alien habitat had set off a battle of jurisdictions in Washington. The dome stood on U.S. Park Service property, but D.C. Police controlled all the access streets, and the U.S. Army was tasked with maintaining a perimeter around it. No agency wanted to surrender a particle of authority to the others. And then there was the polite, well-groomed young man who had introduced himself as "Henry," now sitting in the passenger seat next to her. His neatly pressed suit sported no bulges of weaponry, but she assumed he was CIA.

She now saw method in Frank's madness at calling her so spur-of-the-moment. Her last-minute arrival had prevented anyone from pulling her aside into a cinderblock room for a 'briefing.' Instead, Henry had accompanied her in the bus, chatting informally.

"Say, while you're on the road…"

"No," she said.

"No?"

"The alien's my client. I don't spy on clients."

He paused a moment, but seemed unruffled. "Not even for your country?"

"If I think my country's in danger, I'll get in touch."

"Fair enough," he said pleasantly. She hadn't expected him to give up so easily.

He handed her a business card. "So you can get in touch," he said.

She glanced at it. It said 'Henry,' with a phone number. No logo, no agency, no last name. She put it in a pocket.

"I have to get out here," he said when the bus rolled to halt a hundred yards from the dome. "It's been nice meeting you, Avery."

"Take your bug with you," she said.

"I beg your pardon?"

"The bug you left somewhere in this cab."

"There's no bug," he said seriously.

Since the bus was probably wired like a studio, she shrugged and resolved not to scratch anywhere embarrassing till she had a chance to search. As she closed the door behind Henry, the soldiers removed the roadblock and she eased the bus forward.

It was almost evening, but floodlights came on as she approached the dome. She pulled the bus parallel to the wall and lowered the wheelchair lift. One of the hexagonal panels slid aside, revealing a stocky, dark-haired young man in black glasses, surrounded by packing crates of the same pearly substance as the dome. Avery started forward to help with loading, but he said tensely, "Stay where you are." She obeyed. He pushed the first crate forward and it moved as if on wheels, though Avery could see none. It was slightly too wide for the lift, so the man put his hands on either side and pushed in. The crate reconfigured itself, growing taller and narrower till it fit onto the platform. Avery activated the power lift.

He wouldn't let Avery touch any of the crates, but insisted on stowing them himself at the back of the bus, where a private bedroom suite had once accommodated a touring celebrity singer. When the last crate was on, he came forward and said, "We can go now."

"What about the other passenger?" Avery said.

"He's here."

She realized that the alien must have been in one of the crates—or, for all she knew, *was* one of the crates. "Okay," she said. "Where to?"

"Anywhere," he said, and turned to go back into the bedroom.

Since she had no instructions to the contrary, Avery decided to head south. As she pulled out of the park, there was no police escort, no helicopter overhead, no obvious trailing car. The terms of this journey had been carefully negotiated at the highest levels, she knew. Their security was to be secrecy; no one was to know where they were. Avery's instructions from Frank had stressed that, aside from getting the alien safely where he wanted to go, insuring his privacy was her top priority. She was not to pry into his business or allow anyone else to do so.

Rush hour traffic delayed them a long time. At first, Avery concentrated on putting as much distance as she could between the bus and Washington. It was past ten by the time she turned off the main roads. She activated the GPS to try and find a route, but all the screen showed was snow. She tried her phone, and the result was the same. Not even the radio worked. One of those crates must have contained a jamming device; the bus was a rolling electronic dead zone. She smiled. So much for Henry's bugs.

It was quiet and peaceful driving through the night. A nearly full moon rode in the clear autumn sky, and woods closed in around them. Once, when she had first taken up driving in order to escape her memories, she had played a game of heading randomly down roads she had never seen, getting deliberately lost. Now she played it again, not caring where she ended up. She had never been good at keeping to the main roads.

By 3:00 she was tired, and when she saw the entrance to a state park, she turned and pulled into the empty parking lot. In the quiet after the engine shut off, she walked back through the kitchen and sitting area to see if there were any objections from her passengers. She listened at the closed door, but heard nothing and concluded they were asleep. As she was turning away, the door jerked open and the translator said, "What do you want?"

He was still fully dressed, exactly as she had seen him before, except without the glasses, his eyes were a little bloodshot, as if he hadn't closed them. "I've pulled over to get some sleep," she said. "It's not safe to keep driving without rest."

"Oh. All right," he said, and closed the door.

Shrugging, she went forward. There was a fold-down bunk that had once served the previous owner's entourage, and she now prepared to use it. She brushed her teeth in the tiny bathroom, pulled a sleeping bag from her backpack, and settled in.

MORNING SUN WOKE her. When she opened her eyes, it was flooding in the windows. At the kitchen table a yard away from her, the translator was sitting, staring out the window. By daylight, she saw that he had a square face the color of teak and closely trimmed black beard. She guessed that he might be Latino, and in his twenties.

"Morning," she said. He turned to stare at her, but said nothing. Not practiced in social graces, she thought. "I'm Avery," she said.

Still he didn't reply. "It's customary to tell me your name now," she said.

"Oh. Lionel," he answered.

"Pleased to meet you."

He said nothing, so she got up and went into the bathroom. When she came out, he was still staring fixedly out the window. She started making coffee. "Want some?" she asked.

"What is it?"

"Coffee."

"I ought to try it," he said reluctantly.

"Well, don't let me force you," she said.

"Why would you do that?" He was studying her, apprehensive.

"I wouldn't. I was being sarcastic. Like a joke. Never mind."

"Oh."

He got up restlessly and started opening the cupboards. Frank had stocked them with all the necessities, even a few luxuries. But Lionel didn't seem to find what he was looking for.

"Are you hungry?" Avery guessed.

"What do you mean?"

Avery searched for another way to word the question. "Would you like me to fix you some breakfast?"

He looked utterly stumped.

"Never mind. Just sit down and I'll make you something."

He sat down, gripping the edge of the table tensely. "That's a tree," he said, looking out the window.

"Right. It's a whole lot of trees."

"I ought to go out."

She didn't make the mistake of joking again. It was like talking to a person raised by wolves. Or aliens.

When she set a plate of eggs and bacon down in front of him, he sniffed it suspiciously. "That's food?"

"Yes, it's good. Try it."

He watched her eat for a few moments, then gingerly tried a bite of scrambled eggs. His expression showed distaste, but he resolutely forced himself to swallow. But when he tried the bacon, he couldn't bear it. "It bit my mouth," he said.

"You're probably not used to the salt. What do you normally eat?"

He reached in a pocket and took out some brown pellets that looked like dog kibble. Avery made a face of disgust. "What is that, people chow?"

"It's perfectly adapted to our nutritional needs," Lionel said. "Try it."

She was about to say "no thanks," but he was clearly making an effort to try new things, so she took a pellet and popped it in her mouth. It wasn't terrible—chewy rather than crunchy—but tasteless. "I think I'll stick to our food," she said.

He looked gloomy. "I need to learn to eat yours."

"Why? Research?"

He nodded. "I have to find out how the feral humans live."

So, Avery reflected, she was dealing with someone raised as a pet, who was now being released into the wild. For whatever reason.

"So where do you want to go today?" Avery said, sipping coffee.

He gave an indifferent gesture.

"You're heading for St. Louis?"

"Oh, I just picked that name off a map. It seemed to be in the center."

"That it is." She had lived there once; it was so incorrigibly in the center there was no edge to it. "Do you want to go by any particular route?"

He shrugged.

"How much time do you have?"

"As long as it takes."

"Okay. The scenic route, then."

She got up to clean the dishes, telling Lionel that this was a good time for him to go out, if he wanted to. It took him a while to summon his resolve. She watched out the kitchen window as he approached a tree as if to have a conversation with it. He felt its bark, smelled its leaves, and returned unhappy and distracted.

Avery followed the same random-choice method of navigation as the previous night, but always trending west. Soon they came to the first ridge of mountains. People from western states talked as if the Appalachians weren't real mountains, but they were—rugged and impenetrable ridges like walls erected to bar people from the land of milk and honey. In the mountains, all the roads ran northeast and southwest through the valleys between the crumpled land, with only the brave roads daring to climb up and pierce the ranges. The autumn leaves were at their height, russet and gold against the brilliant sky. All day long Lionel sat staring out the window.

That night she found a half-deserted campground outside a small town. She refilled the water tanks, hooked up the electricity, then came back in. "You're all set," she told Lionel. "If it's all right with you, I'm heading into town."

"Okay," he said.

It felt good to stretch her legs walking along the highway shoulder. The air was chill but bracing. The town was a tired, half abandoned place, but she found a bar and settled down with a beer and a burger. She couldn't help watching the patrons around her—worn-down, elderly people just managing to hang on. What would an alien think of America if she brought him here?

Remembering that she was away from the interference field, she thumbed on her phone—and immediately realized that the ping would give away her location to the spooks. But since she'd already done it, she dialed her brother's number and left a voice mail congratulating him on the concert she was missing. "Everything's fine with me," she said, then added mischievously, "I met a nice young man named Henry. I think he's sweet on me. Bye."

Heading back through the night, she became aware that someone was following her. The highway was too dark to see who it was, but when she stopped, the footsteps behind her stopped, too. At last a car passed, and she wheeled around to see what the headlights showed.

"Lionel!" she shouted. He didn't answer, just stood there, so she walked back toward him. "Did you follow me?"

He was standing with hands in pockets, hunched against the cold. Defensively, he said, "I wanted to see what you would do when I wasn't around."

"It's none of your business what I do off duty. Listen, respecting privacy goes both ways. If you want me to respect yours, you've got to respect mine, okay?"

He looked cold and miserable, so she said, "Come on, let's get back before you freeze solid."

They walked side by side in silence, gravel crunching underfoot. At last he said stiffly, "I'd like to re-negotiate our contract."

"Oh, yeah? What part of the contract?"

"The part about privacy. I..." He searched for words. "We should have asked for more than a driver. We need a translator."

At least he'd realized it. He might speak perfect English, but he was not fluent in Human.

"My contract is with your... employer. Is this what he wants?"

"Who?"

"The other passenger. I don't know what to call him. 'The alien' isn't polite. What's his name?"

"They don't have names. They don't have a language."

Astonished, Avery said, "Then how do you communicate?"

He glowered at her. She held up her hands. "Sorry. No offense intended. I'm just trying to find out what he wants."

"They don't want things," he muttered, gazing fixedly at the moonlit road. "At least, not like you do. They're not... awake. Aware. Not like people are."

This made so little sense to Avery, she wondered if he were having trouble with the language. "I don't understand," she said. "You mean they're not... sentient?"

"They're not conscious," he said. "There's a difference."

"But they have technology. They built those domes, or brought them here, or whatever the hell they did. They have an advanced civilization."

"I didn't say they aren't smart. They're smarter than people are. They're just not conscious."

Avery shook her head. "I'm sorry, I just can't imagine it."

"Yes, you can," Lionel said impatiently. "People function unconsciously all the time. You're not aware that you're keeping your balance right now—you just do it automatically. You don't have to be aware to walk, or breathe. In fact, the more skillful you are at something, the less aware you are. Being aware would just degrade their skill."

They had come to the campground entrance. Behind the dark pine trees, Avery could see the bus, holding its unknowable passenger. For a moment the bus seemed to stare back with blank eyes. She made herself focus on the practical. "So how can I know what he wants?"

"I'm telling you."

She refrained from asking, "And how do *you* know?" because he'd already refused to answer that. The new privacy rules were to be selective, then. But she already knew more about the aliens than anyone else on Earth, except the translators. Not that she understood.

"I'M SORRY, I can't keep calling him 'him,' or 'the alien,'" Avery said the next morning over breakfast. "I have to give him a name. I'm going to call him 'Mr. Burbage.' If he doesn't know, he won't mind."

Lionel didn't look any more disturbed than usual. She took that as consent.

"So where are we going today?" she asked.

He pressed his lips together in concentration. "I need to go to a place where I can acquire knowledge."

Since this could encompass anything from a brothel to a university, Avery said, "You've got to be more specific. What kind of knowledge?"

"Knowledge about you."

"Me?"

"No, you humans. How you work."

Humans. For that, she would have to find a bigger town.

As she cruised down a county road, Avery thought about Blake. Once, he had told her that to play an instrument truly well, you had to lose all awareness of what you were doing, and rely entirely on the muscle memory in your fingers. "You are so in the present, there is no room for self," Blake said. "No ego, no doubt, no introspection."

She envied him the ability to achieve such a state. She had tried to play the saxophone, but had never gotten good enough to experience what Blake described. Only playing video games could she concentrate intensely enough to lose self-awareness. It was strange, how addictive it was to escape the prison of her skull and forget she had a self. Mystics and meditators strove to achieve such a state.

A motion in the corner of her eye made her slam on the brakes and swerve. A startled deer pirouetted, flipped its tail, and leaped away. She continued on more slowly, searching for a sign to see where she was. She could not remember having driven the last miles, or whether she had passed any turns. Smiling grimly, she realized that driving was *her* skill, something she knew so well that she could do it unconsciously. She had even reacted to a threat before knowing what it was. Her reflexes were faster than her conscious mind.

Were the aliens like that all the time? In a perpetual state of flow, like virtuoso musicians or Zen monks in *samadhi*? What would be the point of achieving such supreme skill, if the price was never knowing it was *you* doing it?

Around noon, they came to a town nestled in a steep valley on a rushing river. Driving down the main street, she spied a quaint, cupolaed building with a 'Municipal Library' sign out front. Farther on, at the edge of town, an abandoned car lot offered a grass-pocked parking lot, so she turned in. "Come on, Lionel," she called out. "I've found a place for you to acquire knowledge."

They walked back into town together. The library was quiet and empty except for an old man reading a magazine. The selection of books was sparse, but there was a row of computers. "You know how to use these?" Avery said in a low voice.

"Not this kind," Lionel said. "They're very... primitive."

They sat down together, and Avery explained how to work the mouse and get on the Internet, how to search and scroll. "I've got it," he said. "You can go now."

Shrugging, she left him to his research. She strolled down the main street, stopped in a drugstore, then found a café that offered fried egg sandwiches on Wonder Bread, a luxury from her childhood. With lunch and a cup of coffee, she settled down to wait, sorting email on her phone.

Some time later, she became aware of the television behind the counter. It was tuned to one of those daytime exposé shows hosted by a shrill woman who spoke in a tone of breathless indignation. "Coming up," she said, "Slaves or traitors? Who *are* these alien translators?"

Avery realized that some part of her brain must have been listening and alerted her conscious mind to pay attention, just as it had reacted to the deer. She had a threat detection system she was not even aware of.

In the story that followed, a correspondent revealed that she had been unable to match any of the translators with missing children recorded in the past twenty years. The host treated this as suspicious information that someone ought to be looking into. Then came a panel of experts to discuss what they knew of the translators, which was nothing.

"Turncoats," commented one of the men at the counter watching the show. "Why would anyone betray his own race?"

"They're not even human," said another, "just made to look that way. They're clones or robots or something."

"The government won't do anything. They're just letting those aliens sit there."

Avery got up to pay her bill. The woman at the cash register said, "You connected with that big tour bus parked out at Fenniman's?"

She had forgotten that in a town like this, everyone knew instantly what was out of the ordinary.

"Yeah," Avery said. "Me and my... boyfriend are delivering it to a new owner."

She glanced up at the television just as a collage of faces appeared. Lionel's was in the top row. "Look closely," the show's host said. "If you recognize any of these faces, call us at 1-800-..." Avery didn't wait to hear the number. The door shut behind her.

It was hard not to walk quickly enough to attract attention. Why had she left him alone, as if it were safe? Briefly, she thought of bringing the bus in to pick him up at the library, but it would only attract more attention. The sensible thing was to slip inconspicuously out of town.

Lionel was engrossed in a web site about the brain when she came in. She sat down next to him and said quietly, "We've got to leave."

"I'm not..."

"Lionel. We have to leave. Right now."

He frowned, but got the message. As he rose to put on his coat, she quickly erased his browser history and cache. Then she led the way out and around the building to a back street where there were fewer eyes. "Hold my hand," she said.

"Why?"

"I told them you were my boyfriend. We've got to act friendly."

He didn't object or ask what was going on. The aliens had trained him well, she thought.

The street they were on came to an end, and they were forced back onto the main thoroughfare, right past the café. In Avery's mind every window was a pair of eyes staring at the strangers. As they left the business section of town and the buildings thinned out, she became aware of someone walking a block behind them. Glancing back, she saw a man in hunter's camouflage and billed cap, carrying a gun case on a strap over one shoulder.

She sped up, but the man trailing them sped up as well. When they were in sight of the bus, Avery pressed the keys into Lionel's hand and said, "Go on ahead. I'll stall this guy. Get inside and don't open the door to anyone but me." Then she turned back to confront their pursuit.

Familiarity tickled as he drew closer. When she was sure, she called out, "Afternoon, Henry! What a coincidence to see you here."

"Hello, Avery," he said. He didn't look quite right in the hunter costume: he was too urban and fit. "That was pretty careless of you. I followed to make sure you got back safe."

"I didn't know his picture was all over the TV," she said. "I've been out of touch."

"I know, we lost track of you for a while there. Please don't do that again."

As threats went, Henry now seemed like the lesser evil. She hesitated, then said, "I didn't see any need to get in touch." That meant the country was not in peril.

"Thanks," he said. "Listen, if you turn left on Highway 19 ahead, you'll come to a national park with a campground. It'll be safe."

As she walked back to the bus, she was composing a lie about who she had been talking to. But Lionel never asked. As soon as she was on board he started eagerly telling her about what he had learned in the library. She had never seen him so animated, so she gestured him to sit in the passenger seat beside her while she got the bus moving again.

"The reason you're conscious is because of the cerebral cortex," he said. "It's an add-on, the last part of the brain to evolve. Its only purpose is to monitor what the rest of the brain is doing. All the sensory input goes to the inner brain first, and gets processed, so the cortex never gets the raw data. It only sees the effect on the rest of the brain, not what's really out there. That's why you're aware of yourself. In fact, it's *all* you're aware of."

"Why are you saying 'you'?" Avery asked. "You've got a cerebral cortex, too."

Defensively, he said, "I'm not like you."

Avery shrugged. "Okay." But she wanted to keep the conversation going. "So Mr. Burbage doesn't have a cortex? Is that what you're saying?"

"That's right," Lionel said. "For him, life is a skill of the autonomic nervous system, not something he had to consciously learn. That's why he can think and react faster than we can, and requires less energy. The messages don't have to travel on a useless detour through the cortex."

"Useless?" Avery objected. "I kind of like being conscious."

Lionel fell silent, suddenly grave and troubled.

She glanced over at him. "What's the matter?"

In a low tone he said, "He likes being conscious, too. It's what they want from us."

Avery gripped the wheel and tried not to react. Up to now, the translators had denied that the aliens wanted anything at all from humans. But then it occurred to her that Lionel might not mean humans when he said "us."

"You mean, you translators?" she ventured.

He nodded, looking grim.

"Is that a bad thing?" she asked, reacting to his expression.

"Not for us," he said. "It's bad for them. It's killing him."

He was struggling with some strong emotion. Guilt, she thought. Maybe grief.

"I'm sorry," she said.

Angrily, he stood up to head back into the bus. "Why do you make me think of this?" he said. "Why can't you just mind your own business?"

Avery drove on, listening as he slammed the bedroom door behind him. She didn't feel any resentment. She knew all about guilt and grief, and how useless they made you feel. Lionel's behavior made more sense to her now. He was having trouble distinguishing between what was happening to him externally and what was coming from inside. Even people skilled at being human had trouble with that.

THE NATIONAL PARK Henry had recommended turned out to be at Cumberland Gap, the mountain pass early pioneers had used to migrate west to Kentucky. They spent the night in the campground undisturbed. At dawn, Avery strolled out in the damp morning air to look around. She quickly returned to say, "Lionel, come out here. You need to see this."

She led him across the road to an overlook facing west. From the edge of the Appalachians they looked out on range after range of wooded foothills swaddled in fog. The morning sun at their backs lit everything in shades of mauve and azure. Avery felt like Daniel Boone looking out on the Promised Land, stretching before her into the misty distance, unpolluted by the past.

"I find this pleasant," Lionel said gravely.

Avery smiled. It was a breakthrough statement for someone so unaccustomed to introspection that he hadn't been able to tell her he was hungry two days ago. But all she said was, "Me, too."

After several moments of silence, she ventured, "Don't you think Mr. Burbage would enjoy seeing this? There's no one else around. Doesn't he want to get out of the bus some time?"

"He *is* seeing it," Lionel said.

"What do you mean?"

"He is here." Lionel tapped his head with a finger.

Avery couldn't help staring. "You mean you have some sort of telepathic connection with him?"

"There's no such thing as telepathy," Lionel said dismissively. "They communicate with neurotransmitters." She was still waiting, so he said, "He doesn't have to be all in one place. Part of him is with me, part of him is in the bus."

"In your *head*?" she asked, trying not to betray how creepy she found this news.

He nodded. "He needs me to observe the world for him, and understand it. They have had lots of other helper species to do things for them—species that build things, or transport them. But we're the first one with advanced consciousness."

"And that's why they're interested in us."

Lionel looked away to avoid her eyes, but nodded. "They like it," he said, his voice low and reluctant. "At first it was just novel and new for them, but now it's become an addiction, like a dangerous drug. We pay a high metabolic price for consciousness; it's why our lifespan is so short. They live for centuries. But when they get hooked on us, they burn out even faster than we do."

He picked up a rock and flung it over the cliff, watching as it arced up, then plummeted.

"And if he dies, what happens to you?" Avery asked.

"I don't want him to die," Lionel said. He put his hands in his pockets and studied his feet. "It feels… good to have him around. I like his company. He's very old, very wise."

For a moment, she could see it through his eyes. She could imagine feeling intimately connected to an ancient being who was dying from an inability to part with his adopted human son. What a terrible burden for Lionel to carry, to be slowly killing someone he loved.

And yet, she still felt uneasy.

"How do you know?" she asked.

He looked confused. "What do you mean?"

"You said he's old and wise. How do you know that?"

"The way you know anything unconscious. It's a feeling, an instinct."

"Are you sure he not controlling you? Pushing around your neurotransmitters?"

"That's absurd," he said, mildly irritated. "I told you, he's not conscious, at least not naturally. Control is a conscious thing."

"But what if you did something he didn't want?"

"I don't feel like doing things he doesn't want. Like talking to you now. He must have decided he can trust you, because I wouldn't feel like telling you anything if he hadn't."

Avery wasn't sure whether being trusted by an alien was something she aspired to. But she did want Lionel to trust her, and so she let the subject drop.

"Where do you want to go today?" she asked.

"You keep asking me that." He stared out on the landscape, as if waiting for a revelation. At last he said, "I want to see humans living as they normally do. We've barely seen any of them. I didn't think the planet was so sparsely populated."

"Okay," she said. "I'm going to have to make a phone call for that."

When he had returned to the bus, she strolled away, took out Henry's card, and thumbed the number. Despite the early hour, he answered on the first ring.

"He wants to see humans," she said. "Normal humans behaving normally. Can you help me out?"

"Let me make some calls," he said. "I'll text you instructions."

"No men in black," she said. "You know what I mean?"

"I get it."

WHEN AVERY STOPPED for diesel around noon, the gas station television was blaring with news that the Justice Department would investigate the aliens for abducting human children. She escaped into the restroom to check her phone. The internet was ablaze with speculation: who the translators were, whether they could be freed, whether they were human at all. The part of the government that had approved Lionel's road trip was clearly working at cross purposes with the part that had dreamed up this new strategy for extracting information from the aliens. The only good news was that no hint had leaked out that an alien was roaming the back roads of America in a converted bus.

Henry had texted her a cryptic suggestion to head toward Paris. She had to Google it to find that there actually was a Paris, Kentucky. When she came out to pay for the fuel, she was relieved to see that the television had moved on to World Series coverage. On impulse, she bought a Cardinals cap for Lionel.

Paris turned out to be a quaint old Kentucky town that had once had delusions of cityhood. Today, a county fair was the main event in town. The RV park was almost full, but Avery's E.T. Express managed to maneuver in. When everything was settled, she sat on the bus steps sipping a Bud and waiting for night so they could venture out with a little more anonymity. The only thing watching her was a skittish, half-wild cat crouched behind a trash can. Somehow, it reminded her of Lionel, so she tossed it a Cheeto to see if she could lure it out. It refused the bait.

That night, disguised by the dark and a Cardinals cap, Lionel looked tolerably inconspicuous. As they were leaving to take in the fair, she said, "Will Mr. Burbage be okay while we're gone? What if someone tries to break into the bus?"

"Don't worry, he'll be all right," Lionel said. His tone implied more than his words. She resolved to call Henry at the earliest opportunity and pass along a warning not to try anything.

The people in the midway all looked authentic. If there were snipers on the bigtop and agents on the merry-go-round, she couldn't tell. When people failed to recognize Lionel at the ticket stand and popcorn wagon, she began to relax. Everyone was here to enjoy themselves, not to look for aliens.

She introduced Lionel to the joys of corn dogs and cotton candy, to the Ferris wheel and tilt-a-whirl. He took in the jangling sounds, the smells of deep-fried food, and the blinking lights with a grave and studious air. When they had had their fill of all the machines meant to disorient and confuse, they took a break at a picnic table, sipping Cokes.

Avery said, "Is Mr. Burbage enjoying this?"

Lionel shrugged. "Are you?" He wasn't deflecting her question; he actually wanted to know.

She considered. "I think people enjoy these events mainly because they bring back childhood memories," she said.

"Yes. It does seem familiar," Lionel said.

"Really? What about it?"

He paused, searching his mind. "The smells," he said at last.

Avery nodded. It was smells for her, as well: deep fat fryers, popcorn. "Do you remember anything from the time before you were abducted?"

"Adopted," he corrected her.

"Right, adopted. What about your family?"

He shook his head.

"Do you ever wonder what kind of people they were?"

"The kind of people who wouldn't look for me," he said coldly.

"Wait a minute. You don't know that. For all you know, your mother might have cried her eyes out when you disappeared."

He stared at her. She realized she had spoken with more emotion than she had intended. The subject had touched a nerve. "Sorry," she muttered, and got up. "I'm tired. Can we head back?"

"Sure," he said, and followed her without question.

THAT NIGHT SHE couldn't sleep. She lay watching the pattern from the lights outside on the ceiling, but her mind was on the back of the bus. Up to now she had slept without thinking of the strangeness just beyond the door, but tonight it bothered her.

About 3:00 AM she roused from a doze at the sound of Lionel's quiet footstep going past her toward the door. She lay silent as he eased the bus door open. When he had gone outside she rose and looked to see what he was doing. He walked away from the bus toward a maintenance shed and some dumpsters. She debated whether to follow him; it was just what she had scolded him for doing to her. But concern for his safety won out, and she took a flashlight from the driver's console, put it in the pocket of a windbreaker, and followed.

At first she thought she had lost him. The parking lot was motionless and quiet. A slight breeze stirred the pines on the edge of the road. Then she heard a scuffling sound ahead, a thump, and a soft crack. At first she stood listening, but when there was no more sound, she crept forward. Rounding the dumpster, she saw in its shadow a figure crouched on the ground. Unable to make out what was going on, she switched on the flashlight.

Lionel turned, his eyes wild and hostile. Dangling from his hand was the limp body of a cat, its head ripped off. His face was smeared with its blood. Watching her, he deliberately ripped a bite of cat meat from the body with his teeth and swallowed.

"Lionel!" she cried out in horror. "Put that down!"

He turned away, trying to hide his prey like an animal. Without thinking, she grabbed his arm, and he spun fiercely around, as if to fight her. His eyes looked utterly alien. She stepped back. "It's me, Avery," she said.

He looked down at the mangled carcass in his hand, then dropped it, rose, and backed away. Once again taking his arm, Avery guided him away from the dumpsters, back to the bus. Inside, she led him to the kitchen sink. "Wash," she ordered, then went to firmly close the bus door.

Her heart was pounding, and she kept the heavy flashlight in her hand for security. But when she came back, she saw he was trembling so hard he had dropped the soap and was leaning against the sink for support. Seeing that his face was still smeared with blood, she took a paper towel and wiped him off, then dried his hands. He sank onto the bench by the kitchen table. She stood watching him, arms crossed, waiting for him to speak. He didn't.

"So what was that about?" she said sternly.

He shook his head.

"Cats aren't food," she said. "They're living beings."

Still he didn't speak.

"Have you been sneaking out at night all along?" she demanded.

He shook his head. "I don't know... I just thought... I wanted to see what it would feel like."

"You mean *Mr. Burbage* wanted to see what it would feel like," she said.

"Maybe," he admitted.

"Well, people don't do things like that."

He was looking ill. She grabbed his arm and hustled him into the bathroom, aiming him at the toilet. She left him there vomiting, and started shoving belongings into her backpack. As she swung it onto her shoulder, he staggered to the bathroom door.

"I'm leaving," she said. "I can't sleep here, knowing you do things like that."

He looked dumbstruck. She pushed past him and out the door. She was striding away across the gravel parking lot when he called after her, "Avery! You can't leave."

She wheeled around. "Can't I? Just watch me."

He left the bus and followed her. "What are we going to do?"

"I don't care," she said.

"I won't do it again."

"Who's talking, you or him?"

A light went on in the RV next to them. She realized they were making a late-night scene like trailer-park trash, attracting attention. This wasn't an argument they could have in public. And now that she was out here, she realized she had no place to go. So she shooed Lionel back toward the bus.

Once inside, she said, "This is the thing, Lionel. This whole situation is creeping me out. You can't make any promises as long as he's in charge. Maybe next time he'll want to see what it feels like to kill *me* in my sleep, and you won't be able to stop him."

Lionel looked disturbed. "He won't do that."

"How do you know?"

"I just... do."

"That's not good enough. I need to see him."

Avery wasn't sure why she had blurted it out, except that living with an invisible, ever-present passenger had become intolerable. As long as she didn't know what the door in the back of the bus concealed, she couldn't be at ease.

He shook his head. "That won't help."

She crossed her arms and said, "I can't stay unless I know what he is."

Lionel's face took on an introspective look, as if he were consulting his conscience. At last he said, "You'd have to promise not to tell anyone."

Avery hadn't really expected him to consent, and now felt a nervous tremor. She dropped her pack on the bed and gripped her hands into fists. "All right."

He led the way to the back of the bus and eased the door open as if fearing to disturb the occupant within. She followed him in. The small room was dimly lit and there was an earthy smell. All the crates he had brought in must have been folded up and put away, because none were visible. There was an unmade bed, and beside it a clear box like an aquarium tank, holding something she could not quite make out. When Lionel turned on a light, she saw what the tank contained.

It looked most like a coral or sponge—a yellowish, rounded growth the size of half a beach ball, resting on a bed of wood chips and dead leaves. Lionel picked up a spray bottle and misted it tenderly. It responded by expanding as if breathing.

"*That's* Mr. Burbage?" Avery whispered.

Lionel nodded. "Part of him. The most important part."

The alien seemed insignificant, something she could destroy with a bottle of bleach. "Can he move?" she asked.

"Oh, yes," Lionel said. "Not the way we do."

She waited for him to explain. At first he seemed reluctant, but he finally said, "They are colonies of cells with a complicated life cycle. This is the final stage of their development, when they become most complex and organized. After this, they dissolve into the earth. The cells don't die; they go on to form other coalitions. But the individual is lost. Just like us, I suppose."

What she was feeling, she realized, was disappointment. In spite of all Lionel had told her, she had hoped there would be some way of communicating. Before, she had not truly believed that the alien could be insentient. Now she did. In fact, she found it hard to believe that it could think at all.

"How do you know he's intelligent?" she asked. "He could be just a heap of chemicals, like a loaf of bread rising."

"How do you know *I'm* intelligent?" he said, staring at the tank. "Or anyone?"

"You react to me. You communicate. He can't."

"Yes, he can."

"How? If I touched him—"

"No!" Lionel said quickly. "Don't touch him. You'd see, he would react. It wouldn't be malice, just a reflex."

"Then how do you...?"

Reluctantly, Lionel said, "He has to touch you. It's the only way to exchange neurotransmitters." He paused, as if debating something internally. She watched the conflict play across his face. At last, reluctantly, he said, "I think he would be willing to communicate with you."

It was what she had wanted, some reassurance of the alien's intentions. But now it was offered, her instincts were unwilling. "No thanks," she said.

Lionel looked relieved. She realized he hadn't wanted to give up his unique relationship with Mr. Burbage.

"Thanks anyway," she said, for the generosity of the offer he hadn't wanted to make.

And yet, it left her unsure. She had only Lionel's word that the alien was friendly. After tonight, that wasn't enough.

* * *

NEITHER OF THEM could sleep, so as soon as day came they set out again. Heading west, Avery knew they were going deeper and deeper into isolationist territory, where even human strangers were unwelcome, never mind aliens. This was the land where she had grown up, and she knew it well. From here, the world outside looked like a violent, threatening place full of impoverished hordes who envied and hated the good life in America. Here, even the churches preached self-satisfaction, and discontent was the fault of those who hated freedom—like college professors, homosexuals, and immigrants.

Growing up, she had expected to spend her life in this country. She had done everything right—married just out of high school, worked as a waitress, gotten pregnant at 19. Her life had been mapped out in front of her.

She couldn't even imagine it now.

This morning, Lionel seemed to want to talk. He sat beside her in the co-pilot seat, watching the road and answering her questions.

"What does it feel like, when he communicates with you?"

He reflected. "It feels like a mood, or a hunch. Or I act on impulse."

"How do you know it's him, and not your own subconscious?"

"I don't. It doesn't matter."

Avery shook her head. "I wouldn't want to go through life acting on hunches."

"Why not?"

"Your unconscious... it's unreliable. You can't control it. It can lead you wrong."

"That's absurd," he said. "It's not some outside entity; it's *you*. It's your *conscious* mind that's the slave master, always worrying about control. Your unconscious only wants to preserve you."

"Not if there's an alien messing around with it."

"He's not like that. This drive to dominate—that's a conscious thing. He doesn't have that slave master part of the brain."

"Do you know that for a fact, or are you just guessing?"

"Guessing is what your unconscious tells you. Knowing is a conscious thing. They're only in conflict if your mind is fighting itself."

"Sounds like the human condition to me," Avery said. This had to be the weirdest conversation in her life.

"Is he here now?" she asked.

"Of course he is."

"Don't you ever want to get away from him?"

Puzzled, he said, "Why should I?"

"Privacy. To be by yourself."

"I don't want to be by myself."

Something in his voice told her he was thinking ahead, to the death of his lifelong companion. Abruptly, he rose and walked back into the bus.

Actually, she had lied to him. She *had* gone through life acting on hunches. *Go with your gut* had been her motto, because she had trusted her gut. But of course it had nothing to do with gut, or heart—it was her unconscious mind she had been following. Her unconscious was why she took this road rather than that, or preferred Raisin Bran to Corn Flakes. It was why she found certain tunes achingly beautiful, and why she was fond of this strange young man, against all rational evidence.

As the road led them nearer to southern Illinois, Avery found memories surfacing. They came with a tug of regret, like a choking rope pulling her back toward the person she hadn't become. She thought of the cascade of non-decisions that had led her to become the rootless, disconnected person she was, as much a stranger to the human race as Lionel was, in her way.

What good has consciousness ever done me? she thought. It only made her aware that she could never truly connect with another human being, deep down. And on that day when her cells would dissolve into the soil, there would be no trace her consciousness had ever existed.

THAT NIGHT THEY camped at a freeway rest stop a day's drive from St. Louis. Lionel was moody and anxious. Avery's attempt to interest him in a trashy novel was fruitless. At last she asked what was wrong. Fighting to find the words, he said, "He's very ill. This trip was a bad idea. All the stimulation has made him worse."

Tentatively, she said, "Should we head for one of the domes?"

Lionel shook his head. "They can't cure this... this addiction to consciousness. If they could, I don't think he'd take it."

"Do the others—his own people—know what's wrong with him?"

Lionel nodded wordlessly.

She didn't know what comfort to offer. "Well," she said at last, "it was his choice to come."

"A selfish choice," Lionel said angrily.

She couldn't help noticing that he was speaking for himself, Lionel, as distinct from Mr. Burbage. Thoughtfully, she said, "Maybe they can't love us as much as we can love them."

He looked at her as if the word "love" had never entered his vocabulary. "Don't say us," he said. "I'm not one of you."

She didn't believe it for a second, but she just said, "Suit yourself," and turned back to her novel. After a few moments, he went into the back of the bus and closed the door.

She lay there trying to read for a while, but the story couldn't hold her attention. She kept listening for some sound from beyond the door, some indication of how they were doing. At last she got up quietly and went to listen. Hearing nothing, she tried the door and found it unlocked. Softly, she cracked it open to look inside.

Lionel was not asleep. He was lying on the bed, his head next to the alien's tank. But the alien was no longer in the tank; it was on the pillow. It had extruded a mass of long, cordlike tentacles that gripped Lionel's head in a medusa embrace, snaking into every opening. One had entered an ear, another a nostril. A third had nudged aside an eyeball in order to enter the eye socket. Fluid coursed along the translucent vessels connecting man and creature.

Avery wavered on the edge of horror. Her first instinct was to intervene, to defend Lionel from what looked like an attack. But the expression on his face was not of terror, but peace. All his vague references to exchanging neurotransmitters came back to her now: this was what he had meant. The alien communicated by drinking cerebrospinal fluid, its drug of choice, and injecting its own.

Shaken, she eased the door shut again. Unable to get the image out of her mind, she went outside to walk around the bus to calm her nerves. After three circuits she leaned back against the cold metal, wishing she had a cigarette for the first time in years. Above her, the stars were cold and bright. What was this relationship she had landed in the middle of—predator and prey? father and son? pusher and addict? master and slave? Or some strange combination of all? Had she just witnessed an alien learning about love?

She had been saving a bottle of bourbon for special occasions, so she went in to pour herself a shot.

To her surprise, Lionel emerged before she was quite drunk. She thought of offering him a glass, but wasn't sure how it would mix with whatever was already in his brain.

He sat down across from her, but just stared silently at the floor for a long time. At last he stirred and said, "I think we ought to take him to a private place."

"What sort of private place?" Avery asked.

"Somewhere dignified. Natural. Secluded."

To die, she realized. The alien wanted to die in private. Or Lionel wanted him to. There was no telling where one left off and the other began.

"I know a place," she said. "Will he make it another day?"

Lionel nodded silently.

Through the bourbon haze, Avery wondered what she ought to say to Henry. Was the country in danger? She didn't think so. This seemed like a personal matter. To be sure, she said, "You're certain his relatives won't blame us if he dies?"

"Blame?" he said.

That was conscious-talk, she realized. "React when he doesn't come back?"

"If they were going to react, they would have done it when he left. They aren't expecting anything, not even his return. They don't live in an imaginary future like you people do."

"Wise of them," she said.

"Yes."

THEY ROLLED INTO St. Louis in late afternoon, across the Poplar Street Bridge next to the Arch and off onto I-70 toward the north part of town. Avery knew exactly where she was going. From the first moment Frank had told her the destination was St. Louis, she had known she would end up driving this way, toward the place where she had left the first part of her life.

Bellefontaine Cemetery lay on what had been the outskirts of the city in Victorian times, several hundred acres of greenery behind a stone wall and a wrought-iron gate. It was a relic from a time when cemeteries were landscaped, parklike sanctuaries from the city. Huge old oak and sweetgum trees lined the winding roadways, their branches now black against the sky. Avery drove slowly past the marble mausoleums and toward the hill at the back of the cemetery, which looked out over the valley toward the Missouri River. It was everything Lionel had wanted—peaceful, natural, secluded.

Some light rain misted down out of the overcast sky. Avery parked the bus and went out to check whether they were alone. She had seen no one but a single dog-walker near the entrance, and no vehicle had followed them in. The gates would close in half an hour, and the bus would have to be out. Henry and his friends were probably waiting outside the gate for them to appear again. She returned into the bus and knocked on Lionel's door. He opened it right away. Inside, the large picnic cooler they had bought was standing open, ready.

"Help me lift him in," Lionel said.

Avery maneuvered past the cooler to the tank. "Is it okay for me to touch him?"

"Hold your hand close to him for a few seconds."

Avery did as instructed. A translucent tentacle extruded from the cauliflower folds of the alien's body. It touched her palm, recoiled, then extended again. Gently, hesitantly, it explored her hand, tickling slightly as it probed her palm and curled around her pinkie. She held perfectly still.

"What is he thinking?" she whispered.

"He's learning your chemical identity," Lionel said.

"How can he learn without being aware? Can he even remember?"

"Of course he can remember. Your immune system learns and remembers just about every pathogen it ever met, and it's not aware. Can *you* remember them all?"

She shook her head, stymied.

At last, apparently satisfied, the tendril retracted into the alien's body.

"All right," Lionel said, "now you can touch him."

The alien was surprisingly heavy. Together, they lifted him onto the bed of dirt and wood chips Lionel had spread in the bottom of the cooler. Lionel fitted the lid on loosely, and each of them took a handle to carry their load out into the open air. Avery led the way around a mausoleum shaped like a Greek temple to an unmowed spot hidden from the path. Sycamore leaves and bark littered the ground, damp from the rain.

"Is this okay?" she asked.

For answer, Lionel set down his end of the cooler and straightened, breathing in the forest smell. "This is okay."

"I have to move the bus. Stay behind this building in case anyone comes by. I'll be back."

The gatekeeper waved as she pulled the bus out onto the street. By the time she had parked it on a nearby residential street and returned, the gate was closed. She walked around the cemetery perimeter to an unfrequented side, then scrambled up the wall and over the spiked fence.

Inside, the traffic noise of the city fell away. The trees arched overhead in churchlike silence. Not a squirrel stirred. Avery sat down on a tombstone to wait. Beyond the hill, Lionel was holding vigil at the side of his dying companion, and she wanted to give him privacy. The stillness felt good, but unfamiliar. Her life was made of motion. She had been driving for twenty years—driving away, driving beyond, always a new destination. Never back.

The daylight would soon be gone. She needed to do the other thing she had come here for. Raising the hood of her raincoat, she headed downhill, the grass caressing her sneakers wetly. It was years since she had visited the grave of her daughter Gabrielle, whose short life and death was like a chasm dividing her life into before and after. They had called it crib death then—an unexplained, random, purposeless death. "Nothing you could have done," the doctor had said, thinking that was more comforting than knowing that the universe just didn't give a damn.

Gabrielle's grave lay in a grove of cedar trees—the plot a gift from a sympathetic patron at the café where Avery had worked. At first she had thought of turning it down because the little grave would be overshadowed by more ostentatious death; but the suburban cemeteries had looked so industrial, monuments stamped out by machine. She had come to love the age and seclusion of this spot. At first, she had visited over and over.

As she approached in the fading light, she saw that something was lying on the headstone. When she came close she saw that some stranger had placed on the grave a little terra cotta angel with one wing broken. Avery stood staring at the bedraggled figurine, now soaked with rain, a gift to her daughter from someone she didn't even know. Then, a sudden, unexpected wave of grief doubled her over. It had been twenty years since she had touched her daughter, but the memory was still vivid and tactile. She remembered the smell, the softness of her skin, the utter trust in her eyes. She felt again the aching hole of her absence.

Avery sank to her knees in the wet grass, sobbing for the child she hadn't been able to protect, for the sympathy of the nameless stranger, even for the helpless, mutilated angel who would never fly.

There was a sound behind her, and she looked up. Lionel stood there watching her, rain running down his face—no, it was tears. He wiped his eyes, then looked at his hands. "I don't know why I feel like this," he said.

Poor, muddled man. She got up and hugged him for knowing exactly how she felt. They stood there for a moment, two people trapped in their own brains, and the only crack in the wall was empathy.

"Is he gone?" she asked softly.

He shook his head. "Not yet. I left him alone in case it was me... interfering. Then I saw you and followed."

"This is my daughter's grave," Avery said. "I didn't know I still miss her so much."

She took his hand and started back up the hill. They said nothing, but didn't let go of each other till they got to the marble mausoleum where they had left Mr. Burbage.

The alien was still there, resting on the ground next to the cooler. Lionel knelt beside him and held out a hand. A bouquet of tentacles reached out and grasped it, then withdrew. Lionel came over to where Avery stood watching. "I'm going to stay with him. You don't have to."

"I'd like to," she said, "if it's okay with you."

He ducked his head furtively.

So they settled down to keep a strange death watch. Avery shared some chemical hand-warmers she had brought from the bus. When those ran out and night deepened, she managed to find some dry wood at the bottom of a groundskeeper's brush pile to start a campfire. She sat poking the fire with a stick, feeling drained of tears, worn down as an old tire.

"Does he know he's dying?" she asked.

Lionel nodded. "*I* know, and so he knows." A little bitterly, he added, "That's what consciousness does for you."

"So normally he wouldn't know?"

He shook his head. "Or care. It's just part of their life cycle. There's no death if there's no self to be aware of it."

"No life either," Avery said.

Lionel just sat breaking twigs and tossing them on the fire. "I keep wondering if it was worth it. If consciousness is good enough to die for."

She tried to imagine being free of her self—of the regrets of the past and fear of the future. If this were a *Star Trek* episode, she thought, this would be when Captain Kirk would deliver a speech in defense of being human, despite all the drawbacks. She didn't feel that way.

"You're right," she said. "Consciousness kind of sucks."

The sky was beginning to glow with dawn when at last they saw a change in the alien. The brainlike mass started to shrink and a liquid pool spread out from under it, as if it were dissolving. There was no sound. At the end, its body deflated like a falling soufflé, leaving nothing but a slight crust on the leaves and a damp patch on the ground.

They sat for a long time in silence. It was light when Lionel got up and brushed off his pants, his face set and grim. "Well, that's that," he said.

Avery felt reluctant to leave. "His cells are in the soil?" she said.

"Yes, they'll live underground for a while, spreading and multiplying. They'll go through some blooming and sporing cycles. If any dogs or children come along at that stage, the spores will establish a colony in their brains. It's how they invade."

His voice was perfectly indifferent. Avery stared at him. "You might have mentioned that."

He shrugged.

An inspiration struck her. She seized up a stick and started digging in the damp patch of ground, scooping up soil in her hands and putting it into the cooler.

"What are you doing?" Lionel said. "You can't stop him, it's too late."

"I'm not trying to," Avery said. "I want some cells to transplant. I'm going to grow an alien of my own."

"That's the stupidest—

A moment later he was on his knees beside her, digging and scooping up dirt. They got enough to half-fill the cooler, then covered it with leaves to keep it damp.

"Wait here," she told him. "I'll bring the bus to pick you up. The gates open in an hour. Don't let anyone see you."

When she got back to the street where she had left the bus, Henry was waiting in a parked car. He got out and opened the passenger door for her, but she didn't get inside. "I've got to get back," she said, inclining her head toward the bus. "They're waiting for me."

"Do you mind telling me what's going on?"

"I just needed a break. I had to get away."

"In a cemetery? All night?"

"It's personal."

"Is there something I should know?"

"We're heading back home today."

He waited, but she said no more. There was no use telling him; he couldn't do anything about it. The invasion was already underway.

He let her return to the bus, and she drove it to a gas station to fuel up while waiting for the cemetery to open. At the stroke of 8:30 she pulled the bus through the gate, waving at the puzzled gatekeeper.

Between them, she and Lionel carried the cooler into the bus, leaving behind only the remains of a campfire and a slightly disturbed spot of soil. Then she headed straight for the freeway.

They stopped for a fast-food breakfast in southern Illinois. Avery kept driving as she ate her egg muffin and coffee. Soon Lionel came to sit shotgun beside her, carrying a plastic container full of soil.

"Is that mine?" she asked.

"No, this one's mine. You can have the rest."

"Thanks."

"It won't be him," Lionel said, looking at the soil cradled on his lap.

"No. But it'll be yours. Yours to raise and teach."

As hers would be.

"I thought you would have some kind of tribal loyalty to prevent them invading," Lionel said.

Avery thought about it a moment, then said, "We're not defenseless, you know. We've got something they want. The gift of self, of mortality. God, I feel like the snake in the garden. But my alien will love me for it." She could see the cooler in the rear-view mirror, sitting on the floor in the kitchen. Already she felt fond of the person it would become. Gestating inside. "It gives a new meaning to *alien abduction*, doesn't it?" she said.

He didn't get the joke. "You aren't afraid to become... something like me?"

She looked over at him. "No one can be like you, Lionel."

Even after all this time together, he still didn't know how to react when she said things like that.

THE GREAT DETECTIVE
Delia Sherman

Delia Sherman (www.deliasherman.com) writes short stories and novels for adults and young readers. Several of her short stories have been nominated for the Nebula and World Fantasy Awards, and *The Freedom Maze* received the Andre Norton Award, the Mythopoeic Award, and the Prometheus Award. *Young Woman in a Garden*, a collection of short stories, came out in 20014 from Small Beer Press. Her most recent projects are middle grade novel *The Evil Wizard Smallbone* and three episodes in the Serial Box series *Whitehall*, written with Liz Duffy Adams. She teaches many writing workshops, including Clarion, the Hollins University Program in Children's Literature, and Odyssey. She lives in New York City with her wife Ellen Kushner and many books, most of which at least one of them has read. Besides writing and reading other people's manuscripts, favorite occupations are travel, knitting, cooking, and having adventures, as long as they don't involve actual dragons or wizards of any kind.

November 1880

ON A FOGGY autumn morning, a horseless carriage chugged slowly along a fashionable London street. The carriage was of antique design, steam-driven instead of the more modern clockwork, with a tall chimney pipe that added its acrid mite to the smoky air. A burly footman sat on its box, peering through the gloom at the house numbers. As they passed a pleasant Georgian lodging-house, he hastily pulled the brake and the carriage came to a halt with a long hiss of escaping steam.

The door burst open and a young gentleman sprang out onto the pavement.

He was perhaps twenty-two, tall and knobby, with longish light hair and small, round spectacles. His low-crowned hat was crammed to his ears and his coat was buttoned askew. His careless appearance suggested Bohemian tendencies. The carriage's obviously homemade shaded fog lights revealed a mechanical bent. Not an artisan, not with that coat. A gentleman mechanic, then—possibly an inventor.

The young woman who alit after him was more difficult to parse. She was younger than the gentleman—between eighteen and twenty years of age—and clearly on comfortable terms with him. One would have thought them brother and sister, had there been the slightest resemblance. As it was, she was dark where he was fair, tiny and compact where he was tall and loose-limbed, and her severe mulberry walking costume spoke of a lady's companion rather than a lady. She carried a practical-looking cane that she did not seem to need.

A sulfurous swirl of fog briefly enveloped the pair. When it cleared, they were climbing the lodging-house steps with their footman a few steps behind, bearing in his arms what looked to be a large and elaborate doll clad in china blue.

The young gentleman rang the bell. Above them, a curtain in the first-floor window twitched and a figure retreated into the room beyond.

The game was afoot.

Miss Tacy Gof was in a state of tension so extreme that time slowed almost to a standstill. The ride through the fog from Curzon Street to Pall Mall had taken an age of the world, and another had passed as they waited for an answer to Sir Arthur's ring. Tacy was on the point of reaching for the bell herself when the door snapped open to reveal a small, empty room sealed off from the house itself by a second door.

Sir Arthur stepped in and peered about. "A fog-exhaust!" he exclaimed. "See the fan above the door? I have been longing to see one ever since I read about them in the *London Inventor*!" Then, impatiently: "Come in, come in. There's room enough for all of us!"

There was, though it felt very cramped when the street door swung to, trapping them in a cloud of stinging air. The fan whirred, the air cleared, and the inner door opened, letting them into a hall illuminated by a Smith clockwork lamp.

A lady in black bombazine took one look at Sir Arthur's hat and misbuttoned coat and said, "First floor front, end of the hall."

Sir Arthur sprang up the stairs like a dog on the scent, but Tacy turned, hesitating. "Angharad?"

The doll answered her, its voice tinkling and tuneful as a music box. "Away with you! James and I will follow."

Gratefully, Tacy laid the cane she was holding in the doll's white kid hands and ran up the stairs, reaching the top just as the door to the first floor front opened, revealing quite the largest man she had ever seen. He loomed over Sir Arthur—who was himself a tall man—and was easily twice his girth. Tacy judged him to be perhaps thirty, with a heavy, handsome countenance dominated by a hawklike nose and pale eyes that gave back the light of the Smith lamp like pearls.

Sir Arthur straightened his spine and his spectacles. "Mr. Mycroft Holmes? I am Sir Arthur Cwmlech, of Cwmlech Manor, and I am come to consult your Reasoning Machine on a matter of some importance."

The pale gaze swept past him to the end of the hall, where a musical voice was demanding to be set down *gently*, mind. Turning, Tacy saw the porcelain doll at the stair-head. Quite a picture she made, posed under the Smith with one white kid hand on her silver-topped cane and one white kid boot peeking through the elaborate drapery of her skirt.

"By all that's wonderful," the big man breathed. "It's the Ghost in the Machine."

Although the automaton was indeed haunted by the ghost of Sir Arthur's noble ancestress, she considered the name bestowed on her by the popular press a slight upon her dignity. Tacy had heard her curse an inventor who had addressed her thus in terms that might have distressed him very much, had he been able to understand Welsh. Tacy was relieved when Angharad contented herself with a haughty lift of her molded chin. "I am Mistress Angharad Cwmlech of Cwmlech Manor. And I believe I am as human as yourself."

It was a mild enough rebuke, but Mr. Holmes appeared to feel it extremely. "Your pardon, Mistress Cwmlech. I meant no offense, no offense in the world. I am a firm supporter of mechanical rights—although, of course, you are a special case. Your response to Mr. Justice Booby's denial of your right to testify brought tears to my eyes."

Sir Arthur's nervous cough brought Mycroft Holmes's wandering attention back to the issue at hand. "Ah, yes. A matter of some importance, you say? Then, by all means, come in." He strode down the hall to where Angharad stood, swaying slightly, and gravely offered her his arm. "Mistress Cwmlech—if you will permit me?"

With equal gravity, she accepted his help, though she must reach shoulder-high to do so. *Trust Angharad*, Tacy thought, as she followed Sir Arthur into Mr. Holmes's chambers, *to behave, when every moment is precious, as though time means nothing.* Although perhaps it did not, to a ghost.

The sitting room was a large and airy apartment in the Aesthetic style, hung with Bird and Gear paper from Morris & Co. Green velvet curtains were drawn against the fog and exquisite automata were ranged like statues between glass-fronted cases of curiosities. Tacy's eye was caught by a fist-sized bag constructed from sheets of rubber in one of the cases. "That's never a Peterson's Mechanical Heart!"

"It is," Mr. Holmes said. "You are very observant, Miss—"

"Gof." Having attracted their host's attention, Tacy found that she'd been more comfortable without it.

"You are Welsh," he said, his pale eyes fixing her like a bug on a pin. "A countrywoman, and a blacksmith's daughter, or perhaps sister." He lifted her hand and examined it. "A mechanic... and unmarried. Sir Arthur's apprentice, then, given your tender years."

Startled, Tacy reclaimed her hand. "How did you—? Oh." She touched the iron-and-bronze brooch pinned to her lapel. "This, my old boots, and the stuff of my jacket, is it?"

"And the calluses on forefinger and thumb, the stigmata of our trade." Mr. Holmes displayed his own plump hands, callused precisely as he had described, then waved hospitably towards a cushioned settee, where Angharad sat, her feet dangling some inches above the carpeted floor. "Pray, be seated."

Sir Arthur took the nearest chair and Tacy perched by Angharad, trying not to fidget. Earlier, they had agreed that the story was Sir Arthur's to tell.

Tacy would listen, observe, answer questions if asked, and otherwise keep her tongue firmly behind her teeth.

Mr. Holmes settled himself in a Morris chair facing them.

Sir Arthur began, "It's my Illogic Engine, you see. I—"

The big man lifted a restraining hand. "One moment, if you please." He raised his voice slightly. "Reasoning Machine, engage."

The automaton beside the mantelpiece turned its head and stepped forward.

Never had Tacy seen—or even imagined—a machine so very nearly natural in its gait and movements as Mr. Holmes's Reasoning Machine. Its face was a fine-drawn version of his own countenance—the nose a shade more aquiline, the cheeks narrower, the jaw more sharply cut, the dark hair more abundant. It was almost as tall as the inventor, but much thinner, and its eyes were the same silvery grey. It almost might have been Mr. Holmes's younger brother.

"Exquisite!" Sir Arthur breathed. Angharad reached over and squeezed Tacy's hand painfully.

Mr. Holmes steepled his fingers before his chest. "Order," he said. "Interrogate. Subject: Robbery."

Lowering itself into a wing chair, the Reasoning Machine assumed an attitude the exact mirror of its creator's. "What exactly has been stolen?" The resonant voice was neither metallic nor artificially musical; it would have sounded perfectly natural had it not been so utterly devoid of expression. Tacy shivered.

Sir Arthur leaned forwards, blue eyes intent behind his silver spectacles. "My latest invention, the Illogic Engine."

"What is an Illogic Engine?"

"Ah. Well." Sir Arthur sat back, ready to lecture. "Simply stated, the Illogic Engine is a variation on the Logic Engine that drives intellects such as your own. It is designed to endow mechanicals with those aspects of human intelligence that exist independent of reason."

The Reasoning Machine's fine brows lifted in a parody of surprise. "Engines are, by definition, logical. An Illogic Engine, therefore, cannot exist."

"It does, then," Tacy snapped before she could stop herself. "And functions very well, look you, for a prototype."

After the mechanical's even bass, her voice sounded high and shrill. She fell silent, blushing uncomfortably, though no one seemed to have noticed her outburst.

"Where were you when the theft occurred?" the flat voice went on.

"At a concert. Lord Wolford organized the party. Miss Gof and Mistress Cwmlech accompanied me—and our footman, James, of course. Mistress Cwmlech is unable to climb steps or walk far without assistance."

"And the other servants?"

Sir Arthur glanced at Tacy, who answered in a self-conscious murmur. "The butler, the cook, the kitchen-maid, and the parlor-maid were all in the house." She hesitated. "Also three guard mechanicals in the garden and one in the mews."

"Did any of these persons raise an alarm?"

Persons. Tacy wondered if the Reasoning Machine had meant to include the guard mechanicals in the term. "The servants heard nothing," she said. "The mechanicals were... incapacitated."

And not only the guard mechanicals, she reflected. Every piece of clockwork in the house had been frozen solid as a pond in January, from the hall clock to the toasting machine to the little cleaning mechanicals she had made to polish the workshop windows. It was all very disturbing, particularly as the nature of the sabotage made it unlikely that any common criminal could have been involved. It had to have been a mechanic, working with an inventor—or perhaps an inventor himself.

But who? The inventors of England were a contentious lot: suspicious, secretive, jealous, liable to accusations and lawsuits and plagiarism. From jealousy to theft was not so great a step, if one were unscrupulous as well. The question was, which one of them could it have been?

Tacy returned her attention to the interrogation, which was proceeding with logical precision.

Had there been signs of forced entry? There had not, neither to the house nor the workshop. Who knew about the Illogic Engine? Miss Gof, of course, and Mistress Cwmlech. Miss Gof's father and one Mr. Stanton, who had been his tutor. And Lord Wolford, and perhaps one or two other members of the Royal Society, whose advice Sir Arthur had solicited on one subject or another. "Including," Sir Arthur said, with a bow to Mr. Holmes, "your distinguished creator's."

The inventor, who had been sitting with his eyes closed, as if half-asleep, opened them again. "I was happy to be of assistance," he said graciously. "Well, we have enough to be going on with, I think. Order: Theorize."

The mechanical went very still. Tacy glanced at Sir Arthur, who gazed at it with the air of a dog expecting a treat. He clearly believed Mr. Holmes's mechanical detective capable of pulling the missing Engine from the narrative like a rabbit from a hat. Somewhat to her own surprise, Tacy shared neither Sir Arthur's optimism nor his admiration of the big man's creation. Accustomed to mechanicals from the cradle as she was, she found herself regarding the Reasoning Machine with a discomfort that surprised as much as it distressed her.

The thing is so very nearly human, she thought, and yet it remained a thing, while Angharad, with her obviously mechanical voice, grinding joints, and immovable features, seemed fully human to her. Was it her friendship with Angharad that made the difference?

The Machine's flat voice recalled Tacy's wandering thoughts. "Current data suggest two possibilities. One: A rival inventor or a hireling of such an inventor. Suspects: Lord Wolford, Mr. Jeremiah Stanton, Mr. Arthur Fairleigh, Mr. Mycroft Holmes."

Sir Arthur bridled. "That is impossible! Lord Wolford is a most honorable gentleman. Mr. Holmes is—well—Mr. Holmes, you know! And I would trust both Mr. Fairleigh and Mr. Stanton with anything you care to name. They would never—"

The big man held up a restraining hand. "Lord Wolford is an inventor," he said. "As are Mr. Stanton and Mr. Fairleigh—as am I, come to that. We all stand to gain by stealing your Engine. And Lord Wolford's invitation did take you from home last night."

"He was my father's friend," Sir Arthur said stubbornly. "I will not believe it."

Tacy restrained herself from pointing out that this said more about Sir Arthur's character than Lord Wolford's.

Mr. Holmes shook his head. He seemed about to remonstrate with Sir Arthur when Angharad chimed in, "Order: State second possibility."

After a pause, which Tacy could not help perceiving as startled, the Reasoning Machine said, "Two: A personal enemy. Suspect: Mr. Amos Gotobed."

"Impossible!" Sir Arthur said, and this time, Tacy agreed.

"But he is in prison," she exclaimed. "Thirty years in Dartmoor, the sentence was."

Mr. Holmes shrugged. "Order," he said. "Search newspaper files. Subject: Amos Gotobed."

"Amos Gotobed. Remitted to Dartmoor Prison, August 1880. Escaped from Dartmoor Prison, October 24, 1880."

Escaped! Tacy grew cold. A hand took hers—a mechanical hand, hard and chill under its kidskin covering, but the hand of a friend, and she clutched it desperately. Angharad understood. She had been present in her ghostly form the night Gotobed and his thugs had overturned Sir Arthur's workshop at Cwmlech Manor. With true Cwmlech recklessness, she had leapt into an expensive French automaton Sir Arthur had purchased to study and attacked Gotobed with a hammer. Even though the adventure had ended with the criminal safely locked up in prison, Tacy still woke in the night from dreams of a hulking Gotobed smashing machines and mechanicals and delicate tools as he laughed like the fiend he was.

Oblivious to Tacy's distress, the Reasoning Machine went on, "Scotland Yard have received reports from Newcastle, Maidenhead, and Aberdeen. It is thought that he—"

"Order: Stop," Mr. Holmes said, and the Machine fell silent.

Sir Arthur looked stricken. "I borrowed money from Gotobed, you know, after my father died, leaving me without a feather to fly with. I regretted it almost immediately. It seems I am still to regret it." He lifted his head. "Will you take the case, Mr. Holmes?"

"My dear fellow," the big man said. "Of course we will. We should be at your disposal by this evening—tomorrow forenoon at the latest. In the meantime, I suggest you report the robbery to the police. Inspector Gregson is the man to ask for. He has called us in several times to consult on one affair or another, and understands our methods. You may use my name."

The interview was over.

THAT AFTERNOON, TACY and Angharad sat in the drawing room, waiting for Sir Arthur to return from Scotland Yard. Angharad turned over the cards of a game of patience while Tacy stared blankly at a monograph she'd been meaning to read by one Peter Cantrip, Esq., *DSc(Oxon)*. It concerned the effects of certain sound waves on metal, a subject of deep interest to her, but try as she might, she could not progress past the first paragraph, or say what had been in it.

Tacy laid the monograph aside, collected her wooden whistle from the mantel, and raised it to her lips. There was a whistle in the library, too, and a clarinet in the workshop, for Tacy found music a great aid to thought, as well as a balm to a troubled spirit. She had tootled her way through one Welsh hymn and was beginning another when Angharad said, "Your clarinet I can bear, but 'Llef' upon a pennywhistle is beyond human endurance. Give over, Tacy, my little one, and come watch my play."

Reluctantly, Tacy set down the whistle and sat at the table where Angharad was shuffling for another game. The mechanical fingers creaked like an ancient beldam's as she tapped the cards even. Tacy regretted, not for the first time, that the automaton Angharad haunted was only a rich man's toy, its joints and gears not designed for hard use. The legs had weakened first, then the finger and jaw hinges, so that the rosy mouth always hung slightly ajar.

As Tacy watched, Angharad fumbled the shuffle, spraying the cards broadcast. She cursed blisteringly in Welsh. "Oh, why cannot I have a body like the mechanical detective's, with its joints like oil and its mouth that could smile did the creature only know how?"

"Perhaps Mr. Holmes will make you one," Tacy said.

"More important things to do, he has—playing God on the sixth day, for one. In any case, I do not know how a transfer from one body to another might affect me. I did but jest."

"I know. But perhaps you might let him replace your joints with something better. A pulley more or less cannot make a difference."

Angharad raised a warning hand. "Enough. If I will not suffer you— whom I love and trust as a sister—to lay hands upon this mechanical body, why would I suffer Mr. Mycroft Holmes, who is entirely unknown to me? I haunted Cwmlech Manor for upwards of two hundred years while it crumbled around me. At least in this new ruin I can be seen and heard and go about the world a little."

And that was her last word on the subject. Defeated, Tacy gathered up the cards, shuffled them, and returned them to Angharad, who laid out another hand. As they contemplated the new spread, Sir Arthur burst into the sitting room, accompanied by an acrid whiff of fog and a tall, tow-haired man in a checked coat.

"This is Inspector Gregson of the Metropolitan Police," Sir Arthur said. "Inspector, this is the lady I was telling you of, Miss Tacy Gof."

Inspector Gregson linked his hands behind his back. "Yes. Your *assistant*, I believe you said?"

Something in his voice made Tacy lift her chin. "Sir Arthur is too kind. His apprentice, I am, articled before the Guild of Mechanics."

"I felicitate you," Gregson said. This time the sneer was clearly audible. He turned his deep-set eyes to Angharad. "And this is the famous Ghost in the Machine."

Angharad placed a card with mechanical precision.

"I thought it would move more natural-like," Gregson remarked. "Does it talk?"

"Of course I talk," Angharad said without lifting her head. "Though not, I think, to you."

Sir Arthur's thumb stole to his mouth and he nibbled at it uneasily. Tacy pressed her lips hard to keep from smiling. Gregson flushed brick red, but before he could gather his wits to speak, Sir Arthur's butler appeared with the tea tray.

Swindon had come into Sir Arthur's service from the household of the Marquess of Nether Covington. He was a stately man who, Tacy suspected, felt as if he'd come down in the world. Today, in the wake of a theft, and with police in the house, he had something of the air of an early Christian martyr surrounded by lions. He accepted Gregson's order to gather the servants for questioning with awful courtesy and bowed himself out.

Tacy asked the inspector if he would like tea.

Gregson eyed her with disdain. "This is an investigation, miss, not a tea party. Sir Arthur, if you will show me the workshop, I can get on with my job."

As the door closed behind Sir Arthur and the inspector, Angharad launched into a thoroughly seventeenth-century rodomontade on the subject of the encroaching ways of the lower classes when given the least measure of power.

Tacy let her rant for a while, then said, mildly, "A member of the lower classes I am myself, look you. There's nothing he said that has not been said to you before, by gentlemen of learning. You had your revenge on him. Now let it go."

Angharad lapsed into a sulky silence and Tacy addressed herself to Mrs. Swindon's excellent salmon sandwiches and Mr. Cantrip's monograph. She was lost in the effects of sonic wave-length on various metal alloys when Sir Arthur entered, looking worn.

Angharad lifted her head with a click. "I suppose that fool Gregson has clapped Swindon in prison?"

Sir Arthur sank into a chair and thrust his hands through his hair—not for the first time that day, judging from its wild tangle. "He has not. He has, however, driven both Mrs. Swindon and the parlor-maid into hysterical fits."

"Oh, dear." Tacy handed him a cup of tea. "Did he discover anything of interest?"

"He did. It seems Swindon is in the habit of playing darts at the Running Footman with a man called Albert Norris." He sipped. "Tacy, this tea is cold!"

"Drink it anyway." With an effort, Tacy banished the image of the dignified Swindon at play. "Who is Albert Norris?"

"A coachman, Swindon said. Swindon asked him to supper in the servant's hall, where, as I understand, he was the life and soul of the party. Ethel was quite taken with him."

This meant nothing; the maid Ethel was taken with anything in trousers. "A handsome brute, no doubt."

Sir Arthur set down his cup. "Swindon described him as being of a fleshy habit, tall as a giant and red-faced. Mrs. Swindon mentioned fish eyes and a mouth like a letter-box, but that may be hindsight."

"Gotobed!" Angharad and Tacy exclaimed in chorus.

Sir Arthur shrugged. "That is certainly what Gregson thinks. It seems this Norris appeared at the Running Footman not long after Gotobed's escape from Dartmoor."

It all lined up like ducklings on a pond. After all, Gotobed was a convicted thief. Furthermore, he hated Sir Arthur and would be glad to do him a mischief. Even now, Tacy remembered how the scoundrel had scowled at her and Angharad throughout the trial and how he'd laughed when the judge sentenced him, saying he was sorry that convicts were no longer transported to Australia, as he'd always fancied foreign travel. *A pity for Sir Arthur Cwmlech, too,* he'd added, and smiled meaningfully.

It was not a comfortable memory.

"If it is Gotobed," Sir Arthur said, "he might have been employed by someone else. Swindon mentioned Norris being in the service of one Mr. Peter Cantrip, whoever he may be. Though," he added hopelessly, "I suppose the scoundrel must have been lying."

"Peter Cantrip! I was just reading—" Tacy handed the monograph to Sir Arthur, who glanced at it without much attention.

"Very interesting. I shall certainly show it to Mr. Holmes when he comes. If he comes." He let the pamphlet drop and buried his face in his hands.

Tacy grasped his wrist and shook it gently. "Take heart, my dear. It's tired you are, and no wonder, dealing with mechanicals and police and domestic upheaval, all on top of losing the Engine. We must trust in Mr. Holmes and his mechanical detective, and if they fail us, in our own ingenuity."

TACY WOKE THE next morning to a brisk wind, a clear sky, and a smell of boiling linen rising from the yard where Mrs. Swindon was washing sheets. She dressed quickly and came down to the morning room. After days of fog and rain, it was good to see the sunlight playing over the breakfast table, illuminating the *London Times* Angharad had spread out before her and flashing from the letter knife Sir Arthur plied on the morning's post.

He did not look as though he had slept well.

A glance at the toast rack established that Mrs. Swindon had burnt the toast quite black. Tacy understood this as a sign that the coddled eggs were likely to be hard as rocks, but took one anyway, piled marmalade on the toast to counteract the taste of carbon, and poured herself a cup of lukewarm tea.

"Nothing from Mr. Holmes, I fear," said Sir Arthur, "A letter from Mr. Slovinsky in Budapest, asking if his remarks on escapement pins were useful. I must have forgotten to write and thank him."

Angharad gave a discordant chime. "There's dull you are, Arthur, with your endless mechanics! Can we not speak of something else? The agony column of the *Times* is full of interest this morning." She leaned over the paper. "A gentleman has lost his mechanical dog in the fog, and a lady left her market basket on the Clapham bus. Full of eels it was, all alive-o— at least when she left them. Ah! Here's a wonder: a medical doctor, lately returned from Afghanistan. *Any decent employment considered*, it says. A story there is in that, sure as eggs. Medical men do not easily abandon their Hippocratic oaths."

Sir Arthur, who had been surreptitiously reading his mail, gave a strangled cry and held up a sheet of heavy cream notepaper, his face alight. "From Mr. William Spottiswoode—the president of the Royal Society, you know—an invitation to luncheon! Perhaps he wishes me to speak at the symposium on artificial humanity." He read further, his brow creasing. "This is odd. He most particularly asks me to bring Angharad with me."

Angharad turned her doll-face upon him. "Does he? Well, you may write your Mr. President Spottiswoode and tell him the Ghost in the Machine declines to be questioned and poked at and taken to bits, like as not."

Sir Arthur frowned. "I cannot write that to the president of the Royal Society!" he wailed. "Oh, this invitation could not have come at an unhappier time! What if he wants to see the Illogic Engine? And Mr. Holmes and his Reasoning Machine may be here at any moment!" He turned an anxious blue gaze on Tacy. "What am I to do?"

"Meet Mr. Spottiswoode for lunch, of course," she said briskly. "And you must go with him, Angharad. Nobody who has spoken with you would think of taking you apart, not for any reason."

Angharad was silent, glass eyes glimmering slightly. "Well. I'll charm the old noddlepate—for Arthur's sake, mind. It may be amusing."

Tacy knew a moment of pity for Mr. Spottiswoode. "Not too amusing, I hope. Arthur, pray do not concern yourself over Mr. Holmes and his great detective. I will engage myself to answer any questions they may have."

He smiled at her warmly. "Yes, of course. Bless you, Tacy. We shall go at once."

*   *   *

AFTER PACKING ANGHARAD and Sir Arthur off to Burlington House in the steam carriage, Tacy retired to Sir Arthur's workshop, with the intention of doing a little investigating of her own.

The workshop had been a conservatory when Sir Arthur first took the house, roofed and walled with glass panes, its tile floor cluttered with dying ferns, orange trees in tubs, aspidistra, and sentimental marble statuary. Sir Arthur had replaced it all with bookshelves and tables covered with papers; mechanical instruments; tools; books strayed in from the library; and boxes of assorted gears, springs, escapements, fuses, and fittings. To Ethel, the workshop was a wilderness of tiny objects she was not allowed to move. To Tacy, it was a model of Sir Arthur's mind and hers. She knew precisely where she might lay her hand on any tool or paper she needed. Or at least she *had,* before Inspector Gregson had wantonly reduced it to a chaos of paper, brass, and steel.

Tacy picked up a box containing a set of miniature tools, set it on its shelf, gathered an armful of papers, and began to sort them.

As the clock in the church on the corner struck one, then two, Tacy worked steadily, clearing the floor. By three, with the room restored to its usual state, Tacy set to examining the window latches with a hand lens. By four, when Swindon brought in the tea tray, she was spreading the inward parts of a guard mechanical across a workbench. Her hair had unraveled down her back, her skirt was streaked with oil and dust, and her cuffs were in a high state of grime.

At the clink of china on silver, she turned. "Oh, Swindon, it's you! Is Sir Arthur returned?"

"No, miss."

"Any word from Mr. Holmes?"

"No, miss."

She bit her lip impatiently. "I wonder what is keeping him?"

"I'm sure I don't know, miss."

His tone was repressive, but Tacy was too distracted to notice. "I do wish he'd come. I have more data for him, or at least for that mechanical detective of his." She turned suddenly. "You're a clever man, Swindon. Tell me what you think."

The butler's small eyes widened. "I hardly think, Miss..."

"I've examined everything," she went on, "doors, windows, floor—with a hand lens, look you. But apart from the fact of the missing Engine and its notes, I can find no sign of anyone other than ourselves—and Gregson, of course—having entered the room. Do you not think it curious, Swindon, that a thief should leave no trace at all?"

"No, miss," said Swindon.

"Well, perhaps you are right. Only in romances are thieves so obliging as to leave piles of ash or flecks of mud or monogrammed pocket-handkerchiefs behind them." She rubbed her forehead, smudging it with oil. "And then there's the question of the jammed mainsprings. Every clockwork object in the house, Swindon, saving only the kitchen clock, which runs on a pendulum. How could Gotobed possibly know how to jam them?"

She gazed expectantly at Swindon, who frowned. "Perhaps he learned the trick in prison, miss."

"Perhaps he did. And perhaps he learned patience, as well. For, between the two of us, the Gotobed I knew was a vicious bully. Grievous bodily harm and destruction of property is what I'd expect from him, not a carefully plotted robbery."

Swindon appeared to give the point some thought. "Perhaps Gotobed did not plot it."

"Ah!" said Tacy. "Well-thought-of, Swindon! I wonder..." She fell silent, her eyes fixed on vacancy. Something hovered at the edge of her mind. If only Arthur would return! She always worked better when she was able to talk things over with him. He wasn't particularly clear-headed, but he was brilliantly intuitive. And kind, and dear, and... Oh, where *was* he?

"Will you drink your tea, miss?"

To her surprise, the supercilious butler sounded positively avuncular. She blinked at him. "Oh. Yes. Thank you, Swindon. I expect Sir Arthur and Mistress Angharad will be home any moment. Send them in when they come, will you?" She picked up a tiny turnscrew and bent over the workbench again.

At six, Swindon came to collect the tea tray and inquire whether Mrs. Swindon should hold dinner.

Tacy laid down the clarinet, with which she had been endeavoring to soothe her excited nerves. "Yes—wait, no. I'll take it here on a tray. I confess, I do not know what Sir Arthur is about, to stay so long with Mr. Spottiswoode when the fate of the Illogic Engine is still unknown!"

"As you say, miss."

"Swindon," she said impulsively, "you don't think anything could have happened to them, do you?"

Swindon's mouth tightened. "I shouldn't think so, miss. But I could send Ethel around to the Royal Society to inquire."

Tacy shook her head. "Thank you, but no. I'll wait a little longer."

And wait she did, as the workshop grew cold and her heart grew colder. Would stealing the Illogic Engine satisfy Gotobed's hunger for vengeance? Would he progress to abduction, even murder?

By the time Swindon brought in her tray, Tacy had made up her mind.

"Order a hackney carriage for me, Swindon, please. I am going to Pall Mall to consult Mr. Holmes."

WHEN TACY REACHED Mr. Holmes's lodgings, the landlady informed her that the inventor was not at home. "He and that Reasoning Machine of his went out yesterday, and not a word have I heard since. The gentleman comes and goes like a mouse, with never a word to me. He'll be back when he's back, and not a moment before."

If Tacy had been the kind of woman who wept with frustration, she would have wept then. As it was, she nodded briskly, hailed a mechanical two-wheeler, and directed it to drive her to the headquarters of the Metropolitan Police in Great Scotland Yard. *The police will listen*, she told herself firmly as the hansom whirred across St. James's Park. *They have to listen.*

Listen they did—at least, to the extent of sending her up to Inspector Gregson's office without argument. Inspector Gregson, however, received her story with scant sympathy.

"Sir Arthur's late to dinner, is he?" he said with a rather offensive jollity. "No doubt he's still putting that fancy automaton of his through its paces."

"Mistress Cwmlech is not an automaton," Tacy said hotly. "She is a baronet's daughter and a lady."

Gregson shrugged. "As long as *she* needs to be wound up with a key, she is not a person under the law, and I can take no official note of her absence—unless you wish to report her as stolen property?"

Tacy glared blue murder at him. "And what of Sir Arthur?"

Gregson leaned over his desk. "I will be frank, Miss Gof. Your standing in this matter is uncertain."

"Uncertain!" Tacy exclaimed. "I am Sir Arthur's articled apprentice, sir!"

"Apprentice? Oh, come!" Gregson's tone was jocular. "Pretty young women are not commonly inventors' apprentices—particularly when the inventor's father was a notorious rake."

Shaking with rage, Tacy rose to her feet. "There's a foul, low mind you keep between your ears, Inspector."

"That's as may be," said Gregson. "It's nothing to me if you're his inventive lordship's mistress. My superiors, however, take a dim view of females demanding attention to which they have no right." He picked a piece of paper from the jumble on his desk. "If Sir Arthur and his automaton have not turned up in a day or two, you may send word. In the meantime, Miss Gof, I wish you a very good evening."

THAT NIGHT, THE mystery of Sir Arthur, Angharad, and the Illogic Engine kept Tacy tossing in her bed until, abandoning all thoughts of sleep, she drew a shawl over her night-dress and descended to the workshop. Winding up the heater, she aimed it at Sir Arthur's ratty leather club chair and settled in, determined to think through the case from the beginning.

Annoyingly, her mind drifted to the interview with Inspector Gregson. Mistress, indeed! Was that what the world thought? The idea was ridiculous. Why, Sir Arthur might have been her brother. *No*, she thought, oddly repelled—her cousin. Dear and much loved—as a relative is loved, of course. He and she worked well together, like perfectly balanced gears. If something had happened to him—or to Angharad or the Illogic Engine—she did not know how she would bear it.

All at once, she burst into a fit of weeping like a downpour in the mountains, all wind and water and thunder. When it exhausted itself, she fell into an uneasy doze and awoke at dawn feeling like a wrung-out tea towel.

A bath and breakfast of pheasant pie and porridge did much to revive her, and by half past seven, she was back in the workshop with a fresh pot of tea, a stack of foolscap, and the silver propelling pencil Arthur had given her for her birthday, ready to think about jammed mainsprings.

She began with a sketch of the bust Sir Arthur had made to house the Engine: a male head based on an antique model, articulated to reflect all the human emotions of fear, introspection, joy, anger, and love that the Engine would allow it to feel and express. It was not a beautiful or particularly natural-looking object. Sir Arthur's great gifts as an inventor lay in theory and design rather than aesthetics. Around the bust, she sketched the gears, escapements, springs, pins, pallets, and wheels that made up the Engine itself.

Having filled one sheet with sketches, she took up another for a list of things known to snap, stress, or otherwise wear mainsprings. *Dirt*, she wrote. *Excessive tension. Excessive motion. Sound waves.* She paused. Had she not recently read something on the subject of metallurgy and harmonics? She rubbed her forehead. So much had happened in the last two days. Oh, yes— the monograph. In the sitting room, it had been, waiting for Arthur to return from the Yard. The author was not familiar to her, but she was sure his name began with a C. Cantor? Cuspid?

Thanks to Gregson's sad effect on Ethel, the sitting room had not been dusted and the monograph still lay under the chair. Tacy snatched it up. Ah, yes. "The Effect of Sound Waves on Divers Alloys," by Peter Cantrip, Esq., *DSc(Oxon)*. She carried it triumphantly downstairs and took up a fresh piece of paper.

Some time later, Swindon came in with a tray of sandwiches and fresh tea to find Tacy playing Welsh hymns on her clarinet.

As the tea cooled, Tacy played on, her fingers dancing over the silver keys while the scientific method, Amos Gotobed, revenge, music, theories of harmonics, artificial emotions, the process of building a mechanical, mainsprings, gears, and Angharad's insistence on clinging to her worn body danced through her mind, arranging and rearranging themselves into different patterns.

The clarinet dropped from her lips. Suddenly she knew, as if she had seen it, how the Engine had been stolen, and was a good way towards determining who had stolen it. Not Gotobed, whatever Gregson thought. What she needed was proof, and she thought she knew how she might get it. No inventor, once having the Illogic Engine in his hands, could resist trying to duplicate or even improve it. For that he would need materials, most particularly a certain finely-machined gear made to Sir Arthur's specifications by Steyne & Sons. Number 475-S, it was, the 'S' for the ten tiny sapphires set in it to prevent wear. There were dozens of them in the Illogic Engine—and a pretty penny they'd cost, too. She'd teased Sir Arthur about buying jewels for his mistress until he hardly knew where to look, poor lamb.

A hasty consultation of the London Directory yielded an address for Steyne & Sons in Shoreditch—not a safe place for a lady to walk alone. And Steyne & Sons were unlikely to look with favor upon a request to open their ledgers to her. It seemed Tacy needed a man—a gentleman, by preference. And she needed him quickly.

She rang for Swindon, asked him for the *Times*, then went out to the garden to cut a willow branch. When he returned with the paper, neatly ironed, on a silver tray, she was whittling industriously.

He set the tray at her elbow and Tacy snatched up the paper. "Mistress Angharad found an advertisement yesterday—a military man, it was, seeking employment. Ah, here it is! A doctor, too—even better! Swindon, I will send a telegram."

"Very good, miss."

Some minutes later, Ethel ran to the post office with the following telegram:

DR JOHN WATSON STOP SITUATION AVAILABLE TO
BEGIN ON MUTUAL AGREEMENT STOP REPLY UPON
RECEIPT TACY GOF 9 CURZON STREET STOP

Dr. Watson's reply arrived just as Tacy thought she must run mad with worry. It contained an address on Baker Street, which led her to a cheerful tearoom that smelled deliciously of baking and strawberry jam. Looking about, she saw a lean, slightly shabby figure hunched at a back table and approached it. "Pardon me," she said. A pair of grave brown eyes rose to her face. "I am Miss Tacy Gof. I believe you are here in answer to my telegram."

The man scrambled to his feet, holding out a broad, brown hand. "And I am Dr. John Watson. Please sit down, Miss Gof. Would you like tea?"

Miss Gof would—and some food as well, as it was past noon. As the doctor summoned the waitress, Tacy studied him. He had a pleasant face, she thought, with a firm mouth, though his expression was a little stern. His skin was weathered by the fire of a foreign sun and his mustache was touched with grey, making his age hard to determine.

The luncheon ordered, he turned his attention back to Tacy. "Well, Miss Gof. How do you wish to proceed? I will confess before we start that this is my first interview of this kind."

"Your candor does you credit," Tacy said in a businesslike manner. "You might begin by telling me something of your history. Where, for example, did you train?"

His first answers were short and factual, but gradually he grew more forthcoming. He was the son of a country gentleman who had come to London to train at St. Bartholomew's Hospital. Upon receiving his qualification, he had joined the army and shipped out to Afghanistan as a surgeon. A badly treated bullet wound had led to a fever that so weakened his constitution that he had been sent back to England.

"And why, if I may ask, did you not hang out your shingle? There are not so many good surgeons in England that you would want for patients."

"Most patients prefer an older man—I am only five and twenty. Furthermore," he went on, "I am done with pretending I know anything about healing. My year in Afghanistan left me with an oppressive sense of my own helplessness in the face of the damage artillery can inflict on fragile human bodies. While I was in hospital, I thought I might try my hand at improving the mechanical limbs currently in use by the army. Clumsy, monstrous things they are, forever having to be adjusted. The men hate them."

Tacy smiled encouragingly. "There's a fine ambition. And a practical one."

"Not without extensive training in mechanics, which I can by no means afford. Thus my advertisement."

"Indeed." Tacy made her decision. "The position is yours, should you choose to accept it. That will make a beginning, at any rate. I can at least promise you a mystery, and perhaps even an adventure. But first, I must give you a little background."

Their food arrived, and over Brown Windsor soup and a chop, Tacy recounted everything she thought he needed to know of Angharad and Sir Arthur and the Reasoning Machine. When she had finished, the doctor regarded her with wonder. "An extraordinary story," he said.

"I suppose it is extraordinary," she said, surprised, "if you haven't been living in the thick of it. Just my life, it is to me, nothing out of the way in it at all."

He nodded thoughtfully. "If I understand correctly, you need a kind of bodyguard-cum-fellow-conspirator to help you find your colleague and your friend."

Tacy had not thought of doing the finding herself, but as soon as the doctor suggested it, she knew that was what she wanted. No empty waiting, no fearful imagining, no endless explaining. No Gregson.

Her heart lightened. "That's it in a nutshell, Dr. Watson. Will you do it?"

"I will, if only so I may make the acquaintance of Sir Arthur and Mistress Angharad Cwmlech. What do you need me to do?"

"If you will procure a cab, Dr. Watson, I will tell you as we go."

AFTER THE BRIGHT shops of Baker Street, Shoreditch was unrelieved grey. The sky was grey, the streets were grey, the high walls of the manufactories were grey with smoke and soot. The mechanical hansom dropped Tacy and Dr. Watson at a huddle of grey stone structures built around a yard. A smart sign with the words Steyne & Sons painted on it in gold hung over a shop displaying trays of brightly polished gears.

"Only remember," Tacy said. "Your name is James Watkins, and I am your sister."

The young doctor looked at her gravely. "I know my part, Miss Gof. Do not be anxious."

"I am not anxious," Tacy said. "Should I be caught spying, I will have the vapors. Men can seldom withstand a thoroughgoing fit of the vapors."

Inside the shop, a clerk approached them inquiringly. He was a small, square man, amazingly hairy as to the jaw and eyebrows and bald as to the head. Dr. Watson introduced himself as a neophyte eager to learn. The clerk, a true enthusiast, professed himself glad to answer his questions, and they were soon deep in discussion.

Grateful, for once, for the masculine prejudice that dismisses all females as more or less decorative featherbrains, Tacy wandered to the back of the shop, where a promising-looking ledger stood open upon a high desk. A wary glance forward confirmed two masculine backs bent over a tray. She drew a small notebook and silver pencil from her bag and prepared to snoop.

Alas for her plan, the desk was too high, the light too low, the angle impossible—Tacy could not see the ledger entries, much less examine them. She nipped around the counter and mounted the clerk's platform. Ah, that was better!

As she was running her finger down the column of names, the clerk turned to collect another tray. Hurriedly, she ducked behind the desk and peered cautiously around its side. The clerk was holding a tiny, bright gear up to the light to display its intricacies. She turned back to her task.

The ledger was arranged in a series of columns: date of purchase, client's name and direction, number and description of the items each had purchased. In addition to Sir Arthur's own orders, the delicate and expensive Number 475-S appeared thrice. One box had been sold to a watchmaker by appointment to the Queen, and two boxes each to two individuals: A Mr. Thomas Edison, with an address in New York, America, and a certain Mr. Peter Cantrip.

Breathless with excitement, Tacy wrote down Cantrip's direction. She was making a note of the other addresses when she heard the clerk's voice asking her what she was doing.

Thrusting her notebook in her muff, Tacy stiffened her back and assumed what she hoped was a forbidding expression.

"Well, brother," she said. "Are you finished at last? I feel one of my spasms coming on."

Dr. Watson's face was the picture of brotherly alarm. "To be sure, my dear." Then, man-to-man: "You understand, Mr. Clovelly, I am sure."

Mr. Clovelly's whiskers trembled slightly. "Yes. I mean to say, what are you doing at my desk, miss?"

Tacy gave an awful groan. The doctor hurried over and took her arm. "She is of a hysterical bent," he confided to Mr. Clovelly. "Restless, you know. I had better get her home. Thank you for your advice. It was most helpful."

And he strode from the shop, Tacy clinging to his arm, struggling to stifle her mirth until Steyne & Sons was safely out of sight and sound. "Poor Mr. Clovelly!" she exclaimed as they rounded the corner. "I thought he was going to have a spasm on his own account!"

The doctor smiled. "Indeed. I am much obliged to you, ma'am. Mr. Clovelly has given me a thorough grounding in the science of gears and bearings and drive trains, could I only remember it all. Were you able to procure the information you needed?"

"I think so," Tacy said. "There were three recent orders for the 475-S, but the only one that signified was Mr. Peter Cantrip. Odd it is how his name is constantly turning up, like a worm after rain."

"Odd, indeed. Where does this Cantrip live?"

"In Spitalfields," Tacy said. "What sort of district is Spitalfields?"

Dr. Watson frowned. "Not nearly so respectable as Shoreditch. Ladies do not commonly venture there."

"A blacksmith's daughter, I am." Tacy gave him a sober look. "Have you such a thing as a revolver about you?"

Dr. Watson looked startled. "My service revolver is at my lodgings."

"We will call at your lodgings on the way, then."

WHERE SHOREDITCH SMELLED primarily of smoke and stone, Spitalfields smelled of humanity: poor, cramped, and unhappy. As Tacy and Dr. Watson's hansom churred over the cobbles, rats scampered from its path and hollow-cheeked, ragged men and women stared at it with avid, measuring eyes. At length, the cab turned to enter a barren court, stopping in front of what looked to have been a school, set back behind an iron fence. Its windows were clumsily boarded and its bricks were streaked with moss.

Tacy tapped the hansom's speaking tube. "Will you wait for us?"

"Not in Spitalfields," the mechanical coachman replied.

"Come, come, Miss Gof," said Watson cheerfully. "If you can contemplate with equanimity bearding a mad scientist in his den, the streets of Spitalfields need not alarm you."

"I am not alarmed," said Tacy, with dignity. "Just wondering I was, how we are to get Sir Arthur away, once we've rescued him."

"One problem at a time, Miss Gof," he said. "Before we get away, we must get in."

The iron fence was provided with a stout gate, secured by a bright new chain and lock. Dr. Watson examined it with a businesslike air. "It seems the mysterious Mr. Cantrip does not encourage casual visitors. Have you such a thing as a hairpin about you, Miss Gof?"

"Full of surprises, you are," she said, and drew one out of her coiled hair. As Dr. Watson knelt to address the lock, she saw a movement in the shadows by the door of the building—a misty figure in a white nightdress of antique cut stained down the left side from bosom to hem. It was a figure Tacy had not seen since Angharad had possessed the automaton, and the sight of it filled her with dread.

She seized the bars and called out: "Angharad! What has that Cantrip done to you?"

Angharad waved her question aside impatiently. "Around to the yard with you—there's a door open. 'Ware the rats. *Hurry*, child!"

"Is it Arthur?" Tacy gasped.

Dr. Watson looked around, alarmed. "What is it, Miss Gof? To whom are you speaking?"

Impatiently, Tacy grasped Dr. Watson's sleeve and pulled him towards a narrow and noisome alley that ran along a brick wall to an even more noisome yard. And there she halted, overcome with horror. For between her and the half-open door was a heaving grey swarm of rats the size of small dogs. As if moved by a single mind, they lifted their noses and advanced upon the intruders.

Dr. Watson snatched his revolver from his pocket, pulled back the hammer, and shot the foremost rat between its shining eyes. The resulting explosion of fur, springs, and cogs did nothing to halt the grey tide, which rolled forward, chittering shrilly.

Shuddering with disgust, Tacy drew the willow whistle she'd whittled that morning from her pocket, put it to her lips, and blew. It made no audible sound, though her ears rang slightly.

The rats fell over and were still.

Dr. Watson gaped at her. "Mechanicals," Tacy explained briefly. "I've jammed their mainsprings. Come on!"

Much to Watson's credit, he forbore to question her, but kicked a path through the disabled rats to the door. Soon the pair were standing in a bare and ill-lit corridor, cold as a tomb and smelling strongly of damp and machine oil. At the far end, Tacy could just see Angharad floating above the steps of an iron staircase and beckoning urgently like a specter in a penny dreadful.

Tacy sprang towards her, heart thundering. As she set her foot upon the bottom step, a metallic clatter reached her ears from above, followed by a shriek that froze her to the spot.

Watson dashed past her, straight through Angharad, who swore dreadfully and disappeared.

Shaking off her paralysis, Tacy caught up her skirts and sprang after the doctor. She heard Watson shout, "Stand back, or I shoot!" and then she was at the top of the steps and running down a shadowy hall. When she reached an open door, she plunged through it into an atmosphere permeated with metal, spermaceti oil, and high drama. Under the bright cone of an outsized clockwork lamp, Dr. Watson was holding two tall figures in long leather aprons and magnifying goggles at bay with his revolver. They were surrounded by a dizzying array of machines and devices and at their feet lay the bust that had housed the Illogic Engine, open and empty and dented. Behind them, on a metal table, a figure draped in white linen lay ominously still.

Tacy rushed to the table, her heart clacking like a gear train, and pulled back the sheet to reveal a pair of terrified eyes, lambent as pearls, staring up out of a long, pale face half-obscured by a cloth gag.

She whirled to confront the aproned figures and addressed them furiously. "What is Mr. Holmes's Reasoning Machine doing here? Which of you is Mr. Cantrip? And what have you done with *Arthur*?"

After a moment's hesitation, the slighter of the figures cautiously removed the goggles masking its face.

"Hullo, Tacy," said Sir Arthur Cwmlech.

In the sentimental romances her mother favored, Tacy had often read of a heroine's heart leaping in the presence of her beloved. She had doubted, as a scientifically-minded and rational individual, that an actual human heart would do any such thing. Yet, at the sight of Sir Arthur, his sandy hair in elflocks and his spectacles askew, Tacy's heart leapt—or at least gave a great thump—and she realized that she loved him, not as a cousin or a brother or a friend, but as her own true love.

She burst into tears.

"My dear girl," Sir Arthur said uncomfortably.

Tacy dragged her cuff across her eyes. "Only glad you're safe, I am," she snapped, giving him a look with knives in it. "I was picturing you kidnapped or tortured or worse!"

Sir Arthur fiddled with the goggles. "I *was* kidnapped!"

Realizing that she loved Sir Arthur did not keep Tacy from wanting to shake him until his teeth rattled. "Kidnapped? This does not look like a kidnapping to me."

"If you will allow me to interject," the second figure said, "I think I may be able to shed some light on the subject."

The voice was familiar—urbane, deep, resonant. Tacy had last heard it promising to investigate the theft of the Illogic Engine. "Mr. Holmes!" she exclaimed as the extent of her blindness came clear to her at once. "You're Cantrip!"—and then, bitterly: "And I am the greatest fool in creation!"

The inventor stripped off his goggles. "Not at all, Miss Gof." He shot an irritated look at Dr. Watson, who held his revolver trained steadily upon him. "Please lower your firearm, doctor. There is no danger here."

Dr. Watson frowned. "How did you—?"

"If you wish to abandon your profession, you must stop carrying a stethoscope in your pocket," Tacy snapped. "Oh, put away the pistol, man. The rascal is right. There is no danger in the world—only a pair of clever-boots with more notions than sense. Arthur, tell me plain: What are you doing here, dressed up like a mad scientist in a pantomime?"

Sir Arthur wore the uncertain air of a dog standing over a chewed slipper. "Mr. Holmes has been most hospitable."

Tacy gaped at him, bereft of words.

Watson restored the revolver to his pocket, crossed to the table, and removed the gag from the bound figure's mouth.

"You will regret that," Mr. Holmes remarked.

The Reasoning Machine propped itself on its elbows and gave a bark of laughter. "It's you who'll regret it, Mycroft, when I've told them what you've done."

The voice—wild, half-hysterical—was as far from its previous expressionless tones as possible, putting it beyond all doubt that Mr. Holmes had indeed succeeded in introducing the Illogic Engine into his Reasoning Machine.

Watson unbuckled the straps binding the automaton to the table and helped it to sit on the edge, where it hunched with the sheet clutched around its shoulders, gulping like a frightened child. The doctor laid a soothing hand on its arm, whereupon it buried its face in the astonished man's shoulder with a piteous wail.

Tacy watched this display of unbridled emotion with wonder. The program needed calibration, of course, but there was no doubt that the Illogic Engine worked more or less as she and Sir Arthur had envisioned. Yet, seeing the Reasoning Machine now—distressed, disheveled, and desperate—Tacy could not think of it as a made thing, subject only to the laws of mechanics, but as a living, feeling, suffering fellow-creature.

"I fear my Reasoning Machine is not nearly as reasonable as he was before the introduction of your Illogic Engine," Mr. Holmes observed dryly.

"I warned you it hadn't been tested in a working automaton." Sir Arthur's tone was defensive.

Mycroft Holmes sighed. "So you did. No, the fault is mine, for being impatient."

Tacy rounded upon him. "*Impatient*, you call it? There's lazy you were, and irresponsible and deceitful, and—yes—cruel! Quite apart from what you have done to that poor creature by there, there's you tricking poor Swindon into thinking you were his friend, with your darts and your beer and your good fellowship. Then, to abuse his hospitality so! Can you deny that you took advantage of his invitation to dine with him so that you might take wax impressions of the house keys? The poor man is all but prostrate with shame."

The inventor shrugged his massive shoulders. "There is no shame in succumbing to a superior intelligence."

"And that diabolical whistle you made!" Tacy went on. "Not only did it disable the guard mechanicals, but it froze every mainspring in the house. How could you know it would not destroy the Illogic Engine as well?"

Mr. Holmes eyed her with reluctant respect. "So you know about my whistle, do you? It was a risk, but not a great one. A very little investigation informed me that Sir Arthur procured the springs for the Engine from Messires Baume et Gaulitet. Their alloys, I have reason to know, are particularly resistant to sonic influence. Have you any more crimes to task me with?"

Really, the arrogance of the man was almost past comprehension. "What say you to the charges of theft and kidnapping? What," she said, "of murder?"

"Murder?" For the first time, Mycroft Holmes seemed to be at a loss. Tacy knew a moment of triumph.

"What have you done with Amos Gotobed? Never think to deny it, Mr. Holmes. Having arranged his escape to give the police a convenient red herring to chase, you needed to put him out of the way, in case of blackmail. What surer way than to kill him?"

Holmes's look of bewilderment gave way to one of pure delight. "Well done, Miss Gof! Now I recognize the intelligence behind the elegance of the Illogic Engine's mathematics. " He smiled at her like a mastiff confronted with an angry kitten. "All's fair in love and invention. There was no real harm done by my little deceptions, and perhaps much good. For instance, you may set your mind at rest over the dangerous Mr. Gotobed. I had him conveyed directly from prison to a ship bound for the Antipodes."

Tacy was unmollified. "No harm! What of Angharad?"

Mr. Holmes's pale gaze darted, as if compelled, towards the roof beams. Tacy followed it to Angharad, who was perched gauzily among the rafters, dangling her bare, bloody feet like a small child.

"Angharad!" she exclaimed, relieved.

Sir Arthur brightened. "Am I to understand that Angharad is present? I am extremely relieved to hear it." He peered around him. "You hear that, Angharad? I am very pleased!"

"Would someone," Dr. Watson said plaintively, "have the goodness to tell me what is happening?"

Angharad drifted down to the workshop floor, eyeing the doctor with disfavor. "I do not believe I have been introduced to this gentleman," she announced.

"You know very well he can't hear you, Angharad," Tacy said crossly. "Dr. Watson. May I present to you the ghost of Sir Arthur's ancestress, Mistress Angharad Cwmlech? In front of you, she is," she added as he stared about him, "and a little to the left."

Obediently, Dr. Watson nodded at what he clearly perceived as empty air. "Your servant, ma'am."

The Great Detective lifted his head. "I remember," he exclaimed joyfully. "It was before I began to be interested in things, but I do remember. There was an automaton here—a clumsy, ugly, awkward thing with a voice like a cheap music box. It cursed at Mycroft in Welsh and then it went still and they couldn't make it go again. It had quite broken down. Mycroft was most distressed."

Tacy looked from the inventor's rigid countenance to Angharad. "Do you mean to tell me, then, that he can hear you?"

"See me, too," Angharad said. "*His* ghost I am now, apparently. Got more than he bargained for, look you, when he tried to kidnap me. Oh, he meant well, in his way. Offered me a new body, he did, perfectly and everlastingly beautiful. For what purpose, I know not—and my firm opinion it is that he does not know either."

Holmes's face might have been carved of pink marble.

"I told him what he might do with his body," she went on. "If I am to be some man's chattel, I would sooner it were my great-nephew owned me than yon *coc oen*. Quite heated, I became—too heated, I fear. One moment, I was scolding that pig-headed tub of lard and the next, I was as you see me now."

Her filmy bosom rose in a breathless sigh. "Seventeen years of life I had, with my mam after me day and night to mind my needle and my manners. Then there was the war, and the Roundheads and their rifles sentencing me to two centuries of watching Cwmlechs go about their tedious affairs—in my nightdress, look you, with no hope of a change nor anyone to talk to. And if my mam's rules of ladyhood were burdensome, then those binding a ghost to its curse were more burdensome still. Poor as it was, young Arthur's automaton gave me the only freedom I've ever tasted."

At this pitiful speech, Mr. Holmes abandoned his pretense of deafness. "My dear lady!" he protested. "My fondest wish is to make a body worthy of you. You may design it yourself, if you wish, down to the smallest detail."

"Ha!" Angharad was scornful. "Very well that would be, were that body not your property in law to be turned on and off at your will, displayed, sold, or loaned to an institution, like any other machine."

"Never in the world," the inventor cried. "You have my word."

"The word of a scoundrel and a knave!"

Mr. Holmes pulled himself up to his full considerable height. "How if I see to it that you are granted full personhood under the law? Would you accept a new body, then?"

"I would consider of it," Angharad said with dignity.

"Now that is what I call a handsome offer!" Sir Arthur exclaimed.

Tacy remembered that she was still angry with him. "And I suppose you knew nothing of any of this?"

"My dear girl!" Sir Arthur was indignant. "Of course not! The carriage broke down some way from Berkshire House, so I left James to see to it and hailed a hackney, which drove us here over my strenuous objections. I promise you, I was as distressed as you to discover that Mr. Holmes had engineered the whole."

"Which is why," Tacy observed acidly, "I found you preparing to help him dismember the poor Reasoning Machine."

Sir Arthur raised his thumb to his mouth and nibbled at the nail. "I cannot deny that appearances are against me," he said after a moment. "At first I was indignant, and refused to answer a single question Mr. Holmes put to me. Then Angharad's automaton broke down and I felt obliged to do what I could to fix it—for Angharad's sake, of course. But between working over her together, and his distress when all our efforts failed, and the Reasoning Machine's reaction to the installation of the Illogic Engine—well, one thing led to another."

"I see," Tacy said. And she did. Sir Arthur lived to experiment. For the sake of an untested theory, he would flout convention, bend laws, and fly in the face of common sense. It was this spirit of experimentation that had led him to hire the sixteen-year-old daughter of a blacksmith as his housekeeper, to have her educated and to work with her as a colleague and an equal. It was one of the things she loved in him. "You thought it would be interesting."

Sir Arthur nodded.

"And the experiment did not work quite as you expected."

"It did not." Mr. Holmes, who had been observing all this time, spoke with some feeling.

"Well, you see for yourself." Angharad indicated the Reasoning Machine, who was following the conversation with a painful intensity. "All full of emotions, the poor creature is, and not a notion what to do with them—like a baby, really. Only more clever. The things he called poor Mycroft!"

"Just so," said the inventor. "It is quite unable to control its emotions. After some discussion, Sir Arthur agreed to help me remove the Engine until we could design a better model."

"Mr. Holmes," Sir Arthur added eagerly, "has some very sound ideas about regulation and control, Tacy. It is his opinion that—"

"No!" The Reasoning Machine's voice quivered with terror. "I don't want to be regulated and controlled! They're *my* emotions, and you can't take them away from me!" He clutched at Dr. Watson's arm. "You won't let them take my feelings away, will you?"

The doctor looked alarmed. "My dear chap! Of course it is wrong to deny you your emotions, even temporarily. Yet you must know I have no power to stop Mr. Holmes, should he decide to do so."

"You have a revolver!" the automaton cried. "Threaten him with it, and we will make our escape into the stews of London and live by my wits and your strong arm." A smile blossomed on his lean face. "I shall be the Emperor of Crime, and you shall be my consort!"

His words were met by an astonished silence, broken by Mycroft Holmes's rich laughter.

Her temper in shreds, Tacy turned upon him. "The poor creature has a right to his feelings, look you. Though you forced them upon him, now that he has them, a crime it would be to remove them because you find them inconvenient."

Which, she realized in the silence that followed, could well be said of her feelings as well. Having discovered that she loved Arthur, she could not un-know it again. Nor would she wish to, aware though she was that such an unequal affection must come to nothing. A baronet, even a Welsh baronet, was unlikely to marry a blacksmith's daughter, particularly if she was his apprentice. Particularly if he regarded her in the light of a younger sister. There was nothing for it but to go home to Mam and think how a clever spinster might keep herself. A schoolmistress, perhaps, or a mechanic's secretary. She felt very low indeed.

The Reasoning Machine's pale gaze flicked from her to Sir Arthur. "I do not entirely understand what is happening. But I have a strong feeling that Sir Arthur should kiss Miss Gof without delay."

Tacy gave a little mew and covered her blazing face with her hands.

"Oh," Arthur said. And then, "Oh! Of course," and pulled her awkwardly to him.

Feeling his arms around her and his lips on her hair, Tacy lifted her face, clutched the bib of his apron, and pulled his mouth down to meet hers.

Someone, possibly Dr. Watson, exclaimed "I say!" in a startled tone. She disengaged herself reluctantly.

The Reasoning Machine was wistful. "I wish I had someone to love, too, and a home, and a proper name, like a real person. Jabez would be nice. Or Algernon. Algernon Holmes." He turned to the doctor. "What do you say?"

Watson gave him a wary smile. "I'll give it some thought, old chap. But first things first." He turned his clear brown gaze on the inventor. "You will let him keep his emotions, will you not?"

The big man cast up his hands in defeat. "I will. He must learn to control them, however—he's all but useless as he is." He considered Watson. "Do you think you could undertake to teach him?"

The Machine turned a radiant countenance to the doctor. "The very thing! Oh, do say you will!"

"I..."

"It is settled, then," said Holmes. "In his current state, London is likely to be too much for him. I have a cottage in Sussex, near Bognor Regis, quite sequestered from the world. You shall take him there." He divested himself of his apron and gauntlets. In his shirtsleeves, with his braces showing, he seemed far less formidable, almost human. He fixed Watson with a measuring eye. "Have you any interest in mechanical engineering?"

Dr. Watson looked startled. "Why, yes. Considerable interest."

"Excellent. I shall give you a grounding in basic maintenance before you go."

"And I, myself, shall teach you everything else," the Machine broke in happily. "I know a great deal about mechanical engineering. Do you think there will be bees, Watson? I have a great desire to observe the communal intelligence of bees. Oh, what fun we shall have!"

Here he showed every sign of throwing his arms around Watson and serving him as Tacy had served Sir Arthur. Watson gently deflected the embrace without absolutely spurning it.

Sir Arthur possessed himself of Tacy's hand. "I think," he said, "that I should like to go home now."

But the dawn of reciprocal love had not entirely robbed Tacy of her common sense. "One more question there is to be settled, before we make an end," she said, turning to Mr. Holmes. "You have our prototype and all our notes. Without them, we can neither refine our work, nor present it to the Royal Society, nor apply for a patent. In short, it will be as if the Illogic

Engine was never invented. Unless, perhaps, you intend to present it as your own work?"

The inventor looked shocked. "I may be a thief, Miss Gof, but I am not a scoundrel." He rubbed his face with his well-kept hands. "Well. It seems we have a great deal still to discuss. Doctor, would you be so good as to walk through that door behind you and put the kettle on the hob? I think we could all use a cup of tea."

April 1882

ON A BRIGHT, chilly spring morning, Sir Arthur and Lady Cwmlech sat at breakfast in the cozy morning room of their house on Curzon Street. Sir Arthur was reading a book he had propped up against the saltcellar and absently dripping egg over his waistcoat. Lady Cwmlech, a plate of toast and marmalade at her elbow, was poring over the flimsy sheets of the popular journal, the *Thames-Side Monthly*.

Turning over a page, she uttered an excited squeak. "Here it is at last, Arthur!"

Sir Arthur looked up from his book, pale eyes bleary behind his spectacles. The patent application for the Illogic Engine had kept him up half the night. *Bad as a new baby*, Tacy thought, and smiled. He smiled back wanly. "Here is what, my love?"

"John's account of the Bootlace Murders. Never tell me you've forgotten! Five cobblers strangled with bootlaces and laid out on their benches all neat and tidy, and the police as baffled as sheep at a gate. Last spring it was, just after the wedding."

"After the wedding," Sir Arthur said, "I had more important things to think of than deceased cobblers." He gave Tacy a grin that brought the blood to her cheeks.

"Of course, my dear. But John wrote us about it, remember? Their first case after the move to Baker Street, and so proud he was of how well Sherlock and the police dealt together, after that unfortunate misunderstanding about the purloined letter."

"Damned silly name, Sherlock," Sir Arthur observed.

"No sillier than Mycroft, when all's said and done. None of our concern, in any case." She gave him a wifely look. "Will I read it to you, then, while you wipe the egg off your waistcoat?"

Sir Arthur stared down at the congealed yolk festooning his chest. "Oh, dear," he sighed. "Tacy, do you think...?"

Dipping her napkin in her husband's tea, Tacy dealt with the waistcoat, then rang for Swindon, who bore off the spoiled napery.

"I'm sorry, my love." Sir Arthur said. "I've forgotten what you were saying."

"The Bootlace Murders."

"Ah. The Bootlace Murders. I am all attention. Who did the Great Detective deduce had done 'em?"

"There's pity," Tacy said severely, "to set aside all John's hard work in unfolding the mystery step-by-step, with all the characters of the shoemaker's wife and Inspector Gregson and the man with the limp drawn as clear as life. Furthermore," she went on, "we are to dine with them tonight, before the concert. Churlish, it would be, not to mention his literary debut."

Sir Arthur shook his head. "I dare not, dearest. The patent application—"

"Will be the better for an evening's holiday. A program of Bach, it is. You like Bach."

"I thought Watson preferred Chopin."

"He does. But Madame Neruda plays tonight and Sherlock has conceived a keen interest in the violin. He speaks of learning to play."

"Heaven help us," Arthur said. "Very well. Bach, Neruda, and dinner, it shall be. And the Bootlace Murders. I do not wish to disoblige John."

Tacy had just reached the second murder when Mistress Angharad Cwmlech swept into the room on the arm of Mr. Mycroft Holmes, visible to all and very pretty indeed in a plaid walking dress, with a saucy hat perched on her dark curls. Her lips were soft against Tacy's cheek, if a little chilly.

"Going to a meeting, we are," she announced, "with Rosebery and Ball, about the Bill of Mechanical Rights. Mycroft"—she cast a proprietary glance at the big man—"thinks it possible it may pass, if we can coax the prime minister into speaking in support."

Arthur groaned. "But, my work!"

Mycroft Holmes fixed him with a keen and pearly eye. "This *is* your work,

Arthur—or should be. The patent office will wait—this bill will not."

"Do I not deserve to be a person before the law?" Angharad demanded. "Does not Sherlock?"

"To be sure," Tacy answered her. "And so do all thinking mechanicals."

Sir Arthur sighed and rose to his feet. "You are right, of course. Tacy, ring for the carriage. There is not a moment to be lost."

EVERYONE FROM THEMIS SENDS LETTERS HOME

Genevieve Valentine

Genevieve Valentine's (www.genevievevalentine.com) first novel, *Mechanique*, won the Crawford Award and was nominated for the Nebula the same year. Her second, *The Girls of the Kingfisher Club*, appeared in 2014 to acclaim, and was followed by science fiction novels *Persona* and *Icon*. Valentine's short fiction has appeared in *Clarkesworld*, *Strange Horizons*, *Journal of Mythic Arts*, *Fantasy*, *Apex*, and others, and in the anthologies *Federations*, *The Living Dead 2*, *The Way of the Wizard*, *Teeth*, *After*, and more. Her story "Light on the Water" was a 2009 World Fantasy Award nominee, and "Things to Know about Being Dead" was a 2012 Shirley Jackson Award nominee; several stories have been reprinted in Best of the Year anthologies. Her nonfiction and reviews have appeared at NPR.org, *Strange Horizons*, *Lightspeed*, *Weird Tales*, Tor.com, and *Fantasy Magazine*, and she is a co-author of *Geek Wisdom* (Quirk Books). She has also been known to write *Catwoman* and *Xena: Warrior Princess* comics! Her appetite for bad movies is insatiable.

THE WATER HERE is never going to make good bread. If I'd known, I would have requested sturdier flour—we'll be waiting six years for the next transport pod. Agosti told me today my bread's good for massaging the gums, like he was trying to focus on the positives. Woods threatened to arrest him anyway, which was nice of him.

But that's really the only thing that makes me sad. Otherwise, I promise, I'm getting along here very well. I miss you, too. Every time I'm up late with the dough I imagine you're at the table working, and when I look up it takes me a second to remember. But everyone here is pitching in. Marquez and Perlman and I are figuring out how to cheat an apple tree into producing fruit sooner, and Agosti's building equipment out of our old life support systems. If it works out, we'll have our own cider in two years. ("We can dip the bread in it," Perlman said, and Woods threatened to arrest her, too. Gives him something to do. Imagine being in charge of five people. Good thing he has a knack for building.)

The sun's different than back home—they told us about particles and turbulence on the way over and I was too stupid to understand it and too afraid to tell them, so just pretend I explained and you were really impressed. The planet's locked, so there's really only water on the equator—nothing makes it toward the sun and it's ice by the time you go ten miles further darkside. You're never 100% sure what time it even is, except that it's a little more purple in the daylight for the hour we get it, and at sunset it looks like the whole place was attacked by vampires. It's sunset most of the time. That's not too bad if you can just avoid the river; that river never looks right with the dark coming in.

Agosti and Perlman were up until 3:30 shouting about which route will get us over the mountains, which would be more understandable if there were any mountains. But the movie bank's still broken, so it's just as well. I'm betting on Perlman. If anyone could lead us over imaginary mountains, it's her.

My other entertainment is staying up late, trying to fight the water and make bread that will actually rise, and the bird that sings all night. Samara—Perlman—says we're not supposed to assign characteristics from home to the things we find here until they've been observed and documented and whatever else, but—thrush family.

It's most active during our night hours, and we're working on why (trying to make sure it's not drawn to the lights we brought with us, which would be bad news), but in the meantime it seems happy to sit in the trees outside the kitchen and sing. Three little bursts, then a longer one that's so many notes it sounds like showing off, then a little pause to see if anyone's listening, so it's definitely showing off. If I whistle anything, it tries to repeat it, and it's a fairly good mimic, but nothing I do really takes. It knows what it likes.

It has the same woodwind sound as the one back home, the house I lived in when I was young. Hermit thrush? Wood thrush? Something I used to hear all the time and never thought about, of course. Good news is that now it's just me and this one bird and I'll get to start over again with every new animal. This time I'm going to pay better attention.

Perlman will officially name it—they don't ask the cooks how to classify animal species, that's why the company hauled a biologist out here. But Perlman knows I like it, so maybe she'll consult me. I know it best. That should count for something.

All my love.

PROXIMA CENTAURI PERSONNEL Status Report: Day 1187
Author: Dr. Samara Perlman

Crew Health: Reiterating that as a biologist, I am not in a position to diagnose or treat any major medical issues, am not sure how I was tasked with this position, and am deeply concerned about how soon we can expect a qualified physician rather than a group of people who had slapdash medic training for three days before they left Earth. That said, all six residents currently seem in good health. Carlos Marquez claims a slight cough, but as the scans came back negative, my money's on allergies. If he dies of tuberculosis next week we'll know I was wrong.

Crew Injuries: Anthony Agosti nursing a minor wrist sprain after having punched a wall. Should he resort to violence again I'll be sending him to Officer Woods for a formal report and some time in the brig. We shouldn't build a new planet with the same problems as the old one.

Crew Mental Health: Marie Roland continues to claim she can't see the mountains to the northwest of Themis. No other signs of psychosis appear, and when questioned or shown pictures of the mountains, Roland becomes distracted and mildly agitated. No tendency to violence. Suspect a minor mental block prevents her from fully acknowledging the terrain— homesickness? For now, as she's still willing to train for the mission, there seems to be no point in forcing the issue; have asked Woods to stop pushing it and will let Marie come to it in her own time.

Crew Mission Training: Expedition prep continues. Entire staff follow regimen of five-kilometer runs on hilly terrain every morning, weight lifting three times a week, rock climbing on nearby hills twice a week. Once the snow melts a little off the pass we'll be able to determine the actual level of dexterity required for the climb and train accordingly. Vigil until then.

TO WHOMEVER

there's nothing here left to build and the mountain project is on hold until the thaw and I don't care about sunset please get the movie bank going again before I throw myself in the river full stop

anthony

TO WHOMEVER

there's nothing here left to build and the mountain project is on hold until the thaw and I don't care about sunset please get the movie bank going again before I throw myself in the river full stop

anthony

SORRY SENT IT twice by mistake

wouldn't do that kind of thing if the movie bank worked though probably

anthony

SAMARA AND I did a perimeter walk today, a kilometer out from the camp. I picked almost more plants than I could carry, and I'm fairly sure at least half are edible, which will make meals much more exciting. Samara insisted on running tests for poison, don't worry, but I think if I have to measure one more judicious use of dried black pepper I'm going to scream. I want something that tastes like it grew in the ground.

Samara's amazing. I don't even remember first meeting her; it just feels like I've always known her, which I guess is what close quarters will do to you. We cataloged five species of bird (none of them my bird, so I guess the animals here really can tell day from night and it's something we'll get used to), and she spent a lot more time with insects than I was interested in.

The air here smells just like home. I don't know why—the water's different, so the soil should be different, but it smells exactly like the dirt from my grandmother's garden. It helps stop me from getting lonely, that the soil here might be the same as what we left behind.

Marquez showed us pictures of his children a few nights ago; it's his daughter's birthday. Samara cried, but nobody pushed it. It's strange how much we left behind to be here, and I think no matter how much work you're getting done, sometimes it just hits you how separate you are. We must have really wanted this. I must still.

I know you weren't ready, and you might never be ready. These letters aren't meant to convince you, I promise. It just makes me feel closer to home.

All my love—

DR. MARCH:

Mixed results, as always. Sunset was a little longer than yesterday, so the seasons function is working. None of the subjects have noticed yet that Vivian and Carlos are interfaces, which bodes well for long-term use of constructed intelligence inside Themis. (Suggest we minimize the rock-climbing training until we can work out the uncanny valley problem in the weight distribution. Can the development team extend the thaw?) But overall, investors should be pleased—let me know if you need any demo footage, I have a clip of everyone working on the gardens that should go over well.

Technical glitch, first incident: Anthony's punch should have broken his hand. I'm not sure if the safety settings are appropriately set or too schoolmarmy. We might need to dial them down and get someone to break their leg as a test run for more realistic game play.

Gigantic fucking technical glitch, ongoing: Marie can't see the mountains. I've checked her equipment, and there's no other potential hardware problems (attached is the most recent server diagnostic for your review, but there's nothing in it that would account for it). Either she has an actual mental block that we can't do anything about, or there's a subjectivity issue somewhere in the code for Themis and we have to find it and fix it. I can't tell which one is more likely, because you made me military instead of medical and I can't just put her in jail until she tells me she sees them. Do we have a timetable for getting security clearance on that or are we going to have to settle for imperfect data?

-Woods

WOODS DROPPED INTO the chair in Benjamina's cubicle so hard her BIRDS OF MONTANE ECOSYSTEMS reference chart came loose and sank to the floor.

"You gotta fix those mountains," he said.

"My chart, please."

"It's going to break the sim," he said, scooping it up and smoothing a bent edge. "We'll have done four years of work for nothing because Marie has some synapse you can't outsmart."

"The problem's her head, not the software." After a pointed pause, she turned around. He carried some ego out of a Themis session and it took a day or so to wear off; the faster you could remind him that everyone else was actually busy, the better. "You can see the mountains when you're in Themis, and you know they're not there. Sounds like you should take it up with the psych team."

"I'd have thought you wanted to keep her out of all that." He wasn't quite threatening her; he wasn't quite sympathizing. (The reason Woods got chosen for beta-test jobs was how good he could be at Not Quite.)

Benjamina didn't bother to recite any anonymity bullshit. Woods had been in Themis a long time; they read letters out loud to each other. He knew what she sounded like. "I've been trying."

"They want to test the mountains before we wrap beta."

"We need to look at her file—I can't reverse engineer a synapse misfire."

"They fixed Agosti's color blindness."

"That's different," said Benjamina, picking crumbs off her keyboard. She didn't like that fix, for no particular reason. It was productive; it just itched.

"Listen, I like her, but this is going to kill the beta, and you and I will be under the knife."

"Get the psych team to request Marie's file from the warden. Is Perlman at the same place?"

"Nah, Perlman stabbed her husband, she went someplace serious. Roland's just in a prison for fuckups."

"Fine. So get Dr. March to show me the file. I can port into Carlos for eyes on the ground. Then I'll know what I'm dealing with."

"Nobody in this building's willing to talk to the shrinks but me. That should tell you something." Woods stood up, the little bird poster still in his hands. He was holding the very edges, like it was an expensive library book.

One of the things nobody at Othrys talked about was that the longer you spent in Themis, the weirder physical objects were when you came back. Officially, nobody was talking about it because it was just Woods, and no one liked Woods enough to make him for a martyr of motor-skill dissociation. Unofficially, nobody wanted to think Themis came back with you. Benjamina hoped that wore off, too.

"How are you doing?"

He was smoothing the edges of the chart with the pads of his fingers as he set it down. He looked up at her like he was surprised.

"I'm going to go eat some decent bread," he said finally, and left.

Benjamina's computer pinged. It was waiting for her letter.

AGOSTI CAME BACK from his walk today and did some very elaborate hand gestures about how much snow is left on the mountain pass and pointing to the northwest, and it took me three minutes to realize it wasn't a buildup to a jerkoff joke. Those fucking mountains. Woods told him to knock it off—very sheriffy thing to do, glad he's finding something to lay down the law about—but still. It gets old.

Samara named that bird *Catharus rolandus*. It's useless to be proud of something that has so little to do with actual contributions from you, but I teared up anyway. Plus that genus is apparently very close to the wood thrush after all! I felt like a scientist! Then I baked a shitty loaf of bread and lost that feeling immediately, because a scientist would know how to outsmart this water.

I loved your letter. Not the markets, though—Themis is really good for reminding you of the value of only knowing a few people. The only thing I miss about the night markets is the two of us wearing those giant sweaters with the huge arms we bought as a joke and ended up needing that whole winter and we had to push the sleeves up before we reached for anything. All the fabrics here are sort of flat. They keep you warm, but it's not the same.

All my love

MR. COLLINS:

My name is Dr. Frederick March, and I'm a consulting psychologist for Othrys Games. We've been partnering with your institution to test the latest game from Othrys; I understand you might not have all the details of how the process has gone so far, so first of all, I wanted to thank you, and let you know it's been invaluable. You're assisting us with some truly amazing work about constructed intelligence and full-neuro game play. There are even insights into the human subconscious and stimuli processing that I suspect will have significant implications going forward in other realms of study.

I say all this so you'll understand why I'd so much like to meet to discuss the next steps, since we've had to terminate the study slightly earlier than planned. Your in-house medical team has been exemplary, and we are completely understanding of what happened—immunity to memory suppressants is a risk of repeated exposure and this was discussed prior to beginning. We agree with you that the testing stage has effectively ended—the downside of informed consent.

However, because of this, we would like to work out some visitations with the subjects in question. I understand our team has had some miscommunications with your administration trying to set these up. Let me assure you this is the standard debrief for any long-term player. And in this particular case, I expect that the subjects themselves would benefit from being able to speak with a trained professional about their experience. The amount and type of memories that might be restored have definite in-game applications and are potential data points well within the scope of our contract with your correctional facility. I'm happy to discuss further particulars—please let me know your thoughts.

Sincerely,

Frederick March

*   *   *

Dr. March was already in the VP's office, and Woods wasn't, which meant the worst. Benjamina let the closed-door click echo a moment, trying to decide if looking stoic or penitent would work better. (Women who were too stoic got fired for not caring; women who were too penitent got fired for poor performance.) She forced herself not to ask questions as she sat. Inquisitive women were no better than the other kinds.

"We've had a problem with Themis," the VP said. He looked from one of them to the other. "Frederick knows already."

Of course he did. Benjamina waited.

"It's not the simulation," the VP continued after a moment, as if to put her mind at ease, as if she was concerned that somehow her work wasn't up to par and they would have waited until now to tell her. "In fact, Erytheia—the coders have aliases, it's easier," he explained to Dr. March, "has our lowest fault rate, and has spent the most time working on individual settings for Roland. I think she could be invaluable to us during the postmortem process."

Benjamina blinked. "Postmortem of what?"

Dr. March turned toward her. "Did you know Ms. Roland was a drug addict?"

"No," she said, and her stomach dropped as she considered why the medical side of the experiment wasn't feasible any more. "Did she get any memories back when the drugs stopped working, or is it still a fog?"

"She got them back."

Stoic, she thought. Be stoic. No point being penitent now.

"Are Perlman and Agosti still in beta?" If they were, she'd have to talk to their coders about some in-game reason Marie was gone, though she couldn't think of one they would believe. Marie would never leave Themis. She knew it best. Benjamina might have to port in on a simulation and drop dead in front of them.

"No," said the VP. "We decided to stop beta across the board. Dr. March is trying to get the warden to agree to interviews so we can find out how the, uh— the memory process? Is going. It will probably take a few weeks. Woods will go along and observe, obviously—continuity for them—and then he can circle back with you, so we can bring our findings to the team in a way that isn't so... clinical. No offense."

"Of course," said Dr. March. He was still looking at Benjamina.

"Let me know when," she said, and that was the last thing anyone needed from her.

She drove home with shaking hands, for no good reason—Marie was a test user, they used to have test users at fucking conventions. She'd liked that better; there were plenty of ways to test what players would believe without lying to them at the beginning. Management wanted to test if the environment could fool the mind, but no one had asked Benjamina. None of this had been her idea. Nothing was her fault.

The night was barely cloudy, and she drove past her turnoff and out until there was nothing but the highway on either side, so when she set up the telescope, she could see a glimpse of Proxima Centauri through the haze of light pollution. It blinked back and forth in the lens, and it was so dim. Light from there would never quite suffice.

No one had said anything to the development team—no one ever did unless something was wrong—but she suspected this game was more than a Virtual Experience market maker. There were private companies prepping long-haul spacecraft with stasis technology; they'd want to train their people in the most realistic conditions possible, and they had money to burn.

Normally, she'd write a letter to Marie. Dear Marie, I was looking up at Proxima tonight and I thought about you. Dear Marie, I got your letter. I programmed the thrush to mimic you a little, and you noticed. When the first astronauts land on Proxima Centauri b, maybe there will really be birds. I've studied everything I can, and there's no telling. It might all be a layer of ice. There might be mountains everywhere. They might try to make a new home in a place that's nothing but poison. Dear Marie, I want you to be happy there.

Through the lens, the planet slid around the star.

WOODS,

After you came and talked to us, Samara found out you hadn't even paid us for our time in Themis. Mistake, by the way—if you'd paid us it would have at least looked like you weren't trying to use us like lab rats and get away with it—and I feel like you should have known better. Not the company, but, you. You always seemed like a guy who wanted everything to have a reason.

Samara's got a lawyer, and the company should have papers by now. She told me not to contact you. I'm glad she's suing, because you all deserve it. Go bankrupt.

But I have an offer for whoever's in charge: I can't testify if I'm dead, and I want to go back to Themis permanently. I don't know how long 'permanently' is, since the prison refuses to keep people on life support for things like that and you won't want to bring me to a hospital, so just budget accordingly—a person probably starves to death in a week? So, a week. Unless I've built up such a resistance to the meds that it kills me in a few hours, which I assume would be cheaper.

I don't know who actually made Themis. I'm assuming you were involved, because you had the shortest fuse of anybody there, and at the time I thought that's just what being law enforcement did to people, but it makes more sense if you made it. And I don't know who I was writing to, that whole time. In Themis I just thought I had someone I loved, and he was where my letters went. I didn't know I needed to love someone so badly you could lie to me about it for four years—but that's how it worked, the psychologist said. You made Samara write reports because whatever you managed to do with her, there were some things she wouldn't fall for. I was an idiot and I'd been lonely my whole life. You could do anything to me.

It wasn't you, was it? Was it one person writing me back, or did you reply by committee? One of you must have seen the picture of my arrest, since you gave me long hair in Themis. You talked about missing my braids. Whoever it was, go fuck yourself. I didn't even like it, it was too long, but in Themis I kept it long all that time for your sake. I wanted to cut it—it got so humid in the summers I dreamed of shaving it off, I must have told you, I wrote you so much—but keeping my hair long was like a promise we'd see each other again. So I kept it.

I thought that I couldn't quite picture you because being in stasis on the ship seeped the color out of your dreams. And then it had been a long time, so of course I couldn't really remember you—I looked at your messages and forgot whether you had good posture or not when you typed. I wanted to think you hunched like I did, like that weird pang in the lower back was something we shared 25 trillion miles away. I wondered sometimes why I'd gone to Proxima Centauri if I had someone I loved so much. Not that you can say that to the person you left behind. I never even mentioned it to Samara. But everybody knew Carlos and I had loved ones back home. When there are so few of you, you end up knowing a lot of things that you never talk about.

Carlos isn't real, right? I mean—the doctor told me he wasn't, I know he wasn't. But there wasn't a person pretending to be him? He was just a program that got really excited about apple cider?

I don't even know how to be angry at you—it was the worst hour of my life and I threw up after, but it wasn't You (whoever that is) explaining it, I would have been able to tell. So it still feels like you weren't part of what went wrong, like the program got stuck even after I woke up and you locked me out and I'm still carrying you, someone I love and just forgot—

Anyway, I'm going through withdrawal. The prison definitely doesn't care— they said if I could go through it with the drugs that got me in here I could go through it with whatever they stuck in me to make me forget Themis. But maybe if you read this letter, you still consider me market research and this will be helpful. No appetite, no energy. I have a headache right behind my eyes. I'm always cold, even though Themis was colder than prison so you'd think I wouldn't be. I sleep a lot. I always dream of being back in Themis. Probably good news for you. Sell a million copies. Just give me mine.

And fix the bread. It never worked right, that should be changed.

Let me go home.

Marie

BENJAMINA WAITED UNTIL the office was empty before she crossed the floor to Woods' office. Stoic, not penitent; stoic people didn't skulk over to meet someone they barely liked just to see how interviews had gone with the people they had used.

She'd never been to his office before—he must always have come to her, strange, she'd never even noticed—and it was so blank it startled her into stillness at the threshold.

"Want an invitation?" He was standing, reaching for his coat, like he'd just been waiting for her so they could walk out together. "You look like a vampire."

She didn't say anything, and she didn't move closer; after a second, he cracked a grin. "You're kind of an asshole, Harris."

They walked out in silence, but from the way his thumb brushed the front of his coat lapel over and over, something terrible had happened and they were just waiting to be away from the cameras.

Six blocks later, he said, "It was bad."

She stopped and looked at him.

"She, uh—" He rubbed his hand once, rough, across his forehead. "In Themis, she looked fine. Healthy. It was stupid to assume she'd look the same in person, but I didn't expect... I didn't expect it. Samara's suing us."

It took her a second too long to catch up, and before she could stop it it was out: "Because of how Marie looks?"

"No, if Samara knew how Marie looked she'd have just murdered me." His hands had disappeared into his pockets, fists that pulled against the shoulders and ruined the line of his coat. She'd put that into their last game, the noir murder mystery—the private eye yanked on his coat from the inside that same way. She thought she'd invented it; she'd been proud of herself.

The letter he handed her was on paper so thin she hesitated to touch it.

"It's addressed to me, but trust me, it's for you."

She wanted to take it home and read it where she couldn't embarrass herself, but if Woods sat through three interviews she could manage this. She read it in the wide alley garden between two office buildings, where admin staff ate lunch to pretend they'd gotten away from everything. At some point she started shaking; he stood next to her like they were pretending the wind was cold. She read it again. She put it in her pocket. He didn't argue.

"Will you see her again?"

"I could get arrested for passing her company information. We're getting sued."

"I know."

"Fuck it, I'm hungry," he said.

They found a place far enough away they felt all right sitting down. He ate three pieces of bread out of the plastic basket in the first five minutes. Then he tore a napkin into pieces.

"Samara's skin and bones. Anthony's got insomnia. Dr. Asshole said it was just drug interactions. The prison claims the game damages the cortex. They're probably going to sue each other while Samara and Anthony are suing us."

"But not Marie."

He looked at her. His eyes were very dark; they couldn't quite get them to register in Themis—they coded as black, which always looked flat, so anyone who met him in the game thought his eyes were lighter brown. It must have been a surprise for Marie to see him as he really was.

"We can't do that."

"Are you going to see her again?"

"I'm not passing her a letter, Ben."

"Are you allowed to have an assistant with you, for the interviews? Stenography? Someone has to be holding the recorder."

"You're out of your mind."

Her lips pulled tight across each row of teeth. "I have to do something."

"If you're looking to feel less guilty, stop. No such thing."

He blurred underneath the tears that sprang up. She let them go—too late not to be penitent—so her vision would be clearer for what came next. "Then I'll go myself," she said.

"It's more than your job is worth."

There was nothing to say to that; her job had been worth so little there was no point.

Outside it was not quite dark, and just beginning to be cold; the temperature of Themis, decided by a developer so much her senior she'd never met him.

When she turned toward home, he walked with her.

Halfway there, he said, "We have one more interview with her."

HI MARIE,

My handle on the Themis team is Erytheia. It's not my real name, but it's easier to keep track of who wrote which code this way. Erytheia was one of the daughters of Themis. (I didn't pick it.) When we were getting ready for the dry run they made me your experience specialist so we could concentrate on each user's take on Themis and build as rich a world as possible.

Woods showed me your letter.

I just wanted you to know there wasn't a committee. All your letters came to me, and I read them all. Some of what you told me went into a development memo, like how there weren't enough insects for a landscape with that much standing water and vegetation. But I didn't send my letters to trick you into writing more often, and I didn't discuss anything personal. I answered you because I wanted you to feel like there was a person writing you back. I was the person writing you back.

-E

Hey Marie,

Can you sleep? I can't fucking sleep. My body thinks it's too dark because it's dumb and can only remember one set of things at a time and it's stuck on Themis—like, we were definitely stuck on Themis but you don't have to be such an asshole about it, get used to night and day and let me get some fucking sleep, damn.

And honestly the Themis shit doesn't really bother me. Everything I can remember from there is all of us just doing our best and getting along, so it's not like it was embarrassing. I feel like an idiot for not realizing sooner—now it's so fucking obvious why the movie bank didn't work, because it was too complicated to make it work inside the game or whatever—but actually being there was fine. The part that bothers me is the whole time out here that I thought I was just depressed and dreaming about some random planet is the part that's vanishing, like that's the only part the drugs actually affected once the wall wore off. Can you imagine what we must have looked like to everybody else, hopped up on that stuff?

I'm signing Samara's guy's thing. Are you? You should, they're trying to pay us off but that just means they know they fucked up and want us to keep quiet.

You're not talking to anyone about any of this, right? They told me you're having a rough time and I get that. What wasn't better about Themis than being locked up? But you get killed that way, or they find some reason to extend your sentence twenty years, so zip that shit and just wait for Samara's guy to make us too famous to die.

When we get out we should see if we can get a parole dispensation to cross state lines, it was cool all living together, that was nice. Plus movies work here, that's a reason to stay here. Plus I bet your bread in the real world is amazing.

Keep your cool, Marie. I know you can do this.

-Anthony

* * *

MARIE,

My attorney heard from Othrys Games that you've been in contact with the company, trying to make a deal to get back to Themis. He wanted to send you a cease and desist, but I told him I wanted to talk to you first before we did anything official.

The case we're building downplays the nature of the game as much as possible. It doesn't matter that the game wasn't some battle simulator where we died all the time—it matters that they did it to us without our permission and then hoped people would ignore it because nobody cares about us. If you keep asking to go back in there, they're going to use it as evidence that what they were doing was benign, or helpful, and we're going to have to fight that impression in court, and when the game hits shelves and it's fine, it will look even worse. We're fighting the company—we can't let the game become the thing we're fighting.

This thing is really important—my lawyer says it could be a cornerstone for other cases about prisoners' rights. That's big, Marie. It's bigger than us. Cut it out.

I'm not saying all this to be cruel—I miss it there, too. I could do my work and close doors behind me, of course I fucking miss it. But trying to get back to a lie is only going to hurt us. We need to be free again here. This is our shot. What they did to us was wrong—you can't fix that. Let me fight it.

Flush this letter. They can't find it.

Samara

THE OTHRYS LAWYERS call Benjamina for a deposition, and she sits in a meeting room with no windows with her back to the door—the only other seat, across from the lawyer whose smile is set tight across his face and doesn't get anywhere near his eyes—and tries to ignore that this is all a setup to make her uncomfortable.

She answers fifty questions about the game: its purpose ("Any game's purpose—entertainment"), what game play will be like (it takes ten minutes, and the lawyer's mouth purses the more she talks about how beautiful Themis is), the passage of time ("Four to seven times faster than real time, everybody playing an instance has to agree on the speed if they're playing in the MMORPG rather than single-player," she says, just to watch his jaw tick before he asks for clarification), how long it's been in development (five years), how long the beta test has been going (just over a year), the chance of fatigue ("The same as with any mentally stimulating activity, like a deposition," she says, and the lawyer's lips positively disappear).

"Did you know that Samara Perlman is trying to use the time she spent in Themis as proof of good behavior to reduce her sentence?"

It's an amazing tactic. She keeps her face neutral. "No, I didn't."

"Do you have an opinion on the validity of that?"

"No one who beta tested Themis ever evidenced any antisocial behavior, and as they believed the simulation was real life, their behavior in Themis would be close to real-world behavior."

"If I play a video game and kill a hundred imaginary people, am I a bad person outside the game?"

"Because of killing the video game people, specifically?"

He takes an even breath in and out. "Miss Harris, if you could answer the question."

"I think there's a line between fantasy and reality, but the three subjects who had Themis beta-tested on them weren't aware that line had even been crossed, so the question is kind of useless."

"Please answer it."

"I did."

He closes his eyes and counts to five, this time, which gives her enough time to plant the bug under the table.

She lets the bug run—in for one count of corporate espionage, in for two counts—and siphons out the Othrys talk on her home laptop, with its wallpaper she made from Themis: the view outside the kitchen, where the thrush is singing.

The lawyer hums and taps his pen; in the microphone it sounds like a stone gavel. "Wages we might have to push back on, since I'm not sure we can really count playing video games as 'labor.'"

"Agreed," someone else says. "Plus I see that they're pushing for time served for the passage of time in the game AND asking for wages for physical hours spent using the game. We can probably use that to shut down this thing at both ends. If they can't decide what was more important, how can we?"

"Good point," the lawyer says. "We should get Warden Collins back in here to talk about labor practices. Give him enough rope to hang himself, we can show the only people using these inmates was the prison."

The next day at work, she comes into Woods' office, closes the door behind her.

"They're going to lose."

"I know."

They stand for a little while not looking at each other. He's put up a panorama of Themis on his office wall. It's the geological survey, before they started the naturalist pass and brought people in; the idea of Themis, before anything really happened. The sun is setting. The sun is always setting.

She waits until they lose the case before she visits Marie.

Marie Roland on Themis is nearly six feet tall, has bakers' arms, covers four feet at a stride. She has lines around her eyes from squinting at the sun; they got deeper on Themis, where the sun is safer to look at. Her voice is deep enough that Benjamina had to program the Acomys cahirinus knockoff to startle and bolt when she laughed.

Marie Roland on the other side of the visitation table is someone who— Benjamina has to accept it all at once, there's no point in doing things with best intentions any more—Benjamina's driven into the grave.

She sits down. Marie waits a few seconds to look up at her.

"That was you?" she says, and it's with such disdain that Benjamina almost smiles.

"Yes."

"Have you come to apologize?"

"Yes," she says. "I don't think it will be worth much, but yes."

Marie sits back in her chair. Five seven, maybe five eight; the circles under her eyes are as big as her eyes.

You end up loving the things you make. Benjamina had been prepared for that—she'd seen it happen in other games, she'd seen it happen to Woods, she had braced herself. But Marie was made already; Benjamina can't look her in the eye.

"Samara got to be a biologist. Anthony was an engineer. Was there a reason I wasn't a scientist? Did my file say I was too stupid?"

Benjamina shrugs. "They assigned you to me. I didn't know enough science to code one."

"You don't know how to bake, either," Marie says.

They sit for a moment in quiet. Benjamina leans forward and starts to tell her why she's come, but Marie starts talking, and she freezes.

"I've forgotten a lot of important things," Marie says to the tabletop. "There was—there was a bird, and I know we were trying to make cider but I can't remember how far we got? Was Woods going to arrest us?"

"No. The—uh, the point of the game was to see what people would do with minimal interference."

Marie's gaze is sharp. Benjamina programmed that stare in wholesale, without ever seeing it. In person it feels like a slap.

"So you picked convicts to see what we would do if we thought we could get away with it? Burn in hell."

"I'm wearing a recorder," Benjamina says, "if there's anything you want to get off your chest."

To Penitentiary Staff:

This is a general notice that MARIE ROLAND [ID: 68223-18-0709] should be given a psychiatric evaluation as soon as possible. Recently she has evidenced delusional thinking and bursts of hostility, and a recent visit with a supposed family member left her extremely agitated. All future visits must be approved by the warden's office, and Roland will not be allowed to meet any visitors whatsoever until she has complied with the evaluation and any recommended medication regimen.

Sincerely,

Janet Evanston, on behalf of Christopher Collins, Warden

THE FOLLOWING LETTER to the editor was delivered to our editorial offices by a third party. Upon confirming pertinent facts, the Evening Times considers the letter worthy of publication.

When I was in Themis, I caught a fly.

You'll hear about Themis soon, if they aren't already selling it. It's beautiful there. You'll want to stay in it forever. That's not a threat; I just envy you.

When you stand next to the river and think about vampires, know that I was there first. They sent me without telling me it was virtual. I thought I had been selected to be the first inhabitant of a new planet. I should have known better—the game couldn't make me forget who I was, and no one like me gets selected for something like that—but Themis is hard enough to live in that you believe it's real. It never really feels like night or day and your sleep cycle gets messed up and the terrain is rough for vegetables, so you have to fight the soil for eight months to get anything started. It's not easy. The bread there never baked right. I thought it was the water, for a long time.

I'm currently in the [redacted by editors], which is where Othrys tested Themis on us. I didn't volunteer—I was selected for a sleep study, they said, because I had vivid dreams, and it would get me time off for good behavior if I agreed. They never told us about Themis. For a year, I lived in two places and I didn't know.

I don't know what they gave me to make me forget, but they gave it to me on each end of Themis, on the way in and after I was out. Eventually my body got used to it—side effect of being an addict, which you think they'd have worried about more, but.

Some things I've forgotten—there was a bird I loved, but I couldn't tell you what it looked or sounded like. It's a bird in a dream. But I remember more of it than I was supposed to.

We tried to sue the game company for experimenting on us without our knowledge or permission. It didn't work; we pushed too hard to have it affect our sentences, I guess.

I'm not writing this because I'm surprised. You're probably not surprised, either. Part of me wishes I had it in me to be noble and fight to get us all released because of this—Samara and Anthony deserve their freedom. But I'm writing because I want to live inside Themis until I die, and Othrys says they won't let me.

We lost the lawsuit, so there's no danger in it. It probably looks great to them that I want to go back, anyway. And most people won't live in the same

Themis I built. They're making it more interesting for new people. You'll have cities to live in instead of just shipping-crate mess halls; you'll be able to see the mountains. You'll all be dealing with each other.

Samara's lawyer told me the Themis I lived in was a demo they built just for Anthony and Samara and me—it's not the version on the shelves, so I could live inside it and never come into contact with anyone. You'll have a hard time in Themis, but I'll never be the problem.

They developed that game around us, one thing at a time—the daytime got more purple as we went along and we called it the seasons, and the wildlife filled in in bursts because they didn't think we'd remember what had been there the last time. (We did remember—we just thought nature was getting used to us.) Eventually there were plants with briars and fruit flies that would bother me when I was cooking. Real life. Things you believe. I caught one of them late at night, before it could land on some dough I was rolling out for cookies, and I carried it outside because Samara, our team biologist, had told us to be very careful to preserve everything we found so she could catalog all of it.

It's not real, they forced it on us and we were never meant to keep it, I'm not stupid, but I held the fruit fly in the cup of my hand and felt its wings beating. How can they say that's not mine?

Marie Roland

CORRECTION: AS THE writer of the letter was unavailable for editorial consultation on yesterday's Letter to the Editor, at the advice of legal counsel, it has been removed.

"WHAT THE FUCK did you do?"

Benjamina hands him his coffee. They've told the office they're dating; it explains a lot of time in each other's company.

"I tried to fucking," she looks around, lowers her volume, "help Marie be someone no one could ignore. That's her best chance."

"Her best chance is a legal appeal by people who know what they're doing, not you on a crusade."

She sits back and looks at him, flat. "You think that this time, for sure, three inmates are going to win against two state prisons and Othrys Games by just quietly doing the right thing."

He leans closer; his hand, flat on the table, almost touches her fist.

"I think if anybody realizes you're the problem, you are going to need help and I am not going to be able to give it. What are you thinking?"

She meets his eye. "I saw Marie."

REVIEW: THEMIS IS A WHOLE NEW WORLD
by Sarah McElroy

As a games reviewer, you tend to get jaded about new products. The graphics are increasingly realistic, the plots increasingly dense, and there's a sense that some games are more about one-upsmanship than about providing a transporting experience for players.

Themis is coming to the market nearly three years late, and shrouded in mystery. It was the subject of a lawsuit two years ago, as beta testers complained they hadn't signed on for something as immersive as they got. For normal people, that gives you pause. For gamers, that's the kind of buzz money can't buy. (A one-day-only letter to the editor also appeared in the *Evening Times*; the newspaper didn't respond to requests for comment, so the message-board debate rages on about whether it was a legitimate report from the trenches, or genius advertising.)

And if you've been waiting for Themis as long as I have, it's awkward to realize you understand exactly what those beta testers meant.

In terms of practicalities, Themis isn't very much different from half a dozen other VR immersions that have appeared the last few years. You're part of a hardscrabble crew assigned to terraform Themis, the first colony on Proxima Centauri. If you're looking for more plot, you won't find it: the entire hook of Themis is that the world is, quite literally, what you make it.

But what a world. The eternal sunset casts a rosy glow over the camp, the flies hover over any kill you make. And if you think otherwise, trust me, you'll end up making kills—Themis is about moral questions as much as strategy choices, and your team will have to eat something until the potato harvest. Every herbivore on Proxima Centauri is a take on Earth fauna of the taiga, so if you can't look a reindeer in the eye and fire, you're going to go hungry a lot. And you should think quickly; Themis has admirable ambitions about its much-touted real-time settings, but there's no doubt that the optimal game play occurs at about seven times the speed of life, and at that speed, hunger levels are highly responsive. (Given that your larger goal is simply to cross the mountains and make geological observations about the ice on the dark side of the planet, hunger might be the closest you come to emergency action.)

There have been concerns about the complications of MMORPG when everything is quite so unstructured; it's one thing to put up with creeps when they're a mage avatar in your questing party, and another to deal with them in an environment so sharply realized that it might as well be real. I'm honestly not sure how that setting will develop—when we played it in the Tabula offices, all was well, but the more you open the encampment to strangers, the greater the risk. It's just as well the game has a Private setting, where you and a handful of AI colleagues split the work and develop the colony in contemplative near-silence. You even get to choose your profession. (Medic is so boring as to be childish; go for Cook. Don't worry—there's no achievement bar. You can mess up bread as much as you want.)

These days, to survive in the marketplace, a game can't just be good and survive. It can't even settle for being impressive. It has to be earth-shaking. And for a game that can be explained in a single sentence, Themis really does defy description. I know I'll be seeing copycats for the next ten years; I know none of them will make me feel the way Themis did.

RATING: Must-Have

HELLO SARAH,

I saw your piece about Themis in Tabula. I am a developer at Othrys who worked on the beta testing for Themis and would love to speak with you further. You can contact me at the email above.

Benjamina Harris

* * *

To All Othrys Staff:

Benjamina Harris has been terminated, effective immediately. In the next few days, HR staff may meet with you to ask questions about her performance. We apologize for the inconvenience, and appreciate your cooperation.

Sincerely,

Dan Turpin, CEO

It feels so silly, handing Woods a disk—first time she's handled a physical disk in six years, no bigger than her thumbnail, and still passing it over is like handing him a raw egg.

"I told you I can't help you," he says, but she has her hands in her pockets and after a minute, he slips the thing out of sight.

"Thank you," she says. He's furious with her—that she didn't get out before she was fired, that she's had to create a new identity after everyone's already on alert, that she's making him responsible for backup copies of bugged conversations and stolen correspondence that will get her thrown in prison for fifty years. But he's here when he shouldn't be, and that makes him better than some.

"You won't make it out of the country," he says. "Please just hide closer to home. Yosemite's a thousand square miles."

She could. It would be safer. But living alone in a clearing near the river, birds calling out in the dark, mountains to the northwest—she swallows. It would be stealing.

She says, "I hope it's bad enough that someone finds Marie."

She heads south; the sun sets off the red rocks, and there's no one else for a hundred miles, and she sits in the quiet car and compiles a new geography, and realizes she'll never reach the border.

Still, she drives while she can. The footprint of the mesas is so big it never shifts; she moves like someone in a dream, not quite fast enough.

* * *

EVENING TIMES
OTHRYS WHISTLEBLOWER TELLS ALL ABOUT SHOCKING MEDICAL EXPERIMENTATION: 'THEMIS WASN'T WORTH THE COST'

THE SUNDAY LEDGER
"THE WARDEN KNEW, AND NO ONE STOPPED HIM": HOW 'THEMIS' MUST MARK THE END OF THE PRISON INDUSTRIAL COMPLEX

THE NEW YORK STANDARD
THE ORACLE OF OTHRYS: VIDEO GAME SNITCH BLOWS THE LID OFF VR HORROR

THE LONE CANDLE
THE THEMIS EXPERIMENT: WHY VIRTUAL REALITY MAKES EVERYONE A PRISONER

OWL EYES NEWS
BOSS BATTLE: CHRISTOPHER COLLINS, 'THE VIDEO-GAME WARDEN,' RETIRES WITH $2 MILLION SEVERANCE

TABULA GAMES
WORLD-CLASS: 'THEMIS' BREAKS SALES RECORDS

THE NEW YORK WEEK IN REVIEW
MARIE ROLAND: THE WOMAN WHO CAN NEVER GO HOME

SAMARA, ANTHONY,

This is my last letter. I hope this ends up being of some use to you—make no secret of it, if it will help. I'm happy to be anybody's pawn now.

It was an honor building Themis with you. I'm glad you're not coming, but it won't be the same.

Marie

* * *

SPENT TODAY WALKING downstream a dozen kilometers and recording things. There are more species of cattails in this one stretch than I ever saw on Earth. Saw a lot of teeth marks on them—bodes well for the idea of some Earth-adjacent fauna that have just been scared off by our camp but might eventually be coaxed to come back.

Of course, I shredded my feet and somehow managed to get a giant bruise on my knee without even falling down. (How did they ever let me become a naturalist with a constitution like this?) Listened to a whole chapter of a book while I was soaking in salt water, which is the most salt and the most reading I've gotten since I landed.

You'd think they'd have sent more people, but I guess for a temperate zone you don't really have to. Winters don't kill you here, and it's only a couple of weeks until the pass melts and we can set off for the mountains to do the survey for the second-wave team. (My bet is glacier melt that will sustain a thousand people; Vivian claims there's taiga and we can support twice that. Carlos is holding the money.)

It's winter at home, by now, isn't it? I hope all is well with you. I would love to know for sure.

The bread I made today was edible! The bird outside was very proud of me—he sang along with me all night. I threw him crumbs, at the end of it, and he liked them, and it feels like it will even last the night without going stale. This time next year, I'll have the hang of it for sure.

That bird really does have a lovely song. They said to be careful assigning old observations to what I find here, but: thrush family. I just know it.

All my love—

THOSE SHADOWS LAUGH
Geoff Ryman

Geoff Ryman (www.ryman-novel.com) is the author of *The Warrior Who Carried Life*, the novella "The Unconquered Country", *The Child Garden*, *Was*, *Lust*, and *Air*. His work *253, or Tube Theatre* was published as hypertext fiction and won the Philip K. Dick Memorial Award. He has also won the World Fantasy, Campbell Memorial, Arthur C. Clarke, British Science Fiction Association, Sunburst, James Tiptree, and Gaylactic Spectrum awards. His most recent novel, *The King's Last Song*, is set in Cambodia. Ryman currently lectures in Creative Writing at the University of Manchester in the United Kingdom.

THE TOURIST PRECINCT is owned by Disney.

Though they are very careful to use the Buena Vista branding. The Buena Vista Hotel—it sounds almost local. The tourists are jammed into a thin rind of gravelly coast called the Precinct, one of two places on the island where flat ground meets the sea. There is a container port on the north side but most visas forbid visiting it. Mine did.

Many tourists stay on cruise ships, all white and gold, their lights reflecting on the water. There's a dock, some restaurants, most of them floating. The Precinct's streets are so narrow and they zigzag up the rock face so steeply that the cars edge past each other's mirrors. Turning around at the inevitable dead end is nearly impossible. There is one guarded road up the cliffs onto the plateau—at night narrow vans wobble into the town. Every parking space has a car charger.

The Custom House runs across the mouth of the canyon into the town, a wall of rust-red laterite blocks, the pockmarks ringed with edges so sharp they cut. The Foreign House is crammed next to it, looking more like a prison than a luxury hotel.

My first morning.

I bob down the dock from a merchant ship (much better food than cruise liners and the merchant marine make better company). I see one of the Colinas, holding up a sign in handwritten letters that roll like waves.

Sra Valdez

SINGLEHELIX.

She's tiny, brown, yes bare-breasted, yes with a feather through her nose, and she looks delighted. I catch her eye and wave; she hops up and down. I have to watch where I put my eyes. But luckily (or unluckily) for me, her smile is entrancing.

She greets me traditionally, pressing her forehead against both of my cheeks.

I'd been reading the first explorers' account *En la Tierra de Mujeres* from 1867. The male authors were breathlessly excited about a nation of women who didn't wear many clothes. They cloaked their lust in classical references—'Amazonian' or 'island Cleopatras.' From the text, you get visions of Edwardian actresses done up in modest togas as Clytemnestra or Medea—or maybe Mountain Girl from the Babylon sequence of *Intolerance*, all tomboy exuberance in a leopard skin, headband, a fiery smile—athletic gals vaulting over walls and shooting arrows.

The first engravings of Colinas Bravas were published in *Faro de Vigo* in 1871. The images are filtered through Western eyes—the features European, the locks flowing and curled, the dress rendered modest. But to people of the time the illustrations were a shock.

The giant sandstone-clad temple; the wooden mobile houses carried on pallbearers' rods; the terraces up the slopes that rose like skyscrapers—within a month of the illustrations' publication, scholars were declaring that the main city had been built by Romans or Persians or even Cambodians (all that laterite and sandstone cladding). Little brown women could not have built them.

But the texts on the walls of the temples, particularly the Torre Espiral, turned out to be in their language. It contains the words *hurricano* and *barbeque*. Which means it's Taíno, the language of the Indians whom

Columbus first encountered in my own dear homeland of the Dominican Republic, where they now exist as a genetic trace. Seven hundred years before Columbus, Taíno women sailed west toward the dark continent of Europe and settled an island without a single act of genocide.

At the München Olympics, Leni Riefenstahl's lens could not keep away from the Colinas athletes. They won ten women's gold medals that year, the highest number per head of population of any nation. The German Chancellor Angela Herbort made full propaganda use of them, showed them off at a rally to praise the principles of "health and common ownership."

In the full summer of the American century, the 1960 Rome Olympiad disallowed the Colinas from competition. Their lack of a reproductive cycle was said to be an unfair advantage in training. Colinas were, evidently, not quite women or quite human. The Colinas knew enough of our history to get what happens to people we say are not quite human. That's when they created the Precinct and farmed it out to Disney. They liked the cartoons.

My host tells me her name, though I cannot pronounce or even really hear it. Fouvwetzixityl is one transcription (using Medrano's system). She knows this and tells me in Colina, *You say Evie.*

She takes my hand, and as she leads me toward the Custom House, she starts to skip. I have my rucksack, a small wheelie with my scrubs, and I'm wearing shorts and a tank top. Rumbling behind me, pushed by crewmen from Venezuela, are my battery-powered freezebox, a nanoscope workstation, and a portable extraction suite. The men are allowed only as far as the Custom House. I shake their hands and tip them—but I don't think I will miss men.

At the gate, Evie ducks down into the window, and laughs and does a bit of a dance for the Custom guards who grin enormous gummy smiles, which they hide with their hands. There is such high hilarity that I cannot believe any work is being done. Then, out of nowhere, my passport is returned with a two-page intelligent hologram that looks like the Statue of Liberty. My enormous boxes and I are led through into the City, called simply Ciudad. There isn't another one on the island. The Custom guards wave good-bye to me like I'm going on a school trip.

The public plaza—La Plaza del Pueblo—is crowded with tourists, many of them female couples holding hands and taking snaps. Languages swoop around me like flocks of birds—Spanish of course, but also Chinese, Danish, Yoruba, Welsh, Portuguese, and others I can't identify. The Plaza appears vast. It rears up, rocky cliffs on either side like waves about to break. The main sandstone steps on the south face go up in layers, it is said, to a height of eighty meters. The Torre Espiral looks as old as the pyramids, like a ziggurat only conical, with wide ramps spiraling up it to the flat roof with its giant urn of fire. Tourists are no longer allowed to climb it after a German woman fell off last year. Surrounding the Plaza like a bullring are rows of shops—yes, selling tourist tat—built on two levels, with the Civil Palace on the north side and the National Library on the south next to the main steps. The Library's twelfth-century bas-reliefs in sandstone deserve their fame— joyous scenes of everyday life, women dancing as they pound manioc, or harvesting fields, or throwing mangoes at each other from the trees. And the most famous, a woman giving birth. Beyond the Plaza at the end of the canyon, there's a tumble of boulders, a creek, then a broccoli mass of trees rising up the slope.

Most of Ciudad is in layers on those cliff faces, covered streets winding higher and higher where visitors are not allowed. The houses burrow into the rock. The gardens grow on top of the porches of the houses below them. The effect is like looking at those improbable Art Deco miniatures of cities in silent films. I have to crane my neck at a painful angle. Along the top, wind turbines pirouette on their toes like ballerinas.

They've put my clinic on the ground floor of the Plaza. The sandstone archway is the color of sunset with carved concentric circles that the guidebook says are meant to look like ripples in water. The entrance is clouded with purple bougainvillea spilling down from the roof. Just inside the door is an emergency generator—the islands do import some oil. Also a desk, an operating table, my IT suite, a data projector, screen, and rows of chairs for my seminars.

I'd specified those. Nobody told me Colinas never sit on chairs.

Evie spins round and round, arms outstretched as if all this is hers. She's so delighted I can't stop taking hold of her hand. I should know better, but I am a woman, and I rely on her not being suspicious of me. That makes me feel guilty.

She looks human, but yes, a bit different. Her smile is too wide, her chin too tiny. The Colinas are now recognized as another species within the genus *Homo*. Being parthenogenetic, she ovulates maybe four times in her life. How's this for utopia? Colinas do not have periods. They also do not mate, do not cluster into little paired units. Famously, they are supposed to lack sexual desire.

I ask her, *You have children*? She nods yes and holds up a finger—one. It's customary to only have one.

Aw, what is child name?

Her smile doesn't change but she freezes for a moment and then shakes her head and giggles. She points east and says, *Quatoletcyl Mah*. I know the phrase—'Sad Children Loved.'

I close my eyes with shame. Of course, that's why she's so delighted I'm here. I shouldn't have asked about children. I apologize. Literally I say, *I make mistake*, which is about the closest their language gets to swearing.

She says, *Tomorrow. Tomorrow we see child.*

They have no word for he or she, and in everyday vernacular, no word for me, my, or mine. They can say I, almost like it's a geographical location.

From somewhere a bell sounds. It moans, deeply, like it regrets something.

You leave now, she says, still smiling. Ah. Right. Closing time. She takes my hand again. Hers is sweet and insistent.

Outside thousands of sandaled feet sound like rain or applause as they make their way back to the Custom House, its gates thrown open. On the ocean only seven meters beyond the gate, the sun sits low. The square is flooded with orange, sideways light that makes the temple and terraces the color of overripe apricots. Shadows delineate every carved face or incised word sign. In this light I see that, yes indeed, the lighthouse temple is also a book, the writing in stone all the way up the giddy ramp. It tells the story of how the first Colina mother gave birth.

We know that is a myth, as is her rising out of the sea. There must have been more than one mother—genetically there are five matrilineal lines. Experts argue whether they were expelled or set off across the sea for themselves, looking for somewhere to be.

I look up at the terraces—the houses don't have doors and the rooms are full of a wavering orange light, lit by candles. I want to see inside, be inside, those rooms. I want to know what it is like to live there. I glimpse a donkey being led down toward the main staircase. The woman riding it is brushing her long black hair.

Men are allowed into the Plaza if accompanied by responsible female sponsors. Most of the men have the same expression of delight, a clenched smile, determined to appear benign. Some of the women allow themselves to look pissed off. People traveling in tourist groups or cruise ships often do—they're trapped with each other, and though stuffed full of sights and good food, they have no power. I am happier in my shorts with my rucksack, happier still to have a good working reason for being here.

Evie skips me all the way into the Foreign House. Someone at the entrance invisibly slips her a lei and she drapes the flowers around my neck and claps her hands. The idea of the lei is stolen from Hawaii—they cheerfully admit this. For some reason, the native House staff—in white shirts and black slacks—applaud me. I feel my eyes swell.

They know you help us, Evie says and gives me a forehead kiss. Evie smells of sunlight and honey. I have her for just a moment and she is hot and shivery under my hand. She leaps away, tossing her mane like a horse. One of the staff, looking bone-thin and European, says in perfect Spanish, "She is so proud to be your host."

My room has purple sheets and translucent Colinas chocolate under my pillow. The penthouse suite costs $1,000 a night. No loud music after nine p.m. Unless you want to be locked in with a bunch of rich foreigners getting drunk on whisky that costs $25 a shot (along with the celebs—I have the inestimable privilege of being here the same night as Tom Cruise), there are only two things to do in the House at night. You can watch movies on TV— and only those that contain not a hint of sexual violence or enacted congress. Or something a bit less virtual.

The Foreign House is the only hotel on Colinas Bravas with doors that open into both the Plaza and its harbor—the privilege of being invited or rich.

I step out into the demarcated café space in the very last of the twilight and look up. Lights dance in all the doorways and windows; shadows bend and dip and wave. Those shadows laugh.

The laughter comes from everywhere in gusts. The narrow canyon magnifies the sound and sends it echoing. Songs, too, some of them campfire-simple, some of them complex and formal like choirs, and some amassed, intoning chant like prayer. Strains of music played on reeds and strings sound like an orchestra warming up. It's as if each kind of sound is a different flock of swallows dive-bombing around me. Then, as suddenly as waking up, Ciudad falls silent; the candles go out. There are so many stars!

I turn. I have been observed all this while by the same staff member in American dress—a short-sleeved white shirt, slim black trousers.

Beautiful, I say, flinging up my arms. *Much!*

A happy hour, she says. *Each night.*

And she gestures for me to go back into the hotel. Later, during the night, I am comforted to hear the *sshing* of tropical rain on the courtyard and roof. It must have been a dream but I think I heard that staff member go on to say, *We are easy to love.*

It is a failing of mine that I fall in love with foreigners.

First I fall in love with a country, which means the people in it, and then usually just one of those people to be my partner, my rock, my point of entry. I always do it, and the process is delicious. Though so far, it has also always gone wrong.

I find, for example, that they sleep all the time, or fight all the time, or need a fight to feel passion, or think it's funny to insult me. Or they simply want me to pay for everything. It ends. I go to boring home. Home is the Dominican Republic, sex-tourist destination, Caribbean island with an 11,000-foot-high mountain, miles of beaches, and a national park with hills that look like cupcakes. You've got to have a psychosocial problem with home to find the Dominican Republic dull.

That first night listening to rain, I imagined sitting cross-legged on the floor of one of those high cells, and going to sleep with Evie, and waking up with her at first dawn, of being allowed to stay, of being allowed to love. A harmless fantasy, I thought, and it drifted me off to sleep.

THE NEXT DAY, as promised, I was ready to work at 4:30 a.m. Getting up wasn't difficult—the dawn song of Ciudad is famous and justly so. The people simply get up in the dark and start singing.

It is the aural equivalent of a warm bed—soft, and soothing, and you loll in its sound. But if you have to work, it somehow eases you upright. I washed and looked out of the window of the House to see flashlights and candles like fireflies everywhere among the walkways.

The pavements were made mirrors by the rain, blue and gold puddles. A steady train of women were moving down the steps to set up the shops or open the Library. Evie was waiting for me, holding a candle. I wore my lab trousers and coat. I felt like a native, getting up in drizzle and crossing the Plaza to my place of work. Only, Evie made me veer away from my clinic, steering me toward the Civil Palace where I was to be introduced to the Council, or maybe just a council. I couldn't be too sure.

It was just like *In the Country of Women*. There they sat, as described in 1867—the slim, wise, implacable, and sometimes kindly elders of Colinas Bravas. They, too, wore simple formal clothes made of reed beaten into linen, soft and gray with subtle patterns in the weave or embroidery. The jackets did indeed look like quilts, there were so many pockets. One of the councilors was wearing a tool belt of wrenches, chisels, and a hammer. The elders looked calm, with dim smiles and alert eyes, and their gestures for me to sit were hearty and not to be gainsaid.

"Hello and welcome to Colinas Bravas," said the one in the center, speaking English with an American accent. She had a high, round, polished forehead that reflected light. I gave her the nickname La Señora Luminosa. The name stuck for me. I responded politely, said how glad I was to be there. They asked about my accommodation. Another woman, who spoke with a South African (?) accent, expressed gratitude that I was there, and to SingleHelix for being willing to share etc.

It came down to how long I would need to stay on the island.

"As long as you need me," I said in Spanish, the official second language. I told them that I was unmarried, the head of SingleHelix's Research Division in the Dominican Republic. They nodded glacially. I think they knew what that meant. We in SoloHebra RD do things that Our Friendly Neighbors to the North would rather not do themselves.

They insisted. "How long do you estimate?"

I said six months.

They asked if two might be enough for them to master the basic technology. "*Nos tenemos bíologos en nuestro propio país.*" The technique does not require that all who carry out the procedure need to be microbiologists?

I had to smile. I shook my head. That gesture means nothing to the Colinas. I said, *I stay time you want.* They were very grateful, and they wanted me gone.

It was still dark and cool when we walked in a group to my clinic. Luminosa took my hand and strolled with me as if we were old friends.

"I know this is basically a business proposition for your..." For some reason she had difficulty finding the word company. "But for us, we still experience your visit with deep personal gratitude to you. This is not your home; these are not your people." She stopped and put my hand in both of hers and looked directly into my eyes. "But you help us. We will make sure you see more of us than most foreigners do."

"That would be great honor."

So Luminosa strode on with me, and asked me what I would like to see. I told her that I had read the 1867 text and its sequel about the managed forests—fruit, nuts, hemp all growing as if untended. Is it true that their orange trees stand as high as oaks? The plateau is flat but rolling like England with large forests and open pastures. It is never seen from the air. Its airspace is closed and there is no airport. I hinted I might like to see where the SingleHelix equipment would be made, in the industrial northern port. Her smile didn't change.

That day, my clinic was bigger. The building has movable internal walls. Rows of beds had been added; my fridge preserving the samples buzzed, and I saw that the thermidor's light was on. The operating theatre lights were standing ready.

"Show us how," said Luminosa "No need to do an extraction. We have the two ova ready for you." Evie stepped forward and covered her mouth with both hands, laughing. There is no way to say in her language, "The egg is mine."

I panicked. "We can't do it now! The donor material has to be thawed, inspected, be at the same exact temperature. It has to be from a different matrilineal line...."

Luminosa took my hand again. "We know, we know."

"But you don't understand. If Evie only has one ovum...." I glanced at Evie, looking so innocent. "If anything goes wrong, she'll have lost this chance!"

"Then check everything," said Luminosa, stroking the back of my hand. I went and scanned both sets of donated material, hands shaking. I was annoyed that they had done so much of my work for me, unasked and unsupervised. I didn't like it. I felt rushed. I felt denigrated. I was simultaneously relieved and disgruntled when both ova were fine. "Well, yes, I can start work. Do… does Evie know who the other egg belongs to?"

Luminosa looked blank. "Why would Evie want to know that?"

That brought me up short. Well… but… no need to know who the other mother was?

La Señora swept us on. "No need to explain much to us. We are familiar with the basics. Just show us how to carry out the procedure swiftly and well."

The same images that guided my instruments were shown on the screen. They watched as I micromanaged the translucent needle into the donor ovum, and then slipped the cradle underneath the DNA to carry it out.

"It's just a question of practice," I said. "Hand-eye coordination." The gantry slowly moved between microscope surgeries.

I switched screens. There was Evie's daughter, on the screen unmade, as transparent as a ghost. "This is the delicate bit. Like making lace."

More like joining two halves of a zipper for the first time, link by link. There is always a moment when the two halves somehow snap together and fuse. That's when a new person is created. I told them when it happened. They applauded.

The transfer probe is full of water-based jelly, rich with nutrients. The trick is to gently lower the egg into the very tip, so that it is the first thing presented. I looked around. Evie was already on one of the beds, already naked.

"It's all right," said Luminosa. "No embarrassment. We have no need of that kind of modesty."

I began to feel shivery and a bit sick. I looked down at Evie, at her smile, into her black eyes, and all I saw was trust and hope. I stroked her hair; couldn't help it. I eased stage one into her; stage two was the probe itself extended. I nicknamed the egg Luminosa as well—it was all glowing, the probe has a light. I couldn't watch. I had to. I saw where the egg needed to be placed and lowered it.

"That's it. That's all. We'll know in two days at most." Again, applause.

I had a reaction—the corners of my vision went dark, my legs weak. I needed somewhere to sit, but all my chairs had been pulled back, with the women cross-legged on the tiles. I nearly fell. Luminosa caught me by the shoulder, lowered me to the floor, and as she stroked my shoulder, her eyes asked me a worried question.

"It's a little bit overwhelming," I said, and didn't like to say why. Luminosa kept stroking my shoulder.

Outside, it was still only eight a.m. and cool. We sat on the pavement in the Plaza as the first of the tourists strolled past. One of the councilors brought me a cup of coffee. "Sorry," I kept saying, "sorry." They asked if I wanted to put off our visit, and I said, "No! No!"

After my coffee, as the heat swelled, we made our way to the end of the canyon through its grove of trees, climbing steps along the creek full of rainwater. We attained the plateau surprisingly quickly and I walked out into the shade of giant trees, smelling of citrus blossom. A fleet of Škodas waited for us. They make Škodas here on license; Škodas are everywhere except in Ciudad itself.

I waved the cars away. It was so cool in the shade, shafts of light through the leaves, moss underfoot, even bluebells. All the trees were outsized, huge, lemon bushes the size of mangoes. Yes, there were houses carved out of fallen trunks, left open for anyone who needed them. We went into one for a rest. It had shelves, wooden plates, bowls, serving implements, a working flush toilet, electric lights, dried herbs and spices, even clothes neatly folded.

Evie had slipped in some damp moss that had smeared green down her tunic. She simply stepped out of it front of me, unfolded another tunic from a shelf, and slipped it over her head. I found that so accepting, accepting of me, this galumphing foreigner who smelled so different.

We ate a lunch of raisins, nuts, and about the only cheese they can stand, a very mild sweet cream a bit like mascarpone. Shade-resistant hemp grew on the lower levels. La Señora rolled the leaves into a kind of impromptu cigar and passed it to me. This I had not been expecting. The leaves weren't cured, but were sweet and mild. After lunch, we walked for about an hour, the Škodas rattling indiscreetly behind us.

I don't know what I expected of the *Quatoletcyl Mah*—a wire-mesh fence, perhaps, or confining rooms. Instead I suddenly noticed that Evie was not with me, only La Señora Luminosa. I did hear a sound ahead of us like children playing. And then I saw Evie walking quickly toward me, beaming so pleased, holding the hand of someone almost as tall as she was, but with loping, spidery limbs and a head that looked like the top of it had been cut off. The mouth and chin were outsize as if infected, bristling with teeth.

This is child, Evie said. *Call her Queesi.* She told her daughter my name as they say it: *Mah-ree-rah!* Queesi bellowed my name, gave a belly laugh, and flapped her hands. She liked the name or maybe me, and clumped me with a forehead kiss. Then she darted back and hid her face in her mother's shoulder.

Mahreerah equals elder. She helps us.

Queesi said, *No more sad children.* She knew exactly why I was there, and what she was. Evie was smiling at her daughter with such an expression, mingled kindness and pain.

Sad children were climbing trees picking fruit, or sitting in a circle pounding fibers for linen, or standing on concrete platforms raking what looked like walnuts but which from the smell were surely fermenting cocoa beans, the fruit flesh ragged around them. If the Colinas have a cash crop, it is chocolate. But for them it is a religious drink, unsweetened and used only for the holy days of their religion.

There were thalidomide-like deformities, nearly limbless little things carried on the backs of blind giants. There were tiny ancient-looking crones but with merry grins and goblin eyes, elderly women who were ten years old. Every imaginable genetic disease or infirmity.

Queesi gamboled back to her friends and grabbed a pestle.

Not bad sad children, Evie said. *Not bad.* I took her hand, and she looked up at me, blinking.

Little little sad to see them go, I said.

Little little, she said, and I knew she'd understood what I meant. The sad children were lovely as they were—there was a sadness that there would be fewer of them.

It was now past noon, so we took the Škodas and drove to see one of the mobile towns. Queesi clambered in next to us and bounced up and down on the springed seats.

The cars jostled over the ruts in a causeway between rice paddies. In the distance, we saw people carrying the mobile houses like oversized Arks of the Covenant. One house rested on its carrying rods between the bumpers of two Škodas. Frank Lloyd Wright called the houses architectural masterpieces. What he didn't say or perhaps even know was that each house is also a book, the writings and drawings burned into the wood.

The seasonal rice-harvest town was gathering like a herd of bison. We drove into it past houses radiating outward from one of the conical temples. You see them all across the landscape like factory chimneys. They are made of rocks cleared from fields, each tower centuries old, as rugged as their elders.

The new town was expecting me. My neck was ringed round with leis. There was another lunch—rice, manioc, nuts, and fruit. I was served a boiled duck egg (there were ducks everywhere in the rice fields). I gave a talk about the clinic and the project, mostly in Spanish. When I spoke in Colinas, there was a sigh and applause. I told them how the Council would be setting up clinics all across the country, and how the Council had a license to produce the equipment on the island. After the lecture, Colinas gave me hugs or showed me their babies. Children ran up to me and asked me questions about New York. How did they know I'd lived there? They said New York like they were from north Manhattan.

I've spent a lot of my life battling things—my mom, Santiago de los Caballeros, indeed the whole damn Cibao with its cowboy-hatted men and its shacks and the giant monument Trujillo built to himself and the lies we tell ourselves about our history. This valley looks almost the same as El Cibao, as if I'd remade the DR in a dream.

After lunch Evie and I separated—I was to go on, but she had to drop her daughter off at *Quatoletcyl Mah*. I felt bereft for a minute or two watching her car bounce away, but it was a spectacular drive back—my car zigzagged down the cliff over a sparkling sea with its clusters of bladed turbines marking shallow water, and for one heart-stopping moment down onto Ciudad itself, looking more like garden terraces than a town. It had been a wonderful day. I felt as if I had been given everything I ever wanted all at once. I have been living off that day ever since.

Sometimes countries become your own Magic Kingdom. Every detail of what people wear, how they move and laugh, what they eat, how they eat (with their fingers, scooping up soup with mashed yam or manioc, even sometimes maize), their buildings and the brushed red earth between them, or the sectioned fruit drying in the sun along the unpaved roads, and the way you can pick up the dried plums or apricots with no one to call it stealing. The island is big enough to generate its own rivers, and the water is clean enough to drink from the palm of your hand. There are windmills everywhere, of course—most of the world's windmills are built in Colinas Bravas.

All that electricity. The transatlantic phone cables surfaced here; now there are giant relay towers. Colinas Bravas has the most copious broadband in the world and they hardly use it for anything. They don't talk to us much. They watch wildlife films. And they have a ministry that keeps an eye on world news.

If there was a zombie apocalypse it couldn't get to Colinas Bravas. If the sea levels rise, we might lose the Precinct, but the town itself would climb higher up into the hills. The harbor might even improve. If there is a nuclear war, the prevailing winds will carry most of the radiation away.

THE NEXT MORNING, Evie was waiting for me outside the café. We started work again on another volunteer. Even more people crowded in, looking at the screens or over my shoulders. Too many, perhaps—I made a mess of the extraction. I just about got it out undamaged. Their ova are precious—four in a lifetime—so I said, "Let's leave it. We can wait." But they urged me on. The recipient was sitting up, watching me. They all just watched me—none of them took notes. They appear to have a very different attitude to text and books.

Evie stood next to me as I worked. *You do well well.* It was the strangest thing. She really did have the power to steady my hand. I did it for her. If anything, the next procedure was the neatest extraction and implant I'd ever done.

I kept explaining what I was doing. Right at the end, Luminosa announced, "The children will be knocked clean of genetic faults." And then in Colinas... *This child be not sad.* They don't have a future tense.

My audience had all left; I was turning off the lights and the evening bell was sounding when two tourists walked into my clinic to poke around. They wanted something. They wouldn't leave—a man and a woman, both Italian. Their English was terrible and their Spanish good enough to make bad mistakes, but they understood when I made imploring gestures and shoved my palms toward the doorway. They asked, *"Trabajo?"* and pointed at me. The woman pointed to her husband, to herself, eyes glittering. *"Medico! Medico!"*

Evie came back to fetch me and I signaled for help. She spun away. I said in any language I could think of, "Closed. Cerrado. Chiuso…"

Evie returned with two Colinas wearing thick leather aprons and trousers. Hanging from their shoulders were polished things the color of teak that looked like flutes.

Trouble? they asked me.

I want they go. I pointed my finger.

The flute-things were their guns. Guns were the very first thing the Colinas made once they understood who and what we were.

"Passports," the police demanded. The tourists understood that.

It's ALL IN the sequel that Juan Emmanuel Medrano wrote—*Return to the Country of Women.* He was the most decent of the men who had first landed on the island. Juan Emmanuel fell in love with one of them, a woman nicknamed Zena. Being a man of his time, he thought her lack of interest in sex was natural to all women who had not been corrupted. He was proud of his ability to learn how to do without sex, prescribed it in fact as the straight route to wholesomeness—chastity in marriage.

As for the Colinas, they were already aware that parthenogenesis was accumulating mutations. They have a word that means literally *unfolding snake* for a seed that sheds its skin to become something else. They were aware that their First Mother was a product of an Unfolding Snake and that they all descended from her—or rather what we know, that there must have been at a minimum five women, five different matrilineal lines. It's quite eerie now to read Juan Emmanuel's description of their beliefs. It would appear that they understood everything about DNA save for its double helix shape.

Zena married him in a spirit of self-sacrifice to see if bisexual reproduction brought health. Of course, they could not interbreed. She didn't ovulate for the duration of the marriage.

He really is a brick, poor Juan Emmanuel. He became as much of a Colina as is possible for a man. He waxes syrupy about how Motherhood is the driving engine of Colinas society, how they all dream of being a mother. *Irony alert*: all women dream of nothing but being mothers, and even if they think they don't want to be one, they are overcome with mother love the moment they see the infant. *Irony ends here.*

He never quite got, dear Juan Emmanuel, that Colinas DO have sex, some of them at least, but not just with one person. He drove Zena mad, long after the marriage was over, long after she began to turn her back every time she saw him coming. *Why did you want to be with me all the time?*

"You will come to love me," he responded. "You are my woman." The Colinas have no word for wife or husband or spouse. No one marries.

Poor Juan Emmanuel Medrano. He lived outside the walls on the tiny strip of beach still writing his wife long poems. She moved to a village on the other side of the island. Go home, the Colinas advised him. But Juan Emmanuel couldn't. He loved the place; I believe him when he says he loved Zena. How could you not believe him—look at all he gave up. He became a pathetic figure; forbidden the entire island except for what became the Precinct. He told stories for visitors, set up a hotel, waited out the winter season, and wrote a lexicon and grammar of the Colinas language which is still the best we have. Hollywood made a movie about him starring Humphrey Bogart— he mans the artillery that sink the British gunboats. *Irony alert*: of course those women needed a man to defend them. Ingrid Bergman won an Oscar for playing Zena. In the Foreign House, they still sing that song. Play it for me, Sam.

THAT NIGHT LA Señora invited me to dinner. The room was no bigger than any of the others, a two-chamber hollow in the rock. The walls were covered with beautiful paintings. One of the few things they import from us is oil-based pigments. La Señora explained who had painted what—lots of portraits and bowls of fruit, not great art, but all of it colorful and fun.

They had the money to import something else. Four of the women scurried out and came back laboring under a huge canvas. My breath caught and I sputtered with recognition as if the Queen of England had just walked in—it was one of Monet's giant water lily paintings. I remembered the scandal in France when it had been sold.

It is like us, one of them said, and left it leaning against the wall.

The room had no TV; there was no computer. I asked Luminosa why not. She said they had tried our movies but they were all full of murder or marriage. "We like the cartoons for kids. But in *Wall-E* two robots get married. Why would robots get married? A doll of a cowgirl and a doll of a spaceman get married. Even *things* get married." She shook her head.

The girls started to run in with elaborate clothes. They hauled me to my feet and took off my old khaki. I felt fat and sagging like I needed a scaffolding to hold me up. They pulled over my head a gelabia with black applique. Then a kind of red velvet cape that made me feel like Red Riding Hood. They started swapping clothes, too—butterfly saris, shawls of black lace, Kevlar body armor. Their laughter bounded off the rock and straight into my head.

The Colinas don't own anything.

My DAYS BEGAN to be the same. I asked to be taken up onto the plateau again. I especially wanted to see the container port and the factories. Finally Luminosa said that it was policy not to allow anyone to see their factories.

Luminosa insisted on taking over one of the implants herself, asking me to guide her, and then—without asking me—signaled Evie to try. That was clever of her—I wanted Evie to do well. "*Sí, sí, esa es la manera de hacerlo!*"

Evie and I would walk back to the Foreign House, long after the bell, long after the tourists cleared.

About a week in.

We're walking through dusk and candlelight and all those lovely sounds and I'm holding her hand. But tonight for some reason, fireworks. Tourists are lining the high walls of the Custom House, applauding and raising glasses of champagne.

We're looking up and Evie says, *You write me yes when you go home.*

"Yes yes okay yes."

We have Sky-pee.

And I chuckle. "You use Skype? And Facebook?"

Sky-pee yes. No Facebook No Twits.

"Why not?"

Sky-pee one person, one person. She holds up two fingers.

I can't think of a way to say *Just you and me* in her language. I manage *We talk much* and she giggles and shakes her head, which means yes, but still feels like no to me.

That night I go to bed in the Foreign House and it's like my very bones are humming, and I see her and I see me. I see me taking one half of my DNA and putting it into her egg. I see us having a child together. I'll carry it if they say we can't, that the child might lose parthenogenesis. And she and I will live together with our child in one of those towns, next to forests of oranges, mangoes, and quince, and I'll keep helping their babies to be born.

I felt elated the whole of the next day; I could feel my face make nice shapes; I could see me sparking laughter in other people. That night I asked Evie if she wanted to see my room—that's allowed, she is a Colina, she can go anywhere. The room made her giggle. She ran into the bathroom and flicked the lights, flushed the toilet and turned on the TV—and great, yes, it was *CSI* and they were cutting up a corpse—but for some reason that seemed to be the funniest thing she'd ever seen and she flung herself onto the bed and bounced up and down on it.

Too ripe. Couldn't sleep here.

She stretched out and I couldn't help giving her a kiss. I hugged her and rolled her back and forth, back and forth. She wasn't laughing but looked both troubled and awed, so I kissed her again, open-mouthed this time, and I felt her chest rise up in response.

I would never force myself on anyone. But there are Colinas who want sex. They are not arrested or mocked, but they are regarded as being different. A holdover from the days of change those 1,700 years ago. We didn't do anything adventurous that first night but I couldn't stop myself saying, "I love you." She slipped away and gave a wave with just the tips of her fingers. I watched from my window as she walked through the Plaza at 11:30 p.m.

The next day, Evie looked merry. I thought I had made her happy. She stood up straighter and her eyes looked that bit narrower, as if she had learned something new. She snatched things from people and wagged her hips as if to mock them. Her friends laughed louder or gaped in a caricature of open-mouthed shock, pretending (it seemed to me) to be scandalized. One of the elders came in and clapped her hands and said something outraged and schoolmarmish. I couldn't help but smile and shake my head. The older woman glared at me. *What am I, then, a ringleader? A bad influence?* I dipped my chin, crumpled my lips, and laughed. Evie caught my look, laughed and clapped her hands. *Okay, I am a bad influence, what are you going to do about it?*

That night, long after bedtime, we went for a walk in the Precinct, listening to small waves rolling pebbles back into the water. Out to sea all those floating hotels, container ships, or private yachts. Ciudad was silent now and dark, and Evie's eyes were wide, thrilled but also scared. She insisted we go into a bar.

Immediately two women strode up, wanting to talk. One of them pinned us to the table by saying she'd buy us some drinks. The other squared off with me and asked us outright—how did we meet? How did I know her? They asked her questions about how the Colinas got pregnant and had to be told several times. Twice I explained that Colinas did not form relationships with each other as we understood it. Evie sipped her whisky and hated it, her lips turning down, her nose wrinkling. The two women laughed and one said, "You drink it like this," and knocked the shot back down in one.

The questions didn't stop, of her, of me. What are the houses like inside? What do you mean they don't own anything—they've sewn up the world market in all kinds of things. Other couples shuffled closer, stood in a huddle trying to hear, desperate to actually meet a Colina. Do you go to school? What music do you like? Have you heard of a singer called Mariah Carey?

I said we had to be away. One them said no, stay, the next round's on me. I was worried but Evie seemed to like it. The bar was playing Whitney Houston's "I Wanna Dance with Somebody" and before I knew it, one of the women had made off with my girlfriend. The woman danced like Will Smith making fun of old black men—was she really doing the boogaloo? Evie tried to dance then shook her head, stepped back, and just watched.

"No—come on, you're supposed to join in!"

I got worried. I got mad. I strode up to both of them and said in Colina, *Bedtime. Sleep now.*

Evie smiled and did a head-wobble that I thought meant yes, because it was indeed time to go.

"Spiriting her away, are you?"

As I bundled her off, I told them over my shoulder that Evie had to be up at four and all the other Colinas would be in bed. The woman turned sideways and rumpled her lip at me—*I know what you're up to.*

I felt guilty and sore, like I'd overdone a workout in the gym, and my heartfelt bigger, swollen with misgiving because I was beginning to see that what I wanted would not be possible. I asked Evie to come to my room, and she nodded her head up and down exaggeratedly like a child, which meant no. But I reacted like she'd said yes and pulled her with me. She started to giggle and also to shake, but I got her into the room and hugged her and said, "Stay with me."

We rolled on the bed again and this time I traced her nipples with my tongue down to her joybox and kissed her there. She had a clitoris (though people say they don't) and kissing it had the usual effect. She did not kiss me back—but I thought, give it time. The ache inside was gone: She was mine. More or less fully clothed, I slept. When I woke up again about two, she was gone.

The next day at the clinic she whispered, "I don't see you again." I felt like I just swallowed a barium meal, my throat and esophagus coated all the way to my nauseous stomach.

"I'm sorry. I'm sorry if we went too far."

I thought I knew what the trouble was. Again, no words in Colina. "My intentions are strictly honorable," I said in English as a joke and mimed a chuckle. I couldn't find a light, jokey way to say it even in Spanish.

I told her, *Not that thing only. Good thing.* I had no way to say, "It's not just the sex, I want to be your partner." She sighed and looked back at me glumly and seemed to shrink.

I had to say it in Spanish. 'I... want... to... marry... you.' I hammered each word like a nail.

She stared blankly, eyes on the floor, and then abruptly streamed out through the archway.

I thought I was in love; I thought this was it; I thought we'd have a child; I thought I'd live here—I saw it all in front of me, a beautiful new life. And I'd lost it. I hated myself for having sex. I held my head in my hands and paced and called myself stupid. Why ruin everything for sex, when what I wanted was a wife? I had completely misunderstood the problem.

In the morning, full of determination, I went to the Civil Palace to see La Señora Luminosa and declare myself. It was still dark, but the stars seemed to make a promise. I could hear the waves and seagulls and slippered feet. It was early even for them. I knew what I was going to do and felt solemn, determined, even brave.

In the Palace, Luminosa was lighting candles, her face a bit puffy from having just woken up. Another elder shuffled forward and yawned.

"I've done a terrible thing," I said. "I... Evie and me..."

"She was in your room and you had sex. Not so terrible." She didn't even look at me.

"No. You don't understand. I didn't force myself on her or anything. But I'm not sure she was ready for it."

Luminosa said Evie's Colina name in surprise. "Eouvwetzixityl? If she didn't want it, it wouldn't happen." The old woman looked amused. "She was curious, I think. And I believe she likes it." Luminosa stood up and looked straight at me, a half-smile on her face. "So have you confessed enough?"

"I want you to know, I wasn't just toying with her, or exploiting her."

"You couldn't."

"I want to marry her."

Both women stopped, looked at each other, and then started to laugh. The elder made a kind of squawk, covered her mouth, and had to turn her back. Luminosa groaned, "Oh no!"

"I... I... I... could live here. I... we... we could have a child. You know, me contribute to the gene pool." That was my attempt to join in with what I thought was a robust and hearty reaction.

Luminosa shook her head. "Women do this, too?"

"We fall in love, yes."

The elder woman howled with laughter and ran off, calling out names.

Luminosa sighed. "You can't marry. We have no such category in law. And there is no question of you being able to stay and live with us. It was in your contract."

I began to feel cold, but with sweat along my hairline. "Well, well, I think we ought to hear from Evie."

"We will." She went back to lighting candles. I began to hear from outside cries and shouts, doors slamming and the usual morning sounds of running feet, perhaps with more laughter than usual.

The Colinas gawped at me feverishly, eyes glistening. They chattered and roared with laughter. Evie strode in, her back rigid, eyes wide, hands clasped in front of her like a choirboy trying to make the toilet in time.

Luminosa said, her voice going brassy, *Foreigner wants to do Medrano with you.*

Bouquets of faces crammed through the doorway, and they all roared with laughter. Evie looked mortified and also weary at the same time. At that moment, my only concern was for her.

Why do this? she asked me. *You want me inside you like a baby!* I remember that phrase because it was so strange. But she had no word for ownership. She couldn't say: *Why do you want to own me?* Both hands were curled into claws of frustration. She spun on her heel and pushed her way through the throng.

I began to realize just how big a catastrophe this was.

They would tell me to leave; they would tell SingleHelix the reason why. It's part of our ethos never to proposition the single women we help all over the world. I would have to leave the company, maybe the country: Santo Domingo has very few jobs in the field.

"Start today's clinic," advised Luminosa.

Evie did not visit that day or the next. No one said much else about it, though some of the students' jaws swelled with suppressed laughter. *How you have baby with Evie she has baby coming?* one of them asked. *Why Evie want three babies?* Each time one of them asked a question like that there was shrill, speeded-up laughter as if flowers had learned how to chuckle.

Nobody asked me to climb the hill again or to eat with them. When the evening bell tolled, I had to vacate the Plaza. I went to the Foreign House and waited in that downstairs bar, pacing, clutching a gin, staring out at the Plaza. It looked empty but rang with laughter and that made me wonder if they were telling jokes about me. I hoped Evie would come. I waited long after nine p.m. when all was still and dark, thinking that she might slip away when she thought nobody could see. Finally the barista said I should get some sleep, as she folded the big iron shutters and slipped bolts into the floor.

Two days later I was asked to attend a breakfast in the Palace. I knew what it was about. There were nuts and fruit and cheese. The elders thanked me for a job well done. They said they were particularly pleased by my teaching and all the efforts I had made to fit in, and to show interest in and respect for their culture. I was to receive a ten thousand dollar bonus.

"And don't worry—we have said not a thing about Evie to your... your... owners." Luminosa's smile was like the Mona Lisa's.

I spent another night pacing in the bar, listening to that sound of laughter, singing, prayer—nightmarish. It wasn't just losing Evie. I was losing that sound, I was losing a country. I couldn't believe that I would have to go back to Santo Domingo and the Agora Mall, with its McDonald's and its Apple Store and its pharmacy that sold ultraviolet toothbrush sterilizers for fifty bucks. The world felt like an apple withering with age.

That night was fireworks again and the hotel's doors were open, and I glanced about me as the sky boomed and battered and kept blossoming out like flowers, and I gathered myself up, darted around the black cloth partitions that separated us from the Plaza. And I ran. I pounded across the pavement, imagining that I was being chased. I ran past the bougainvillea front of what had been my clinic, up the main steps, and then along each of the terraces, as if in panic, looking through each open archway, checking rooms full of flickering light and surprised faces. No Evie, no Luminosa, room after room.

Finally I found Luminosa sitting on the floor playing poker with three others. I collapsed at their feet and sobbed, "Please let me stay. Please. I'll be good. I'll stay away from Evie. She won't ever see me again. Send me out to a town on the plateau. Send me to the north. I can help sell machines. I speak the language. Only let me stay, please, please let me stay." I kept it up until even I couldn't make sense of what I was saying. All that time, Luminosa stroked my hair and hugged me. Finally I calmed down, and, exhausted, I let myself be led away.

But I didn't leave.

Now I work in the Precinct for the Disney Corporation in their big hotel at the end of the strip. Classy, with facades made of the local sandstone, vast interiors with polished marble floors and lots of locked doors. I speak Spanish, English, and of course Colina, and I have a charming little story to tell of how I came here and fell in love with the place, only I don't mention that I am not allowed back in. The guests sit rapt with attention. "Oh, I would love to see inside one of their homes." And I correct them with pained tolerance. "Oh, that is the thing. They don't have homes. They really don't own anything."

On fireworks nights I get to stand on the wall and look out over the Plaza with its steps and songs and chants and running feet and those lights darting about like fireflies, and I always marvel how it is that you almost never see them.

Or I sit in my room at the Buena Vista Hotel where the broadband is amazing and I see every episode of *Mad Folk* and *Game of Thrones*. Evie never answers my calls on Skype. Sometimes I crunch along the beach after even the Precinct has gone to bed, except for the odd drunken tourist, sometimes men looking shaken, miserable, fists bunched. They teach me, those men, the cost of desire.

Last night I had a dream: I was hiking again with Dad. He used to take me up into the mountains—a two-day trek to Pico Duarte where it's cold, and frost dances in the air and breaks the sunlight up into rainbows.

Only this time we were walking in Colinas Bravas, and I was overjoyed they'd let him in, and then I realized that this was actually the Cibao, but a different Cibao, a Cibao that they ruled. As if somehow world history had been reversed and the Taíno still ruled Española and Europe had been settled by them. Dad and I sat on top of a cliff and let the wind blow over us.

I didn't get along with my mother. She hated how I turned out, but so often we become like our parents, don't we? She was a good Catholic who believed in original sin. Have I made up that she once said those women of Colinas must be a different species because they don't know original sin?

If she did, then I think my mother was right.

Original sin is having two sexes, one of whom doesn't carry the child, who needs to know the child is HIS and in so doing needs to know the woman is HIS, and in time, since it's a deal, he has to be HERS as well. If you absolutely must own the person you love most, then how important is owning everything else you love or like? Your book, your designer evening gown, your phone, your knife and fork (even just for the duration of the meal!), your piece of bacon, your slice of orange, your car, your home, your room, your bed, your individual sock with the green toes, let alone your own child. Owning becomes the culture, possession nine points of the law.

Except in Colinas Bravas.

They love the name Colinas Bravas, it chimes with how they see their country and perhaps themselves: the brave hills. But their own name for the place is the third person of their verb to be—"*Ser*" in Spanish. Transcription: *Xix*. The land just is. Not even the land is theirs. It's not England or even Herland.

The opposite of original sin is faith and here's mine.

I am, despite everything, a good person and soon they will see that. I've become a visibly better person living here. I don't need to own Evie, I don't need to own anything. I love this place and will do all I can to help it, out of love.

I write to La Señora Luminosa with ideas—your people love telling stories, I say. Why don't you let me record them, write them down, publish them in English, in Spanish. You tell them on your radio station. Let me put a satellite radio in the cover of the book so that people can listen and read at the same time? A tablet in the cover so that they can see more about you? Why don't you run your own TV station so that you can finally watch things on it that are made for you? Let me do a website for you. Let me help sell your windmills all over the Americas in Spanish and in English.

I work to become like them.

I lie awake and listen to pebbles hiss on that beach and I try to cast off owning. I have only my rucksack and khaki and my hotel slacks and shirt. Over and over I visualize my womb, my ovum, imagine a jink in my belly and that a snake unfolds inside me, and I see myself marching to Luminosa chaste but pregnant and saying "behold." I establish a sixth matrilineal line. I imagine this and as I drift off to sleep, I hear that sound, the waves of laughter.

One day, they will let me back in.

SEASONS OF GLASS AND IRON
Amal El-Mohtar

Amal El-Mohtar (amalelmohtar.com) is a writer, editor and critic. Her short fiction has won the Locus Award and been nominated for the Nebula, World Fantasy and Aurora awards, while her poetry has won the Rhysling award three times. Her work has appeared in *Lightspeed*, *Strange Horizons*, *Uncanny*, and *The Djinn Falls in Love & Other Stories*. She reviews books for NPR, edits Goblin Fruit, and lives in Ottawa with her partner and two cats.

For Lara West

TABITHA WALKS, AND thinks of shoes.

She has been thinking about shoes for a very long time: the length of three and a half pairs, to be precise, though it's hard to reckon in iron. Easier to reckon how many pairs are left: of the seven she set out with, three remain, strapped securely against the outside of the pack she carries, weighing it down. The seasons won't keep still, slip past her with the landscape, so she can't say for certain whether a year of walking wears out a sole, but it seems about right. She always means to count the steps, starting with the next pair, but it's easy to get distracted.

She thinks about shoes because she cannot move forward otherwise: each iron strap cuts, rubs, bruises, blisters, and her pain fuels their ability to cross rivers, mountains, airy breaches between cliffs. She must move forward, or the shoes will never be worn down. The shoes must be worn down.

It's always hard to strap on a new pair.

Three pairs of shoes ago, she was in a pine forest, and the sharp green smell of it woke something in her, something that was more than numbness, numbers. (*Number? I hardly know 'er!* She'd laughed for a week, off and on, at her little joke.) She shivered in the needled light, bundled her arms into her fur cloak but stretched her toes into the autumn earth, and wept to feel, for a moment, something like free—before the numbers crept in with the cold, and *one down, six to go* found its way into her relief that it was, in fact, possible to get through a single pair in a lifetime.

Two pairs of shoes ago, she was in the middle of a lake, striding across the deep blue of it, when the last scrap of sole gave way. She collapsed and floundered as she undid the straps, scrambled to pull the next pair off her pack, sank until she broke a toe in jamming them on, then found herself on the surface again, limping toward the far shore.

One pair of shoes ago, she was by the sea. She soaked her feet in salt and stared up at the stars and wondered whether drowning would hurt.

She recalls shoes her brothers have worn: a pair of seven-league boots, tooled in soft leather; winged sandals; satin slippers that turned one invisible. How strange, she thinks, that her brothers had shoes that lightened their steps and tightened the world, made it small and easy to explore, discover.

Perhaps, she thinks, it isn't strange at all: why shouldn't shoes help their wearers travel? Perhaps, she thinks, what's strange is the shoes women are made to wear: shoes of glass; shoes of paper; shoes of iron heated red-hot; shoes to dance to death in.

How strange, she thinks, and walks.

Amira makes an art of stillness.

She sits atop a high glass hill, its summit shaped into a throne of sorts, thick and smooth, perfectly suited to her so long as she does not move. Magic girdles her, roots her stillness through the throne. She has weathered storms here, the sleek-fingered rain glistening between glass and gown, hair and skin, seeking to shift her this way or that—but she has held herself straight, upright, a golden apple in her lap.

She is sometimes hungry, but the magic looks after that; she is often tired, and the magic encourages sleep. The magic keeps her brown skin from burning during the day, and keeps her silkshod feet from freezing at night—

so long as she is still, so long as she keeps her glass seat atop her glass hill.

From her vantage point she can see a great deal: farmers working their land; travelers walking from village to village; the occasional robbery or murder. There is much she would like to come down from her hill and tell people, but for the suitors.

Clustered and clamoring around the bottom of her glass hill are the knights, princes, shepherds' lads who have fallen violently in love with her. They shout encouragement to one another as they ride their warhorses up the glass hill, breaking against it in wave after wave, reaching for her.

As they slide down the hill, their horses foaming, legs twisted or shattered, they scream curses at her: the cunt, the witch, can't she see what she's doing to them, glass whore on a glass hill, they'll get her tomorrow, tomorrow, tomorrow.

Amira grips her golden apple. By day she distracts herself with birds: all the wild geese who fly overhead, the gulls and swifts and swallows, the larks. She remembers a story about nettle shirts thrown up to swans, and wonders if she could reach up and pluck a feather from them to give herself wings.

By night, she strings shapes around the stars, imagines familiar constellations into difference: suppose the great ladle was a sickle instead, or a bear? When she runs out of birds and stars, she remembers that she chose this.

TABITHA FIRST SEES the glass hill as a knife's edge of light, scything a green swathe across her vision before she can look away. She is stepping out of a forest; the morning sun is vicious, bright with no heat in it; the frosted grass crunches under the press of her iron heels, but some of it melts cold relief against the skin exposed through the straps.

She sits at the forest's edge and watches the light change.

There are men at the base of the hill; their noise is a dull ringing that reminds her of the ocean. She watches them spur their horses into bleeding. Strong magic in that hill, she thinks, to make men behave so foolishly; strong magic in that hill to withstand so many iron hooves.

She looks down at her own feet, then up at the hill. She reckons the quality of her pain in numbers, but not by degree: if her pain is a six it is because it is cold, blue with an edge to it; if her pain is a seven it is red, inflamed, bleeding; if her pain is a three it has a rounded yellow feel, dull and perhaps draining infection.

Her pain at present is a five, green and brown, sturdy and stable, and ought to be enough to manage the ascent.

She waits until sunset, and sets out across the clearing.

AMIRA WATCHES A mist rise as the sun sets, and her heart sings to see everything made so soft: a great cool hush over all, a smell of water with no stink in it, no blood or sweat. She loves to see the world so vanished, so quiet, so calm.

Her heart skips a beat when she hears the scraping, somewhere beneath her, somewhere within the mist: a grinding, scouring sort of noise, steady as her nerves aren't, because something is climbing the glass hill and this isn't how it was supposed to work, no one is supposed to be able to reach her, but magic is magic is magic and there is always stronger magic—She thinks it is a bear, at first, then sees it is a furred hood, glimpses a pale delicate chin beneath it, a wide mouth twisted into a teeth-gritting snarl from the effort of the climb.

Amira stares, uncertain, as the hooded, horseless stranger reaches the top, and stops, and stoops, and pants, and sheds the warm weight of the fur. Amira sees a woman, and the woman sees her, and the woman looks like a feather and a sword and very, very hungry.

Amira offers up her golden apple without a word.

TABITHA HAD THOUGHT the woman in front of her a statue, a copper ornament, an idol, until her arm moved. Some part of her feels she should pause before accepting food from a magical woman on a glass hill, but it's dwarfed by a ravenousness she's not felt in weeks; in the shoes, she mostly forgets about her stomach until weakness threatens to prevent her from putting one foot in front of the other.

The apple doesn't look like food, but she bites into it, and the skin breaks like burnt sugar, the flesh drips clear, sweet juice. She eats it, core and all, before looking at the woman on the throne again and saying—with a gruffness she does not feel or intend—"Thank you."

"My name is Amira," says the woman, and Tabitha marvels at how she speaks without moving any other part of her body, how measured are the mechanics of her mouth. "Have you come to marry me?"

Tabitha stares. She wipes the juice from her chin, as if that could erase the golden apple from her belly. "Do I have to?"

Amira blinks. "No. Only—that's why people try to climb the hill, you know."

"Oh. No, I just—" Tabitha coughs, slightly, embarrassed. "I'm just passing through."

Silence.

"The mist was thick, I got turned around—"

"You climbed"—Amira's voice is very quiet—"a glass hill"—and even—"by accident?"

Tabitha fidgets with the hem of her shirt.

"Well," says Amira, "it's nice to meet you, ah—"

"Tabitha."

"Yes. Very nice to meet you, Tabitha."

Further silence. Tabitha chews her bottom lip while looking down into the darkness at the base of the hill. Then, quietly: "Why are you even up here?"

Amira looks at her coolly. "By accident."

Tabitha snorts. "I see. Very well. Look." Tabitha points to her iron-strapped feet. "I have to wear the shoes down. They're magic. I have a notion that the stranger the surface—the harder it would be to walk on something usually—the faster the sole diminishes. So your magical hill here..."

Amira nods, or at least it seems to Tabitha that she nods—it may have been more of a lengthened blink that conveyed the impression of her head's movement.

"... it seemed like just the thing. I didn't know there was anyone at the top, though; I waited until the men at the bottom had left, as they seemed a nasty lot—"

It isn't that Amira shivers, but that the quality of her stillness grows denser. Tabitha feels something like alarm beginning a dull ring in her belly.

"They leave as the nights turn colder. You're more than welcome to stay," says Amira, in tones of deepest courtesy, "and scrape your shoes against the glass."

Tabitha nods, and stays, because somewhere within the measured music of Amira's words she hears please.

*   *   *

AMIRA FEELS HALF-asleep, sitting and speaking with someone who isn't about to destroy her, break her apart for the half kingdom inside.

"Have they placed you up here?" Tabitha asks, and Amira finds it strange to hear anger that isn't directed at her, anger that seems at her service.

"No," she says softly. "I chose this." Then, before Tabitha can say anything else, "Why do you walk in iron shoes?"

Tabitha's mouth is open but her words are stopped up, and Amira can see them changing direction like a flock of starlings in her throat. She decides to change the subject.

"Have you ever heard the sound geese make when they fly overhead? I don't mean the honking, everyone hears that, but—their wings. Have you ever heard the sound of their wings?"

Tabitha smiles a little. "Like thunder, when they take off from a river."

"What? Oh." A pause; Amira has never seen a river. "No—it's nothing like that when they fly above you. It's... a creaking, like a stove door with no squeak in it, as if the geese are machines dressed in flesh and feathers. It's a beautiful sound—beneath the honking it's a low drone, but if they're flying quietly, it's like... clothing, somehow, like if you listened just right, you might find yourself wearing wings."

Without noticing, Amira had closed her eyes while speaking of the geese; she opens them to see Tabitha looking at her with curious focus, and feels briefly disoriented by the scrutiny. She isn't used to being listened to.

"If we're lucky," she says softly, turning a golden apple around and around in her hands, "we'll hear some tonight. It's the right time of year."

TABITHA OPENS HER mouth, then shuts it so hard her back teeth meet. She does not ask how long have you been sitting here, that you know when to expect the geese; she does not ask *where did that golden apple come from? Didn't I just eat it?* She understands what Amira is doing and is grateful; she does not want to talk about the shoes.

"I've never heard that sound," she says instead, slowly, trying not to look at the apple. "But I've seen them on rivers and lakes. Hundreds at a time, clamoring like old wives at a well, until something startles them into rising, and then it's like drums, or thunder, or a storm of winds through branches. An enormous sound, almost deafening—not one to listen closely for."

"I would love to hear that," Amira whispers, looking out toward the woods. "To see them. What do they look like?"

"Thick, dark—" Tabitha reaches for words. "Like the river itself is rising, lifting its skirts and taking off."

Amira smiles, and Tabitha feels a tangled warmth in her chest at the thought of having given her something.

"WOULD YOU LIKE another apple?" offers Amira, and notes the wariness in Tabitha's eye. "They keep coming back. I eat them myself from time to time. I wasn't sure if—I thought it was meant as a prize for whoever climbed the hill, but I suppose the notion is they don't go away unless I give them to a man."

Tabitha frowns, but accepts. As she eats, Amira feels Tabitha's eyes on her empty hands, waiting to catch the apple's reappearance, and tries not to smile—she'd done as much herself the first fifty or so times, testing the magic for loopholes. Novel, however, to watch someone watching for the apple.

As Tabitha nears the last bite, Amira sees her look confused, distracted, as if by a hair on her tongue or an unfamiliar smell— and then the apple's in Amira's hand again, feeling for all the world like it never left.

"I don't think the magic lets us see it happen," says Amira, almost by way of apology for Tabitha's evident disappointment. "But so long as I sit here, I have one."

"I'd like to try that again," says Tabitha, and Amira smiles.

FIRST, TABITHA WAITS. She counts the seconds, watching Amira's empty hands. After seven hundred seconds, there is an apple in Amira's hand. Amira stares at it, looking from it to the one in Tabitha's.

"That's—never happened before. I didn't think there could be more than one at a time."

Tabitha takes the second apple from her but bites into it, counting the mouthfuls slowly, watching Amira's hands the while. After the seventh bite, Amira's hands are full again. She hands the third apple over without a word.

Tabitha counts—the moments, the bites, the number of apples—until there are seven in her lap; when she takes an eighth from Amira, the first seven turn to sand.

"I think it's the magic on me," says Tabitha thoughtfully, dusting the apple sand out of her fur. "I'm bound in sevens—you're bound in ones. You can hold only one apple at a time—I can hold seven. Funny, isn't it?"

Amira's smile looks strained and vague, and only after a moment does Tabitha realize she's watching the wind-caught sand blowing off the hill.

AUTUMN CRACKLES INTO winter, and frost rimes the glass hill into diamonds. By day, Amira watches fewer and fewer men slide down it while Tabitha sits by her, huddled into her fur; by night, Tabitha walks in slow circles around her as they talk about anything but glass and iron. While Tabitha walks, Amira looks more closely at her shackled feet, always glancing away before she can be drawn into staring. Through the sandal-like straps that wrap up to her ankle, Amira can see they are blackened, twisted ruins, toes bent at odd angles, scabbed and scarred.

One morning, Amira wakes to surprising warmth, and finds Tabitha's fur draped around her. She is so startled she almost rises from her seat to find her— has she left? Is she gone?—but Tabitha walks briskly back into her line of sight before Amira can do anything drastic, rubbing her thin arms, blowing on her fingers. Amira is aghast.

"Why did you give me your cloak? Take it back!"

"Your lips were turning blue in your sleep, and you can't *move*—"

"It's all right, Tabitha, please—" The desperation in Amira's voice stops Tabitha's circling, pins her in place. Reluctantly, she takes her fur back, draws it over her own shoulders again. "The apples—or the hill itself, I'm not sure— keep me warm enough. Here, have another."

Tabitha looks unconvinced. "But you looked so cold—"

"Perhaps it's like your feet," says Amira, before she can stop herself. "They look broken, but you can still walk on them."

*   *   *

TABITHA STARES AT her for a long moment, before accepting the apple. "They feel broken too. Although"—shifting her gaze to the apple, lowering her voice—"less and less, lately."

She takes a bite. While she eats, Amira ventures, quietly, "I thought you'd left."

Tabitha raises an eyebrow, swallows, and chuckles. "Without my cloak, in winter? I like you, Amira, but—" *Not that much* dies on her tongue, as she tastes the lie in it. She coughs. "That would be silly. Anyway, I wouldn't leave you without saying good-bye." An uncertain pause then. "Though, if you tire of company—"

"No," says Amira, swiftly, surely. "No."

SNOW FALLS, AND the last of the suitors abandon their camps, grumbling home. Tabitha walks her circles around Amira's throne by day now as well as night, unafraid of being seen.

"They won't be back until spring," says Amira, smiling. "Though then they keep their efforts up well into the night as the days get longer. Perhaps to make up for lost time."

Tabitha frowns, and something in the circle of their talk tightens enough for her to ask, as she walks, "How many winters have you spent up here?"

Amira shrugs. "Three, I think. How many winters have you spent in those shoes?"

"This is their first," says Tabitha, pausing. "But there were three pairs before this one."

"Ah. Is this the last?"

Tabitha chuckles. "No. Seven in all. And I'm only halfway through this one."

Amira nods. "Perhaps, come spring, you'll have finished it."

"Perhaps," says Tabitha, before beginning her circuit again.

WINTER THAWS, AND everything smells of snowmelt and wet wood. Tabitha ventures down the glass hill and brings Amira snowdrops, twining them into her dark hair. "They look like stars," murmurs Tabitha, and something in Amira creaks and snaps like ice on a bough.

"Tabitha," she says, "it's almost spring."

"Mm," says Tabitha, intent on a tricky braid.

"I'd like—" Amira draws a deep, quiet breath. "I'd like to tell you a story."

Tabitha pauses—then, resuming her braiding, says, "I'd like to hear one."

"I don't know if I'm any good at telling stories," Amira adds, turning a golden apple over and over in her hands, "but that's no reason not to try."

ONCE UPON A time there was a rich king who had no sons, and whose only daughter was too beautiful. She was so beautiful that men could not stop themselves from reaching out to touch her in corridors or following her to her rooms, so beautiful that words of desire tumbled from men's lips like diamonds and toads, irresistible and unstoppable. The king took pity on these men and drew his daughter aside, saying, Daughter, only a husband can break the spell over these men; only a husband can prevent them from behaving so gallantly toward you.

When the king's daughter suggested a ball, that these men might find husbands for themselves and so be civilized, the king was not amused. You must be wed, said the king, before some guard cannot but help himself to your virtue.

The king's daughter was afraid, and said, Suppose you sent me away?

No, said the king, for how should I keep an eye on you then?

The king's daughter, who did not want a husband, said, Suppose you chose a neighboring prince for me?

Impossible, said the king, for you are my only daughter, and I cannot favor one neighbor over another; the balance of power is precarious and complicated.

The king's daughter read an unspeakable conclusion in her father's eye, and in a rush to keep it from reaching his mouth, said, Suppose you placed me atop a glass hill where none could reach me, and say that only the man who can ride up the hill in full armor may claim me as his bride?

But that is an impossible task, said the king, looking thoughtful.

Then you may keep your kingdom whole, and your eye on me, and men safe from me, said his daughter.

It was done just as she said, and by her will. And if she's not gone, she lives there still.

* * *

WHEN AMIRA STOPS speaking, she is taken aback to feel Tabitha scowling at her.

"That," growls Tabitha, "is *absurd*."

Amira blinks. She had expected, she realizes, some sympathy, some understanding. "Oh?"

"What father seeks to protect men from their pursuit of his daughter? As well seek to protect the wolf from the rabbit!"

"I am not a rabbit," says Amira, though Tabitha, who has dropped her hair and is pacing, incensed, continues.

"How could it be your fault that men are loutish and ill mannered? Amira, I promise you, if your hair were straw and your face dull as dishwater, men— bad men—would still behave this way. Do you think the suitors around the hill can see what you look like, all the way up here?"

Amira keeps quiet, unsure what to say—she wonders why she wants to apologize with one side of her mouth and defend herself with the other.

"You said you chose this," Tabitha spits. "What manner of choice was that? A wolf's maw or a glass hill."

"On the hill," says Amira, lips tight, "I want for nothing. I do not need food or drink or shelter. No one can touch me. That's all I ever wanted—for no one to be able to touch me. So long as I sit here, and eat apples, and do not move, I have everything I want."

Tabitha is silent for a moment. Then, more gently than before, she says, "I thought you wanted to see a river full of geese."

Amira says nothing.

Tabitha says, still more gently, "Mine are not the only iron shoes in the world."

Still nothing. Amira's heart grinds within her, until Tabitha sighs.

"Let me tell you a story about iron shoes."

ONCE UPON A time, a woman fell in love with a bear. She didn't mean to; it was only that he was both fearsome and kind to her, that he was dangerous and clever and could teach her about hunting salmon and harvesting wild honey, and she had been lonely for a long time. She felt special with his eyes on her, for what other woman could say she was loved by a bear without being torn between his teeth? She loved him for loving her as he loved no one else.

They were wed, and at night the bear put on a man's shape to share her bed in the dark. At first he was gentle and kind, and the woman was happy; but in time the bear began to change—not his shape, which she knew as well as her own, but his manner. He grew bitter and jealous, accused her of longing for a bear who was a man day and night. He said she was a terrible wife who knew nothing of how to please bears. By day he spoke to her in a language of thorns and claws, and by night he hurt her with his body. It was hard for the woman to endure, but how can one love a bear entirely without pain? She only worked harder to please him.

In the seventh year of their marriage, the woman begged her husband to allow her to go visit her family. He consented to her departure on the condition that she not be alone with her mother, for surely her mother would poison her against him. She promised—but the woman's mother saw the marks on her, the bruises and scratches, and hurried her into a room alone. In a moment of weakness, the woman listened to her mother's words against her husband, calling him a monster, a demon. Her mother insisted that she leave him—but how could she? He was still her own dear husband in spite of it all—she only wished him to be as he had been when she first married him. Perhaps he was under a curse, after all, and only she could lift it?

Burn his bear skin, said her mother. Perhaps that is his curse. Perhaps he longs to be a man day and night but is forbidden to say so.

When she returned to her husband, he seemed to have missed her, and was kind and sweet with her. In the night while he slept next to her in his man's shape, she gathered up his bear skin as quietly as she could, built up the fire, and threw it in.

The skin did not burn. But it began to scream.

It woke her husband, who flew into a great rage, saying she had broken her promise to him. When the woman wept that she had only wanted to free him from his curse, he picked up the skin, tossed it over her shoulders, and threw a bag of iron shoes at her feet. He said that the only way to make him a man day and night was to wear his bear's skin while wearing out seven pairs of iron shoes, one for each year of their marriage.

So she set out to do so.

* * *

AMIRA'S EYES ARE wide and rimmed in red, and Tabitha flushes, picks at a burr caught in her husband's fur.

"I knew marriage was monstrous," says Amira, "but I never imagined—"

Tabitha shrugs. "It wasn't all bad. And I broke my promise—if I hadn't seen my mother, I would never have thought to try and burn the skin. Promises are important to bears. This, here"—she gestures at the glass hill—"this is monstrous: to keep you prisoner, to prevent you from moving or speaking—"

"Your husband wanted to keep you from speaking! To your *mother*!"

"And look what happened when I did," says Tabitha stiffly. "It was a test of loyalty, and I failed it. You did nothing wrong."

"That's funny," says Amira, unsmiling, "because to me, every day feels like a test: Will I move from this hill or not, will I grasp at a bird or not, will I toss an apple down to a man when I shouldn't, will I speak too loudly, will I give them a reason to hurt me and fall off the hill, and every day I don't is a day I pass—"

"That's different. That's dreadful."

"I don't see the difference!"

"You don't love this hill!"

"I love you," says Amira, very softly. "I love you, and I do not understand how someone who loves you would want to hurt you, or make you walk in iron shoes."

Tabitha chews her lips, trying to shape words from them, and fails.

"I told my story poorly," she says, finally. "I told it selfishly. I did not speak of how good he was—how he made me laugh, the things he taught me. I could live in the iron shoes because of his guidance, because of knowing the poison berry from the pure, because he taught me to hunt. What happened to him, the change in him"—Tabitha feels very tired—"it must have had to do with me. I was meant to endure it until the curse broke, and I failed. It's the only thing that makes sense."

AMIRA LOOKS AT Tabitha's ruined feet.

"Do you truly believe," she says, with all the care she pours into keeping her spine taut and straight on her glass seat, "that I had nothing to do with those men's attentions? That they would have behaved that way no matter what I looked like?"

"Yes," says Tabitha firmly.

"Then is it not possible"—hesitant, now, to even speak the thought—"that your husband's cruelty had nothing to do with you? That it had nothing to do with a curse? You said he hurt you in both his shapes."

"But I—"

"If you've worn your shoes halfway down, shouldn't you be bending your steps toward him again, that the last pair be destroyed near the home you shared?"

In the shifting light of the moon both their faces have a bluish cast, but Amira sees Tabitha's go gray.

"When I was a girl," says Tabitha thickly, as if working around something in her throat, "I dreamt of marriage as a golden thread between hearts—a ribbon binding one to the other, warm as a day in summer. I did not dream a chain of iron shoes."

"Tabitha"—and Amira does not know what to do except to reach for her hand, clutch it, look at her in the way she looks at the geese, longing to speak and be understood—"you did nothing wrong."

Tabitha holds Amira's gaze. "Neither did you."

They stay that way for a long time, until the sound of seven geese's beating wings startles them into looking up at the stars.

THE DAYS AND nights grow warmer; more and more geese fly overhead. One morning Tabitha begins to walk her circle around Amira when she stumbles, trips, and falls forward into Amira's arms.

"Are you all right?" Amira whispers, while Tabitha clutches at the throne, shaking her head, suddenly unsteady.

"The shoes," she says, marveling. "They're finished. The fourth pair. Amira." Tabitha laughs, surprises herself to hear the sound more like a sob. "They're done."

Amira smiles at her, bends forward to kiss her forehead. "Congratulations," she murmurs, and Tabitha hears much more than the word as she reaches, shaky, wobbling, for the next pair in her pack. "Wait," says Amira quietly, and Tabitha pauses.

"Wait. Please. Don't—" Amira bites her lip, looks away. "You don't have to—you can stay here without—"

Tabitha understands, and returns her hand to Amira's. "I can't stay up here forever. I have to leave before the suitors come back."

Amira draws a deep breath. "I know."

"I've had a thought, though."

"Oh?" Amira smiles softly. "Do you want to marry me after all?"

"Yes."

Amira's stillness turns crystalline in her surprise.

TABITHA IS TALKING, and Amira can barely understand it, feels Tabitha's words slipping off her mind like sand off a glass hill. Anything, anything to keep her from putting her feet back in those iron cages—

"I mean—not as a husband would. But to take you away from here. If you want. Before your suitors return. Can I do that?"

Amira looks at the golden apple in her hand. "I don't know—where would we go?"

"Anywhere! The shoes can walk anywhere, over anything—"

"Back to your husband?"

Something like a thunderclap crosses Tabitha's face. "No. Not there."

Amira looks up. "If we are to marry, I insist on an exchange of gifts. Leave the fur and the shoes behind."

"But—"

"I know what they cost you. I don't want to walk on air and darkness if the price is your pain."

"Amira," says Tabitha helplessly, "I don't think I can walk without them anymore."

"Have you tried? You've been eating golden apples a long while. And you can lean on me."

"But—they might be useful—"

"The glass hill has been very useful to me," says Amira quietly, "and the golden apples have kept me warm and whole and fed. But I will leave them—I will follow you into woods and across fields, I will be hungry and cold and my feet will hurt. But if you are with me, Tabitha, then I will learn to hunt and fish and tell the poison berry from the pure, and I will see a river raise its skirt of geese, and listen to them make a sound like thunder. Do you believe I can do this?"

"Yes," says Tabitha, a choking in her voice, "yes, I do."

"I believe you can walk without iron shoes. Leave them here—and in exchange, I will give you my shoes of silk, and we will fill your pack with seven golden apples, and if you eat from them sparingly, perhaps they will help you walk until we can find you something better."

"But we can't climb down the hill without a pair of shoes!"

"We don't need to." Amira smiles, stroking Tabitha's hair. "Falling's easy—it's keeping still that's hard."

Neither says anything for a time. Then, carefully, for the hill is slippery to her now, Tabitha sheds her fur cloak, unstraps the iron shoes from her feet, and gives them and her pack to Amira. Amira removes the three remaining pairs and replaces them with apples, drawing the pack's straps tight over the seventh. She passes the pack back to Tabitha, who shoulders it.

Then, taking Tabitha's hands in hers, Amira breathes deep and stands up.

THE GLASS THRONE cracks. There is a sound like hard rain, a roar of whispers as the glass hill shivers into sand. It swallows fur and shoes; it swallows Amira and Tabitha together; it settles into a dome-shaped dune with a final hiss.

Hands still clasped, Amira and Tabitha tumble out of it together, coughing, laughing, shaking sand from their hair and skin. They stand, and wait, and no golden apple appears to part their hands from each other.

"Where should we go?" whispers one to the other.

"Away," she replies, and holding on to each other, they stumble into the spring, the wide world rising to meet them with the dawn.

THE ART OF SPACE TRAVEL
Nina Allan

Nina Allan's (www.ninaallan.co.uk) stories have appeared in numerous magazines and anthologies, including *Best Horror of the Year #6*, *The Year's Best Science Fiction and Fantasy 2013*, and *The Mammoth Book of Ghost Stories by Women*. Her novella *Spin*, a science fictional re-imagining of the Arachne myth, won the BSFA Award in 2014, and her story-cycle *The Silver Wind* was awarded the Grand Prix de L'Imaginaire in the same year. Her debut novel *The Race* was a finalist for the 2015 BSFA Award, the Kitschies Red Tentacle, and the John W. Campbell Memorial Award. A new novel, *The Rift*, is due in 2017.

MAGIC SPELLS ARE chains of words, nothing more. Words that help you imagine a different future and create a shape for it, that help you see what it might be like, and so make it happen. Sometimes when I read about our struggle to land people on Mars, that's how the words seem to me—like an ancient incantation, and as deeply unfathomable, a set of mystical words, placed carefully in order and then repeated as a magical chant to bring about a future we have yet to imagine.

The Edison Star Heathrow has sixteen floors, 382 bedrooms, twenty private penthouse apartments, and one presidential suite. It is situated on the northern stretch of the airport perimeter road, and operates its own private shuttle bus to ferry patrons to and from the five terminals. We have a press lounge and a flight lounge and conference facilities. As head of housekeeping, it's my job to make sure things run smoothly behind the scenes. My job is hard work but I enjoy it, by and large. Some days are more demanding than others.

It was all just rumours at first, but last week it became official: Zhanna Sorokina and Vinnie Cameron will be spending a night here at the hotel before flying out to join the rest of the Mars crew in China. Suddenly the Edison Star is the place to be. The public bar and the flight lounge have been jammed ever since the announcement. There's still a fortnight to go before the astronauts arrive, but that doesn't seem to be putting the punters off one little bit. It's cool to be seen here, apparently. Which is ironic, given that we weren't even the mission sponsors' first choice of hotel. That was the Marriott International, only it turned out that Vinnie Cameron had his eighteenth here, or his graduation party or something. He wanted to stay at the Edison Star and so that's what's happening.

I guess they thought it would be churlish to deny him, considering.

The first result of the change of plan is that the Marriott hates us. The second is that Benny's on meltdown twenty-four hours a day now instead of the usual sixteen. I can't imagine how he's going to cope when the big guns arrive.

"Perhaps he'll just explode," says Ludmilla Khan—she's the third-floor super. A dreamy expression comes into her eyes, as if she's picturing the scene in her mind and kind of liking it. "Spontaneous combustion, like you see in the movies. The rest of us running around him flapping like headless chickens."

She makes me laugh, Ludmilla, which is a good thing. I think there's every chance that Benny would drive me over the edge if I didn't see the funny side. Benny's a great boss, don't get me wrong—we get on fine most of the time. I just wish he wasn't getting so uptight about the bloody astronauts. I mean, Jesus, it's only the one night and then they'll be gone. Fourteen hours of media frenzy and then we're last week's news.

Probably I'm being mean, though. This is Benny's big moment, after all, when he gets to show off the Edison Star to the world at large and himself as the big guvnor man at the heart of it all. There's something a bit sad about Benny underneath all his bullshit. I don't mean sad in the sense of pathetic, I mean genuinely sad, sorrowful and bemused at the same time, as if he'd been kidnapped out of one life and set to work in another. And it's not as if he doesn't work hard. He's beginning to show his age now, just a little. He's balding on top, and his suits are getting too tight for him. He wears beautiful suits, Benny does, well cut and modern and just that teeny bit more expensive than he can really afford. Benny might be manager of the Edison Star, but you can tell by his suits that he still wishes he owned it. You can see it every time he steps out of the lift and into the lobby. That swagger, and then the small hesitation.

It's as if he's remembering where he came from, how far there is to fall, and feeling scared.

My mother, Moolie, claims to know Benny Conway from way back, from the time he first came to this country as a student, jetting in from Freetown or Yaoundé, one of those African cities to the west that still make it reasonably easy for ordinary civilians to fly in and out.

"He had a cardboard suitcase and an army surplus rucksack. He was wearing fake Levis and a gold watch. He sold the watch for rent money the first day he was here. He still called himself Benyamin then, Benyamin Kwame."

When I ask Moolie how she can know this, she clams up, or changes her story, or claims she doesn't know who I'm talking about. I don't think it's even Benny she's remembering, it can't be, or not the Benny Conway who's my boss, anyway. She's confusing the names, probably, getting one memory mixed up with another the way she so often does now.

Either that, or she just made it up.

Benny slips me extra money sometimes. I know I shouldn't accept it but I do, mainly because he insists the money is for Moolie, to help me look after her. "It must be tough, having to care for her all by yourself," Benny says, just before he forces the folded-over banknotes on me, scrunching them into my hands like so many dead leaves. How he came to know about Moolie in the first place, I have no idea. There's a chance Ludmilla Khan told him, I suppose, or Antony Ghosh, the guy who oversees our linen contract. Both of them are friends of mine, but you can imagine the temptation to gossip in a fish tank like this. I take the money because I tell myself I've earned it and I can't afford not to, also because maybe Benny really is just sorry for Moolie and this is his way of saying so, even though I've told him enough times that it's not so much a question of looking after Moolie as looking out for her. Making sure she remembers to eat, stuff like that. It's the ordinary stuff she forgets, you see. During her bad patches her short-term memory becomes so unreliable that every day for her is like the beginning of a whole new lifetime.

It's not always like that, though. She can look after herself perfectly well most of the time, she just gets a bit vague. She can't do her work anymore, but she's still interested in the world, still fascinated by what makes things tick, by aeroplanes and rivers and metals, the rudiments of creation. Those are her words, not mine—*the rudiments of creation*. Moolie used to be a physicist. Now she sounds more like one of those telly evangelists you see on the late-night news channels, all mystery and prophecy and lights in the sky. But when it comes down to it, she's interested in the same things she's always been interested in—who we are and how we came here and where the bloody hell we think we're going.

If you didn't know her how she was before, you wouldn't necessarily spot that there's anything wrong with her.

It's all still inside, I know it—everything she was, everything she knows, still packed tight inside her head like old newspapers packed into the eaves of an old house. Yellowing and crumpled, yes, but still telling their stories.

For me, Moolie is a wonder and a nightmare, a sadness deep down in my gut like a splinter of bone. Always there, and always worrying away at the living flesh of me.

The doctors say there's nothing to stop her living out a normal lifespan but I think that's bollocks and I think the doctors know it's bollocks, too. Moolie was fifty-two last birthday, but sometimes she's bent double with back pain, as bad as a woman of eighty or even worse. Other times she burbles away to herself in a made-up language like a child of four. Her whole system is riddled with wrongness of every kind. The doctors won't admit it, though, because they're being paid not to. No one wants to be liable for the compensation. That's why you won't find any mention of the *Galaxy* air crash in Moolie's medical file, or the sixteen lethal substances that were eventually identified at the crash site, substances that Moolie was hired to isolate and analyse.

There were theories about a dirty bomb, and it's pretty much common knowledge now that some of the shit that came out of that plane was radioactive. But ten years on and the report Moolie helped to compile still hasn't been made public. The authorities say the material is too sensitive, and they're not kidding.

The medics have given Moolie a diagnosis of early-onset Alzheimer's. If you believe that then I guess, well, you know how it goes.

When Moolie dies I'll be free. Free to move away from the airport, free to look for another job, free to buy a one-way ticket to Australia and make a new life there. I lie awake at night sometimes, scheming and dreaming about these things, but in the morning I wonder how I'll manage. Moolie is like a part of me, and I can't imagine how the world will feel without her in it.

When she goes, all her stories will go with her, the ones she makes up as well as the ones that happen to be true.

Once she's gone, I'll never discover which were which.

I THINK ABOUT the astronauts a lot. Not the way Benny would like me to be thinking of them, I bet—with Benny it's all about scanning the rooms for bugging devices, checking the kitchens for deadly pathogens, making sure the PA system in the press lounge hasn't blown a gasket.

I know these things are important. If we cock up it won't just be Benny who looks an idiot, and the last thing I want to see is some kid in the catering department getting fired because someone forgot to tell them to stock up on mixers. I check and recheck, not for Benny's sake but because it's my job, and my job is something I care about and want to do well. But every now and then I catch myself thinking how crazy it is really, all this preparation, all this fussing over things that don't actually matter a damn. When you think about what Zhanna Sorokina and Vinnie Cameron and the rest of them are actually doing, everything else seems juvenile and pointless by comparison.

They're going to Mars, and they won't be coming back.

I wonder if they know they're going to die. I mean, I know they know, but I wonder if they think about it, that every one of them is bound to cop it much sooner than they would have done otherwise, and probably in a horrible way. It's inevitable, isn't it, when you consider the facts? There's no natural air on Mars, no water, no nothing. There's a good chance the whole crew will wind up dead before they can even set up a base there, or a sealed habitat, or whatever it is they're supposed to be doing when they arrive.

How do they cope with knowing that? How does anyone begin to come to terms with something that frightening? I can't imagine it myself, and I have to admit I don't try all that hard, because even the thought of it scares me, let alone the reality.

In interviews and articles I've read online, they say that learning to cope with high-risk situations is all part of the training, that anyone with insufficient mental stamina is weeded out of the selection process more or less straightaway. I'm still not sure I understand, though. Why would anyone volunteer for something like that in the first place?

Ludmilla Khan is especially upset because one of the women astronauts is a mother. We all know her name—Jocelyn Tooker. Her kids are five and three. They've gone to live in Atlanta, with their grandmother.

"How can she bear it? Knowing she'll never see them grow up, that she'll never hear their voices again, even?"

"I don't know," I say to Ludmilla. "Perhaps she thinks they'll be proud of her." The way Ludmilla talks, you'd think Jocelyn Tooker had murdered both her kids and chucked their bodies down a well. One of the male crew, Ken Toh, has an eight-year-old son, but people don't go on about that nearly as much as they do about Jocelyn Tooker.

Ludmilla has two little ones of her own, Leila and Mehmet, so I can see how Jocelyn Tooker's decision might weigh on her mind. I've thought about it over and over, and the only thing I can come up with that makes sense of it is that the crew of the *Second Wind* look upon going to Mars not as a one-way ticket to an early exit but as a way of cheating death altogether. I mean, everyone aboard that spacecraft is going to live forever—in our hearts and minds, in our books and stories and films, and in thousands of hours of news clips and documentaries. Even if they crash and burn like the crew of the *New Dawn*, we'll never stop talking about them, and speculating, and remembering.

If you look at it that way it's a straight trade: fifty years or so of real life now against immortality. I can see why some people might think that's not such a bad deal.

In a way, the men and women who go into space are our superheroes. Ten years from now, some journalist will be asking Jocelyn Tooker's children what it feels like to have a superhero for a mum.

Who is Ludmilla Khan, or me or anyone else for that matter, to try and guess at how those kids will judge her, or what they'll say?

*   *   *

MY NAME IS Emily Clarah Starr. The Starr is just a coincidence. Clarah is for my grandmother, whom I can't remember because she died when I was three. There's a photo of us, Moolie and Clarah and me, out by the King George VI Reservoir before it was officially declared to be toxic and cordoned off. Moolie has me in one of those front-loading carry-pouch things—all you can see is the top of my head, a bunch of black curls. Grandma Clarah is wearing a hideous knitted blue bobble hat and a silver puffer jacket, even though it's May in the photo and the sun is shining, reflecting itself off the oily water like electric light.

"Your grandma never got used to the climate," Moolie told me once. "She always felt cold here, even though she came over with her aunts from Abuja when she was six."

Moolie in the photograph is tall and thin, elegant and rather aloof, unrecognisable. She seems full of an inner purpose I cannot divine. She says it was my father who chose the name Emily for me. I don't know if I should believe that story or not.

I have no idea who my father is, and Moolie's account varies. I went through a phase of pestering her about him when I was younger, but she refused to tell me anything, or at least not anything I could rely on.

"Why should it matter who your dad is? What did fathers ever do for the world in any case, except saddle unsuspecting women with unwanted children?"

"Unwanted?" I gaped at her. The idea that Moolie might not have wanted me had never occurred to me. I simply *was*, an established fact, *quod erat demonstrandum*. But that's the ego for you—an internalized life support system, and pretty much indestructible.

"Oh, Emily, of course I wanted you. You were a bit of a shock to the system, though, that's all I'm saying."

"What did Dad say, when he found out?"

"Don't call him Dad, he doesn't deserve it."

"My father, then. And if the guy was such an arsehole why did you shag him?"

I was about fourteen then, and going through a stroppy phase. When rudeness didn't get me anywhere I started hitting Moolie with psychological claptrap instead—all this stuff about how I had a right to know, that it would damage my self-esteem if she kept it from me. You know, the kind of rubbish you read in magazines. The situation stood at stalemate for a while, then finally we had this massive row, a real window-shaker. It went on for hours. When we'd been round in circles one time too many, Moolie burst into tears and said the reason she wouldn't tell me anything was that she didn't know. She'd had several boyfriends back then. Any one of them could be my father.

"We can do a ring-round, if you want," she said, still sniffing. "Drop a few bombshells? Destroy a few households? What do you reckon?"

What I reckoned was that it was time I shut up. For the first time in my life I was feeling another person's pain like it was my own. For the first time ever I was seeing Moolie as a person in her own right, someone whose life could have taken a whole different path if little Emily hadn't come along to mess things up.

It was a shock, to put it mildly. But it was good, too, in the long run, because it brought Moolie and me together and made us real friends. I stopped caring about who my dad was, for a long time. Then when Moolie started getting ill I didn't want to make things worse by dragging it all up again.

Then Moolie said what she said about the book, and everything changed.

THE BOOK IS called *The Art of Space Travel* by Victoria Segal. I remember the book from when I was a little kid because of the star maps. The maps fold out from between the normal pages in long, concertina-like strips. They're printed in colour—dark blue and yellow—on smooth, glossy paper that squeaks slightly when you run your finger across it. I always thought the star maps were beautiful. Moolie would let me look at the book if I asked but she would never leave me alone with it—I suppose she thought I might accidentally damage it.

As I grew older I had a go at reading it every once in a while, but I always gave up after a chapter or two because it was way over my head, all the stuff about quasars and dark matter and the true speed of light. I would soldier on for a couple of pages, then realise I hadn't actually understood a word of it.

As well as the star maps, the book is filled with beautiful and intricate diagrams, complicated line drawings of planetary orbits, and the trajectories of imaginary spacecraft, rockets that never existed but one day might. I always loved the thought of that, that they one day might.

The book's shiny yellow cover is torn in three places.

The day Moolie drops the bombshell is a Tuesday. I don't know why I remember that, but I do. I come in from work to find Moolie looking sheepish, the look she gets now when she's lost something or broken something or forgotten who she is, just for the moment. I've learned it's best not to question her when she gets like that because it makes her clam up, whereas if you leave her alone for a while she can't resist sharing. So I pretend I haven't noticed anything and we have supper as usual. Once we've finished eating, Moolie goes into the front room to watch TV and I go upstairs to do some stuff on my computer.

After about half an hour, Moolie appears in the doorway. She's holding *The Art of Space Travel*, clasping it to her chest with both arms as if she's afraid it might try to get away from her. Then she dumps it down on my bed like a brick. It makes a soft, plump sound as it hits the duvet. A small puff of air comes up.

"This belonged to your father," Moolie says. "He left it here when he went."

"When he went where?" I say. I'm trying to keep my voice low and steady, as if we're just having a normal conversation about nothing in particular.

My heart is thumping like a road drill, like it wants to escape me. It's almost painful, like the stitch in your side you get from running too far and too fast.

"Your dad was an astronaut," Moolie says. "He was part of the *New Dawn* mission."

My hands are shaking, just a bit, but I'm trying to ignore that. "Moolie," I say to her. Moolie is what I called her when I was first learning to talk, apparently. It made her and Grandma Clarah laugh so much they never tried to correct me. Moolie's actual name is Della—Della Starr. She was once one of the most highly qualified metallurgists in the British aerospace industry. "What on Earth are you talking about?"

"He knew I was pregnant," Moolie says. "He wanted to be involved—to be a father to you—but I said no. I didn't want to be tied to him, or to anyone. Not then. I've never been able to make up my mind if I did the right thing or not."

She nods at me, as if she's satisfied with herself for having said something clever, and then she leaves the room. I stay where I am, sitting at my desk and staring at the open doorway Moolie just walked out of, wondering if I should go after her and what I'm going to say to her if I do.

When I finally go downstairs, I find Moolie back in the living room, curled up on the sofa, watching one of her soaps. When I ask her if she was telling the truth about my dad being an astronaut she looks at me as if she thinks I've gone insane.

"Your father wasted his dreams, Emily," she says. "He gave up too soon. That's one of the reasons I told him to go. Life's hard enough as it is. The last thing you want is to be tied to someone who's always wishing he'd chosen a different path."

When a couple of days later I ask her again about *The Art of Space Travel*, she says she doesn't have a clue where it came from. "It was here in the house when we moved in, I think," she says. "I found it in the built-in wardrobe in your bedroom, covered in dust."

I've been through the book perhaps a thousand times, searching for a sign of my father—a name on the flyleaf, a careless note, scribbled comments in the margin, underlinings in the text, even. There's nothing, though, not even a random inkblot. Aside from being yellowed and a bit musty-smelling, the pages are clean. There's nothing to show who owned the book, who brought it to this house, that it was ever even opened before we had it.

I want to find Dad. I tell myself it's because Moolie is dying, that whoever the man is and whatever he's done, he has a right to know the facts of his own life. I know it's more than that, though, if I'm honest. I want to find him because I'm curious, because I've always been curious, and because I'm afraid that once Moolie is gone I'll have nobody else.

Our house is on Sipson Lane, in the borough of Hillingdon. It was built in the 1970s, almost a hundred years ago now to the year. It's a shoddy little place, one of a row of twenty-two identical boxes flung up to generate maximum profit for the developer with a minimum of outlay. It's a wonder it's lasted this long, actually. Some of the other houses in the row are in a terrible state—the metal window frames rusted and buckling, the lower floors patchy with mildew. The previous owner put in replacement windows and a new damp-proof course, so ours isn't as bad as some. It's dry inside, at least, and I used some of the extra cash from Benny to put up solar panels, which means we can afford to keep the central heating on all the time.

Moolie's like Clarah now—she can't stand the cold.

Sipson is a weird place. Five hundred years ago it was a tiny hamlet, surrounded by farmland. Since then it's evolved into a scruffy housing estate less than half a mile from the end of the second runway at Heathrow Airport. Moolie bought the Sipson Lane house because it was cheap and because it was close to her job, and the best thing about it is that it's close to my job too, now. It takes me less than half an hour to walk into work, which not only cuts down on expenses, it also means I can get home quickly if there's an emergency.

The traffic on the perimeter road is a constant nightmare. In the summer, the petrol and diesel fumes settle over the airport like a heavy tarpaulin, a yellowish blanket of chemical effluent that is like heat haze, only thicker, and a lot more smelly.

When you walk home in the evenings, though, or on those very rare winter mornings when there's still a hard frost, you could take the turning into Sipson Lane and mistake it for the entrance to another world: The quiet street, with its rustling plane trees, the long grass sprouting between the kerbstones at the side of the road. The drawn curtains of the houses, like gently closed eyelids, the soft glow behind. Someone riding past on a bicycle. The red pillar box opposite the Sipson Arms. You'd barely know the airport even existed.

It's like an oasis in time, if there is such a thing. If you stand still and listen to the sound of the blackbirds singing, high up in the dusty branches of those plane trees, you might almost imagine you're in a universe where the *Galaxy* air crash never happened.

They had planes flying in and out of here again within the hour, of course. The airport authorities, backed by the government, insisted the main damage was economic and mostly short term. They claimed the rumours of ground contamination and depleted uranium were just so much scaremongering, that the whole area within the emergency cordon had been repeatedly tested and repeatedly found safe.

A decade on they say that even if the toxicity levels were a bit on the high side in the first year or so after the crash, they're well within the accepted safety limits now.

THE FIRST QUESTION I have to ask myself is this: Is there any possibility at all that it's true? What Moolie told me about my father and the *New Dawn* mission, I mean?

My first instinct is to dismiss it as just another fraction of Moolie craziness. One of the features of Moolie's illness is that it's often hard to know whether she's talking about stuff that really happened to her or stuff she's dreamed or read about or seen on TV. Her mind can't tell the difference now, or not all the time. Just seeing the Mars team on television might be enough to land her with a complete fantasy scenario, indistinguishable from her life as she's actually lived it.

But the thing is—and I can hardly believe I'm saying this—there is a very small chance that her story might turn out to be real. The dates fit, for a start. I was born in March 2047, just three months before the *New Dawn* was launched on its mission to Mars. And before you roll your eyes and say, *Yes, but so were about three hundred thousand other kids*, just consider this: Moolie did a lot of specialist placements early on in her career. One of them was in Hamburg, at the University of the European Space Programme, where she spent the better part of 2046 helping to run strength tests on prototypes of some of the equipment designed to be used aboard the *New Dawn*. Some of the Mars team were in residency in Hamburg at around the same time, eight of them in all, five women and three men. Moolie would have come into direct contact with every one of them.

I know, because I've looked up the details. I even have a file now, stuff I've found online and printed off. If you think that's creepy, just try having an unknown dad who might have died in an exploding rocket and see how *you* get on. See how long it takes before you start a file on him.

* * *

TOBY SOYINKA WAS second communications officer aboard the *New Dawn*, the one who just happened to be outside the vehicle when the disaster occurred. His body was thrown clear of the wreckage, and was recovered three months later by an unmanned retrieval pod launched by the crew of the Hoffnung 3 space station. Toby's body was shipped back to Earth at enormous expense, not so much for the sake of his family as to be subjected to a year-long post mortem.

The mission scientists wanted to know if Toby was still alive when he floated free, and if so then for how long. Knowing that would tell them all kinds of things, apparently—important information about the last moments of the *New Dawn* and why she failed.

According to the official reports, Toby Soyinka was killed in the primary explosion, the same as the rest of the crew. As you might expect, the conspiracy theorists went bonkers. Why would Soyinka be dead if his suit was undamaged? How come only a short section of the official post mortem has ever been released into the public sphere?

There are people who claim that Toby was alive up there for at least three hours after the rocket exploded—depending on individual physiology, his suit's oxygen tanks would have contained enough air for between three and four hours.

Toby's suit was also fitted with a radio communicator, but it was short-range only, suitable for talking with his colleagues back on board the *New Dawn* but not powerful enough to let him speak with Mission Control.

Would he have wanted to, though, even if he could have? Knowing that he was going to die, and everyone on the ground knowing there was fuck all they could do about it?

I mean, what could one side of that equation possibly have to say to the other?

Well, I guess this is it, Tobes. Sorry, old chap. Hey, did anyone remember to send out for muffin?

I think about that, and I think of Toby Soyinka thinking about that, and after the terror what comes through to me most strongly is simple embarrassment.

If it had been me in that floating spacesuit I reckon I'd have switched my radio off and waited in silence. Listed my favourite movies in order from one to a hundred and gazed out at the stars.

At least Toby died knowing he'd done something extraordinary, that he'd seen sights few human beings will ever see.

And Toby Soyinka is a hero now, don't forget that. Perhaps that's what the crew of the *Second Wind* are telling themselves, even now.

In the movies when something goes wrong and one of the crew is left floating in space with no hope of rescue, the scene almost always ends with the doomed one taking off his or her helmet, making a quick and noble end of it rather than facing a slow and humiliating death by asphyxiation.

Would anyone really have the guts to do that, though? I don't think I would.

Toby Soyinka was born in Nottingham. Toby's dad was a civil engineer—he helped design the New Trent shopping village—and his mum was a dentist. Toby studied physics and IT at Nottingham Uni, then went on to do postgraduate work at the UESP in Hamburg, where he would have met Moolie. Most of the photos online show Toby at the age of twenty-eight, the same age he was when he died, and when he and the rest of the crew were all over the media. He looks skinny and hopeful and nervous, all at once. Sometimes when I look at pictures of Toby I can't help thinking he seems out of his depth, as if he's wondering what he signed up for exactly, although that's probably just my imagination.

Once, when I was browsing through some stuff about Toby online, Moolie came into the room and sneaked up behind me.

"What are you looking at?" she said. I hadn't heard her come in. I jumped a mile.

"Nothing much," I said. I hurried to close the window but it was too late, the photos of Toby were staring her in the face. I looked at her looking, curious to see what her reaction would be, but Moolie's eyes slid over his features without even a single glimmer of recognition. He might have been a tree or a gatepost, for all the effect he had on her.

Was she only pretending not to recognise him? I don't think so. I always know when Moolie's hiding something, even if I don't know what it is she's hiding.

I DON'T BELIEVE that Toby Soyinka was my father. It would be too much like a tragic fairy tale, too pat.

*　　*　　*

"How's your mum?" Benny says to me this morning.

"She's fine, Benny," I reply. "She's getting excited about the mission, same as you." I grin at him and wink, firstly because I can never resist taking the piss out of Benny, just a little bit, and secondly because it's true. Moolie has barely been out of the living room this past week. She has the television on all day and most of the night, permanently tuned to the twenty-four-hour news feed that's supposed to be the official mouthpiece of the mission's sponsors. The actual news content is pretty limited but since when has that ever been a deterrent in situations like this? They squeeze every last ounce of juice out of what they have—then they go back to playing the old documentaries, home video footage, endlessly repetitive Q&As with scientists and school friends.

Moolie watches it all with equal attention, drinking it down like liquid nutrient through a straw. She doesn't get to bed till gone three, some nights, and when I ask her if she's had anything to eat she doesn't remember. I make up batches of sandwiches and leave them in the fridge for her. Sometimes she scoffs the lot, sometimes I go down in the morning and find them untouched.

She's immersed in the Mars thing so deeply that sometimes it seems like Moolie herself is no longer there.

What is it that fascinates her so much? When she first started watching I felt convinced it had to do with my father, that all the talk of the *Second Wind* was bringing back memories of what happened to the *New Dawn*. I'm less sure of that now—why should everything have to be about me and my father? Moolie is—was—a scientist, and the Mars mission is just about the most exciting scientific experiment to be launched in more than a decade, perhaps ever. Of course she'd be interested in it. You could argue that her obsession with the news feed is the best evidence I have that she is still herself.

She seems so engaged, so invigorated, so *happy* that I don't want to question it. I want her to stay like this for as long as she can.

"Well, tell her I asked after her," Benny says. I glance at him curiously, wondering if he's serious. I've always found it strange, this spasmodic concern of his for a person he's never met. At the same time, though, it's just so Benny. It's no wonder he's never made it to the top. To make it to the top you need to be a heartless bastard, pretty much. On the heartless bastard scale, Benny Conway has never figured very high up.

I nod briskly. "I will," I say. I never feel comfortable talking with him about Moolie—it's all too close to home. I'd rather stick to work, any day. "What's on today?"

Benny immediately looks shifty. A moment later I understand why. "There's another news crew dropping by," he says. "They want to do an interview. With you."

"With me? What the hell for? Oh, for God's sake, Benny, what are they expecting me to say?"

"You're head of housekeeping at the Edison Star, Emily. That's an important and responsible position. They just want to ask you what it's been like, preparing for such an important occasion. There's nothing for you to be anxious about, I promise you. They've said it shouldn't take more than ten minutes, fifteen at the most."

"I'm not anxious, I'm pissed off," I say. "You could at least have asked me first." Benny looks hurt and just a little bit surprised. I know I've overstepped the mark and I wouldn't normally be so rude but just for the moment I feel like killing him. It's all right for Benny—he loves all this shit. Benny's great with the press, actually, he's what you might call a people person. Put him in front of a camera and he's away.

Me? I just want to be left alone to get on with my job. The idea of being on TV leaves me cold. There's Moolie to be considered, too—seeing me up on the screen like that, it might warp her sense of reality more than ever.

It's done now, though, isn't it? There's not much sense in kicking off about it. Best to get the whole thing over and done with and then forget it.

I GUESS IT'S mainly because of Benny that I'm still here. Working at the hotel, I mean. I certainly never planned on staying forever. It was supposed to be a holiday job, something to bring in some money while I went through college. I started out studying for a degree in natural sciences, following in Moolie's footsteps, I suppose, which was madness. I failed my first-year exams twice. It should have been obvious to anyone that I wasn't cut out for it.

"You're such a dreamer, Emily," Moolie said to me once. "Head in the stars." She cracked a kind of half-smile, then sighed. She was paying for extra tutorials for me at the time, trying to give me a better shot at the re-sits. It must have felt like flushing money down the toilet. When I told her I'd been offered a permanent job at the Edison Star and had decided to take it she gave me such an odd look, like I'd announced I was running away to join the circus or something. But she never questioned it or gave me a hard time, or tried to talk me out of it the way a lot of parents would have.

It was a relief to her, most likely, that I'd finally found something I could do, that I was good at, even. It also meant I stayed close to home. First of all because it was convenient, and then later, with Moolie's illness, because it became necessary. I've never regretted it. I regret some of the things that might have been, but the regret has always taken second place to the desire not to have things change. I don't think it's just because of Moolie, either. Sometimes I believe it's the airport itself, and Sipson, both the kind of non-places that keep you addicted to transience, the restless half-life of the perpetual traveller who never goes anywhere.

The idea of settling for anything too concrete begins to seem like death, so you settle for nothing.

Benny Conway's never married, which probably seems strange to you, given that he's such a people person, but I can imagine that being with him day in and day out would drive anyone nuts.

Beneath the confidence and sunny bravado, Benny's actually quite needy and insecure. One of the downsides of working in a close environment is that you often get to know more about the people you work with than you strictly want to.

I SPEND THE morning checking the inventories and trying not to get too worked up about the stupid interview. At 1:30 I go down to the lobby. What passes for the news crew is already there—a camera guy and a college kid, sent along by some backroom satellite outfit most likely, one of the countless pirate stations that don't have the clout to get themselves an invite for what Ludmilla and I have snarkily begun to call the Day of Judgement.

These two have to make do with me instead. I begin to feel sorry for them. The student who interviews me is called Laura—I never learn her surname—a tiny thing dressed in a black pantsuit and with her copper-red hair cut close to her head. She reminds me of Pinocchio, or one of those Pierrot dolls that my school friends were so crazy about when I was a kid. I like her immediately—she seems so earnest!—and so I find myself relaxing into the process and even enjoying it. I'm expecting the questions Laura asks me to be work-related—what will the astronauts be having for supper, how do you keep the hotel running normally and still maintain security, that kind of thing. Some of her actual questions catch me off guard.

"It's thirty years since the crew of the *New Dawn* lost their lives," Laura says. "Do you think it's right that we should risk another Mars mission?"

"I think in a way we're doing it for them," I say. "The astronauts who died, I mean." I'm stumbling over my words, because I haven't planned this. It's strange to hear myself saying these things, thoughts I never really knew I was thinking until now. "I think we should ask ourselves what they would have wanted. Would they have wanted us to try again? I think they would have. So I think we should, too. I believe we have to try again, for their sakes."

Laura looks delighted and surprised, as if what I said in reply to her question was the kind of answer she wanted but didn't expect. Not from the likes of me, anyway. She wraps up the interview soon after—she wants to quit while she's ahead, most likely.

"That was great," she says to me, off-camera. She exchanges a couple of words with the camera guy, who's preoccupied with packing away his equipment. After a moment Laura turns back to me. She's smiling, and I think she's about to say goodbye. But then her expression becomes serious again and she asks me another question. "Your mum was here when the *Galaxy* flight came down, wasn't she?"

I'm so surprised I can't answer at first. I glance across at the camera guy, wondering if he's somehow still filming this, but he's moved away from us slightly, towards the reception desk. I see him checking his mobile. "She was working here, yes," I say. My throat feels dry and I swallow. What's this about? "She was part of the forensic investigation team that went out to the crash site. She was an expert in metal fatigue."

Laura has moved to stand in front of me, blocking my view of the rest of the lobby and clearly expecting me to say more, but I'm not sure what I should say, whether I should say anything, even.

I can't imagine why she's asking me this question now, when the camera is off. It has nothing to do with the astronauts or with the hotel, and I'm asking myself what it does have to do with, exactly. Is this the question Laura wanted to ask me all along? And if so, why?

"There was an awful smell," I say, and then suddenly I'm remembering that smell, jet fuel thickened by dust, ignited by anguish, and the way it hung over the airport and over our village for weeks, or so it seemed, longer even than that, so long that in the end you understood it was all in your mind, it had to be, that no real smell lingers that long. Even the stench of combusted bodies fades eventually.

I haven't thought of these things in years, not like this, not precisely enough to bring back that smell.

But can I tell Laura any of this? She would have been about ten when it happened; she might not even remember it as a real event. Children don't take much notice of the news unless it affects them directly. Everything she knows about the crash will come from old TV footage, the slew of documentaries and real-time amateur video that followed after.

Everything from the acknowledged facts to the certifiably crazy.

What would she say if I told her that Moolie worked alongside the black box recovery unit and the token medics and the loss adjusters? That she was out there for almost three weeks, picking over what was essentially radioactive trash, trying to come up with a reasonable theory of what had happened and who was responsible?

Of that original forensic team, two are still working and seem in good health, three have died of various cancers, and four are like Moolie.

There is an ongoing legal enquiry, but the way things are going the remaining witnesses will all be dead before any decision is made on liability.

I bet that's what the authorities are hoping, anyway.

"Here's my number," Laura says. She delves into her jacket pocket and then hands me a card, a glossy white oblong printed with an email address and cell number in cool grey capitals.

Quaint, I think, and rather classy, if you're into retro.

"Give me a call, if you feel like talking about it. I'd really like to do a story on your mother, if you think she'd be up for it." Laura hesitates, uncertain suddenly, a precocious child in front of an audience of hostile strangers.

"Think about it, anyway."

"I will," I say, and slip the card into my pocket. Later, after Laura is gone, I try to imagine her with Moolie, asking her questions.

Does Moolie remember the *Galaxy*, even?

Some days, probably.

The whole idea of her doing an interview is insane.

Of the three male astronauts Moolie had dealings with at the UESP in Hamburg, only Toby Soyinka actually went on to get picked as flight crew. The two other guys involved with the *New Dawn* mission ended up working on the ground in IT and comms. Angelo Chavez was born in Queens, New York City. His exceptional talent for mathematics was spotted in nursery school. At the age of six he won a place at a specialist academy for gifted children. Angelo did well, and seemed well adjusted, until his father began an affair with a work colleague and buggered off. Angelo's mother relocated with Angelo to Chicago to be closer to family.

Angelo was bullied at his new school. He began truanting, then moved on to shoplifting and dealing cannabis on high school premises. By the time he turned fourteen he was regularly in trouble with the police. It was a youth worker at a juvenile detention centre who helped get Angelo back on track by asking him to help out with the centre's computer system. Later, when Angelo applied for a place at MIT, the man acted as his sponsor and referee. Angelo achieved perfect scores in three out of his five first-year assignments. He graduated with one of the highest averages of that decade.

After graduation, he began working as a games designer for a Tokyo-based franchise, and landed a junior post at NASA just eighteen months later. Three years after joining NASA, Angelo went to Hamburg for six months to work as a visiting lecturer at the UESP. While he was there, he met and fell in love with the Dutch astrophysicist Johan Wedekin. They became civil partners in July 2048.

They've been together now for almost thirty years. I suppose it's possible that Angelo was shagging Moolie in Hamburg as well as Johan, but I think it's unlikely.

Marlon Habila was born in Lagos, the son of two teachers. He speaks six languages fluently, and has a solid working knowledge of eight others. He wrote his postgraduate thesis on the acquisition of language in bilingual children. He was initially employed by the UESP to help develop a more straightforward method for teaching Mandarin to trainee astronauts, and became interested in the *New Dawn* mission while he was there. After a number of years in Hamburg, Marlon was headhunted by NASA as a senior communications technician and relocated to Austin, Texas, where he still lives today.

He was in Hamburg at the same time as Moolie, though, no doubt about it. When I look at photographs of Marlon Habila, it's like looking into a mirror.

I once showed Moolie a photo of Marlon and asked if she remembered him. She was in one of her lucid patches at the time, so I thought there might be a chance I'd get something resembling a straight answer out of her. I reckoned it was worth a try, anyway. You never know with Moolie, how she's going to react. Sometimes during her good phases you can chat with her and it'll feel almost like the old times.

On the other hand, it's often during these good times that she's at her most evasive. Ask Moolie her own name then and there's no guarantee you'll get the answer you were expecting.

When I showed her the picture of Marlon, her eyes filled with tears. Then she snatched it out of my hands and tore it in two.

"Don't talk to me about that boy," she hissed at me. "I've told you before."

"No you haven't," I persisted. "Can you tell me anything about him? Do you know what he's called?"

She gave me a look, boiling over with impatience, as if I'd asked her if the world was flat or round.

"You know damn well what he's called," she said. "Stop trying to trick me. I'm not brain-dead yet, you know." She stomped out of the room, one foot dragging slightly because of the muscle wastage that had already begun to affect her left side. I stared stupidly down at the two torn pieces of the photograph she had thrown on the floor, then picked them up and put them in the waste bin. An hour or so later I went upstairs to check on Moolie and she was fine again, completely calm, sitting up in bed and reading softly aloud to herself from J. G. Ballard's *Vermilion Sands*.

I asked her if she wanted anything to eat or drink and she shook her head. The next time I looked in on her she was sound asleep.

* * *

Do I REALLY believe that Marlon Habila is my dad? Some days I feel so certain it's like knowing for sure. Other days I think it's all bullshit, just some story I've constructed for myself so the world doesn't feel so crazy and out of control. It's a well-known fact that kids who grow up not knowing who their parents are—or who one parent is—always like to imagine they're really a princess, or the son of a Polar explorer who died bravely in tragic circumstances, or some such junk. No one wants to be told their daddy is really a dustman who got banged up for petty thieving and who never gave a shit.

"Daddy was a spaceman" sounds so much better.

The thing is, even if I knew for an absolute certainty that Marlon Habila was my birth father, it's still not obvious what—if anything—I should do about it.

I found contact details for Marlon online—it wasn't difficult—and I've lost count of the number of emails I've started to write and then deleted. *Dear Marlon, Dear Dr Habila, Dear Marlon* again. *You don't know me, but I think I might be your daughter.*

Just like in those old TV miniseries Moolie enjoys so much, those overblown three-part dramas about twins separated at birth, or men of God who fall illicitly in love, or lost survivors of the *Titanic*, stories that unfold in a series of unlikely coincidences, all tied together with a swooning orchestral soundtrack. They're pretty naff, those stories, but they do draw you in. When Moolie's going through one of her bad times she'll watch them all day long, five of the things in a row, back to back.

I suppose the reason people like stories like that is that no matter how confused the plot seems at the start, things always work out. By the time the film's over you always understand what happened, and why. There's always a proper ending, with people hugging each other and crying, if you see what I mean.

In the case of Marlon Habila, the proper ending is that he moved to Texas. A year after the *New Dawn* tragedy he married Melissa Sanberg, one of the senior operatives working on what they call the shop floor of Mission Control. They have two sons and one daughter—Aaron, Willard, and little Esther. Eighteen, sixteen, and nine.

In the photos they look happy. I mean, *really* happy. I have to ask myself what might happen to that happiness if I sent my email.

I can't help thinking about what Moolie said that time, about dropping bombshells.

In a way it would be easier if my father turned out to be Toby Soyinka after all. Dead is safe, nothing would change, and hey, at least I would know my dad was a hero. People would look at me with sympathy, and fascination. It would make a good miniseries, actually. You can imagine the ending—me and Toby's relatives hugging and crying as we hand round the old photographs for the umpteenth time and saying, *If only he knew* in choked-up voices. I'd watch it, anyway, I wouldn't be able to help myself. I'd blub at the end too, probably. Another Saturday night in with Moolie, a supply of tissues and a box of chocolates on the sofa between us.

Who doesn't want a story that makes sense?

I've made up my mind that if the *Second Wind* launches safely I'm going to send that email.

THE BIGGEST HEADACHE with having astronauts staying at the Edison Star is the incessant press coverage. Sorokina and Cameron themselves are the least of our worries—they're just two extra guests; to put it bluntly, they're hardly going to send us into a tailspin no matter how picky they might be about their food or the ambient room temperature. We've had to take on extra security just for that week, but aside from that it'll be business pretty much as usual. The problem is that it will be business under intense scrutiny, and until the astronauts actually arrive, the press hounds have nothing to do except sit and bitch. You can bet your life that if one of them happens to spot a rat in the garbage store it'll be headlining as a major news story within the hour.

You're never more than six feet from a rat: Getting up close and personal with the Edison Star's new temp staff.

It's enough to give Benny a coronary. Which means no rats, no undercooked turkey, no tide marks on the bathtubs, no financial mismanagement, no corporate bribery, no spree killings.

Not until this astronaut business is safely behind us, at any rate.

What it mostly means for me is a lot of overtime, but I don't mind. I'm enjoying myself quite a bit, to tell the truth. I know how this place works, you see, I've even grown to love it over the years. The only problem is winding down, switching off. Even when I'm at home I'm constantly running through mental checklists, trying to head cock-ups off at the pass before they happen. Sometimes I find myself lying awake into the small hours. If I'm not careful I'm going to end up like Moolie.

WILL THERE BE children born on Mars, I wonder? Martian children, who think of the planet Mars as their one true home?

It is strange to think of, and rather wonderful, too, that we might come to that. What will our Earth seem like to them, our built-in atmosphere and water on tap, our border controls and health and safety laws, our wars over patches of land that we like to call countries?

Will we seem like kings to them, or tyrants, or simply fools?

I have brought *The Art of Space Travel* into work with me this morning. I wrapped it inside a supermarket carrier bag for protection, then stuffed it into the back of my locker with the trainers I wear for walking in and my rucksack and my spare cardigan. I have this silly idea, that when Zhanna Sorokina and Vinnie Cameron arrive I'll get them both to sign it. I know the book was written long before they were born, that it has no connection with them, but I would like to have something of theirs, all the same, something of theirs joined with something of mine. Something to keep once they are gone, that will remind me that although they're Martians now, they started out from here.

It will be a way of keeping them safe, maybe. I know how crazy that sounds.

IT'S STRANGE, BUT each time I think of something happening to them it's not the *New Dawn* I think of but the *Galaxy*, that doomed aeroplane, fireballing out of the sky over Heathrow.

I was in school when it happened, almost ten miles away, but all of us heard the crash, even from there.

*   *   *

WHEN THE CALL comes through, I'm in the middle of signing off the bulk orders for cleaning supplies—Dettox, Ajax, Glasene, Pledge—we get through tens of gallons of each on a monthly basis. I prefer staff to keep their mobiles switched off while they're on shift because they're so distracting, but I have to keep mine by me because of Moolie. Weeks and sometimes months go by without it ever ringing but you never know. When I see her number flashing onscreen I pick up at once.

I speak her name, only it's not her on the line after all, it's our neighbour, Allison Roberts, from next door.

"She was out the front, just lying there," Allison says. Moolie's phone was lying there too, apparently, which I suppose was lucky.

I can't remember the last time Moolie went outside by herself.

I call Benny on his private line, the one that never gets diverted. I know he's chairing a meeting but I don't care, I don't give a shit suddenly, and Benny must realise it's urgent because he knows I wouldn't disturb him otherwise, and so he picks up immediately.

"I have to go," I gasp. I explain what's happened the best I can and he says okay. I'm running for the lifts by then. I need to get to the basement, where the staff lockers are. When I reach the lockers I can't get my key card to work, and then when it finally does everything comes pouring out in a tidal wave. My clobber's everywhere, suddenly. It's the last thing I need. My chest is so high and tight I feel like screaming.

"For fuck's sake!" I'm seconds away from bursting into tears. I'm still trying to scoop everything together when Benny appears. I realise he must have left his meeting to come down, which is so bloody unlike him that all I can think is that he's here to give me a bollocking.

He doesn't, though.

"Don't worry about this," he says. "Just take what you need and get going. I've called a taxi for you—it'll be out the front in five minutes. I'll take care of your things." He makes a gesture towards the stuff on the floor, and of course I can't help thinking how downright weird all this is, but I don't have time to dwell on it. I need to get moving.

Allison said that Moolie was having difficulty breathing when she found her. The paramedics soon got her stabilized but it's still very worrying.

"Are you sure about this?" I say to Benny. "I'm really sorry."

"Quite sure," Benny says. "Call me if you need me, okay?"

I take a moment to wonder if Benny is losing it, if the strain is finally getting to him, but I know that now is not the time to go looking for answers to that question.

"I will," I say. "Thanks." I grab my rucksack and shove on my trainers and then I'm gone.

MOST OF THE things that are wrong with Moolie—the decreasing short-term memory and loss of appetite, the insomnia, the restlessness—none of these are life-threatening. Not in and of themselves, anyway. But every now and then she'll have an attack of apnoea, and these are much more frightening. What apnoea means, basically, is that Moolie can't breathe. The first time she had an attack, the doctors kept asking me if she smoked. Each time I said no they looked at me with doubt. It was obvious they thought I was lying.

In fact the apnoea is caused by the thousands of microscopic mushroom-like growths that have colonized the lining of Moolie's lungs. Most of the time these growths remain inactive and appear to do no harm, but periodically they flare up or inflate or expand or whatever—hence the apnoea.

"It's definitely not cancer," the medics insist. There's a real sense of triumph in their voices as they say this, as if the growths' non-cancerous nature is something they've seen to personally. But when I ask them what it is if it's not cancer they never seem to give me a direct answer and I don't think they have one. I don't think anyone really knows what it is, to be honest. It's a whole new disease.

Whatever it is, it seems to have the advantage of being slow-growing. Moolie might die of old age before the growths clutter up her bronchial tubes, or fill her lungs with spores, or find some other, quicker way of preventing her from breathing entirely. In the meantime, the doctors stave off the attacks by giving Moolie a shot of adrenaline and then supplementing her oxygen for an hour or so. The enriched oxygen seems to kill the mushroom things off, or make the growths subside, or something. Whatever it does it works, and surprisingly quickly. By the time I come on to the ward, Moolie is sitting up in bed with a cup of tea.

"What are you doing here?" she says to me.

"I might ask you the same question." I can't tell yet if she's being sarcastic or if she's genuinely confused. Sometimes when she comes round after an attack she's delusional, or delirious, whatever you want to call it when the brain gets starved of oxygen for any length of time.

Moolie seems okay, though—this time, anyway. She's sipping her tea as if she's actually enjoying it. There's a biscuit in the saucer, too, with a bite taken out of it—Moolie eating something without being reminded is always a good sign.

I notice that one of the nurses has brushed her hair. She looks—very nearly—the way she does in that old photograph, her and me and Grandma Clarah out by the reservoir.

"I'm fine, Emily," she says, neatly sidestepping my actual question, which is so typical of her that I am tempted to believe her. "There was no need for you to leave work early. I know Benny needs you more than I do at the moment." She takes another sip of tea. "You could have come in afterwards, if you wanted to. They say I can probably go home tomorrow, in any case."

She's peeping at me over the rim of her teacup, grinning like a naughty schoolgirl—See what I did. Trying to boss me about like any normal mother. She can be like this after the treatments—it's as if the rarefied oxygen cleans out her brain, or something. I know it won't last, but it makes me feel like crying, nonetheless.

Just to have her back again.

Sometimes I forget how much I miss her.

I sit down on the plastic chair at the side of the bed. "I'm here now," I say. "You're not getting rid of me that easily." I reach for her free hand across the bedcovers and she lets me take it. After a couple of minutes one of the ward staff brings me a cup of tea of my own. It's good just to sit, to not feel responsibility or the need for action. The mechanics of this place are unknown to me, and therefore the urge to do, to change, to control is entirely absent.

Moolie begins telling me about the TV programme she was watching before she had her turn. Yet another documentary about the Mars mission—no surprises there. I'd rather she told me what it was that made her go outside by herself, but she waves my question away like an importunate fly.

"That girl," she says instead. "That girl, Zhanna. She's twenty-six tomorrow, did you know that? She says she doesn't want children, that her work is enough for her. She'll be dead before she's forty, more than likely. She doesn't know what she's doing."

"You were younger than she is when you had me, Mum," I say. "Did you know what you were doing?"

Moolie shakes her head slowly and deliberately from side to side. "No, I didn't," she says. "I didn't have a clue."

Then she says something strange.

"I won't always get better, Emily. The day will come when I don't come home. You should have a talk with Benny, before that day comes. There's no point in us pretending. Not anymore."

The mug of tea is still warm between my hands but in spite of this I suddenly feel cold all over. When I ask Moolie what she's talking about she refuses to answer.

By THE TIME I leave the hospital my shift has been over for ages. I decide to go back to the hotel anyway, just in case anything cropped up after I left. I check in with housekeeping and when I've satisfied myself that no major disasters have occurred in my absence I go in search of Benny. I find him in his office. There's a semicircle of empty chairs in front of his desk, the ghost of a meeting. Benny is alone, sitting very still in his chair, reading something—a book?—by the light of his desk lamp. He seems miles away, absent in a manner that is most unlike him.

When he realises I'm there he jerks upright, and there's an expression on his face—panic, almost—as if I've caught him out in a secret. He slams the book shut, making a slapping sound.

It's pointless him trying to hide it, though. I'd know the book anywhere, because it belongs to us, to Moolie and me. It's *The Art of Space Travel*.

"Emily," Benny says. He's watching my face for signs of disaster and at the same time he still looks guilty. It's a weird combination, almost funny. "I wasn't expecting you back. How's your mother?"

"Moolie's fine," I say. "They're letting her out tomorrow. What are you doing with that?"

I am talking about the book, of course, which I can't stop staring at, the way

Benny is holding it to him, like a shield. All of a sudden there's this noise in my ears, a kind of roaring sound, and I'm thinking of Moolie and Moolie telling me that I should talk to Benny.

I'm thinking of the way Benny is always asking after Moolie, and what Moolie said before, such a long time ago, about Benny arriving in this country with a cardboard suitcase and fake Levis, and a gold watch that he had to sell to get the money to rent a room.

"Emily," Benny says again, and the way he says my name—like he's apologising for something—makes me feel even weirder. He unfolds the book again across his lap, opening it to the centre, where I know there's a double-page colour spread of the Milky Way, with its billions of stars, all buzzing and fusing together, cloudy and luminous, like the mist as it rises from the surface of the George VI Reservoir.

Benny runs his fingers gently across the paper. It makes a faint squeaking sound. I know exactly how that paper feels: soft to the touch, slightly furry with impacted dust, old.

Benny is touching the book as if it is his.

My stomach does a lurch, as if the world is travelling too fast suddenly, spinning out of control across the blackly infinite backdrop of the whole of space.

"One of my schoolteachers gave me this book," Benny says. "His name was Otto Okora. His parents brought him here to London when he was six years old. They never returned to Africa, but Otto did. He came back to teach high school in Freetown and that's where he stayed. He said that England was too cold and too crowded, and that the sky here was never black enough to see the stars. He had this thing about Africa being closer to outer space than any other continent. 'We never lost our sense of life's mysteries,' was what he used to say. Otto was crazy about outer space. He would sit us down in the long hot afternoons and tell us stories about the first moon landings and the first space stations, the first attempts to map the surface of Mars. It was like poetry to me, Emily, and I could never get enough of it. I learned the names of the constellations and how to see them. I knew by heart the mass and volume and composition of each of the planets in our solar system. I even learned to draw my own star maps—impossible journeys to distant planets that no one in a thousand of our lifetimes will ever see. I saw them, though. I saw them at night, when I couldn't sleep. Instead of counting chickens I would count stars, picking them out from my memory one by one, like diamonds from a black silk handkerchief."

Like diamonds from a black silk handkerchief.

I want to hug him. Even in the midst of my confusion I want to hug him and tell him that I feel the same, that I have always felt the same, that we are alike.

That we are alike, of course we are.

The truth has been here in front of me, all the time. How stupid am I?

There's a kind of book called a grimoire, which is a book of spells. I've never seen one—I don't know if such a thing really exists, even—but *The Art of Space Travel* has always felt to me like it had magic trapped in it. Like you could open its pages and accidentally end up somewhere else. All those dazzling ropes of stars, all those thousands of possible futures, and futures' futures.

All those enchanted luminous pathways, blinking up at us through the darkness, like the lights of a runway.

I clear my throat with a little cough. I haven't a single clue what I ought to say.

"Your mother did her nut when you first got a job here," Benny says quietly. "She called me on the phone, tore me off a strip. She said I wasn't to breathe a word, under pain of death. That was the first time we'd spoken to one another in ten years."

"I WAS SUPPOSED to study medicine," Benny says to me later. "My heart was never in it, though. I didn't know what I wanted, only that I wanted to find a bigger world than the world I came from. I remember it as if it was yesterday, standing there on the tarmac and looking up at this hotel and just liking the name of it. I gazed up at the big lit-up star logo and it was as if I could hear Otto Okora saying, *You go for it, Benny boy, that's a good omen*. I liked the people and I liked the bustle and I liked the lights at night. All the taking off and landing, the enigma of arrival. There's a book with that name—your mother gave me a copy right back at the beginning, when she still believed in me and things were good between us. I never got round to reading it, but I loved that title. I loved it that I'd finally discovered something I was good at.

"Would she mind very much, do you think?" Benny says. "If I went to see her?"

"It's your funeral," I say, and shrug. I try and picture it as it might happen on TV, Benny pressing Moolie's skinny hand to his lips while she smiles weakly up from the pillows and whispers his name. You see how funny that is, right? "Only don't go blaming me if she bites your head off."

ZHANNA SOROKINA IS shorter than she appears on television. She has short mouse-brown hair, and piercing blue eyes. She looks like a school kid.

When I ask her if she'll sign *The Art of Space Travel* she looks confused. "But I did not write this," she says.

"I know that," I say. "But it's a book about space. My dad gave it to me. It would mean a lot to me if you would sign it. As a souvenir."

She uses the pen I give her, a blue Bic, to sign the title page. She writes her name twice, first in the sweeping Cyrillic script she would have learned at school and then again underneath in spiky Latin capitals.

"Is this okay?" she asks.

"Very," I reply. "Thank you."

Sorokina smiles, very briefly, and then I see her awareness of me leak from her eyes as she moves away towards the lift that will take her up to the tenth-floor news suite and the waiting cameras, the media frenzy that will surround her for the remainder of her time here on Earth. Her bodyguard moves in to shield her.

It's the last and only time I will see her close to.

In leaving this world, she makes me feel more properly a part of it.

I WISH I had a child I could one day tell about this moment. I've never felt like this before, but suddenly I do.

BENNY WOULD KILL me if he knew I was down here. I'm supposed to be upstairs, in the news suite, making sure they're up and running with the drinks trolleys. That there are three different kinds of bottled beer, instead of the two that would be usual for these kinds of occasions.

WHISPER ROAD (MURDER BALLAD NO. 9)
Caitlín R. Kiernan

Caitlín R. Kiernan (www.caitlinrkiernan) is a two-time recipient of both the World Fantasy and Bram Stoker awards, and the *New York Times* has declared her 'one of our essential writers of dark fiction.' Her recent novels include *The Red Tree* and *The Drowning Girl: A Memoir*, and, to date, her short stories have been collected in thirteen volumes, including *Tales of Pain and Wonder, A is for Alien, The Ammonite Violin & Others*, and the World Fantasy Award winning *The Ape's Wife and Other Stories*. Currently she's editing her fourteenth and fifteenth collections—*Houses Under the Sea: Mythos Tales* and *Dear Sweet Filthy World*. She has recently concluded *Alabaster*, her award-winning, three-volume graphic novel for Dark Horse Comics. She is currently working on her next novel, *Interstate Love Song*, based on the story that appeared in last year's volume. She lives in Providence, Rhode Island.

IT MAKES ME think of skipping stones, the way the pale red light skips along above the tree tops. It makes me think of finding a cobble on the beach, slate or granite or schist, no more than half the size of my palm, smoothed by ages of weather and not ground quite entirely flat. I put my thumb *here*, and I put my middle finger *here*, the weight of the stone cradled by my index finger. The stone hits the water, though the pale red light does not quite seem to touch the tops of the trees growing out beyond the edges of the cornfields. There is no moon tonight, no clouds, but no moon, either, and the light is very bright, silhouetted against the southern July sky. I ask Easter if she sees it, too. It's always good to be sure I'm not the only one. All too often I have found that I am the only one. Easter is messing around with the radio, looking for a station that isn't country music or preaching or hip hop, and she asks, "What? Do I see what?" I say, "If you'd look, you'd know what." Or she wouldn't, but, whichever way, I'd still have my answer. It skips like a grey slate cobble, that light, not moving smoothly along in its course, but buffeted from below, and I think how striking air and striking water are not necessarily so very different. Easter raises her head, and by the dashboard lights her bottle-blue eyes almost glow. It was her eyes that got me first; not her ass or her tits or the promise of what's between her legs, but those startling blue eyes. I take my right hand off the steering wheel and point out the open driver's side window. "Real low," I tell her. "Right above the treetops. If you see it, you'll know. If you see it, just tell me, so I know it isn't only me." And I know right away from her expression that she does, indeed, see the pale red light skimming along almost like a skipping stone on the waters of West Cove or Mackerel Cove or Hull Cove. But I still want to hear her say it out loud. She left the radio tuned to a blur of static, and I almost reach over and switch it off, but then she says, "Yeah, I see it. Don't you think it's probably an airplane? Or maybe a helicopter?" No, I reply, because it looks a lot more like a stone bouncing across water than it looks like either a helicopter or a plane, and, honestly, it doesn't *look* anything at all like a skipping stone. The comparison only comes to mind because of the way it's moving. *Behavior,* I think, *is not appearance.* "Then what is it?" Easter wants to know, as if I have the answer. And I catch a dull sliver of anxiety dug into her voice. That's hardly surprising, since the thing above the trees can't be too much more than half a mile away from us, half a mile from the edge of Tuckertown Road to that black wall of maples and oaks and pines. It can't be much more than a hundred feet above the treetops; maybe not even that. So, I don't fault her for sounding just a little bit nervous. Here it is past midnight, and we're the only car in sight. After that ugly piece of business back at the farm, we're both certainly worse for the wear, and now there's this thing that I'm pretty sure isn't a helicopter or an airplane, and she says, "I can't hear it. That close, don't you think we ought to be able to hear it, whatever it is?" I tell her I need a cigarette, please, and so she lights one and sets it between my lips. I breathe in smoke, willing the nicotine to clear my head, trying to concentrate on the road, because we just passed a yellow, diamond-shaped sign with the stark black outline of a buck printed on it.

Wouldn't that be hilarious, a fucking deer dashes out in front of us, and we're both staring at a light in the sky. Next thing you know, bam, we're dead in the proverbial ditch, so there's our comeuppance. If you subscribe to notions of karma and fair play and the witches' threefold law, well, that would be our ironic just reward. "How fast are we going?" asks Easter, and I say, "You've got eyes, don't you?" But I glance at the speedometer, anyway, and the needle is sitting right at seventy. "Maybe you ought to slow down," she tells me. Maybe I should, I tell myself, because getting stopped for speeding would be almost as funny as hitting a deer. I ease my foot off the gas pedal, and the speedometer needle promptly retreats to sixty-five, sixty, fifty-five. "Hey, Chaz," says Easter, "it's slowing down, too," and when I look I see that she's right. Out there across the field, the pale red light hasn't moved on ahead of us, like it should have. We aren't trailing along behind, as we should now be doing. "What the fuck," she says. "What the fuck would do that?" Like I should know. Like I do know, but I've decided at this late date to start keeping secrets from her. "Can you please find a station?" I ask. "The static's getting on my nerves. I hate that sound. I've always hated that sound. It's like hearing ants." Easter switches off the radio, and I say fine, yeah, that works, too. We pass a turnoff for some or another nameless dirt road and a couple of big trees very briefly block our view of the thing in the sky. "Maybe we should stop," she says, and I ask her what good she thinks that would do. "It might keep going, Chaz. It might pass us by, if we were to stop now. You could pull over there," and she points through the windshield towards a place up ahead where the shoulder is a little wider and paved with gravel. "You could just pull over, and we could see if it keeps going." She sounds a lot more afraid than she did only a minute before, that strained brittleness that comes before panic starts to creep into her voice. And I realize that I find this more disconcerting than the sight of the thing in the sky, because Easter is the one who never loses her shit. Not really. I couldn't count all the times she's talked me down. I wouldn't care to try. Back at the farm, when the dogs started barking and I reached for my gun, she was there to say, "No, no, Chaz. It's okay. They're just dogs. People will think it was a coyote set them off. Or just a skunk. Or a raccoon. There are lots of things out here to make dogs bark at night. No one even notices. No one gives it hardly more than a passing thought." But barking dogs are one thing, and that pale red light skimming along above the trees, well, that's another altogether. I don't pull over, and we rush past the gravelly place at the side of the road. Easter makes a small, uneasy noise, and she takes the cigarette from my mouth and sits smoking and watching the strange light out beyond the cornfield. "Just a little farther," I tell her. "That Jehovah's Witness church, that's not too far from here. I can pull over there, if you'd like." The tip of the cigarette flares in the dark, and she exhales a grey cloud; the wind through the open windows pulls it apart. "They don't believe in blood transfusions. Jehovah's Witnesses, I mean. Did you know that?" she asks me, and I say no, I didn't. "Well, it's true. They don't. They believe that blood is sacred, so it's some sort of blasphemy or something, some kind of unholy desecration, to get a blood transfusion. So, they'll just let their people bleed to death and shit. No, I don't think we should stop there. We should find somewhere else to stop." And fine, I tell her. We won't stop at the church. We'll keep going. "They won't allow organ transplants, either," she says. "Because, when you get someone else's heart, or their liver, or their kidneys, you're inevitably gonna get some of their blood in the bargain. It can't be helped, and so they're also against organ transplants. They'd rather let people die." I take my eyes off the road long enough to see that the red light is still out there, pacing us. Skipping. Skimming. And then the landscape on my left abruptly changes, and the fields are replaced by a merciful tangle of trees growing too closely together, grape vines, greenbriers, bracken, and I actually breathe a sigh of relief. *Now it can't see us,* I think. *Now it'll get bored and go away, find some other car to follow.* For a moment, neither I nor Easter says a word. I don't look at her, but I can feel her blue, blue eyes staring past me at the open driver's side window, staring towards the welcome, concealing sanctuary of the woods outside the window. "You okay?" I finally ask her, more to break the silence than anything else. She laughs a not entirely convincing sort of laugh and says, "Jesus in Heaven, what the fuck is wrong with us? Sure, that was weird. That was really fucking weird, but what the fuck is wrong with us, freaking out like that over a goddamn airplane or a helicopter." And I tell her it's just we're both still keyed up after the scene back at the farm. That it's probably nothing but the adrenaline making us jump at shadows. "Well, we gotta calm down," she says. "We're not ever gonna to get to Hartford, or anywhere else, if we don't we don't get a grip and our shit together." I tell her we'll be fine, everything's gonna be right as rain, and now she's opening the glove compartment, digging around for the bottle of Percocet she keeps stashed in there. Back at the farm on Whisper Road, she was the one dolling out calm and reassurances, and the comforting words sound funny coming from me, as unconvincing as that laugh of hers. She finds the bottle and dry swallows two of the pastel yellow pills; she offers me one, but I say no. Not when I'm driving. When I'm driving I don't drink and I don't smoke weed and I don't take pills, and Easter says, "Suit yourself. " And then she says, "There's a place you can pull over at Worden's Pond. It's not much farther, a little parking lot with a dock for fishermen and kayaks and stuff. We can stop there, just long enough to catch our breath." That sounds good, I reply. That sounds perfect. So, we'll stop at Worden's Pond. Easter puts the prescription bottle back into the glove compartment and slams it shut, because the latch is busted and if you don't slam it, the door doesn't stay closed. She flicks the cigarette butt out the window. In the rearview, I see it hit the road and die in a bouncing flurry of orange sparks. "Maybe it was a drone," she says. "I've never seen one at night, so maybe that's what it was. I don't know what they'd look like in the dark, but they might look like that. I was reading a magazine article about using drones to catch illegal deer hunters. You know, poachers. And to spot forest fires and check on power lines—all sorts of other everyday things you might not know about drones getting used for. I bet that's what it was. I bet it was just a drone." Maybe so, I tell her. Maybe that's exactly what it was. And I'm also thinking, *I expect the police use them, too,* but I keep that to myself. The police aren't looking for us. No one's looking for us. Not yet. No one saw us, and, besides, it'll be at least another day or two before anyone goes poking around the farm and calls the cops. It might have been longer, if she'd let me kill the dogs. Those dogs get hungry, they'll attract attention, no matter what Easter says about no one out here paying any mind to barking dogs. But when I told her I was going to kill them, the beagle and the German Shepherd, she said she'd leave me if I did. She helped me tie up the man and the woman, and she watched me cut their throats, but then when I say I need to put down a couple of mutts to save our hides, to buy us time, and she tells me she'll walk if I do. I don't know if she really meant it, but I didn't kill the fucking dogs. "Isn't it crueler to leave them here to starve?" I asked her, and she replied, "They won't starve. Someone will find them." And then someone will be looking for us, only I didn't say that. "We used to swim in Worden's Pond," says Easter, "when we were kids, my brothers and me. My brothers used to catch turtles and water snakes there." We pass the church—the Kingdom Hall, according the sign hanging out front—and the woods on our left give way to open fields again. I taste foil, and for a few seconds my heart is a long-distance runner thudding in my chest. "Don't look," Easter tells me, as if I have some choice in the matter. Of course I look, but there isn't anything out there to see. No pale red phantom skipping along. Nothing but dry-stone walls and alfalfa and more rows of tall corn, then a black line of trees to mark the boundary of someone's toil, marking off the southern edge of the fields. I think about how those cornstalks would rustle out there in the dark, whenever the wind stirs, and it gives me a shiver. "It's gone," I say, not feeling even half as relieved as I should. "Whatever it was, it's gone now. Relax. Find something on the radio." Easter turns her head to see for herself, cause maybe after the way things went back on Whisper Road, my word isn't good enough for her anymore. I said no one was gonna get hurt, and then they did, and so I can't exactly blame her for losing faith. But I want to, whether blaming her is right or wrong. It'll be a long, long time before I'm over losing her trust. "It's gone," she says, like an echo, and I say, "Like I told you, huh?" She turns away from me then, turning head and shoulders to stare at the summer night from the vantage point of her own window. "We should stop anyway," she says. "Just to clear our heads." I nod and tell her, "Fine, sure, we'll stop anyway," even though I only want to keep driving. The tires are making music, the steady lullaby hum of rubber against asphalt, and what matters now is putting as many miles behind us as quickly as possible—get out of Rhode Island, get up to Hartford, ditch this car, get some fucking sleep, then figure out what comes next. Easter has friends in Hartford, people she says will be sympathetic to our situation—for the right price. She switches the radio on again, and this time it only takes her a moment to find the college station out of Kingston. They're playing the Rolling Stones, "Start Me Up," a song I know from my father's old records. "Leave it there," I say to her. "That's good. You sure we need to stop now? Can't be more than twenty, twenty-five miles from here to the state line. We could stop then, stop and piss and top off the tank. Get some coffee." But she stubbornly shakes her head, no, "No, I need to stop *before* that, I need to get some air." As if all the air in South County isn't blowing in through her open window, whipping at her long hair, roaring in our ears. I can smell the ocean on that air, the ocean and cooling tar and fresh-cut hay. And then she adds, "I need to wash my hands." Easter looks down at her open palms. She washed her hands back at the farm after I killed those two, washed her hands twice in the kitchen sink with scalding hot water and liquid dishwashing soap, Palmolive or Dawn or Joy or something like that. I finally had to tell her to stop it, that she was gonna scrub all the skin off if she didn't, and we needed to get the fuck out of there. I couldn't have her going all Lady Macbeth on me, especially when she wasn't the one who held the knife and there wasn't a drop of blood on her anywhere. I check the speedometer, the gas gauge, the odometer, the clock. I almost tell her she can wait to wash her hands again, that it won't kill her to wait, but then I lose my nerve. I'm a goddamn coward when it comes to Easter. "It wasn't necessary," she says, "what you did." And I tell her, "Well, it seemed pretty necessary at the time. But now it's done, and there's no point being sorry for something that can't be undone. That's just what happened. That's just the way it went." She rubs her palms together, wrings her hands, then glances past me at the place where the pale red light isn't skipping along beneath the sky and above the trees. "They got kids," she says. "I saw photographs. Kids and grandkids, and all I'm saying is it wasn't necessary, and you promised no one would get hurt. I've never done anything like that before, that's all. I'd never seen anything like that done." I say, "You've seen it in the movies, lots of times. You've seen it on TV." And she says, "That isn't the same. That isn't the same at all." She's absolutely fucking right, of course, but I don't tell her so, and I don't apologize, either. Instead, I say "Don't pretend you didn't know what I am." She takes another cigarette from the half-empty pack on the dash, lights it, and at first I think she's staring at me, but really she's only staring at the place where the pale red light isn't. In the darkness, her face is like a painting on black velvet. "Don't you even feel anything?" she asks. "Anything at all?" Before I can reply, she says, "There's a little cemetery off over there, on the far side of that pasture. There's a dozen or so marble headstones, but the dates are mostly worn away. Acid rain, you know, it ruins the marble. Acid rain from pollution, makes the stone soft. Makes it rot." She pauses, takes a drag, holds in the smoke a moment, exhales. "I haven't ever killed anything, much less anyone." We pass a few houses lined up neatly on either side of Tuckertown Road, and the night is briefly interrupted by streetlights and porch lights and lamps still burning in windows, unsuspecting people asleep and dreaming in their beds or up late or maybe even already awake again and getting ready for tomorrow. Tidy rows of mailboxes. Tidy yards and tidy fences. "You knew," I say, and "Yeah, Chaz, I knew," she replies. "But knowing isn't the same thing as seeing, and it certainly isn't the same thing as being a party to it." And now the houses are behind us, along with whatever comfort might be found in the cold white electric glow of all those lights, whatever dim sanctuary. The night takes us back. The night is a jealous bitch, but she's also forgiving. I'm driving too fast again, my foot too heavy on the accelerator, and I'm trying to decide if the speed is worth the risk of cops and hitting deer when I smell sulfur. Before I can ask Easter if she smells it, she says. "Jesus, did you hear that?" and I see she's got both her hands clapped over her ears. "No," I tell her. "I didn't hear anything." And she asks, "Is that the car? Jesus, is it the *car* making that noise?" The stink of sulfur is suddenly overwhelming, and my stomach rolls like I'm getting seasick, like I'm stuck on the ferry from Galilee to Block Island. "Is it Morse code?" she wants to know. *I'm going to puke,* I think. *I'm seasick without even being near the sea, and I'm going to fucking puke right here on the steering wheel and in my lap if I don't get off the road right now.* I put my foot on the brake, slowing down and looking for some safe place to pull over. But there are steep shoulders on the left and on the right of us, steep shoulders and deep, weed-filled ditches. Then I finally hear whatever it is Easter's hearing, only it isn't loud at all, and certainly it's nothing that would ever make you want to cover your ears. In fact, it seems very far away, a muted, indistinct *beep-beep-beeping.* Maybe it does sound like Morse code. Maybe that's exactly what it sounds like, but I wouldn't know. I can tie forty different knots, every single one in the Boy Scout handbook, but I don't know shit about Morse code. "There's something wrong," Easter says, hands still over her ears, and if she sounded scared before, now she sounds terrified. "There's something wrong with the sky. Don't slow down. Don't stop. Please, don't stop." And back at the farm on

Whisper Road, hardly even an hour and a half ago, she's watching me tie up the man and his wife with lengths of strong jute rope I bought that afternoon down in Wakefield. Easter asked me if duct tape wouldn't be easier and faster, and I told her easier and faster is sloppy, and sloppy is how people get caught. Sloppy is what the sheriffs and police detectives are always counting on. "Like this," I say, standing at an angle so she can see my hands. "Over and under and around." The man and woman are silent. I haven't gagged them, and I keep expecting him to make threats. I keep expecting her to beg or start crying. But they don't do either. I wish they would; it would be so much easier if they would, if I were angry. Anger takes the edge off everything. Anger is better than whisky or cocaine when I need to steady my nerves. "Can't you talk, old lady?" I ask the woman, looping the rope about her skinny ankles, cinching it tightly. "Cat got your tongue?" Easter tells me to leave her alone. "We got what we came for, didn't we? There's no point being cruel." And I see then that the old woman is watching her, not me. So is the man, and I know they're both thinking how Easter's the weak one in this equation, how whatever slim hope they might have of seeing daylight and getting out of this alive resides there in her startling blue eyes. Hell, from where they're sitting right now, Easter probably looks as sweet as the Divine Baby Jesus wrapped up safe in Mother Mary's arms. It's her eyes. Her eyes have mercy in them. When we first met, I told her I'd never seen eyes that shade of blue, and that's when she told me it was called cornflower blue. "It's just a weed that grows wild in cornfields," she said. "Cornflowers, I mean. They bloom in June and flower all summer long." So, that's what I'm thinking, there in the farmhouse, in that that old couple's bedroom, looping rope round and round, that these two see God in my lover's cornflower eyes. "Did you hear that?" Easter wants to know, and when I ask, "Did I hear what?" she shakes her pretty head and turns away. "Just hurry," she tells me. "Finish tying them up and let's get out of here." I reply, "Hurrying is just as bad as being sloppy. Hurrying *makes* you sloppy." Easter, she glances at the alarm clock ticking away the night on the little table beside the bed. The clock's face is washed with soft green light, like dashboard light, like the light on Easter's face when she reaches for a cigarette or opens the glove compartment or wanders the radio dial looking for a station that suits her fancy. "Sunrise is at 5:16," she says, "and we're expected in Hartford before

noon. I'm not saying be sloppy, but we can't hang around here all night."
And right here I feel the spark of anger I was hoping for, right fucking here,
and I say, "Okay, fine. My bad. Let's get this the fuck over with and get back
on the road." I reach down and pull the butterfly knife out of my right boot,
flip it open, and Easter just stands there watching me while I cut their throats.
I open their carotids and the arterial spray paints the floor and walls. Neither
of them makes a sound. They don't beg. They don't whimper. They don't cry
out in fear or pain. And I think that's fucking creepy, that's goddamn fucking
eerie, and I can't help but wonder if this whole thing's gone south on us. I let
go of the old woman's body, and it pitches forward, landing face down in its
own blood. *Her* own blood. "You didn't have to do that," says Easter, just
barely loud enough for me to hear. "You promised me no one was going to
get hurt." Then she looks down at her hands, then back to the bodies, then
back at her hands again. That's when she goes downstairs to the kitchen
sink. I stand there in the bedroom a few minutes longer, staring at the dead
woman and her husband, not really giving a shit that they're dead, but pissed
off that Easter made me kill them. Pissed off that she's pissed at me, when it
was her fault, when she's the one that threw that bright copper spark that set
me on fire. I wipe the knife clean on the nubby white chenille bedspread, fold
the blade closed, and stick it back into my boot. I go downstairs and find her
at the sink. "I didn't mean to do that," I tell her. "I didn't come in here
meaning to kill anyone." She doesn't look up, just squirts more soap from
the green plastic bottle into her hands and says, "I never said you did. But
they're still dead, regardless." I tell her that we need to go, and Easter says
go on ahead, she's coming, she'll be right behind me, she just has to wash her
hands first. And this is when the dogs in the pen out back start barking. I
reach for the pistol tucked into the waistband of my jeans, but she stops me.
"Why is it they call you Easter, anyway?" I asked her, the first night we met,
and she told me, "When I was a little girl, I used to raise rabbits. My daddy,
he started calling me Easter when I was a kid, and it just sorta stuck." And I
said, "Rabbits? For what? For the skins? For the meat?" And she made a
face and said no, just for pets. She never let anyone kill one of her rabbits.
No one ever tried. And there in the farmhouse on Whisper Road she puts her
hands on mine, her hands all wet and soapy, hands that have never been
stained with the blood of rabbits or human beings. She tells me how I'm not

going to shoot those dogs, because there's no need, because people out here are used to hearing dogs barking at night, and they'll just think it's because there's a skunk or a coyote or a raccoon poking about the garbage cans, getting them stirred up. "No more killing," she says, "not tonight. Not if you want me to stay." And then she looks back over her shoulder at the steam rising from the sink because she left the tap on, steam fogging the windowpane above the sink, and she says, "Chaz, did you hear that?" I ask her did I hear what, because all I heard is the damn dogs, and she says, "I don't know. I don't know what it was. Was it Morse code?" And she must have shut off the water before we left the house, but, if so, I can't remember her doing it. I can't remember walking back up the dirt road to where I'd left the car parked in the shade of two huge oak trees, either. And there must be a word for this, when you suddenly realize that you can't remember something you should, something that's just fucking happened. "Is that the *car* making that noise?" she wants to know. We were standing in the kitchen, and the dogs were barking, and everything smelled like dishwashing liquid and blood, and then we're driving down Tuckertown Road, and when I turn my head I see that pale red light skipping along above the treetops. "No," Easter insists, "there was something else, something in between there, after the kitchen, but before you asked me to look and tell you what I saw." And I say, "I don't think I'd know Morse code if I heard it." I can't remember getting back into the car or turning the key in the ignition. I can't remember stowing the box from the old couple's basement in the trunk of the car, but I know that's exactly where I put it. "Dots and dashes," says Easter. She's standing alone at the far end of the dock jutting out into Worden's Pond. I'm looking north, and on my right the sky's beginning to brighten. On my left, the night is as dark as night can be. There's a mist rising up off the water and from the tall grass and cattails growing all along the shore. There's a canoe tied up at the end of the dock, and Easter says, "A lot of people think the first time anyone used S.O.S. to call for help was when the *Titanic* sank, but that's a myth." I'm sitting on the hood of the car, watching her, trying to remember what happened after I smelled sulfur and she heard Morse Code, how we got from there to the pond. That must be half a mile or more I've forgotten, and now the sun is coming up, even though the last time I checked the clock on the dash it was only a little past two thirty. I've forgotten half a mile and more than two and a half hours. "How's that even possible?" I ask her, and that's when I see the light, way out over the water, hovering just a few feet above the steaming surface of the pond. "Three dots," says Easter, "three dashes, then three more dots. Three short, three long, three short. Some people think it stands for something, like 'save our ship' or 'save our souls,' but the truth is it doesn't stand for anything at all." She's holding my pistol in her right hand, holding it down at her side, staring out across the water at the light that isn't skipping or skimming, but just hanging there like a fat butchered hog. "You should come back," I say. "You shouldn't get so close to that thing. We don't know what it wants." And I think then how the hood of the car is cold, how the engine block isn't popping and pinging the way it does when it's cooling off, and I tell Easter again that she should come back. "We don't even know what it is," I say. I'm amazed at how perfectly, utterly calm I sound. "Come back over here, and tell me more about the *Titanic* and Morse code. I don't know where you learn all this stuff." She shakes her head, and when she does I imagine that the pale red light sort of bobs along in unison. It isn't making any sound whatsoever. "No, Chaz," she says. "I think I'm exactly where I'm supposed to be. You promised me no one would get hurt tonight. You promised me, and then you killed them, anyway. You didn't need to do that." And it occurs to me that someone's standing there beside her, someone or only the *shadow* of someone. *Get up,* I think. *Get the fuck up off your ass and go get her.* But I don't move. I'm not even sure I can move, my arms and legs feel so heavy, like lead weights, like marble headstones etched by years and years of acid rain. Out on the pond, the pale red light waits impatiently, and there on the dock, Easter raises the pistol and presses the barrel beneath her chin. *Get up. Get the fuck up and do something.* But then the shadow leans in close, and I imagine that it's whispering to Easter secret words that only she's supposed to hear, truths and revelations that I'll never know. She squeezes the trigger, and thunder blooms and rumbles and rolls away like sunrise, dashing the night apart upon the hateful shingle of the coming day.

RED DIRT WITCH
N.K. Jemisin

N.K. Jemisin (www.nkjemisin.com) lives and writes in Brooklyn, New York.
Her work has been nominated for the Hugo (three times), the Nebula (four
times), and the World Fantasy Award (twice); shortlisted for the Crawford,
the Gemmell Morningstar, and the Tiptree; and she has won a Locus Award
for Best First Novel and *Romantic Times'* Reviewer's Choice Award (three
times). In 2016, she became the first black person to win the Best Novel
Hugo for *The Fifth Season*. Jemisin has published seven novels, including the
Inheritance trilogy and Dreamblood duology, and the first two in the Broken
Earth trilogy—Hugo winner *The Fifth Season* and *The Obelisk Gate*. The
final book in the series is due out in 2017. Jemisin's short fiction has been
published in *Clarkesworld, Postscripts, Strange Horizons, Baen's Universe*,
and various print anthologies. She also currently writes a *New York Times*
book review column, Otherworldly, in which she covers the latest in science
fiction and fantasy.

THE WAY TO tell the difference between dreams that were prophecy and dreams
that were just wasted sleep was to wait and see if they came three times.
Emmaline had her third dream about the White Lady on the coldest night ever
recorded in Alabama history. This was actually *very* cold—ten degrees below
zero, on a long dark January Sabbath when even the moon hid behind a veil
of shadow.

Emmaline survived the cold the way poor people everywhere have done
since the dawn of time: with a warm, energetic friend. Three patchwork quilts
helped too. The friend was Frank Heath, who was pretty damn spry for a man
of fifty-five, though he claimed to be forty-five so maybe that helped. The quilts

were Em's, and it also helped that one of them had dried flowers (Jack-in-the-pulpits) and a few nuggets of charcoal tucked under each patch of leftover cloth. That made for a standing invitation to warmth and the summertime, who were of course welcome to pay a visit and stay the night anytime they liked. Those *had* come a-calling to the children's beds, at least, for which Emmaline was grateful; the children slept soundly, snug and comfortable. That left Em and Frank free to conduct their own warmthmaking with an easy conscience.

After that was done, Emmaline closed her eyes and found herself in the Commissary Market down on Dugan. Dusty southern daylight, bright and fierce even in winter, shone slanting onto the street alongside the market, unimpeded by cars or carts—or people. Pratt City wasn't much of a city, being really just the Negro neighborhood of Birmingham, but it was a whole place, thriving and bustling in its way. Here, though, Emmaline had never seen the place so empty in her life. As if to spite the cold, the market's bins tumbled over with summer produce: watermelons and green tomatoes and peaches and more, along with a few early collards. That meant that whatever this dream meant to warn her of, it would come with the heat of the mid-months.

Out of habit, Em glanced at the sign above these last. Overpriced again; greedy bastards.

"Why, greed's a sin," said a soft, whispery voice all around her. "Be proper of you to punish 'em for it, wouldn't it?"

This was one of the spirits that she'd tamed over the years. They liked to test her, though, so it was always wise to be careful with 'em. "Supposin' I could," she said in reply. "But only the store manager, since the company too big to go after. And I can't say's I truly blame the manager, either, since he got children to feed same as me."

"Sin's sin, woman."

"And let she who is without sin cast the first stone," Em countered easily. "*As you well know.*" Then she checked herself; no sense getting testy. Ill-wishing opened doors for ill winds to blow through—which was probably why the voice was trying to get her to do it.

The voice sighed a little in exasperation. It was colorless, genderless, barely a voice at all; that sigh whispered like wind through the stand of pines across the street. "Just tellin' you somebody comin', cranky old biddy."

"Who, Jesus Christ? 'Bout time, His slow ass."

Whispery laughter. "Fine, then—there a White Lady a-comin', a *fine* one, and she got something special in mind for you and yours. You ready?"

Em frowned to herself. The other two dreams had been more airy-fairy than this—just collections of symbols and hints of a threat, omens and portents. It seemed fate had finally gotten impatient enough to just say plain what she needed to hear.

"No, I ain't ready," Em said, with a sigh. "But ain't like that ever made no mind to some folk. Thank you for the warning."

More laughter, rising to become a gale, picking Emmaline up and spinning her about. The Market blurred into a whirlwind—but through it all, there were little ribbons that she could see edging into the tornado from elsewhere, whipping about in shining silken red. Truth was always there for the taking, if you only reached out to grasp it. Thing was, Em didn't *feel* like grasping it; she was tired, Lord have mercy. The world didn't change. If she just relaxed, the dream would let her back into sleep, like she wanted.

But... well. Best to be prepared, she supposed.

So Em stretched out a hand and laid hold of one of the ribbons. And suddenly the street that ran through the market was full of people. *Angry* people, most of 'em white and lining the road, and marching people, most of 'em black and in the middle of the road. The black ones' jaws were set, their chins high in a way that always meant trouble when white folks were around, because Lord didn't they hate seeing pride. "Trouble, trouble," sang-song the voice—and before the marchers appeared a line of policemen with billy clubs in their hands and barking dogs at their sides. Emmaline's guts clenched for the blood that would almost surely be spilled. Pride! Was it worth all that blood?

Yet when she opened her mouth to shout at the marchers for their foolishness, the whispery voice laughed again, and she spun again, the laughter chasing her out of dreams and up to reality.

Well, this was what she'd wanted, but she didn't much like it because reality was dark and painfully cold on her mouth and chin, which she'd stuck outside the covers to breathe. Her teeth were chattering. She reached back.

"Ain't time to get up," muttered Frank at her stirring, half-dreaming himself.

"You got Sunday to rest," said Emmaline. "You want to live 'til then, you get to work."

His low, rich laugh warmed her more than his body ever could. "Yes ma'am," he said, and did as he was bid.

And because they had set to, Emmaline missed that her only girlchild Pauline got up and walked the hall for awhile, disturbed by bad dreams of her own.

SINCE THE SPIRITS had given her a full season's warning, Em spent the time preparing for the White Lady's arrival. This meant she finished up as much business as possible in the days right after the dream. The cold passed quickly, as cold was wont to do in Alabama. And as soon as the weather was comfortable again, Emmaline set Pauline to grinding all the herbs she'd laid in since November, then had her boy Sample put her shingle out by the mailpost, where it read HERBS AND PRAYERS, FOR ALL AND SUNDRY. This brought an immediate and eager stream of customers.

First there was Mr. Jake, who'd gotten into a spat with his cousin over Christmas dinner and had wished death on him, and now was regretting it because the cousin had come down with a wet cough. Emmaline told him to take the man some chitlins made with sardine oil and extra garlic. Then she handed him a long braid of garlic heads, ten in all, from her own garden.

"*That* much garlic?" Jake had given her a look of pure affront; like most men of Pratt City, he was proud of his cooking. "I look Eye-talian to you?"

"All right, let him die, then." This elicited a giggle from Pauline, who sat in on most of Em's appointments these days.

So, grumbling, Jake had bought the garlic from Emmaline and gone off to make his amends. People talked about Jake's stanky, awful chitlins 'til the day he died—but his cousin ate some of the peace offering, and he got better.

And there was Em's cousin Renee, who came by just to chat, and conveniently told Emmaline all the goings-on in and around Pratt City. There was trouble brewing, Renee said, *political* trouble; whispers in the church pews, meetings at the school gym, plans for a boycott or two or ten. Way up in Virginia, folks were suing the government about segregation in the schools. Em figured it wouldn't come to nothing, but all the white folks was up like angry bees over the notion of their precious children sitting next to Negro children, competing next to Negro children, befriending Negro children. It was going to get ugly. Many evils came riding in on the tails of strife, though—so here, Emmaline suspected, would be their battleground.

Then there was Nadine Yates, a widow who like Emmaline had done what she had to do to keep herself and her children alive through the cold and not-so-cold days. Nadine was afraid she might be pregnant again. "I know it's a sin," she said in her quiet, dignified voice while Emmaline fixed her some tea. For this one, she'd sent Pauline off to the market with her brothers; Pauline was still just a girl, and some things were for grown women's ears only. "Still, if you could help me out, I'd be grateful."

"Sin's makin' a world where women got to choose between two children' eatin' and three children starvin'," Emmaline said, "and you sure as hell didn't do that. You made sure he wasn't some fool who'll spread it all over, didn't you?"

"He got a wife and a good job, and he ain't stupid. Gave my boys new coats just last week."

A man who knew how to keep a woman-on-the-side properly. But then wouldn't it be simple enough for him to just take care of the new child too? Emmaline frowned as a suspicion entered her mind. "He white?"

Nadine's nearer jaw flexed a little, and then she lifted her chin in fragile defensiveness. "He is."

Emmaline sighed, but then nodded toward the tea cooling in Nadine's hand. "Drink up, now. And it sound like he can afford a guinea-hen, to me."

So a few days later, after the tea had done its work, Nadine dropped by and handed Emmaline a nice fat Guinea fowl. It was a rooster, but Em didn't mind. She pot-roasted it with dried celery and a lot of rosemary from her garden, and the rind of an orange that Pauline had found on the road behind a market truck. Emmaline had smacked the girl for that, because even though 'finding' wasn't 'stealing', white folks didn't care much for making distinctions when it came to little colored girls. But Pauline—who was smart as a whip and Em's pride—had glared at her mother after the blow. "Momma, I followed the truck to a stop sign and offered to give it back. I knew that white man wouldn't want it 'cause I touched it, and he didn't! So there!"

Smart as a whip, but still just a child, and innocent yet of the world's worst ugliness. Emmaline could only sigh and thank God the truck driver hadn't been the kind who'd have noticed how pretty Pauline was becoming. As an apology for the smack, she'd let Pauline have half the orange while the boys got only a quarter each. Then she'd sat the girl down for a long talk about how the world worked.

And so it was, as the brief winter warmed toward briefer spring and began the long slow march into Southern summer. By the time the tomato plants flowered, Em was as ready as she could be.

"Oh, Miss Emmaline!" called a voice from outside. An instant later Jim and Sample, Emmaline's boys, ran into the kitchen.

"It's a red lady outside," Sample gushed.

"Well, go figure," Emmaline said. "Ain't like you ain't a quarter red yourself." Her papa had been Black Creek, his hair uncut 'til death.

"Not *that* kinda red," said Sample, rolling his eyes enough to get a hard look from Emmaline. "She askin' for you."

"Is she, now?" Emmaline turned from the pantry and handed Sample a jar of peach preserves. "Open that for me and you can have some." Delighted to be treated like a man, Sample promptly sat down and began wrestling with the tight lid.

"I don't like this one," said Jim, and since Jim was her artist—none of the dreaming in him, but he saw things others didn't—Emmaline knew the time had come. She wiped her hands on a cloth and went out onto the porch to meet the White Lady.

She smelled the lady before she saw her: a thick waft of magnolia perfume, too cloying to be quite natural. Outside, the perfume wasn't as bad, diminished and blended in among the scents of Em's garden and the faint sulfurous miasma that was omnipresent in Pratt City on still days like this—that from the Village Creek, polluted as it was with nearly a century's worth of iron and steel manufacturing waste. The woman to whom the perfume belonged stood on the grassy patch in front of Em's house, fastidiously away from the red dirt path that most people walked to reach her front porch. Why, this lady was just as pretty as a flower in a full-skirted dress of cotton print, yellow covered in white-and-green lilies. No crinoline, but nearly as old-fashioned, with layers separated by bunched taffeta and edged in lace. Around the heart-shaped bodice, her skin was white as pearl—so white that Em figured she'd have burned up in a minute if not for the enormous parasol positioned over her head. And here was why Sample had called her red: the confection of her hair, spun into an elegant chignon behind her head and topped with a crown of white flowers, was nearly as burgundy as good wine.

It was all Em could do not to feel inadequate, given that she wore only an old faded housedress, with her own hair done up in plaits and hidden away beneath a wrap. But she drew herself up anyway, and reminded herself that she needed no parasol to keep her skin fine; the sun did that itself, and black didn't crack beneath its blessing. Those were just surface things, anyway. The White Lady was nearly *all* surface; that was the nature of her kind. That was how this meeting would go, then: an appearance of grace and gentility, covering the substance of battle.

"Why, I've come to see 'bout you, Miss Emmaline," the White Lady said, as if they were in the middle of a conversation and not the beginning. Her voice was light and sweet, as honeyed as her yellow eyes. "You know me?"

"Yes, ma'am," Em said, because she knew the children were watching and it wouldn't do for them, 'specially the boys, to think they could smart off to white ladies. Even if this one wasn't really a white lady. "Heard here and there you was coming."

"Did you, now!" She simpered, dimples flashing, and flicked at her skirts. As she did this, Em caught a glimpse of a figure behind her: a little black girl, couldn't have been more than seven, crouched and holding the pole of the great big parasol over the woman's head. The little girl's feet were bare beneath the simple white shift she wore, and her eyes were still and empty.

"I suppose I shouldn't be surprised that you heard," the White Lady said, unfolding a little lace fan and fluttering it at herself. "Figured you'd have your ways. Could I trouble you for some tea or lemonade, though, Miss Emmaline? It's always almighty hot in this land. Not that that bothers your kind like it does mine."

"Mighty hot indeed," Emmaline agreed evenly. She nodded to Pauline, who stood beside her trembling a little. Even a half-trained girlchild knew power when she saw it. Pauline jumped, but went inside. "This land made its natural

435

people brown for a reason, though, ma'am, long before either your'n or most of mine came along. Seems to me you could make yourself fit the land better—if you wanted, of course."

The woman extended one long, thin arm and ran her fingers up the pearly skin, looking almost bemused to find such flesh upon herself. "I *should*, I suppose, but you know there's more reward than price comes with this skin."

Em did indeed know. "Pauline's gone to fetch some tea for you, ma'am. No lemonade, I'm afraid; lemons cost too dear when you got three children and no husband, see."

"Ah, yes! About those children of yours."

As much as Emmaline thought she had braced herself, she still couldn't help tensing up when the White Lady's yellow eyes shifted to dance over the faces of Jim and Sample. Lord, but she should've guessed! America wasn't the Old Country; these days the White Folk didn't bother with silly tricks or living in mounds, and they didn't stay hidden, for why should they? But the one thing they still did, in spades here in this land of cheap flesh, was steal children. And if they kept to children of a certain hue, why, the police didn't even ask after them. Emmaline set her jaw.

The woman's eyes lingered on Jim long enough to be worrying. Jim, smart one that he was, had gone still and quiet, looking down at his feet, knowing better than to meet any white woman's gaze. Sample was all a-bristle, not liking the way the woman was eyeballing his little brother; ah, damnation, Emmaline never should've picked for Sample's father a man who liked to fight. Boy was gonna get himself in trouble some day.

Em had a feeling, though, that this was a feint. Then Pauline came back onto the porch with a big sweating glass of iced tea... and sure enough, the White Lady's gaze landed on the girl with much more than greed for a cool drink.

Pauline stopped there, with her eyes narrowed, because like Emmaline, she knew what was beneath the surface. The woman laughed prettily at the look on the girl's face.

"*Trouble comin' tell*," the White Lady sang, still grinning. "*Trouble comin' fine! Nought to pay the price but sweet blood like fine wine.*" She had a beautiful voice—lilting and hymn-reverberant and high as birds flew. Hardly sounded human, in fact, which was fitting enough.

Em raised a hand in praise anyway, because beauty was meant to be acknowledged, and to deny it would just invite her further in. "Trouble always coming, ma'am," she replied to the song. "Some'a us, this world made of trouble. Not that you folk help."

"Aww, Miss Emmaline, don't be like that. Come on here, girl, with that tea. It's powerful hot."

Em glanced at Pauline; Pauline nodded once, tightly. Then she walked down the steps to the bottommost slat—no further—and held forth the glass.

The White Lady sighed, throwing a look at Em. "Ought to raise your children to show some respect, Miss Emmaline."

"Lots of ways to show respect, ma'am."

The White Lady sniffed. Then she turned her head, and the little girl who'd been holding the parasol straightened and came around her. The parasol stayed where it was, holding itself up against the ground. As the child moved forward, Em's skin came all over goosebumps. Wasn't right, seeing a child who should've been lively so empty of life and magic. The little girl twitched a little while she walked, as if with a palsy, or as if jerked on strings. She stopped before Pauline and held her hands up, and Em didn't blame Pauline at all for her grimace as she pushed the glass into the child's hands.

"Whose was she?" Emmaline asked, as the little girl twitched and moved to bring the tea back to her mistress.

"Nobody who matters, Miss Em, don't you mind." The White Lady took the glass of tea, then smoothed a hand over the child's soft cap of hair with an almost fond smile. "Such a lovely girl, though, isn't she? Everybody says you folk can't be beautiful, but that's just not true. Where else would I be able to get this?" She preened, smoothing a hand over one unblemished, shining cheek.

"She had power," Pauline said then. Em started; she was used to Pauline keeping her mouth shut around white folks, like a good sensible girl should. But Pauline was still staring at the little girl in horror. Her expression hardened, though, from shock into disgust. "She had *power*, and you *took* it. Like a damn thief."

The White Lady's eyebrows looked to have climbed into her red hair for a moment. Emmaline was right there with her, shocked at Pauline's cheek. She snapped without thinking, "Pauline Elizabeth, shut your mouth before I shut it."

Pauline shut up, though Emmaline could see the resentful flex of muscle along her jaw. But the White Lady let out a soft laugh, chilling them both into silence.

"Well! I can't say I think much of how you're raising your children, Miss Emmaline. Negro children never can sit still and be quiet, I suppose. Of course I took her power, girl; not like *she* could do anything with it. Now. I think I'm owed an apology, don't you?"

Damnation. Stiffly, Emmaline said, "I'm sorry for my daughter's foolishness, ma'am. I'll see to her when we're done talking."

"Oh, but that isn't enough, Miss Em." The White Lady tilted her head, long red lashes catching the light. "Honestly, how's she going to learn respect if you do all the apologizing for her?"

Pauline spoke tightly, with a darting glance at Emmaline for permission to speak. "I'm sorry too, ma'am."

"Now, see? That wasn't so hard." The White Lady gestured with the tinkling glass of tea at Pauline, beaming. "But don't you think you owe me a bit more, after smarting off like that? Why, I'm *wounded*. You called me a thief! And even if I am, it's the principle of the thing." She stepped forward. "I think you should come with me for a while, and learn respect. Don't you?"

"No, ma'am," Emmaline snapped, before Pauline could dig herself further into trouble. "I don't think she owes you a thing beyond what you've had."

"Oh, now, be reasonable." The White Lady stepped forward once more, almost to the porch steps—but then she paused, her smile fading just a little. When she glanced off to the side, she spied the rosemary bush at last, growing scraggly in the summer heat. Growing, though, still, and by its growth weaving a bit of protection around the house. Beginning to frown, the woman glanced to the other side; there was plenty of sage, too, thriving in the heat unlike the rosemary.

Eyes widening, the woman finally turned about, spying at last the prize of Emmaline's yard: the sycamore fig. It grew in an arc over on the far side of the yard, because many years ago some neighborhood children had played on it and nearly broken its trunk. It had survived, though—through the heat, through the breaking, and through isolation, for it was nearly the only one of its kind in America. By the stories Emmaline's own mother had told of its planting, the seed-fig had been smuggled over from Africa herself, tucked into some poor soul's wound to keep it safe and living through the Middle Passage.

"Supposed to be rowan, thorn, and ash," said the White Lady. All at once she sounded sulky.

Emmaline lifted her chin. "That'd work too," she said, "'cause Lord knows I got some Scots Irish in me from my poor slave foremothers' travails. But this ain't the soil of Eire; red Alabama dirt roots different protectors. And you ain't the same as your'n back in the Old Country neither, not after all these years of drinking Negro blood, so rosemary, sage, and fig will do for *you*."

The White Lady let out a huffy little sound... but then she took a dainty step back. She started to raise the glass of tea, then paused, focusing sharply on it; her lip curled. Then she glared at Pauline.

"Just a little bit of acorn flour, ma'am," Pauline said, with such exaggerated innocence in her voice that Emmaline had to stifle a smile in spite of herself. "For flavor?"

"Rosemary, sage, and fig to bind," said the White Lady. It was clear now that she was furious, as she held the glass of tea out from herself and then dropped it. The tea spilled into the grass, and the glass split into three pieces. She drew in a deep breath, visibly mastering temper. "And *oak* to strike the blow. Well, Miss Emmaline, I'll grant you won this one, but it leaves us in a bit of a fix. You can't keep yours safe everywhere, and I can't be chasing after 'em all damn day and night." She thought a moment. "How 'bout a deal?"

"Ain't enough water in the river Jordan," Emmaline snapped.

"Sure?" The White Lady's grin crept back, like a dog badly banished. "Safety and prosperity for the rest, if you give me but one?"

"I done told you *no*," Emmaline said. She was forgetting to pretend polite; well, Sample hadn't gotten it only from his father. "How many more times I got to—"

"What kind of safety?" asked Pauline.

"Lord, have mercy, I'mma have to kill this girl," Emmaline could not help muttering. But Pauline had set her jaw in that tight, stubborn way that meant she didn't care if she got a smack for it. She persisted: "How much prosperity?"

Oh, and if that didn't spread the White Lady's grin nearly from ear to ear. "Why, *lots*, sugar. Bless your heart!"

"Girl, shut your *mouth*," Emmaline snapped. But the White Lady held up a hand, and all at once Emmaline found herself unable to speak. Oh, Mercy! Em knew, then. Stupid, *stupid* girl.

"Pauline, don't!" blurted Jim, but the White Lady eyed him too, and he was shut up as firmly as Emmaline herself. Sample just stared from one to the other of his siblings and from them to the White Lady, his hands flexing as if he wanted to hit somebody, but wasn't sure where to start.

"Children should be seen and not heard," said the White Lady, gesturing gracefully with the fan. "But *ladies* with that blood like wine, sweet and high and so fine, get some choices in the matter 'til it's taken from them. What say you, *Miss* Pauline?"

Pauline, to her credit, glanced at Emmaline again. Her belligerence had faded by now, and her small face was properly anxious and afraid. Then, though, her jaw firmed, and she faced the White Lady squarely. "You said trouble was comin'."

"Oh, indeed." The White Lady let her gaze drip left and right, syruping all over the boys. "So much trouble! Folks getting uppity from here to the Carolinas. De-seg-gregation! Non-discrim-ination! And don't you know them bullnecks will be hitting back fast, beating y'all back into your place." She stopped her gaze on hotheaded Sample; Sample set his jaw. "Hitting back *hard*, I tell you, on boys who think to be called men."

Pauline caught her breath. Then, though, thank the Lord, she bit her bottom lip. "I want to speak to my mother."

There was a moment's long, pent pause. Then the White Lady flipped her fan back up into a blurring wave, dropping into a mocking curtsy. The servant child moved jerkily back behind her, taking hold of the parasol again. "Seeking counsel is wise, and within the rules besides," the White Lady admitted. "Not too much counsel, though, little miss. Some deals don't last long."

With that, she flounced off with the child in tow—though Emmaline noted that she skirted wide around the sycamore fig before passing behind a pine tree and vanishing.

The instant Emmaline could speak and move she did, hurrying over to

Pauline and slapping the tar out of the girl before she could speak. "Didn't I tell you about folks like that?" she demanded, pointing with a shaking hand after the White Lady. "Didn't I *tell* you they'll put a pretty orange in your hand and snatch it back with the hand attached?"

It had been happening more and more lately that Pauline defied her—but then, this was only proper, was it not? A girl coming into her womanhood, and her adult power, should speak her mind sometimes. "I know, Momma," Pauline said, without a trace of apology. Her voice was so calm and strong and even that Emmaline blinked. "But I had dreams."

"Well, you should've told me! And you should've told me about the blood coming, I know how to make you safe for at least a bit of time, and—"

"You *can't* make me safe, Momma." Pauline said it so sharp, her gaze so hard, that Emmaline could only flinch back. "That's why you told me what to be scared of, ain't it? So I could make myself safe. And I know, 'cause you taught me, that it's a woman's job to fight for hers."

"That's a man's job," Jim said, scowling—though he too should've been quiet, cowed by the slap. Sample nodded fiercely. Emmaline groaned and put a hand in the air for strength; all of her children had forgotten how to mind, all at once.

"Decent folks' job, then," Pauline said back, with a little heat. "But Momma, I *saw* it in the dream. People marching! Big ol' redneck bulls, standing up like men, holding dogs and billy clubs. Blood everywhere." Emmaline's skin went all a-prickle with remembered fear. Yet there was no fear in Pauline's face as she went on, her voice rising in excitement. "At the end of it, though, Momma, at the end... I saw white children and black children sitting by each other in school. It was yellow and brown and red children there, too! Black people at the front of a bus! Momma..." Pauline bit her lip, then leaned forward to whisper, though there was no one to hear but family. "I saw *a black man in a big white house.*"

There were always black men in the big white houses of downtown Birmingham. Who else was going to tend their gardens or wash their cars? And yet... there was a fervor in Pauline's gaze that warned Emmaline there was something more to her daughter's dreams.

Didn't matter, though. The world didn't change. And somebody had to protect her fool children from themselves.

Seething with pent-up anger and fear, Emmaline herded the children inside. She made them go to bed early, with no supper for smarting off, because they had to *learn*—Pauline especially. Wasn't no prosperity worth a girlchild's soul and what little innocence life allowed her. Wasn't no safety for black boys beyond what humility bought them, little as that was.

And while they slept, Emmaline burned sage, and she prayed to every ancestor of three continents who might listen, and then she set herself up in a chair before the door with her grandmother's old musket across her knees. She would stay up day and night, if she had to, for her children's sake.

After a few hours had passed in slow and taut silence, and the candles burned low, and the weight of drowsiness pressed on the back of her head like a blanket, Emmaline got up to keep herself awake. She peeked in the boys' room: they were snoring, curled up, though Jim had a half-eaten peach still in his hand, sneaked out from some hiding place or another against just such an occasion of their mother's wrath.

Pauline's room, though, was cold from the open window wafting sharp bitter wind over the girl's empty bed.

THERE WOULD BE only one place the girl could have gone: the Fairgrounds, in the shadow of Red Mountain.

Emmaline ran to Renee's house, since Renee had the only working phone on the street. There she called Frank, who came over bringing his mule. The mule ran like it knew what was at stake, so fast and hard that Emmaline's bottom was raw long before she reached the place.

The Fairgrounds were only Fairgrounds once a year. The rest of the time it was just a fallow field, occasionally used for harness racing. Long ago, though, it had been the breaking ground of a plantation—the place where new slaves, freshly force-marched up from the port of Mobile, got branded and stripped of name and spirit before being sent into the fields. As Emmaline halted the mule and slid off its back, she felt all that old blood there in the ground, mixed with old tears and the red dirt beneath her feet. White Folk fed on that sort of magic. This would be a place of power for them.

As Em reached the top of the hill, she saw that Pauline stood beneath a pine that was being strangled by a carpet of kudzu. Before her stood the White

Lady—shining even more now, her skin catching the moon's gleam in the way of her people, ears gone to points and mouth too wide and full of sharp fangs. They both turned as Emmaline thumped up, out of breath, her legs shaking from holding so tight to the mule's sides. Still, she moved to stand between them, in front of Pauline and facing the White Lady. "I ain't gon' let you!"

"Deal's done, Miss Emmaline," said the White Lady, looking amused. "Too late."

Emmaline turned to Pauline, shaking, horrified. Pauline, though, lifted her chin. "I saw it, Momma," she said. "One life for three. Trouble coming whether we want it or not, but if I go, you and the boys will get through it."

In a wordless fury, Emmaline flung herself at the White Lady. She did this without using her body, and the White Lady met her without hers, taking her *up* and *out* and *through* and *into* dreaming. Thing was, dreaming wasn't a thing mortal folks did so well when they were awake, so Emmaline tumbled, helpless, lashing out ineffectually. And in the perverse way of her kind—who loved to lie, but liked it best of all when truth became their weapon—the White Lady showed Emmaline the future that Pauline had bought. She saw:

Markets full of melons and greens and peaches, all artificially fresh and reeking of chemicals in the dead of winter. Long elevated strips of road carving up Negro towns and neighborhoods all over the country. Gray, looming schools isolating bright black minds and breaking their spirits and funneling them into jails. Police, everywhere, killing and killing and *killing*. This? Emmaline fought nausea and despair, lest she strengthen her enemy— but it was nearly impossible not to feel something. Oh, Lord, her baby had given up her freedom for *this*?

And yet. All at once Emmaline was not alone in her tumbling. Pauline, new and raw and woman-strong, pushed at Emmaline, helping her straighten up. Then Pauline pointed, snatching more truth from the White Lady's dream than even she wanted shown; the White Lady hissed into their minds like ice on a griddle. Pauline ignored this and said, "Look, Momma!"

And then Em saw the rest.

Marching black people, attacked by dogs. But still marching. Children— Sample!—struck by the blasts of fire hoses, the torrent peeling off clothes and tearing skin. *Still marching.* Joined by dozens, hundreds, thousands, hundreds of thousands.

Still. Marching.

Before these marches, prayers and church-plate dinners. *Emmaline, sprinkling a little fire into the chicken and dumplings to warm the marchers against the cold hose water to come.* Young women refusing to be ordered out of their bus seats to go sit in the back. *Emmaline braiding a donkey's stubbornness into their hair.* Children holding their heads high through crowds of shouting, jeering white teenagers and adults. *Emmaline trimming a few figs from the sycamore to make jam, sweetening the children's mouths with the taste of heritage and survival.*

And so much more. Brown faces in space! Emmaline could only stare at the stars, and savor the impossible possibility. Brown men on the Supreme Court! Then she saw the white house that Pauline had mentioned. *The* White House, nestled amid statues and obelisks and the mirror pools of Washington, D.C., a place of power in itself. She saw a man standing on its steps, brown as fig jam. And then a woman, black as molasses, her gaze hard and high and proud. And then another woman, and another brown man, and *so many more*, their frequency increasing with the spinning of the sun.

Still marching. Never stopping, 'til freedom was won.

Pauline's single sacrifice could set all of it in motion. But—

"No!" Emmaline fought her way back toward wakefulness. "I can't—it can't be me who stays!" She didn't believe! She had taught her children to bow their heads, not lift them up high. "I'm not what they need!"

You gon' be all they get, sugar, said the White Lady into the dream, in a laughing whisper.

No. No, she damn well would *not* be.

The dream still spun around her. Emmaline set her jaw and plunged her hand into it, grabbing wildly this time, and pulling back... the jar of sycamore jam.

"Sin's sin," she snapped. The top of the jar was tight, but she wrestled it off and plucked out a dripping, soft sycamore fig to brandish against the churning dark. "A deal's a deal. But one kind of prey the same as another to you lot, ain't it? You like children's beauty, but a woman's don't hurt you none. You like innocence, but you'll take foolishness. So here mine: *I can't believe the world will ever change.*

"I can't hope. It ain't in me. Spent too long making it easier for people to live downtrodden. I know how to survive, but I ain't got the fight for change in me—not like my baby does. So take me, and leave her."

"No!" Pauline shouted, but Emmaline had enough control to drown her out with the sound of chanting, marching crowds.

The shape of the White Lady had blurred into the dream, but she was a sharp-toothed presence amid the swirl. *Take you both, child and fool, all mine.*

Emmaline grinned. "Greed's a sin." The dream cracked a little beneath good Christian truth, allowing Em to summon the whiff of burned sage. The White Lady flinched hard enough to slow the whirlwind of the dream, for the smell carried with it lamentations for stolen lands, stolen children, and the stolen lives of Em's Creek forbears. Emmaline set that in place opposite the jar of figs. "Your bargain was one for three, not two for two."

Images of marchers warped and twisted around them, the White House dissolving into the foxy face of the White Lady. "True enough," she said, conjuring up her fan again. "Still, I'd rather the child if you don't mind. Or even if you do."

Here Emmaline faltered. She had not dreamt of rosemary. Frantically she rifled through images, tossing away the fish she'd dreamt of before each of her children, shoving aside the green tomatoes and the collards of the market. Lord! Had she never once dreamt of baking chicken?

She had not. But then, through the tittering laughter of the White Lady and her cronies, Emmaline smelled a dream of pot-roasted guinea-rooster, with orange peel... and rosemary. That had been the first time Emmaline accorded her daughter the respect of a fellow woman—oh, and Pauline had been savoring that feeling, all this time! There was a bit of innocence attached to it, too, lost after Emmaline's explanation about white men's oranges; the perfect sweetening to lure in a hungry fey. And indeed, the White Lady paused, lifting her face a little and half-closing her eyes in pleasure at the toothsome aroma. But then she stiffened as she caught the rosemary's perfume.

"Rosemary, sage, and fig," said Pauline, in a tone of satisfaction. "Now let my Momma—"

"Take me," Emmaline said. *Commanded*, now, because she could. She had bound the White Lady by both the ancient rules of the Old Country and the newer rules of flesh and blood. The deal had been made, one innocent life for three lives protected and prosperous, but Emmaline had control over which life the White Men got to keep, at least.

"Momma!" Pauline, her beautiful powerful Pauline, abruptly resolved out of the dream's swirl and turned to her. "Momma, you can't."

"Hush." Emmaline went to her, held her close, kissed her cornrowed head. "I done told you a million times that the world doesn't change—but I was wrong, and I'm sorry for that. You got a big fight ahead of you, but you can win it. And you're better suited for that fight than I'll ever be." She hugged the girl tight. "Be strong, baby. Tell your brothers the same. I know y'all are anyway."

Pauline clutched at her. "But Momma, I, you can't, I didn't want—"

The White Lady closed the dream around Emmaline, and whisked her away.

IN THE MORNING, Pauline woke up on the ground of the Fairgrounds wet with dew and weeping. Her brothers, who had come up to the Fairgrounds to find her, came quietly to her side to hold her tight.

COUSIN RENEE TOOK the children in, of course, for blood was blood. She sent them one by one to Alabama State for their learning, so they were there when the Freedom Rides began. Naturally all three joined up. Through the dark times that followed, the foretold dogs and hoses and beatings—and the unforseen lynchings and assassinations and bombings—there were white folk aplenty doing evil... but no White Folk. The fey did not go again where they had been bested once, and in any case, their time was waning. The dirt of Alabama was red for many reasons, not the least of which that it was full of iron ore. Took a lot of power to overcome that much iron... and the times were changing such that not even black children could be stolen with impunity any more.

The White Folk kept their promise, at least: Jim got his arm bitten by a dog during a protest, but it did not tear his throat out. Hard-headed Sample dated a white woman and only had to flee town; the men who meant to chain him up behind their truck and drag him to death did not catch him. Pauline got married, dreamt of fish, and made her own daughters to carry on the family legacy. After a few more years, she ran for city council and won, and nobody strung her up. Then she ran for mayor, and won that too. All the while she turned a tidy profit from her sideline barbecue business. The greens had a little extra warmth in them that made everyone feel better towards each other, so she called them Freedom Greens, mostly as a joke.

But one year the black man Pauline had dreamt of in the White House passed through town, and he decided to come all the way to Pratt City to have some of Pauline's Famous Freedom Greens. Folks went wild. Somebody paid her to write a book about her life. Somebody optioned the film rights. Companies called and asked to franchise her recipe—but Pauline said no, instead hiring a small staff of Pratt City dwellers and leasing a commercial kitchen to fill all the thousands of orders for greens herself.

In every can, mind, there was a sprinkle of rosemary, sage, and a tiny dab of sycamore fig. Just to cut the bitterness a bit.

AND LATE ONE cold winter's night, Pauline dreamt again of the White Folk. She saw how lean and poorly they were looking these days, deprived of their easy prey, and as the hate of the world dwindled and left them hungry. But as she fought the urge to smile at their misfortune—for ill-wishing would only make them stronger—she caught a glimpse of a painfully familiar black face among their foxy whiteness, strong and proud and shining in its own way. A face that was smiling, and satisfied, and full of motherly pride.

So the world changed. And so Pauline woke up and went to hold her oldest granddaughter close, whispering to her of secrets and savory things and dreams yet to come—and of Great Grammy Em, never to be forgotten, who would one day also be free.

RED AS BLOOD AND WHITE AS BONE
Theodora Goss

Theodora Goss (www.theodoragoss.com) was born in Hungary and spent her childhood in various European countries before her family moved to the United States. Although she grew up on the classics of English literature, her writing has been influenced by an Eastern European literary tradition in which the boundaries between realism and the fantastic are often ambiguous. Her publications include the short story collection *In the Forest of Forgetting*; *Interfictions*, a short story anthology coedited with Delia Sherman; and *Voices from Fairyland*, a poetry anthology with critical essays and a selection of her own poems. Her most recent book is *The Thorn and the Blossom: A Two-sided Love Story*. She has been a finalist for the Nebula, Crawford, and Mythopoeic Awards, as well as on the Tiptree Award Honor List, and has won the World Fantasy and Rhysling Awards. Her debut novel, *The Strange Case of the Alchemist's Daughter,* will be published in 2017.

I AM AN orphan. I was born among these mountains, to a woodcutter and his wife. My mother died in childbirth, and my infant sister died with her. My father felt that he could not keep me, so he sent me to the sisters of St. Margarete, who had a convent farther down the mountain on which we lived, the Karhegy. I was raised by the sisters on brown bread, water, and prayer.

This is a good way to start a fairy tale, is it not?

When I was twelve years old, I was sent to the household of Baron Orso Kalman, whose son was later executed for treason, to train as a servant. I started in the kitchen, scrubbing the pots and pans with a brush, scrubbing the floor on my hands and knees with an even bigger brush. Greta, the German cook, was bad-tempered, as was the first kitchen maid, Agneta. She had come from Karberg, the big city at the bottom of the Karhegy—at least it seemed big, to such a country bumpkin as I was then. I was the second kitchen maid and slept in a small room that was probably a pantry, with a small window high up, on a mattress filled with straw. I bathed twice a week, after Agneta in her bathwater, which had already grown cold. In addition to the plain food we received as servants, I was given the leftovers from the baron's table after Greta and Agneta had picked over them. That is how I first tasted chocolate cake, and sausages, and beer. And I was given two dresses of my very own. Does this not seem like much? It was more than I had received at the convent. I thought I was a lucky girl!

I had been taught to read by the nuns, and my favorite thing to read was a book of fairy tales. Of course the nuns had not given me such a thing. A young man who had once stayed in the convent's guesthouse had given it to me, as a gift. I was ten years old, then. One of my duties was herding the goats. The nuns were famous for a goat's milk cheese, and so many of our chores had to do with the goats, their care and feeding. Several times, I met this man up in the mountain pastures. (I say *man*, but he must have been quite young still, just out of university. To me he seemed dreadfully old.) I was with the goats, he was striding on long legs, with a walking stick in his hand and a straw hat on his head. He always stopped and talked to me, very politely, as he might talk to a young lady of quality.

One day, he said, "You remind me of a princess in disguise, Klara, here among your goats." When I told him that I did not know what he meant, he looked at me in astonishment. "Have you never read any fairy tales?" Of course not. I had read only the Bible and my primer. Before he left the convent, he gave me a book of fairy tales, small but beautifully illustrated. "This is small enough to hide under your mattress," he said. "Do not let the nuns see it, or they will take it from you, thinking it will corrupt you. But it will not. Fairy tales are another kind of Bible, for those who know how to read them."

Years later, I saw his name again in a bookstore window and realized he had become a poet, a famous one. But by then he was dead. He had died in the war, like so many of our young men.

I followed his instructions, hiding the book under my mattress and taking it out only when there was no one to see me. That was difficult at the convent, where I slept in a room with three other girls. It was easier in the baron's house, where I slept alone in a room no one else wanted, not even to store turnips. And the book did indeed become a Bible to me, a surer guide than that other Bible written by God himself, as the nuns had taught. For I knew nothing of Israelites or the building of pyramids or the parting of seas. But I knew about girls who scrubbed floors and grew sooty sleeping near the hearth, and fish who gave you wishes (although I had never been given one), and was not Greta, our cook, an ogress? I'm sure she was. I regarded fairy tales as infallible guides to life, so I did not complain at the hard work I was given, because perhaps someday I would meet an old woman in the forest, and she would tell me that I was a princess in disguise. Perhaps.

The day on which *she* came was a cold, dark day. It had been raining for a week. Water poured down from the sky, as though to drown us all, and it simply did not stop. I was in the kitchen, peeling potatoes. Greta and Agneta were meeting with the housekeeper, Frau Hoffman, about a ball that was to take place in three days' time. It would celebrate the engagement of the baron's son, Vadek, to the daughter of a famous general, who had fought for the Austro-Hungarian emperor in the last war. Prince Radomir himself was staying at the castle. He had been hunting with Vadek Kalman in the forest that covered the Karhegy until what Greta called this unholy rain began. They had been at school together, Agneta told me. I found it hard to believe that a prince would go to school, for they never did in my tales. What need had a prince for schooling, when his purpose in life was to rescue fair maidens from the dragons that guarded them, and fight ogres, and ride on carpets that flew through the air like aeroplanes? I had never in my life seen either a flying carpet or an aeroplane: to me, they were equally mythical modes of transportation.

I had caught a glimpse of the general's daughter when she first arrived the day before, with her father and lady's maid. She was golden-haired, and looked like a porcelain doll under her hat, which Agneta later told me was from Paris. The lady's maid had told Frau Hoffman, who had told Greta, and the news had filtered down even to me. But I thought a Paris hat looked much like any other hat, and I had no interest in a general's daughter. She did not have glass slippers, and I was quite certain she could not spin straw into gold. So what good was she?

I was sitting, as I have said, in the kitchen beside the great stone hearth, peeling potatoes by a fire I was supposed to keep burning so it could later be used for roasting meat. The kitchen was dark, because of the storm outside. I could hear the steady beating of rain on the windows, the crackling of wood in the fire. Suddenly, I heard a *thump, thump, thump* against the door that led out to the kitchen garden. What could it be? For a moment, my mind conjured images out of my book: a witch with a poisoned apple, or Death himself. But then I realized it must be Josef, the under-gardener. He often knocked on that door when he brought peas or asparagus from the garden and made cow-eyes at Agneta.

"A moment," I cried, putting aside the potatoes I had been peeling, leaving the knife in a potato near the top of the basket so I could find it again easily. Then I went to the door.

When I pulled it open, something that had been leaning against it fell inside. At first I could not tell what it was, but it moaned and turned, and I saw that it was a woman in a long black cloak. She lay crumpled on the kitchen floor. Beneath her cloak she was naked: her white legs gleamed in the firelight. Fallen on the ground beside her was a bundle, and I thought: *Beggar woman. She must be sick from hunger.*

Greta, despite her harshness toward me, was often compassionate to the beggar women who came to our door—war widows, most of them. She would give them a hunk of bread or a bowl of soup, perhaps even a scrap of meat. But Greta was not here. I had no authority to feed myself, much less a woman who had wandered here in the cold and wet.

Yet there she lay, and I had to do something.

I leaned down and shook her by the shoulders. She fell back so that her head rolled around, and I could see her face for the first time. That was no cloak she wore, but her own black hair, covering her down to her knees, leaving her white arms exposed. And her white face... well. This was a different situation entirely. It was, after all, within my area of expertise, for although I knew nothing at all about war widows, I knew a great deal about lost princesses, and here at last was one. At last something extraordinary was happening in my life. I had waited a long time for this—an acknowledgment that I was part of the story. Not one of the main characters of course, but perhaps one of the supporting characters: the squire who holds the prince's horse, the maid who brushes the princess's hair a hundred times each night. And now story had landed with a thump on the kitchen floor.

But what does one do with a lost princess when she is lying on the kitchen floor? I could not lift her—I was still a child, and she was a grown woman, although not a large one. She had a delicacy that I thought appropriate to princesses. I could not throw water on her—she was already soaking wet. And any moment Greta or Agneta would return to take charge of my princess, for so I already thought of her. Finally, I resorted to slapping her cheeks until she opened her eyes—they were as deep and dark as forest pools.

"Come with me, Your Highness," I said. "I'll help you hide." She stood, stumbling a few times so that I thought she might fall. But she followed me to the only place I knew to hide her—my own small room.

"Where is..." she said. They were the first words she had said to me. She looked around as though searching: frightened, apprehensive. I went back to the kitchen and fetched her bundle, which was also soaked. When I handed it to her, she clutched it to her chest.

"I know what you are," I said.

"What... I am? And what is that?" Her voice was low, with an accent. She was not German, like Frau Hoffman, nor French, like Madame Francine, who did the baroness's hair. It was not any accent I had heard in my short life.

"You are a princess in disguise," I said. Her delicate pale face, her large, dark eyes, her graceful movements proclaimed who she was, despite her nakedness. I, who had read the tales, could see the signs. "Have you come for the ball?" *What country did you come from?* I wanted to ask. *Where does your father rule?* But perhaps that would have been rude. Perhaps one did not ask such questions of a princess.

"Yes... Yes, of course," she said. "What else would I have come for?"

I gave her my nightgown. It came only to her shins, but otherwise fitted her well enough, she was so slender. I brought her supper—my own supper, it was, but I was too excited to be hungry. She ate chicken off the bone, daintily, as I imagined a princess would. She did not eat the potatoes or cabbage—I supposed they were too common for her. So I finished them myself.

I could hear Greta and Agneta in the kitchen, so I went out to finish peeling the potatoes. Agneta scolded me for allowing the fire to get low. There was still meat to roast for the baron's supper, while Greta made a cream soup and Agneta dressed the cucumber salad. Then there were pots and pans to clean, and the black range to scrub. All the while, I smiled to myself, for I had a princess in my room.

I finished sweeping the ancient stone floor, which dated back to Roman times, while Greta went on about what we would need to prepare for the ball, how many village women she would hire to help with the cooking and baking for that night. And I smiled because I had a secret: My princess was going to the ball, and neither Greta nor Agneta would know.

When I returned to my room, the princess was fast asleep on my bed, under my old wool blanket that was ragged at the edges. I prepared to sleep on the floor, but she opened her eyes and said, "Come, little one," holding the blanket open for me. I crawled in and lay next to her. She was warm, and she curled up around me with her chin against my shoulder. It was the warmest and most comfortable I had ever been. I slept soundly that night.

The next day, I woke to find that she was already up and wearing my other dress.

"Today, you must show me around the castle, Klara," she said. Had she heard Greta or Agneta using my name the night before? The door was not particularly thick. She had not told me her name, and I did not have the temerity to ask for it.

"But if we are caught," I said, "we will be in a great deal of trouble!"

"Then we must not be caught," she said, and smiled. It was a kind smile, but there was also something shy and wild in it that I did not understand. As though the moon had smiled, or a flower.

"All right," I said. I opened the door of my room carefully. It was dawn, and light was just beginning to fall over the stones of the kitchen, the floor and great hearth. Miraculously, the rain had stopped overnight. Greta and Agneta were—where? Greta was probably still snoring in her nightcap, for she did not rise until an hour after me, to prepare breakfast. And Agneta, who also rose at dawn, was probably out fetching eggs and vegetables from Josef. She liked to take her time and smoke a cigarette in the garden. None of the female servants were allowed to smoke in the castle. I had morning chores to do, for there were more potatoes to peel for breakfast, and as soon as Agneta returned, I would need to help her make the mayonnaise.

But when would I find such a good opportunity? The baron and his guests would not be rising for hours, and most of the house servants were not yet awake. Only the lowest of us, the kitchen maids and bootblack, were required to be up at dawn.

"This way," I said to my princess, and I led her out of the kitchen, into the hallways of the castle, like a great labyrinth. Frightened that I might be caught, and yet thrilled at the risk we were taking, I showed her the front hall, with the Kalman coat of arms hanging from the ceiling, and then the reception room, where paintings of the Kalmans and their horses stared down at us with disapproval. The horses were as disapproving as their masters. I opened the doors to the library, to me the most magical room in the house—two floors of books I would never be allowed to read, with a spiral staircase going up to a balcony that ran around the second floor. We looked out the windows at the garden arranged in parterres, with regular paths and precisely clipped hedges, in the French style.

"Is it not very grand?" I asked.

"Not as grand as my house," she replied. And then I remembered that she was a princess and likely had her own castle, much grander than a baron's.

Finally, I showed her the ballroom, with its ceiling painted like the sky and heathen gods and goddesses in various states of undress looking down at the dancers below.

"This is where you will dance with Prince Radomir," I said.

"Indeed," she replied. "I have seen enough, Klara. Let us return to the kitchen before you get into trouble."

As we scurried back toward the kitchen, down a long hallway, we heard voices coming from one of the rooms. As soon as she heard them, the princess put out her hand so I would stop. Softly, she stepped closer to the door, which was partly open.

Through the opening, I could see what looked like a comfortable parlor. There was a low fire in the hearth, and a man was sprawled on the sofa, with his feet up. I moved a few inches so I could see his face—it was Vadek Kalman.

"We'll miss you in Karelstad," said another man, sitting beyond where I could see him. "I suppose you won't be returning after the wedding?"

Had they gotten up so early? But no, the baron's son was still in evening dress. They had stayed up all night. Drinking, by the smell. Drinking quite a lot.

"And why should I not?" asked Vadek. "I'm going to be married, not into a monastery. I intend to maintain a social life. Can you imagine staying here, in this godforsaken place, while the rest of you are living it up without me? I would die of boredom, Radomir." So he was talking to the prince. I shifted a little, trying to see the prince, for I had not yet managed to catch a glimpse of him. After all, I was only a kitchen maid. What did he look like?

"And if your wife objects? You don't know yet—she might have a temper."

"I don't know a damn thing about her. She hasn't said two words to me since she arrived. She's like a frightened mouse, doing whatever her father the general tells her. Just the same as in Vienna. I tell you, the whole thing was put together by her father and mine. It's supposed to be a grand alliance. Grandalliance. A damn ridiculous word..."

I heard the sound of glass breaking, the words "God damn it all," and then laughter. The princess stood perfectly still beside me. She was barely breathing.

"So he thinks there's going to be another war?"

"Well, don't you? It's going to be Germany this time, and Father wants to make sure we have contacts on the right side. The winning side."

"The Reich side, eh?" said the prince. I heard laughter again, and did not understand what was so funny. "I wish my father understood that. He doesn't want to do business with the Germans. Karel agrees with him—you know what a sanctimonious ass my brother can be. You have to, I told him. Or they'll do business with you. And to you."

"Well, if you're going to talk politics, I'm going to bed," said Vadek. "I get enough of it from my father. Looks like the rain's finally stopped. Shall we go for a walk through the woods later today? That other wolf is still out there."

"Are you sure you saw it?"

"Of course I'm sure. It was under the trees, in the shadows. I could swear it was watching you. Anyway, the mayor said two wolves had been spotted in the forest, a hunting pair. They're keeping the children in at night in case it comes close to the village. You know what he said to me when I told him you had shot one of them? *It's bad luck to kill the black wolves of the Karhegy,* he said. I told him he should be grateful, that you had probably saved the life of some miserable village brat. But he just shook his head. Superstitious peasant."

"Next time, remind him that he could be put in prison for criticizing the crown prince. Things will be different in this country when I am king, Vadek. That I can tell you."

I heard appreciative laughter.

"And what will you do with the pelt? It's a particularly fine one—the tanner said as much, when he delivered it."

"It will go on the floor of my study, on one side of my desk. Now I need another, for the other side. Yes, let's go after the other wolf—if it exists, as you say."

The princess pulled me away.

I did not like this prince, who joked about killing the black wolves. I was a child of the Karhegy, and had grown up on stories of the wolves, as black as night, that lived nowhere else in Europe. The nuns had told me they belonged to the Devil, who would come after any man that harmed them. But my friend the poet had told me they were an ancient breed, and had lived on the mountain long before the Romans had come or Morek had driven them out, leading his tribesmen on their small, fierce ponies and claiming Sylvania for his own.

Why would my princess want to marry him? But that was the logic of fairy tales: The princess married the prince. Perhaps I should not question it, any more than I would question the will of God.

She led me back down the halls—evidently, she had learned the way better than I knew it myself. I followed her into the kitchen, hoping Greta would still be asleep—but no, there she stood, having gotten up early to prepare a particularly fine breakfast for the future baroness. She was holding a rolling pin in her hand.

"Where in the world have you been, Klara?" she said, frowning. "And who gave you permission to wander away? Look, the potatoes are not yet peeled. I need them to make pancakes, and they still need to be boiled and mashed. Who the devil is this with you?"

I looked over at my princess, frightened and uncertain what to say. But as neatly as you please, she curtsied and said, "I've come from the village, ma'am. Father Ilvan told me you need help in the kitchen, to prepare for the ball."

Greta looked at her skeptically. I could tell what she was thinking—this small woman with her long, dark hair and accented voice. Was she a Slav? A gypsy? The village priest was known equally for his piety and propensity to trust the most inappropriate people. He was generous to peddlers and thieves alike.

But she nodded and said, "All right, then. Four hands are faster than two. Get those potatoes peeled."

That morning we peeled and boiled and mashed, and whisked eggs until our arms were sore, and blanched almonds. While Greta was busy with Frau Hoffman and Agneta was gossiping with Josef, I asked my princess about her country. Where had she come from? What was it like? She said it was not far, and as beautiful as Sylvania, and yes, they spoke a different language there.

"It is difficult for me to speak your language, little one," she said. We were pounding the almonds for marzipan.

"Do you tell stories there?" I asked her.

"Of course," she said. "Stories are everywhere, and everyone tells them. But our stories may be different from yours. About the Old Woman of the Forest, who grants your heart's desire if you ask her right, and the Fair Ladies who live in trees, and the White Stag, who can lead you astray or lead you home..."

I wanted to hear these stories, but then Agneta came in, and we could not talk again about the things that interested me without her or Greta overhearing. By the time our work was done, long after supper, I was so tired that I simply fell into bed with my clothes on. Trying to stay awake although my eyes kept trying to close, I watched my princess draw the bundle she had brought with her out from the corner where I had put it. She untied it, and down came spilling a long black... was it a dress? Yes, a dress as black as night, floor-length, obviously a ball gown. It had been tied with its own sleeves. Something that glittered and sparkled fell out of it, onto the floor. I sat up, awake now, wanting to see more clearly.

She turned and showed me what had fallen—a necklace of red beads, each faceted and reflecting the light from the single bare bulb in my room.

"Do you like it?" she asked.

"They are... what are they?" I had never seen such jewels, although I had read about fabulous gems in my fairy tale book. The beads were each the size of a hummingbird's egg, and as red as blood. Each looked as though it had a star at its center. She laid the dress on my bed—I reached over and felt it, surreptitiously. It was the softest velvet imaginable. Then she clasped the necklace around her neck. It looked incongruous against the patched dress she was wearing—my second best one.

"Wait, where is..." She looked at the floor where the necklace had fallen, then got down on her knees and looked under the bed, then searched again frantically in the folds of the dress. "Ah, there! It was caught in a buttonhole." She held up a large comb, the kind women used to put their hair up in the last century.

"Will you dress my hair, Klara?" she asked. I nodded. While she sat on the edge of my bed, I put her hair up, a little clumsily but the way I had seen the baroness dress her hair, which was also long, not bobbed or shingled. Finally, I put in the comb—it was as white as bone, indeed probably made of bone, ornately carved and with long teeth to catch the hair securely.

"There," I said. "Would you like to look in a mirror?" I held up a discarded shaving glass I had found one morning on the trash heap at the bottom of the garden. I used it sometimes to search my face for any signs of beauty, but I had found none yet. I was always disappointed to find myself an ordinary girl.

She looked at herself from one side, then the other. "Such a strange face," she said. "I cannot get used to it."

"You're very beautiful," I said. And she was, despite the patched dress. Princesses are, even in disguise. That's how you know.

"Thank you, little one. I hope I am beautiful enough," she said, and smiled.

That night, she once again slept curled around me, with her chin on my shoulder. I dreamed that I was wandering through the forest, in the darkness under the trees. I crossed a stream over mossy stones, felt the ferns brushing against my shins and wetting my socks with dew. I found the little red mushrooms that are poisonous to eat, saw the shy, wild deer of the Karhegy, with their spotted fawns. When I woke, my princess was already up and dressed.

"Potatoes," she said. "Your life is an endless field of potatoes, Klara." I nodded and laughed, because it was true.

That day, we helped prepare for the ball. We were joined by Marta, the daughter of the village baker, and Anna, the groom's wife, who had been taking odd jobs since her husband was kicked by one of the baron's horses. He was bedridden until his leg was fully healed, and on half-salary. We candied orange and lemon peels, and pulled pastry until it was as thin as a bedsheet, then folded it so that it lay in leaves, like a book. We soaked cherries in rum, and glazed almonds and walnuts with honey. I licked some off my fingers. Marta showed us how to boil fondant, and even I was permitted to pipe a single icing rose.

All the while, we washed dishes and swept the floor, which quickly became covered with flour. My princess never complained, not once, even though she was obviously not used to such work. She was clumsier at it than I was, and if we had not needed the help, I think Greta would have dismissed her. As it was, she looked at her several times, suspiciously. How could any woman not know how to pull pastry? Unless she was a gypsy and spent her life telling fortunes, traveling in a caravan...

There was no time to talk that day, so I could not ask how she would get to the ball. And that night, I fell asleep as soon as my head touched the pillow.

The next day, the day of the ball, we were joined by the two upstairs maids: Katrina, who was from Karberg like Agneta, and her cousin, whose name I have forgotten. They were most superior young women, and would not have set foot in the kitchen except for such a grand occasion. What a bustle there was that day in the normally quiet kitchen! Greta barking orders and Agneta barking them after her, and the chatter of women working, although my princess did not chatter of course, but did her work in silence. We made everything that could not have been made ahead of time, whisking the béchamel, poaching fish, and roasting the pig that would preside in state over the supper room, with a clove-studded orange in its mouth. We sieved broth until it was perfectly clear, molded liver dumplings into various shapes, and blanched asparagus.

Nightfall found us prepared but exhausted. Greta, who had been meeting one last time with Frau Hoffman, scurried in to tell us that the motorcars had started to arrive. I caught a glimpse of them when I went out to ask Josef for some sprigs of mint. Such motorcars! Large and black and growling like dragons as they circled around the stone courtyard, dropping off guests. The men in black tails or military uniforms, the women in evening gowns, glittering, iridescent. How would my princess look among them, in her simple black dress?

At last all the food on the long kitchen table—the aspics and clear soup, the whole trout poached with lemons, the asparagus with its accompanying hollandaise—was borne up to the supper room by footmen. It took two of them to carry the suckling pig. Later would go the cakes and pastries, the chocolates and candied fruit.

"Klara, I need your help," the princess whispered to me. No one was paying attention—Katrina and her cousin had already gone upstairs to help the female guests with their wraps. Marta, Anna, and Agneta were laughing and gossiping among themselves. Greta was off doing something important with Frau Hoffman. "I need to wash and dress," she said. And indeed, she had a smear of buttery flour across one cheek. She looked as much like a kitchen maid as a princess can look, when she has a pale, serious face and eyes as deep as forest pools, and long black hair that kept escaping the braid into which she had put it.

"Of course," I said. "There is a bathroom down the hall, beyond the water closet. No one will be using it tonight."

No one noticed as we slipped out of the kitchen. My princess fetched her dress, and then I showed her the way to the ancient bathroom shared by the female servants, with its metal tub.

"I have no way of heating the water," I said. "Usually Agneta boils a kettle, and I take my bath after her."

"That's all right," she said, smiling. "I have never taken a bath in hot water all my life."

What a strict regimen princesses followed! Never to have taken a bath in hot water... not that I had either, strictly speaking. But after Agneta had finished with it, the bathwater was usually still lukewarm.

I gave her one of the thin towels kept in the cupboard, then sat on a stool with my back to the tub, to give her as much privacy as I could while she splashed and bathed.

"I'm finished," she said finally. "How do I look, little one?"

I turned around. She was wearing the black dress, as black as night, out of which her shoulders and neck rose as though she were the moon emerging from a cloud. Her black hair hung down to her waist.

"I'll put it up for you," I said. She sat on the stool, and I recreated the intricate arrangement of the other night, with the white comb to hold it together. She clasped the necklace of red beads around her neck and stood.

There was my princess, as I had always imagined her: as graceful and elegant as a black swan. Suddenly, tears came to my eyes.

"Why are you crying, Klara?" she asked, brushing a tear from my cheek with her thumb.

"Because it's all true," I said.

She kissed me on the forehead, solemnly as though performing a ritual. Then she smiled and said, "Come, let us go to the ballroom."

"I can't go," I said. "I'm just the second kitchen maid, remember? You go... you're supposed to go."

She smiled, touched my cheek again, and nodded. I watched as she walked away from me, down the long hallway that led to other parts of the castle, the parts I was not supposed to enter. The white comb gleamed against her black hair.

And then there was washing-up to do.

It was not until several hours later that I could go to my room, lie on my bed exhausted, and think about my princess, dancing with Prince Radomir. I wished I could see her... and then I thought, *Wait, what about the gallery?* From the upstairs gallery one could look down through a series of five roundels into the ballroom. I could get up to the second floor using the back stairs. But then I would have to walk along several hallways, where I might meet guests of the baron. I might be caught. I might be sent back to the nuns—in disgrace.

But I wanted to see her dancing with the prince. To see the culmination of the fairy tale in which I had participated.

Before I could take too long to think about it, I sneaked through the kitchen and along the back hallway, to the staircase. Luckily, the second-floor hallways were empty. All the guests seemed to be down below—as I scurried along the gallery, keeping to the walls, I could hear the music and their chatter floating upward. On one side of the gallery were portraits of the Kalmans not important enough to hang in the main rooms. They looked at me as though wondering what in the world I was doing there. Halfway down the other side were the roundels, circular windows through which light shone on the portraits. I looked through the first one. Yes, there she was—easy to pick out, a spot of black in the middle of the room, like the center of a Queen Anne's lace. She was dancing with a man in a military uniform. Was he... I would be able to see better from the second window. Yes, the prince, for all the other dancers were giving them space. My princess was dancing with the prince—a waltz, judging by the music. Even I recognized that three-four time. They were turning round and round, with her hand on his shoulder and her red necklace flashing in the light of the chandeliers.

Were those footsteps I heard? I looked down the hall, but they passed—they were headed elsewhere. I put my hand to my heart, which was beating too fast, and took a long breath in relief. I looked back through the window.

My princess and Prince Radomir were gone. The Queen Anne's lace had lost its center.

Perhaps they had gone into the supper room? I waited, but they did not return. And for the first time, I worried about my princess. How would her story end? Surely she would get her happily ever after. I wanted, so much, for the stories to be true.

I waited a little longer, but finally I trudged back along the gallery, tired and despondent. It must have been near midnight, and I had been up since dawn. I was so tired that I must have taken a wrong turn, because suddenly I did not know where I was. I kept walking, knowing that if I just kept walking long enough through the castle hallways, I would eventually end up somewhere familiar. Then, I heard her voice. A door was open—the same door, I suddenly realized, where we had listened two days ago.

She was in that room—why? The door was open several inches. I looked in, carefully. She stood next to the fireplace. Beside her, holding one of her hands, was the prince. She was turned toward him, the red necklace muted in the dim light of a single lamp.

"Closer, and farther, than you can guess," she said, looking at him, with her chin raised proudly.

"Budapest? Perhaps you come from Budapest. Or Prague? Do you come from Prague? Tell me your name. If you tell me your name, I'll wager I can guess where you come from in three tries. If I do, will I get a kiss?"

"And if you don't?"

"Then you'll get a kiss. That's fair, isn't it?"

He drew her to him, circling her waist with his arm. She put her arm around his neck, so that they stood clasped together. He still held one of her hands. It was a private moment, and I felt that I should go—but I could not. In my short life, I had never been to a play, but I felt as audience members feel, having come to a climactic moment. I held my breath.

"My name is meaningless in your language," she said. He laughed, then leaned down and kissed her on the lips. They stood there by the fireplace, his lips on hers, and I thought, *Yes, this is how a fairy tale should end.*

I sighed, although without making a noise that might disturb them. Then with the arm that had been around his neck, she reached back and took the intricately carved comb out of her hair, so that it tumbled down like nightfall. With a swift motion, she thrust the sharp teeth of the comb into the side of his neck.

The prince threw back his head and screamed, like an animal in the forest. He stumbled back, limbs flailing. There was blood down his uniform, almost black against the red of his jacket. I was so startled that for a moment I did nothing, but then I screamed as well, and those screams—his maddened with pain, mine with fear—echoed down the halls.

In a moment, a footman came running. "Shut up, you," he said when he saw me. But as soon as he looked into the room, his face grew pale, and he began shouting. Soon there were more footmen, and the baron, and the general, and then Father Ilvan. Through it all, my princess stood perfectly still by the fireplace, with the bloody comb in her hand.

When they brought the prince out on a stretcher, I crouched by the wall, but no one was paying attention to me. His head was turned toward me, and I saw his eyes, pale blue. Father Ilvan had not yet closed them.

They led her out, one footman on each side, holding her by the upper arms. She was clutching something. It looked like part of her dress, just as black, but bulkier. She did not look at me, but she was close enough that I could see how calm she was. Like a forest pool—deep and mysterious.

Slowly, I walked back to the kitchen. In my room, I drew up my knees and hugged them, then put my chin on my knees. The images played in my head, over and over, like a broken reel at the cinema: him bending down to kiss her, her hand drawing the comb out of her hair, the sharp, quick thrust. I had no way of understanding them. I had no stories to explain what had happened.

At last I fell asleep, and dreamed those images over and over, all night long.

In the morning, there was breakfast to prepare. As I fried sausages and potatoes, I heard Greta tell Agneta what had happened. She had heard it from Frau Hoffman herself: A foreign spy had infiltrated the castle. At least, she was presumed to be a foreign spy, although no one knew where she came from. Was she Slovakian? Yugoslavian? Bulgarian? Why had she wanted the prince dead?

She would not speak, although she would be made to speak. The baron had already telephoned the Royal Palace, and guards had been dispatched to take her, and the body of the prince, to Karelstad. They would arrive sometime that afternoon. In the meantime, she was locked in the dungeon, which had not held prisoners for a hundred years.

After breakfast, the baron himself came down to question us. The servants had been shown a sketch of a small, pale woman with long black hair, made by Father Ilvan. Katrina had identified her as one of the village women who had helped in the kitchen, in preparation for the ball. Why had she been engaged?

Because Father Ilvan had sent her, said Greta. But Father Ilvan had no knowledge of such a woman. Greta and Agneta were told to pack their bags. What had they been thinking, allowing a strange woman to work in the castle, particularly when the crown prince was present? If they did not leave that day, they would be put in the dungeon as well. And no, they would not be given references. I was too frightened to speak, to tell the baron that I had been the one to let her in. No one paid attention to me—I was too lowly even to blame.

By that afternoon, Marta, the baker's daughter, was the new cook, and I was her kitchen maid. In two days, I had caused the death of the prince and gotten promoted.

"Klara," she said to me, "I have no idea how we are to feed so many people, just the two of us. And Frau Hoffman says the royal guards will be here by dinnertime! Can you imagine?"

Then it was now or never. In an hour or two, I would be too busy preparing dinner, and by nightfall my princess—my spy?—would be gone, taken back to the capital for trial. I was frightened of what I was about to do, but felt that I must do it. In my life, I have often remembered that moment of fear and courage, when I took off my apron and sneaked out the door into the kitchen garden. It was the first moment I chose courage over fear, and I have always made the same choice since.

The castle had, of course, been built in the days before electric lights. Even the dungeon had windows. Once, Josef had shown them to me, when I was picking raspberries for a charlotte russe. Holding back the raspberry canes, he had said, "There, you see, little mouse, is the deep dark dungeon of the castle!" Although as far as I could tell it was just a bare stone room, with metal staples in the walls for chains. From the outside, the windows were set low into the castle wall, but from the inside they were high up in the wall of the dungeon—high enough that a tall man could not reach them. And they were barred.

It was late afternoon. Josef and the gardener's boy who helped him were nowhere in sight. I crawled behind the raspberry canes, getting scratched in the process, and looked through one of the barred windows.

She was there, my princess. Sitting on the stone floor, her black dress pooled around her, black hair hanging down, still clutching something black in her arms. She was staring straight ahead of her, as though simply waiting.

"Princess!" I said, low in case anyone should hear. There must be guards? But I could not see them. The dungeon door was barred as well. There was no way out.

She looked around, then up. "Klara," she said, and smiled. It was a strange, sad smile. She rose and walked over to the window, then stood beneath it, looking up at me, her face pale and tired in the dim light. Then I could see what she had been clutching: a wolf pelt, with the four paws and eyeless head hanging down.

"Why?" I asked. And then, for the first time, I began to cry. Not for Prince Radomir, but for the story. Because it had not been true, because she had allowed me to believe a lie. Because when Greta said she was a foreign spy, suddenly I had seen life as uglier and more ordinary than I had imagined, and the realization had made me sick inside.

"Klara," she said, putting one hand on the wall, as far up as she could reach. It was still several feet below the window. "Little one, don't cry. Listen, I'm going to tell you a story. Once upon a time—that's how your stories start, isn't it? Quietly, so the guards won't hear. They are around the corner, having their dinners. I can smell the meat. Once upon a time, there were two wolves who lived on the Karhegy. They were black wolves, of the tribe that has lived on the mountain since time out of mind. The forest was their home, dark and peaceful and secure. There they lived, there they hoped to someday raise their children. But one day, a prince came with his gun, and he shot one of the wolves, who was carried away by the prince's men for his fine pelt. The other wolf, who was his mate, swore that she would kill the prince."

I listened intently, drying my face with the hem of my skirt.

"So she went to the Old Woman of the Forest and said, 'Grandmother, you make bargains that are hard but fair. I will give you anything for my revenge.' And the Old Woman said, 'You shall have it. But you must give me your beautiful black pelt, and your dangerous white teeth, and the blood that runs in your body. For such a revenge, you must give up everything.' And the wolf agreed. All these things she gave the Old Woman, who fashioned out of them a dress as black as night, and a necklace as red as blood, and a comb as white as bone. The old woman gave them to the wolf and said, 'Now our bargain is complete.' The wolf took the bundle the Old Woman had given her and stumbled out of the forest, for it was difficult walking on only two legs. On a rainy night, she made her way to the castle where the prince was staying. And the rest of the story, you know."

I stared down at her, not knowing what to say. Should I believe it? Or her? Common sense told me that she was lying, that she was a foreign spy and I was a fool. But then, I have never had much common sense. And that, too, has stood me in good stead.

"Klara, put your hand through the bars," she said.

I hesitated, then did as I was told.

She put the pelt down on the floor beside her, carefully as though it were a child, then unclasped the necklace of red beads. "Catch!" she said, and threw it up to me. I caught it—and then I heard boots echoing down the corridor. "Go now!" she said. "They're coming for me." I drew back my hand with the necklace in it and crawled away from the window. The sun was setting. It was time for me to return to the kitchen and prepare dinner. No doubt Marta was already wondering where I was.

When I got back to the kitchen, I learned that the royal guards had arrived. But they were too late—using the metal staples on the walls, my princess had hanged herself by her long black hair.

When I was sixteen, I left the baron's household. By that time, I was as good a cook as Marta could teach me to be. I knew how to prepare the seven courses of a formal dinner, and I was particularly skilled in what Marta did best: pastry. I think my pâté à choux was as good as hers.

In a small suitcase, I packed my clothes, and my fairy tale book, and the necklace that my wolf-princess had given me, which I had kept under my mattress for many years.

Perhaps it was not wise, moving to Karelstad in the middle of the German occupation. But as I have said, I am deficient in common sense—the sense that keeps most people safe and out of trouble. I let bedraggled princesses in out of the rain. I pack my suitcase and move to the capital with only a fortnight's wages and a reference from the baroness. I join the Resistance.

Although I did not know it, the café where I worked was a meeting-place for the Resistance. One of the young men who would come to the café, to drink coffee and read the newspapers, was a member. He had long hair that he did not wash often enough, and eyes of a startling blue, like evening in the mountains. His name was Antal Odon, and he was a descendent of the nineteenth-century poet Amadeo Odon. He would flirt with me, until we became friends. Then he did not flirt with me any longer, but spoke with me solemnly, about Sylvanian poetry and politics. He had been at the university until the Germans came. Then, it no longer seemed worthwhile becoming a literature professor, so he had left. What was he doing with himself now, I asked him?

It was he who first brought me to a meeting of the Resistance, in the cellar of the café where I worked. The owner, a motherly woman named Malina who had given me both a job and a room above the café, told us about Sylvanians who had been taken that week—both Jews and political prisoners. The next day, I went to a jeweler on Morek Stras, with my necklace as red as blood. How much for this? I asked him. Are these beads worth anything?

He looked at them through a small glass, then told me they would be worth more individually. Indeed, in these times, he did not know if he could find a purchaser for the entire necklace. He had never seen such fine rubies in his life.

One by one, he sold them off for me, often to the wives of German officers. Little did they know that they were funding the Resistance. I kept only one of the beads for myself, the smallest. I wear it now on a chain around my neck. So you can see, Grandmother, that my story is true.

As a member of the Resistance, I traveled to France and Belgium and Denmark. I carried messages sewn into my brassiere. No one suspects a young girl, if she wears high heels and red lipstick, and laughs with the German officers, and looks down modestly when they light her cigarette. Once, I even carried a message to a small town in the Swiss mountains, to a man who was introduced to me as Monsieur Reynard. He looked like his father, as far as one can tell from official portraits—one had hung in the nunnery schoolroom. I was told not to curtsy, simply to shake his hand as though he were an ordinary Sylvanian. I did not tell him, *I saw your older brother die. I hope that someday you will once again return to Sylvania, as its king.*

With my friend Antal, I smuggled political refugees out of the country. By then, we were more than friends... We hoped someday to be married, when the war was over. But he was caught and tortured. He never revealed names, so you see he died a hero. The man I loved died a hero.

When the war ended and the Russian occupation began, I did not know what to do with myself. I had imagined a life with Antal, and he was dead. But there were free classes at the university, for those who had been peasants, if you could pass the exams. I was no longer a peasant exactly, but I told the examiners that my father had been a woodcutter on the Karhegy, and I passed with high marks, so I was admitted. I threw myself into work and took my degree in three years—in Sylvanian literature, as Antal would have, if he had lived. I thought I would find work in the capital, but the Ministry of Education said that teachers were needed in Karberg and the surrounding area, so I was sent here, to a school in the village of Orsolavilag, high in the mountains. There I teach students whose parents work in the lumber industry, or at one of the hotels for Russian and Austrian tourists.

When I first returned, I tried to find my father. But I learned that he had died long ago. He had been cutting wood while drunk, and had struck his own leg with an axe. The wound had become infected, and so he had died. A simple, brutal story. So I have no one left in the world. All I have left is my work.

I teach literature and history to the children of Orsolavilag... or such literature and history as I am allowed. We do not teach fairy tales, which the Ministry of Education thinks are decadent. We teach stories of good Sylvanian boys and girls who learn to serve the state. In them, there are no frogs who turn into princes, no princesses going to balls in dresses like the sun, moon, and stars. No firebirds. There are no black wolves of the Karhegy, or Fair Ladies who live in trees, or White Stag that will, if you are lost, lead you home. There is no mention even of you, Grandmother. Can you imagine? No stories about the Old Woman of the Forest, from whom all the stories come.

Within a generation, those stories will be lost.

So I have come to you, whose bargains are hard but fair. Give me stories. Give me all the stories of Sylvania, so I can write them down, and so our underground press in Karberg, for which we could all be sent to a prison camp, can publish them. We will pass them from hand to hand, household to household. For this, Grandmother, I will give you what my princess gave so long ago: whatever you ask. I have little left, anyhow. My only possession of value is a single red bead on a chain, like a drop of blood.

I am a daughter of these mountains, and of the tales. Once, I wanted to be in the tales themselves. When I was young, I had my part in one—a small part, but important. When I grew older, I had my part in another kind of story. But now I want to become a teller of tales. So I will sit here, in your hut on goose legs, which sways a bit like a boat on the water. Tell me your stories, Grandmother. I am listening...

TERMINAL

Lavie Tidhar

Lavie Tidhar (lavietidhar.wordpress.com) is the author of the Jerwood Fiction Uncovered Prize winning and Premio Roma nominee *A Man Lies Dreaming* (2014), the World Fantasy Award winning *Osama* (2011) and the critically-acclaimed *The Violent Century* (2013). His latest novel is *Central Station* (2016). He is the author of many other novels, novellas and short stories.

FROM ABOVE THE ecliptic the swarm can be seen as a cloud of minute bullet-shaped insects, their hulls, packed with photovoltaic cells, capturing the sunlight; tiny, tiny flames burning in the vastness of the dark.

They crawl with unbearable slowness across this small section of near space, beetles climbing a sheer obsidian rock face. Only the sun remains constant. The sun, always, dominates their sky.

Inside each jalopy are instrument panels and their like; a sleeping compartment where you must float your way into the secured sleeping bag; a toilet to strap yourself to; a kitchen to prepare your meal supply; and windows to look out of. With every passing day the distance from Earth increases and the time-lag grows a tiny bit longer and the streaming of communication becomes more echoey, the most acute reminder of that finite parting as the blue-green egg that is Earth revolves and grows smaller in your window, and you stand there, sometimes for hours at a time, fingers splayed against the plastic, staring at what has gone and will never come again, for your destination is terminal.

There is such freedom in the letting go.

*　　*　　*

THERE IS THE music. Mei listens to the music, endlessly. Alone she floats in her cheap jalopy, and the music soars all about her, an archive of all the music of Earth stored in five hundred terabytes or so, so that Mei can listen to anything ever written and performed, should she so choose, and so she does, in a glorious random selection as the jalopy moves in the endless swarm from Earth to Terminal. Chopin's Études bring a sharp memory of rain and the smell of wet grass, of damp books and days spent in bed, staring out of windows, the feel of soft sheets and warm pyjamas, a steaming mug of tea. Mei listens to Vanuatu string band songs in pidgin English, evocative of palm trees and sand beaches and graceful men swaying in the wind; she listens to Congolese kwasa kwasa and dances, floating, shaking and rolling in weightlessness, the music like an infectious laugh and hot tropical rain. The Beatles sing "Here Comes the Sun," Mozart's Requiem trails off unfinished, David Bowie's "Space Oddity" haunts the cramped confines of the jalopy: the human race speaks to Mei through notes like precise mathematical notations, and, alone, she floats in space, remembering in the way music always makes you remember.

She is not unhappy.

At first, there was something seemingly inhuman about using the toilets. It is like a hungry machine, breathing and spitting, and Mei must ride it, strapping herself into leg restraints, attaching the urine funnel, which gurgles and hisses as Mei evacuates waste. Now the toilet is like an old friend, its conversation a constant murmur, and she climbs in and out without conscious notice.

At first, Mei slept and woke up to a regiment of day and night, but a month out of Earth orbit, the old order began to slowly crumble, and now she sleeps and wakes when she wants, making day and night appear as if by magic, by a wave of her hand. Still, she maintains a routine, of washing and the brushing of teeth, of wearing clothing, a pretence at humanity which is sometimes hard to maintain being alone. A person is defined by other people.

Three months out of Earth and it's hard to picture where you'd left, where you're going. And always that word, like a whisper out of nowhere, Terminal, Terminal...

Mei floats and turns slowly in space, listening to the Beach Boys.

*　　*　　*

"I HAVE TO do this."

"You don't have to," she says. "You don't have to do anything. What you mean is that you want to. You want to do it. You think it makes you special but it doesn't make you special if everyone else is doing it." She looks at him with fierce black eyes and tucks a strand of hair, clumped together in her perspiration, behind her ear. He loves her very much at that moment, that fierce protectiveness, the fact someone, anyone, can look at you that way, can look at you and feel love.

"Not everyone is doing it."

They're sitting in a café outdoors and it is hot, it is very hot, and overhead, the twin Petronas Towers rise like silver rockets into the air. In the square outside KLCC, the water features twinkle in the sun and tourists snap photos and waiters glide like unenthusiastic penguins amongst the clientele. He drinks from his kopi ice and traces a trail of moisture on the face of the glass, slowly. "You are not *dying*," she says, at last, the words coming as from a great distance. He nods, reluctantly. It is true. He is not dying, not immediately anyway; only in the sense that all living things are dying, that there is a trajectory, the way a jalopy makes its slow but finite way from Earth to Mars. Speaking of jalopies, there is a stand under the awnings, for such stands are everywhere now, and a man shouting through the sound system to come one, come all and take the ultimate trip—and so on, and so forth.

But more than that, implicit in her words is the question: is he dying? In the more immediate sense? "No," he says. "But."

That word lies heavy in the hot and humid air.

She is still attractive to him, even now: even after thirty years, three kids now grown and gone into the world, her hair no longer black all over but flecked with strands of white and grey, his own hair mostly gone, their hands, touching lightly across the table, both showing the signs of gravity and age. And how could he explain?

"Space," he tries to say. "The dark starry night which is eternal and forever, or as long as these words mean something in between the beginning and the end of spaceandtime." But really, is it selfish, is it not inherently *selfish* to want to leave, to go, up there and beyond—for what? It makes no sense, or no more sense than anything else you do or don't.

"Responsibility," she says. "Commitment. Love, damn it, Haziq! You're not a child, playing with toys, with, with... with *spaceships* or whatever. You have children, a family, we'll soon have grandkids if I know Omar, what will they do without you?"

These hypothetical people, not yet born, already laying demands to his time, his being. To be human is to exist in potentia, unborn responsibilities rising like butterflies in a great big obscuring cloud. He waves his hand in front of his face, but whether it is to shoo them away or because of the heat, he cannot say. "We always said we won't stand in each other's way," he begins, but awkwardly, and she starts to cry, silently, making no move to wipe away the tears, and he feels a great tenderness but also anger, and the combination shocks him. "I have never asked for anything," he says. "I have... Have I not been a good son, a good father, a good husband? I never asked for anything—" and he remembers sneaking away one night, five years before, and wandering the Petaling Street Market with television screens blaring and watching a launch, and a thin string of pearls, broken, scattered across space... Perhaps it was then, perhaps it was earlier, or once when he was a boy and he had seen pictures of a vast red planet unmarred by human feet...

"What did I ask," she says, "did I complain, did I aspire, did I not fulfil what you and I both wanted? Yes," she says, "yes, it is selfish to want to go, and it is selfish to ask you to stay, but if you go, Haziq, you won't come back. You won't ever come back."

And he says, "I know," and she shakes her head, and she is no longer crying, and there is that hard, practical look in her eyes, the one he was always a little bit afraid of. She picks up the bill and roots in her purse and brings out the money and puts it on the table. "I have to go," she says, "I have an appointment at the hairdresser's." She gets up and he does not stand to stop her, and she walks away; and he knows that all he has to do is follow her; and yet he doesn't, he remains seated, watching her weaving her way through the crowds, until she disappears inside the giant mall; and she never once looks back.

BUT REALLY, IT is the sick, the slowly dying, those who have nothing to lose, those untied by earthly bonds, those whose spirits are as light as air: the loners and the crazy and worst of all the artists, so many artists, each convinced in his or her own way of the uniqueness of the opportunity, exchanging life for immortality, floating, transmuting space into art in the way of the dead, for they are legally dead, now, each in his or her own jalopy, this cheap mass-manufactured container made for this one singular trip, from this planet to the next, from the living world to the dead one.

"Sign here, initial here, and here, and here—" and what does it feel like for those everyday astronauts, those would-be Martians, departing their homes for one last time, a last glance back, some leaving gladly, some tearfully, some with indifference: these Terminals, these walking dead, having signed over their assets, completed their wills, attended, in some instances, their very own wakes: leaving with nothing, boarding taxis or flights in daytime or night, to the launch site for rudimentary training with instruments they will never use, from Earth to orbit in a space plane, a reusable launch vehicle, and thence to Gateway, in low Earth orbit, that ramshackle construction floating like a spider web in the skies of Earth, made up of modules, some new, some decades old, joined together in an ungainly fashion, a makeshift thing.

... HERE WE ARE all astronauts. The permanent staff is multinational, harassed; monkey-like, we climb heel and toe heel and toe, handholds along the walls no up no down but three-dimensional space as a many splendored thing. Here the astronauts are trained hastily in maintaining their craft and themselves, and the jalopies extend out of Gateway, beyond orbit, thousands of cheap little tin cans aimed like skipping stones at the big red rock yonder.

Here, too, you can still change your mind. Here comes a man now, a big man, an American man, with very white face and hands, a man used to being in control, a man used to being deferred to—an artist, in fact; a writer. He had made his money imagining the way the future was, but the future had passed him by and he found himself spending his time on message boards and the like, bemoaning youth and their folly. Now he has a new lease on life, or thought he had, with this plan of going into space, to Terminal Beach: six months floating in a tin can high above no world, to write his masterpiece, the thing he is to be remembered by, his *novel*, damn it, in which he's to lay down his entire philosophical framework of a libertarian bent: only he has, at the last moment, perhaps on smelling the interior of his assigned jalopy, changed his mind. Now he comes inexpertly floating like a beach ball down the shaft, bouncing here and there from the walls and bellowing for the agent, those sleazy jalopymen, for the final signature on the contract is digital, and sent once the jalopy is slingshot to Mars. It takes three orderlies to hold him, and a nurse injects him with something to calm him down. Later, he would go back down the gravity well, poorer yet wiser, but he will never write that novel: space eludes him.

Meanwhile, the nurse helps carry the now-unconscious American down to the hospital suite, a house-sized unit overlooking the curve of the Earth. Her name is Eliza and she watches day chase night across the globe and looks for her home, for the islands of the Philippines to come into view, their lights scattered like shards of shining glass, but it is the wrong time to see them. She monitors the IV distractedly, feeling tiredness wash over her like the first exploratory wave of a grey and endless sea. For Eliza, space means always being in sight of this great living world, this Earth, its oceans and its green landmasses and its bright night lights, a world that dominates her view, always, that glares like an eye through pale white clouds. To be this close to it and yet to see it separate, not of it but apart, is an amazing thing; while beyond, where the Terminals go, or farther yet, where the stars coalesce as thick as clouds, who knows what lies? And she fingers the gold cross on the chain around her neck, as she always does when she thinks of things alien beyond knowing, and she shudders, just a little bit; but everywhere else, so far, the universe is silent, and we alone shout.

"HELLO? IS IT me you're looking for?"

"Who is this?"

"Hello?"

"This is jalopy A-5011 sending out a call to the faithful to prayer—"

"This is Bremen in B-9012, is there anyone there? Hello? I am very weak. Is there a doctor, can you help me, I do not think I'll make it to the rock, hello, hello—"

"This is jalopy B-2031 to jalopy C-3398, bishop to king 7, I said bishop to king 7, take that Shen you twisted old fruit!"

"Hello? Has anyone heard from Shiri Applebaum in C-5591, has anyone heard from Shiri Applebaum in C-5591, she has not been in touch in two days and I am getting worried, this is Robin in C-5523, we were at Gateway together before the launch, hello, hello—"

"Hello—"

Mei turns down the volume of the music and listens to the endless chatter of the swarm rise alongside it, day or night, neither of which matter or exist here, unbound by planetary rotation and that old artificial divide of darkness and the light. Many like Mei have abandoned the twenty-four hour cycle to sleep and rise ceaselessly and almost incessantly with some desperate need to *experience* all of this, this one-time-only journey, this slow beetle's crawl across trans-solar space. Mei swoops and turns with the music and the chatter, and she idly wonders of the fate to have befallen Shiri Applebaum in C-5591: is she merely keeping quiet or is she dead or in a coma, never to wake up again, only her corpse and her cheap little jalopy hitting the surface of Mars in ninety more days? Across the swarm's radio network, the muezzin in A-5011 sends out the call to prayer, the singsong words so beautiful that Mei stops, suspended in mid-air, and breathes deeply, her chest rising and falling steadily, space all around her. She has degenerative bone disease, there isn't a question of starting a new life at Terminal, only this achingly beautiful song that rises all about her, and the stars, and silent space.

TWO DAYS LATER Bremen's calls abruptly cease. B-9012 still hurtles on with the rest towards Mars. Haziq tries to picture Bremen: what was he like? What did he love? He thinks he remembers him, vaguely, a once-fat man now wasted with folded awkward skin, large glasses, a Scandinavian man maybe, Haziq thought, but all he knows or will ever know of Bremen is the man's voice on the radio, bouncing from jalopy to jalopy and on to Earth where jalopy-chasers scan the bands and listen in a sort of awed or voyeuristic pleasure.

"This is Haziq, C-6173..." He coughs and clears his throat. He drinks his miso soup awkwardly, suckling from its pouch. He sits formally, strapped by Velcro, the tray of food before him, and out of his window he stares not back to Earth or forward to Mars but directly onto the swarm, trying to picture each man and woman inside, trying to imagine what brought them here. Does one need a reason? Haziq wonders. Or is it merely that gradual feeling of discomfort in one's own life, one's own skin, a slowly dawning realisation that you have passed like a grey ghost through your own life, leaving no impression, that soon you might fade away entirely, to dust and ash and nothingness, a mild regret in your children's minds that they never really knew you at all.

"This is Haziq, C-6173, is there anyone hearing me, my name is Haziq and I am going to Terminal"—and a sudden excitement takes him. "My name is Haziq and I am going to Terminal!" he shouts, and all around him the endless chatter rises, of humans in space, so needy for talk like sustenance, "We're all going to Terminal!" and Haziq, shy again, says, "Please, is there anyone there, won't someone talk to me. What is it like, on Terminal?"

BUT THAT IS a question that brings down the silence; it is there in the echoes of words ords rds and in the pauses, in punctuation missing or overstated, in the endless chess moves, worried queries, unwanted confessionals, declarations of love, in this desperate sudden *need* that binds them together, the swarm, and makes all that has been before become obsolete, lose definition and meaning. For the past is a world one cannot return to, and the future is a world none has seen.

Mei floats half-asleep half-awake, but the voice awakens her. Why *this* voice, she never knows, cannot articulate. "Hello. Hello. Hello..." And she swims through the air to the kitchenette and heats up tea and drinks it from the suction cup. There are no fizzy drinks on board the jalopies, the lack of gravity would not separate liquid and gas in the human stomach, and the astronaut would wet-burp vomit. Mei drinks slowly, carefully; all her movements are careful. "Hello?" she says, "Hello, this is Mei in A-3357, this is Mei in A-3357, can you hear me, Haziq, can you hear me?"

A pause, a micro-silence, the air filled with the hundreds of other conversations through which a voice, his voice, says, "This is Haziq! Hello, A-3357, hello!"

"Hello," Mei says, surprised and strangely happy, and she realises it is the first time she has spoken in three months. "Let me tell you, Haziq," she says, and her voice is like music between worlds, "let me tell you about Terminal."

* * *

IT WAS RAINING in the city. She had come out of the hospital and looked up at the sky and saw nothing there, no stars no sun, just clouds and smoke and fog. It rained, the rain collected in rainbow puddles in the street, the chemicals inside it painted the world and made it brighter. There was a jalopy vendor on the corner of the street, above his head a promotional video in 3D, and she was drawn to it. The vendor played loud K-pop and the film looped in on itself, but Mei didn't mind the vendor's shouts, the smell of acid rain or frying pork sticks and garlic or the music's beat which rolled on like thunder. Mei stood and rested against the stand and watched the video play. The vendor gave her glasses, embossed with the jalopy sub-agent's logo. She watched the swarm like a majestic silver web spread out across space, hurtling (or so it seemed) from Earth to Mars. The red planet was so beautiful and round, its dry seas and massive mountain peaks, its volcanoes and canals. She watched the polar ice caps. Watched Olympus Mons breaking out of the atmosphere. Imagined a mountain so high, it reached up into space. Imagined women like her climbing it, smaller than ants but with that same ferocious dedication. Somewhere on that world was Terminal.

"Picture yourself standing on the red sands for the very first time," she tells Haziq, her voice the same singsong of the muezzin at prayer, "that very first step, the mark of your boot in the fine sand. It won't stay there forever, you know. This is not the moon, the winds will come and sweep it away, reminding you of the temporality of all living things." And she pictures Armstrong on the moon, that first impossible step, the mark of the boots in the lunar dust. "But you are on a different world now," she says, to Haziq or to herself, or to the others listening, and the jalopy-chasers back on Earth. "With different moons hanging like fruit in the sky. And you take that first step in your suit, the gravity hits you suddenly, you are barely able to drag yourself out of the jalopy, everything is labour and pain. Who knew gravity could hurt so much," she says, as though in wonder. She closes her eyes and floats slowly upwards, picturing it. She can see it so clearly, Terminal Beach where the jalopies wash ashore, endlessly, like seashells, as far as the eye can see the sand is covered in the units out of which a temporary city rises, a tent city, all those bright objects on the sand. "And as you emerge into the sunlight they stand there, welcoming you, can

479

you see them? In suits and helmets, they extend open arms, those Martians, *Come*, they say, over the radio comms, *come*, and you follow, painfully and awkwardly, leaving tracks in the sand, into the temporary domes and the linked-together jalopies and the underground caves which they are digging, always, extending this makeshift city downwards, and you pass through the airlock and take off your helmet and breathe the air, and you are no longer alone, you are amongst people, real people, not just voices carried on the solar winds."

She falls silent then. Breathes the limited air of the cabin. "They would be planting seeds," she says, softly, "underground, and in greenhouses, all the plants of Earth, a paradise of watermelons and orchids, of frangipani and durian, jasmine and rambutan..." She breathes deeply, evenly. The pain is just a part of her, now. She no longer takes the pills they gave her. She wants to be herself; pain and all.

In jalopies scattered across this narrow silver band, astronauts like canned sardines marinate in their own stale sweat and listen to her voice. Her words, converted into a signal inaudible by human ears, travel across local space for whole minutes until they hit the Earth's atmosphere at last, already old and outdated, a record of a past event; here they bounce off the Earth to the ionosphere and back again, jaggedy waves like a terminal patient's heart monitor circumnavigating this rotating globe until they are deciphered by machines and converted once more into sound:

Mei's voice speaking into rooms, across hospital beds, in dark bars filled with the fug of electronic cigarettes' smoke-like vapoured steam, in lonely bedrooms where her voice keeps company to cats, in cabs driving through rain and from tinny speakers on white sand beaches where coconut crabs emerge into sunset, their blue metallic shells glinting like jalopies. Mei's voice soothes unease and fills the jalopy-chasers' minds with bright images, a panoramic view of a red world seen from space, suspended against the blackness of space; the profusion of bright galaxies and stars behind it is like a movie screen.

"Take a step, and then another and another. The sunlight caresses your skin, but its rays have travelled longer to reach you, and when you raise your head the sun shines down from a clay-red sun, and you know you will never again see the sky blue. Think of that light. It has travelled longer and faster than you ever will, its speed in vacuum a constant 299,792,458 meters per second. Think of that number, that strange little fundamental constant, seemingly arbitrary: around that number faith can be woven and broken like silk, for is it a randomly created universe we live in or an ordained one? Why the speed of light, why the gravitational constant, why Planck's? And as you stand there, healthy or ill, on the sands of Terminal Beach and raise your face to the sun, are you happy or sad?"

Mei's voice makes them wonder, some simply and with devotion, some uneasily. But wonder they do, and some will go outside one day and encounter the ubiquitous stand of a jalopyman and be seduced by its simple promise, abandon everything to gain a nebulous idea, that boot mark in the fine-grained red sand, so easily wiped away by the winds.

And Mei tells Haziq about Olympus Mons and its shadow falling on the land and its peak in space, she tells him of the falling snow, made of frozen carbon dioxide, of men and women becoming children again, building snowmen in the airless atmosphere, and she tells him of the Valles Marineris, where they go suited up, hand in gloved hand, through the canyons whose walls rise above them, east of Tharsis.

Perhaps it is then that Haziq falls in love, a little bit, through walls and vacuum, the way a boy does, not with a real person but with an ideal, an image. Not the way he had fallen in love with his wife, not even the way he loves his children, who talk to him across the planetary gap, their words and moving images beamed to him from Earth, but they seldom do, any more, it is as if they had resigned themselves to his departure, as if by crossing the atmosphere into space he had already died and they were done with mourning.

It is her voice he fastens onto; almost greedily; with need. And as for Mei, it is as if she had absorbed the silence of three months and more than a hundred million kilometres, consumed it somehow, was sustained by it, her own silence with only the music for company, and now she must speak, speak only for the sake of it, like eating or breathing or making love, the first two of which she will soon do no more and the last of which is already gone, a thing of the past. And so she tells the swarm about Terminal.

*   *   *

BUT WHAT IS Terminal? Eliza wonders, floating in the corridors of Gateway, watching the RLVs rise into low Earth orbit, the continents shifting past, the clouds swirling, endlessly, this whole strange giant spaceship planet as it travels at 1,200 kilometres an hour around the sun, while at the same time Earth, Mars, Venus, Sun and all travel at nearly 800,000 kilometres per hour around the centre of the galaxy, while *at the same time* this speed machine, Earth and sun and the galaxy itself move at 1,000 kilometres per *second* towards the Great Attractor, that most mysterious of gravitational enigmas, this anomaly of mass that pulls to it the Milky Way as if it were a pebble: all this and we think we're *still*, and it makes Eliza dizzy just to think about it.

But she thinks of such things more and more. Space changes you, somehow. It tears you out of certainties, it makes you see your world at a distance, no longer of it but apart. It makes her sad, the old certainties washed away, and more and more she finds herself thinking of Mars; of Terminal.

To never see your home again; your family, your mother, your uncles, brothers, sisters, aunts, cousins and second cousins and third cousins twice removed, and all the rest of them: never to walk under open skies and never to sail on a sea, never to hear the sound of frogs mating by a river or hear the whooshing sound of fruit bats in the trees. All those things and all the others you will never do, and people carry bucket lists around with them before they become Terminal, but at long last everything they ever knew and owned is gone and then there is only the jalopy confines, only that and the stars in the window and the voice of the swarm. And Eliza thinks that maybe she wouldn't mind leaving it all behind, just for a chance at... what? Something so untenable, as will-o'-the-wisp as ideology or faith and yet as hard and precisely defined as prime numbers or fundamental constants. Perhaps it is the way Irish immigrants felt on going to America, with nothing but a vague hope that the future would be different from the past. Eliza had been to nursing school, had loved, had seen the world rotate below her; had been to space, had worked on amputations, births, tumour removals, fevers turned fatal, transfusions and malarias, has held a patient's hand as she died or dried a boy's tears or made a cup of tea for the bereaved, monitored IVs, changed sheets and bedpans, took blood and gave injections, and now she floats in freefall high above the world, watching the Terminals come and go, come and go, endlessly, and the string of silver jalopies extends in a great horde from Earth's orbit to the Martian surface, and she imagines jalopies fall down like silver drops of rain, gently they glide down through the thin Martian atmosphere to land on the alien sands.

She pictures Terminal and listens to Mei's voice, one amongst so many but somehow it is the voice others return to, it is as though Mei speaks for all of them, telling them of the city being built out of cheap used bruised jalopies, the way Gateway had been put together, a lot of mismatched units joined up, and she tells them, you could fall in love again, with yourself, with another, with a world.

"Why?" Mei says to Haziq, one night period, several weeks away from planetfall. "Why did you do it?"

"Why did I go?"

She waits; she likes his voice. She floats in the cabin, her mind like a calm sea. She listens to the sounds of the jalopy, the instruments and the toilet and the creaks and rustle of all the invisible things. She is taking the pills again, she must, for the pain is too great now, and the morphine, so innocent a substance to come like blood out of the vibrant red poppies, is helping. She knows she is addicted. She knows it won't last. It makes her laugh. Everything delights her. The music is all around her now, Lao singing accompanied by a khene changing into South African kwaito becoming reggae from PNG.

"I don't know," Haziq says. He sounds so vulnerable then. Mei says, "You were married."

"Yes."

Curiosity compels her. "Why didn't she come with you?"

"She would never have come with me," Haziq says, and Mei feels her heart shudder inside her like a caged bird, and she says, "But you didn't ask."

"No," Haziq says. The long silence is interrupted by others on the shared primitive radio band, hellos and groans and threats and prayers, and someone singing, drunk. "No," Haziq says. "I didn't ask."

* * *

ONE MONTH TO planetfall. And Mei falls silent. Haziq tries to raise her on the radio but there is no reply. "Hello, hello, this is Haziq, C-6173, this is Haziq, C-6173, has anyone heard from Mei in A-3357, has anyone heard from Mei?"

"This is Henrik in D-7479, I am in a great deal of pain, could somebody help me? Please, could somebody help me?"

"This is Cobb in E-1255, I have figured it all out, there is no Mars, they lied to us, we'll die in these tin cans, how much air, how much air is left?"

"This is jalopy B-2031 to jalopy C-3398, queen to pawn 4, I said queen to pawn 4, and check and mate, take that, Shen, you twisted old bat!"

"This is David in B-1201, jalopy B-1200, can you hear me, jalopy B-1200, can you hear me, I love you, Joy. Will you marry me? Will you—"

"Yes! Yes!"

"We might not make it. But I feel like I know you, like I've always known you, in my mind you are as beautiful as your words."

"I will see you, I will know you, there on the red sands, there on Terminal Beach, oh, David—"

"My darling—"

"This is jalopy C-6669, will you two get a room?" and laughter on the radio waves, and shouts of cheers, congrats, mazel tov and the like. But Mei cannot be raised, her jalopy's silent.

NOT JALOPIES BUT empty containers with nothing but air floating along with the swarm, destined for Terminal, supplements for the plants, and water and other supplies, and some say these settlers, if that's what they be, are dying faster than we can replace them, but so what. They had paid for their trip. Mars is a madhouse, its inmates wander their rubbish heap town, and Mei, floating with a happy distracted mind, no longer hears even the music. And she thinks of all the things she didn't say. Of stepping out onto Terminal Beach, of coming through the airlock, yes, but then, almost immediately, coming out again, suited uncomfortably, how hard it was, to strip the jalopies of everything inside and, worse, to go on corpse duty.

She does not want to tell all this to Haziq, does not want to picture him landing, and going with the others, this gruesome initiation ceremony for the newly arrived: to check on the jalopies no longer responding, the ones that didn't open, the ones from which no one has emerged. And she hopes, without reason, that it is Haziq who finds her, no longer floating but pressed down by gravity, her fragile bones fractured and crushed; that he would know her, somehow. That he would raise her in his arms, gently, and carry her out, and lay her down on the Martian sand.

Then they would strip the jalopy and push it and join it to the others, this spider bite of a city sprawling out of those first crude jalopies to crash-land, and Haziq might sleep, fitfully, in the dormitory with all the others, and then, perhaps, Mei could be buried. Or left to the Martian winds.

She imagines the wind howling through the canyons of the Valles Marineris. Imagines the snow falling, kissing her face. Imagines the howling winds stripping her of skin and polishing her bones, imagines herself scattered at last, every tiny bit of her blown apart and spread across the planet.

And she imagines jalopies like meteorites coming down. Imagines the music the planet makes, if only you could hear it. And she closes her eyes and she smiles.

"I HOPE IT'S you..."

"SIGN HERE, INITIAL here, and here, and here."

The jalopyman is young and friendly, and she knows his face if not his name. He says, perhaps in surprise or in genuine interest, for they never, usually, ask, "Are you sure you want to do it?"

And Eliza signs, and she nods, quickly, like a bird. And she pushes the pen back at him, as if to stop from changing her mind.

"I HOPE IT'S you..."

"Mei? Is that you? Is that you?"

But there is no one there, nothing but a scratchy echo on the radio; like the sound of desert winds.

FOXFIRE, FOXFIRE
Yoon Ha Lee

Yoon Ha Lee's (*www.yoonhalee.com*) first novel, *Ninefox Gambit*, was published to critical acclaim in 2016. The first in the Machineries of Empire series, it will be followed in 2017 by *Raven Stratagem*. Lee is the author of more than forty short stories, some of which have appeared in *Tor. com*, *Lightspeed*, *Clarkesworld*, and *The Magazine of Fantasy and Science Fiction*. Lee's first short story collection is *Conservation of Shadows*. He lives in Louisiana with his family and has not yet been eaten by gators.

IF I'D LISTENED to the tiger-sage's warning all those years ago, I wouldn't be trapped in the city of Samdae during the evacuation. Old buildings and new had suffered during the artillery battle, and I could hear the occasional wailing of sirens. Even at this hour, families led hunched grandmothers and grandfathers away from their old homes, or searched abandoned homes in the hopes of finding small treasures: salt, rags, dried peppers. As I picked my way through the streets tonight, I saw the flower-shaped roof tiles for which Samdae was known, broken and scattered beneath my feet. Faraway, blued by distance, lights guttered from those skyscrapers still standing, dating to the peninsula's push to modernization. It had not done anything to prevent the civil war.

I had weighed the merits of tonight's hunt. Better to return to fox-form, surely, and slip back to the countryside; abandon the purpose that had brought me to Samdae all those years ago. But I only needed one more kill to become fully human. And I didn't want to off some struggling shopkeeper or midwife. For one thing, I had no grudge against them. For another, I had no need of their particular skills.

No; I wandered the Lantern District in search of a soldier. Soldiers were easy enough to find, but I wanted a nice strapping specimen. At the moment I was posing as a prostitute, the only part of this whole affair my mother would have approved of. Certain human professions were better-suited to foxes than others, she had liked to say. My mother had always been an old-fashioned fox.

"Baekdo," she had said when I was young, "why can't you be satisfied with chickens and mice? You think you'll be able to stop with sweet bean cakes, but the next thing you know, it will be shrimp crackers and chocolate-dipped biscuits, and after that you'll take off your beautiful fur to walk around in things with buttons and pockets and rubber soles. And then one of the humans will fall in love with you and discover your secret, and you'll end up like your Great-Aunt Seonghwa, as a bunch of oracle bones in some shaman's purse."

Foxes are just as bad at listening to their mothers as humans are. My mother had died before the war broke out. I had brought her no funeral-offerings. My relatives would have been shocked by that idea, and my mother, a traditionalist, would have wanted to be left to the carrion-eaters.

I had loved the Lantern District for a long time. I had taken my first kill there, a lucky one really. I'd crept into a courtesan's apartment, half-drunk on the smells of quince tea and lilac perfume. At the time I had no way of telling a beautiful human from an ugly one—I later learned that she had been a celebrated beauty—but her layered red and orange silks had reminded me of autumn in the forest.

Tonight I wore that courtesan's visage. Samdae's remaining soldiers grew bolder and bolder with the breakdown in local government, so only those very desperate or stubborn continued to ply their trade. I wasn't worried on my own behalf, of course. After ninety-nine kills, I knew how to take care of myself.

There. I spotted a promising prospect lingering at the corner, chatting up a cigarette-seller. He was tall, not too old, with a good physique. He was in uniform, with the red armband that indicated that he supported the revolutionaries. Small surprise; everyone who remained in Samdae made a show of supporting the revolutionaries. Many of the loyalists had fled overseas, hoping to raise support from the foreign powers. I wished them luck. The loyalists were themselves divided between those who supported the queen's old line and those who wished to install a parliament in place of the Abalone Throne. Fascinating, but not my concern tonight.

I was sauntering toward the delicious-looking soldier when I heard the cataphract's footsteps. A Jangmi 2-7, judging from the characteristic whine of the servos. Even if I hadn't heard it coming—and who couldn't?—the stirring of the small gods of earth and stone would have alerted me to its approach. They muttered distractingly. My ears would have flattened against my skull if they could have.

Superstitious people called the cataphracts ogres, because of their enormous bipedal frames. Some patriots disliked them because they had to be imported from overseas. Our nation didn't have the ability to manufacture them, a secret that the foreigners guarded jealously.

This one was crashing through the street. People fled. No one wanted to be around if a firefight broke out, especially with the armaments a typical cataphract was equipped with. It was five times taller than a human, with a stride that would have cratered the street with every step, all that mass crashing down onto surprisingly little feet if not for the bargains the manufacturers had made with the small gods of earth and stone.

What was a lone cataphract doing in this part of the city? A scout? A deserter? But what deserter in their right mind would bring something as easy to track as a cataphract with them?

Not my business. Alas, my delicious-looking soldier had vanished along with everyone else. And my bones were starting to hurt in the particular way that indicated that I had sustained human-shape too long.

On the other hand, while the cataphract's great strides made it faster than I was in this shape, distances had a way of accommodating themselves to a fox's desires. A dangerous idea took shape in my head. Why settle for a common soldier when I could have a cataphract pilot, one of the elites?

I ducked around a corner into the mouth of an alley, then kicked off my slippers, the only part of my dress that wasn't spun from fox-magic. (Magical garments never lasted beyond a seduction. My mother had remarked that this was the fate of all human clothes anyway.) I loved those slippers, which I had purloined from a rich merchant's daughter, and it pained me to leave them behind. But I could get another pair of slippers later.

Anyone watching the transformation would only have seen a blaze of coalescing red, like fire and frost swirled together, before my bones resettled into their native shape. Their ache eased. The night-smells of the city sharpened: alcohol, smoke, piss, the occasional odd whiff of stew. I turned around nine times—nine is a number sacred to foxes—and ran through the city's mazed streets.

The Lantern District receded behind me. I emerged amid rubble and the stink of explosive residue. The riots earlier in the year had not treated the Butterfly District kindly. The wealthier families had lived here. Looters had made short work of their possessions. I had taken advantage of the chaos as well, squirreling away everything from medicines to salt in small caches; after all, once I became human, I would need provisions for the journey to one of the safer cities to the south.

It didn't take long to locate the cataphract. Its pilot had parked it next to a statue, hunched down as if that would make it less conspicuous. Up close, I now saw why the pilot had fled—whatever it was they were fleeing. Despite the cataphract's menacing form, its left arm dangled oddly. It looked like someone had shot up the autocannon, and the cataphract's armor was decorated by blast marks. While I was no expert, I was amazed the thing still functioned.

The statue, one of the few treasures of the district to escape damage, depicted a courtesan who had killed an invading general a few centuries ago by clasping her arms around him and jumping off a cliff with him. My mother had remarked that if the courtesan had had proper teeth, she could have torn out the general's throat and lived for her trouble. Fox patriotism was not much impressed by martyrs. I liked the story, though.

I crouched in the shadows, sniffing the air. The metal reek of the cataphract overpowered everything. The small gods of earth and stone shifted and rumbled. Still, I detected blood, and sweat, as well as the particular unappetizing smell of what the humans called Brick Rations, because they were about as digestible. Human blood, human sweat, human food.

A smarter fox would have left the situation alone. While dodging the cataphract would be easy, cataphract pilots carried sidearms. For all I knew, this one would welcome fox soup as an alternative to Brick Rations.

While cataphract-piloting didn't strike me as a particularly useful skill, the pilots were all trained in the more ordinary arts of soldiering. Good enough for me.

I drew in my breath and took on human-shape. The small gods hissed their laughter. This time, when the pain receded, I was wrapped in a dress of green silk and a lavender sash embroidered with peonies. My hair was piled atop my head and held in place by heavy hairpins. The whole getup would have looked fashionable four generations ago, which I knew not because I had been alive then (although foxes could be long-lived when they chose) but because I used to amuse myself looking through Great-Aunt Seonghwa's collection of books on the history of fashion.

I'd hoped for something more practical, but my control of the magic had slipped. I would have to make the best of it. A pity the magic had not provided me with shoes, even ugly ones. I thought of the slippers I had discarded, and I sighed.

Carefully, I stepped through the street, pulse beating more rapidly as I contemplated my prey. A pebble dug into my foot, but I paid it no heed. I had endured worse, and my blood was up.

Even in human-shape, I had an excellent sense of smell. I had no difficulty tracking the pilot. Only one; I wondered what had happened to her copilot. The pilot lay on her side in the lee of a chunk of rubble, apparently asleep. The remains of a Brick Ration's wrapper had been tossed to the side. She had downed all of it, which impressed me. But then, I'd heard that piloting was hungry work.

I crouched and contemplated the pilot, taut with anticipation. At this distance, she reeked worse than her machine. She had taken off her helmet, which she hugged to her chest. Her black hair, cropped close, was mussed and stringy, and the bones of her face stood out too prominently beneath the sweat-streaked, dirty skin.

She'd also taken off her suit, for which I didn't blame her. Cataphracts built up heat—the gods of fire, being fickle, did an indifferent job of masking their infrared signatures—and the suits were designed to cool the pilot, not to act as armor or protect them against the chilly autumn winds. She'd wrapped a thermal blanket around herself. I eyed it critically: effective, but ugly.

No matter what shape I took, I had a weapon; there is no such thing as an unarmed fox. I wondered what the magic had provided me with today. I could feel the weight of a knife hanging from my inner sash, and I reached in to draw it out. The elaborate gilt handle and the tassel hanging from the pommel pleased me, although what really mattered was the blade.

I leaned down to slit the pilot's throat—except her eyes opened and she rolled, casting the helmet aside. I scrambled backwards, but her reflexes were faster, a novelty. She grabbed my wrist, knocking the knife out of my hand with a clatter, and forced me down.

"Well-dressed for a looter," the pilot said into my ear. "But then, I suppose that goes with the territory."

I had no interest in being lectured before my inevitable addition to a makeshift stewpot. I released human-shape in a flutter of evanescent silks, hoping to wriggle out of her grip.

No such luck. Almost as if she'd anticipated the change, she closed her hands around my neck. I snapped and clawed, to no effect. I had to get free before she choked the life out of me.

"*Gumiho*," the pilot breathed. Nine-tailed fox. "I thought all your kind were gone."

My attempt at a growl came out as a sad wheeze.

"Sorry, fox," the pilot said, not sounding sorry in the least.

I scrabbled wildly at the air, only half paying attention to her words.

"But I bet you can speak," she went on as I choked out a whine. "Which means you're just as likely to snitch to my pursuers as something fully human."

She was saying something more about her pursuers, still in that cheerful conversational voice, when I finally passed out.

I WOKE TRUSSED up as neatly as a rabbit for the pot. The air was full of the strange curdled-sweet smell of coolant, the metal reek of cataphract, the pilot's particular stink. My throat hurt and my legs ached, but at least I wasn't dead.

I opened my eyes and looked around at the inside of the cockpit. The blinking lights and hectic status graphs meant nothing to me. I wished I'd eaten an engineer along the way, even though the control systems were undoubtedly different for different cataphract models. I'd been tied to the copilot's seat.

Cataphracts could be piloted solo if necessary, but I still wondered if the copilot had died in battle, or deserted, or something else entirely.

The cockpit was uncomfortably warm. I worked my jaw but couldn't get a good purchase on the bindings. Worse, I'd lost the knife. If I couldn't use my teeth to get out of this fix—

"Awake?" the pilot said. "Sorry about that, but I've heard stories of your kind."

Great, I had to get a victim who had paid attention to grandmothers'-tales of fox spirits. Except now, I supposed, *I* was the victim. I stared into the pilot's dark eyes.

"Don't give me that," the pilot said. "I know you understand me, and I know you can speak."

Not with my muzzle tied shut, I can't, I thought.

As if she'd heard me, she leaned over and sawed through the bonds on my muzzle with a combat knife. I snapped at the knife, which was stupid of me. It sliced my gums. The familiar tang of blood filled my mouth.

"You may as well call me Jong," the pilot said. "It's not my real name, but my mother used to call me that, after the child and the bell in the old story. What shall I call you?"

I had no idea what story she was talking about. However, given the number of folktales living in small crannies of the peninsula, this wasn't surprising. "I'm a fox," I said. "Do you need a name for me beyond that?" It wasn't as though we planned on becoming friends.

Jong strapped herself in properly. "Well, you should be grateful you're tied in good and tight," she said as she manipulated the controls: here a lever, there a button, provoking balletic changes in the lights. "The straps weren't designed with a fox in mind. I'd hate for you to get splattered all over the cockpit when we make a run for it."

"So kind of you," I said dryly. *Sorry,* I thought to my mother's ghost. *I should have listened to you all those years ago.* Still, Jong hadn't eaten me yet, so there was hope.

"Oh, kindness has nothing to do with it." The cataphract straightened with a hiss of servos. "I can't talk to the gods of mountain and forest, but I bet you can. It's in all the stories. And the mountains are where I have to go if I'm going to escape."

Silly me. I would have assumed that a cataphract pilot would be some technocrat who'd disdain the old folktales. I had to go after one who knew enough of the lore to be dangerous. "Something could be arranged, yes," I said. Even as a kit my mother had warned me against trusting too much in gods of any kind, but Jong didn't need to know that.

"We'll work it out as we go," she said distantly. She wasn't looking at me anymore.

I considered worrying at the bonds with my teeth, even though the synthetic fibers would taste foul, but just then the cataphract shuddered awake and took a step. I choked back a yip. Jong's eyes had an eerie golden sheen that lit up their normal brown; side-effect of the neural interface, I'd heard, but I'd never seen the effect up close before. If I disrupted the connection now, who knew what would happen? I wasn't so desperate that I wanted the cataphract to crash into uselessness, leaving me tied up inside it while unknown hostiles hunted us. Inwardly, I cursed Jong for getting me involved; cursed myself for getting too ambitious. But recriminations wouldn't help now.

For the first hour, I stayed silent, observing Jong in the hopes of learning the secrets of the cataphract's operation the old-fashioned way. Unfortunately, the closest thing to a cataphract pilot I'd ever eaten had been a radio operator. Not good enough. No wonder Great-Aunt Seonghwa had emphasized the value of a proper education, even if I had dismissed her words at the time. (One of her first victims had been a university student, albeit one studying classical literature rather than engineering. Back then, you could get a comfortable government post by reciting maxims from *The Twenty-Three Principles of Virtuous Administration* and tossing off the occasional moon-poem.) The ability to instantly absorb someone's skills by ingesting their liver had made me lazy.

"Why are they after you?" I asked, on the grounds that the more information I could extract from Jong, the better. "And who are they, anyway?"

She adjusted a dial; one of the monitors showed a mass of shapes like tangled thread. "Why are they after anyone?"

Not stupid enough to tell a stranger, then. I couldn't fault her. "How do I know you won't use me, then shoot me?"

"You don't. But I'll let you go after I get away."

Unsatisfying, as responses went. "Assuming you get away."

"I have to." For the first time, Jong's cheerfulness faltered.

"Maybe we can bargain," I said.

Jong didn't respond for a while, but we'd entered a defile and she was presumably caught up making sure we didn't tumble over some ledge and into the stony depths. I had difficulty interpreting what I saw. For one thing, I wasn't used to a vantage point this high up. For another, I couldn't navigate by scent from within the cockpit, although I was already starting to become inured to the mixed smells of grubby human and metal.

"What bargain can you offer?" Jong said when she'd parked us in a cranny just deep enough in the defile that the cataphract wouldn't be obvious except from straight above.

I wondered if we had aerial pursuit to worry about as well. Surely I'd hear any helicopters, now that the cataphract had powered down? I knew better than to rely on the small gods of wind and storm for warning; they were almost as fickle as fire.

Jong's breathing became unsteady as she squinted at a scatterfall of glowing dots. She swore under her breath in one of the country dialects that I could understand only with difficulty. "We'll have to hope that they're spreading themselves too thin to figure out which way we've gone," she said in a low voice, as though people could hear her from inside the cockpit. "We'll continue once I'm sure I can move without lighting up their scanners."

Carefully, I said, "What if I swear on the spirits of my ancestors to lead you where you need to go, with the aid of the small gods to mask your infrared signature?" This was a guess on my part, but she didn't correct me, so I assumed it was close enough. "Will you unbind me, at least?"

"I didn't think foxes worshiped ancestors," Jong said, eyeing me skeptically. She fished a Brick Ration out of a compartment and unwrapped it with quick, efficient motions.

My mouth watered despite the awful smell. I hadn't eaten in a while. "Foxes are foxes, not gods," I said. "What good is worship to a fox? But I remember how my mother cared for me, and my other relatives. Their memory means a lot to me."

Jong was already shaking her head. A crumb of the Brick Ration fell onto her knee. She picked it up, regarded it contemplatively, then popped it into her mouth.

A ration only questionably formulated to sustain humans probably wouldn't do me much good in fox-form, but it was difficult not to resent my captor for not sharing, irrational as the sentiment was.

"I need a real guarantee that you'll be helpful, not a fox-guarantee," Jong said.

"That's difficult, considering that I'm a fox."

"I don't think so." Jong smiled, teeth gleaming oddly in the cockpit's deadened lights. Her face resembled a war-mask from the old days of the Abalone Throne. "Swear on the blood of the tiger-sages."

My heart stuttered within me. "There are no tiger-sages left," I said. It might even have been true.

Jong's smile widened. "I'll take that chance."

WHEN I WAS a young fox, almost adult, and therefore old enough to get into the bad kind of trouble, my mother took me to visit a tiger-sage.

Until then, I had thought all the tiger-sages had left the peninsula. Sometimes the humans had hunted them, and more rarely they sought the tigers' advice, although a tiger's advice always has a bite in it. I'd once heard of hunters bringing down an older tiger in a nearby village, and I'd asked my mother if that had been a sage. She had only snorted and said that a real sage wouldn't go down so easily.

Tiger-sages could die. That much I knew. But their deaths had nothing to do with shotguns or nets or poisoned ox carcasses. A tiger-sage had to be slain with a sword set with mirror-jewels or arrows fletched with feathers stolen from nesting firebirds. A tiger-sage had to be sung to death in a game of riddles during typhoon season, or tricked into sleep after a long game of *baduk*—the famously subtle strategy game played upon a board of nineteen-by-nineteen intersecting lines, with black stones and white. A tiger-sage had to consent to perish.

We traveled for days, because even a fox's ability to slice through distance dwindled before a tiger-sage's defenses. My mother was more nervous than I'd ever seen her. I, too stupid to know better, was excited by the excursion.

At last we approached the tiger-sage's cave, high upon a mountain, where the trees grew sideways and small bright flowers flourished in the thin soil.

Everything smelled hard and sharp, as though we lingered dangerously close to the boundary between *always* and *never*.

The cave had once served as a shrine for some human sage. A gilded statue dominated the mouth of the cave, lovingly polished. It depicted a woman sitting cross-legged, one palm held out and cupping a massive pearl, the other resting on her knee. The skull of some massive tusked beast rested next to the statue. The yellowing bone had been scored by claw-marks.

The tiger-sage emerged from the cave slowly, sinuously, like smoke from a hidden fire. Her fur was chilly white except for the night-black stripes. She was supposed to be the last of the tiger-sages. One by one they had departed for other lands, or so the fox-stories went. Whether this one remained out of stubbornness, or amusement at human antics, or sheer apathy, my mother hadn't been able to say. It didn't matter. It was not for a fox to understand the motivations of a sage.

"Foxes," the tiger rumbled, her amber eyes regarding us with disinterest. "It is too bad you are no good for oracle bones. Fox bones always lie. The least you could have done was bring some incense. I ran out of the good stuff two months ago."

My mother's ears twitched, but she said only, "Venerable sage, I am here to beg your counsel on my son's behalf."

I crouched and tried to look appropriately humble, having never heard my mother speak like this before.

The tiger yawned hugely. "You've been spending too much time with humans if you're trying to fit all those flowery words in your mouth. Just say it straight out."

Normally my mother would have said something deprecating—I'd grown up listening to her arguing with Great-Aunt Seonghwa about the benefits of human culture—but she had other things on her mind. That, or the tiger's impressive display of sharp teeth reminded her that to a tiger, everything is prey. "My son hungers after human-shape," my mother said. "I have tried to persuade him otherwise, but a mother's words only go so far. Perhaps you would be willing to give him some guidance?"

The tiger caught my eye and smiled tiger-fashion. I had a moment to wonder how many bites it would take for me to end up in her belly. She reared up, or perhaps it was that she straightened. For several stinging moments, I could not focus my vision on her, as though her entire outline was evanescing.

Then a woman stood where the tiger had been, or something like a woman, except for the amber eyes and the sharp-toothed smile. Her hair was black frosted with white and silver. Robes of silk flowed from her shoulders, layered in mountain colors: dawn-pink and ice-white and pale-gray with a sash of deepest green. At the time I did not yet understand beauty. Years later, remembering, I would realize that she had mimicked the form of the last legitimate queen. (Tigers have never been known for modesty.)

"How much do you know of the traditional bargain, little fox?" the tiger-woman asked. Her voice was very little changed.

I did not like being called little, but I had enough sense not to pick a fight with a tiger over one petty adjective. Especially since the tiger was, in any shape, larger than I was. "I have to kill one hundred humans to become human," I said. "I understand the risk."

The tiger-woman made an impatient noise. "I should have known better than to expect enlightenment from a fox."

My mother held her peace.

"People say I am the last of the tiger-sages," the tiger-woman said. "Do you know why?"

"I had thought you were all gone," I said, since I saw no reason not to be honest. "*Are* you the last one?"

The tiger-woman laughed. "Almost the last one, perhaps." The silk robes blurred, and then she coiled before us in her native shape again. "I killed more than a hundred humans, in my time. Never do anything by halves, if you're going to do it. But human-shape bored me after a while, and I yearned for my old clothing of stripes and teeth and claws."

"So?" I said, whiskers twitching.

"So I killed and ate a hundred tiger-sages from my own lineage, to become a tiger again."

My mother was tense, silent. My eyes had gone wide.

The tiger looked at me intently. "If the kit is serious about this—and I can smell it on him, that taint is unmistakable—I have some words for him."

I stared at the tiger, transfixed. It could have pounced on me in that moment and I wouldn't have moved. My mother made a low half-growl in the back of her throat.

"Becoming human has nothing to do with flat faces and weak noses and walking on two legs," the tiger said. "That's what your people always get wrong. It's the hunger for gossip and bedroom entanglements and un-fox-ish loyalties; it's about having a human heart. I, of course, don't care one whit about such matters, so I will never be trapped in human-shape. But for reasons I have never fathomed, foxes always lose themselves in their new faces."

"We appreciate the advice," my mother said, tail thumping against the ground. "I will steal you some incense." I could tell she was desperate to leave.

The tiger waved a paw, not entirely benevolently. "Don't trouble yourself on my account, little vixen. And tell your aunt I warned her, assuming you get the chance."

Two weeks after that visit, I heard of Great-Aunt Seonghwa's unfortunate demise. It was not enough to deter me from the path I had chosen.

"COME ON, FOX," Jong said. "If your offer is sincere, you have nothing to fear from a mythical tiger."

I refrained from snapping that 'mythical' tigers were the most frightening of all. Ordinary tigers were bad enough. Now that I was old enough to appreciate how dangerous tiger-sages were, I preferred not to bring myself to one's attention. But remaining tied up like this wasn't appealing, either. And who knew how much time I had to extract myself from this situation?

"I swear on the blood of the tiger-sages," I said, "that I will keep my bargain with you. No fox tricks." I could almost hear the tiger-sage's cynical laughter in my head, but I hoped it was my imagination.

Jong didn't waste time making additional threats. She unbuckled herself and leaned over me to undo my bonds. I admired her deft hands. *Those could have been mine,* I thought hungrily; but I had promised. While a fox's word might not be worth much, I had no desire to become the prey of an offended tiger. Tiger-sages took oaths quite seriously when they cared to.

My limbs ached, and it still hurt when I swallowed or talked. Small pains, however, and the pleasure of being able to move again made up for them. "Thank you," I said.

"I advise being human if you can manage it," Jong said. I choked back a snort. "The seat will be more comfortable for you."

I couldn't argue the point. Despite the pain, I was able to focus enough to summon the change-magic. Magic had its own sense of humor, as always. Instead of outdated court dress, it presented me in street-sweeper's clothes, right down to the hat. As if a hat did anything but make me look ridiculous, especially inside a cataphract.

To her credit, Jong didn't burst out laughing. I might have tried for her throat if she had, short-tempered as I was. "We need to"—yawn—"keep moving. But the pursuers are too close. Convince the small gods to conceal us from their scan, and we'll keep going until we find shelter enough to rest for real."

Jong's faith in my ability to convince the small gods to do me favors was very touching. I had promised, however, which meant I had to do my best. "You're in luck," I said; if she heard the irony in my voice, she didn't react to it. "The small gods are hungry tonight."

Feeding gods was tricky business. I had learned most of what I knew from Great-Aunt Seonghwa. My mother had disdained such magic herself, saying that she would trust her own fine coat for camouflage instead of relying on gods, to say nothing of all the mundane stratagems she had learned from her own mother. For my part, I was not too proud to do what I had to in order to survive.

The large gods of the Celestial Order, who guided the procession of stars, responded to human blandishments: incense (I often wondered if the tiger I had met lit incense to the golden statue, or if it was for her own pleasure), or offerings of roast duck and tangerines, or bolts of silk embroidered with gold thread. The most powerful of the large gods demanded rituals and chants. Having never been bold enough to eat a shaman or magician, I didn't know how that worked. (I remained mindful of Great-Aunt Seonghwa's fate.) Fortunately, the small gods did not require such sophistication.

"Can you spare any part of this machine?" I asked Jong.

Her mouth compressed. Still, she didn't argue. She retrieved a screwdriver and undid one of the panels, joystick and all, although she pocketed the screws. "It's not like the busted arm's good for anything anymore," she said. The exposed wires and pipes of coolant looked like exposed veins. She grimaced, then fiddled with the wires' connectors until they had all been undone. "Will this do?"

I doubted the small gods knew more about cataphract engineering than I did. "Yes," I said, with more confidence than I felt, and took the panel from her. I pressed my right hand against the underside of the panel, flinching in spite of myself from the metal's unfriendly warmth.

This is my offering, I said in the language of forest and mountain, which even city foxes spoke; and my mother, as a very proper fox, had raised me in the forest. *Earth and stone and—*

Jong's curse broke my concentration, although the singing tension in the air told me that the small gods already pressed close to us, reaching, reaching.

"What is it?" I said.

"We'll have to fight," Jong said. "Buckle in."

I had to let go of the panel to do so. I had just figured out the straps—the cataphract's were more complicated than the safety restraints found in automobiles—and the panel clanked onto the cockpit's floor as the cataphract rumbled awake. The small gods skittered and howled, demanding their tribute. I was fox enough to hear them, even if Jong showed no sign of noticing anything.

The lights in the cockpit blazed up in a glory of colors. The glow sheened in Jong's tousled hair and reflected in her eyes, etched deep shadows around her mouth. The servos whirred; I could have sworn the entire cataphract creaked and moaned as it woke.

I scooped up the panel. Its edges bit into my palms. "How many?" I asked, then wondered if I should be distracting Jong when we were entering combat.

"Five," she said. "Whatever you're doing, finish it fast."

The machine lurched out of the crevice where we'd been hiding, then broke into its version of a run. My stomach dropped. Worse than the jolting gait was the fact that I kept bracing for the impact of those heavy metal feet against the earth. I kept expecting the cataphract to sink hip-deep. Even though the gods of earth and stone cushioned each stride, acting as shock-absorbers, the discrepancy between what I expected and what happened upset my sense of the world's equilibrium.

The control systems made noises that had only shrillness to recommend them. I left their interpretation to Jong and returned my attention to the small gods. From the way the air in the cockpit eddied and swirled, I could tell they were growing impatient. Earth and stone were allied to metal, after all, and metal, especially when summoned on behalf of a weapon, had its volatile side.

The magic had provided me not with a knife this time but with a hat pin. I retrieved it and jabbed my palm with the pointy end. Blood welled up. I smeared it onto the cataphract's joystick. *Get us out of here,* I said to the small gods. Not eloquent, but I didn't have time to come up with anything better.

The world tilted askew, pale and dark and fractured. Jong might have said something. I couldn't understand any of it. Then everything righted itself again.

More, the small gods said in voices like shuddering bone.

I whispered stories to them, still speaking in the language of forest and mountain, which had no words except the evocation of the smell of fallen pine needles on an autumn morning, or loam worked over by the worms, or rain filling paw prints left in the mud. I was still fox enough for this to suffice.

"What in the name of the blistering gods?" Jong demanded. Now even she could hear the clanging of distant bells. Music was one of the human innovations that the small gods had grown fond of.

"They're building mazes," I said. "They'll mask our path. *Go!*"

Her eyes met mine for a moment, hot and incredulous. Then she nodded and jerked a lever forward, activating the walk cycle. The cataphract juddered. The targeting screen flashed red as it locked on an erratically moving figure: another cataphract. She pressed a trigger.

I hunched down in my seat at the racket the autocannon made as it fired four shots in rapid succession, like a damned smith's hammer upon the world's last anvil. The small gods rumbled their approval. I forced myself to watch the targeting screen. For a moment I thought Jong had missed. Then the figure toppled sideways.

"Legged them," Jong said with vicious satisfaction. "Don't care about honor or kill counts, it's good enough to cripple them so we can keep running."

We endured several hits ourselves. While the small gods could confuse the enemies' sensors, the fact remained that the cataphract relied on its metal armor to protect its inner mechanisms. The impacts rattled me from teeth to marrow. I was impressed that *we* hadn't gone tumbling down.

And when had I started thinking of us as 'we,' anyway?

"We're doomed," I said involuntarily when something hit the cataphract's upper left torso—by then I'd figured out the basics of a few of the status readouts—and the whole cockpit trembled.

Jong's grin flickered sideways at me. "Don't be a pessimist, fox," she said, breathless. "You ever hear of damage distribution?"

"Damage what?"

"I'll explain it to you if we—" A shrill beep captured her attention. "Whoops, better deal with this first."

"How many are left?"

"Three."

There had been five to begin with. I hadn't even noticed the second one going down.

"If only I weren't out of coolant, I'd—" Jong muttered some other incomprehensible thing after that.

In the helter-skelter swirl of blinking lights and god-whispers, Jong herself was transfigured. Not beautiful in the way of a court blossom but in the way of a gun: honed toward a single purpose. I knew then that I was doomed in another manner entirely. No romance between a fox and a human ever ended well. What could I do, after all? Persuade her to abandon her cataphract and run away with me into the forest, where I would feed her rabbits and squirrels? No; I would help her escape, then go my separate way.

Every time an alert sounded, every time a vibration thundered through the cataphract's frame, I shivered. My tongue was bitten almost to bleeding. I could not remember the last time I had been this frightened.

You were right, Mother, I wanted to say. Better a small life in the woods, diminished though they were from the days before the great cities with their ugly high-rises, than the gnawing hunger that had driven me toward the humans and their beautiful clothes, their delicious shrimp crackers, their games of dice and *yut* and *baduk*. For the first time I understood that, as tempting as these things were, they came with a price: I could not obtain them without also entangling myself with human hearts, human quarrels, human loyalties.

A flicker at the edge of one of the screens caught my eye. "Behind us, to the right!" I said.

Jong made a complicated hooking motion with the joystick and the cataphract bent low. My vision swam. "Thank you," she said.

"Tell me you have some plan beyond 'keep running until everyone runs out of fuel,'" I said.

She chuckled. "You don't know thing one about how a cataphract works, do you? Nuclear core. Fuel isn't the issue."

I ignored that. Nuclear physics was not typically a fox specialty, although my mother had allowed that astrology was all right. "Why do they want you so badly?"

I had not expected Jong to answer me. But she said, "There's no more point keeping it a secret. I deserted."

"Why?" A *boom* just ahead of us made me clutch the armrests as we tilted dangerously.

"I had a falling out with my commander," Jong said. Her voice was so tranquil that we might have been sitting side by side on a porch, sipping rice wine. Her hands moved; moved again. A roaring of fire, far off. "Just two left. In any case, my commander liked power. Our squad was sworn to protect the interim government, not—not to play games with the nation's politics." She drew a deep breath. "I don't suppose any of this makes sense to you."

"Why are you telling me now?" I said.

"Because you might die here with me, and it's not as if you can give away our location any *more*. They know who I am. It only seems fair."

Typically human reasoning, but I appreciated the sentiment. "What good does deserting do you?" I supposed she might know state secrets, at that. But who was she deserting *to*?

"I just need to get to—" She shook her head. "If I can get to refuge, especially with this machine more or less intact, I have information the loyalists can make use of." She was scrutinizing the infrared scan as she spoke.

"The Abalone Throne means that much to you?"

Another alert went off. Jong shut it down. "I'm going to bust a limb at this rate," she said. "The Throne? No. It's outlived its usefulness."

"You're a parliamentarian, then."

"Yes."

This matter of monarchies and parliaments and factions was properly none of my business. All I had to do was keep my end of the bargain, and I could leave behind this vexing, heartbreaking woman and her passion for something as abstract as *government*.

Jong was about to add something to that when it happened. Afterwards I was only able to piece together fragments that didn't fit together, like shards of a mirror dropped into a lake. A concussive blast. Being flung backwards, then sideways. A sudden, sharp pain in my side. (I'd broken a couple ribs, in spite of the restraints. But without them, the injuries would have been worse.) Jong's sharp cry, truncated. The stink of panic.

The cataphract had stopped moving. The small gods roared. I moved my head; pain stabbed all the way through the back of my skull. "Jong?" I croaked.

Jong was breathing shallowly. Blood poured thickly from the cut on her face. I saw what had happened: the panel had flown out of my hands and struck her edge-on. The small gods had taken their payment, all right; mine hadn't been enough. If only I had foreseen this—

"Fox," Jong said in a weak voice.

Lights blinked on-off, on-off, in a crazed quilt. The cockpit looked like someone had upended a bucket full of unlucky constellations into it. "Jong," I said. "Jong, are you all right?"

"My mission," she said. Her eyes were too wide, shocky, the red-and-amber of the status lights pooling in the enormous pupils. I could smell the death on her, hear the frantic pounding of her heart as her body destroyed itself. Internal bleeding, and a lot of it. "Fox, you have to finish my mission. Unless you're also a physician?"

"Shh," I said. "Shh." I had avoided eating people in the medical professions not out of a sense of ethics but because, in the older days, physicians tended to have a solid grounding in the kinds of magics that threatened shape-changing foxes.

"I got one of them," she said. Her voice sounded more and more thready. "That leaves one, and of course they'll have called for reinforcements. If they have anyone else to spare. You have to—"

I could have howled my frustration. "I'll carry you."

Under other circumstances, that grimace would have been a laugh. "I'm dying, fox, do you think I can't tell?"

"I don't know the things you know," I said desperately. "Even if this metal monstrosity of yours can still run, I can't pilot it for you." It was getting hard to breathe; a foul, stinging vapor was leaking into the cockpit. I hoped it wasn't toxic.

"Then there's no hope," she whispered.

"Wait," I said, remembering; hating myself. "There's a way."

The sudden flare of hope in Jong's eyes cut me.

"I can eat you," I said. "I can take the things you know with me, and seek your friends. But it might be better simply to die."

"Do it," she said. "And hurry. I assume it doesn't do you any good to eat a corpse, or your kind would have a reputation as grave-thieves."

I didn't squander time on apologies. I had already unbuckled the harness, despite the pain of the broken ribs. I flowed back into fox-shape, and I tore out her throat so she wouldn't suffer as I devoured her liver.

The smoke in the cockpit thickened, thinned. When it was gone, a pale tiger watched me from the rear of the cockpit. It seemed impossible that she could fit; but the shadows stretched out into an infinite vast space to accommodate her, and she did. I recognized her. In a hundred stolen lifetimes I would never fail to recognize her.

Shivering, human, mouth full of blood-tang, I looked down. The magic had given me one last gift: I wore a cataphract pilot's suit in fox colors, russet and black. Then I met the tiger's gaze.

I had broken the oath I had sworn upon the tiger-sage's blood. Of course she came to hunt me.

"I had to do it," I said, and stumbled to my feet, prepared to fight. I did not expect to last long against a tiger-sage, but for Jong's sake I had to try.

"There's no 'have to' about anything," the tiger said lazily. "Every death is a choice, little not-a-fox. At any step you could have turned aside. Now—" She fell silent.

I snatched up Jong's knife. Now that I no longer had sharp teeth and claws, it would have to do.

"Don't bother with that," the tiger said. *She* had all her teeth, and wasn't shy about displaying them in a ferocious grin. "No curse I could pronounce on you is more fitting than the one you have chosen for yourself."

"It's not a curse," I said quietly.

"I'll come back in nine years' time," the tiger said, "and we can discuss it then. Good luck with your one-person revolution."

"I needn't fight it alone," I said. "This is your home, too."

The tiger seemed to consider it. "Not a bad thought," she said, "but maps and boundaries and nationalism are for humans, not for tigers."

"If you change your mind," I said, "I'm sure you can find me, in nine years' time or otherwise."

"Indeed," the tiger said. "Farewell, little not-a-fox."

"Thank you," I said, but she was gone already.

I secured Jong's ruined body in the copilot's seat I had vacated, so it wouldn't flop about during maneuvers, and strapped myself in. The cataphract was damaged, but not so badly damaged that I still couldn't make a run for it. It was time to finish Jong's mission.

ELVES OF ANTARCTICA
Paul McAuley

Paul McAuley (www.unlikelyworlds.co.uk) worked as a research biologist and university lecturer before becoming a full-time writer. He is the author of more than twenty novels, several collections of short stories, a *Doctor Who* novella, and a BFI Film Classic monograph on Terry Gilliam's film *Brazil*. His fiction has won the Philip K. Dick Memorial Award, the Arthur C. Clarke Award, the John W. Campbell Memorial Award, the Sidewise Award, the British Fantasy Award and the Theodore Sturgeon Memorial Award. His latest novel, *Into Everywhere*, was published by Gollancz in 2016; *Austral*, a novel about the post-global warming Antarctica featured in this story, is scheduled for 2017.

MIKE TORRES SAW his first elf stone three weeks after he moved to the Antarctic Peninsula. He was flying helos on supply runs from Square Bay on the Fallieres Coast to kelp farms in the fjords to the north, and in his free time had taken to hiking along the shore or into the bare hills beneath Mount Diamond's pyramidal peak. Up there, he had terrific views of the rugged islands standing in the cold blue sea under the high summer sun, Mount Wilson and Mount Metcalf rising beyond the south side of the bay, and the entirety of the town stretched along the shore below. Its industrial sprawl and grids of trailer homes, the rake of its docks, the plantations of bladeless wind turbines, and the airfield with helos coming and going like bees, two or three blimps squatting in front of their hangars, and the runway where a cargo plane, an old Airbus Beluga maybe, or a Globemaster V with its six engines and tail tall as a five-storey building, might be preparing to make its lumbering run towards the sky. All of it ugly, intrusive and necessary: the industrial underbelly of a project that was attempting to prevent the collapse of Antarctica's western ice sheet. It was serious business. It was saving the world. And Mike Torres was part of it.

He was a second-generation climate change refugee, born into the Marshall Islands diaspora community in Auckland. A big, quiet guy who'd survived a tough childhood—his father drinking himself to death, his mother taking two jobs to raise him and his sisters in their tiny central city apartment. Age sixteen, Mike had been part of a small all-city crew spraying tags everywhere on Auckland's transport system; after his third conviction for criminal damage (a big throwie at Remuera Railway Station), a sympathetic magistrate had offered him a spell of workfare on a city farm instead of juvenile prison. He discovered that he loved the outdoor life, earned his helicopter pilot's licence at one of the sheep stations on the high pastures of North Island, where little Robinson R33s were used to muster sheep, and five years later went to work for Big Green, one of the transnational ecological remediation companies, at the Lake Eyre Basin project in Australia.

Desalinated seawater had been pumped into the desert basin to create an inland sea, greening the land around it and removing a small fraction of the excess water that had swollen the world's oceans; Big Green had a contract to establish shelter-belt forests to stabilise and protect the edge of the new farmland. Mike loved watching the machines at work: dozers, dumper trucks and 360 excavators that levelled the ground and spread topsoil; mechanical planters that set out rows of tree seedlings at machine-gun speed, and truck spades that transplanted semi-mature fishtail, atherton and curly palms, acacia, eucalyptus and sheoak trees. In one direction, stony scrub and fleets of sand dunes stretched towards dry mountains floating in heat shimmer; in the other, green checkerboards of rice paddies and date and oil palm plantations descended stepwise towards the shore of the sea. The white chip of a ferry ploughing a wake in blue water. A string of cargo blimps crossing the sky. Fleets of clouds strung at the horizon, generated by climate stations on artificial islands. Everything clean and fresh. A new world in the making.

Mike hauled supplies to the crews who ran the big machines and the gangers who managed the underplanting of shrubs and grasses, brought in engineers and replacement parts, flew key personnel and VIPs to and fro. He sent most of his pay packet home, part of it squirrelled into a savings account, part supporting his mother and his sisters, part tithed to the Marchallese Reclamation Movement, which planned to rebuild the nation by raising artificial islands above the drowned atoll of Majuro. A group of reclaimers had established a settlement there, occupying the top floors of the President's house and a couple of office buildings they had storm-proofed. Mike religiously watched their podcasts, and trawled archives that documented life before the flood, rifling through clips of beach parties, weddings, birthdays and fishing trips from old family videos, freezing and enlarging glimpses of the bustle of ordinary life. A farmer's market, a KFC, a one-dollar store, a shoal of red taxis on Majuro's main drag, kids playing football on a green field at the edge of the blue sea. Moments repossessed from the gone world.

He watched short films about exploration of the drowned ruins, feeds from web cams showing bright fish patrolling the reefs of sunken condos and shops. The reclaimers were attempting to construct a breakwater with fast-growing edited corals, and posted plans for the village of floating houses, the next stage of the project. Mike dreamed of moving there one day, of making a new life in a new land, but places in the reclaimer community were fiercely contested. He'd had to dig into his savings to get his mother the stem cell therapy she needed for a heart problem, and one of his sisters became engaged, soon there would be a wedding to pay for... So when the contract at Lake Eyre finished, Mike signed up for a new project in the Antarctic Peninsula.

Lake Eyre had created a place where refugees from the drowning coasts could start afresh. The engineering projects run out of the Antarctic Peninsula were part of an attempt to preserve the continent's last big ice sheet and prevent another catastrophic rise in ocean levels, the loss of half-drowned cities and land reclaimed from previous floods, and the displacement of more than sixty per cent of the world's population. Factories and industrial plants on the peninsula supported a variety of massive geoengineering projects, from manufacturing fleets of autonomous high-albedo rafts that would cool ocean currents by reflecting sunlight, to creating a thin layer of dust in the lower stratosphere that would reflect a significant percentage of the sun's light and heat back into space. One project was attempting to cool ice sheets by growing networks of superconducting threads that would syphon away geothermal heat. Another was attempting to protect glaciers from the heat of the sun by covering them in huge sheets of thermally reflective material.

Square Bay's factories used biomass supplied by the kelp farms to manufacture the tough thin material used in the thermal blanket project. As a bonus, the fast-growing edited strains of kelp sequestered carbon dioxide from the atmosphere, contributing to attempts to reverse the rise in levels that had driven the warming in the first place. It was good work, no doubt, the sharp end of a massive effort to ameliorate the effects of two centuries of unchecked industrialisation and fossil carbon burning, but many thought that it was too little, too late. Damage caused by the great warming was visible everywhere on the Antarctic Peninsula. Old shorelines drowned by rising sea levels, bare bones of mountains exposed by melting snow and ice, mines and factories, port cities and settlements spreading along the coast... There were traces of human influence everywhere Mike walked. Hiking trails with their blue markers and pyramidal cairns, scraps of litter, the mummified corpse of an albatross with a cache of plastic scraps in its belly, clumps of tough grasses growing between rocks, fell field meadows of mosses and sedge—even a few battered stands of dwarf alder and willow. Ecopoets licensed by the Antarctic Authority were spreading little polders and gardens everywhere as the ice and snow retreated. They had introduced arctic hares, arctic foxes and herds of reindeer and musk oxen further south. Resurrected dwarf mammoths, grazing tussock tundra in steep valleys snaking between the mountains.

Change everywhere.

One day, Mike followed a long rimrock trail to a triangulation point at a place called Pulpit Peak, fifteen kilometres south of the town. The pulpit of Pulpit Peak was a tall rock that stood at the edge of a cliff like the last tooth in a jaw, high above the blue eye of a meltwater lake. There was the usual trample of footprints in the apron of sandy gravel around it, the usual cairn of stones at the trail head, and something Mike hadn't seen before, a line of angular characters incised into one face of the rock, strange letters or mathematical symbols with long tails or loops or little crowns that reminded him of something he couldn't quite recall. And the triangulation point, a brass plate set in the polished face of a granite plinth, stated that it was thirty metres due north of its stated location 'out of respect to local religious custom.'

"I checked it with my phone's GPS," Mike told his friend Oscar Manu that evening. They were at the Faraday Bar 'n' Barbeque after a six-a-side soccer match, sitting on the terrace with their teammates under an awning that cracked like a whip in the chill breeze. "Sure enough, it was exactly thirty metres north of where it was supposed to be. And that writing? It's elvish. A guy I knew back home, old roustabout there, had a tattoo in the same kind of script. Back in the day, he was an extra in those old fantasy movies, had it done as a memento."

Mike's phone had translated the inscription. *The Place of the Meeting of Ice and Water.* A reference, maybe, to the vanished glaciers that had flowed into Square Bay.

"One of the sacred elf stones is what it is," Oscar said.

Oscar was from Tahiti, which had had its own share of troubles during the warming, but was in better shape than most Pacific Islands nations. One of its biotech firms had engineered the fast-growing, temperature-tolerant strain of staghorn coral the reclaimers were using to rebuild the reefs of Majuro. He was drinking Pangaea beer; Mike, who knew all too well that he was his father's son, was on his usual Lemon & Paeroa, saying, "You're telling me there are people here who believe in elves?"

"Let's put it this way: the road between Esperanza and O'Higgins has a kink where it swings around one of those stones," Oscar said.

"You're kidding," Mike said, because Oscar was famous for his patented wind-ups.

"Go see for yourself the next time you're up north," Oscar said. "It's just past the twenty kilometre marker."

Adi Mara chipped in, saying that a couple of Icelanders she knew took that kind of shit very seriously. "They have elves back home. The Huldufólk— the hidden people."

"Elf elves?" Oscar said. "Pointy ears, bad dress sense, the whole bit?"

"They look like ordinary people who just happen to be invisible most of the time," Adi said. "They live under rocks, and if you piss them off they can give you bad frostbite or sunburn, or cause accidents. Icelanders reckon some big rocks are actually disguised elvish churches or chapels. Building work and road construction can be held up if someone discovers that a place sacred to elves is right in the way."

"They don't sound that scary," Oscar said.

"Scary isn't the point," Adi said. She was their goalie, smaller than Mike, Oscar and the other guys, but fearless in the goal mouth. She punted every save way down the field, regardless of the positions of her teammates, and would tear you a new one if you didn't make good use of her passes. "The point is, Iceland is pretty bleak and tough, so it's only natural that Icelanders believe in forces stronger than they are, try to humanise the landscape with stories about folk who own it. And it's the same here."

Mike said that maybe it was the other way around. "Maybe the stones are reminders that Antarctica isn't really a place where ordinary people should be living."

"Back in the day that might have been true," Oscar said. "But look around you, Torres. We have Starbucks and McDonald's. We have people who are bringing up kids here. And we have beer," he said, draining his glass and reaching for the communal jug. "Any place with beer, how can you call it inhospitable?"

The talk turned to rumours of feral ecopoets who were supposed to be living off the land and waging a campaign of sabotage against construction work. Roads and radio masts and other infrastructure damaged, trucks and boats hijacked, sightings of people where no people should be. Freddie Aata said he knew someone who'd seen a string of mammoths skylighted on a ridge with a man riding the lead animal, said that the Authority police had found several huts made of reindeer bones and antlers on the shore of Sjörgen Inlet, on the east coast.

"Maybe they're your elves," Freddie told Mike. "Bunch of saboteurs who want to smack us back into the Stone Age, chiselling rocks with runes to mark their territory."

Mike still hadn't seen much of the peninsula. After arriving at O'Higgins International Airport he'd been flown directly to Square Bay in the hold of a cargo plane, catching only a few glimpses of snowy mountains rising straight up from the sea. There were vast undiscovered territories beyond the little town and the short strip of coast where he tooled up and down on service runs. Places as yet untouched by human mess and clutter. He found a web site with a map and a list of GPS coordinates of elf stones, realised that it gave him a shape and purpose to exploration, and started hitching helo and boat rides out into the back country to find them. There really was a stone, *The Church of the Flat Land*, on the road between Esperanza and O'Higgins, the two big settlements at the northern end of the peninsula. There was a stone at the site of an abandoned Chilean research station on Adelaide Island. *The Embassy of the Sea Swimmers*. There were stones standing stark on hilltops or scree slopes. A boulder in a swift meltwater river. A boulder balanced on another boulder on a remote stony shore on the Black Coast. *The Land Dances*. A stone on a flat-topped nunatak in an ice field in the Werner Mountains, the most southerly location known. *The Gate to the Empty Country*.

They were all found pieces, incised with their names but otherwise unaltered. Markers that emphasised the emptiness of the land in which they stood, touching something inside Mike that he couldn't explain, even to himself. It was a little like the feeling he had when he paged through old images of the Marshall Islands. A plangent longing, deeper than nostalgia, for a past he'd never known. As if amongst the stones he might one day find a way back to a time not yet despoiled by the long catalogue of Anthropocene calamities, a Golden Age that existed only in the rearview mirror.

He had quickly discovered that visiting elf stones was a thing some people did, like birders ticking off species or climbers nailing every hard XS route. They posted photos, poems, diaries of the treks they had made, and fiercely squabbled about the origin of the stones and their meaning. No one seemed to know how old the stones were or who had made them, if it was a single person or a crew, if they were still being made. Most stoners agreed that the oldest was a tilted sandstone slab just a short steep hike from a weather station on the Wilkins Coast. *The House of Air and Ice*. It was spattered with lichens whose growth, according to some, dated it to around a century ago, long before the peninsula had been opened to permanent settlement. But others disputed the dating, pointing out that climate change meant that lichen growth could no longer be considered a reliable clock, and that in any case establishment of lichen colonies could be accelerated by something as simple as a yoghurt wash.

There were any number of arguments about the authenticity of other stones, too. Some were definitely imitations, with crudely carved runes that translated into mostly unfunny jokes. *Gandalf's Hat. Keep Out: Alien Zone. Trespassers Will Be Shot*. There was a stone with a small wooden doorway fitted into a crack in its base. There was a stone painted with the tree-framed doorway to the Mines of Moria. There was a miniature replica of Stonehenge. There were miniature replicas of elf stones hidden on roofs of buildings in O'Higgins and Esperanza.

And even stones that most stoners considered to be the real deal were disputed by the hardcore black-helicopter conspiracy freaks who squabbled over the precise dimensions of runes, or looked for patterns in the distribution of the stones, or believed that they were actually way points for a planned invasion by one of the governments that still claimed sovereignty over parts of Antarctica, or some kind of secret project to blanket the peninsula with mind-controlling low-frequency microwaves, and so forth.

Oscar Manu found a website run by some guy in O'Higgins who looked a bit like a pantomime elf, with a Santa Claus beard and a green sweater, sitting at a desk littered with books and papers, a poster-sized photo of *The Gate to the Empty Country* on the wall behind him. Apparently he gave a course in elven mythology that included a visit to the stone set on the shoulder of a pebble bar north of the town's harbour, and awarded certificates to his pupils.

"Maybe he knows who made the things," Oscar said. "Maybe, even, *he* made them. You should go talk to him, Torres. You know you could ace that test and get yourself certified."

But as far as Mike was concerned, it wasn't really about elves, the whole fake history of aboriginal inhabitants. It was the idea that the essence of the land had survived human occupation and climate change, ready to re-emerge when the warming was reversed. The stones were an assertion of primacy, like the pylons set by the reclaimers around the perimeter of Majuro, marking the atoll's shape in the rolling waves that had drowned it. One of those pylons had Mike's name engraved on it, near the top of a list of sponsors and donors.

Despite their isolation and the stark splendour of the stones' settings, people couldn't help despoiling them. 'Robbo' had carved his tag at the base of *The Church of the Flat Land*. When Mike visited Deception Island, a three-day trip that included a stopover in O'Higgins (he ticked off the stone north of the harbour, but didn't visit the elf university), there was a cruise ship at anchor in the natural harbour of the island's flooded caldera, and he had to wait until a tourist group had finished taking selfies and groupies in front of a gnarled chimney of lava carved with a vertical line of runes, *Here We Made With Fire*, before he could have a few minutes alone with it. Someone had planted a little garden of snow buttercup and roseroot around *The Embassy of the Sea Swimmers*. There'd been some kind of party or gathering at *The Land Dances*, leaving a litter of nitrous oxide capsules and actual tobacco cigarette butts, illegal on three continents. And people had tucked folded slips of paper, prayers or petitions, amongst the small pyramid of stones, each marked with a single rune, of *Our High Haven*, on an icy setback high in the Gutenko Mountains.

Mike had made a short detour to find that last site after dropping off a party of geologists. It was a beautiful day. The blue dome of the sky unmarked except for the trail of a jet plane crawling silently northeast. Hardly any wind. In the absolute stillness he could hear the tide of blood in his ears, the faint sigh of air in his nostrils. Looking out across the pure white expanse of the Dyer Plateau towards mountain peaks sawtoothing the horizon he could imagine that the view was exactly as it had been before anyone had set foot on the continent. Ice and rock and snow and sky. Except that he remembered something one of the geologists had said as they'd unloaded their gear—that in the permanent dark of winter people heloed up to the plateau for wild skiing under the Antarctic moon and stars, using GPS to navigate from ice lodge to ice lodge. The snow here was fantastic, the geologist had said, a lot more of it than there used to be because the warmer air transported more moisture and caused more precipitation. Part of the expedition's work was measuring erosion caused by increased rainfall and snowmelt.

Change everywhere.

By now, it was long past midsummer. Christmas had come and gone. The weeks of 24-hour sunlight were over and nights were lengthening inexorably. The first snow had fallen at Square Bay. As the research season ended, Mike and the other helo pilots were kept busy retrieving people from far-flung science camps, and Mike had a brief fling with one of the scientists. Sarah Conway, an English palaeontologist eight years older than him, part of a team which had been working on a rich seam of fossils in a sedimentary layer high in the Eternity Range. They met at one of the social nights in the town's two-lane bowling alley, where the pins were painted to resemble penguins and an ancient jukebox played K-pop from the last century. Sarah was a good-looking big-boned blonde with the kind of unassailable confidence and ambition, founded on good old-fashioned middle-class privilege, that Mike knew he should resent, but she was smart, funny and vivid, and when he saw how other men looked at her he felt a fierce pride that she had chosen him instead of any of them.

"She's a fine woman," Oscar said, "but you do know she's only into you for just the one thing."

"We're just having a little fun before she goes back to the World," Mike said.

"I have plenty of experience of short-term romances is all I'm saying," Oscar said. "Have fun, sure, but don't let her go breaking your heart."

Mike knew that Oscar was right, knew that he should keep it cool, fool around but keep a certain distance, but one day he told Sarah about the elf stones, and when she expressed an interest he took her up into the hills to show her the one at Pulpit Peak.

At first, she seemed to get it, saying that she understood why he hadn't documented the stones in any way. "It's about the moment. The connection you make through the stones. The journey you make to find them changes you. And when you actually see them, you're changed again. It makes you see their context afresh," she said, her broad smile showing the gap between her front teeth that Mike found terrifically attractive.

But then he tried to explain his idea that the stones had been sited in places that reminded people of what had been lost, the ice and the snow, the empty quiet of unpopulated Nature that would one day come again, and everything went north.

"This was all forest ten million years ago," Sarah said. "And a hundred million years before that, in the Cretaceous, it was even warmer. Covered by rainforest, inhabited by dinosaurs and amphibians and early mammals. Some big non-flying dinosaurs survived here after the asteroid impact wiped them out everywhere else. We found a nest with ankylosaur eggs this season that we think definitely post-dates the extinction event. And last season we found a partial hypsilophodont skull with enlarged eye sockets. It confirms the dinosaurs lived here all year around, and had acute night vision that helped them to hunt during the polar night. The point being, choosing one state over another, ice over forest, is completely subjective."

"But this time the change isn't natural. Antarctica should be covered in ice and snow," Mike said, "and we fucked it up."

"I'm just taking the long view. Nothing lasts forever. But that doesn't mean that when the Anthropocene passes it will be replaced by a replica of the immediate past. As my grandfather used to like saying, you can't unring a bell. There'll be something else here. Something different."

"It will come back if we help it," Mike said.

"Are we talking about Antarctica or your lost island home?"

"That doesn't have anything to do with the stones," Mike said, although of course it did. He was angry, but mostly with himself. He shouldn't have told her about the reclaimers. He shouldn't have shared his stupid ideas about the stones. He'd said too much, he'd opened his heart, and she was repaying his trust with a lecture.

"Antarctica could freeze over again, but it won't ever be what it once was," Sarah said. "And you can build new islands, but it won't bring back what you've lost. It will be something new. You can't hate change. It's like hating life."

"I can hate the wrong kind of change, can't I?" Mike said, but he could see that it was no good. She was a scientist. She had all the answers, and he was just a dumb helo pilot.

So they broke up on a sour note. A few days later, while Mike was out on a supply run to one of the kelp farms, Sarah caught a plane to New Zealand, leaving him with the feeling that he'd somehow fucked up.

"You definitely fucked up a perfectly good lay with that obsession of yours," Oscar said.

"I'm not obsessed."

Oscar laid a finger alongside his broad flat nose, pulling down his lower eyelid and staring straight at Mike. "I've been watching you Torres. The time you spend chasing those stones. The time you spend talking about chasing them, or what you found when you ran one down. You think it's more important than anything else. And anyway, she's right."

"What do you mean, she's right?"

"She's right about bringing back the past. You can't. You drop a glass, it breaks on the floor. No way the pieces are going to leap up and fit themselves back again."

"You could glue them back together," Mike said, trying to turn it into a joke.

"You can't beat time, dude," Oscar said. "It only runs in one direction, and there's only one way out of this world."

"I didn't realise that you are a nihilist."

"I'm a realist. Instead of than trying to go against the current, I go with the flow. Don't fuck it up with ideas about rewinding clocks, Torres. Don't hang your hopes on some dream," Oscar said, half-singing that last sentence, having fun. "Don't, in a nutshell, be so fucking *serious* about what you can't get back."

Mike wondered unhappily if Sarah was right. If Oscar was right. If he'd become obsessed about bringing back what had been lost. Yearning for something he'd never known, something he could never have. Obsessing, yeah, over his romantic ideas about the stones. Because who knew what they really meant? What they meant to the person who had chosen and named them, and carved them with runes?

But he was too stubborn to give all that up so easily. Rootless and unsettled, he hitched a helo ride north to the Danco Coast, landing at the end of a fjord pinched between steep ridges and hiking up a shallow winding river towards the site of a stone, one of the last on his list. If he got back into his groove, he told himself, maybe everything would be okay. Maybe everything would become clear, and he'd think of the things he should have said to Sarah and the things that he needed to say to Oscar, to himself.

And as he picked his way between boulders alongside the river, cold clean air blowing through him and clear water chattering over and around rocks and dropping in little waterfalls, with the steep sides of the U-shaped valley rising on either side to bare ridges stark against the empty blue sky and snow-capped mountains standing ahead, he did feel lifted out of himself, the slough of his merely human problems.

There was change here, like everywhere else—the river fed by melting ice, with kerbs of pillow moss along its stony banks, stretches of sedges and cotton grass, some kind of bird, a kite or hawk, rising in lazy circles on a thermal above a scree slope starred with yellow flowers, amazing to see a land-based predator in a place where a century ago every animal species had depended on the ocean for food—but the land was empty and its silence profound, and he was part of it, absorbed in it, in the rhythm of walking, with a goal ahead of him and everything else dwindling into insignificance.

The river grew shallower and slower, breaking up into still pools and streams trickling between shoals and banks of pebbles, and there was the elf stone, an oval ice-smoothed boulder three metres high bedded in black gravel, with runes carved around its waist. *The Navel of Our Kingdom Under the Ice.*

Once upon a time, not so long ago, a glacier had flowed through the valley, debouching onto the ice shelf that had filled the fjord. But warm sea currents had undercut and broken up the ice, and the glacier had retreated to the 300-metre contour. The elf stone was one of many erratics deposited by its retreat, and the face of the glacier was a kilometre beyond: a pitted cliff of dirty ice that loomed over a tumble of ice blocks and pools of chalky meltwater.

After pitching his tent on a shoulder of sandy gravel, Mike lay awake a long time, listening to the whisper of water over stone and the distant retorts and groans of the glacier. When he woke, the air had turned to freezing milk. An ice fog had descended, whiting everything out. The sun was a diffuse glow low in the east; there was a rime of ice on tufts of moss and grass; every sound was muffled.

Mike brewed coffee on his efficient little Tesla stove, ate two granola bars and a cup of porridge with honey and a chopped banana stirred into it, and broke camp and started the hike back along the river, taking it slowly in the thick chill fog. He wasn't especially worried. Either the fog would lift and the helo would return and pick him up, or it wouldn't, and he'd be stuck here for a day or two until a bigger helo with Instant Flight Rules equipment could be diverted. No big deal. He had enough supplies to wait it out, told himself that it was a kind of adventure, even though he could call for help on his phone at any time, and GPS meant that he couldn't really get lost. Actually, he didn't even need GPS. All he had to do was follow the river.

He had been hiking for a couple of hours when he heard movement behind and above him. A soft heavy tread, a sudden sough of breath. He stood still, listening intently. The tread grew closer, shadows loomed out of the fog, bigger than any man, and Mike felt a spike of unreasoning fear. Then the wind shifted, the fog swirled aside, and he saw the first of them.

The high forehead and small brown eyes, the tear-drop ears with their elongated hair-rimmed lobes. The questing trunk. The shaggy pelt blended from shades of auburn and chocolate. Sturdy legs footing carefully on loose stones.

One by one, the SUV-sized mammoths trod past, five, seven, ten of them. At the end of the procession came a female with her young calf trotting beside her, trunk curled like a question mark, dissolving like the rest into the mist, leaving behind a musky scent and dinnerplate-sized footprints slowly filling with water in the gravel along the edge of the river.

And now another figure materialised out of the thinning fog, and a man's voice said, "Are you lost, friend?"

"I know exactly where I am," Mike said, resenting the implication that he was somehow trespassing. "What about you?"

"At the moment, I'm following the mammoths." The figure resolved into a slight man in his sixties, dressed in a red parka with a fur-trimmed hood, wind-proof trousers, boots. He had some kind of British accent, a neat salt-and-pepper beard, skin darkened by sun exposure but still pale at the roots of his widow's peak.

"You're in charge of them?" Mike said, wondering if the man was an ecopoet, wondering if there were others like him nearby.

"Oh, hardly," the man said, and introduced himself: Will Colgate. "May we walk on? My friends are getting away."

As they walked alongside the river, Will Colgate explained that he was studying the mammoths' behaviour, what they ate, where they went, and so on. "They need to eat a lot, so they cover a lot of territory. Yesterday they were ten kilometres south of here. Tomorrow they'll be ten kilometres north. Or more."

"So you're a scientist," Mike said. He hadn't been scared, not exactly, but he felt a little knot in his chest relax.

"Oh, no. No, I'm just an amateur. A naturalist, in the old tradition. Back in O'Higgins I'm a plumber," Will Colgate said. Adding: "I think I know why you're here."

"You do?"

"Only one reason why people would come here. To such an out-of-the-way place. You're a stoner."

"I'm interested in them," Mike admitted. "Why they are where they are. What they mean."

"Figured that out yet?"

Will Colgate had a sharp edge to his grandfatherly air.

"I think maybe they're memorials," Mike said. "Markers commemorating what was, and what will come again."

"Interesting. I once met someone, you know, who claimed she'd made them. She was a member of one of the seed-bombing crews. They take balls of clay and nutrients and seeds, so-called green bullets, and scatter them as they walk. Most of the seeds never germinate, of course, and most of the ones that do soon die. But enough thrive... Some of those willows might be theirs," Will Colgate said, pointing to a ghostly little island of shrubs standing knee-high in the river's flow.

"This woman you met—she really made the stones?"

"That's what she said. But she isn't the only one to lay claim to them, so who knows?"

Mike said shyly, "I think he or she may have been a helo pilot."

Will Colgate seemed to like the idea. "Of course, an awful lot of people use helicopters here. They're like taxis. When I was a geologist, back in the day, working for Rio Tinto, I was flown everywhere to check out likely lodes. Gave that up and went native, and here I still am. Place can get under your skin, can't it?"

"Yeah, it can."

They walked on for a while in companionable silence. Mike could hear, faintly, the tread of the mammoths up ahead. More a vibration coming up through the soles of his boots than actual sound.

Will Colgate said, "If you were going to mark up one of those stones with runes, all you'd need is an automatic cutter. Neat little thing, fits into a rucksack. Programme it, tack to it in place, it would do the job in twenty minutes. Chap I know in O'Higgins uses one to carve gravestones."

"You'd also need to know which places to choose, which stones," Mike said. "How each relates to the other."

"Mmm. But perhaps it started as a joke that slowly became serious. That gained its meaning in the making. The land will do that to you."

The river broadened, running over a pavement of rock deeply scored by the ice. Mike smelt the sea on the fog, heard a splashing of water and a distant hoarse bugling that raised hairs on the back of his neck. And then he and Will Colgate arrived at the place where the river tumbled down a stony shore, and saw, dimly through thick curtains of mist, that the mammoths had waded waist-deep into the sea. Several were squirting water over themselves; others grazed on kelp, tugging long slippery strands from a jut of black rocks, munching them like spaghetti.

"The place of the meeting of ice and water," Will Colgate said. "As it once was. By the time I got here, the river was already running, although back then the ice was about where that elf stone is now."

"Are you really a plumber?"

"Fully certified. Although I've done all kinds of work in my time."

"Including making gravestones?"

"People are mostly cremated now. When they aren't shipped back to the World. Laser engraved brass markers, or modded resin with soulcatcher chips that talk to your phone. It isn't the same," Will Colgate said, and stepped towards the edge of the sea and turned back and called out gleefully. "Isn't that a lovely sight?"

"Yes. Yes, it is."

The mammoths were intruders, creatures from another time and place, but the sight of them at play lifted Mike's heart. While the old man videoed them, walking up and down at the water's edge to get better angles, Mike called the helo crew. They were grounded. Everyone along the coast without IFR was grounded, waiting for the fog to lift. Mike told them it didn't matter. He squatted on coarse black sand rucked by the tread of heavy feet, strangely happy. After a while, Will came back and rummaged in his backpack and set a pan of water on a little hotplate.

"Time for a cuppa, I think."

They drank green tea. Will said that there was a theory that the mammoths bathed in the sea to get rid of parasites. "Another claims that seaweed gives them essential minerals and nutrients they can't find on land. But perhaps they come here to have fun. I mean, that's what it looks like, doesn't it?"

"Are there other people like you?"

Will gave the question serious consideration, said, "Despite the warming, you know, it is still very difficult to live off the land. Not impossible with the right technology, but you can't really go the full primitive. You know, as in stories about feral ecopoets. Stone-tipped spears and such. I suppose it might be possible in a hundred or so years, when it will be warmer and greener, but why would anyone want to do such a foolish thing?"

"Maybe by then the ice will have come back."

"Despite all our heroic efforts, I don't think we will be able to preserve the ice cap. Not all of it. Not as it is. In a thousand years, yes, who knows, the ice may return. But right now we have the beginnings of something new. We've helped it along. Accelerated it. We've lost much along the way, but we've gained much, too. Like the mammoths. Although, of course, they aren't really mammoths, and mammoths never lived in the Antarctic."

"I know," Mike said, but Will was the kind of earnest pedagogue who couldn't be derailed.

"They are mostly elephant, with parts of the mammoth genome added," he said. "The tusks, the shaggy coat, small ears to minimise heat loss, a pad of fat behind the skull to insulate the brain and provide a store of food in winter, altered circadian clocks to cope with permanent darkness in winter, permanent day in summer... Traits clipped from a remnant population of dwarf mammoths that survived on an island in the Siberian Arctic until about four thousand years ago. The species hasn't been reborn, but it has contributed to something new. All of this is new, and precious, and fragile. Which is why we shouldn't try to live out here just yet."

"Who is this 'we'?"

"Oh, you know, people like me," Will said vaguely. "Natural history enthusiasts you might say. We live in cities and settlements, spend as much time as we can in the wild, but we try not to disturb or despoil it with our presence. The mammoths aren't ours, by the way. They're an Authority project, like the arctic hares and foxes. Like the reindeer. But smaller things, insects and plants, the mycorrhizal fungi that help plant roots take up essential nutrients, soil microbes, and so on—we try to give a helping hand. Bees are a particular problem. It's too early for them, some say, but there's a species of solitary bee from the Orkneys, in Scotland, that's quite promising..." Will blinked at Mike. "Forgive me. I do rattle on about my obsessions sometimes."

Mike smiled, because the guy really was a little like a pixie from a children's storybook. Kindly and fey, a herder of bees and ants, friend of magical giants, an embodiment of this time, this place.

"I have trouble accepting all the changes," he said. "I shouldn't really like the mammoths. But I can't help thinking they seem so at home."

And with a kind of click he realised that he felt at home too. Here on the foggy beach, by one of the rivers of Antarctica, with creatures got up from a dream sporting in the iceless sea. In this new land emerging from the deep freeze, where anything could be possible. Mammoths, bees, elves... Life finding new ways to live.

Presently, the mammoths came up from the water, out of the fog, long hair pasted flat, steam rising from the muscular slopes of their backs as they used their trunks to grub at seaweed along the strandline. Will followed them with his camera as they disappeared into the fog again, and Mike stood up and started to undress. Leave on his skinsuit? No, he needed to be naked. The air was chill on his skin, the stones cold underfoot as he walked towards the water. He heard Will call out to him, and then he was running, splashing through icy water, the shock of it when he plunged into the rolling waves almost stopping his heart. He swam out only a little way before he turned back, but it was enough to wash himself clean.

THE WITCH OF ORION WASTE AND THE BOY KNIGHT

E. Lily Yu

E. Lily Yu (elilyyu.com) received the 2012 John W. Campbell Award for Best New Writer. Her fiction has appeared in *McSweeney's*, *Boston Review*, *Uncanny*, and *The Magazine of Fantasy and Science Fiction*, among others, and has been nominated for the Hugo, Nebula, World Fantasy, Sturgeon, and Locus Awards.

ONCE, ON THE edge of a stony scrub named for a star that fell burning from Orion a hundred years ago, there stood a hut with tin spangles strung from its rafters and ram bones mudded in its walls. Many witches had lived in the hut over the years, fair and foul, dark and light, but only one at any particular time, and sometimes no one lived there at all.

The witch of this story was neither very old nor very young, and she had not been born a witch but had worked, once she was old enough to flee the smashed bowls and shrieks of her home, as a goose girl, a pot scrubber, then a chandler's clerk. On the days when she wheedled the churchwomen into buying rosewater and pomanders, the chandler declared himself fond of her, and on other days, when she asked too many questions, or wept at the abalone beauty of a cloud, or refused to take no for an answer, he loudly wished her back among her geese.

On a Monday like any other, the chandler gave her two inches of onion peel scrawled with an order, and precise instructions to avoid being turned into a toad, and shortly thereafter the clerk carried a packet of pins and three vials of lavender oil the three heathery miles from the chandler's shop to the hut on Orion Waste.

The white-haired crone who lived in the hut opened the door, took the basket, and looked the clerk up and down. She spat out a small object and said, "You will do."

"I beg your pardon?"

"I have a proposition for you," the crone said. "It is past time for me to leave this place. There is a city of women many weeks' travel away, and it sings in my mind like a young blue star. Would you like to be a witch?"

Here was something better than liniment for the hurts confided to her, better than candles for warding off nightmares.

"I would," the clerk said.

"Mind, you must not meddle in what is none of your business, nor help unless you are asked."

"Of course," the clerk said, her thoughts full of names.

"Too glib," the crone said. "The forfeit is three years' weeping." She rummaged in her pockets and placed a brass key beside the book on the squat table. "But you won't listen."

The clerk tilted her head. "I heard you clearly."

"Hearing's not listening. You learned to walk by falling, and you'll stir a hornet's nest and see for yourself. I was just as foolish at your age." The crone shook a blackthorn stick under the clerk's nose. "I would teach you to listen, if I had the time. Here is the key. Here is the book. Here is the bell. Be careful who you let through that door."

Grasping the basket and her stick, the crone sneezed twice and strode off into other stories without a backwards glance.

And the clerk sat down at the table and leafed through the wormy tome of witchcraft, dislodging mushrooms pressed like bookmarks and white moths that fluttered into the fire. Bent over the book, by sunlight and candlelight, she traced thorny letters with her fingertips and committed the old enchantments, syllable by syllable, to heart.

The villagers who came with bread, apples, mutton, and the black bottles of cherry wine the old witch favored were surprised by news of the crone's departure and doubtful of the woman they knew as goose girl and chandler's clerk. Their doubts lasted only until she compounded the requested charms for luck, for gout, for biting flies, for thick, sweet cream in the pail. For all its forbidding appearance, the Waste provided much of what the book prescribed: gnarled roots that she picked and spread on a sunny cloth, bark peeled in long curls and bottled, snake skins cast in the shade of boulders and tacked to the rafters.

Certain of her visitors traveled farther, knowing only the hundred-year-old tale of a witch on the Waste. They came stealthily at night and asked for poison, or another's heart, or a death, or a crown, and the witch, longing for the simple low-necked hissing of geese, shut the door in their faces.

A few of these were subtler than the rest, and several lied smoothly. But the crone had left a tongueless bell, forged from cuckoo spit, star iron, and lightning glass, which if warmed in the mouth showed, by signs and symbols, true things. In this way the witch could discern the dagger behind the smile. But the use of it left her sick and shuddering for days, plagued with bad dreams and waking visions, red and purple, and she only resorted to the bell in great confusion.

Three years from when she first parted its covers, the witch turned the last page of the book, read it, and sat back with a sigh. Someone had drawn in the margin a thorny archway, annotated in rusty red ink in a language she did not recognize, but apart from that, she knew all the witchcraft that the book held. The witch felt ponderous with knowledge and elastic with powers.

But because even arcane knowledge and occult powers do not properly substitute for a bar of soap and a bowl of soup, she washed her face and ate.

Loud knocking interrupted her meal. She brushed the crumbs from her lap, wiped the soup from her chin, and opened the door.

A knight stood upon her doorstep, a black horse behind him. A broken lance lay in his arms. He was tall, with a golden beard, and his eyes were as green as ferns.

"Witch," said the knight. "Do you have a spell for dragons?"

"I might," she said.

"What will it cost me? I am sworn to kill dragons, but their fire is too terrible and their strength too great."

"Do you have swan down and sulfur? Those are difficult to find."

"I do not."

"A cartful of firewood?"

"I have no cart and no axe, or I would."

"Then a kiss," the witch said, because she liked the look of him, "and I will spell your shield and your sword, your plate and your soft hair, to cast off fire as a duck's feather casts off rain."

The knight paid her the kiss with alacrity and not, the witch thought, without enjoyment. He sat and watched as she made a paste of salamander tails and serpentine, adding to this a string of ancient words, half hummed and half sung. Then she daubed the mixture over his armor and sword and combed it through his golden hair.

"There you go," she said. "Be on your way."

The knight set his chin upon his fists. "These dragons are formidable," he said. "Larger than churches, with cruel, piercing claws."

"I have never seen one," the witch said, "but I am sure they are."

"I am too tired and bruised to face dragons today. With your permission, I shall sleep outside your house, guard you from whatever creeps in the dark, and set forth in the morning."

"As you wish," the witch said. She shared with him her supper of potatoes, apples, and brookweed and the warmth of her hearth, though the hut was small with him in it, and he told her stories of the court he rode from, of its high bright banners and its king and queen.

In the morning the knight was slow to buckle on his plate. The witch came to the door to bid him farewell, bearing a gift of butternuts knotted in a handkerchief. He raised his shield reluctantly, as if its weight pained him.

"Dragons are horrible in appearance," he said. "Those who see them grow faint and foolish, and are quickly overtaken and torn limb from limb."

"That sounds likely," the witch said.

"They gorge on sheep and children and clean their teeth with men's bones. In their wake they leave gobbets of meat that the crows refuse."

"You have seen dreadful things," the witch said.

"I have." The knight tucked his helmet under his arm and pondered a dandelion growing between his feet. "And the loneliness is worse."

"Perhaps it would be better to have a witch with you."

"Will you come? I carry little money, only promises of royal favor. But I'll give kisses generously and gladly, and swear to serve you and defend you."

"I have never seen a dragon except in books," the witch said. "I would like to."

The knight smiled, a smile so luminous that the sun seemed to rise in his face, and paid her an advance as a show of good faith.

The witch took a warm cloak, the brass key, and at the last moment, on an impulse, the glass-and-iron bell, then locked the hut behind her. The knight helped her onto his horse, and together they rode across the Waste and beyond it. Grasshoppers flew up before them, and quail scattered. Wherever they went, the witch gazed about her with delight, for she had never traveled far from her village or the hut on the Waste, and everything she saw gleamed with newness.

They rode through forests and meadows that had no names the witch knew, singing and telling stories to pass the time. In the evenings the witch gathered herbs and dowsed for water, and the knight set snares for rabbits and doves. The knight had a strong singing voice and a laugh like a log crumbling in a fire, and the days passed quickly, unnumbered and sweet.

Before long, however, the land grew parched, and the wind blew hot and sulfurous. The witch guessed before the knight told her that they had passed into the country of dragons.

Late one evening they arrived at a deep crater sloped like a bowl, its edges black and charred. The bitter smoke drifting from the pit stung their eyes. Down at the center of the crater, something shifted and settled.

"Is that a dragon?" the witch said.

"It is," the knight said, his face long.

"Will you ride into battle?"

"Dragons hunt at night, and their sight is better than a cat's. It would devour me in two bites before I saw it, then my horse, and then you."

Clicking his tongue, the knight turned the charger. They rode until they reached the scant shelter of a dry tree among dry boulders, where they made camp.

The witch scratched together a poor meal of nuts and withered roots. The knight did not tell stories or sing. At first, the witch tried to sing for the both of them, her voice wavering up through the darkness. But no matter what she said or sang, the knight stared into the fire and sighed, and soon she too lapsed into silence.

The next morning, the witch said, "Will you fight the dragon today?"

"It is stronger than me," the knight said, gazing into his reflection on the flat of his sword. "It breathes the fires of hell, and no jiggery-pokery from a midwife's pestle could endure those flames. Tomorrow I shall ride back to my king, confess my failure, and yield my sword. My enemies will rejoice. My mother will curse me and drink."

The witch said nothing to this, but sat and thought.

The sun scratched a fiery path across the sky, hot on the back of her neck, and the air rasped and seethed with the sound of distant dragons.

When it was dark, and the knight was sound asleep, the witch drew his sword from its sheath and crept to the black horse. She swung herself up into its saddle, soothing it when it whickered, and with whispers and promises of sugar, she coaxed it across the sand to the edge of the crater. There she dismounted and descended in silence.

The dragon waited at the bottom of the pit, its eyes bright as mirrors.

It was not the size of a church, as the knight had said, only about the size of her hut on the Waste, but its teeth were sharp and serrated, its claws long and hooked, and gouts of flame dripped from its gullet as it slithered toward her.

The dragon drew a breath, its sides expanding like a bellows, and the fire in its maw brightened. Sharp shadows skittered over the ashes.

"You are no more frightening than my father," the witch said, with more courage than she felt. "And no less. But I have faced foxes and thumped them, and I shall thump you."

Flames flowered forth from its fangs, and as the witch leapt aside, a third of her hair smoldered and shriveled.

The narrow snout swayed toward her, but the witch shouted two words of binding that sent her staggering backwards with their force, and the dragon's jaws clamped shut.

The dragon thrashed its head from side to side, white smoke rising from its nostrils, clawing at its mouth.

Then it charged her, and she ran.

As ashes floated thick around her, and skulls and thighbones broke and scattered under her feet, the witch looked over her shoulder and gasped a word of quenching.

At once the smoke of its breath turned to a noxious steam. The dragon lurched and fell. Although it could not stir, it glared, and its hate was hot on her skin.

The witch lifted the knight's sword, and with tremendous effort, and twelve laborious strokes, she cut off its head.

At dawn she woke the knight, signing because her throat was raw and her lips were cracked, and led him to the scaly black carcass in the crater. The knight stared, then exclaimed and kissed her, and this kiss was sweeter than all that had come before.

"My lovely witch, my darling! With you beside me, why should I fear dragons?"

Although she ached all over, and a tooth felt loose in its socket, the witch blushed and brightened.

They continued into the land of dragons. Water grew more and more elusive, and the pools and damp patches the witch located were brackish and bitter, so when they reached a shallow river, they followed its course. The water was warm and brown, and tadpoles squirmed in it.

One afternoon, as the sun slanted down and strewed diamonds on the river, the witch saw the second dragon. This one was the length of a watchtower and red as dried blood, and it crouched in a muddy wallow, half hidden by dead brush. When she called the knight's attention to it, he wheeled the horse around.

"Are you frightened?" she said.

There was no reply.

"Are you upset?"

He lowered his visor.

"Did I do something wrong?"

His eyes glittered out of his helmet, but he did not say a word.

The witch twined her fingers in the horse's mane and named the birds and burdocks they passed, then prattled about the weather, and still the knight said nothing.

Some hours later, over their supper of frogs, he broke his silence. "This one is viler than the last," he said. "Even you could not vanquish it. Me it would swallow in a snap, sword and all."

"It did not look so terrible," the witch said, light-headed with relief.

"But it is."

"You are a brave and valiant knight, and I am sure you will succeed."

"Of course you'd say that," the knight said, frowning. "It's not you who will die a nasty death, all teeth and soupy tongue."

"But your sword arm is strong, and your blade is trusty and well kept. Besides, I have enchanted your sword and your armor."

"As you like. I shall challenge it in the morning, and it will eat toasted knight for breakfast. Farewell." The knight turned his back to her, pillowed his head on his hands, and soon was snoring.

The witch had grown fond of the knight, in her way. His fear soured her stomach, and she tossed and turned, unable to sleep for thoughts of his death. In the middle of the night, she arose and sought the dragon.

The reeds were trodden and crushed in a wide swathe where it couched, and dead fish and birds lay all about. Its red scales were gray in the dim starlight, and it snuffed and snorted at subtle changes in the wind, finally fixing its eyes upon her. This dragon was heavy and sluggish, unlike the last, but poison dripped in black strings from its jaws. It lifted itself from the muck and lumbered forward.

"You are no more poisonous than my mother," the witch said, swallowing her fear. "And no less. But I have turned biting lye into soap, and I shall render you down as well."

She spoke the words of binding, but the dragon shrugged off her spell like so many flung pebbles. She shouted a word of quenching, and its jaws widened in a mocking grin. As she coughed on the word, her own throat burning, the dragon lunged and snapped.

The mud sucked at her feet as she fled, and marsh vapors wavered and tore as she ran through them. She tried words of severing and words of sickening, tasting blood on her lips, to no avail.

Bit by bit, the subtle gases of the dragon's breath slowed and stupefied her. The world spun. Then a root thrusting out of the mire hooked her ankle.

She skidded and slid.

Across the oozy earth the dragon crawled, bubbling and hissing. As its jaws opened to swallow her, the witch, her voice dull, spoke a word of cleansing.

The syllables slipped between scales into the dragon's veins and curdled the deadly blood. The dragon shuddered, its black eyes rolling back. Its snout scraped her leg, and then its long bulk splashed into the mud and lay still.

The witch limped to where the river flowed, languid and wide, and washed off, as best she could, the muck, the rot, the black blood and the red.

The sound of plackart clinking against pauldron woke her in the morning. Her knight—for she was beginning to think of him as hers—was grimly and glumly donning his gear.

No need, the witch wished to say, but her throat hurt as much as if she had swallowed a fistful of pins.

"Wait here," the knight said. "I do not want you to witness my shameful death. When I am crisped and crunched, ride swiftly to the court of Cor Vide and tell them their youngest knight is dead."

He spurred his horse and set off. Within the hour, he returned, his face dark.

"Witch, did you do this?" he said. "Did you kill that dragon while I slept?"

The witch nodded, unable to speak. The knight did not kiss her. He let her clamber onto the horse without offering his arm, and they rode all that day and the next in an ugly silence.

On the third day, when her throat had healed somewhat, the witch rasped, "Are you angry with me?"

"I am never angry, for anger is wicked and poisonous. But what will the court call a knight who lets women slay his dragons?"

"You seemed afraid."

"I wasn't afraid, witch."

"I wanted to help."

"You did more harm than good."

"I am sorry," she said.

"Do not do it again."

The river they were following dwindled to a stream, then to dampness, and then the earth split and cracked, but they continued in the same direction, in hopes that the stream ran underground and sprang up again somewhere.

By and by, their mouths parched, they came to a crooked tower with a broken roof and a great golden serpent wrapped many times around its base. The witch, knight, and horse were the only things that moved upon the barren plain, and they raised a great cloud of dust. While they were still at a distance, the serpent began unwinding itself from the tower.

"Stay, witch," the knight said, looking pale. "My sword is but a lucifer to this creature. Its fire will shrivel me, and the steel of my armor will drip over my bones. I'll die, but I'll die honorably. Remember me. I did love you."

And the witch watched, anxious, as her knight trudged on foot toward the tower, sheets of air around him shimmering with heat.

The serpent's eyes were red jewels, and its forked tongue lashed in and out of its mouth as the knight approached. Rearing up, the serpent spat a feathering jet of fire. The shield rose to meet it. Flames broke on its boss and poured off, harmless.

The knight laughed. His sword flashed.

But its edge rebounded from the scales without cutting, once, twice, and in a trice the serpent had tangled him in its coils and suspended him upside down.

His helmet tumbled off. His sword slipped from his mailed hand. He hung in midair, his golden curls loose, his face exposed.

The serpent squeezed, and he screamed.

The witch screamed too: a word of unraveling. The serpent's loops slackened, and the knight crashed to the ground. She screamed a word of piercing, and the serpent's eyes ran liquid and useless from their sockets. The serpent flailed, blind and enraged, battering the tower. Stones loosened from their mortar and fell. One crushed the knight's shield into splinters.

Finding his footing again, the knight slipped under the thrashing coils and sank his sword into one emptied eye, up to the hilt.

With a roar of agony, and spasms that shook down the upper third of the tower, the dragon expired.

The knight did not stand and savor his triumph. He whirled on the witch.

"I saw you. You goaded it—you spurred it to rage. You were trying to kill me!"

No, the witch would have said, if she were able.

But her lips were blistered and her tongue numb.

She pointed instead, in mute appeal.

A woman had emerged from the tower. She had watched what the witch had done; she could speak to her innocence. Her gown was green, and her smile, which she turned on them, was brilliant as an emerald. Several golden objects on her girdle swung and glittered as she approached, stepping delicately around the pools of smoking blood.

"Did you do this, good knight?" she said. "Have you freed me from this place?"

The knight bowed, then stood taller. "I did, though I did not know you were here. Where shall I bring you? Where will you be safe? You must have friends somewhere."

"Northeast," she said. "A long way."

"However far it is, I will accompany you."

"There is treasure in that tower, if you seek treasure. I stopped to play with rings, crowns, and necklaces, admiring myself in a golden glass. I did not realize that it was a dragon's hoard, and that the possessor would return. He gnawed my palfrey to the hooves and guarded me greedily from that time on. What I search for is not there, but that hoard will pay for your time."

"What gold could outshine the copper of your hair? You shall ride behind me, and this witch shall walk beside. For you look like a lady, and your feet are too soft for the road."

The lady's eyes danced. "Oh no, the witch shall ride. Both of us together, if you insist. I have met witches before, and they grow ugly if spited. This one is quite ugly already, and that smock does her no favors."

The witch, her breast burning, could not meet the lady's eyes. She looked instead at her rich green gown, stiff with gilt embroidery. Hanging from her girdle were toys of tin and wood, painted gold: a carved dog, a jumping acrobat, a wind-up man.

"Let me help you up," the knight said.

"First tie my hands behind me," the lady said. "I am under a curse. What I touch is mine and ever after shall be."

"A strange curse," the knight said, but obliged. He lifted her onto the horse in front of the witch. Her red hair blew into the witch's mouth. For sport, the lady leaned to one side, then the other, pretending to topple.

"Don't let her fall," the knight said to the witch. "I know you are jealous and would love nothing better. But if harm comes to her, I will cut off your head."

They proceeded more slowly after that, the knight leading the horse, the witch holding the reins, and the strange lady smiling in the witch's arms. As they rode, the witch wept, but very softly, for whenever the knight heard, he looked at her with disgust.

"Stop," he said. "Enough. You have no reason to cry."

Then her tears fell hotter and faster into the lady's red hair.

In the lengthening evenings, while the witch foraged, the knight and lady talked together and laughed. With her hands bound, the lady could do little for herself, and so the knight fed her, slid her silken slippers from her feet, and waited on her every wish.

The knight kissed the witch for the food and water she brought them, briefly and without interest, and apologized to the lady after. At night the lady nuzzled her head into the crook of the knight's arm and spread her long hair over them. The witch lay awake, watching the stars until they blurred and ran together.

"Why do you never sing anymore?" the knight said one evening, as the witch turned a rabbit over the fire. "Sing for us."

"He says you have a fine voice, for a witch. Do let me hear it."

"I don't anymore," the witch rasped. The lady grimaced. "I burned it to cinders for him. It hurts to speak."

"You'll heal," the knight said.

"I might, or I might not. The words of power I used were dear, and I am paying."

"You want me to feel guilty," the knight said.

"No, I wanted—"

"I don't want to hear about it." He folded his arms. "There was never any point in talking to you, anyway."

The lady laughed and laid her head against his shoulder.

Another evening, as the witch returned with chanterelles and hedgehog mushrooms in her skirt, she heard the knight say, "She's bewitched me, you know. That's why I hunt dragons—for her sport. That's why I kiss her every night—I am forced."

"Such a glorious knight, under the thumb of a lowly thing like her. How awful," the lady said.

"It is awful."

"Why don't you strike her head off while she sleeps?"

"I'm ensorcelled, remember. I cannot kill her. My father, a lord and a haughty man, would have strangled her for her insolence, but I am nothing like him."

"Indeed you are not," the lady said.

"You are kinder than she ever was. I've told you more than I've ever told her. Can you free me, as I have freed you?"

"Say the word, and I shall prick her with poisoned needles while she rides. She will die of that, slowly, unsuspecting, and then you shall be free."

"Do, and I shall follow you faithfully."

"Then pluck the air between the two of you as we go, as if you are pulling petals, and put them in this purse. You'll not see or feel what you gather, as your senses are not so fine, but I shall decoct what is there to a poison."

"I knew it," the knight said. "She has a foul and invisible power over me."

"A strange influence, certainly."

The witch stepped into the firelight, balancing their supper in her muddy skirt, and both the knight and the lady fell quiet and averted their eyes.

The moon waxed and waned, and the witch wearied of weeping. She was sick of holding the lady, sick of suffering her pinpricks, sick of watching the knight play with the lady's russet hair. Her pain had grown tedious and stale, but she was far from home and bewildered, for sometimes, still, the knight smiled at her with swift and sudden fondness, and it was as though he was again the knight she had set forth with, many and many a month ago.

Late one night, as she covered herself with her muddy cloak, she heard a clinking in its folds. In its pocket she found the key to her hut and the tongueless bell, which in her misery she had forgotten about.

The witch put the bell in her mouth, and the world shone.

First she looked upon the sleeping knight. In his place she saw a small boy, much beaten and little loved, his face wet from crying. He writhed in his sleep with fear. Around his limbs wound a silver spell, older than the witch and wrought with greater art than hers, and when the witch strummed the strands of it with a nail, she heard in their hum that they would break and let him grow only when he had slain three dragons by his own hand.

Then the witch saw how she had wronged him by killing the black dragon, the red, and the gold. She would have kissed his forehead and asked forgiveness, but a black asp crept out of his mouth and hissed at her, and she was afraid.

She turned to the lady who slept at his side. A hole gaped in her breast, its torn edges fluttering. The witch stuck her hand in but found nothing: not a bone, not a thread, not corners, nor edges either. It howled with hunger, that hole. The woman who wore it would wander the world, snatching and grasping and thrusting into that aching emptiness everything within reach, forever trying to fill it, and failing.

The witch grieved for her too.

The three of them had camped beside a pool of water, and now the witch knelt on its mossy margin. In the light of the half moon she saw how her limbs were shriveled and starved for love, her bones riddled with cracks from bearing too much too soon. She sat there for hours, until she knew herself, and the fractures and hollow places within her, and the flame that burned, small and silent, at her core.

And when the witch understood that nothing kept her weeping on the black horse but herself, that the sorcery that had imprisoned her and blinded her was her own, she spat out the bell, dashed her reflection into a million bright slivers, and laughed.

With a whistle, the witch rose into the air, and whistling, she flew. When she stopped for breath, her feet sank softly to the earth. In this manner she traveled over the country of dragons, through nameless meadows and woods, and across the Orion Waste.

Once in all that time, when her heart gave a sharp pang, the witch put the bell in her mouth and looked back.

Far away, the knight was unknotting the cord around the lady's wrists, first with fingers, and then, when it proved stubborn, with teeth. When her arms were free, he clasped her to his breast and buried his face in her hair.

But in the moment of their embrace, the knight began to shrink. The lady's arms tightened around him. Faster and faster the knight diminished, armor and all, until he was no taller than a chess piece and stiff and still.

The lady caught him between forefinger and thumb. She studied the leaden knight, her expression pleased, then puzzled, then disappointed. At last, shaking her head, she tied him to her girdle between the wooden dog and painted acrobat. Between one knot and the next, she flinched and sucked her finger, as if something had bitten her.

Then she mounted the black horse and rode slowly onward, searching for that which would fill her lack.

After that the witch flew without pause, without eating or drinking, and the wind dried her tears to streaks of salt.

Just as her strength gave out, the hut on Orion Waste rose like a star on the horizon. The witch unlocked the door and collapsed onto her narrow bed. There she remained, shivering with fever, for the better part of a month.

One or two people from the village, seeing the light in her window across the scrub, came with eggs and bread and tea, left them silently, and went away again.

One day, in a wave of sweat, the fever broke. The witch crawled to her feet, unlatched the window, and saw the Waste covered in white and yellow wildflowers.

The book of witchcraft lay open on the table, though she was sure no one had touched it. In the margin of the last page, wild roses peppered the tangle of thorns.

A week later, the witch returned to the village, her few belongings in hand, and asked the chandler if he might allow her to mind the shop again. He agreed gladly, for he was old and stiff, and she was quick and could climb the ladder to the highest shelves for him.

There she lived for a year, content, sweeping the floor, mending the shelves, and stirring a little magic into her soaps, so they cleaned better than others, and gave hope besides. She did not speak much, for her voice frightened children, but she listened carefully, and closely, and no one seemed to mind.

And there she would have stayed, growing gray and wise, had not a peddler with a profitable knack for roaming between stories rung the shop bell.

Looking over the wares he had spread on a cloth, all polished and gleaming, the witch and the shopkeeper chose combs, mirrors, scissors, and ribbons to buy. When the silver had been counted out and poured into his hands, and the goods collected, the peddler grinned a gapped grin and dug from his pack a pair of dancing shoes, cut from red leather and pricked all over with an awl.

"For you," he said to the witch. "Secondhand, and a few bloodstains, but pretty, no? *Some* angels don't like to see the poor dance, and the last lass had a heart too clean and Christian to wear them for long, but your heart's spotted, and these are just your size."

"Thank you," the witch said, "but I don't know how to dance. I know how to fly, and slay dragons, and make good soap, but dancing is a mystery."

"Then you should learn," the peddler said.

The shopkeeper sighed, because he could guess what was coming. When the witch approached him three days later, with a request, and a promise, he sent her on her way with a bag containing three cakes of soap, three spools of thread, three needles, a mirror, and a comb, cursing the peddler under his breath.

That night, as the stars glistened overhead, and the frogs and crickets sang a joyful Mass from their secret places, the witch locked up the hut, laced on the red shoes, whistled, and flew.

SEVEN BIRTHDAYS
Ken Liu

Ken Liu (*http://kenliu.name*) is an author and translator of speculative fiction, as well as a lawyer and programmer. A winner of the Nebula, Hugo, and World Fantasy Awards, he has been published in *The Magazine of Fantasy & Science Fiction, Asimov's, Analog, Clarkesworld, Lightspeed,* and *Strange Horizons*, among other places. His debut novel, *The Grace of Kings*, the first in a silkpunk epic fantasy series was published in 2015, and was followed by sequel *The Wall of Storms* in late 2016. Debut collection *The Paper Menagerie and Other Stories* was also published in 2016. In addition to his original fiction, Ken is also the translator of numerous literary and genre works from Chinese to English. He lives with his family near Boston, Massachusetts.

7:

THE WIDE LAWN spreads out before me almost to the golden surf of the sea, separated by the narrow dark tan band of the beach. The setting sun is bright and warm, the breeze a gentle caress against my arms and face.

"I want to wait a little longer," I say.

"It's going to get dark soon," Dad says.

I chew my bottom lip. "Text her again."

He shakes his head. "We've left her enough messages."

I look around. Most people have already left the park. The first hint of the evening chill is in the air.

"All right." I try not to sound disappointed. You shouldn't be disappointed when something happens over and over again, right? "Let's fly," I say.

Dad holds up the kite, a diamond with a painted fairy and two long ribbon tails. I picked it out this morning from the store at the park gate because the fairy's face reminded me of Mom.

"Ready?" Dad asks.

I nod.

"Go!"

I run toward the sea, toward the burning sky and the melting, orange sun. Dad lets go of the kite, and I feel the *fwoomp* as it lifts into the air, pulling the string in my hand taut.

"Don't look back! Keep running and let the string out slowly like I taught you."

I run. Like Snow White through the forest. Like Cinderella as the clock strikes midnight. Like the Monkey King trying to escape the Buddha's hand. Like Aeneas pursued by Juno's stormy rage. I unspool the string as a sudden gust of wind makes me squint, my heart thumping in time with my pumping legs.

"It's up!"

I slow down, stop, and turn to look. The fairy is in the air, tugging at my hands to let go. I hold on to the handles of the spool, imagining the fairy lifting me into the air so that we can soar together over the Pacific, like Mom and Dad used to dangle me by my arms between them.

"Mia!"

I look over and see Mom striding across the lawn, her long black hair streaming in the breeze like the kite's tails. She stops before me, kneels on the grass, wraps me in a hug, squeezing my face against hers. She smells like her shampoo, like summer rain and wildflowers, a fragrance that I get to experience only once every few weeks.

"Sorry I'm late," she says, her voice muffled against my cheek. "Happy birthday!"

I want to give her a kiss, and I don't want to. The kite line slackens, and I give the line a hard jerk like Dad taught me. It's very important for me to keep the kite in the air. I don't know why. Maybe it has to do with the need to kiss her and not kiss her.

Dad jogs up. He doesn't say anything about the time. He doesn't mention that we missed our dinner reservation.

Mom gives me a kiss and pulls her face away, but keeps her arms around me. "Something came up," she says, her voice even, controlled. "Ambassador Chao-Walker's flight was delayed and she managed to squeeze me in for three hours at the airport. I had to walk her through the details of the solar management plan before the Shanghai Forum next week. It was important."

"It always is," Dad says.

Mom's arms tense against me. This has always been their pattern, even when they used to live together. Unasked for explanations. Accusations that don't sound like accusations.

Gently, I wriggle out of her embrace. "Look."

This has always been part of the pattern too: my trying to break their pattern. I can't help but think there's a simple solution, something I can do to make it all better.

I point up at the kite, hoping she'll see how I picked out a fairy whose face looks like hers. But the kite is too high up now for her to notice the resemblance. I've let out all the string. The long line droops gently like a ladder connecting the Earth to heaven, the highest segment glowing golden in the dying rays of the sun.

"It's lovely," she says. "Someday, when things quiet down a little, I'll take you to see the kite festival back where I grew up, on the other side of the Pacific. You'll love it."

"We'll have to fly then," I say.

"Yes," she says. "Don't be afraid to fly. I fly all the time."

I'm not afraid, but I nod anyway to show that I'm assured. I don't ask when "someday" is going to be.

"I wish the kite could fly higher," I say, desperate to keep the words flowing, as though unspooling more conversation will keep something precious aloft. "If I cut the line, will it fly across the Pacific?"

After a moment, Mom says, "Not really… The kite stays up only because of the line. A kite is just like a plane, and the pulling force from your line acts like thrust. Did you know that the first airplanes the Wright Brothers made were actually kites? They learned how to make wings that way. Someday I'll show you how the kite generates lift—"

"Sure it will," Dad interrupts. "It will fly across the Pacific. It's your birthday. Anything is possible."

Neither of them says anything after that.

I don't tell Dad that I enjoy listening to Mom talk about machines and engineering and history and other things that I don't fully understand. I don't tell her that I already know that the kite wouldn't fly across the ocean—I was just trying to get her to talk to me instead of defending herself. I don't tell him that I'm too old to believe anything is possible on my birthday—I wished for them not to fight, and look how that has turned out. I don't tell her that I know she doesn't mean to break her promises to me, but it still hurts when she does. I don't tell them that I wish I could cut the line that ties me to their wings—the tugging on my heart from their competing winds is too much.

I know they love me even if they no longer love each other; but knowing doesn't make it any easier.

Slowly, the sun sinks into the ocean; slowly, the stars wink to life in the sky. The kite has disappeared among the stars. I imagine the fairy visiting each star to give it a playful kiss.

Mom pulls out her phone and types furiously.

"I'm guessing you haven't had dinner," Dad says.

"No. Not lunch either. Been running around all day," Mom says, not looking up from the screen.

"There is a pretty good vegan place I just discovered a few blocks from the parking lot," Dad says. "Maybe we can pick up a cake from the sweet shop on the way and ask them to serve it after dinner."

"Um-hum."

"Would you put that away?" Dad says. "Please."

Mom takes a deep breath and puts the phone away. "I'm trying to change my flight to a later one so I can spend more time with Mia."

"You can't even stay with us one night?"

"I have to be in D.C. in the morning to meet with Professor Chakrabarti and Senator Frug."

Dad's face hardens. "For someone so concerned about the state of our planet, you certainly fly a lot. If you and your clients didn't always want to move faster and ship more—"

"You know perfectly well my clients aren't the reason I'm doing this—"

"I know it's really easy to deceive yourself. But you're working for the most colossal corporations and autocratic governments—"

"I'm working on a technical solution instead of empty promises! We have an ethical duty to all of humanity. I'm fighting for the eighty percent of the world's population living on under ten dollars—"

Unnoticed by the colossi in my life, I let the kite pull me away. Their arguing voices fade in the wind. Step by step, I walk closer to the pounding surf, the line tugging me toward the stars.

49:

THE WHEELCHAIR IS having trouble making Mom comfortable.

First the chair tries to raise the seat so that her eyes are level with the screen of the ancient computer I found for her. But even with her bent back and hunched-over shoulders, she's having trouble reaching the keyboard on the desk below. As she stretches her trembling fingers toward the keys, the chair descends. She pecks out a few letters and numbers, struggles to look up at the screen, now towering above her. The motors hum as the chair lifts her again. Ad infinitum.

Over three thousand robots work under the supervision of three nurses to take care of the needs of some three hundred residents in Sunset Homes. This is how we die now. Out of sight. Dependent on the wisdom of machines. The pinnacle of Western civilization.

I walk over and prop up the keyboard with a stack of old hardcover books taken from her home before I sold it. The motors stop humming. A simple hack for a complicated problem, the sort of thing she would appreciate.

She looks at me, her clouded eyes devoid of recognition.

"Mom, it's me," I say. Then, after a second, I add, "Your daughter, Mia."

She has some good days, I recall the words of the chief nurse. *Doing math seems to calm her down. Thank you for suggesting that.*

She examines my face. "No," she says. She hesitates for a second. "Mia is seven."

Then she turns back to her computer and continues pecking out numbers on the keyboard. "Need to plot the demographic and conflict curves again," she mutters. "Gotta show them this is the only way…"

I sit down on the small bed. I suppose it should sting—the fact that she remembers her outdated computations better than she remembers me. But she is already so far away, a kite barely tethered to this world by the thin strand of her obsession with dimming the Earth's sky, that I cannot summon up the outrage or heartache.

I'm familiar with the patterns of her mind, imprisoned in that swiss-cheesed brain. She doesn't remember what happened yesterday, or the week before, or much of the past few decades. She doesn't remember my face or the names of my two husbands. She doesn't remember Dad's funeral. I don't bother showing her pictures from Abby's graduation or the video of Thomas's wedding.

The only thing left to talk about is my work. There's no expectation that she'll remember the names I bring up or understand the problems I'm trying to solve. I tell her the difficulties of scanning the human mind, the complications of recreating carbon-based computation in silicon, the promise of a hardware upgrade for the fragile human brain that seems so close and yet so far away. It's mostly a monologue. She's comfortable with the flow of technical jargon. It's enough that she's listening, that she's not hurrying to fly somewhere else.

She stops her calculations. "What day is today?" she asks.

"It's my—Mia's birthday," I say.

"I should go see her," she says. "I just need to finish this—"

"Why don't we take a walk together outside?" I ask. "She likes being out in the sun."

"The sun... It's too bright..." she mutters. Then she pulls her hands away from the keyboard. "All right."

The wheelchair nimbly rolls next to me through the corridors until we're outside. Screaming children are running helter-skelter over the wide lawn like energized electrons while white-haired and wrinkled residents sit in distinct clusters like nuclei scattered in vacuum. Spending time with children is supposed to improve the mood of the aged, and so Sunset Homes tries to recreate the tribal bonfire and the village hearth with busloads of kindergarteners.

She squints against the bright glow of the sun. "Mia is here?"

"We'll look for her."

We walk through the hubbub together, looking for the ghost of her memory. Gradually, she opens up and begins to talk to me about her life.

"Anthropogenic global warming is real," she says. "But the mainstream consensus is far too optimistic. The reality is much worse. For our children's sake, we must solve it in our time."

Thomas and Abby have long stopped accompanying me on these visits to a grandmother who no longer knows who they are. I don't blame them. She's as much a stranger to them as they're to her. They have no memories of her baking cookies for them on lazy summer afternoons or allowing them to stay up way past their bedtime to browse cartoons on tablets. She has always been at best a distant presence in their lives, most felt when she paid for their college tuition with a single check. A fairy godmother as unreal as those tales of how the Earth had once been doomed.

She cares more about the idea of future generations than her actual children and grandchildren. I know I'm being unfair, but the truth is often unfair.

"Left unchecked, much of East Asia will become uninhabitable in a century," she says. "When you plot out a record of little ice ages and mini warm periods in our history, you get a record of mass migrations, wars, genocides. Do you understand?"

A giggling girl dashes in front of us; the wheelchair grinds to a halt. A gaggle of boys and girls run past us, chasing the little girl.

"The rich countries, who did the most polluting, want the poor countries to stop development and stop consuming so much energy," she says. "They think it's equitable to tell the poor to pay for the sins of the rich, to make those with darker skins stop trying to catch up to those with lighter skins."

We've walked all the way to the far edge of the lawn. No sign of Mia. We turn around and again swerve through the crowd of children, tumbling, dancing, laughing, running.

"It's foolish to think the diplomats will work it out. The conflicts are irreconcilable, and the ultimate outcome will not be fair. The poor countries can't and shouldn't stop development, and the rich countries won't pay. But there is a technical solution, a hack. It just takes a few fearless men and women with the resources to do what the rest of the world can't do."

There's a glow in her eyes. This is her favorite subject, pitching her mad scientist answer.

"We must purchase and modify a fleet of commercial jets. In international airspace, away from the jurisdiction of any state, they'll release sprays of sulfuric acid. Mixed with water vapor, the acid will turn into clouds of fine sulfate particles that block sunlight." She tries to snap her fingers but her fingers are shaking too much. "It will be like the global volcanic winters of the 1880s, after Krakatoa erupted. We made the Earth warm, and we can cool it again."

Her hands flutter in front of her, conjuring up a vision of the grandest engineering project in the history of the human race: the construction of a globe-spanning wall to dim the sky. She doesn't remember that she has already succeeded, that decades ago, she had managed to convince enough people as mad as she was to follow her plan. She doesn't remember the protests, the condemnations by environmental groups, the scrambling fighter jets and denunciations by the world's governments, the prison sentence, and then, gradual acceptance.

"... the poor deserve to consume as much of the Earth's resources as the rich..."

I try to imagine what life must be like for her: an eternal day of battle, a battle she has already won.

Her hack has bought us some time, but it has not solved the fundamental problem. The world is still struggling with problems both old and new: the bleaching of corals from the acid rain, the squabbling over whether to cool the Earth even more, the ever-present finger-pointing and blame-assigning. She does not know that borders have been sealed as the rich nations replace the dwindling supply of young workers with machines. She does not know that the gap between the wealthy and the poor has only grown wider, that a tiny portion of the global population still consumes the vast majority of its resources, that colonialism has been revived in the name of progress.

In the middle of her impassioned speech, she stops.

"Where's Mia?" she asks. The defiance has left her voice. She looks through the crowd, anxious that she won't find me on my birthday.

"We'll make another pass," I say.

"We have to find her," she says.

On impulse, I stop the wheelchair and kneel down in front of her.

"I'm working on a technical solution," I say. "There is a way for us to transcend this morass, to achieve a just existence."

I am, after all, my mother's daughter.

She looks at me, her expression uncomprehending.

"I don't know if I'll perfect my technique in time to save you," I blurt out. *Or maybe I can't bear the thought of having to patch together the remnants of your mind.* This is what I have come to tell her.

Is it a plea for forgiveness? Have I forgiven her? Is forgiveness what we want or need?

A group of children run by us, blowing soap bubbles. In the sunlight the bubbles float and drift with a rainbow sheen. A few land against my mother's silvery hair but do not burst immediately. She looks like a queen with a diadem of sunlit jewels, an unelected tribune who claims to speak for those without power, a mother whose love is difficult to understand and even more difficult to misunderstand.

"Please," she says, reaching up to touch my face with her shaking fingers, as dry as the sand in an hourglass. "I'm late. It's her birthday."

And so we wander through the crowd again, under an afternoon sun that glows dimmer than in my childhood.

343:

ABBY POPS INTO my process.

"Happy birthday, Mom," she says.

For my benefit she presents as she had looked before her upload, a young woman of forty or so. She looks around at my cluttered space and frowns: simulations of books, furniture, speckled walls, dappled ceiling, a window view of a cityscape that is a digital composite of twenty-first-century San Francisco, my hometown, and all the cities that I had wanted to visit when I still had a body but didn't get to.

"I don't keep that running all the time," I say.

The trendy aesthetic for home processes now is clean, minimalist, mathematically abstract: platonic polyhedra; classic solids of revolution based on conics; finite fields; symmetry groups. Using no more than four dimensions is preferred, and some are advocating flat living. To make my home process a close approximation of the analog world at such a high resolution is considered a wasteful use of computing resources, indulgent.

But I can't help it. Despite having lived digitally for far longer than I did in the flesh, I prefer the simulated world of atoms to the digital reality.

To placate my daughter, I switch the window to a real-time feed from one of the sky rovers. The scene is of a jungle near the mouth of a river, probably where Shanghai used to be. Luxuriant vegetation drape from the skeletal ruins of skyscrapers; flocks of wading birds fill the shore; from time to time, pods of porpoises leap from the water, tracing graceful arcs that land back in the water with gentle splashes.

More than three hundred billion human minds now inhabit this planet, residing in thousands of data centers that collectively take up less space than old Manhattan. The Earth has gone back to being wild, save for a few stubborn holdouts who still insist on living in the flesh in remote settlements.

"It really doesn't look good when you use so much computational resources by yourself," she says. "My application was rejected."

She means the application to have another child.

"I think two thousand six hundred twenty-five children are more than enough," I say. "I feel like I don't know any of them." I don't even know how to pronounce many of the mathematical names the digital natives prefer.

"Another vote is coming," she says. "We need all the help we can get."

"Not even all your current children vote the same way you do," I say.

"It's worth a try," she says. "This planet belongs to all the creatures living on it, not just us."

My daughter and many others think that the greatest achievement of humanity, the re-gifting of Earth back to Nature, is under threat. Other minds, especially those who had uploaded from countries where the universal availability of immortality had been achieved much later, think it isn't fair that those who got to colonize the digital realm first should have more say in the direction of humanity. They would like to expand the human footprint again and build more data centers.

"Why do you love the wilderness so much if you don't even live in it?" I ask.

"It's our ethical duty to be stewards for the Earth," she says. "It's barely starting to heal from all the horrors we've inflicted on it. We must preserve it exactly as it should be."

I don't point out that this smacks to me of a false dichotomy: Human vs. Nature. I don't bring up the sunken continents, the erupting volcanoes, the peaks and valleys in the Earth's climate over billions of years, the advancing and retreating icecaps, and the uncountable species that have come and gone. Why do we hold up this one moment as natural, to be prized above all others?

Some ethical differences are irreconcilable.

Meanwhile, everyone thinks that having more children is the solution, to overwhelm the other side with more votes. And so the hard-fought adjudication of applications to have children, to allocate precious computing resources among competing factions.

But what will the children think of our conflicts? Will they care about the same injustices we do? Being born *in silico*, will they turn away from the physical world, from embodiment, or embrace it even more? Every generation has its own blind spots and obsessions.

I had once thought the Singularity would solve all our problems. Turns out it's just a simple hack for a complicated problem. We do not share the same histories; we do not all want the same things.

I am not so different from my mother after all.

2,401:

THE ROCKY PLANET beneath me is desolate, lifeless. I'm relieved. That was a condition placed upon me before my departure.

It's impossible for everyone to agree upon a single vision for the future of humanity. Thankfully, we no longer have to share the same planet.

Tiny probes depart from *Matrioshka*, descending toward the spinning planet beneath them. As they enter the atmosphere, they glow like fireflies in the dusk. The dense atmosphere here is so good at trapping heat that at the surface the gas behaves more like a liquid.

I imagine the self-assembling robots landing at the surface. I imagine them replicating and multiplying with material extracted from the crust. I imagine them boring into the rock to place the mini-annihilation charges.

A window pops up next to me: a message from Abby, light-years away and centuries ago.

Happy birthday, Mother. We did it.

What follows are aerial shots of worlds both familiar and strange: the Earth, with its temperate climate carefully regulated to sustain the late Holocene;

Venus, whose orbit has been adjusted by repeated gravitational slingshots with asteroids and terraformed to become a lush, warm replica of Earth during the Jurassic; and Mars, whose surface has been pelted with redirected Oort cloud objects and warmed by solar reflectors from space until the climate is a good approximation of the dry, cold conditions of the last glaciation on Earth.

Dinosaurs now roam the jungles of Aphrodite Terra, and mammoths forage over the tundra of Vastitas Borealis. Genetic reconstructions have been pushed back to the limit of the powerful data centers on Earth.

They have recreated what might have been. They have brought the extinct back to life.

Mother, you're right about one thing: We will be sending out exploration ships again.

We'll colonize the rest of the galaxy. When we find lifeless worlds, we'll endow them with every form of life, from Earth's distant past to the futures that might have been on Europa. We'll walk down every evolutionary path. We'll shepherd every flock and tend to every garden. We'll give those creatures who never made it onto Noah's Ark another chance, and bring forth the potential of every star in Raphael's conversation with Adam in Eden.

And when we find extraterrestrial life, we'll be just as careful with them as we have been with life on Earth.

It isn't right for one species in the latest stage of a planet's long history to monopolize all its resources. It isn't just for humanity to claim for itself the title of evolution's crowning achievement. Isn't it the duty of every intelligent species to rescue all life, even from the dark abyss of time? There is always a technical solution.

I smile. I do not wonder whether Abby's message is a celebration or a silent rebuke. She is, after all, my daughter.

I have my own problem to solve. I turn my attention back to the robots, to breaking apart the planet beneath my ship.

16,807:

IT HAS TAKEN a long time to fracture the planets orbiting this star, and longer still to reshape the fragments into my vision.

Thin, circular plates a hundred kilometers in diameter are arranged in a lattice of longitudinal rings around the star until it is completely surrounded. The plates do not orbit the star; rather, they are statites, positioned so that the pressure from the sun's high-energy radiation counteracts the pull of gravity.

On the inner surface of this Dyson swarm, trillions of robots have etched channels and gates into the substrate, creating the most massive circuits in the history of the human race.

As the plates absorb the energy from the sun, it is transformed into electric pulses that emerge from cells, flow through canals, commingle in streams, until they gather into lakes and oceans that undulate through a quintillion variations that form the shape of thought.

The backs of the plates glow darkly, like embers after a fierce flame. The lower-energy photons leap outward into space, somewhat drained after powering a civilization. But before they can escape into the endless abyss of space, they strike another set of plates designed to absorb energy from radiation at this dimmer frequency. And once again, the process for thought-creation repeats itself.

The nesting shells, seven in all, form a world that is replete with dense topography. There are smooth areas centimeters across, designed to expand and contract to preserve the integrity of the plates as the computation generates more or less heat—I've dubbed them seas and plains. There are pitted areas where the peaks and craters are measured by microns, intended to facilitate the rapid dance of qubits and bits—I call them forests and coral reefs. There are small studded structures packed with dense circuitry intended to send and receive beams of communication knitting the plates together—I call them cities and towns. Perhaps these are fanciful names, like the Sea of Tranquility and Mare Erythraeum, but the consciousnesses they power are real.

And what will I do with this computing machine powered by a sun? What magic will I conjure with this matrioshka brain?

I have seeded the plains and seas and forests and coral reefs and cities and towns with a million billion minds, some of them modeled on my own, many more pulled from *Matrioshka*'s data banks, and they have multiplied and replicated, evolved in a world larger than any data center confined to a single planet could ever hope to be.

In the eyes of an outside observer, the star's glow dimmed as each shell was constructed. I have succeeded in darkening a sun just as my mother had, albeit at a much grander scale.

There is always a technical solution.

117,649:

HISTORY FLOWS LIKE a flash flood in the desert: the water pouring across the parched earth, eddying around rocks and cacti, pooling in depressions, seeking a channel while it's carving the landscape, each chance event shaping what comes after.

There are more ways to rescue lives and redeem what might have been than Abby and others believe.

In the grand matrix of my matrioshka brain, versions of our history are replayed. There isn't a single world in this grand computation, but billions, each of them populated by human consciousnesses, but nudged in small ways to be better.

Most paths lead to less slaughter. Here, Rome and Constantinople are not sacked; there, Cuzco and V nh Long do not fall. Along one timeline, the Mongols and Manchus do not sweep across East Asia; along another, the Westphalian model does not become an all-consuming blueprint for the world. One group of men consumed with murder do not come to power in Europe, and another group worshipping death do not seize the machinery of state in Japan. Instead of the colonial yoke, the inhabitants of Africa, Asia, the Americas, and Australia decide their own fates. Enslavement and genocide are not the handmaidens of discovery and exploration, and the errors of our history are averted.

Small populations do not rise to consume a disproportionate amount of the planet's resources or monopolize the path of its future. History is redeemed.

But not all paths are better. There is a darkness in human nature that makes certain conflicts irreconcilable. I grieve for the lives lost but I can't intervene. These are not simulations. They cannot be if I respect the sanctity of human life.

The billions of consciousnesses who live in these worlds are every bit as real as I am. They deserve as much free will as anyone who has ever lived and must be allowed to make their own choices. Even if we've always suspected that we also live in a grand simulation, we prefer the truth to be otherwise.

Think of these as parallel universes if you will; call them sentimental gestures of a woman looking into the past; dismiss it as a kind of symbolic atonement.

But isn't it the dream of every species to have the chance to do it over? To see if it's possible to prevent the fall from grace that darkens our gaze upon the stars?

823,543:

THERE IS A message.

Someone has plucked the strings that weave together the fabric of space, sending a sequence of pulses down every strand of Indra's web, connecting the farthest exploding nova to the nearest dancing quark.

The galaxy vibrates with a broadcast in languages known, forgotten, and yet to be invented. I parse out a single sentence.

Come to the galactic center. It's reunion time.

Carefully, I instruct the intelligences guiding the plates that make up the Dyson swarms to shift, like ailerons on the wings of ancient aircraft. The plates drift apart, as though the shells in the matrioshka brain are cracking, hatching a new form of life.

Gradually, the statites move away from one side of the sun and assume the configuration of a Shkadov thruster. A single eye opens in the universe, emitting a bright beam of light.

And slowly, the imbalance in the solar radiation begins to move the star, bringing the shell-mirrors with it. We're headed for the center of the galaxy, propelled upon a fiery column of light.

Not every human world will heed the call. There are plenty of planets on which the inhabitants have decided that it is perfectly fine to explore the mathematical worlds of ever-deepening virtual reality in perpetuity, to live out lives of minimal energy consumption in universes hidden within nutshells.

Some, like my daughter Abby, will prefer to leave their lush, life-filled planets in place, like oases in the endless desert that is space. Others will seek the refuge of the galactic edge, where cooler climates will allow more efficient computation. Still others, having re-captured the ancient joy of living in the flesh, will tarry to act out space operas of conquest and glory.

But enough will come.

I imagine thousands, hundreds of thousands of stars moving toward the center of the galaxy. Some are surrounded by space habitats full of people who still look like people. Some are orbited by machines that have but a dim memory of their ancestral form. Some will drag with them planets populated by creatures from our distant past, or by creatures I have never seen. Some will bring guests, aliens who do not share our history but are curious about this self-replicating low-entropy phenomenon that calls itself humanity.

I imagine generations of children on innumerable worlds watching the night sky as constellations shift and transform, as stars move out of alignment, drawing contrails against the empyrean.

I close my eyes. This journey will take a long time. Might as well get some rest.

A very, very long time later:

THE WIDE SILVERY lawn spreads out before me almost to the golden surf of the sea, separated by the narrow dark band that is the beach. The sun is bright and warm, and I can almost feel the breeze, a gentle caress against my arms and face.

"Mia!"

I look over and see Mom striding across the lawn, her long black hair streaming like a kite's tails.

She wraps me in a fierce hug, squeezing my face against hers. She smells like the glow of new stars being born in the embers of a supernova, like fresh comets emerging from the primeval nebula.

"Sorry I'm late," she says, her voice muffled against my cheek.

"It's okay," I say, and I mean it. I give her a kiss.

"It's a good day to fly a kite," she says.

We look up at the sun.

The perspective shifts vertiginously, and now we're standing upside down on an intricately carved plain, the sun far below us. Gravity tethers the surface above the bottoms of our feet to that fiery orb, stronger than any string. The bright photons we're bathed in strike against the ground, pushing it up. We're standing on the bottom of a kite that is flying higher and higher, tugging us toward the stars.

I want to tell her that I understand her impulse to make one life grand, her need to dim the sun with her love, her striving to solve intractable problems, her faith in a technical solution even though she knew it was imperfect. I want to tell her that I know we're flawed, but that doesn't mean we're not also wondrous.

Instead, I just squeeze her hand; she squeezes back.

"Happy birthday," she says. "Don't be afraid to fly."

I relax my grip, and smile at her. "I'm not. We're almost there."

The world brightens with the light of a million billion suns.

THE VISITOR FROM TAURED
Ian R. MacLeod

Ian R. MacLeod (www.ianrmacleod.com) has been writing and selling (as opposed to writing and not selling, which he says he's been doing for much longer) for almost 30 years. Amongst many accolades, his work has won the Arthur C. Clarke Award, the World Fantasy Award (twice) and the Sidewise Award for alternate history (three times). He took a Law degree and drifted into the English Civil Service, but writing was always his first love and ambition. He has recently released a short story collection, *Frost on Glass*, and has a new novel, *Red Snow*, due out shortly. He lives in the riverside town of Bewdley in what he insists is still, currently, the United Kingdom. The 'original' visitor from Taured is a genuine urban myth, and is well worth Googling, but he says the genesis of this story came from a fear that books are losing out to other forms of entertainment, and some odd ideas he has about the nature of reality.

1.

THERE WAS ALWAYS something otherwordly about Rob Holm. Not that he wasn't charming and clever and good-looking. Driven, as well. Even during that first week when we'd arrived at university and waved goodbye to our parents and our childhoods, and were busy doing all the usual fresher things, which still involved getting dangerously drunk and pretending not to be homesick and otherwise behaving like the prim, arrogant, cocky and immature young assholes we undoubtedly were, Rob was chatting with research fellows and quietly getting to know the best virtuals to hang out in.

Even back then, us young undergrads were an endangered breed. Many universities had gone bankrupt, become commercial research utilities, or transformed themselves into the academic theme-parks of those so-called 'Third Age Academies'. But still, here we all were at the traditional redbrick campus of Leeds University, which still offered a broad-ish range of courses to those with families rich enough to support them, or at least tolerant enough not to warn them against such folly. My own choice of degree, just to show how incredibly supportive my parents were, being Analogue Literature.

As a subject, it already belonged with Alchemy and Marxism in the dustbin of history, but books—and I really do mean those peculiar, old, paper, physical objects—had always been my thing. Even when I was far too young to understand what they were, and by rights should have been attracted by the bright, interactive, virtual gewgaws buzzing all around me, I'd managed to burrow into the bottom of an old box, down past the stickle bricks and My Little Ponies, to these broad, cardboardy things that fell open and had these flat, two-dee shapes and images that didn't move or respond in any normal way when I waved my podgy fingers in their direction. All you could do was simply look at them. That, and chew their corners, and maybe scribble over their pages with some of the dried-up crayons which were also to be found amid those predigital layers.

My parents had always been loving and tolerant of their daughter. They even encouraged little Lita's interest in these ancient artefacts. I remember my mother's finger moving slow and patient across the creased and yellowed pages as she traced the pictures and her lips breathed the magical words that somehow arose from those flat lines. She wouldn't have assimilated data this way herself in years, if ever, so in a sense we were both learning.

The Hungry Caterpillar. The Mister Men series. *Where The Wild Things Are.* Frodo's adventures. Slowly, like some archaeologist discovering the world by deciphering the cartouches of the tombs in Ancient Egypt, I learned how to perceive and interact through this antique medium. It was, well, the *thingness* of books. The exact way they *didn't* leap about or start giving off sounds, smells and textures. That, and how they didn't ask you which character you'd like to be, or what level you wanted to go to next, but simply took you by the hand and led you where they wanted you to go.

Of course, I became a confirmed bibliophile, but I do still wonder how my life would have progressed if my parents had seen odd behaviour differently, and taken me to some paediatric specialist. Almost certainly, I wouldn't be the Lita Ortiz who's writing these words for whoever might still be able to comprehend them. Nor the one who was lucky enough to meet Rob Holm all those years ago in the teenage fug of those student halls back at Leeds University.

2.

So. Rob. First thing to say is the obvious fact that most of us fancied him. It wasn't just the grey eyes, or the courtly elegance, or that soft Scottish accent, or even the way he somehow appeared mature and accomplished. It was, essentially, a kind of mystery. But he wasn't remotely stand-offish. He went along with the fancy dress pub crawls. He drank. He fucked about. He took the odd tab.

One of my earliest memories of Rob was finding him at some club, cool as you like amid all the noise, flash and flesh. And dragging him out onto the pulsing dance floor. One minute we were hovering above the skyscrapers of Beijing and the next a shipwreck storm was billowing about us. Rob, though, was simply there. Taking it all in, laughing, responding, but somehow detached. Then, helping me down and out, past clanging temple bells and through prismatic sandstorms to the entirely non-virtual hell of the toilets. His cool hands holding back my hair as I vomited.

I never ever actually thanked Rob for this—I was too embarrassed—but the incident somehow made us more aware of each other. That, and maybe we shared a sense of otherness. He, after all, was studying astrophysics, and none of the rest of us even knew what that was, and had all that strange stuff going on across the walls of his room. Not flashing posters of the latest virtual boy band or porn empress, but slow-turning gas clouds, strange planets, distant stars and galaxies. That, and long runs of mek, whole arching rainbows of the stuff, endlessly twisting and turning. My room, on the other hand, was piled with the precious torn and foxed paperbacks I'd scoured from junksites during my teenage years. Not, of course, that they were actually needed. Even if you were studying something as arcane as narrative fiction, you were still expected to download and virtualise all your resources.

The Analogue Literature Faculty at Leeds University had once taken up a labyrinthine space in a redbrick terrace at the east edge of the campus. But now it had been invaded by dozens of more modern disciplines. Anything from speculative mek to non-concrete design to holo-pornography had taken bites out of it. I was already aware—how couldn't I be?—that no significant novel or short story had been written in decades, but I was shocked to discover that only five other students in my year had elected for An Lit as their main subject, and one of those still resided in Seoul, and another was a post-centenarian on clicking steel legs. Most of the other students who showed up were dipping into the subject in the hope that it might add something useful to their main discipline. Invariably, they were disappointed. It wasn't just the difficulty of ploughing through page after page of non-interactive text. It was linear fiction's sheer lack of options, settings, choices. Why the hell, I remember some kid shouting in a seminar, should I accept all the miserable shit that this Hardy guy rains down his characters? Give me the base program for *Tess of the d'Urbervilles*, and I'll hack you fifteen better endings.

I pushed my weak mek to the limit during that first term as I tried to formulate a tri-dee excursus on *Tender Is The Night*, but the whole piece was reconfigured out of existence once the faculty ais got hold of it. Meanwhile, Rob Holm was clearly doing far better. I could hear him singing in the showers along from my room, and admired the way he didn't get involved in all the usual peeves and arguments. The physical sciences had a huge, brand new faculty at the west end of campus called the Clearbrite Building. Half church, half-pagoda and maybe half spaceship in the fizzing, shifting, headachy way of modern architecture, there was no real way of telling how much of it was actually made of brick, concrete and glass, and how much consisted of virtual artefacts and energy fields. You could get seriously lost just staring at it.

My first year went by, and I fought hard against crawling home, and had a few unromantic flings, and made vegetable bolognaise my signature dish, and somehow managed to get version 4.04 of my second term excursus on *Howard's End* accepted. Rob and I didn't became close, but I liked his singing, and the cinnamon scent he left hanging behind in the steam of the showers, and it was good to know that someone else was making a better hash of this whole undergraduate business than I was.

"Hey, Lita?"

We were deep into the summer term and exams were looming. Half the undergrads were back at home, and the other half were jacked up on learning streams, or busy having breakdowns.

I leaned in on Rob's doorway. "Yeah?"

"Fancy sharing a house next year?"

"Next year?" Almost effortlessly casual, I pretended to consider this. "I really hadn't thought. It all depends "

"Not a problem." He shrugged. "I'm sure I'll find someone else."

"No, no. That's fine. I mean, yeah, I'm in. I'm interested."

"Great. I'll show you what I've got from the letting agencies." He smiled a warm smile, then returned to whatever wondrous creations were spinning above his desk.

3.

WE SETTLED ON a narrow house with bad drains just off the Otley Road in Headingley, and I'm not sure whether I was relieved or disappointed when I discovered that his plan was that we share the place with some others. I roped in a couple of girls, Rob found a couple of guys, and we all got on pretty well. I had a proper boyfriend by then, a self-regarding jock called Torsten, and every now and then a different woman would emerge from Rob's room. Nothing serious ever seemed to come of this, but they were equally gorgeous, clever and out of my league.

A bunch of us used to head out to the moors for midnight bonfires during that second winter. I remember the smoke and the sparks spinning into the deep black as we sang and drank and arsed around. Once, and with the help of a few tabs and cans, I asked Rob to name some constellations for me, and he put an arm around my waist and led me further into the dark.

Over there, Lita, up to the left and far away from the light of this city, is Ursa Major, the Great Bear, which is always a good place to start when you're stargazing. And there, see close as twins at the central bend of the Plough's handle, are Mizar and Alcor. They're not a true binary, but if we had decent binoculars, we could see that Mizar really does have a close companion. And there, that way, up and left his breath on my face, his hands on my arms maybe you can just see there's this fuzzy speck at the Bear's shoulder? Now, that's an entire, separate galaxy from our own filled with billions of stars, and its light has taken about twelve million years to reach the two of us here, tonight. Then Andromeda and Cassiopeia and Canus Major and Minor... Distant, storybook names for distant worlds. I even wondered aloud about the possibility of other lives, existences, hardly expecting Rob to agree with me. But he did. And then he said something which struck me as strange.

"Not just out there, either, Lita. There are other worlds all around us. It's just that we can't see them."

"You're talking in some metaphorical sense, right?"

"Not at all. It's part of what I'm trying to understand in my studies."

"To be honest, I've got no real idea what astrophysics even means. Maybe you could tell me."

"I'd love to. And you know, Lita, I'm a complete dunce when it comes to, what *do* you call it two-dee fiction, flat narrative? So I want you to tell me about that as well. Deal?"

We wandered back toward the fire, and I didn't expect anything else to come of our promise until Rob called to me when I was wandering past his room one wet, grey afternoon a week or so later. It was deadline day, my hair was a greasy mess, I was heading for the shower, and had an excursus on John Updike to finish.

"You *did* say you wanted to know more about what I study?"

"I was just..." I scratched my head. "Curious. All I do know is that astrophysics is about more than simply looking up at the night sky and giving names to things. That isn't even astronomy, is it?"

"You're not just being polite?" His soft, granite-grey eyes remained fixed on me.

"No. I'm not absolutely."

"I could show you something here." He waved at the stars on his walls, the stuff spinning on his desk. "But maybe we could go out. To be honest, Lita, I could do with a break, and there's an experiment I could show you up at the Clearbrite that might help explain what I mean about other worlds... But I understand if you're busy. I could get my avatar to talk to your avatar and—"

"No, no. You're right, Rob. I could do with a break as well. Let's go out. Seize the day. Or at least, what's left of it. Just give me…" I waved a finger toward the bathroom. "… five minutes."

Then we were outside in the sideways-blowing drizzle, and it was freezing cold, and I was still wet from my hurried shower, as Rob slipped a companionable arm around mine as we climbed the hill toward the Otley Road tram stop.

Kids and commuters got on and off as we jolted toward the strung lights of the city, their lips moving and their hands stirring to things only they could feel and see. The Clearbrite looked more than even like some recently arrived spaceship as it glowed out through the gloom, but inside the place was just like any other campus building, with clamouring posters offering to restructure your loan, find you temporary work, or get you laid and hammered. Constant reminders, too, that Clearbrite was the only smartjuice to communicate in realtime to your fingerjewel, toejamb or wristbracelet. This souk-like aspect of modern unis not being something that Sebastian Flyte, or even Harry Potter in those disappointing sequels, ever had to contend with.

We got a fair few hellos, a couple of tenured types stopped to talk to Rob in a corridor, and I saw how people paused to listen to what he was saying. More than ever, I had him down as someone who was bound to succeed. Still, I was expecting to be shown moon rocks, lightning bolts or at least some clever virtual planetarium, but instead he took me into what looked like the kind of laboratory I'd been forced to waste many hours in at school, even if the equipment did seem a little fancier.

"This is the physics part of the astro," Rob explained, perhaps sensing my disappointment. "But you did ask about other worlds, right, and this is pretty much the only way I can show them to you."

I won't go too far into the details, because I'd probably get them wrong, but what Rob proceeded to demonstrate was a version of what I now know to be the famous, or infamous, Double Slit Experiment. There was a long black tube on a workbench, and at one end of it was a laser, and at the other was a display screen attached to a device called a photo multiplier a kind of sensor. In the middle he placed a barrier with two narrow slits. It wasn't a great surprise even to me that the pulses of light caused a pretty dark-light pattern of stripes to appear on the display at the far end. These, Rob said, were ripples of the interference pattern caused by the waves of light passing through the two slits, much as you'd get if you were pouring water. But light, Lita, is made up individual packets of energy called photons. So what would happen if, instead of sending tens of thousands of them down the tube at once, we turned the laser down so far that it only emitted one photon at a time? Then, surely, each individual photon could only go through one or the other of the slits, there would be no ripples, and two simple stripes would emerge at the far end. But, hey, as he slowed the beep of the signal counter until it was registering single digits, the dark-light bars, like a shimmering neon forest, remained. As if, although each photon was a single particle, it somehow became a blur of all its possibilities as it passed through both slits at once. Which, as far as anyone knew, was pretty much what happened.

"I'm sorry," Rob said afterwards when we were chatting over a second or third pint of beer in the fug of an old student bar called the Eldon which lay down the road from the university, "I should have shown you something less boring."

"It wasn't boring. The implications are pretty strange, aren't they."

"More than strange. It goes against almost else we know about physics and the world around us—us sitting here in this pub, for instance. Things exist, right? They're either here or not. They don't flicker in and out of existence like ghosts. This whole particles-blurring into wave business was one of the things that bugged me most when I was a kid finding out about science. It was even partly why I chose to study astrophysics—I thought there'd be answers I'd understand when someone finally explained them to me. But there aren't." He sipped his beer. "All you get is something called the Copenhagen Interpretation, which is basically a shoulder shrug that says, hey, these things happen at the sub-atomic level, but it doesn't really have to bother us or make sense in the world we know about and live in. That, and then there's something else called the many worlds theory..." He trailed off. Stifled a burp. Seemed almost embarrassed.

"Which is what you believe in?"

"Believe isn't the right word. Things either are or they aren't in science. But, yeah, I do. And the maths supports it. Simply put, Lita, it says that all the possible states and positions that every particle could exist in are real that they're endlessly spinning off into other universes."

"You mean, as if every choice you could make in a virtual was instantly mapped out in its entirety?"

"Exactly. But this is real. The worlds are all around us—right here."

The drink, and the conversation moved on, and now it was my turn to apologise to Rob, and his to say no, I wasn't boring him. Because books, novels, stories, they were *my* other worlds, the thing I believed in even if no one else cared about them. That single, magical word, *Fog*, which Dickens uses as he begins to conjure London. And Frederic Henry walking away from the hospital in the rain. And Rose of Sharon offering the starving man her breast after the Joab's long journey across dustbowl America, and Candide eating fruit, and Bertie Wooster bumbling back across Mayfair...

Rob listened and seemed genuinely interested, even though he confessed he'd never read a single non-interactive story or novel. But, unlike most people, he said this as if he realised he was actually missing out on something. So we agreed I'd lend him some of my old paperbacks, and this, and what he'd shown me at the Clearbrite, signalled a new phase in our relationship.

4.

IT SEEMS TO me now that some of the best hours or my life were spent not in reading books, but in sitting with Rob Holm in my cramped room in that house we shared back in Leeds, and talking about them.

What to read and admire, but also—and this was just as important—what not to. *The Catcher in the Rye* being overrated, and James Joyce a literary show-off, and *Moby Dick* really wasn't about much more than whales. Alarmingly, Rob was often ahead of me. He discovered a copy of *Labyrinths* by Jorge Luis Borges in a garage sale, which he gave to me as a gift, and then kept borrowing back. But he was Rob Holm. He could solve the riddles of the cosmos, and meanwhile explore literature as nothing but a hobby, and also help me out with my mek, so that I was finally able produce the kind of arguments, links and algorithms for my piece on *Madame Bovary* that the ais at An Lit actually wanted.

Meanwhile, I also found out about the kind of life Rob had come from. Both his parents were engineers, and he'd spent his early years in Aberdeen, but they'd moved to the Isle of Harris after his mother was diagnosed with a brain-damaging prion infection, probably caused by her liking for fresh salmon. Most of the fish were then factory-farmed in crowded pens in the Scottish lochs, where the creatures were dosed with antibiotics and fed on pellets of processed meat, often recycled from the remains their own breed. Which, just as with cattle and Creutzfeldt-Jakob Disease a century earlier, had resulted in a small but significant species leap. Rob's parents wanted to make the best of the years Alice Holm had left, and set up an ethical marine farm—although they preferred to call it a ranch—harvesting scallops on the Isle of Harris.

Rob's father was still there at Creagach, and the business, which not only produced some of the best scallops in the Hebrides, but also benefited other marine life along the costal shelf, was still going. Rob portrayed his childhood there as a happy time, with his mother still doing well despite the warnings of the scans, and regaling him with bedtime tales of Celtic myths, which was probably his only experience before meeting me of linear fictional narrative.

There were the kelpies, who lived in lochs and were like fine horses, and then there were the Blue Men of the Minch, who dwelt between Harris and the mainland, and sung up storms and summoned the waves with their voices. Then, one night when Rob was eleven, his mother waited until he and his father were asleep, then walked out across the shore and into the sea, and swam, and kept on swimming. No one could last long out there, the sea being so cold, and the strong currents, or perhaps the Blue Men of the Minch, bore her body back to a stretch of shore around the headland from Creagach, where she was found next morning.

Rob told his story without any obvious angst. But it certainly helped explain the sense of difference and distance he seemed to carry with him. That, and why he didn't fit. Not here in Leeds, amid the fun, mess and heartbreak of student life, nor even, as I slowly came to realise, in the subject he was studying.

He showed me the virtual planetarium at the Clearbrite, and the signals from a probe passing through the Oort Cloud, and even took me down to the tunnels of a mine where a huge tank of cryogenically cooled fluid had been set up in the hope of detecting the dark matter of which it had once been believed most of our universe was made. It was an old thing now, creaking and leaking, and Rob was part of the small team of volunteers who kept it going. We stood close together in the dripping near-dark, clicking hardhats and sharing each other's breath, and of course I was thinking of other possibilities—those fractional moments when things could go one of many ways. Our lips pressing. Our bodies joining. But something, maybe a fear of losing him entirely, held me back.

"It's another thing that science has given up on," he said later when we were sitting at our table in the Eldon. "Just like that ridiculous Copenhagen shoulder-shrug. Without dark matter, and dark energy, the way the galaxies rotate and recede from each other simply doesn't make mathematical sense. You know what the so-called smart money is on these days? Something called topographical deformity, which means that the basic laws of physics don't apply in the same way across this entire universe. That it's pock-marked with flaws."

"But you don't believe that?"

"Of course I don't! It's fundamentally unscientific."

"But you get glitches in even the most cleverly conceived virtuals, don't you? Even in novels, sometimes things don't always entirely add up."

"Yeah. Like who killed the gardener in *The Big Sleep*, or the season suddenly changing from autumn to spring in that Sherlock Holmes story. But this isn't like that, Lita. This isn't..." For once, he was in danger of sounding bitter and contemptuous. But he held himself back.

"And you're not going to give up?"

He smiled. Swirled his beer. "No, Lita. I'm definitely not."

5.

PERHAPS INEVITABLY, ROB'S and my taste in books had started to drift apart. He'd discovered an antique genre called Science Fiction, something which the AIs at An Lit were particularly sniffy about. And even as he tried to lead me with him, I could see their point. Much of the prose was less than luminous, the characterisation was sketchy, and, although a great deal of it was supposedly about the future, the predictions were laughably wrong.

But Rob insisted that that wasn't the point, that SF was essentially a literature of ideas. That, and a sense of wonder. To him, wonder was particularly important. I could sometimes—maybe as that lonely astronaut passed through the stargate, or with those huge worms in that book about a desert world—see his point. But most of it simply left me cold.

Rob went off on secondment the following year to something called the Large Millimetre Array on the Atacama Plateau in Chile, and I, for want of anything better, kept the lease on our house in Headingley and got some new people in, and did a masters on gender roles in George Eliot's *Middlemarch*. Of course, I paid him virtual visits, and we talked of the problems of altitude sickness and the changed assholes our old uni friends were becoming as he put me on a camera on a Jeep, and bounced me across the dark-skied desert.

Another year went—they were already picking up speed—and Rob found the time for a drink before he headed off to some untenured post, part research, part teaching, in Heidelberg that he didn't seem particularly satisfied with. He was still reading—apparently there hadn't been much else to do in Chile—but I realised our days of talking about Proust or Henry James had gone.

He'd settled into, you might almost say retreated, a sub-genre of SF known as alternate history, where all the stuff he'd been telling me about our world continually branching off into all its possibilities was dramatised on a big scale. Hitler had won World War Two—a great many times, it seemed—and the South was triumphant in the American Civil War. That, and the Spanish Armada had succeeded, and Europe remained under the thrall of medieval Roman Catholicism, and Lee Harvey Oswald's bullet had grazed past President Kennedy's head. I didn't take this odd obsession as a particularly good sign as we exchanged chaste hugs and kisses in the street outside the Eldon, and went our separate ways.

I had a job of sorts, thanks to Sun-Mi my fellow An Lit student from Korea, teaching English to the kids of rich families in Seoul, and for a while it was fun, and the people were incredibly friendly, but then I grew bored, and managed to wrangle an interview with one of the media conglomerates which had switched physical base to Korea in the wake of the California Earthquake. I was hired for considerably less than I was getting paid teaching English, and took the crowded commute every morning to a vast half-real, semi-ziggurat high-rise mistily floating above the Mapo District, where I studied high res worlds filled with headache-inducing marvels, and was invited to come up with ideas in equally headache-inducing meetings.

I, an Alice in these many virtual wonderlands, brought a kind of puzzled innocence to my role. Two, maybe three, decades earlier, the other developers might still have known enough to recognise my plagiarisms, if only from old movies their parents had once talked about, but now what I saying seemed new, fresh and quirky. I was a thieving literary magpie, and became the go-to girl for unexpected turns and twists. The real murderer of Roger Ackroyd, and the dog collar in *The Great Gatsby*. Not to mention what Little Father Time does in *Jude the Obscure*, and the horror of Sophie's choice. I pillaged them all, and many others. Even the strange idea that the Victorians had developed steam-powered computers, thanks to my continued conversations with Rob.

Wherever we actually were, we got into the habit of meeting up at a virtual recreation of the bar of Eldon which, either as some show-off feat of virtual engineering, or a post-post-modern art project, some student had created. The pub had been mapped in realtime down to the atom and the pixel, and the ghosts of our avatars often got strange looks from real undergrads bunking off from afternoon seminars. We could actually order a drink, and even taste the beer, although of course we couldn't ingest it. Probably no bad thing, in view of the state of the Eldon's toilets. But somehow, that five-pints-and-still-clear-headed feeling only added to the slightly illicit pleasure of our meetings. At least, at first.

It was becoming apparent that, as he switched from city to city, campus to campus, project to project, Rob was in danger of turning into one of those ageing, permanent students, clinging to short-term contracts, temporary relationships and get-me-by loans, and the worst thing was that, with typical unflinching clarity, he knew it.

"I reckon I was either born too early, or too late, Lita," he said as he sipped his virtual beer. "That was even what one of the assessors actually said to me a year or so ago when I tried to persuade her to back my project."

"So you scientists have to pitch ideas as well?"

He laughed, but that warm, Hebridean sound was turning bitter. "How else does this world work? But maths doesn't change even if fashions do. The many worlds theory is the only way that the behaviour of subatomic particles can be reconciled with everything else we know. Just because something's hard to prove doesn't mean it should be ignored."

By this time I was busier than ever. Instead of providing ideas other people could profit from, I'd set up my own consultancy, which had thrived, and made me a great deal of money. By now, in fact, I had more of the stuff than most people would have known what to do with. But *I* did. I'd reserved a new apartment in a swish high-res, high-rise development going up overlooking the Han River, and was struggling to get the builders to understand that I wanted the main interior space to be turned into something called a *library*. I showed them old walk-throughs of the Bodleian in Oxford, and the reading room of the British Museum, and the Brotherton in Leeds, and many other lost places of learning. Of course I already had a substantial collection of books in a secure, fireproofed, climate-controlled warehouse, but now I began to acquire more.

The once-great public collections were either in storage or scattered to the winds. But there were still enough people as rich and crazy as I was to ensure that the really rare stuff—first folios, early editions, hand-typed versions of great works—remained expensive and sought-after, and I surprised even myself with the determination and ruthlessness of my pursuits. After all, what else was I going to spend my time and money on?

There was no grand opening of my library. In fact, I was anxious to get all the builders and conservators, both human and otherwise, out of the way so I could have the place entirely to myself. Then I just stood there. Breathing in the air, with its savour of lost forests and the dreams.

There were first editions of great novels by Nabokov, Dos Passos, Stendhal, Calvino and Wells, and an early translation of Cervantes, and a fine collection of Swift's works. Even, in a small nod to Rob, a long shelf of pulp magazines with titles like *Amazing Stories* and *Weird Tales*, although their lurid covers of busty maidens being engulfed by intergalactic centipedes were generally faded and torn. Not that I cared about the pristine state of my whispering pages. Author's signatures—yes the thrill of knowing Hemingway's hands had once briefly grasped this edition, but the rest didn't matter. At least, apart from the thrill of beating others in my quest. Books, after all, were old by definition. Squashed moths. Old bus tickets. Coffee cup circles.

Exclamations in the margin. I treasured the evidence of their long lives.

After an hour or two of shameless gloating and browsing, I decided to call Rob. My avatar had been busy as me with the finishing touches to my library, and now it struggled to find him. What it did eventually unearth was a short report stating that Callum Holm, a fish-farmer on the Isle of Harris, had been drowned in a boating accident a week earlier.

Of course, Rob would be there now. Should I contact him? Should I leave him to mourn undisturbed? What kind of friend was I, anyway, not to have even picked up on this news until now? I turned around the vast, domed space I'd created in confusion and distress.

"Hey."

I span back. The Rob Holm who stood before me looked tired, but composed. He'd grown a beard, and there were a few flecks of silver now in it and his hair. I could taste the sea air around him. Hear the cry of gulls.

"Rob!" I'd have hugged him, if the energy field permissions I'd set up in this library had allowed. "I'm so, so sorry. I should have found out, I should have "

"You shouldn't have done anything, Lita. Why do you think I kept this quiet? I wanted to be alone up here in Harris to sort things out. But..." He looked up, around. "What a fabulous place you've created!"

As I showed him around my shelves and acquisitions, and his ghost fingers briefly passed through the pages of my first edition *Gatsby,* and the adverts for X-Ray specs in an edition of *Science Wonder Stories,* he told me how his father had gone out in his launch to deal with some broken tethers on one of the kelp beds, and been caught by a sudden squall. His body, of course, had been washed up, borne by to the same stretch of shore where Rob's mother had been found.

"It wasn't intentional," Rob said. "I'm absolutely sure of that. Dad was still in his prime, and proud of what he was doing, and there was no way he was ever going to give up. He just misjudged a coming storm. I'm the same, of course. You know that, Lita, better than anyone."

"So what happens next? With a business, there must be a lot to tie up."

"I'm not tying up anything."

"You're going to stay there?" I tried to keep the incredulity out of my voice.

"Why not? To be honest, my so-called scientific career has been running on empty for years. What I'd like to prove is never going to get backing. I'm not like you. I mean…" He gestured at the tiered shelves. "You can make anything you want become real."

6.

ROB WASN'T THE sort to put on an act. If he said he was happy ditching research and filling his father's role as a marine farmer on some remote island, that was because he was. I never quite did find the time to physically visit him in Harris—it was, after all, on the other side of the globe—and he, with the daily commitments of the family business, didn't get to Seoul. But I came to appreciate my glimpses of the island's strange beauty. That, and the regular arrival of chilled, vacuum-packed boxes of fresh scallops. But was this really enough for Rob Helm? Somehow, despite his evident pride at what he was doing, and the funny stories he told of the island's other inhabitants, and even the occasional mention of some woman he'd met at a cleigh, I didn't think it was. After all, Creagach was his mother and father's vision, not his.

Although he remained coy about the details, I knew he still longed to bring his many worlds experiment to life. That, and that it would be complicated, controversial and costly to do so. I'd have been more than happy to offer financial help, but I knew he'd refuse. So what else could I do? My media company had grown. I had mentors, advisors and consultants, both human and AI, and Rob would have been genuinely useful, but he had too many issues with the lack of rigour and logic in this world to put up with all glitches, fudges and contradictions of virtual ones. Then I had a better idea.

"You know why nothing ever changes here, don't you?" he asked me as our avatars sat together in the Eldon late one afternoon. "Not the smell from the toilets or the unfestive Christmas decorations or that dusty Pernod optic behind the bar. This isn't a feed from the real pub any longer. The old Eldon was demolished years ago. All we've been sitting in ever since is just a clever formation of what the place would be like if it still existed. Bar staff, students, us, and all."

"That's..." Although nothing changed, the whole place seemed to shimmer. "How things are these days. The real and the unreal get so blurry you can't tell which is which. But you know," I added, as if the thought had just occurred to me, "there's a project that's been going the rounds of the studios here in Seoul. It's a series about the wonders of science, one of those proper, realtime factual things, but we keep stumbling over finding the right presenter. Someone fresh, but with the background and the personality to carry the whole thing along."

"You don't mean me?"

"Why not? It'd only be part time. Might even help you promote what you're doing at Creagach."

"A scientific populariser?"

"Yes. Like Carl Sagan, for example, or maybe Stephen Jay Gould."

I had him, and the series—which, of course, had been years in development purgatory—came about. I'd thought of it as little more than a way of getting Rob some decent money, but, from the first live-streamed episode, it was a success. After all, he was still charming and persuasive, and his salt-and-pepper beard gave him gravitas—and made him, if anything, even better looking. He used the Giant's Causeway to demonstrate the physics of fractures. He made this weird kind of pendulum to show why we could never predict the weather for more than a few days ahead. He swam with the whales off Tierra del Fuego. The only thing he didn't seem to want to explain was the odd way that photons behaved when you shot them down a double-slotted tube. That, and the inconsistencies between how galaxies revolved and Newton's and Einstein's laws.

In the matter of a very few years, Rob Holm was rich. And of course, and although he never actively courted it, he grew famous. He stood on podiums and looked fetchingly puzzled. He shook a dubious hand with gurning politicians. He even turned down offers to appear at music festivals, and had to take regular legal steps to protect the pirating of his virtual identity. He even finally visited me in Seoul, and experienced the wonders of my library at first hand.

At last, Rob had out-achieved me. Then, just when I and most of the rest of the world had him pigeon-holed as that handsome, softly accented guy who did those popular science things, his avatar returned the contract for his upcoming series unsigned. I might have forgotten that getting rich was supposed to be the means to an end. But he, of course, hadn't.

"So," I said as we sat together for what turned out to be the last time in our shared illusion of the Eldon. "You succeed with this project. You get a positive result and prove the many worlds theory is true. What happens after that?"

"I publish, of course. The data'll be public, peer-reviewed, and—"

"Since when has being right ever been enough?"

"That's..." He brushed a speck of virtual beer foam from his grey beard. "... how science works."

"And no one ever had to sell themselves to gain attention? Even Galileo had to do that stunt with the cannonballs."

"As I explained in my last series, that story of the Tower of Pisa was an invention of his early biographers."

"Come on, Rob. You know what I mean."

He looked uncomfortable. But, of course, he already had the fame. All he had to do was stop all this Greta Garbo shit, and milk it.

So, effectively I became PR agent for Rob's long-planned experiment. There was, after all, a lot for the educated layman, let alone the general public, or us so-called media professionals, to absorb. What was needed was a handle, a simple selling point. And, after a little research, I found one.

A man in a business suit had arrived at Tokyo airport in the summer of 1954. He was Caucasian, but spoke reasonable Japanese, and everything about him seemed normal apart from his passport. It looked genuine, but was from somewhere called Taured, which the officials couldn't find in any of their directories. The visitor was as baffled as they were. When a map was produced, he pointed to Andorra, a tiny but ancient republic between France and Spain, which he insisted was Taured. The humane and sensible course was to find him somewhere to sleep while further enquiries were made. Guards were posted outside the door of a secure hotel room high in a tower block, but the mysterious man had vanished without trace in the morning, and the Visitor from Taured was never seen again.

Rob was dubious, then grew uncharacteristically cross when he learned that the publicity meme had already been released. To him, and despite the fact that I thought he'd been reading this kind of thing for years, the story was just another urban legend, and would further alienate the scientific establishment when he desperately needed their help. In effect, what he had to obtain was time and bandwidth from every available gravitational observatory, both here on Earth and up in orbit, during a crucial observational window, and time was already short.

It was as the final hours ticked down in a fervid air of stop-go technical problems, last minute doubts, and sudden demands for more money, that I finally took the sub-orbital from Seoul to Frankfurt, then the skytrain on to Glasgow, and some thrumming, windy thing of string and carbon fibre along the Scottish west coast, and across the shining Minch. The craft landed in Stornoway harbour in the Isle of Lewis—the northern part of the long landmass of which Harris forms the south—where I was rowed ashore, and eventually found a bubblebus to take me across purple moorland and past scattered white bungalows, then up amid ancient peaks.

Rob stood waiting on the far side of the road at the final stop, and we were both shivering as we hugged in the cold spring sunlight. But I was here, and so was he, and he'd done a great job at keeping back the rest of the world, and even I wouldn't have had it any other way. It seemed as if most of the niggles and issues had finally been sorted. Even if a few of his planned sources had pulled out, he'd still have all the data he needed. Come tomorrow, Rob Holm would either be a prophet or a pariah.

7.

HE STILL SLEPT in the same narrow bed he'd had as a child in the rusty-roofed cottage down by the shore at Creagach, while his parents' bedroom was now filled with expensive processing and monitoring equipment, along with a high-band, multiple-redundancy satellite feed. Downstairs, there was a parlour where Rob kept his small book collection in an alcove by the fire—I was surprised to see that it was almost entirely poetry; a scatter of Larkin, Eliot, Frost, Dickinson, Pope, Yeats and Donne and standard collections amid a few Asimovs, Clarkes and Le Guins—with a low tartan divan where he sat to read these works. Which, I supposed, might also serve as a second bed, although he hadn't yet made it up.

He took me out on his launch. Showed me his scallop beds, and the glorious views of this ragged land with its impossibly wide and empty beaches, and there, just around the headland, was the stretch of bay where both Rob's parents had been found, and I almost hear the Blue Men of the Minch calling to us over the sigh of the sea. There were standing stones on the horizon, and an old whaling station at the head of a loch, and a hill topped by a medieval church filled with the bodies of the chieftains who had given these islands such a savage reputation through their bloody feuds. And meanwhile, the vast cosmic shudder of the collision of two black holes was travelling toward us at lightspeed.

There were scallops, of course, for dinner. Mixed in with some fried dab and chopped mushroom, bacon and a few leaves of wild garlic, all washed down with malt whisky, and with whey-buttered soda bread on the side, which was the Highland way. Then, up in the humming shrine of his parents' old bedroom, Rob checked on the status of his precious sources again.

The black hole binaries had been spiralling toward each other for tens of thousands of years, and observed here on earth for decades. In many ways, and despite their supposed mystery, black holes were apparently simple objects—nothing but sheer mass—and even though their collision was so far off it had actually happened when we humans were still learning how to use tools, it was possible to predict within hours, if not minutes, when the effects of this event would finally reach Earth.

There were gravitational observatories, vast-array laser interferometers, in deep space, and underground in terrestrial sites, all waiting to record this moment, and Rob was tapping into them. All everyone else expected to see—in fact, all the various institutes and faculties had tuned their devices to look for—was this... Leaning over me, Rob called up a display to show a sharp spike, a huge peak in the data, as the black holes swallowed each other and the shock of their collision flooded out in the asymmetrical pulse of a gravitational wave.

"But this isn't what I want, Lita. Incredibly faint though that signal is—a mere ripple deep in the fabric of the cosmos—I'm looking to combine and filter all those results, and find something even fainter.

"This..." He dragged up another screen. "Is what I expect to see." There was the same central peak, but this time it was surrounded by a fan of smaller, ever-decreasing, ripples eerily reminiscent of the display Rob had once shown me of the ghost-flicker of those photons all those years ago in Leeds. "These are echoes of the black hole collision in other universes."

I reached out to touch the floating screen. Felt the incredible presence of the dark matter of other worlds.

"And all of this will happen tonight?"

He smiled.

8.

THERE WAS NOTHING else left to be done—the observatories Rob was tapping into were all remote, independent, autonomous devices—so we took out chairs into the dark, and drank some more whisky, and collected driftwood, and lit a fire on the shore.

We talked about books. Nothing new, but some shared favourites. Poe and Pasternak and Fitzgerald. And Rob confessed that he hadn't got on anything like as well as he'd pretended with his first forays into literature. How he'd found the antique language and odd punctuation got in the way. It was even a while before he understood the obvious need for a physical bookmark. He'd have given up with the whole concept if it hadn't been for my shining, evident faith.

"You know, it was *Gulliver's Travels* that finally really turned it around for me. Swift was so clever and rude and funny and angry, yet he could also tell a great story. That bit about those Laputan astronomers studying the stars from down in their cave, and trying to harvest sunbeams from marrows. Well, that's us right here, isn't it?"

The fire settled. We poured ourselves some more whisky. And Rob recited a poem by Li Po about drinking with the Moon's shadow, and then we remembered those days back in Leeds when we'd gone out onto the moors, and drank and ingested far more than was good for us, and danced like savages and, yes, there had even been that time he and I had gazed up at the stars.

We stood up now, and Rob led me away from the settling fire. The stars were so bright here, and the night sky was so black, that it felt like falling merely to look up. Over there in the west, Lita, is the Taurus Constellation. It's where the Crab Nebula lies, the remains of a supernova the Chinese recorded back in 1054, and it's in part of the Milky Way known as the Perseus Arm, which is where our dark binaries will soon end their fatal dance. I was leaning into him as he held his arms around me, and perhaps both of us were breathing a little faster than was entirely due to the wonders of the cosmos.

"What time is it now, Rob?"

"It's…" He checked his watch. "Just after midnight."

"So there's still time."

"Time for what?"

We kissed, then crossed the shore and climbed the stairs to Rob's single bed. It was sweet, and somewhat drunken, and quickly over. The earth, the universe, didn't exactly move. But it felt far more like making love than merely having sex, and I curled up against Rob afterwards, and breathed his cinnamon scent, and fell into a well of star-seeing contentment.

"ROB?"

The sky beyond the window was already showing the first traces of dawn as I got up, telling myself that he'd be next door in his parents' old room, or walking the shore as he and his avatar strove to deal with a torrent of interview requests. But I sensed that something was wrong.

It wasn't hard for me to pull up the right screen amid the humming machines in his parents' room, proficient at mek as I now was. The event, the collision, had definitely occurred. The spike of its gravitational wave had been recorded by every observatory. But the next screen, the one where Rob had combined, filtered and refined all the data, displayed no ripples, echoes, from other worlds.

I ran outside shouting Rob's name. I checked the house feeds. I paced back and forth. I got my avatar to contact the authorities. I did all the things you do when someone you love suddenly goes missing, but a large part of me already knew it was far too late.

Helicopter arrived. Drones circled. Locals gathered. Fishermen arrived in trawlers and skiffs. Then came the bother of newsfeeds, all the publicity I could ever have wished for. But not like this.

I ended up sitting on the rocks of that bay around the headland from Creagach as the day progressed, waiting for the currents to bear Rob's body to this place, where he could join his parents.

I'm still waiting.

9.

FEW PEOPLE ACTUALLY remember Rob Holm these days, and if they do, it's as that good-looking guy who used to present those slightly weird nature—or was it science?—feeds, and didn't he die in some odd, sad kind of way? But I still remember him, and I still miss him, and I still often wonder what really happened on that night when he left the bed we briefly shared. The explanation given by the authorities, that he'd seen his theory dashed and then walked out into the freezing waters of the Minch, still isn't something I can bring myself to accept. So maybe he really was like the Visitor from Taured, and simply vanished from a universe which couldn't support what he believed.

I read few novels or short stories now. The plots, the pages, seem over-involved. Murals rather than elegant miniatures. Rough-hewn rocks instead of jewels. But the funny thing is that, as my interest in them has dwindled, books have become popular again. There are new publishers, even new writers, and you'll find pop-up bookstores in every city. Thousands now flock to my library in Seoul every year, and I upset the conservators by allowing them to take my precious volumes down from their shelves. After all, isn't that exactly what books are for? But I rarely go there myself. In fact, I hardly ever leave the Isle of Harris, or even Creagach, which Rob, with typical consideration and foresight, left me in his will. I do my best with the scallop farm, pottering about in the launch and trying to keep the crabs and the starfish at bay, although the business barely turns a profit, and probably never did.

What I do keep returning to is Rob's small collection of poetry. I have lingered with Eliot's Prufrock amid the chains of the sea, wondered with Hardy what might have happened if he and that woman had sheltered from the rain a minute more, and watched as Silvia Plath's children burst those final balloons. I just wish that Rob was here to share these precious words and moments with me. But all there is is you and I, dear, faithful reader, and the Blue Men of the Minch calling to the waves.

FABLE
Charles Yu

Charles Yu is the author of *How to Live Safely in a Science Fictional Universe, Sorry Please Thank You,* and *Third Class Superhero* and worked as a storyboard editor on *Westworld*. He received the National Book Foundation's 5 Under 35 Award and was a finalist for the PEN Center USA Literary Award. His work has been published in *The New York Times, Playboy, The New Yorker,* and *Slate,* among other periodicals. Yu lives in Los Angeles with his wife, Michelle, and their two children where he is currently working on his next novel, *The Book of Wishing*.

ONCE UPON A time, there was a man whose therapist thought it would be a good idea for the man to work through some stuff by telling a story about that stuff.

The man lived in a one-bedroom efficiency cottage all by himself, in a sort of dicey part of town. One day, the man woke up and realized that this was pretty much it for him. It wasn't terrible. But it wasn't great, either. And not likely to improve. The man was smart enough to realize this, yet not quite smart enough to do anything about it. He lived out the rest of his days and eventually died. The end. Happy now?

The man could see that his therapist was not amused.

A rather unsatisfactory ending, the therapist opined, and suggested that the man could do better. The man thought, Is she really serious about this? But he didn't say anything out loud. The man was not convinced that he needed to be talking to the therapist at all, but he had tried so many other things (potions, spells, witches), and spent so much of his copper and silver, with absolutely nothing to show for it, that he figured why the hell not.

So how do I do this? he asked.

Why don't you start again? the therapist replied. And, instead of rushing to the end, try to focus on the details.

O.K., the man said.

Once upon a time, there was a man who did not know how to use a sword and was also very afraid of dragons, so he took the L.S.A.T., did pretty well, and ended up getting into a decent law school. There he learned useful skills. Skills that would allow him to earn a living in the village and to court the women of that village.

But what the man came to find soon after graduation was that, in this particular village, there were many people with the same skills. Many, many people. Really hard to overstate how many lawyers there were in that village. Accordingly, despite the man's efforts the local maidens were not overly impressed. And, after all that schooling, the man was ashamed to admit the sad fact that he still did not know how to use a sword.

But the man was fine with this. Totally cool with it. Did not feel inadequate whatsoever. He landed a job with a medium-sized firm. The pay was a bit below market, and the position wasn't exactly his first choice. Top three, maybe. Top fiveish. Somewhere in there. Nevertheless, again, the man could have done worse. Competently plying his trade afforded him a very livable existence. Allowed him to enjoy the company of loved ones. His parents were both gone now, and his sister lived in another kingdom, on the other side of the sea. But it wasn't like he didn't have friends. He totally had friends. People he could call to get the occasional beer or catch a movie. It was just that, well, there were those nights. Nights when the moon was new and the sky was dark, and the hour before dawn stretched out before him, threatening never to end. On those endless nights, he would lie in his cottage alone, looking through the window, up at the starless sky, and wondering, Was there a life for him out there in the world? Someone who would love him? Or could learn to love him or, at least, let herself be loved by him?

He thought about enchanting some young lady, but he had no talent for magic so that was not really an option. If he was going to find a fair maiden to marry him, he would have to do it the old-fashioned way: trick her into it. Kidding. No, he was going to have to find a woman with sufficiently low standards so as to give himself a fighting chance.

He eventually found such a woman, the only daughter of the candlemaker, a girl whom everyone thought of as plain. Also sad. Quite sad. Not until they had been married for many years would the man come to understand how sad she truly was.

But the man was getting ahead of himself. For now, the point was the man knew that he had to marry the candlemaker's daughter. Because unlike everyone else in the village, including the candlemaker himself, the man could see one thing: the young lady was not plain at all. She simply possessed a very mild form of magic, which she used for the purpose of hiding her loveliness. The man told the girl that he knew her secret. She denied it, and he told her that he knew she would deny it. Of course she had to deny that she was, in actuality, the most fetching maiden in the village—maybe in the entire realm. The girl looked confused. Her face flushed with embarrassment. She searched his eyes, trying to understand. Was the man teasing her? But the man did not smile. He seemed earnest. Told her that he knew why she used her magic to hide her beauty: it was in order to protect herself. But, for some reason, he (and only he) could see through it. Now the girl started to cry, because surely the man was trying to humiliate her, wasn't he? But she saw that he remained earnest. And, after a while, she stopped crying and, her face slick with tears, kissed the man softly on the lips.

The man asked the candlemaker for his daughter's hand in marriage. Her father asked that the man slay a dragon to prove his devotion. Even though the man was in decent shape, totally respectable shape, especially considering that he didn't have time to go to the gym, he still wasn't strong enough to swing a two-handed broadsword. So, being nothing if not practical, he sought out the smallest dragon he could find.

After a long search, he found one not much bigger than a wild fowl. Possibly a baby. If we're being honest, the dragon looked sickly. It had scared, wet eyes, and as the man raised his sword above his head to slay it his betrothed said to him, Don't. Please. That's dumb. You don't need to kill a baby dragon just to prove something to me. All right, the man said, barely hiding his relief. He lowered his sword, petted the young dragon on the head, and sent it back to the cave or wherever. The candlemaker was angry, or maybe not angry—he was a fairly gentle soul—but definitely miffed. Still, he wanted his daughter married off, so, grudgingly, he gave his blessing. The man had found his wife.

He said to her, I will provide you with a good life. Pretty good, at least. She said, Quit talking and let's go before my father changes his mind.

And so they did.

And the man loved his wife. To the extent that he knew how to love, anyway. The man had a clumsiness about him, in his hands and in his heart. He fumbled words, missed chances, and, despite his best intentions, was prone to mishandling fragile things. Together they shared a quiet existence that was defined by well-managed expectations. Perhaps not the stuff of legends. Not quite deserving of 'once upon a time.' But it was comfortable and honest.

HE WONDERED ALOUD, ahem, if this was really worth his and the therapist's time.

But the man was coming to understand that his therapist was not going to let him out of this exercise until he had navigated his way along

(1) an emotionally honest path to

(2) an unexpected

(3) yet inevitable destination.

Whatever that meant. The man sighed loudly and continued.

Once upon a time, there was a guy who couldn't swing a sword and nearly peed his pants whenever he saw even a toddler-size dragon, so he went to law school, where he learned a bunch of very useful skills, and when he graduated he became a lawyer, and he was pretty O.K. at that, and it allowed him to build a life, try to build a life.

Great. The therapist liked where this was going.

But he had dreams of more. He told his wife this, as they lay in their cold stone hut at night.

Oh? she said, hopeful. A little surprised. What do you dream of? Being a hero?

No, he said sheepishly. Deep down in his heart, what he dreamed of was not to be a lawyer, or a hero, but a blacksmith. A silly dream, he knew, so he had never told anyone. He waited for her to laugh, but she didn't. She said that it was a lovely thing to dream of.

But, having said this, the man was already talking himself out of it. Blacksmithing was old-fashioned and hardly anyone actually made a living at it anymore. He would, of course, keep his job as a lawyer. Would always provide for her. And the candlemaker's daughter said, I know you will.

It was cold, so they spooned. Made love under the nearly empty night sky. Through the window, the man saw a single star. It hung low, twinkling at them.

This was kind of how they did things for a while. Talked at night, made love, and then the man would fall asleep and his wife would listen to him snore and worry about him. He seemed tired, overworked. She would worry well past the witching hour, and at some point drift off into her own restless half-sleep, just before dawn. She had anxiety and took potions for it, and herbs, and other things from the apothecary. All of it was prescription—it wasn't like she was self-medicating or anything. But the potions didn't help, or maybe helped a little—they caused her to have spells of forgetfulness, to lose an hour here or there, but nothing really could lessen her dread. It turned out that she was right to feel dread.

One night, in the very short time during which both she and her husband were asleep, a sorceress from far away, whom they didn't know, put a spell on their home, for some reason they would never understand. They would not ever be blessed with the gift of a child. That one star hung in the sky, and it would never fall to Earth for them.

The couple handled this news in different ways. The candlemaker's daughter did research, read books about it. Found a local support group that met on Tuesdays. The man, unsure of what to say, tried not to talk about it. Stopped blacksmithing for a while. Started grinding his teeth at night. A distance grew between them. The man wanted to touch his wife, to be with her, but it hurt too much.

Still, they loved each other. After work one day, the man came home with two bottles of good wine and they opened both bottles and sat on the floor in the middle of the living room in their hut and drank all the wine and ate an entire loaf of hard bread and laughed at each other and at themselves, tried to see the silver lining in being cursed by a malevolent force and, in the morning when they woke up, they felt a little better.

They made a list. There was always adoption. Which took time and money and patience and luck. But they were in no rush, were they? Plus, while they waited they could enjoy each other. Take more vacations. If they could save up enough copper coins, maybe even go all the way to the seashore. Eventually. Why not? They were staying glass half full about it all.

And then, out of nowhere, boom. Just like that. Just when the man had given up, you know? One day the star did fall from the sky into the belly of the man's wife. And there it burned for six weeks until it had a heartbeat. At twelve weeks, they told family, friends. At eighteen weeks, they found out: it would be a boy. Their boy. And the lawyer-blacksmith and the candlemaker's daughter were overjoyed. They didn't want to question why it had happened now, or whether it had anything to do with them finally letting go. They just thanked the heavens and the earth and whatever little magic might be left in the world.

It wasn't the easiest pregnancy. There were nights when the invisible wolf, carried along by the fire wind, would come and snatch at the child with its jaws, try to take it away and carry it back into the hills. The wolf came at thirty weeks. At thirty-two weeks, it came again, and the sage elder mages were worried and had the man's wife spend the night, just for observation. Just a precaution.

Fortune was smiling, though, and they made it to thirty-five weeks. The mages still had concerns. They looked into their crystal balls or whatever. Behind closed doors, they talked in hushed tones. They nodded their sage heads sagely, stroked their beards, gave the lawyer-blacksmith grim and ponderous looks. Ugh, the mages were really kind of awful about the whole thing. So when the child was finally born the man and his wife wept with joy and relief. Two arms and two legs. Two eyes, a nose and a mouth, color in his cheeks. Head covered with wisps of soft, almost invisible hair.

It was a few weeks later that the man's wife first noticed it.

Something about their baby.

Difficult to see at first, because the boy looked fine. He acted fine. Nursed. Slept.

For the first two months, the blacksmith and his wife would frequently stop what they were doing, pause, and look at each other. As if to say, We did it.

Six months in, they didn't look at each other anymore; instead, each of them silently studied their boy. Afraid to say anything to the other, lest they make it real by uttering out into the world what was, day by day, increasingly hard to ignore. Saying only generally positive things, vague expressions of hope. No reason to worry yet. Don't jump to any conclusions.

At twelve months, they said nothing. There was no need to say anything.

The man and his wife took the boy back to the mage who had brought him into the world. At first, the old wizard refused to see them. He shook his head gently. The man's wife begged. Fell to her knees and pleaded. The lawyer-blacksmith tried to pull her up by the arms. But she wouldn't move. She cried there in front of the mage's tower for three brutally hot days and three painfully cold nights, the man watching over her the whole time.

On the morning of the fourth day, the mage emerged, on his way to somewhere else, and was alarmed and scared as he stumbled over the candlemaker's daughter, still waiting there. He could not let this go on any longer.

Your son, he said. He will never be of this world.

Now the man's wife broke down with fresh tears. The man stared at the mage and said, What do you mean? What does that mean? I know you're a mage and that's how you talk, but you can't say something like that and then just stand there.

The boy's spirit, the mage explained, what some might call his soul—it is trapped. You can think of it as being inside a small box, and that box is inside another box, and that box in another, and so on.

Is this because of the curse?

Could be. Hard to say. It is possible that the child is afraid to come into the world, or that he is not fully allowed to, owing to the persistent dark energy that was attached to his creation.

Dark energy. At this phrase, the man's skin turned cold. He feared. He knew. Something in him had caused all of this. He had no way of proving it, but the man knew it was his fault, could not even look at his wife, afraid that just one look and she would instantly understand.

But if his wife did have any such thoughts she did not betray them. She took the man's hand in hers and pressed the mage for options. What could they do? Tell us what to do.

The answer, the mage said, may be hidden deep within him. Too deep to retrieve safely. You will never know him. But you will care for him, love him, see that he has everything a child needs.

As soon as the lawyer-blacksmith heard these words, he knew that they were true. He wondered what insurance would cover; he worried about the large deductible, the high cap on out-of-pocket expenses. Ahead of him, the lawyer-blacksmith saw many years of therapists, of special schools, of helpers. No birthday parties. No playdates or friends. No playing baseball with his son.

At sixteen months, the boy stood up once, clapped his hands.

At twenty months, a word: Bye. Bye-bye.

Then, at two years, more words, all in rapid succession: Mama, baby, Dada, sorry.

Why sorry?

Maybe he heard it often.

At three, he said, What's that? And, Who's that? And, Where are we going?

When he was five, the lawyer-blacksmith's son said, Dad is my best friend. He said this from very far away, from a place deep inside himself. The man could barely hear his son. The boy was sitting on the ground and looked confused, and from his mouth came a terrible sound. An old sound, a pain trapped in there. The boy looked out the window at other boys running. He wanted to run. But his legs wouldn't work right.

His father said, They do work, son. Your legs are just fine.

And the son said, Then why do I feel stuck?

His father said, We will get you unstuck. Those are nice legs, good legs. Don't be mad at your legs. Look at me. Look at Mommy. We will figure this out. We gave you those legs. We are sorry. I am sorry. But it is not your fault. And you will get to run.

The boy eventually did run. Sort of. It looked funny, and other boys laughed at him. So after a few tries the boy stopped running.

WAS THE MAN O.K.? Did he need a moment?

The man was fine.

A glass of water, perhaps?

No, the man said. I'm fine.

Deep breath, O.K.?

In other ways, things were going pretty well. As it turned out, the man did have a talent for blacksmithing. Not a great talent. He would not make swords for knights and princes. But he had something. And people noticed. They started to bring him stuff to smith, and he could smith the heck out of that stuff. He hammered stuff and flattened other stuff and made stuff, stuck stuff in the fire, and stuff. What had started out as a thing on the side turned into a little bit of a cottage industry.

He had time to do this because he had quit his job at the firm and now worked as a lawyer in local government. No bonus, but good benefits. And the hours were so much better. Now the man was home most nights for dinner. He and his wife and son moved to a slightly bigger cottage, just outside the village. The lawyer-blacksmith was still no knight or lord, of course, but he could provide for his family. They were never hungry. Things were fine, mostly, although sometimes when they went down to the village for a harvest festival, other families would look at them, and they hated the way they were looked at. Sympathy, mixed with something else. Something like, I admire you, but don't touch me or I might catch your plague of misfortune. Sympathy, as in, I sympathize, my heart goes outward to you— outward to you, as in, You over there, stay over there, don't come any closer. I will admire you from a distance. The man knew that look well. The man's wife said, Don't be so hard on people. They mean well. But the man said, Meaning well is for shit. Oh, he knew that look and how he hated that look. The presumptuousness of it. Those other families didn't say anything. That was the worst part. Except when they did say something. And that was even worse: So inspiring. You must be so strong, selfless. Now, that was a fairy tale. The idea of selfless people. As if their lives were somehow different, as if they didn't have flaws and urges, didn't ever want to have a couple of drinks, or three, or ten. As if having a kid like theirs made them into some kind of charmed species, some imaginary fairytale type of nonhuman humans, people who never got bored or tired or horny. But the blacksmith-lawyer, as much as he resented these strangers with their heartfelt looks, couldn't blame them. So he ignored them.

He was up for a promotion to managing attorney of his department. By now his son was eight. No, closer to ten. Now fifteen. The years were getting away from him. The boy still had no friends, and though it hurt the man every time his son asked why not, it hurt more on the day that his son stopped asking. That was years ago now. Things were still fine. The cottage felt small, so they bought another one. Not great timing, because a month later the blacksmith-lawyer was passed over for the better job. Something about his not having the right attitude. He'd heard back-channel whispers throughout the village that the higher-ups in the department all liked him, but they wondered if he could commit to the additional responsibility. Given, well, his circumstances. They knew he had a kid at home who required extra care. That was all maybe a nice way for them to not say what the problem really was. Maybe that they found it kind of depressing to be around him. They all felt for him, though. His lovely wife, his special-needs kid or whatever. They would never fire him, he knew. He could have a job there for as long as he wanted, doing land surveys on local fiefdoms. Dividing up the realm for lesser lords and vassals, assessing taxes on men far richer than he could ever dream of being. Drawing a steady stream of copper into his accounts. A stable life, a life for his family. That was the right thing to do.

So he did it. He was angry at his wife, even though she had never asked him to do it. He began staying out late, for work, at first, and then not for work. His wife made ever more frequent trips to the apothecary. Began to learn the trade. Soon she had perfected a potion of her own. An elixir for relaxation, she called it. Just to get through the day.

Their son continued to grow. His body did, anyway. The rest of him, it was harder to tell. At times, he seemed like a soul trapped inside a mind trapped inside a brain trapped inside a body. A body that turned into a man's body, while somewhere in there, flitting around like a moth, without any direction or understanding, was a child. A baby. Their baby.

FUCK, MAN, DO I have to do this? I don't know if I can keep doing this.

Keep going. This is good.

What's good?

The therapist said that this was serious progress. The man was finally getting somewhere.

The man didn't know what else to say. His armpits were sweaty, his back hurt, his ass was sore from the therapist's lumpy couch. He had to take a piss. He was tired of narrating.

O.K., then. He could have a break, drink some water, and then, whenever he was ready, start again.

The man didn't want to start again. But the therapist cast a meaningful gaze at the clock and the man understood that his time was almost up, and so he started again. Once upon a time, there was a therapist who had no idea what she was doing.

The man waited for a reaction, but the therapist didn't take the bait. She didn't say anything. She nodded, and leaned forward, and waited for him to continue.

Once upon a time, there was a therapist who wasn't going to do any good and cost too much, and it's not like the man was made of money. He did all right, but this was not exactly in the budget, and, anyway, they weren't the kind of people who hired therapists. That was for rich people. It was his wife's idea, soon to be ex-wife, maybe, and what kind of crap was this, imposing conditions on him, to save his marriage, like he deserved this, after all he had done—conditions. Conditions! Like he was the only one who was broken. Like he was the only one who had maybe got a little too angry at the kid, the man-child, never violent but just a little mean. But, God damn it, he didn't know where the meanness came from. He couldn't help it, really, when it started rising up in him, the blood and heat, climbing into his face, and he could feel it—he was going to say something that he couldn't take back, he was going to say something that was the opposite of what he wanted to say, when all he wanted to do was stroke the boy's cheek and say—

SORRY. SHIT. SORRY. I'm all over the place.

It's O.K. Take a moment. Take as long as you need.

I don't know.

What don't you know?

I don't know if I can do this.

Have a sip of water.

The man took a sip of ice-cold water.

Once upon a time, there was an angry guy, who hated the story he was in. All right? He was angry, O.K.? Once upon a time, there was a guy who wasn't allowed to start a story with 'once upon a time.' Because it wasn't once upon a time. It was a specific time. And he wasn't a blacksmith—he was just a regular guy who lived in the forest. He waited maybe too long to get married, but the thing was, he had his mom to take care of, never felt it was time, all those years, watching her body shrivel up. His mom, who deserved better. He worked days, and at night he looked after her, and then, when she was gone, he got married. A little later in life. Maybe too late. But he'd wanted his own story. Just a simple one. That was all he and his wife wanted, and the obgyn told them about the elevated risks, the witch's curse and all that. But whatever. They had the boy anyway. The man and his wife and the boy who laughed and clapped but didn't talk or run. It was a family. His family. His wife—she was good, she was a better person than he was. She showed him how to love the boy. He loved the hell out of the boy.

And they moved even deeper into the forest. They wanted to be far from everything else. They didn't want to see other people anymore. Wanted to find another forest, another village, another once upon a time, where they'd be safe from potions, and spells, and anything else. Dragons. Werewolves. Curses. A place without magic. Wherever that might be.

The guy and his wife built their house to be strong, fortifying it with wood, sticks, mud, stones, whatever they could find. They lived carefully, quietly, didn't even look at each other most days. They'd had enough of living in a half-assed fairy tale. Enough bloodshed, enough potions and elixirs, enough of that for a lifetime. They figured if they didn't talk, didn't try to understand it all, then the story would just go away. Would stop trying to mean something, would stop trying to break their broken hearts.

So they stopped thinking. At night, they stopped dreaming. From their heads, they carved out the parts that had made dreams and fed them to wild animals. Scattered their dream-stuff on the ground, to be pecked at, gnawed at, chewed up. Waking, sleeping without dreams, working. Like this, they passed many days. Years.

The boy grew. But he didn't, really. Then one day the man looked at his wife across the breakfast table. She was putting a strawberry into their son's mouth. Their son was smiling. Dumb, unknowing, a grown man's face with the eyes of a child. The smile of an idiot.

This was the most beautiful thing the man had ever seen.

For a moment, he was happy.

He went out to gather wood and, in his happiness, walked much farther from his home than he had in a long time. He came upon a stream, over which there had once been a bridge, whose wooden planks had now rotted away. And there he discovered a curious sight.

On the other side of the ruined bridge, sitting there alone, was his son. What are you doing out here? He asked. How did you get here?

The boy said he didn't know. He started to moan. A horrid sound. A grown man crying like a baby. I'm sorry, he said, I'm so sorry.

O.K., the man said. O.K. Don't cry. Tell me, sorry for what, little dude? What are you sorry for?

For all the trouble. For messing up your life.

Oh, God, the man said. No.

The man was the one who should apologize. How could he possibly explain that he wasn't strong enough, or good enough, to be the boy's father?

The boy said that he was trapped, wasn't he? Trapped over here, on this side of the bridge. He started to cry again.

From across the distance, the man tried to soothe his son. Hummed to him, a song from when he was a baby. The boy stopped sobbing for a moment, long enough to say, Dad, tell me a story.

But what kind of story could the man tell? The man wasn't a good enough storyteller. He'd had a kind of allegorical thing going for him once, but he'd lost the trail. No map, no legend. He no longer knew what stood for what.

He looked around. He was in the darkest part of the forest. He didn't know this area. The cottage, the clearing in the woods, it was all so small, and so far from everything. The sounds coming from the trees were frightening. The man realized now what he had done. He had tried to ignore the story. He and his wife had tried to go on with their days, not speaking or thinking too hard. But the story had never gone away. Neglect and time had done their work. While the man wasn't looking, this place had fallen apart.

He turned to see where he had come from and saw that the trail back to the cottage led nowhere. A few yards from him, it just sort of faded into the surroundings. Behind him, no way to retrace his steps. In front of him, a bridge to his son that had long since rotted. If he tried to cross, it wouldn't hold his weight. He couldn't get from here to there.

So, instead, he turned away from both, away from home and from his son. And he just ran. He ran as fast as he could, flat out running through the unknown forest. And then his wife was running beside him. And every ghoul, every beast, every horrible thing, corporeal, immaterial, every thing that had ever hunted or haunted the man and the woman, was now right behind them, pressing. And leading them all was their son, their son, asking, Don't you want to be my parents? Why not? Why not? Soon they couldn't remember if they'd ever done anything but run. Their lives had been one long chase.

No, the man said, this isn't fair.

And his wife said, We have no time for fair.

And the man said, Why are we running? We're in our own story. We don't have to run.

Then he looked down at his body, and he saw that he was not a hero, not a blacksmith, or anything else. He looked over at his wife and saw that she was not a damsel in distress, not a candlemaker's daughter. He barely knew her anymore. But he knew that she was Rachel. She was whoever was inside of Rachel. She was the mother of their child. Their boy. He looked at the boy. A grownup man now. Still a boy. A lovable boy trapped inside a smelly man, and he knew that he would wipe the boy's nose and ass and anything else for as long as he needed to, because that's what blacksmiths do. That's what fairy-tale heroes do. They become government lawyers. They buy groceries. They shave their son three times a week, and feed him pudding, and sing to him once in a while.

This was not a dream, not a fairy tale. This was all there was, all there would be.

Once upon a time, there was a fable, and maybe at one point things corresponded, one for one, or close enough, but somewhere along the way it had twisted, and now he wasn't sure what it was.

THE MAN WAS out of ideas. He heard the clock ticking: tick tick tick tick tick tick tick tick tick. He looked at his therapist, wondering if he was already overtime. The therapist didn't say anything. The man understood that he was in a new territory. He'd reached the edge of the forest. There was nowhere left to run.

He took a breath, realized that he was still sweating. Was this what the therapist had wanted? A lawyer-blacksmith in her office, sweating all over her couch, slowly losing his grip? Did she know how to help him? Could she help him remember how to get from here to there?

Time's up, she said. It's a start.

A start?

Yes.

The man looked at his therapist. Wondering if she could possibly be serious.

His lunch hour was over. The man got up to leave. On his way out the door, he said, See you next week, and the therapist said, Maybe. He turned to look at her. She said, Let's see where you go from here.

The man went down the hall, relieved himself, washed his hands, splashed water on his face. As he stepped back out into the hallway, that was when he saw it. It looked like—but come on, no way. He was just seeing things now. But. Could it be?

In the carpet, the faintest outline.

A trail.

Where did it lead? Was it a way out? Or a way in?

And the man said to himself, All right, then, maybe she's right. If this is where your story starts, then so be it.

HONOURABLE MENTIONS: 2016

"Rager in Space", Charlie Jane Anders (*Bridging Infinity*)

"Because Change Was the Ocean and We Lived By Her Mercy", Charlie Jane Anders (*Drowned Worlds*)

"Panic City", Madeline Ashby (*CyberWorld*)

"Fifty Shades of Grays", Steven Barnes (*Lightspeed, 06/16*)

"Mars Abides", Stephen Baxter (*Obelisk*)

"The Story of Kao Yu", Peter S. Beagle (*Tor.com*)

"Waking in Winter", Deborah Biancotti (*PS Publishing*)

"The Voice in the Cornfield, the Word Made Flesh", Desirina Boskovich (*F&SF, 9-10/16*)

"Martian Triptych", James Bradley (*Dreaming in the Dark*)

"The House That Jessica Built", Nadia Bulkin (*The Dark, 11/16*)

"Six Degrees of ~~Separation~~ Freedom", Pat Cadigan (*Bridging Infinity*)

"Nesters", Siobhan Carroll (*Children of Lovecraft*)

"A Dead Djinn in Cairo", P. Djèli Clark (*Tor.com, 10/05/16*)

"The Lost Child of Lychford", Paul Cornell (*Tor.com Publishing*)

"Pearl", Aliette de Bodard (*The Starlit Wood*)

"The Life and Times of Angel Evans", Meredith Debonnaire (*Booksmugglers, 9/13/16*)

"The Sound That Grief Makes", Kristi DeMeester (*The Dark #17 10/16*)

"Breadcrumbs", Malcolm Devlin (*Interzone 264, 5-6/16*)

"The Adventure of the Extraordinary Rendition", Cory Doctorow (*Echoes of Holmes*)

"Induction", Thoraiya Dyer (*Bridging Infinity*)

"Where the Pelican Builds Her Nest", Thoraiya Dyer (*In Your Face*)

"The Bridge of Dreams", Gregory Feeley (*Clarkesworld 114, 3/16*)

"Not Without Mercy", Jeffrey Ford (*Conjunctions 69: Other Aliens*)

"Lazarus and the Amazing Kid Phoenix", Jennifer Giesbrecht (*Apex, 7/16*)

"Tower of the Rosewater Goblet", Nin Harris (*Strange Horizons*)

"Little Widow", Maria Dahvana Headley (*What the #@&% Is That?*)

"Origins", Carlos Hernandez (*The Grim Future*)

"The Magical Properties of Unicorn Ivory", Carlos Hernandez (*The Assimilated Cuban's Guide to Quantum Santeria*)

"Snapshot, 1988", Joe Hill (*Cemetery Dance #74/75*)

"The City Born Great", N.K. Jemisin (*Tor.com, 09/28/16*)

"The Dream Quest of Vellitt Boe", Kij Johnson (*Tor.com Publishing*)

"The Seventh Gamer", Gwyneth Jones (*To Shape the Dark*)

"Empty Planets", Rahul Kanakia (*Interzone 262, 1-2/16*)

"Breathe", Cassandra Khaw (*Clarkesworld 116, 5/16*)

"Hammers on Bone", Cassandra Khaw (*Tor.com Publishing*)

"Excerpts for an Eschatology Quadrille", Caitlín R. Kiernan (*Children of Lovecraft*)

"The Line Between the Devil's Teeth (Murder Ballad No. 10)", Caitlín R. Kiernan (*Sirenia Digest 130, 12/16*)

"Kit: Some Assembly Required", Kathe Koja & Carter Scholtz (*Asimov's, 8/16*)

"The One Who Isn't", Ted Kosmatka (*Lightspeed, 07/16*)

"Postcards from Natalie", Carrie Laben (*The Dark, 7/16*)

"The Finest, Fullest Flowering", Marc Laidlaw (*Nightmare 45*)

"Masked", Rich Larson (*Asimov's, 7/16*)

"Sparks Fly", Rich Larson (*Lightspeed, 03/16*)

"The Ballad of Black Tom", Victor LaValle (*Tor.com Publishing*)

"Shadows Weave", Yoon Ha Lee (*Beneath Ceaseless Skies, 05/25/16*)

"Discards", David D. Levine (*Tor.com, 3/30/16*)

"Dispatches from the Cradle: The Hermit—Forty-Eight Hours in the Sea of Massachusetts", Ken Liu (*Drowned Worlds*)

"The Snow Train", Ken Liu (*Genius Loci*)

"Ozymandias", Karin Lowachee (*Bridging Infinity*)

"My Body, Herself", Carmen Maria Machado (*Uncanny 9-10/16*)

"In the Ruins of Mohenjo-Daro", Usman T. Malik (*The Mammoth Book of Cthulhu*)

"The Wreck at Goat's Head", Alexandra Manglis (*Strange Horizons 11/16*)

"Something Happened Here, But We're Not Quite Sure What It Was", Paul McAuley (*Tor.com, 07/20*)

"Ye Highlands and Ye Lowlands", Seanan McGuire (*Uncanny 10, 5-6/16*)

"This Census-taker", China Mieville (*Del Rey*)

"Last Gods", Sam J. Miller (*Drowned Worlds*)

"Only Ten Shopping Days Left Until Ragnarok", James Morrow (*Drowned Worlds*)

"Cold Comfort", Pat Murphy & Paul Doherty (*Bridging Infinity*)

"Pair of Ugly Sisters, Three of a Kind", Garth Nix (*The Grim Future*)

"With Her Diamond Teeth", Pear Nuallak (*The Dark, 11/16*)

"Afrofuturist 419", Nnedi Okorafor (*Clarkesworld 122, 11/16*)

"The Charge and the Storm", An Owomoyela (*Asimov's, 6/16*)

"Unauthorized Access", An Owomoyela (*Lightspeed, 09/16*)

"Between Dragons and Their Wrath", An Owomoyela & Rachel Swirsky (*Clarkesworld 113, 2/16*)

"Ten Poems for the Mossums, One for the Man", Suzanne Palmer (*Asimov's, 8/16*)

"Ash", Susan Palwick (*F&SF, 05-06/16*)

"Blind Spot", Paul Park (*Conjunctions 69: Other Aliens*)

"The Devil You Know", K.J. Parker (*Tor.com Publishing*)

"Told by an Idiot", K.J. Parker (*Beneath Ceaseless Skies, 02/04/16*)

"Spells Are Easy If You Have the Right Psychic Energy", Dominica Phettaplace (*F&SF, 07-08/16*)

"Project Symmetry", Dominica Phetteplace (*Asimov's, 6/16*)

"Project Empathy", Dominica Phetteplace (*Asimov's, 3/16*)

"Sooner or Later Everything Falls Into the Sea", Sarah Pinsker (*Lightspeed, 02/16*)

"Under One Roof", Sarah Pinsker (*Uncanny*)

"Left Behind", Cat Rambo (*Clarkesworld*)

"Parables of Infinity", Robert Reed (*Bridging Infinity*)

"Sixteen Questions for Kamala Chatterjee", Alastair Reynolds (*Bridging Infinity*)

"The Iron Tactician", Alastair Reynolds (*Newcon Press*)

"Between Nine and Eleven", Adam Roberts (*Crises and Conflicts*)

"And Then, One Day, the Air Was Full of Voices", Margaret Ronald (*Clarkesworld 117, 6/16*)

"The Bog Girl", Karen Russell (*The New Yorker, 06/20/16*)

"The Tale of Mahliya and Mauhub and the White-Footed Gazelle", Sofia Samatar (*The Starlit Wood*)

"Prodigal", Gord Sellar (*Analog, 12/16*)

"Inheritance, or the Ruby Tear", Priya Sharma (*Black Static 53*)

"Vulcanization", Nisi Shawl (*Nightmare Magazine, 1/16*)

"The Best Story I Can Manage Under the Circumstances", Robert Shearman (*Five Stories High*)

"Finnegan's Field", Angela Slatter (*Tor.com, Jan-16*)

"Under She Who Devours Suns", Benjanun Sriduangkaew (*Beneath Ceaseless Skies, 07/21/16*)

"Sgt. Augmento", Bruce Sterling (*Terraform, 8/17/16*)

"The Process Is a Process All Its Own", Peter Straub (*Conjunctions 69: Other Aliens*)

"Front Row Seat to the End of the World", E.J Swift (*Now We Are Ten*)

"Drowned", Lavie Tidhar (*Drowned Worlds*)

"The Vanishing Kind", Lavie Tidhar (*F&SF, 07-08/16*)

"Snow Day", Catherynne M. Valente (*Uncanny 11, 7-8/16*)

"The Limitless Perspective of Master Peek; or, The Luminescence of Debauchery", Catherynne M. Valente (*Beneath Ceaseless Skies, 05/25/16*)

"Familiaris", Genevieve Valentine (*The Starlit Wood*)

"That Game We Played During the War", Carrie Vaughn (*Tor.com, 03/16*)

"The Mind Is Its Own Place", Carrie Vaughn (*Asimov's, 9/16*)

"Dragon Brides", Nghi Vo (*Lightspeed, 04/16*)

"Only Their Shining Beauty Was Left", Fran Wilde (*Shimmer 09/16*)

"A Taste of Honey", Kai Ashante Wilson (*Tor.com Publishing*)

"The Metal Demimonde", Nick Wolven (*Analog, 6/16*)

"A Fist of Permutations in Lightning and Wildflowers", Alyssa Wong (*Tor. com, 03/02/16*)

"Secondhand Bodies", J Y Yang (*Lightspeed, 01/16*)

COPYRIGHT

EDITED BY JONATHAN STRAHAN

THE BEST SCIENCE FICTION & FANTASY OF THE YEAR

VOLUME EIGHT

INCLUDING STORIES BY **K J PARKER** // **NEIL GAIMAN**
GEOFF RYMAN // **GREG EGAN** // **M JOHN HARRISON**
CAITLÍN R KIERNAN // **E LILY YU** // **MADELINE ASHBY**
TED CHIANG // **JOE ABERCROMBIE** // **IAN MCDONALD**

THE BEST SCIENCE FICTION & FANTASY OF THE YEAR
VOLUME EIGHT

From the inner realms of humanity to the far reaches of space, these are the science fiction and fantasy tales that are shaping the genre and the way we think about the future. Multi-award winning editor Jonathan Strahan continues to shine a light on the very best writing, featuring both established authors and exciting new talents.

Within you will find twenty-eight incredible tales, showing the ever growing depth and diversity that science fiction and fantasy continues to enjoy. These are the brightest stars in our firmament, lighting the way to a future filled with astonishing stories about the way we are, and the way we could be.

FEATURING:

GREG EGAN • YOON HA LEE • NEIL GAIMAN • E LILY YU
K J PARKER • GEOFF RYMAN • M BENNARDO • RAMEZ NAAM
TED CHIANG • PRIYA SHARMA • RICHARD PARKS • LAVIE TIDHAR
M JOHN HARRISON • JOE ABERCROMBIE • JAMES PATRICK KELLY
CHARLIE JANE ANDERS • THOMAS OLDE HEUVELT • VAL NOLAN
BENJANUN SRIDUANGKAEW • ELEANOR ARNASON • ROBERT REED
IAN R MACLEOD • SOFIA SAMATAR • IAN MCDONALD • KARIN TIDBECK
• MADELINE ASHBY • CAITLÍN R KIERNAN • AN OWOMOYELA

 WWW.SOLARISBOOKS.COM

Follow us on Twitter! www.twitter.com/solarisbooks

EDITED BY JONATHAN STRAHAN

THE BEST SCIENCE FICTION & FANTASY OF THE YEAR

VOLUME NINE

FEATURING STORIES BY
LAUREN BEUKES
PAOLO BACIGALUPI
JOE ABERCROMBIE
K. J. PARKER
KEN LIU
GARTH NIX
ELIZABETH BEAR
KAI ASHANTE WILSON
RACHEL SWIRSKY
CAITLÍN R. KIERNAN
GENEVIEVE VALENTINE
AND MANY MORE

THE BEST SCIENCE FICTION & FANTASY OF THE YEAR

VOLUME NINE

Science fiction and fantasy has never been more diverse or vibrant, and 2014 has provided a bountiful crop of extraordinary stories. These stories are about the future, worlds beyond our own, the realms of our imaginations and dreams but, more importantly, they are the stories of ourselves. Featuring best-selling writers and emerging talents, here are some of the most exciting genre writers working today.

Multi-award winning editor Jonathan Strahan once again brings you the best stories from the past year. Within you will find twenty-eight amazing tales from authors across the globe, displaying why science fiction and fantasy are genres increasingly relevant to our turbulent world.

FEATURING:

KELLY LINK • HOLLY BLACK • KEN LIU • USMAN T. MALIK
LAUREN BEUKES • PAOLO BACIGALUPI • JOE ABERCROMBIE
GENEVIEVE VALENTINE • NICOLA GRIFFITH • CAITLÍN R. KIERNAN
GREG EGAN • K. J. PARKER • RACHEL SWIRSKY • ALICE SOLA KIM
GARTH NIX • KARL SCHROEDER • ELLEN KLAGES • PETER WATTS
KAI ASHANTE WILSON • MICHAEL SWANWICK • ELEANOR ARNASON
JAMES PATRICK KELLY • IAN MCDONALD • AMAL EL-MOHTAR
TIM MAUGHAN • ELIZABETH BEAR • THEODORA GOSS

 WWW.SOLARISBOOKS.COM

Follow us on Twitter! www.twitter.com/solarisbooks

EDITED BY JONATHAN STRAHAN

THE BEST SCIENCE FICTION & FANTASY OF THE YEAR

VOLUME TEN

INCLUDING STORIES BY
PAOLO BACIGALUPI
ELIZABETH BEAR
GREG BEAR
JEFFREY FORD
NEIL GAIMAN
NALO HOPKINSON
ALASTAIR REYNOLDS
GENEVIEVE VALENTINE
CAITLÍN R. KIERNAN
CATHERYNNE M. VALENTE
GEOFF RYMAN
ANN LECKIE
IAN MCDONALD
KAI ASHANTE WILSON
AND MANY MORE

THE BEST SCIENCE FICTION & FANTASY OF THE YEAR
VOLUME TEN

Jonathan Strahan, the award-winning and much lauded editor of many of genre's best known anthologies, is back with his tenth volume in this fascinating series, featuring the best science fiction and fantasy from 2015. With established names and new talent, this diverse and ground-breaking collection will take the reader to the outer reaches of space and the inner realms of humanity with stories of fantastical worlds and worlds that may still come to pass.

FEATURING:

NEIL GAIMAN • ELIZABETH BEAR • GREG BEAR
NISI SHAWL • IAN MCDONALD • PAOLO BACIGALUPI • KELLY LINK
GEOFF RYMAN • ANN LECKIE • JEFFREY FORD • NALO HOPKINSON
ALYSSA WONG • TAMSYN MUIR SIMON INGS • GWYNETH JONES
ALASTAIR REYNOLDS • USMAN T. MALIK • NIKE SULWAY
CAITLÍN R. KIERNAN • ROBERT REED • KELLY ROBSON
CATHERYNNE M. VALENTE • KIM STANLEY ROBINSON
GENEVIEVE VALENTINE • VONDA N. MCINTRYE
SAM J. MILLER • KAI ASHANTE WILSON

REACH FOR INFINITY

EDITED BY JONATHAN STRAHAN

HUMANITY AMONG THE STARS

What happens when we reach out into the vastness of space?
What hope for us amongst the stars?

Multi-award winning editor Jonathan Strahan brings us fourteen
new tales of the future, from some of the finest science fiction
writers in the field.

'A strong collection of stories that readers of science
fiction will certainly enjoy.' - Locus Magazine on
Engineering Infinity

'Stands as a solid and at times striking contribution to
the ongoing discussion about what science fiction is in
the 21st century.' - The Speculative Scotsman

'If you want science fiction, rather than space opera,
this is for you.' - Total SciFi Online

FEATURING:

GREG EGAN • ALIETTE DE BODARD • IAN MCDONALD
KARL SCHROEDER • PAT CADIGAN • KAREN LORD
ELLEN KLAGES • ADAM ROBERTS • LINDA NAGATA
HANNU RAJANIEMI • KATHLEEN ANN GOONAN • KEN MACLEOD
ALASTAIR REYNOLDS • PETER WATTS

 WWW.SOLARISBOOKS.COM

Follow us on Twitter! www.twitter.com/solarisbooks

EDGE OF INFINITY

EDITED BY **JONATHAN STRAHAN**

ONE GIANT LEAP FOR MANKIND

Those were Neil Armstrong's immortal words when he became the first human being to step onto another world. All at once, the horizon expanded; the human race was no longer Earthbound.

Edge of Infinity is an exhilarating new SF anthology that looks at the next giant leap for humankind: the leap from our home world out into the Solar System. From the eerie transformations in Pat Cadigan's "The Girl-Thing Who Went Out for Sushi" to the frontier spirit of Sandra McDonald and Stephen D. Covey's "The Road to NPS," and from the grandiose vision of Alastair Reynolds' "Vainglory" to the workaday familiarity of Kristine Kathryn Rusch's "Safety Tests," the thirteen stories in this anthology span the whole of the human condition in their race to colonise Earth's nearest neighbours.

'One of the year's most exciting anthologies.' - io9

FEATURING:

**HANNU RAJANIEMI • ALASTAIR REYNOLDS • JAMES S. A. COREY
JOHN BARNES • STEPHEN BAXTER • KRISTINE KATHRYN RUSCH
PAUL MCAULEY • SANDRA MCDONALD • STEPHEN D. COVEY
ELIZABETH BEAR • PAT CADIGAN • GWYNETH JONES
AN OWOMOYELA • BRUCE STERLING**

 WWW.SOLARISBOOKS.COM

Follow us on Twitter! www.twitter.com/solarisbooks

MEETING INFINITY

EDITED BY **JONATHAN STRAHAN**

FEATURING STORIES BY GREGORY BENFORD • JAMES S.A. COREY • NANCY KRESS
ALIETTE DE BODARD • KAMERON HURLEY • MADELINE ASHBY • SIMON INGS
JOHN BARNES • GWYNETH JONES • IAN MCDONALD • YOON HA LEE • RAMEZ NAAM
AN OWOMOYELA • BENJANUN SRIDUANGKAEW • BRUCE STERLING • SEAN WILLIAMS

'Revel in stories that speak to both head and heart.' ★★★★★'
SFX Magazine on *Engineering Infinity*

THE FUTURE IS OURSELVES

The world is rapidly changing. We surf future-shock every day, as the progress of technology races ever on. Increasingly we are asking: how do we change to live in the world to come?

Whether it's climate change, inundated coastlines and drowned cities; the cramped confines of a tin can hurtling through space to the outer reaches of our Solar System; or the rush of being uploaded into cyberspace, our minds and bodies are going to have to drastically alter.

Multi-award winning editor Jonathan Strahan brings us another incredible volume in his much praised science-fiction anthology series, featuring stories by Madeline Ashby, John Barnes, James S.A. Corey, Gregory Benford, Benjanun Sriduangkaew, Simon Ings, Kameron Hurley, Nancy Kress, Gwyneth Jones, Yoon Ha Lee, Bruce Sterling, Sean Williams, Aliette de Bodard, Ramez Naam, An Owomoyela and Ian McDonald.

'[The *Infinity* series] has gone from strength to strength.'
Tor.com

FEATURING:

**GREGORY BENFORD • JAMES S.A. COREY • NANCY KRESS
ALIETTE DE BODARD • KAMERON HURLEY • MADELINE ASHBY
SIMON INGS • JOHN BARNES • GWYNETH JONES • IAN MCDONALD
BENJANUN SRIDUANGKAEW • BRUCE STERLING • SEAN WILLIAMS
YOON HA LEE • RAMEZ NAAM • AN OWOMOYELA**

 WWW.SOLARISBOOKS.COM

Follow us on Twitter! www.twitter.com/solarisbooks